RECONSTRUCTION

DESTRUCTION 3

BETHANY A PERRY

To Addy and Jack.
Endings are hard. I love you both.
Thank you for letting me tell your story, my friends.

Warnings: this book contains the following content:

Amputation
Forced captivity
Medical procedures
Murder
Needles (medical use)
Pregnancy trauma
PTSD
Discussion of sexual assault
Suicidal ideations
Suicide

*Additional disturbing content due to the nature of a zombie/horror story

THE BREAK

CHAPTER 1

The helicopter touched down, and Melinda's feet hit the soil above the Molehill for the first time in five years.

"Good to be home, huh, Mama?" Hector bumped her with his shoulder, black eyes smiling. All his dark hair stood on end.

She glared, clutching the satchel. "It is. I wonder if it's changed while we've been gone."

He shook his head. "What would they do different?"

"You got me, Heck. You got me."

Grinning, he ignored the path and ran down the hill through the tall grass.

That evil imp hopping through the sunny grass could have killed her whole family. And what would she have left? Just what was in this satchel. Pieces of Jack.

"Let's go, Mama!" Hector waved from the bottom of the hill, smiling into the sun.

Following the brick path down the hill, taking the steps one careful foot at a time, she descended. Wouldn't do to get sloppy and lose the samples now. Or the research.

Warmth spread through her. The research.

She smiled.

Hector opened the door within the hill. "What's that smile for?"

"My research. From Shanti Station. It should all be here." She shook her head. "I told Tim I deleted it, but in reality, I transmitted it all here. I'd forgotten." Her smile grew. So many things to be happy about. Before walking in, she met his eyes. "You were instrumental in that. I don't know if I ever thanked you. Releasing those remnants was a stroke of genius."

His lips split in a grin that rivaled the sun. He waved her in.

The door closed behind her, locking them into the earthen smell she'd been away from for so long. It didn't feel like dying here, and yet it didn't feel like living. But it did smell like wet earth, and there could be few more pleasant scents in the world.

Hector followed on her heels. "You think they still kept our rooms?"

She led the way through the labyrinth of tunnels. "I do. Our things are probably still there as well." It would be something to see her old music collection again. The DVDs she'd located over time. Her telescope.

But first.

"I've got to report in, Heck. Why don't you go ahead and see if your room has changed."

Without another word, the boy ran off down another corridor. The dark swallowed him.

Sure, tile and brick lined the hallways. But the electric and phone cables didn't have conduit and the lamps only shone in a three-foot circle. Spaced at least five feet apart as they were, it didn't make for the brightly lit hallways she'd become accustomed to in Magnolia, or in Shanti Station, for that matter. And the light tapered off entirely about twenty feet out. Something about all the earth surrounding them, most likely.

Compared to this place, the Big House on Harkers was nothing as far as confusing hallways went. But her feet found their way. Tapping on the door with her knuckles, she clutched the satchel in the other hand and waited.

Swinging open, the heavy metal door creaked. A full-figured woman revealed herself behind it, nodding to Melinda with a sideways smile. "General. So good to see you again."

"Ilasha, your perfect hair has not changed," Melinda said, brushing through the door.

Ilasha closed the door, smiling. Leaning out of a shadow, her dark brown skin and high cheekbones shone. "You wouldn't believe the hell I go through to keep it that way, ma'am."

Melinda snickered. "Ma'am. Please, Lash. Don't start with me. Where is he?" Eyes wide, she glanced around the room as though the man she sought would somehow reveal himself. Like a magician in what used to be Vegas.

Lash held out a hand. "Where else? Things don't change much around here, Em."

"After you."

Affecting a stronger Southern accent than the one she already had, Lash fluttered the long lashes framing her deep brown eyes. "Don't you be lookin' at my ass, white woman." Swinging her hips, she led Melinda across the anteroom where Lash's desk and a couple chairs sat. Before leading her into the office beyond a second set of doors, a nameplate reading "Charles Anthony" glued to the center, she leaned over and lowered her voice. "He ain't been in the greatest mood lately, hon. Watch yourself."

She'd been able to handle him before she left. Shouldn't be any different now, even though it'd been a few years.

Clearing her throat, Lash stepped into the room, tugging Melinda's elbow. "Look what the cat dragged in, sir." Fingers in the small of her back, she gave Melinda a gentle push. And before Melinda could say another word, she disappeared.

Melinda rolled her shoulders. "Mister Anthony, sir, I can't believe I'm standing here again. After all these years, I—"

"Are you bringing me a vaccine, General?" Behind a great oak desk, he sifted through paper. Mounds of it.

"You received my transmission from Shanti Station?"

He snorted. "Your own Tranquility Base. Yes, my dear. I did. That was nearly a year ago." Laying a paper down, he glared over the top of his glasses. Hawkish blue eyes, set wide in his pale face, pierced her, pinning her to the spot. "Are you telling me you've made no progress since then?"

"I. Yes. I have." She held up the satchel and cleared her throat. "Using my test vaccine, we may have synthesized immunity."

He stood so fast the chair rolled into the wall with a bang. "You what?" With three large steps, he rounded the desk.

She straightened her shoulders and held the flinch inside. "It's not a hundred percent," she said, the satchel falling a tick, "but I witnessed it, Charles. Immunity in a living, breathing person." She cleared her throat again.

Arms crossed, he leaned against the desk. "Immunity. Huh. And what is it you have there?" he asked, bony finger pointing at the satchel.

She clutched it close. "My research. Samples. Half the clean biological component from the immune person. Some of their blood."

"Half. Some. Samples. Doesn't sound like much, General." He paused and removed his glasses. Cleaning them on his shirt, he glared. "What can you do with this half-assed science you've brought me?"

Her stomach curled. She grimaced. "Give me a few days. We need human eggs. I can synthesize some embryos."

"Ah. So that's the half you've brought? The father of this immune person? Is this person a child?"

"A newborn."

"Even better," he said, slapping the desk. The flat of his hand echoed off the wood.

Melinda jumped, clutching the case. "I am almost certain this was the first human born with it, sir."

Waving a hand, he slid the glasses up his nose. "Do it again, Melinda. Then we'll talk."

* * *

Dean twitched, jerked, and started fighting with the sheet.

Adelaide sat up so fast, she fell off the front of the chair. On her way to the floor, hardwood flying at her face, she had time to smile. It might've taken a week, but he'd finally woken. Fought his way out of the coma of blood loss, death, and rebirth.

Smashing her mouth into the ground never felt better.

"Adelaide! No!" Dean shouted through hoarse, underused vocal cords. His raspy voice echoed off the ceiling and walls of the Harkers Island infirmary.

She wiped her mouth, tasted blood, and popped up beside the bed. The relief coursing through her, that he'd woken and the first thing he shouted was her name, overpowered her leg muscles. On her knees, she grabbed his hand. "I'm right here,

Dean," she said, her cheeks cramping from the smile splitting her lips.

Gripping her hand, his head fell into the pillow. "Thank god, Addy. Oh, thank god. I thought. I thought you were." He stopped, eyes closed, and squeezed her fingers together hard enough to break bone.

Right. While he was dead, she'd tried to get him to bite her so he wouldn't be alone. A flawed choice her dad saved her from.

"I'm right here, Dean. I'm OK. And so are you."

"It's a miracle," Doctor Huxley said, weaving through the beds.

"You patch me up, doc?" Dean asked, facing the doctor.

Addy sat on the side of the bed.

Dean snaked his hand around her waist and pulled her closer.

The adrenaline her relief had produced now mixed with heat and light. It all pooled in her stomach. Throwing up might be an option.

"Although I am no medical doctor, I did, mister Ross. I did. It was Adelaide here," Hux said, angling his forehead at Addy, "whose quick thinking saved your life. I've never seen someone lose so much blood, turn, and yet be brought back to life." He paused, hand on his chin. "If you'd asked me a month ago, I would have told you it was impossible."

Addy mouthed the next sentence along with him.

"And I'm a leading expert in the virus."

Dean grimaced and gazed at Addy. "If you're an expert, doc, then it sounds like I owe you and Addy my life. But you took a hell of a risk, sweetheart. I remember that." He closed his eyes. "I do remember that."

She flushed, the blood tightening the skin of her forehead.

Dean frowned. "When do you think I can get out of here?"

Huxley motioned to the other doctor. "Doctor Larter says it will be another week before you can leave here. We must give that artery time to heal properly. You should do as little as possible until then. And of course, you must heal from the virus. That will take significantly longer."

Addy twisted her fingers. As long as he was alive, they could get through his recovery together.

Dean hacked, coughed, hacked some more, and spat a clump of blood and mucus into a tissue.

She snagged the trash can beside his bed and held it up.

He threw the wadded tissue inside with a grunt.

Huxley cleared his throat. "Significantly longer."

"You're the expert." Dean reclined on the pillow again and stared at Addy. Taking in a few deep breaths, he didn't move his eyes from her.

Without another word, Hux crossed the room again and sat next to Doc Larter.

"I'm so glad you're OK," Dean said, squeezing Addy again.

She swallowed, the urge to puke passing. "The feeling is mutual." She hadn't stopped smiling. Her cheeks were going numb.

"How's everyone else? Your dad, Jane, Mike?"

"They're OK." She shook her head and splayed her fingers on her thigh. "They've pretty much worked everything out. I've been here a lot, so I haven't seen much of them."

"What about all the others? Matt, Ella?"

Her insides headed for the hills. Center hollow, a tear collected in the corner of her eye and dropped. "You don't remember." More statement than question. Addy'd been told it was hard to remember before and after being turned.

Easing to his side, he rubbed her back. "No, sweetie, I'm sorry, I don't. Something happen to them?"

"Ella's dead. Ricardo shot her. And Matt. Well. He's here on the island. But he won't talk to anyone."

"Ricardo? What the hell?"

She explained what she'd been able to get out of Matt. Ricardo was another one of her mom's "adopted" kids, but since he used a fake name and Matt didn't see him until the second before Ric pulled the trigger, no one knew. He'd surprised them all, and Ella paid the price.

"Damn." His hand slipped off her back. "Anyone else?"

"You remember Paul?" Reliving all the death and torment that followed their escape from Magnolia wasn't high on the to-do list, but he needed her. She couldn't run away from it, no matter how much she might want to. He needed her.

"He's the last one I remember losing, yeah."

Another tear falling splashed on the side of his arm and rolled back, soaking into her shirt. "Mom shot Burke, Ric shot Ella, and as Mom flew away, one of them threw a grenade at us. You're the only one it killed, but Matt got a nasty cut from it. Dad and Jane and the baby were too far away. Everybody else, and Celia and Mike, they're fine." She glanced at him. "Yaz stayed back, and Renzo is going back soon to help with cleanup. Some more people from the island are going too."

"Yeah. They've got a horde to clean up, huh."

"It's a mess, Dean."

"Me too, honey. Me too." One hand stayed on her arm, his thumb rubbing back and forth.

Sitting with him until his breathing evened out, she watched his chest rise and fall. The artery in his neck, not unlike the one in his leg, beat in time with his living heart.

"Sweetie," he croaked.

Hypnotized by his rubbing thumb, his breathing, his beating artery, she almost fell again. She clutched the side of the bed and chuckled. "You scared me."

He opened his eyes to slits. "No, Addy. You scared *me*."

"What do you mean, like, right now? That was—"

"Addy," he said, pushing himself to his elbows with a flinch, "I don't remember much about getting from there to here. I couldn't see much more than the ceiling of the train. And." He stopped and dropped his eyes. "I remember your face. I wanted to—" With a scowl, he stopped again. A hacking cough emanated from deep in his lungs, turning his face red.

Jumping up, Addy reached for the tissues. Water. Something to help him.

He waved his hand at her, stretching to snatch a tissue himself. After hacking until she was sure he'd lose all the oxygen stored in his brain, he spat into the tissue and leaned over the bed to drop it into the trash.

Thunk.

Face cooling, red easing into pale and sweaty, he shook his head. "I remember what you did, Adelaide. You tried to let me bite you." Eyes wide, he caught hers and didn't let go. "And I wanted to."

She broke eye contact first and tapped her toes together. "I did. I couldn't let you be alone. Not after. Not after everything." With a shrug, she looked up at him again.

His glare softened, and the corners of his mouth turned down, dimpling his cheeks. "I get it." Laying back on the pillow, he laced his fingers across his chest and stared into her eyes. "I need you."

She opened her mouth to tell him how much she needed him too. How beyond happy she was he'd survived. How much she loved him.

But he cleared his throat and went on before she got any of it out. "I need you to leave. I can't." Covering his eyes with one hand, his frown bit further into his cheeks. "I can't be responsible for you doing something like that."

If the hollow feeling when she talked about Ella was immense, this was the Grand Canyon of empty.

"Dean, what are you saying?"

He did her the favor of meeting her eyes with those emeralds of his again. "Leave. Don't come back. If what we had caused you to do something like that. We." He exhaled. "We can't have it anymore."

Standing so fast the blood rushed away from her head, she wobbled on her feet. "Wait. What?"

Crossing his arms over his chest, he looked away. A tear rolled out the side of his eye, but his voice hardened. "I can't be with you anymore, Addy."

She tried to ask him what again, but there was no air to do it with.

* * *

Jack crossed his arms over his stomach, ocean spray wetting his face.

The magnetic, full of life feeling it gave him was nothing but a shell of its former self. He'd been looking for some solitude. A way to wrap his mind around who he was now. But Jane asked to come see the ocean, and how could he refuse? She wanted to dip her toes in the primordial waters of the planet's creation. He couldn't refuse her the moment simply because he felt sorry for himself.

So now the three of them walked down the beach, Jack picking up seashells smoothed by the tides, little Katie strapped to Jane's chest.

"You ought to show me how to do that sometime," he said, angling his chin at the wrap and the snuggly baby warm and asleep inside. Her head lolled to that uncomfortable angle newborns got. Like her neck was about to snap right off.

Kissing Katie's fuzzy hair, Jane slipped her fingers around his forearm and tugged until his hand popped loose. She enfolded it in her own. "You never learned with Mike or Addy?"

Palm sweaty, he shook his head. Talking about Mike and Adelaide as babies also brought up his ex-wife. He couldn't look at the memory head-on. It'd been tainted. Like film with developing solution spilled over it. He stuck his other hand in his pocket and ran the pad of his thumb over the sharp edge of a broken shell, eyes following the sand as it disappeared behind his feet. "I didn't. No. I didn't."

She squeezed his hand. "I'd be happy to show you, Jack. You'll like it."

He smiled at the baby. Such a pretty, innocent thing. Already, he found himself head over heels in love with her. "I'm sure I would." Sneaking a peek at Jane's eyes, turned to him with such love and trust, he bit the inside of his cheek and cast about for something else to say. "Addy killed a few 'Heads on this beach, did she tell you?"

"To save the horses, she said."

He stopped. "She said she was up in the lighthouse." He turned to find it, Jane keeping hold of his hand and spinning in a circle around him like a moon. His restless legs dragged him toward it. "Wanna go up there?"

Running her hand along the baby's back, Jane nodded. "Addy said the stairs were intact."

"That she did."

The ocean to his back, he crossed the beach with Jane in tow. When they reached the deeper sand, the loose piles of it above the tide line baked to a temperature just less than melted glass, he dug his feet in as far as they'd go. The molten sand seared his ankles. The pain, immediate and exquisite, flamed through his calves and ignited adrenaline.

"You think Dean's going to be all right?"

"He's strong. He'll pull through."

"Not what I asked."

Stepping into the shadow cast by the western-leaning sun, Jack stared up at the tower. Like Addy had said, the paint was chipped and peeling, but you could still see the outline of the black and white diamonds that once adorned her cylindrical sides. Still staring up the tower, he spoke from the side of his mouth. "Eventually. Melin… Well, I guess it's not an easy thing to recover from."

"You're right. He's strong. He'll be all right," Jane said, tugging him. They went around and came to the door.

He turned the handle, but the door didn't budge. With a frown, he gave it a nudge with his shoulder. Still, it remained shut.

Jane rammed it with her shoulder.

It popped open, and she righted herself. "There we go." She stepped inside.

"You won't let me get the door for you, at least let me check for 'Heads," Jack said, hand on her shoulder. The other on the haft of his holstered knife.

Without waiting for a response, he squeezed past her into the lighthouse. Ears open, he peeked behind the door, about the only place in the room they could hide. If they were.

One could hope.

But no. The place was dead silent. Nothing to fight. Nothing to die over.

After Jane walked in, he shut the door behind her and searched for something to bar it. Again, nothing. He gave it a few shoves with his shoulder for good measure. If any Dead Heads made it onto the island, and into this room, it'd take them hours to climb the stairs. And that was only if they smelled food at the top.

Staring up the spiral stairs, he doubted they could be smelled that far away.

One hand on the baby, the other on the rail, Jane started up the stairs. Her hips, still wider than before but not as wide as a week ago, twitched back and forth as she climbed.

"Jane," he said, catching up to her and casting for something to say, again. "Have you thought about what you want to do when Katie gets older?"

"What do you mean?" She slowed as they neared the halfway point. Sweat dripped down the back of her neck.

"As in, did you want to stay home with her? Or do something else? Island living has its perks. You can do whatever you want."

"I know that, Jack. And you know I will." She stopped and faced him. "What do you think?"

"I get a vote?"

"Yeah. I think." She smirked. "It's like we talked about. We're a team, right?"

"We are," he said, corners of his mouth turned up. He might question everything now, about himself or his capabilities or his place in the world, but one thing he didn't have to question was that she elevated him. He was better for being part of her team.

Starting back up the stairs, she grinned over her shoulder. "Right. So, though it goes against my nature, you get a say."

At the top, he insisted on going up into the lantern room first.

"I want to check the floor and the room, make sure it's safe for you guys. There's not much I can do right, but I'll do that." He started up the narrow stairs. More like a ladder, really. It—

"Hang on," she said, reaching for his arm. "What do you mean there's not much you do right? You do plenty, Jack." She caught and held his eyes, the fine line between her brows deep.

Heart beating in his throat, he tried not to flinch. "You're right. Sorry. I just, um…"

She took his hand, wrapping her fingers around his. "If you're talking about Andrew, sometimes I feel like it was my fault too. If we hadn't been talking, they might not have taken him away." She kissed Katie's forehead. "Sometimes I dream about that night, but I can never change what happened. They always take him away."

The fact he hadn't thought of Andrew in weeks, that he'd been talking about something completely different, and he had no idea she blamed herself, crowded his throat. He pulled her into a hug and whispered into her hair. "It wasn't your fault."

She stepped back. "Sure. Anyway. Get up there and check it out."

How did you not know she still thought about that? Why didn't you ever bother to ask?

Poking his head into the lens room, he took in the round space. One of the six-foot panes, which Addy said were all intact when she came up here with Dean, had been broken. They'd missed hurricane season while they'd been in the Virginia mountains. It must've happened then. Otherwise, the room was clear.

"Come on up, Jane," he said, climbing the rest of the way into the room. As he waited for her to mount the stairs, he stepped closer to the broken window. Jagged edges of glass poked from the sides of its frame. They gleamed. The gaping hole let in the heat and the light like the windows. But it also welcomed the outside in, with its breath and tears.

The sudden desire to drag his forearm against one of the edges invaded his thoughts. See if it was as easy as it looked to break the skin and slice the artery beneath.

Jane smiled out one of the intact windows. "I don't know if I've ever looked out a window this high. Do you think we could see Emerald Isle from here? The prison where we got little Katie?" She kissed the baby on the head. Without taking her eyes from the sight below, she held a hand out to him.

He glanced at the broken window again. If he needed it, the possibility of stepping out of it and just continuing to walk could always hang out in the back of his mind.

For now, he pushed it away and took her hand, gazing across the sound and looking with her for the place where it was all OK. Before that woman ruined everything.

Holding his girls close, he breathed.

CHAPTER 2

Surprised both feet lifted from the ground high enough to take steps, Addy wandered the island.

It couldn't be real, what Dean said. Couldn't be with her? Like, break up? How the hell did that make sense? Did he not love her anymore? Was that what he meant?

It was just the virus. He didn't know what he was saying. That's all.

She sidestepped a tree at the last moment.

Arms crossed, she stopped. "The hell am I?" She spun a circle. She'd been headed for the long wooden dock that went through the swamp, where they first landed on this island, forever ago. Almost a year now.

Mumbling under her breath, she turned around. "Unless I want to get in one of those boats and paddle out to the lighthouse, I may as well go back." Better than wandering through the swamp.

Although she forced her thoughts away from the lighthouse, she couldn't find anything to distract her from Dean. From his obviously ill-formed ideas. He was definitely being influenced by his death. Couldn't think straight. It was literally the only explanation. He couldn't mean to break up with her.

"It's just plain idiotic," she said, little louder than a whisper.

"What is?"

With a start, she drew her machete.

Expression listless, Matt frowned. "Sure. That's as good an idea as any."

With a grimace, she reseated the blade. "Nothing. Don't sneak up on me like that."

"I was walking like an elephant, Addy. Not my fault you didn't hear me." He brushed past her, out of the swamp.

With a sigh, she caught up to him. "How are you? How's your back?"

"Fine. Great." Deep lines on either side of his mouth pointed down.

"So, the first one was a lie. How's your back, really?"

He looked up. Not a complete eye roll, but its cousin. "It's fine. You don't have to mother me."

"I know that, Matt. I'm trying to be your friend, not your mom."

He shook his head.

"Friends look after each other, that's all," she said. "How's your back?"

"You're nothing if not insistent. It's fine." He scratched at his shoulder blade. "Itchy." Stopping, he let his mouth turn up on one side. "You know where I can find one of those old back scratchers?"

She tried to grin. "Do you need help with the dressing? Or is it healed enough to go without?"

Smiling, he closed his eyes. Stumbled a step.

She gripped his shoulder and steadied him, taking in details she should have noticed. The sweaty skin of his face was paler than usual. He'd lost weight, his cheeks sucking in. His hair stuck out at all angles instead of lying down with the almost military precision he usually used on it. "Are you sure it's all right?"

He shook his head.

"Where are you staying?"

Pointing, he shuffled his feet. "It's up here."

They stopped in front of a large building. It may have once been a barn or a storage building but now housed a number of apartments where a lot of the single guys lived.

She led him inside. "Where's your room?"

"Upstairs." The longer they walked, the more his legs trembled.

"Great. Good. How did you even make it downstairs?"

He stumbled again, and when she reached for his arm, his jacket fell open, and she clutched exposed skin.

Heat baked into her hand.

"Fuck's sake. You're burning up," she said, hauling him up the stairs. She laid a wrist on the hot skin of his forehead. "Did the doctor give you anything to take?"

He shook his head. "Yes."

Unable to decipher the double meaning, she shook him. "You just. What?"

"Yes. But I haven't been taking it." He stopped, gripping the banister, eyes half-lidded. "I deserve the pain. I shouldn't dull it."

"That's all well and good." They resumed the climb. "But if it was antibiotics he gave you, you need to take them. Or you could die. You clearly have an infection."

He chuckled, tripping up the last stair and onto the landing. "That's like the coffee. How do we even still have that crap?"

"You ask the wildest questions. How should I know?"

Pointing to a door, he sagged. He let her drag him inside and flopped on the bed. As he landed on his back, he pulled air over his teeth in a sharp inhale.

"Let me see your back."

He slapped her hand. "I do not need your help, Adelaide Cooke."

"Christ, Matt. You're as bad as El—"

She stopped, air sucked from her lungs like she'd been punched in the gut. How could she think to speak the name of Matt's dead girlfriend with the wound so fresh? She'd loved Ella too, and the pain of losing her was nearly as bad as whatever just happened with Dean. Cheeks at least magenta, she turned her back. "Where are your pills?"

"Second drawer," he said, voice thick.

Digging them out, she ignored the fact she'd almost made both of them cry. She read the handwritten instructions the doc tucked inside the bottle, fished out a pill, and filled a glass from the kitchenette sink. "Take this. Take another tomorrow. And the next day. Until they're gone."

He took the pill and dry swallowed it. Pointing his red-rimmed eyes at the door, he grunted. "Fine. Can you leave now?"

She set the water on the end table next to him. "Look. I'm sorry. I didn't mean to."

He lifted his eyes and that same side of his mouth. "I know. It's OK. Well"—his throat worked—"it's not OK. But it's OK." Laying back, he covered his eyes with his forearm. "I'll take my pills. Promise."

"And redress that once a day too."

He waved his hand in the air. "Don't need a mother hen, Addy."

She left him to his own devices.

* * *

A knock on Addy's door roused her from overheated dreams of running.

Rubbing her eyes, she stumbled to the door and unbarred it. The addition of the bar had been a nice thing Dad had done while she was in the hospital, waiting for Dean to wake.

Oh, fucking hell. Dean.

Those few seconds of forgetting had been nice. But the weight settled around her heart again as she opened the door.

"Hey, lady," Jane said, sketching a wave, baby bundled in a wrap of cloth against her chest.

"Hey yourself. Get in here." Addy held the door wide.

Dipping in a brief curtsy, Jane stepped into the house and unwrapped the baby. "Thought it was about time you officially meet your baby sister. She's almost three weeks old already," she said, cradling the baby as she dropped the mound of cloth on a chair. Her hair fell in her face, and she whipped her head to get it out of the way.

"Where's your needles?"

"She likes to play in my hair when she's eating. I thought it probably wouldn't be good if she grabbed one. Don't worry." She showed Addy her back. "Till I get her trained, I got it covered."

Indeed she did. She'd fashioned some kind of back holster for no less than four knives. A leather and cloth contraption crossed her shoulder blades.

Addy grinned. "Of course you do."

"Works good for nursing too." Stroking the baby's face with a finger, she whispered in her ear. "Hey angel, wake up and meet your big sister."

The baby stirred, her toothless mouth open in a yawn. She made a spitting noise Addy associated with two things. Cats and newborns.

"You worked in the nursery here before, right?"

Addy held her hands out for the baby. "I did. It was fun. Not as hard as I thought."

Jane passed the baby and sat on the couch, cocking an elbow onto the arm. "The lack of sleep thing is for the birds though."

"Come on," Addy said, booping the baby's nose, "there have been plenty of nights we didn't get enough sleep."

"Those days are in the long-forgotten past."

"Yes. Five years is so very long ago." Addy chuckled, thinking back to how long they'd been in the village before this crazy trip began. What had now become this crazy relocation. She'd come to accept her cat and the memory stick with all her *Trek* were gone forever.

"Closing in on six now. But don't trust me about calendars and shit." Her eyes slipped closed.

Addy sat and propped her arm, Katherine a warm ball in her elbow. Such a snuggle queen already. Almost enough of a comfort to forget about Dean for more than five minutes.

Knives jabbed her in the gut. Sawed into the walls of her heart and spilled blood. She choked.

Eyes popping open, Jane sat up. "You OK?"

Addy frowned. "Yes. How's Dad? Where is he?"

She side-eyed Addy. "Distant. That's how he is. He's out there, right now, convincing Michael it's about time they redo the entire surface of the dock. But first he needs to reroof our house. And update the fence."

"Is he ever home?" Addy could see him out there, swinging a hammer. He'd built a lot of things for them in the years they'd lived without all this modern convenience. He'd been good at it.

"Oh yeah. He's home enough to help out. He takes care of the kitchen and the cooking and all. Just lets me rest with this little angel." She chuckled. "He even wakes up in the night when she does. He gets me water and fusses around for a few minutes, checks the windows and doors, every time."

"Sounds great." Addy shoved thoughts of Dean doing the same for her in some imagined—and now impossible—future as far away as they'd go. Goddammit. What the hell was wrong with him?

"Speaking of water, want some?"

Addy stood, handing her sister back to Jane. "I'll get it." Wandering through the kitchen door, she spotted Data's bowls in the corner. Another punch in the gut. Even her dog had gone away.

Eyes stinging, she pushed those thoughts away too and shuffled back to the living room. "What do you mean distant?" Sitting, she handed Jane her glass.

"Well. It's not like Jack is the biggest talker. We know that."

Addy nodded.

Chuckling, Jane went on. "But, I mean, we. You know. You've got Dean. In a relationship, it's not just talking. There's closeness. It doesn't need words. But it's there." She paused, taking a drink. "I can see him trying, but it's not there. I don't know what happened."

Swallowing tears, Addy tried not to choke on the water she drank to cover them.

Jane noticed. Of course.

"Hey," she said, setting her glass down, "what's wrong? Is it, I don't know, is it me and Jack?"

Smiling, tears she couldn't stop seeping into the corner of her mouth, she waved her hand. "No. No. That's fine, Jane. Any issues I had with you guys are so far in the past I don't even know what they look like anymore."

"Then what is it? It's not Dean? Is he going to be OK?" She searched Addy's face, a line between her brows.

Ah hell. The tears wouldn't stop. With Ella being dead and her mom being gone, again, Dean leaving her was too much. The weight so heavy she couldn't lift the blanket. And the blanket was wet.

"He's going to be fine. If Dad doesn't kill him, I guess."

"Oh, fuck," Jane said. "Fuck's sake Addy. No." Sliding down the couch, she settled Katie into the crook of one arm and threw the other around Addy's shoulders.

Closing her eyes, Addy let the tears she'd tried so hard to deny soak her in an ocean of them. Now if only they would wash away how worthless it all felt, maybe she could recover.

* * *

Jack pulled a chair out and sat at Paul's round kitchen table. A bubbling kettle sat on the stove, slow wisps of steam escaping from the edges of the lid.

"I hate having to do this," Scott said, staring out the window over the sink.

"Do you do it with everyone who, um, who doesn't come back?"

Scott bobbed his silver head. "I do." He faced Jack, his lone arm crooked across his stomach as though it folded over its missing companion. "You know I don't ever get out of the office, and I know there's a lot of people on this island who think I'm not good for much." What few lines his face earned over the years deepened.

"No they don't, Scott," Jack said, shaking his head. "They respect you. You always make the right decisions for them."

"They're not often easy to make. There was a time when." He stopped and shifted his eyes to the kettle. "A time when I thought we'd never keep this island away from all the people out there with designs on it." Catching Jack's eyes, he frowned. "There were a lot of them."

"Had a lot of houses to settle up after that, didn't you?"

"We did."

"I understand why you don't leave much. The house or the island."

"Is that right?"

"Yeah, I do. If I'd had a place like this for my kids, I wouldn't want to leave either." He stood, the faces of his children at the front of his mind. "And I'd do anything to protect it."

"Would you go as far as this Mann woman your daughter told me about?"

He removed the kettle from the heat a moment before it whistled. All Paul had left was green tea, and Jack's dad taught him to stop the water just before boiling. He measured the leaves into filters and filled two cups.

Settling back down at the table, he shook his head. "I don't know. I'd like to say no, but I don't like lying."

Scott took the opposite chair and smiled. He took a breath, lifted an eyebrow, and shook his head. "Understood. All too well."

In silence, they drank their tea.

Jack took in the kitchen, pushing the thought of that damned hospital in the mountains out of his head. What should be quiet reflection in memory of his friend, and sometimes father figure, shattered with thoughts of hordes and hospitals.

He stood and packed the magnets and knickknacks from around the fridge. Each one telling some kind of story Jack would never get to know.

"Thank you for coming to help," Scott said. "I usually do this alone."

"Why do you do it?" Jack asked, opening a trinket box. Inside, Paul had stuffed it to the brim with shells, smooth rocks, and in the midst of them, a pink hair ribbon. Whether it belonged to Paul's wife or daughter, Jack couldn't guess. It'd been tied around his wrist in the prison when they first met. Why hadn't he ever asked him about it? With a sniff, he closed the lid and settled it into the larger box.

Scott stood and glanced in at the trinket box. "I think you know. It serves as a good reminder the people I have here are that. People. Not numbers. Not something to be sacrificed when needed. People. And some of them," he said, caressing the side of the trinket box with a finger, "some of them people I wish I'd known better." He waved his hand around the room. "Looking at their things, seeing their life as they left it, helps me understand them that much better."

Swallowing, throat tight, Jack nodded. The only words he had seemed inadequate.

"I honestly think it should be Addy helping me, not you."

"Why is that?" He checked the top of the fridge. Spic and span, apart from the months of dust buildup.

"She'll take over this island from me at some point, I'm sure."

Jack choked on spit and coughed. "That could be. Where is she?"

Scott closed the box. "She refused to meet me here. She did not look good. Is she all right?"

"I. Well. I don't know," Jack said. Guilt, his ever-present friend, popped out of his chest and dug out a nice, deep hole for itself. "I guess I haven't talked to her in a few days."

"Say hi for me next time you do. I don't think she wants much to do with her former role as lieutenant, but she was spectacular at the job. Best Lou I've had."

Jack turned, heading into the living room to pack up in there.

But Scott reached out and stopped him. "Are *you* all right, Jack? You seem off your footing."

"Just doing this. I kinda liked the old guy. I didn't get to say goodbye."

And about a billion other things, but that's enough.

"If you want to talk, my door is always open."

* * *

Letting herself into Yasuo's house, Addy wrinkled her nose at the musty smell. They'd been gone close to half a year. She'd left the windows open in her house a few days to get the smell out.

She leaned her staff next to the door and set about opening Yaz's windows. Still in Magnolia, he'd called twice. With the commander dead and her mother fled, their concern about IRF monitoring their phone calls dropped to zero. Let them listen.

The first time Yaz called, he let them know everyone was all right. The second, while Dean was still in the hospital, to tell her they needed reinforcements. Fast. The fight was going, but it was not going well.

"These Magnolia people are great, Addy," he said, "but there's not enough of them. I don't know if we can get this done. And…" He lowered his voice, whispering into the phone. Static crackled. "The Emerald Isle people are like horses in a tornado. I'm afraid they're going to bolt any day now. And right into the tornado."

"We'll send some people to help, Yaz." She paused, his breath whistling on the other end of the phone, and stared at the outside of the infirmary door.

Dean lay in there in a coma, but alive. Alive. Desperate to get back to his side so she'd be sure to be there when he woke, she hesitated. This conversation with Yaz could take a turn, and she'd be on the phone for forever.

But she'd learned a lot from him, and one of the things was to choose how you wanted to react to things like fear. Even though he'd failed at his own lesson.

She bit her lip and spoke low into the phone. "How are you, though? With the horde and everything?"

His sharp exhale blew across the phone's mic, echoing like a gale-force wind. "It's hard, Addy. I'm not going to lie. I know that's difficult for you, especially because we talked about stuff like this."

"You did kinda seem to have it all under control. I figured if you taught me how to be like that, well." She nodded into the phone. "It's been hard to accept you being afraid."

"I'm sorry, Addy. I feel like I've failed you. Failed me."

What she'd done on the train flashed through her mind. Trying to get Dean to bite her, so he wouldn't be alone. "We all fuck up, Yaz."

"Yeah, well, it feels like a pretty big one." He grunted, as though he'd flopped into a chair. A dog growled from somewhere nearby.

"That my dog?" Catching her breath, she held it and listened for more.

"It is. You wanna say hi?"

Pushing the door with the big red cross on it open a crack, she peeked in on Dean. Close to the doc's station, no privacy walls around him since he was the only patient left, he lay on his back. Still, but breathing.

"No, Yaz. I need to get back to Dean. But listen. I think I get it. And even if I don't, I certainly don't think any less of you. Don't let this get you down," she said, easing the door closed. She sat at the same table where she'd once sat across from Tim. Listening to him talk about IRF and her father and Dean.

She shuddered.

Yaz blew into the receiver again. "We've made some progress, but if we had more help, we could get this horde over the wall. Get this town cleaned up."

"I'll get Renzo and some others on it. We'll get them stocked and up there as quick as we can."

"Be careful, Adelaide. Don't try to save everyone while I'm gone."

She smiled. "I'll do what I damn well please."

"I know you will," he said, grin coming through his voice.

After they'd hung up, conversation feeling final in some way, she'd returned to Dean. It'd taken another day for him to wake. And lose his damn mind.

Either way, Yaz also said he wanted to come back as soon as the horde was run out of Magnolia. So here she was, opening his windows and getting the house aired out. Renzo would be leaving to go up there soon.

When she opened the back door, Yaz's fat orange ball of fur raced into the house. Smacking into her ankles, he all but knocked her over.

"Jesus, Cliff, watch it." She tromped into the living room to get the food she brought, letting the mystery of how long the cat'd been waiting by the door go. Cliff followed, twisting around her ankles. "We're going outside to eat. I don't know when I'll be back next time, kitty." She snatched up the bag, located his bowls, and walked it all to the porch. As she filled the food bowl, he scarfed so fast she was afraid he'd choke. How did you Heimlich a cat?

Grabbing the water bowl, she spun to go inside.

The image of Dean standing too close, of running into his midsection with a bowl full of cat water, hit her with an immediate wave of red pain. Gripped her heart and squeezed like it was trying to juice her.

Like orange juice.

Ella and her mimosas.

Going from zero to shock in less time than it took to drop the bowl and the bag of food, she fell into the doorjamb.

What she wouldn't give to wail. Sob. Scream.

Instead, she got nothing. Eyes dry as the desert. Insides numb as a sleeping limb. No pins and needles. No nothing.

And the Grand Canyon returned, its vast expanse a deep hole carved by a river that still surged and rushed through the bottom. Continuing to erode the sides, even now.

How to dam such a torrent?

Closing the house up, she left the staff by the front door.

CHAPTER 3

"I think, at some point, we should go back to that island," Mike said. He handed Jack another board.

"That so?" Jack laid it next to the one he'd just nailed into place.

"For one thing, we should make sure it's safe for when the Emerald Isle people come back. It's likely we missed some 'Heads."

Standing, Jack pulled four nails from the tool pouch hanging on his fancy new belt. Jane offered to make him one, but they'd been able to find a perfectly good one in an old tool store across the sound. He'd even found a couple 'Heads to kill. It'd been a good day.

"Dad?"

"Sorry, Mike," he said, lifting the nails. "It's a good idea." Not that he wanted to ever see that island again. When he arrived, prisoner or not, things had been pretty OK. But when he left. Boy. Were they ever not.

And it got worse from there.

He stuck the nails in his mouth and bent to hammer the board in. He'd settled for resurfacing and replacing only the damaged boards on the small dock. The large one would have to wait, Jane needed a new roof.

"Let me hold the nails. You take this." Mike held a sucker at eye level.

Mystery flavor. The boy knew him. He did always like a mystery.

He traded three nails for the sucker. He saved one back to hammer into place, but first he unwrapped the sucker and stuck it in his mouth.

The sticky sweet flavor crowded his tongue. Made it seem larger than it was. His saliva harder to swallow. Taking another nail from Mike, he popped the sucker out. Without any preamble, a memory hit him with all the force of a Mack truck.

After a successful raid on a grocery store, Michael, no more than five, sat with a bag full of suckers just like this in his lap. Grinning down at it, he caressed it. Jack helped him open it, and Mike gave one to him and one to his pregnant Mom. That was the first time he'd given out candy, and the first time any of them had had any since they'd left their apartment over a year prior.

And that silly happy memory full of sugar and sweetness was now ruined too. Because there she was, as she had been. But over her smiling face, he superimposed the grin she'd worn as she'd told him he'd enjoyed it. As she stared into his eyes, reminding him she owned him.

With a shudder he disguised under a cough, he finished nailing down the new board, and they moved on to the next repair. By the time they finished the dock, he'd been able to get past any real thoughts and concentrated on the physical strain. His back wasn't happy about all the bending over, and after a while he ended up crouching on the pier as Mike handed the boards to him. Even his ankles hurt when they were done, but it was the good and solid ache one got from manual labor.

Mike carrying the bulk of the tools and the rest of the boards, they walked back from the end of the pier. "Tomorrow, you want to go to Emerald Isle?"

"I don't know, son. I'd kind of like to start on the roof."

Mike bumped him. "Let the roof wait. We should check the island."

Jack stopped, eyelids drooping. "You're right. We'll do it first." His mouth stretched into a real smile. "Hey, Mike."

"Hey, Dad?"

"I'm glad we got past that whole thing. I don't know if there's enough apologies in the world, but—"

"But you've already said all the ones you need to say," Mike interrupted. "That's days gone by. No more apologies needed." He shuffled his foot. "I can't blame you for my mistakes. That's not very grown-up of me. If anyone owes apologies, it's me."

Since Mike's hands were full, Jack threw his arm around his shoulders and pulled him in. "You're a good man, Michael Cooke."

"I learned from the best," he said, leaning his face into Jack's shoulder.

After dropping Mike at his house, Jack dragged his tired feet along to his own. He'd kept the one Scott gave him. Though he'd spent only one night in it, it had its own perimeter fence and bars inside the doors. All of them. Someone like him once lived here. Maybe he should ask Scott about that.

Maybe not.

As he opened the front door, Jane's laughter crowded his ears.

He hung his tool belt by the door and followed her laughter through the house until he found her upstairs in the baby's room. Since little Katie still slept in the same bed with them, and was still too small to do, well, much of anything, they didn't spend much time in this room.

"Hey honey," Jane said, without looking up, "look what I got from the nursery."

A swing, no taller than his knee, rocked with the baby inside. Two toys, stuffed parrots, hung in front of her face. She stared at them, taking the occasional swipe. Looking for all the world like a kitten. Jane giggled each time she did.

"Mike and I are going to get a group together, go over to Emerald Isle tomorrow or the next day." He eased down onto the rocker and removed one boot. "Gonna make sure it's clean of 'Heads and ready for anyone who wants to come home."

Jane spun on her ass to face him. Knees drawn up to her chest, she wrapped her arms around them. "You guys are good, then?"

"We are, Jane. We really are." He pried the other boot off and wiggled his toes. Nice to let them breathe.

"Good." After sliding the baby out of the swing, she stood. "Come out here. We got a surprise for you."

Her hip sway mesmerizing, he followed her out of the room. The house settled with comfortable warmth, and the mellow creaking of worn hardwood followed with them as well.

She laid the baby in a playpen in the living room and stroked the side of her head. "Be right back, littles." She grabbed Jack's hand and tugged him toward the kitchen. "Come see."

On the stove, two pots sat on the burners. One with a red streak down the side, drying the way blood did. Flaky and deepening from red to rust.

The sight put him in mind of 'Heads and bleeding, but the scent wafting from the pots pulled him by the nose. He flashed on his favorite cartoon rabbit once upon a time, floating through the air at the smell of carrots.

Lifting the lid of the pot without the red stain, she waved her hand across the top, wafting the scent closer to him. "I know you like to do the cooking, but I wanted to make you something. Addy helped, so I'm sure it'll be both edible and palatable."

He peeked in the pot. Long noodles, red sauce, some wild mushrooms. Grinning, he met her eyes. "Where'd you get the tomatoes? It's not their season."

"Come on, Jack," she said, lowering the lid to the counter, "you know we can get more than we need here, any time of year. These guys are well practiced at having a stock of preserves on hand." She opened a cabinet. "Bowl or plate?"

Stepping closer, he ran his hand up her back and leaned his face into her shoulder. For the first time in weeks, he didn't consider what he was doing before he touched her, and the warmth of her spread from his chest outward.

With a smile, she twisted around and leaned against the counter. Hooking two fingers in his belt loop, she tugged.

Pressing her against the counter, and before anything else intruded, he kissed her. The silky lips that tasted like Jane. Felt like Jane. Her balanced reply giving him as much as he gave her. He drifted with her, the goose bumps dancing up his spine when she sank her hand into his hair and cupped the back of his head.

But the powerful scent of the spaghetti sauce climbed into his nose. Her arms encircled him. And the heat rushed through him. The sensation of being trapped, by the smells, her arms, his own self, it overpowered him.

Choking down a whimper, he grimaced and stepped back. Fighting the urge to turn away from her altogether, he settled for looking at the floor.

"What's wrong?"

Frown going deeper into his cheeks, he cast about for a reason.

Say something, idiot. She's going to worry.

"It, uh, hasn't been four weeks yet, has it?"

A slow grin crossing her lips, she stepped closer. "The doc did say we only had to wait until I was ready. Four weeks was a suggestion." Taking a handful of his shirt in her fist, she closed the distance again. "I don't think four weeks is set in stone. In fact," she said, kissing him under the jaw, "Three is plenty. More than enough."

He closed his eyes. He could imagine nothing better than to be with her.

And nothing worse.

Say something, man. Anything. Get out of it.

He kissed her on the forehead. "I'm twelve kinds of wiped out from today, baby. Can I get a rain check?" Gripping the hand holding his shirt, he winced at his sweaty palms.

Hopefully she wouldn't notice.

One side of her mouth lifted. "Course you can." Standing on tiptoe, she kissed him on the cheek. "Let me get you a plate."

As she turned her back, he clutched his stomach. The fact he hadn't curled into a ball of righteous self-pity the way he had on the train was a small milestone in itself. Maybe he'd be OK. Maybe.

* * *

The voice came from the door. "It's been a little more than a week, Melinda," a man said. "Are we having any luck?"

"Did you get me some incubators?" Melinda asked, eyes glued to the microscope in front of her.

"The medical equipment kind or the human kind?" He slid a stool across the floor. Its metal legs scraped with a high-pitched squeal.

She winced. "The human kind, Cormac. I need the human kind. These embryos will not grow in a machine."

Cormac, brown eyes set deep in his pale, almost sallow face, leaned on the table and crossed one knee over the other. He tapped his knee with one slender finger. "Do you think these will be immune?"

Sighing, she stood. How much to tell the prick? "Statistical analysis shows a good chance."

"What, fifty-fifty? That's what it seems like to me." He poked his lip out, lifting the hand he'd been tapping his knee with, and tapped his teeth instead.

Setting Melinda's own on edge.

"You know what, Cormac McNamara, you didn't do the analysis, so get your skinny ass out of it," Lash said, sauntering through the door.

God, she looked as good as she had when Melinda left. But they hadn't parted on the best of terms, and while Lash had been cordial this last week, and a couple times downright friendly, she hadn't offered to come visit. Then again, Melinda hadn't offered the opposite, so whose move was it? Were there any moves to be made after so much had happened in the last few years?

"You know, Ilasha," Cormac said, "I get pretty tired of your attitude. Especially coming from a glorified secretary. I should go tell Anthony about it. He's your boss, ain't he?" He stood, arms crossed. Although he was no taller than Melinda herself, he puffed out his chest in an attempt to intimidate.

Melinda fought a giggle. Nobody was intimidating either woman in this room.

Lash held the door open. "Well, boy, don't let the door hit you on the way."

With a chuffing sound, Cormac smoothed his slick hair and stalked through the door. "One of these fuckin' days, Lash," he began.

"You won't do shit," Melinda said, beating Lash to the punch. "And you know it."

Ilasha flashed her a heart-melting glance. Gratitude mixed with admiration mixed with affection. A cat-like grin crossing her lips, she closed the door in Cormac's face with deliberation.

Grinning wider, she faced Melinda and leaned against it. "Got some successful embryos?"

Taking a few deep breaths, slowing her racing heart, Melinda nodded. "Think so. We'll need to freeze these until that idiot gets me some incubators." Thanking Lash for her help on the tip of her tongue, instead she sat on her stool and went back to the microscope. She wouldn't be the first to crack.

Lash pulled up the same stool Cormac had, legs scraping across the floor again. But she pulled it up far closer. Her knee brushed Melinda's thigh. "We gonna talk or not?"

Melinda swallowed. Blinking fast before her eyes clouded, she frowned. Getting what she wanted was easy, as long as she knew what she wanted.

With Lash, she was never sure.

Well, that was a lie. She was sure. Just afraid. Not a sensation she was used to.

She didn't look up from the scope. "It's what we're doing right now, isn't it?"

"You know that's not what I mean." Lash sighed. "I heard about Burke."

Melinda's head snapped up. Eyes fighting to adjust to the quick change from bright microscope light to harsh fluorescents, she blinked. "What do you mean?"

"I see you blushing. What I mean," she said, laying a hand on Melinda's knee, "is I heard you killed him. You know who he was, right?"

"I guess not." She shook her head. Of course, Lash knew why she blushed. The woman kept her ear to the ground. Being the entirety of the secretary pool for the Molehill had its advantages, one of them being access to information about absolutely everything that went on both inside and out. Though who, besides her family and their friends, knew she killed Burke was a question that would need answering. Someone had to have told Lash. It got back here somehow.

"Well, he was pretty high up in IRF. Pretty high."

"So?"

"So"—she leaned in—"I hear IRF feels like it might be time to go to war. We need to get this vaccine thing worked out, Em."

Melinda choked around the heart that'd found its way to her throat. "I need those incubators. If we can synthesize immunity, we'll blow IRF out of the water."

"Do they have your vaccine research?"

"Some of it. As little as I needed to share with them so they'd allow me free rein to study the girl and her baby."

Lash chuckled. "The girl has a name. Jane Doe, right? Or is it Cooke, now?"

Clearing her throat, Melinda grimaced.

"That's your husband she's with, right? How's that sit with you?"

A lie crossed her mind. But it didn't matter. She'd never been able to lie to her. "I don't even want him back. But it sits with me like an overturned cement truck. Heavy, sideways, and wrecked."

"Well damn, Em. Come over later. You know where I am. We'll see if we can't right the truck."

Despite what she'd said earlier, Melinda watched Ilasha swing her ass as she walked out.

* * *

An insistent knock rattled Addy's front door. She didn't know how long she'd sat staring out the window, but she clutched the pillow next to her and threw it across the room. The pillow that had, until recently, been Dean's.

It smacked into a large shell she found one of the days she and Mom went fishing. What Mom had called a lightning whelk. The shell fell to the floor and broke. A piece skidded away.

"Crap," she muttered, rubbing her face and stumbling to the door. She yanked it open. She hadn't bothered with the damned bar.

"Hello, Adelaide. Hope I'm not disturbing you," Scott said.

"Fine. Come in." Without waiting for him to enter, she headed for the kitchen.

He caught the screen before it slammed back into the frame and closed the front door. The metal of the bar scraped against the hooks as he lowered it in.

"What do you want, Scott?" She sat her percolating coffee pot on the stove. It wasn't as efficient as the press, but something about the press made her think of Dean. In some roundabout way. So she'd gone back to the percolator. "Be damned if he's going to ruin coffee for me, the son of a bitch."

A chair scraped away from the table. "What was that?"

"Nothing. Want some coffee?"

"I'll take a cup."

Addy started the coffee. She imagined him sitting there with his hand under his chin, watching her with those bright grey-blue eyes of his. Probably smiling a little, because whatever he was here to ask for, he was sure to get his way.

That's what he thinks.

Addy sat two cups on the counter. She leaned against it and crossed her arms. "Since you neglected to answer me. What do you want?"

"Let's have coffee first, then we can talk about it. Are you going to get another dog?" he asked, glancing at Data's bowls.

"Fuck's sake Scott, just tell me what you're here for." She yanked a chair to two legs and huffed into it.

He lifted his missing arm. "I can't do this job for much longer, Addy."

"You're quitting?"

"Not right now. But soon, yes."

Dread settled over her brow and worked its way down. "Why?"

He massaged his shoulder. "Considering my injury, I am still capable of administrative duties, but not much more. A leader who cannot fight with his people is no leader at all."

The dread wormed its way into her stomach and settled there like a stone. "One, that's complete and utter self-pitying bullshit, and you know it. And two, who's going to replace you?"

He deliberately ignored her first statement and skipped on to the second. "I haven't worked that through yet. The coffee's done," he said, pointing his forehead at the stove.

Gulping, she stood and pulled the pot off the burner. The piping hot coffee half poured, half steamed out of the pot and into their cups.

A month ago she would have already told him no. Knowing full well she'd do it.

This was not a month ago.

Holding her breath, she sat again and folded her arms over her stomach. Considered asking him not to ask. But all her assertiveness dried up and left. Chipped away by Ella's and Dean's blood. Mingling on the ground and sucking the life right out of her. Yasuo's fear like a vampire of the spirit. Mom yanking her heart through her chest as she flew away, leaving them one, last, terrible gift. And as though the universe was never out of jokes, Dean punched a hole into the empty heart and pulled out the flesh remaining.

She had nothing left to give.

And yet, here was Scott.

"You know who I'd like it to be." He blew across the top of his coffee.

She stared at her own coffee, the steam floating away in slow wisps, the oils on the surface swirling in circles. Her head shook from side to side. She didn't ask it to. It just did.

"Adelaide, please consider it. You know how everyone here feels about you."

Eyes fixed on the coffee, her head continued to shake.

"It doesn't have to be right away," he went on. "I'd ease you into it. First, you can be my lieutenant again. I'll teach you the additional work required over time."

"I can't, Scott." She cleared her throat. On the tip of her tongue rested, well, everything the last couple weeks brought her. It bunched up in her gut with the dread.

"I heard about what happened with Dean," he said, laying his hand over hers. "I'm sorry. I am certain it was...ill-advised."

She laughed without humor. "That's one way to put it."

He patted her hand. "There's my Lou. Look, I know it's been a tough few weeks. I won't ask for your decision right now."

"I won't do it."

He swallowed the rest of his coffee. "Get back to me when you think you're ready. You make the best coffee on the island, Addy. Has anyone told you that?"

"Why don't you ever listen when I talk?" She shook her head. One side of her mouth turned up.

"That is untrue, and you know it. I listen perfectly well. Come see me next week, all right?" He headed for the front door. "Get some exercise. Walk. It's good for the soul. See you soon."

And he was gone.

CHAPTER 4

Celia plunked down next to Addy and motioned over the bar. "Hey, Christian, whatever she's having."

The taciturn bartender reached behind the bar and pulled down the vodka. Measuring out a shot, he dumped it over ice and poured some cranberry juice over both.

Taking it, Celia nodded to him and spoke to Addy. "Heavy drinks tonight, huh?"

"Don't give me shit." She tapped Celia's glass with her own. "Just drink."

Eyebrows turned up, Celia drank and shook her head. "Goddamn, Christian, distill this yourself?"

The bald bartender wandered over and leaned on the bar. "I did. Problem?"

Celia coughed. "No, no problem. Strong. Good job."

He made a finger gun at her and walked away, smiling.

"Man knows his liquor," Celia said, sipping her drink again.

"How?" Addy asked.

"What's that?"

"How does he know? Who taught him?"

Celia shook her head. "When I first got here, there was another guy. I don't remember his name, that was a long time ago. I guess he taught Christian. He's the one who found this." She waved her hand at the bar top and large mirrored back. "That's his old radio, if I remember right."

Addy leaned on her hand. "How long ago was that?"

Heavy-lidded eyes narrowed. "You asking when I moved here? Trying to dig up my back story?"

Grinning, Addy sipped. "I've known you forever, Celia. Till a year ago, I didn't even know you came from the East Coast.

Cut me some slack," she said, leaning over. She bumped Celia with her shoulder. "I'm curious."

Chuckling, Celia took another drink and called Christian over once again. "When did I get here, Christian?"

He laughed. "Weren't more than a little spit. Meaner than —"

"A wolverine," Addy interrupted.

Christian gripped the towel over his shoulder. "She ain't changed much, just got bigger. Couldn't have been more than eleven or twelve."

"There you go. A kid. Thanks." She waved Christian away.

He side-eyed her and walked off, pretending to wipe a spot down the bar. Eavesdropping, for sure.

"You're not from here," Addy said. "Where are you from, then?"

"North of here. It was a rough time. My parents. Well." She took a drink, grimacing as it went down. "I ran away from home." She shrugged. "The virus hit. Here I am."

Addy took a drink. "Did you never see your parents again?"

"No, I did not. I wasn't about to go back to that big city after the virus hit. Then, I don't know." She punched Addy in the shoulder. A playful tap. "I found new people. They're probably dead, anyway, my parents."

Celia was right, they probably were. Addy scratched at a spot on the bar.

Christian leaned on the bar in front of them. "Ladies, I hate to interrupt. But." He pointed behind them with his eyes.

Addy turned, attempting to follow his gaze. She squinted to look past all the people gathered in the middle of the bar, laughing and talking and smoking and drinking. After the sun went down, it almost always got crowded in the room. Surely, that wasn't what Christian was pointing out.

As her vision narrowed, a shape coalesced in the far corner. The light diffused before it got there, but a man sat deep in the corner of the room, nursing a beer.

"Go and get him, Addy," Celia said. "Don't let him drink alone."

Addy scoffed. "I'm not his babysitter." She spun back to the bar, before he looked up and caught her staring.

"OK."

Exhaling, Addy smiled. "Thank you. There's no sense in—"

Celia stood and walked away before she finished.

Great.

Back to the room, Addy polished off her drink and asked Christian for another.

Staring at her through the glass he'd been drying, he lifted his lips in half a grin. "Might want to slow down, Lou."

"Don't fucking call me that. Get me a drink." She stared at a spot on the bar.

Without another word, Christian poured the drink and walked away.

She sipped, still staring at the spot, regret seeping up her cheeks in red splotches she could see in the mirror.

Celia sat next to her again. Matt pulled the stool up on Cee's other side and sat his beer on the bar. Christian served him another and left before Addy had a chance to make her apology.

"Fine," she muttered, taking another drink.

"Hi, Matt. Thanks for joining us," Celia said, leaning onto Addy's shoulder and speaking in a falsetto. She switched to Matt's shoulder and lowered her voice a register. "Thanks for having me, Addy." She sat up straight and swigged her vodka. "Now that's settled, can we loosen up, please? This is a bar, not a funeral home."

Addy frowned. "A what what?"

"Girl. I don't know how I feel about you not knowing that one. Moving on. Are the guys treating you all right, Matt?"

He shrugged, trying to hide a wince with a pull from his beer.

"How's your back?" Addy asked. "You still have a fever?"

Narrowing his eyes, he pressed his lips together and glared.

Brow scrunched into an angular V, Addy opened her mouth to tell him she was, once again, trying to look out for her friend. Not baby him.

Celia unsnapped her knife and laid it on the bar. "Here, we'll cut the tension with this. Last one standing doesn't have to be nice."

Addy deflated. "Sorry, Cee. Long day."

"You're telling me. Tomorrow's going to be even longer."

"Why is that?" Matt asked.

"Addy's brother wants to take a team over to Emerald Isle. Make sure it's all cleaned up for when the residents come back from Virginia."

Matt jumped, eyes closing for a split second. He polished off the beer. "I take it you're going."

"You know. Mike asked. I know the place. Might as well." She grinned. "That reminds me. Hey, Addy, why don't we tell him about the time we cleaned out a whole block for us and Jane and her parents?"

Addy chuckled. "Me and Mike whined for days about wanting a roof for a while. So Dad made it happen. Seems like we had just met Cee. It was the first time we went on a raid like that with her," she said, leaning around Celia and speaking to Matt.

He sat forward. "What happened?"

"Got the damn place clear and slept there for weeks." Celia laughed. "I found out real quick how these people could get whatever they put their minds to."

Drinking and laughing, Celia and Addy swapped stories from Addy's teens for hours. Matt laughed along, asking questions here or there but mostly listening. His smile came easier as time went on, and as it did, so did Addy's.

At the end of one particularly rousing story during which Celia ended up standing on the bar and thrusting into the air with her knife as illustration, she hopped down and wobbled. Her lids drooped. "I gotta find my bed, y'all."

Addy laughed. "Cee, you never say y'all. You definitely need sleep."

"Need help getting home?" Matt asked, half standing.

Celia waved a hand. "No. I got it." She pointed to Christian. "Yo. Christian. Lates." She wobbled out the door and into the night. Moonlight bounced off her shiny dark hair before the door closed on her drunk ass.

"You kinda let me and Cee take up the whole night with our exploits."

He twirled his beer bottle. "My teen years were a bit different from yours, Addy."

She sipped her own drink. "You got to look at the stars with her. Was it fun?"

"Was it fun for you, when you were a kid?" He slid onto Cee's stool, dragging the empty bottle with him.

"Course. She used to tell me about all the constellations and all the galaxies we couldn't see. And the one we can." She named it.

"Andromeda," Matt said, speaking at the same time as her.

She laughed. "She always talked about how much people could do when they worked together. How we could change the world."

He rolled the bottle between his fingers. "She didn't just talk about it. I watched her do it. She's not a one-woman show. It took a whole team of people to come as far as they have." He snuck a peek at Addy. "With perfecting the Cure. And the vaccine. She's one piece of the machine."

"I don't want to talk about that right now," Addy said, finishing her drink, the weight of that day on the hospital lawn, when her mother left her bleeding in the snow, heavy in her stomach with the alcohol. "Can we talk about something else?"

Matt asked Christian for another drink. Swallowing half of it in one go, he glanced at Addy with the side of his eye. Lower lid red.

Oh good lord, no. They couldn't talk about Ella.

She blurted the first thing that came to mind that wasn't Dean or Ella. "Did Mom ever show you *Star Trek*?"

He laughed. "Cheese central? Yeah, of course. Who do you think showed it to, um…" He stopped and cleared his throat.

But instead of lingering on the name of the ghost on his lips, she pushed forward. "What? Cheese? You don't like it?"

And until Christian told them it was time to pack it up, they debated the virtues and downfalls of *Star Trek*, sci-fi, and television in general. What little experience either of them had with it.

Booted out into the night, Addy opened her nostrils wide and took in the odor of the sound.

"Extra fishy tonight," Matt said. "But at least the moon is full."

"That makes up for the smell."

Chatting about the island, the moon, and anything but the people they'd lost, they made their way to Addy's.

Halfway up the walk, she stopped. "Make sure you change those bandages."

From the road, Matt sketched a salute. "And take my antibiotics. Yes, ma'am."

Addy gave him half a curtsy and stumbled the rest of the way up the walk. As she reached the steps, Matt called her name.

She turned slow enough to keep from falling over. "What's up?"

"You gonna take that lieutenant job everybody here says you're so good at?"

She shook her head. "Can't."

"Yeah." He shuffled a foot. "Night."

After waving at his back, she tottered up the stairs and let herself in the house.

* * *

Katherine whimpered, jerking Jack from sleep.

"Shh, baby. It's OK," Jane whispered. The whimpering stopped, and the baby began taking long, regular breaths. Sucking from deep within her mouth. "There you go," Jane said, sleep taking her voice over again.

Laying a hand on her hip, Jack sat up. "You need anything?"

"No, honey. Go back to sleep." The full moon shining through the window illuminated the side of her face, her closed eyes.

He eased from under the covers. "I'll get you some water."

Jane exhaled through her nose, short and sharp. "I'll be asleep before you get back. Don't bother, really."

"It'll just take a second. You need water to replace what the baby's taking," he said, feet landing on the cold floor. It froze them from the bottom up, and he took a moment to relish the painful pricks racing along the soles.

He crept down the stairs and through the house, checking every window. After ensuring both doors remained chained and barred, the yard and street silent and still, he shuffled to the kitchen. He stared through the window over the kitchen sink, the water cracking the ice as it passed over it. The sound gave him no joy. No satisfaction. It was just ice.

Glass in hand, he toured the living room again, checking the windows once more. He'd have to check upstairs as well. Couldn't be too careful.

But there on the end table, he'd lain his clean gun. He'd cleaned it tonight as Jane sat knitting and the baby kicked her little feet in her swing. A fire crackled merrily in the fireplace too, and he'd come close to something like happiness as they all sat together in silence.

Fresh oil gleamed on the outside of the gun's barrel. He stepped to it, putting the glass down next to it and picking it up, its weight heavy in his hand. Not as heavy as some he'd carried, like the revolver, but the black .45 got the job done every time. Few firearms had been as true to him as this one.

He turned it over, considering the weight. Its easy-pull trigger. How the oil would taste.

"Jack?"

From far away, her voice echoed into the dark room. He rubbed a finger over the engraving on the barrel, tracing the tip of his thumb along the esses.

"Jack?" From the top of the stairs. "You coming back?"

Her voice held no fear; no whine tinged it. But there was need. Like there'd been the first time he'd heard her shouting his name as she closed in on him like a freight train. The night they'd been abducted together. Like when she'd called him back from the dark as he nearly got eaten by a fresh 'Head, one of his own friends. Over and over, she called him back.

As quiet as he could, he laid the gun on the table and wiped his hand on his shorts. Picking up her water, he headed for the stairs.

She stood halfway down the staircase, her legs pale in the silver moonlight. "Everything all right?"

He met her halfway up. When she slid her hands around his shoulders, he let her pull him in. Still a step below her, he laid his head on her breast. And smiled at the milky scent.

"Are you all right?"

Reluctant to speak a lie, he answered her question with a question. "Why?"

"I don't know." In the dark, her wide green eyes flitted across his face. "You talk to me if you need to, OK? It's what I'm here for."

Hand in her hair, he stood on his toes and kissed her. Quickly. Before she felt him tremble. If she hadn't woken, what would he have done?

Living like this was impossible.

"Come on back to bed, before Katie gets cold," he said, handing her the glass. Hand in the small of her back, he followed her up the stairs, and when she grasped his hand and pulled him into the bedroom, he slipped under the covers with her without checking the windows as he'd planned. She curled around the baby, and he curled around her, arm squeezing her waist and face buried in her hair.

He whispered he loved her a hundred times before falling back to sleep, safe and warm and rescued from the cold. For at least one more night.

* * *

Sitting on the top of the prison wall, feet hanging over the side, Jack watched the group as they exterminated the rest of the 'Heads. Dozens had fallen into the moat at some point or another, like it collected them. Some of them got so waterlogged from the constant filling and draining of the moat with the tide, they couldn't get to their feet anymore. After Celia, Addy, and Jane took out a significant portion of them with their arrows, the rest of the group crawled down into the moat to take care of the rest.

Mike sat next to him. "That's about it, Dad."

Jack jerked his chin. "How's your sister?"

Mike scratched his jaw. "OK, I guess. Think it was good for her to come along. She ordered some people around, you know."

Jack watched her, down in the muck. She almost smiled as she and Celia sliced and diced. Gathering up their arrows as they went.

A small grin stretched his mouth. "I know. Leading them whether she wants to or not." Fingers steepled, he shoved both hands between his knees. "How's Dean?"

"Better than he was a couple days ago. Refuses to see her."

"Shit. I hope he'll change his mind once he gets to feeling better."

"So does she."

His eyes drifted to the window of the cell where he'd first been with Jane.

What a night.

Before Melinda came along and ruined everything.

A smile thought about touching his lips. Three sentiments he wouldn't have expected, even a year ago. Yet here he was.

The smile slipped away.

Feet crunched the sand next to him.

Keeping his eyes on Addy and Celia, he didn't lift his head. Jane's bowstring twanged, and the 'Head behind Addy dropped.

"I'm dead on my feet." She sat next to him and draped her feet over the wall.

He leaned his head on her shoulder. "You were only here for half of it."

"Yeah, well, look at all these people you got to help you," she said, waving her arm. "I remember the seven of us cleaned up a whole block in less time once."

He sat up and grinned.

Flushing, she smiled back. A large, happy thing he hadn't seen on her in weeks.

"We got soft," Mike said, crunching a hard candy. His teeth squealed over it, popping and cracking the candy to bits. "Plus, this island is a few miles long."

Leaning in front of Jack, she pinched her lips and narrowed her eyes. "That wasn't long after I met you guys." She pointed her forehead at Mike and spoke from beneath her brow. "You were already soft."

He chuckled, kicking the wall and gazing off across the surf.

"You weren't," she said, catching Jack's eyes. Her own eyes sparkled. "I mean, Mike wasn't really, either, I was teasi—"

Jack caught her in a kiss. He floated away for a few moments, and when he let her go, her cheeks and the tip of her nose were red. He brushed a hair from her forehead. "Tomorrow, why don't we take Katie out to the beach for a bit?"

"What, you mean you'll stop killing 'Heads or working on the roof for two seconds so I can see you?"

He nodded.

"Sounds good, love." She stood, holding a hand out to him.

He took it. Standing and ineffectively brushing sand from his pants, he turned to help Mike up.

Who'd disappeared.

It was a shame. He would like to have seen him one more time. But some things couldn't be helped.

He leaned into Jane's ear. "Maybe when I get back, I can take you up on that rain check too."

She kissed him in the soft space behind his jaw. Her lips light as a hummingbird. "Sounds even better."

Hand in hand, they walked down to the beach with everyone else.

Next to the surf, he kissed her on the cheek. "I'll see you there."

The fine line appeared between her brows. "You're not coming with us?"

"I'll take one of the canoes they left here last year. We could always use the extra boats."

She took a step toward him. "I'll come with you then."

"No, you go with them. They've got the motorboats, and you should get back to Katie." He peeked at her breasts. "Looks like you need to feed her soon."

She cocked a grin. "You just wanted to look at my tits."

"True. But—"

"You're right. I do. I'll see you at home," she said, raising to her toes to kiss him on the temple.

As Addy and Celia walked past, Jane squeezed his shoulder before quick-stepping to catch them.

Adelaide glanced over her shoulder, tired eyes drooping. Raising a hand to him, she kept walking.

Though she didn't see it, he raised a hand and fought the urge to run to her. Gather his little girl in his arms and tell her everything was OK.

It most certainly was not OK. He used to be able to lie to her about it, it's what you did as a dad, but he couldn't anymore. He'd lost his usefulness in that department.

And in so many other ways.

Watching until they all disappeared around the curve of the island, he listened to the ocean crash against the sand. The great living thing that'd once tried to swallow him whole. He'd been ready to let it, if it chose to, but that hadn't been in the plan. Nor had it been in the cards.

The ocean released him. And that was OK. He couldn't sully her with his death. It wouldn't be fair to her beauty. She deserved better. Brave sailors. Swarthy pirates. Dreamy explorers.

Not the likes of him.

He trudged back up the beach and into the prison. His limp slight, he descended the stairs Renzo once forced him down. That limp and the permanent bullet in his leg constant reminders of the hospital that'd become his own endless prison.

The tide had already come in. Soon, the water in the moat would be several feet deep. Even though all these 'Heads were dead, again, most people wouldn't come into deep water with bodies floating in it. It went against their nature.

He'd promised Jane he'd be back soon. Even made plans with her so she'd go ahead and head back. He'd have hours to himself out here. Not that he'd need them. But it'd be at least that long until they found him.

The gun hung heavy at his side all day. Trying to chase the thought off, he'd thrown himself into cleaning up the island. He'd forget about it just long enough to remember her face instead, stomach revolting. Fists clenching. Teeth grinding so hard they nearly broke. Just being on the island was enough to remind him of that woman.

And the guilt. Good lord.

There were times when he forced himself to think of Andrew because it elevated the guilt to something manageable. At least that had a handle on it he could grab.

Slogging through the water and muck in the moat, legs wet to his calves, he remembered the damned jumpsuit. The one that'd been two sizes too small. The legs rode up to somewhere on his calf. It'd still be dry right now.

He chuckled. Such a good night. Before Melinda came back to life.

You know what you should have done, Jack? Should have made sure she was dead in the first place. Should have gone back to bury her.

Anything that happened because she'd been brought back from that day at the sporting goods store where she died was solely his fault.

The experiments she'd been doing when he found her. All the people she'd killed or turned into half Dead Head, half human. Coming between him and Jane, breaking Mike's heart. Even Dean's and Ella's deaths could be laid at her feet. Countless others.

In the end, what she'd done to him—what he'd let her do— was inconsequential compared to that.

He looked up. He'd made his way into the cell where he'd last been unaware she was alive. Where, in so many ways, his life had changed for good. He didn't have to look down to know the weight in his hand, the way it lay across his palm all smooth and heavy, was his .45.

The sun had almost set. The day done, black water lapped against the walls of the moat. The only ones not out of reach now, the dead who floated out there. Everyone else, too far away to help. Too far away to stop him.

At least, if he did it right, he'd never have to wake up again.

CHAPTER 5

As she closed the cryo door on the last of the embryos, Melinda kissed her fingertips and laid them on the outside of the door. With the other hand, she set the temperature on the digital meter next to the drawer to keep the embryos in stasis until she was ready for them.

"Sleep well, babies," she whispered. "You're going to save the world. Just wanted you to know."

Smiling, she glided down the hall. She might not have been able to get Jack back, she might never, but she'd always have a piece of him.

Her lopsided grin slid off the edge of her mouth.

He's the father of your children. How could you.

"What?" Her voice echoed off the rounded walls. She jumped.

Straightening her shoulders, she glanced up at the next intersection of sloping hallways. Lash didn't say she'd moved, so her room must still be down...

Melinda inspected the halls to her left and right.

"Last time I was here, they didn't all look so much alike," she muttered.

"Shouldn't talk to yourself, General. People will begin to wonder," a voice said behind her.

Heart leaping into her throat, she frowned. "Sorry, sir. It's been a while. I got turned around."

Clasping his hands behind his back, Anthony filled the hallway. "Never happened to you before." He leaned left. "Walk with me, Melinda."

She hurried to catch up as he strode down the hall, hands still clasped behind his back.

"I suppose you know we know about what happened with Burke."

"It was necessary to facilitate my escape from the compound. I do not regret it."

"I'm sure you don't. But it was regrettable." He stopped, staring ahead. "We could have used him to gain information from IRF." He glared at her from the side of his eye. "And, we could have used him to have our test population escorted back to their home on the island. Now, we've lost them. Even if they return to the island, I suspect your facilities there will be of little future use. No," he said, walking on, "your presence on Emerald Isle is at an end."

She caught up to him and matched his pace. "I have newer vaccine research. And twenty-three successful embryos. I need incubators and we can get started synthesizing immunity."

He stopped again, grin lifting one corner of his mouth.

His flat eyes threw her off-balance. Throat tight, she waited for him to speak again. He had something to say, it was all over his face.

"You bring me one sample of the immune blood. One tiny, stinking vial. And expect me to think you can do it again."

"I can," she said, standing straight and clasping her own hands behind her back. She leaned into his space. "You know I can."

He shook his head. "What can you tell me about the immune child? The collection method of your donor sperm? Your proposal to create immunity was interesting, I will admit."

So he saw the merit of her plan, after all. Crafty bastard, trying to get her off her footing.

She smiled, the corners of her mouth lifting independent of each other. "Twenty incubators. Fifty percent control. Fifty percent given the vaccine prior to implantation. Twenty-five percent infected with live virus at six months." Taking another step closer, she widened her eyes and trapped his. "We can create immunity. I am certain." Backing up a step, she lowered her head. "I've done it once already. I can do it again."

Anthony blew a breath out his lips. "You don't even have a perfect vaccine."

"It's now approaching ninety-eight percent efficacy. That's incredible for a vaccine."

Stepping into her space, Anthony grasped her shoulder. Warm hand, but a firm grip. "You keep working on the vaccine. Someone else will handle the embryos."

"What?" Her shrill shout bounced off the walls and drilled into her ears. "You can't do that, Charles. This is my study. Those are my embryos. You have no idea what I went through to get them."

His fingers dug into her shoulder. Clipped and manicured nails pinched the skin, the joint creaking under his grip.

She fought a grimace and won.

"Those are Talus's eggs. These are their facilities. Of which, I am in charge. And my orders stand as I have stated." He pinched harder. "Do you have a problem with that, General?"

Yes. Yes, I do. Those are my *babies.*

She glared at him but didn't protest again.

He released her, smoothing her shirt. "Take a week off, General. You deserve it." Walking away, he spoke over his shoulder. "You've done so much for us. Don't ever think we've forgotten."

She stood, rooted to the center of the corridor, as he disappeared into the dark.

* * *

Dragging her feet across the dock, Addy headed for home.

"Adelaide."

Stopping, she looked up. In the dusky light, she made out broad shoulders. Of course, only one person had shoulders that broad. "Hey, Renzo. What's going on?"

"Listen, I've got supplies rounded up. People too. I talked to Scott." He crossed his arms. "He told me you won't take the lieutenant job."

A wave of people coming in from Emerald Isle broke as they went around the two of them.

"If you're not going to take the job here, why don't you come with us? We could sure use your help."

"Hey, Renzo," Matt said, walking past, "how are things?" He stuck out his hand, those parenthetical smile lines of his framing his mouth.

The big man shook. "About ready to go. You coming to Magnolia with us?"

Dropping his hand like it was on fire, Matt shook his head so hard his short hair flew. "No can do, man. Sorry." He started to walk away.

For a bare moment, Addy considered stopping him. But why? She didn't want to go either. Back to that place? Where they'd lost Ella? Where they'd lost Dean?

And she'd lost her mom again, and again, and again in that place.

She followed Matt. "I can't help you, Renzo. I'm sorry."

Renzo's feet hit the dirt as he jogged to catch up to her. "You sure? What else are you going to do?"

"Fuck, Zo, I have no goddamned clue," she said, voice raised more than she'd intended. Impossible to recapture the words and stuff them back in her mouth, she let them hang out there.

Matt turned and walked backward. "Hey, um. We can't go to the mountains, Renzo. Not because we don't want to, but because we already have something we've got to do."

Renzo looked between them both. "That right?"

Matt stopped and waited for them to catch up. When they did, he fell into step with them. "Look," he said, leaning in front of Addy and lowering his voice, "we're not supposed to talk a lot about it. Hush-hush, you know?"

Just as clueless as Renzo, Addy leaned in to listen as well. Whatever yarn he was spinning, it sounded more interesting than sitting around the island twiddling her thumbs.

"I know where the Molehill is. There's a city not far from there. I can't go into details, but we've got to get there and infiltrate the Molehill. It's kinda top-secret work, so," he said, glancing at Addy, "only a couple operatives can go. I shouldn't be talking about it."

Addy grinned. The feeling of tumblers locking into place didn't happen often, but it was a feeling to chase when it did.

The tumblers fell with a great metallic clang, so, lie or no, she chased. "Sorry I yelled at you Zo, I should have told you."

He shrugged. "I get it, Addy. I could come with you guys instead, if you need."

Addy's brownzel eyes met Matt's blues. They shook their heads in unison.

"This is mostly reconnaissance. Pretty boring stuff," Addy said. "I don't think we'll get into too much trouble."

Renzo chuckled. "Lies. But suit yourself. Be seeing you." He stopped and clapped Matt on the shoulder. "Still sorry about your girl."

Matt swallowed, jaw bunching. When he opened his mouth and no sound escaped, he closed it and nodded.

Standing on tiptoes, Addy hugged the big man. "Stay safe. Say hi to the girl and her dog."

Squeezing her bones together in a tight hug, Renzo grunted. "You got it. You stay safe too." He trotted off.

Addy frowned. "Well, that was—"

Matt's retreating back greeted her.

She sighed. "Matthew, I—"

He stopped, eyes wide, face red. Throat working, he stepped toward her. "Don't. Don't call me that, Addy."

Eyes focused on the sweat that'd popped on his brow, she realized what she'd done. Only Ella ever called him by his full name. "Fuck, Matt. I'm sorry. It was an accident."

"Whatever," he said, walking again. His face still red.

She caught up to him. "You're right about the Molehill. You were bullshitting, but I think it's a good idea we gather some intel."

"What the hell. Why not?"

"All right. Don't leave without me. I'll talk to Dad and Scott first thing."

* * *

The door to the cell creaked. A foot scraped across a sandy patch, rasping the sole of the shoe. Only one person would have trudged through the deep water, bodies floating all around.

Jack wanted to smile, though it came out more like a frown. "I know you're there," he whispered, eyes glued to the gun in his hand. The last golden relics of day bounced into the cell, glinting off the shiny metal barrel.

She stepped around the side of the archway. "Jack."

Chest hollow, guilt compounding itself that she'd found him like this, he kept his head lowered. Though, in his mind, he replayed the way he'd crossed the cell to her, once upon a time. "Jane."

Soft feet padded across the stone floor. She knelt next to him. "Are we gonna keep pretending nothing is wrong? Or are you gonna put that gun down and tell me what the hell?"

His fingers went limp, and the gun clattered to the floor. Covering his face instead, the scent of gun oil light in his nose, he closed his eyes.

He'd carried a cloak the last few weeks and it lay over everything, stealing the color from the world and dampening all but the guilt. The world tasted like nothing.

The only things with any flavor were the guilt and the gun oil.

When she slid her arm around his shoulders, tugging, he leaned on her.

The sun sank below the horizon, dragging the cloak with it. Dragging it off his shoulders and down, deep, beneath the ground.

He took a moment to consider that killing himself would have been easier than what he faced now. Telling the truth. Admitting his own weakness. But those were his options.

"We've got a few hours, Jack." Resting her cheek on his head, she brushed the hair away from the side of his neck. "The question is, why?"

"Why what?"

"Why are we here? Why were you ready to eat that gun? Why have you been lying to me?"

He sat up. "What have I lied about?"

"'I'm fine, Jane.' Yeah. You forget how long I've known you. I can see you lying from a mile away."

"What do you want me to say?" He cast his eyes at the floor.

"Tell me why."

Might as well tell her. Maybe she'll do you the favor of shooting you herself.

"I slept with Melinda, Jane."

"When we were split up? I know."

"No. At the hospital. In Magnolia."

Her breath stopped. She stiffened. "You what?"

"I'm sorry. I can't explain how sorry."

She stood. Crossing her arms, she paced. "So why are we here? In this place?"

His shoulders raised and fell an inch. "I saw it sitting down here today, and it seemed like. I don't know. This was the first place you and I were together," he said, unable to look at her as she paced, "and it was the last place we were together before she ruined everything." Avoiding Jane, he took in the walls. Cold water wept between the stones. "Before I left this room that day, she was still perfect. The memory I'd molded in the image of a goddess."

Stopping, Jane stood in the archway, her back to him. "What does that have to do with it?"

Casting his eyes about, unable to take her in, his gaze fell on the gun again.

Climbing to his feet, knees popping and cracking, he took a few steps toward her. Not close enough to touch her. "I didn't. I didn't want to."

She took one large step, erasing the rest of the space between them, her eyes spitting fire. "But you did anyway? In some kind of chivalrous attempt to save me? That's a piss poor excuse, Jack."

"I didn't want to," he whispered, shoulders falling. Poor excuse, indeed. And still, he couldn't look at her.

She ducked, following his sight line until she met it. "I think you need to explain this to me."

Swallowing, he pulled his brows together. "Why? Isn't that enough?" Voice breaking, he turned away from her again.

"Because the people I love end up dead. This might be worse. And I need to know why." Strong as a statue, she didn't break like he had. She stood, defiant, and demanded a reason.

His scalp crawled away from his face, taking the hair with it, and sweat popped out on his forehead.

But when he caught sight of her, arms folded over herself, staring with her fire-breathing eyes and waiting for him to explain, he sank to the floor and told her, from beginning to end, what happened.

How his mind screamed no. How he'd told her no. Begged her. Pleaded with her to stop.

How, despite that, his body betrayed him.

How she'd gotten her samples.

"So," he said, clearing his throat and closing his eyes, "clearly I wanted it. I mean, she couldn't force me, if I hadn't wanted her to."

At some point during the telling, Jane leaned a flashlight against the wall and sat on the cold stone floor with him. Legs crossed, she'd listened, eyes widening. Mouth twisting.

He retrieved the gun and held it out to his furious woman. The one with murder in her eyes.

He assumed. He hadn't looked at her during the whole thing. Not for more than a second or two.

Gentle hands took the gun from him. She slid closer.

He peeked at her, ready to turn his eyes away, but she caught him with her own.

It wasn't murder in them. No, not at all.

She laid the gun in the floor and gave it a push.

It slid into the opposite wall.

Her hands cold, she took one of his in both of hers. Running her thumbs over the top, she tugged. "Look at me, Jack."

He did as he was told.

"What happened to you was not your fault."

"Of course it was. No kind of man would allow that. She must've been right. I wanted—" He stopped. Couldn't finish.

"Jack," she said, tugging his hand again, "there's no other word for it. She raped you."

His breath caught. The coiled spring in his chest loosened enough to release some blood to his brain. "How can you say that? I'm a man, Jane. It's different." He narrowed his eyes. "Isn't it?" The first fluttering of doubt flapped its wings.

Long and slow, she exhaled between tight lips. "I ever tell you why my hermit parents took up with you and your kids?"

Brow furrowed, he shook his head. He opened his mouth to ask why but found the words had dried up.

It didn't matter. She went on. "I was what? Fourteen when we met? Less?"

He asked the guilt to take a hike. He didn't have time to feel bad about their age disparity. Not right now, for Chrissakes.

It slunk around the edges, looking for a way in.

"Just before we met you all, we'd spent a week in this kind of community camp. Kinda weird for Bill and Nancy. You know they weren't that fond of people." When she reached for it, he let her take his other hand. Her hands had warmed now.

And his had stopped sweating.

She blew another breath through her lips. "Haven't talked about this in a while." Favoring him with a crooked smile, she scooted closer. "Anyway. They went down to the river to do some laundry. I stayed at the camp. There were these two boys. I'd seen them around. I guess they were about my age or a little older."

The words to make her stop got stuck in his throat. He didn't want to imagine her, just the girl she was when he met her, going through what she was about to tell him.

How had he never known?

"The second one didn't even have to hold me down. By then, I'd crawled into that place in my mind. Just like you talked about, Jack. Just like it." She met his eyes. "I blamed myself for a long time too. Thought I must've wanted it, since I didn't defend myself. I just. I froze. Thought if I let them do it, they'd leave me alone when they were done." A tear dropped from one eye. "But if Bill and Nancy hadn't packed me up that very night and left, I would have either been raped again or slit those boy's throats in their sleep. Even money." The corner of her mouth turned up. Not a smile. But not a grimace. "Then we met you. And they saw how you were with your kids and saw you could use some help. Same way they could." She glanced around the cell and chuckled. "So. Here we are."

Again, he tried to speak. But so many things wanted to spill out, they all got bottlenecked in his mouth.

"It wasn't my fault." She stopped until she caught his eyes again. "What happened to you, it wasn't your fault. We start there." Releasing his hand, she stroked his cheek. "We work outward from that. I've been through this, Jack. Why do you think I read all those damned dry psychology books?"

He chuckled. The words finally found their way out. "People have different ideas of fun."

"Come here," she said, opening her arms.

He fell into them and crushed her to him. Giving in to her embrace, as much as she gave in to his.

She cradled his head. "We'll get through this."

CHAPTER 6

The rising sun shot daggers into Addy's eyes. Shading them, she stepped onto the porch and locked the door behind her.

"You talk to Scott and Jack?" Matt asked. Pack on his back, he stood at the bottom of the steps with his arms crossed. Rifle hanging on one shoulder.

She answered his question with a question. "Is that my Bowie knife?" She angled her forehead at the knife holstered on his hip.

"You mean my knife?"

Poking out her bottom lip, she puffed out a breath. "Whatever." She hefted her own pack onto her shoulder.

He followed her down the walk. "Did you?"

"I did catch Scott before he went to sleep. If he ever sleeps. You know," she said, with half a grin, "I'm not entirely sure he does."

"He seems the type. What about Jack?"

She frowned. "He wasn't home last night. I just called him. They're down at the dock right now, trying to scare up some breakfast. I gotta make a quick stop first." Her feet angled toward the Big House.

As they approached the front door, Matt slowed. "You think this is a good idea?"

She stopped. "No. You gonna stop me?"

"I'll never get closure, Addy. You go and get yours."

Telling him to take his closure and shove it up his ass one of the many things bouncing around her brain, she left him at the bottom of the walk.

The hallway to the infirmary had always been impossibly long. As she approached the doors with their big, red crosses, her heart beat in her mouth, pounding her brain, and sent the

63

blood hurtling through arteries and veins and capillaries. It took a thousand steps to get to the doors, and when she did, she stopped.

"You can do this, Addy," she whispered, sitting at the table across the hall. Sliding the pack from her shoulders, she took a breath. "You can." Her voice trembled, but it was louder. She stood.

Arm stiff, she shoved the door.

It swung inward and hit someone.

"Oof."

She gave the door a gentle push.

Of course. Because of course.

Dean stood on the other side of it, holding his nose and glaring. The other hand leaned on a cane.

When his eyes fell on her face, his glare relaxed. He paled, breathing shallow. "Addy. Are you OK?"

"Sorry, I. Sorry. Is your nose all right?" Easing the door the rest of the way open, she leaned against it. His wide green eyes never looked so beautiful.

He lowered his hand and looked at it. "No blood. I'm OK." Limping with the cane, he wobbled through the door.

She followed him into the hallway. Her heart grew wings and flew away, leaving her center hollow. Empty. "Are you leaving the infirmary?"

Sitting at the table, he shook his head. "No. Doc wanted me to practice walking with the cane a bit. Wanted me to stretch my legs. Took me a couple days to make it this far. But it's getting better." He gestured at her pack. "Going somewhere?"

"I. Um. Yeah," she said, sitting across from him. "Gonna see what kind of intel I can gather on the Molehill."

Eyes on the floor, he spun the cane in his hands. "Oh." He met her eyes.

She held her breath.

"Be careful." He stood and hobbled down the hall.

As he passed, she couldn't help it. "Ask me to stay." Her voice more of a whine than she'd intended.

"I can't do that," he said, stopping. "I won't."

She stood, invading his space. It was all she could do not to grab him and hold him. "I can't let you go, Dean. Don't ask me to."

On uncertain feet, he backed up a step. "You don't have a choice." He dropped his eyes, lips pinched. "Be careful out there," he repeated.

"Fucking bullshit."

"Addy—"

"It's bullshit, Dean," she said, spinning. Her hair flew into her face, sticking to her cheek. Whenever it was she'd started crying. Again. "You know it is. You still love me."

Mouth a fine white line, he stared. Silent.

"Don't you?" Less whiny than she feared.

He broke eye contact. "You know I do."

"Then what the hell? I mean, I—"

"It's over, Adelaide." He limped away from her.

A flower vase sat on the table. Innocent. Ready to be picked up and hurled at the wall, where it'd shatter into a million pieces.

Instead, fists clenched, she grabbed her pack, twisted on a heel, and stalked back down the hall, out the front door, and past Matt.

He jogged to catch up and fell into step with her. "Get what you wanted?"

Swiping at her face, she brushed the tears from her cheeks with such force one hit him and soaked into his sleeve. "Bullshit. It's bullshit, Matt."

"I'm not gonna argue that. But did you get what you were looking for?"

"I don't fucking know," she said, her heart settling into its accustomed place. The muscles in her thighs threatened to lock up, trembling with adrenaline that had nowhere to go.

"Going to check in with your dad and then we're out of here, right?"

Her feet carried her autonomous of her brain. "Why are you so anxious to leave?"

He adjusted the rifle over his shoulder. "Feel like I'm not really fitting in."

"Sorry."

"I'm used to it. Just seemed like doing something useful like this is better than sitting on my hands and waiting for the guys to haze me."

She chuckled. "Guys do that?"

"You have no idea, Addy. In some places, it's worse than others. I didn't have to worry about it in California too bad."

"Why not?"

"Well, once Ella heard about it, she..." Feet slowing, he trailed off.

Addy stopped and bit her lip. Get him to talk about her, or let it go? Half a grin hit her. It'd be nice to hear more about Ella. She hadn't known enough about her. "She what?"

"Not important," he said, catching up to her. He cleared his throat. "Christian makes good drinks, but that's about the best thing I can say about this place." He paused, grinning. "And Scott. He's a good guy. Too pretty. And too good of a liar. But a good guy."

Addy rolled her eyes. "You'd know about liars." She laughed.

He chuckled, dimples deep. "Yeah."

They rounded a bend, the dock coming into sight. Jane stood at the head of it, baby in her arms, speaking with Hux and Mike. Dad hung his legs off the side, fishing.

And for as peaceful as it was, all Addy wanted to do was get this conversation over with so they could get the hell off this island.

* * *

Feet dangling over the side of the dock, Jack eyed the line. The fish didn't bite much in the winter, but it was worth a shot. And after the night he and Jane had had—the talk, rowing back in the canoe—the peace of fishing seemed too good to be true.

Jane stood out of earshot, speaking with Hux and Mike.

Addy and Matt came around the corner, both carrying packs.

Uh-oh. What was she planning?

She walked onto the dock, Matt trailing her.

"Dad."

He stood, one eye on the line, and gave her half a hug. "Hey, little girl. What's going on?"

She jiggled her pack and swiped at her nose. "I'm leaving to try and get some intel on the Molehill."

Matt caught his eyes. "We. I know where it is, you know."

"I remember."

Matt cleared his throat but didn't say more.

Addy touched Jack on the shoulder. "What about you?"

One eye still on the line, he crossed his arms. "Mike suggested we check out the Library of Congress."

Matt scoffed. "No shit?"

"What's that?" Addy asked.

"It's in DC," Jack answered. "When I was young, it was the greatest repository of knowledge in the world. It broke my heart to think it could have been destroyed, but Hux thinks it may still be intact."

"Oh, yeah," Matt said. "IRF has lots of intel about it. They couldn't get in, but it's still there, all right."

IRF, not allowed in? Then who controlled the library? And how were they using it?

Talk about powerful currency.

The line swished back and forth. Jack tugged, picking up the pole with the other hand and yanking.

"We'll leave you to it, Dad."

He almost let the fish go. Instead, he held out one arm and his little girl stepped into it. He kissed her on the forehead. "I love you, kid."

"I love you too. Be safe."

He nodded, noncommittal.

"Matt," he said, grabbing the pole with both hands. "Watch yourself out there." He considered adding something about not trusting him, or making sure Addy didn't get hurt, or some foolish nonsense, but he basically did trust the guy, and Addy could very well take care of herself.

"I will, Jack."

As they said their goodbyes to Hux, Jane, and Michael, Jack turned his full attention to the fish.

The line thrummed, the hooked fish fighting to get away. Caught on the hook, with no way to rescue itself.

Not unlike he'd been.

Rather than shove the thought away, he practiced what Jane said. Accepting fear as a normal response to what happened. Apparently, according to her, he couldn't get through it if he fought against it.

He murmured under his breath and reeled the fish in. "It's a normal response. It's all right to have fear." Pulling the hooked fish from the water, he rolled his shoulders. "You're not there now. Relax, Jack."

He grabbed the reeled-in fish and squeezed. Not too hard. But the damn thing had to stop flapping so he could get the hook out.

Inside his head, the echo of teeth squeaking together resounded.

Loosening his jaw, he freed the hook from the fish's mouth.

Fresh fish, the best thing about living on the coast. His mouth filled with saliva just thinking about roasting it.

It flapped once, its weak tail hitting the back of his hand, giving one last gasp to escape.

Something he'd hardly allowed himself, frozen as he was with the fear. In defeat. And something Jane wanted to give back to him, something she said she could find in the books in that library. Healing.

He threw the fish in the water and stood, gathering his pole and tackle.

After speaking with Mike, Jane met him on the dock, sticking a hand out for him.

How many times had she pulled him from the edge? Four now? Five? Who could keep track. The woman was a goddamned miracle.

He kissed the side of her forehead. "When are we leaving?"

Hux cleared his throat. "I would think tomorrow or the next day. I'd like Mr. Ross to come with us. And—"

"Celia refuses to let us leave without her," Mike said, crossing his arms.

"Why do we need Dean again?" Jack frowned at the doctor. Dean was not his favorite person right now. Besides. "Is he fully healed?"

"A few reasons, Mr. Cooke."

"Jack."

Huxley cleared his throat again. "Jack. He does have some healing from the virus still to do, though his leg is more or less intact. I believe he'll do best under my care. Also, I, uh. I need to study his recovery. His is a unique case." He smiled, buck teeth poking out over his lip. "Your family seems to be full of unique cases."

The correction about Dean on the edge of his lips, Jack backed off. Yes, Dean had broken up with Addy. Broken her heart like it'd never been. The chance she'd taken on him balled up and thrown away like garbage.

But making one grievous mistake didn't mean he wasn't family. Like it or not, he was part of the crew now.

"I would ask why we're leaving so soon, but my woman here is chomping at the bit to see this library. Better not keep her waiting." He leaned forward, lowering his voice. "It's not good for your health to keep her waiting."

Mike chuckled. "Truth." He gave her a grin, cheek dimpling.

"What did I tell you, Michael Cooke," Celia said, popping out of nowhere.

Mike jumped, face blazing red. "I already told them, Cee."

"When are we leaving?" she asked, hands on her hips. Staring through Jack.

Like most conversations with Celia, the door to "you should stay here" land was already closed.

"Tomorrow. Noon," Jack said, glancing around the circle. "We taking Dean's train?"

"Yep. We're going over to the mainland to get her all ready after I leave here."

"I'll come with you," Celia said. "About time I learned how to drive the thing."

Mike opened his mouth.

Jack chuckled. Could have written the script for what was about to happen.

Before Mike had a chance to respond, to even think about telling her no, Celia walked away. "See you there," she called over her shoulder. "Shag your ass, pretty boy."

Mike took his leave, mumbling something about getting Dean across the sound.

Jack angled for home, Jane beside him. The good doctor on her other side. "Have you spoken to Scott, Huxley?"

His dandelion hair bounced. "He expects you'll see him before you leave."

"I expect I will. Tomorrow." It'd been a long day, and curling up beside the fire for one more night sounded like about the closest one could get to heaven. And he'd take every ounce of that he could get.

CHAPTER 7

"How far would you say we got today?" Matt asked, dropping his pack to the ground. He sat, slumping against it and digging for his canteen.

"Not far enough," Addy said, doing the same. She laid her bow on the ground beside her. "Twenty miles or more."

"You're a hell of a taskmaster, Addy." Taking three large gulps from the canteen, he laid his head against the pack and closed his eyes.

The sun set through the trees. A day's grueling walk from the island, yet she hadn't walked off the rage, the hurt, the disappointment.

He inhaled a sharp breath through his nose and sat up. "I'll get some wood. You want the first watch?"

She cupped her elbows. "Jesus, Matt. This whole plan is awful."

He stood. "Meaning?"

"It's February. It's freezing out here. And." She picked at the toe of her boot. It'd started to come apart from the sole.

"And?"

Shrugging, she squinted up at him. "It's like we don't have much to talk about except shit we don't want to talk about."

"Yeah." Shoving his hands in his pockets, he kicked at the ground. "We did pretty good today, I thought."

"True." They'd gone over best fights with other people, the craziest things they'd seen other people doing, and favorite 'Head kills.

"I still think the time I lined up three 'Heads on one spear was better than yours," he said.

She exhaled a laugh. "You cannot beat hitting five with the same bullet."

"You sure that was you? I never see you carry a gun."

"Just because you've never seen it, doesn't mean it didn't happen."

He laughed. "I'll get the wood. You clear a spot for a fire. Did either of us bring a tent?"

And in fact, she'd rolled up a two-person tent in her pack. She shoved her arm in and dug for it. "Good call. I'll get it set up. You want me to take the first watch?"

"We'll flip for it when I get back," he said, disappearing into the trees.

After sweeping the ground clear of sticks and rocks, she unrolled the tent and had started to string it up when he shouted.

"Adelaide!" His voice echoed off the trees.

Unsheathing her machete as she ran through the woods, bouncing off a tree or two, she burst into a clearing.

Matt stood from a pile of bottles and trash. "Oh, good. Put that away and help me carry these." He nodded at the machete.

She sheathed it and joined him. "The hell? Sounded like you were dying."

He rolled his eyes. "Sure. Grab some stuff, would you?"

"Why do we want someone's trash?"

He grinned with one side of his mouth and shoved some bottles and random junk into her arms. "Trust me. Take these."

Wrapping her arms around the stuff before it fell, she let him pile a little more on top. "You didn't have to shout. I bet you called every 'Head for six miles."

"It wasn't that loud. Don't overreact."

"Don't treat me like a child, Matt. I'm not Ella."

Too late to pull that comment back in, genius. Shit.

He stopped, jaw working. His own arms loaded with bottles, he headed back to camp.

"Shit," Addy said aloud. "Wait. I'm sorry. It slipped. I didn't mean—"

"It's fine. You're right. I'm sorry." He wove through the trees until he arrived back at the spot where they'd stopped, off the highway they'd been following west. "Let me get some wood and I'll show you my plan about the bottles and stuff."

She helped him gather up kindling and sticks for the fire. As the sun set and the temperature plummeted, her breath plumed before her. The fire was going to be about all that kept them alive tonight.

Cuddling up to Dean would have been perfect on a night like this.

As she set up the fire and finished the tent, she watched Matt circle the campsite over and over, going farther out each time. It took her a few rounds to work out what he was doing, but once she did, she understood neither of them would need to lose sleep tonight.

Which was good. She wasn't sure what would be worse. Taking the first watch, or being woken in the cold depths of the night to keep watch over a waning fire and a snoring man.

He settled down next to her in front of the fire, their backs to the tent.

She handed him a stick. "Here."

Taking the meat she held out, he spiked it to the end of the stick and held it over the fire. "Gotta admit, this is a little odd for me."

"What?"

"Sleeping in a camp. Eating food cooked over an open fire."

Inhaling the smoky wood scent, Addy's mouth watered. "My favorite way to cook. All this town living keeps trying to make me soft."

"It doesn't have far to go." He took a bite of the meat and side-eyed her.

"Yeah, yeah. You're already there. Stringing up the bottles and crap for an early-warning system was a good idea though. I'll give you that."

"Thanks. I couldn't see staying up half the night if I didn't have to. All that town living has made me soft. I'll admit it." He smiled. "She liked things to be comfortable."

An image of Ella, honey-colored hair flying over her shoulder, brow raised, snuck into Addy's mind. "I'll bet."

Matt removed the meat from the stick and took a bite. Chewing, he leaned back and threw an arm behind his head. "Hey, look," he said, pointing into the sky.

Addy followed his pointing finger and caught sight of Cassiopeia. The Seven Sisters and the Winter Triangle were up there somewhere too, but the trees obscured most of it. "One of the things I love about the west. You can see everything at once."

"She always used to tell me the light pollution from before made it almost impossible to see the Pleiades most nights."

They'd switched from one "she" to another, but Addy was no more eager to name this one aloud. The light and the heat from that deadly grenade splashed across the inside of her eyelids. "Dad said she used to say that was one of the best things about the apocalypse. No more light pollution."

"She must hate the Queen City."

"Is that the city you talked about?" Addy asked, leaning on an elbow and resting her head in her hand.

"Yeah," he said, copying her. "It's not far from the Molehill. They keep their distance now, but they used to be a lot friendlier. It's like a real city, I guess. I haven't been there in a few years. Not since she sent me west." He scraped the ground with his thumb. The dying flames bounced off his face. Frowning, he stood and offered Addy a hand, breath clouding the space in front of his mouth. "This fire is turning to embers. Let's build it back up and get in the tent. At least we'll be out of the cold."

Taking his hand, she stood and helped him stoke the fire. "You sure about the bottles?"

"You know there's not many real hordes left. They congregate. The one at the ocean pulls them all there like a big magnet."

"Why is that?"

"I ask the silly questions around here." He unzipped the tent. "Ladies first."

She crawled in, freeing her machete and sliding into the sleeping bag. Glancing at the sides of the tent, she bit her lip. She'd planned on sleeping in here alone, with him taking a watch. It seemed such a small space for two people.

He slid in feet first and zipped the flap. "I'll try not to kick you in the face," he said, unsheathing her knife.

His knife. Whatever.

"Well. I'm armed. So know you'll probably lose a foot if you do."

* * *

The train crawled to a halt. Jack stood. "Something on the tracks again?"

"You should let me help you with this one," Dean said.

"You'll rip those stitches," Jack said, not looking at him. It'd been harder than he wanted to admit, forgiving the man. Even after three days on the train, in close quarters like this. Seemed hurting his kids physically wasn't the only thing he couldn't stomach.

"I won't. Come on, let me help." Dean limped to the door and pulled a baseball bat from the stand. "I'll watch your back. You can do all the heavy lifting, I promise."

Dragging his eyes to Dean's, he held them. "Stay here. Michael."

Mike stood, floor creaking under his heels. No one spoke.

"Take this." Jack held his hand out for the bat. "Celia, you're with us."

Dean laid the handle of the bat in Jack's palm, shoulders drooping. "I'll keep the train ready in case we need to make a quick getaway."

Mike took the bat and glanced at Celia. "How are we doing this?"

She crossed her arms and leveled her heavy lids at Jack.

Jack opened the door and poked his head out. The eastern Virginia evening greeted him. Crisp, wet, late-February air blew across his face. Otherwise, the sun sank in silence. Though the nights still dipped below freezing, and the bugs hadn't woken yet, the air tasted fresh. No decay on the breeze.

"Smells all right. Let's start with what's blocking the tracks and go from there. Celia," he said, stepping onto the porch, "ask Dean to turn on the lights. It's on its way to dark out here."

Behind him, two people collided and spoke over each other.

"Sorry, Cee."

"Mike. What the hell." She clicked her tongue. "Dean, lights."

Lights turned on, flooding all sides of the train with so many lumens, it hurt his eyes.

"Looks good to me, Jack," Celia said, peering out the window over the bed. "We doing this while we're still young, or?"

"Too late for some of us." Long blade in one hand, he pulled his gun for the other. Just in case. For no good reason, Paul's voice echoed in his head. *Be lucky if you get as old as me, whippersnapper.*

He just collected dead people these days.

As he crept to the front of the train, Celia and Mike silent behind him, he idly thought it would have been better if Melinda had stayed that way.

His jaw clenched, teeth squeaking together.

With no time to replay the entirety of their complicated relationship, he pushed it all aside. In the open like this, seconds mattered. Dead Head activity was minimal lately, but that was no reason to get complacent.

Rolling his shoulders, he stepped around the front of the train, Celia and Mike following.

"Damn, Dad. That's a hell of a tree. We're gonna need a chainsaw or something."

Lifting the machete, Jack looked between the tree and his blade. "Yeah. Do you think Dean has anything big enough for this?"

"Jack," Dean whispered from above.

He cranked his neck.

Dean's head stuck out the window. "We can chain it to the engine and pull it off the track. Might be better to do it in the light though."

"Where's the chain?"

"There's a compartment in the back. Hang on." Dean's head disappeared from the window.

"Stay here," Jack said, walking past Mike and Celia. "Keep your eyes open."

The door of the train squeaked.

Jack winced. "Needs oil, Dean."

"That it does. Here, the compartment is below the thing." He took each stair one ginger step at a time. "These storage compartments aren't standard. Added them myself a couple years back."

Hand sliding down the side of the train, he wobbled.

Jack grabbed him under the arm and steadied him. "Easy. Don't hurt yourself."

"In case you need to know," he said, easing his ass to the dirt, "the top one has more weapons. The bottom one has chain and other tools. Hand tools and stuff. Both use the same key." He dug a ring out of his pocket and held up the right one.

Staring, Jack took in the details of its teeth. The shape and size of its head. "Got it. But you'll be here to unlock it next time. And the time after that." He knelt. "Don't think I'm going to let anything happen to you now, Dean."

Dean slid the key home and stopped. "I wish I could tell you I'm sorry."

"I'm not going to be caught between you two. You did what you thought was right. The fact no one else agrees with you is no reason to apologize to me. I won't bring it up if you won't."

Dean unlocked the compartment. Thick lengths of chain rested on top of one another inside. He reached for it.

Jack put a hand on his shoulder. "Stop. You're definitely going to hurt yourself if you strain to pick that up. Let me." He turned his head. "Michael!"

Holding the side of the train for support, Dean stood. "Well anyway. Remember which key it is. For the weapons too. I'll get the train ready for hauling. What we can do is wrap the chain around it and pull. Once it gets sideways enough, I should be able to ease past. I'd still rather do this in the daylight. Could be all kinds of stuff under that tree."

"Sorry, but we're not stopping here," Jack said, shaking his head. He pulled the chain from the compartment, coiling it on the ground next to him. "What if IRF came to clear the tracks tonight? They'd run smack into us. I don't think that's a great idea. After." He paused, teeth clenched.

"After Magnolia. Yeah. You're right. Let's get this done." He hopped up the stairs and disappeared into the train.

Now. Where was Mike?

He checked behind him again. Neither Mike nor Celia stood next to the train where he'd left them.

Goose bumps raised on his arm. He hadn't heard anything. "Mike? Celia?" He stood, leaving the coil of chain on the ground and stepping toward the front of the train. Called his boy again.

Backing into the circle of light in front of the train, Mike tripped over the rail and fell on his ass. Disheveled and bloody. His wide eyes fell on Jack.

Yanking his gun from its holster with one hand, Jack unsheathed the machete again with the other and sprinted to Mike. "You all right?"

Mike opened his mouth.

"Fine," Celia answered, stepping into the light, her blade bloody and her clothes stinking with coagulated fluids. "But one of these days *I'm* going to get to be the damsel instead of you people."

"There was half a dozen or so over there," Mike said, pointing as he stood. He pulled a sucker out of his pouch and offered one to Celia. "Your favorite."

Shaking her head, she took it. "How do you know that?"

"Observation. Dad?"

Jack shook his head, declining the sucker. "Half a dozen?"

"Less, now," Celia said, sheathing her blade. "Half a one."

Chuckling, Jack waved them toward the train. "I've got the chain. Help me haul it up here, and watch my back while I get it secure. We'll get this tree out of the way and head on down the tracks."

* * *

Ilasha opened the door.

Fists clenched and stuffed into her elbows, Melinda barged in.

"Come in, dear," Lash said, closing and locking the door. "You're late." She settled into her overstuffed couch, which had been reupholstered at least twice since Melinda had known her. The woman liked things to be neat and tidy, even living in a glorified hole in the ground.

"I forgot how to get here," Melinda said, sinking into a green velvet wingback chair. She pulled her feet up and peered over her knees as Lash chuckled.

"Hope you were better at lying when you were out there with those people, Em. Otherwise I'm sure they know all your secrets already."

Melinda slid her hand down the arm of the chair. "You always have the best furniture, Lash." She smiled. "A girl could get jealous."

"Please. Yours is just as nice. Maybe not so stylish," she said, lips curving, "but nice."

"We never had things like this chair." She ran her other hand down the arm.

"It was a long time ago you were that wandering woman. You've been either here or in houses for what. Ten years?"

"More," Melinda agreed. She folded her fingers together.

"You saw your family out there."

Above wide eyes, Melinda pinched her mouth closed. She hadn't talked to anyone, confided in anyone, about them. Not since she'd first seen them, back on Emerald Isle.

Lash stood. "I'll get drinks."

After pouring some red wine and serving, Lash clinked her glass to Melinda's. "Spill."

"There's not much to tell." There was so much to tell. But how to get a finger under the corner of it? Every time she tried to grab the pain, it squirted away.

"Last time I saw you, we talked about your man. How he's with someone else?"

"So he says."

Ilasha curled up in the arm of the couch, leaning closer. Bright brown eyes urged Melinda to continue.

"Hell, Lash. You know. He hasn't been my man in years. He left me there to die. If he'd come back to kill me—" She stopped, staring at her knee.

"You're still on about that. After all this time. You've gotta let that go." When Melinda didn't answer, she went on. "How are your kids?"

"Loyal to their father."

"Yeah, but how *are* they?"

"Strong." Melinda smiled. "Confident. Adelaide can be impressive. They're beautiful children. I'm sorry I missed the last decade. They turned into adults."

"Why didn't they come with you?" She refilled the glasses.

Melinda drank. Swiped at an eye. "They could be dead for all I know. Heck threw a grenade at them to cover our escape."

"Damn. Hopefully we can find out. Let me put my ear to the ground."

Melinda picked at the seam on the arm of the chair, silent.

Lash narrowed her eyes. "You've got something on your mind, babe. Tell me."

Melinda finished off her drink and refilled it. "You always have the smoothest wine."

Lash watched as she settled into the chair, her eyes still narrowed.

"Anthony kicked me off the immunity project," Melinda said, standing to pace. "That son of a bitch."

"Ah, see. There's the real problem." Smiling, she cupped her glass with two fingers and waved it at Melinda. "Tell me about it."

"Those are my embryos, Ilasha. You don't know what I went through to get them."

Ilasha opened her mouth.

Melinda walked all over whatever Lash might have said. "First of all, I had to follow that *girl* from Shanti Station. She was the only one to survive the vaccine trial. I had to watch her."

Lash drank. Eyes round over the rim of the glass.

"When she turned up pregnant, I knew. I saw the way she looked at him. How could I not?"

"You used to look at him that way."

"Fucking A right I did. But." She pointed her index finger in the air. "I was fascinated by the possibilities. To have given the girl the vaccine, after fertilization but before implantation?"

"I hate to be a stickler, but how do you know it was after fertilization?"

A rock settled into her gut. "A mistake. I waited too long, there was a mix-up at the prison. And. Well." She shrugged. Opening her mouth to speak, her throat clenched. She swallowed and tried again. "I lost him. I was on the verge of getting him back, and he was gone."

Lash snuck a warm hand onto her knee. "Thought you didn't care."

"Fuck, Ilasha. I don't know."

The hand on her knee squeezed. "Damn near twenty years and two kids? Of course you don't. But, Em." She pointed between them. "You moved on, too, right?"

Breathing shallow, Melinda laid her hand over Lash's. "I thought I had. Then you stayed here when I left. You broke my heart."

"I don't think we need to retread that water. I stayed because I had to." Setting the glass down, Lash took Melinda's hand in both of hers. "And I don't know where that leaves us."

"Me neither."

Lash's thumb slid across her hand. Back and forth. Back and forth. Hypnotized, she told Lash most of the rest of the story. About Jack making a fool of himself in front of their children, about surrendering herself so the girl could get care at the hospital, knowing she could work it around to her advantage, about discovering the child was immune.

"And you think it's because of the vaccine?"

"I know it is. I know it."

"How'd you convince your man to contribute to your study?"

Refilling their glasses, Melinda clinked. "That, my dear Ilasha, is a story for another time."

CHAPTER 8

"Hang back a minute, Addy," Matt said, gripping her shoulder. "We're close to the perimeter."

"Wow, already?"

Matt scoffed. "Already. We've been walking like a week. I don't remember it being so far." He offered her his canteen.

She took it and sipped. "How far are we from the city?"

"About fifteen miles, I think."

"You think?" Capping the canteen, she wiped her mouth and returned it. "Guessing, or…?"

He unscrewed the lid and polished off what was left. "Kinda, yeah." He grinned.

She stared at the horizon and could make out the city skyline. "How much of it is still standing? Are you sure it's safe?"

"I haven't been here in like, six years or so, but it was good last time I was here. They'd started to tear down the walls."

If she'd still been drinking, she would have spit water everywhere. She cursed instead. "Do what to the who?"

"Tear down the walls. These people are something else, Addy. Like you," he said, bumping her with his shoulder. "You'll like them."

She leaned away. "What's that supposed to mean?"

"They're good people. Smart. Don't back down for anything." He stared across the horizon. "She would have liked them too."

Addy's chest squeezed in like a bellows, pressing the air out between her lips. "That does not help my confidence."

He smiled with one side of his mouth.

Oh, dear lord. Over the last week, he'd brought up Ella at least five times a day. Never by name. But what began as a sideways smile always ended in a melancholy man who didn't speak for an hour. *If* she let him wallow in it.

Considering the last couple months, wallowing was inevitable. But dammit. She didn't want to join him right now.

She took a step. "You said we're not far. Why don't we get a move on? I'd like to get down there before the sun sets, at least."

Slinging the canteen strap over his shoulder, he pointed north. "I suggest we take the road. We don't want them to think we're sneaking up on them."

"That wouldn't do."

They walked up a small incline and stepped through a broken guardrail onto a cracked and lumpy surface. Addy kicked at a shin-high bump in the asphalt. "Not terribly well maintained."

"There's better roads. Just not this one."

Addy caught sight of rusted heaps beside the road. "Someone cleared it at some point." She pointed.

Matt nodded. "Ahead of us is the QC."

"Why the QC?"

"Why call it that?"

"Yeah."

"Used to be its nickname. The Queen City, or something."

"Whatever that means."

He chuckled. "What you said. It's been here at least as long as the Molehill. At one point, they all worked together to clean up the city."

Mom. Her stomach fell. "What happened?"

Stepping over a hillock growing in the road, he shook his head. "Talus isn't very friendly. You know that."

Cheeks no doubt an interesting shade of fire-engine red, Addy grimaced. "So, what—"

"Halt!"

They stopped.

Matt raised both hands in the air.

Watching the direction from which the voice had come, Addy raised her own hands. Her bowstring cut into her chest.

A woman stepped out onto the road, rifle leveled at them. "Lay your weapons on the ground, please."

Addy didn't twitch. "We're not here to hurt an—"

The male voice came from behind the bare trees again. "Put them on the ground. We don't want to hurt you. We have to check your things."

"For what?" Addy asked, laying her bow down. She unsnapped the machete.

"Slow," the woman said, approaching. "Unsheathe it slow." Five feet away, the end of the gun never wavered.

Matt laid his rifle down and slipped her Bowie knife from his scabbard. "It's all right, Addy." He laid the gleaming blade next to the rifle and stood, wide smile deepening the dimples around his mouth. "Been a while since I've been to the QC. How's she holding up?"

The rifle-wielding woman shrugged. "Good. Who do you work for?"

"No one," Addy said. "Why do we have to work for someone?"

A tall man cleared the trees. He approached, and Addy made out a touch of grey in his beard. Would Mike have grey in his beard if he grew it out? He was about the same age as this guy.

"Most people do, Addy was it? Pack on the ground, please."

Slipping the pack from her shoulders, she held a hand out. "Adelaide Cooke."

He shook. "Ryan," he said, giving her a nice up and down pump. Good and firm. A lock of hair fell over his ear. Pushing it back, he stuck his hand out to Matt.

Matt lowered his pack and did the same. "Matt Lyburn."

Ryan narrowed his eyes. "You guys moving here? Heard it was a good place to raise kids or something?"

Reddening again, Addy stammered.

Matt saved her. "Nah, man. My girl wouldn't approve of me looking at other women. She's waiting for me." He angled his chin in a vague direction that could have been construed as the city.

The blood that had rushed to Addy's cheeks drained to her toes. Ella stood there, between them, transparent as a memory. Real as a ghost.

"Waiting in town?"

Addy tried on half a smile. The best she could ask for. "She's out there, all right."

Seeming satisfied, Ryan bent over and emptied their packs, pulling the entire contents out onto the broken asphalt. He paused on a couple things—Addy's phone, Matt's extra ammo—but didn't seem too concerned. His face maintained a pleasant neutrality as he bared their belongings to the world.

The last thing he pulled from Matt's pack was a book. *Welcome to the Universe: An Astrophysical Tour.*

When he finished emptying Addy's bag, he laid her book right next to his. *Metamorphosis.* The book with Data on the cover.

She glanced at Matt.

His face pale, his eyelids low, he frowned.

She almost wanted to hug him. Ella gave them those books at Addy's first Christmas. Now it was all either of them had of her.

After looking over the stuff strewn across the ground one more time, Ryan stuck a thumb in the air. "They're clean."

The woman lowered her rifle. "Welcome to the QC, guys." Her freckled nose bobbed when she smiled. "You'll like it here. I hope you see your girl soon."

Matt picked up the book and squeezed it so hard his knuckles turned white. "I'm sure I will."

Ryan clapped him on the shoulder and shook Addy's hand again. "I'll radio to the next checkpoint. You shouldn't have any more trouble getting in. Once you get to the edge of town, some guys will escort you to the bank building. Sly should be on duty when you get there. He'll get you settled tonight."

Addy paused gathering her things. "A bed? Tonight?"

"We got plenty." He smiled.

They repacked their bags, strapped on their weapons, and headed toward town.

* * *

Morning streamed through the giant windows of their room and baked Addy's still-closed eyelids, turning them red. She inhaled through her nose, filling her lungs with the scent of this place. Something beneath the odd recycled-air scent permeating the high-rise tickled her senses.

It was all the people. The sound of them aside, the air smelled like them. Like fresh soap and dirt ground in wherever it could. Both at once. But also, like skin, and sweat, and that indefinable scent people exhaled from inside living lungs. Wet, but bloodless. Fresh. Clean.

The opposite of the dead.

She smiled as Matt pulled in that first "just woke up" breath through his nose. They'd been holed up in the same third-floor room. For accountability, according to their hosts, but also by their own choice. Addy wasn't about to lose sight of her only friend on the first night. In this strange place, with all these people everywhere, he was all she had.

"Sleep good?"

"No."

Opening her eyes, she turned her head.

Across the room, he sat up and swung his feet to the floor. "Not anymore, Addy. I can't get away from her." He slid his hand under the pillow and pulled out the Bowie knife. "I don't know why I'm telling you this. But every time I close my eyes, I see Hector. Right before he shot her. I see her hair flying over her shoulder like it's in slow motion." He glanced at her, eyes hooded. "She was smiling. Just before she left me. That 'I won this one' smile." The corners of his mouth raised, but when he looked up again, they fell. Couldn't sustain the fight against gravity. "I don't know why I told you that."

"Because I'm the only one left who cared about her besides you. You want to talk about her, I'll listen. But," she said, standing, machete in hand, "you're gonna have to listen to me whine about Dean from time to time."

"About that." He sheathed the knife and joined her at the door. "I don't get it. It still doesn't make any sense. He had to have known how lucky he was." He held the door open for her.

Blood tingling in her cheeks, she let the compliment slide. How did you respond to that? Thank you? You're right? Flattery will get you everywhere? Nothing sounded good in her head.

Matt closed the door behind them. "Who's that guy we met last night? I was so wiped by the time we got here, I can't even remember what he looked like."

"His name's Sly. He said he'd still be on duty for a couple hours before shift change this morning. He should be downstairs." She matched his gait as they made their way to the stairwell. They went down one flight on the stairs and finished descending the last two floors via rope ladder suspended in the defunct elevator shaft.

Addy didn't need to be told how indefensible these sorts of buildings were. High-rise death traps. No doubt a wide variety of security measures had been taken to keep the dead out.

A radio echoed up the elevator shaft as they descended the ladder. Words obscured.

"You tell patrol three to get their asses back to their assigned lane," a voice said from the lobby. "I find out they've been going off course again, they'll figure out why you don't mess with me. Ficking stable duty for a week. Mucking out ficking stalls. I am not going to have this."

The response came back clear. "*10-4, boss. Will advise.*"

Plastic clattered. "Fickin too right you will."

Addy stepped out of the elevator, Matt following. "Sly."

The boy turned. Face darkened by a smattering of freckles crossing his nose and cheeks, not unlike Dean's, tired eyes smiled above them. "Hey, new people. Addy. And Mark?"

"Matt."

Addy chuckled.

"Sorry, I'm usually better with names. Long couple days. And it's almost time to sleep." He yawned, shoving shaggy brown hair out of the way and wiping his face with one hand. "And these fickin fuckin idiots and their stupid games. I swear. They're gonna get taken off rotation, they keep this up."

Matt adjusted the rifle over his shoulder. "What's the problem?" His official voice. Captain of the guard voice.

Sly crossed his arms. "These two on patrol together on thirds, Howe and Enoch. I know perfectly well what they're sneaking off to do together. But you'd think while they were on duty they'd be able to actually mind their duties. It's just a few hours, for god's sake." He smoothed his manicured mustache down over his lip. "If I have to take them off the route, you want it?"

Matt shook his head. "Patrols? On third? Ha. No."

Sly looked Addy up and down. "Suit yourself. I'm about off shift. I'll take you to the boss. He'll want to meet you two."

Addy started, heart tripping. "Why would some boss want to meet us? We're just here to, uh."

"Heard it was a good place to raise kids," Matt interjected.

Addy's heart tripped again. Fell over its own feet.

Sly chuckled, unchaining and opening the front door. "Really?"

"No," Matt said, laughing.

Emerging from the building into the sun, rays focused by all the buildings made of glass, Addy shielded her eyes and blinked around.

Although they stood in the heart of the city, trees grew thick on every corner and lined every block. The city itself—what Addy had seen of it—had an older feel, something that had broken a little but still stood against time the way her trees did.

Sly's replacement slipped through the door and buttoned-up the building after.

"Two young, healthy people," Sly said. "No kids. Heavily armed." He nodded at Addy's bow. "Boss is gonna want to meet you. Find out what you're about."

* * *

Jack expected barriers. Guard posts. Chains. Something.

Anything.

The creeping silence accompanying the train ride through town left his nerves on edge. Like the calm before the storm.

Jane, cradling Katherine with one arm while she tucked her breasts away with the other, watched him out of the side of her eye. "You all right? You seem a little jumpy."

He shook his head. "It's too quiet."

"Agreed," Dean said, leaning close to the window over the bed. "There should be people. Or 'Heads. Or something. This used to be the capital."

"Of?" Jane lifted the baby, patting her back.

"The country," Jack said, sinking down next to her. She'd grown fond of the spot behind the chair, across from the bed. Tucked in the corner where she could be close to the door. Or maybe it was that he'd grown fond of the spot, and she'd followed.

"Oh, right. Think I heard this one. Washington?"

Dean continued to stare out the window. His breath fogged the glass. "DC. We're nearing downtown. Oh. That's a shame."

Mike slowed the train and spoke over his shoulder. "Dad."

Finally. The trouble he'd been expecting. The coil in his chest unraveled.

He stared out the window with Dean. "What's a shame?"

"The Washington monument's gone. Used to be right there."

Jack shrugged. "As long as the damn library is intact."

"Dad."

He wobbled to the front of the train as it continued to slow. "What's going on?" He took in the screens. Some blinking red on the one he'd memorized as the proximity display. Nothing alarming, just something to keep an eye on. "This place is too damned quiet," he said, leaning over Mike's shoulder. Speaking low, as though he'd wake whatever slept.

"We crossed all the bridges fine. The track is even. It's been maintained. But." Mike pointed.

Jack recognized what looked like a map. "But?"

"We're heading underground."

"Dean," Jack called. "Need you."

One of Dean's feet dragged heavy as he made his way up front. *Scrape, thump. Scrape, thump.* He stood on the other side of Mike and leaned over. "Yeah."

"What do you know about this city? And what can you tell me about what the proximity screens say about these underground tunnels?"

"Scooch," he said, bumping Mike's shoulder.

Mike stood.

Dean sat, leaning forward to adjust the screens. The map screen went flat, showing the track in front of them in sharp reality. Track lines projected over the picture, an illustration of where they were going. They closed in on the tunnel.

Jack gripped the Captain's Chair, clenching his fists and teeth. Going into the tunnel seemed like a horrible idea. But the even calm of the city wore against his nerves. Getting out and walking was worse than using the tunnels.

Though the scent of the air itself was fresh, something smelled wrong here.

"All right," Dean said, punching up another overhead map and displaying it below the one with the tracks. He scrolled the screen with his finger. "The tunnels start here. We go a little ways…"

Seeing someone operate a touch screen again both exciting and unnerving, Jack continued to clench his teeth.

"We come out here," Dean went on, pointing. He pinched and zoomed the proximity screen over the sparse red dots. "This is concerning. But I think it's OK."

As Jack went to speak, he found his jaw stuck together. He pried it open.

Jane laid a hand on his shoulder and spoke at the same time. "Breathe," she whispered, pressed against his arm. "You can't control everything. Just breathe."

He exhaled, loosening his jaw and working it back and forth. Let his fingers relax, peeling the fingernails out of the palm of the one not clutching the chair. Once he'd taken a couple deep breaths, he tried again. "Can this thing see all the way to the end of the tunnel?"

Dean frowned. Making some adjustments in the panel next to his thigh, he narrowed his eyes at the screen and double-tapped it with a fingertip. "No. Almost. But not quite."

Jack paced to the back of the train. Maybe someone should scout ahead on foot.

Dean was out.

Celia stood next to Mike, both of them peering out the tiny front window.

Hux sat curled up in the front corner, making notes in a small notebook that'd conformed itself to the shape of his hip pocket.

Jane still stood by the Captain's Chair, watching him with her eyes slitted and Katie in one arm.

The only other option was himself.

He shook his head. Sticking together was the safest bet. "Let's batten down the hatches and go for it. We're gonna waste a lot of time getting to this fancy library if we stop at every tunnel."

As they locked and barred the door, pulling the drapes and arming themselves with all the ranged weapons they could put their hands to, Dean rolled the train forward.

"It is odd we haven't seen many people, Mr. Cooke," Huxley said. "The last I'd heard, Washington was still densely populated."

"Densely for who?" Jack asked, peeking around the rear curtain. A couple 'Heads wandered out there. Tripping over tracks as they passed.

"About ten thousand, at last count."

"That many," Celia said, from her perch nearby. "Why?"

"Why what, young lady?"

"Why would they want to stay in this shithole." Not a question.

Socially awkward the doctor may be, he sometimes knew when to shut the fuck up. This time, he did so.

They crept through the tunnel, the occasional bump coming from the front wheels. And again as they ran over old, dry bones with the rear ones.

"Just 'Heads," Dean whispered, each time.

After years inched by, or at least hours made of tightly stretched rubber bands, Dean spoke over his shoulder again. "Proximity sensors say the rest of the way is clear."

Jack relaxed an inch. He'd been clenching again, but at least there were no half-moons in his palm this time. And he hadn't cracked any teeth. He'd take the win. "How many more tunnels between us and the library?"

"Five or six, according to these old maps."

As the train reentered the sunlight and the caboose filled with yellow light again, Jack crept to the front. "Good job, Dean."

Dean smiled. His eyes didn't crinkle, but his mouth turned up. And that was more than yesterday. "Thanks."

Jack patted him on the shoulder. "Let's play it a bit by ear. I'd like to see the area surrounding this library. Doc, do we access it from above or below ground?"

Pocketing his small book, Huxley stood. "I am, ah, uncertain, Mr. Cooke. What little I know about the city, I have exhausted. The rest is conjecture."

"And you're sure the Library of Congress is still there?"

"All those books," Jane said, from the back. "I can't imagine."

A real grin stretched Jack's tight lips. "It'll be a sight to behold, that's for sure. Dean, get us through the next handful of tunnels, and then find a place for us to settle in for a spell and see what we can see."

CHAPTER 9

Following Sly into some sort of tunnel made of brick, Addy and Matt walked in silence. Sly rambled about the town, sounding for all the world like he was trying to keep himself awake at this point.

"So yeah, the city's been here for like fifteen years or something. Got about twenty, thirty thousand people now. We started knocking down the wall a few years ago." Swaying on his feet, he grinned and pointed between them. "Boss's name is Morgan. You guys'll like him. He's good people."

"How do you know we are?" Addy asked as Sly resumed walking and talking.

"You're good with those weapons you got. I know that."

"Makes you say that?" Matt asked.

"Most people, they still carry, but some of them only do it because they're supposed to. They twitch when they walk, handle a gun like they haven't picked one up in years. Let's face it, most of them haven't." He shrugged. "You carry like you mean it. Boss is gonna like you."

Addy ducked under a low-hanging limb as they made their way to the edge of town. They'd passed a fortress-looking thing with giant statues of cats out front. Huge cats made of the same green metal she'd seen all over the South as they'd traveled.

In Dean's train.

She shook her head. "What can you tell us about the area?"

Matt bumped her arm and gave her the side-eye. Shook his head a micrometer to the left and right.

Yeah, yeah, Matt. I know. I'm not about to ask about the damn Molehill. I'm not an idiot.

"It's nice. Peaceful. Been a long time since we saw a horde. Got a few issues with other people, though, so the guard is as tight as ever."

A man strolled out from under the awning of a half-crumbled brick building. "What are you telling these kids, Sly?"

Sly shook his head. "Boss, this is Addy and Mark."

"Matt."

"Sorry, man. Matt." Sly grinned. "They're new. Thought you'd like to meet 'em."

"Morgan," he said, extending his hand to Addy. Above his short white beard, brown eyes twinkled. Hair still more pepper than salt ruffled in the light breeze. "Addy?"

"Adelaide. Cooke." A firm handshake, this one. Not overly smooth, but also not clumsy. A lot like her dad's, truth be told. Judging by the deep crow's feet and smile lines, he was maybe a couple years older.

He winked at her and traded her hand for Matt's. "And Matt. Short for Matthew?"

He winced. "Just Matt, sir."

A wave of sadness hit Addy. That she should be standing here, in this great city with all these living people, the bright sun beating down on her head as it tried to chase winter away, it wasn't fair Ella wasn't standing between them.

And Dean by her side.

But they were both there, weren't they?

Morgan waved Sly off. "Thanks, Sly. Appreciate you bringing them over. Why don't you guys come with me?"

Addy and Matt flanked Morgan as he walked them through the city. "You've seen a lot of the city so far. You stayed the night in the bank building?"

"I think that's what they called it," Matt said. He cleared his throat.

Did he know that from before? Or did he really remember what they said? She didn't.

"You guys passed the stadium, a good portion of the houses, a couple of parks. What do you think of our fair town?"

"A lot of people to defend and no wall to do it." He adjusted the rifle over his shoulder, frown lines pointed down.

Addy piggybacked off his sentiment. "Sly said you hadn't seen a horde in a while, but is that any reason to get complacent about having a wall?"

Morgan stopped and faced them, smile crinkling the edges of his eyes.

Not unlike... *Give it a rest, Addy. He's talking and you're missing it.*

"—something I'd like to show you." He tilted his head. "Follow me."

Hooking his thumbs into his belt, he walked with a swagger Addy hadn't seen in years. If ever.

Dad would probably throw out a few questions here. What would he want to know?

"Morgan," she said.

He inclined his head.

"Who runs this place? You?"

He chuckled. "No, Addy. Not me. I'm, for lack of a better word, the general of the guard. But I'm not in charge here."

"Who is?"

"There's a council. So long as I have enough women and men for my security force, and those men and women are fed, clothed, and housed, I don't stick my nose in."

Sounded like her kind of person.

"You mean you don't pay attention to the council?" Matt asked.

"That's the last thing I mean, Matt. I mean, I don't tell them what to do. They don't tell me what to do." He stopped, crossing his arms, and faced Matt. "We've got a good relationship. The weight we pull is in keeping everyone safe from 'Heads. Everyone appreciates that. Including the council." He started walking again. "Let me show you why that's especially important. I want to introduce you to some of my favorite people."

Addy's stomach growled.

Matt's lips raised, dimples touching his cheeks for the first time today. "Me too."

Pointing down a street lined with blocky, redbrick buildings, Morgan grinned. "We'll get you taken care of. Right up here. Sorry about that. Not the first impression I would have liked you to have. Being hungry, that is."

"I've had worse," Addy said, kicking a rock. It bounced into a gutter and clanked away down the sewer.

"If you guys decide to stay here with us, and work for me, you won't have to worry about that again."

"You want us to be in the guard?" Matt asked. "You sure about that?"

Morgan stopped, hands on his hips. He looked him up and down. "There'll be a trial period, of course." He gave Addy the same up and down, twinkle in his eye. "A buffer for both of us. We'll call it a 'getting to know you' period." He held a finger skyward. "First, you should meet these people."

Turning down a street, he led them one building down. A blocky building, made of cinder blocks, had worn paint on the side showing three letters, "T R E." They followed him through a latched chain-link fence that listed to the outside. Silent, they crossed the yard.

Addy stopped and laid her hands on a loading dock with no stairs, the only access to get inside. It came up to her chin. She bent her knees to jump, but a hand landed between her shoulder blades.

"Here," Matt said. Lacing his hands together, he lowered them to knee height.

She stepped into the cradle, and he lifted her. Pushing off with her other foot, she flew to the top of the loading dock like she'd jumped off a coiled spring. Once she was up, she stuck a hand out to him.

He took it, scrambling up the side of the dock. They both leaned down to help Morgan.

"I could do it without you," he said, walking up the side of the dock, "but it's a lot better with you. Thanks, guys." Leading them through an oversized door in the side of the building, he inhaled.

Addy did the same and caught a few things. Beer, bacon, and coffee.

Well. Can't get much better than that.

Matt's stomach made itself known this time.

Mouth watering, Addy grinned.

Behind the bar, a man popped up. About five-foot-nothing, with a mop of curly hair, aviator shades, and a hand-rolled cigarette hanging out of his mouth, he grinned. "Morgan, my man. What brings you down to the Tree?"

Morgan gestured to Matt and Addy. "These are my new friends. Get them some food, would you, Jim?" He pointed at the stools lining the bar. "Have a seat. We'll get you fed, then I'll introduce you to the rest of the Troupe."

* * *

Pushing the curtains aside, Jack peeked out the window. "That's the library?"

Huxley breathed next to his ear. Smelled like he'd recently eaten garlic, though how that could be possible without him knowing, Jack couldn't be sure.

"That's it. That's where we need to go." Hux pressed his face closer to the window, pulling his jaw back and emphasizing his overbite. In danger of his teeth hitting the window, he stopped short and instead fogged it up with hot breath on cold glass. "It looks clear."

"Sure," Jack said. Still holding the curtain up with a single finger, he worked his jaw, trying to get it to loosen. This was no time to have a panic attack. Something he hadn't wanted to admit he'd been having.

Along with night terrors. At least the bouts of rage and deep depression had begun to loosen their hold. Thanks to Jane helping him talk through it. Think through it. Remember now. Which was useful in close quarters with others like this.

The street was clear all the way to the library. Too clear.

"I hate this, it's too quiet," he said. "You're sure we need to go there?"

Hux exhaled through his nose, fogging the glass again. He spoke to the window. "I saw a documentary once about the Black Death. You know about the plagues, right?"

Jack considered. School had been years and years ago, but of course he'd learned about it.

"I saw a documentary once. So long ago," Huxley said, not waiting for Jack to answer. He sat on the bed. The picture of Dean and his little brother hanging over the bed rattled as Hux leaned on the wall. "Your son is quite the great problem solver. I've never had a better lab assistant for helping me with thinking problems." Grinning in the vague direction of the front, his eyes glazed. "He's something special, your son."

Jack opened his mouth. To agree? To be humble? To say thank you? Was it a compliment? Mike had always been, well, Mike. Different in his own bright, cheery way. If nothing else, a set of tiny fluttery wings brushed up against Jack. That his son had found a niche had to be some kind of blessing he'd never hoped for. Not in the world in which he'd raised him.

"We got to talking about immunity. And the plague." Eyes alight, Huxley gripped Jack's shoulder. "Did you know, according to this television documentary, some people developed a natural immunity to the plague?"

Jack's eyes snapped back to the doc. "What?"

"Mmm. Natural immunity. Biological. Human. Granted, the plagues were bacterial, not viral. But this virus…" He paused, taking a breath through tight lips and seeming to taste it. "This virus behaves unusually. At times, not like a virus at all. We've been able to treat it like one, but reanimating dead bodies…" He watched Jack through the corner of his eye. "You must admit, that is unusual."

Jack nodded, mouth dry.

Hux went on, his eyes clamped to Jack's. "I must find out the truth about this immunity to the plague. And if it is true, what the conditions were. If they can be recreated, if they even have to." He gripped Jack's shoulder. "Mr. Cooke, there could be nothing more to your daughter's immunity than biology. I must get into that library to find out."

Jack stood. The idea of Katie's immunity being natural swirled through his head. Even if it were true, the doctor needed more information. Melinda needed to be stopped. Besides all that, Jane desperately wanted in the library. Had her own research to do. And he hadn't seen that many books in one place together since high school. It'd be nice.

"Dean," he said, creeping to the front of the train. "Get us closer. It's still too quiet out there. Be ready to throw this thing in reverse at the first sign of trouble. We'll go underground and circle around on foot if needed."

Dean released the brake. "You got it."

Jack patted him on the shoulder. "I'll take point." He eased up to the only front window, on the right side of the train, and leaned into it. So still. So quiet.

Light fingers landed on his shoulder. A few weeks ago she would have slipped an arm around his waist from behind. Now, she approached him a bit like one did a horse. Slow, within their line of sight, light but firm touches to let them know where you were. Never from behind without warning.

He frowned. "We ready to do this?"

She laid one hand on the baby's back where she'd been strapped to her chest again. "This little girl is going to be awake for most of it though. She's already taken like four naps today. She's wide the hell awake."

"I know it's difficult. Just keep her as quiet as you can." He kissed Katie on the head.

"Don't have to tell me twice," Jane said. She caught him before he stood and brushed her lips across his cheek.

One hand balled into a fist, but goose bumps didn't race up his spine. The adrenaline didn't begin its immediate pumping. He'd take the blessings where they came.

He caught her chin with two fingers and gave her one short kiss. Not chaste, but not porn. Something in-between. And about as much physical contact as he could handle at this point.

She smiled. "Watch the road, lover boy." Swinging her hips, she took up her bow and arrow and peeked out the back window.

Jack knelt in front of the window, gun drawn.

The train eased forward. The scenery remained still. Not even the dead moved out there. It was as though there was some kind of movement force-field around the library.

Jack idly wondered if they could punch through.

Dean stopped the train. "I don't like it. It's not right, Jack. I vote underground."

Jane traded between the window and Jack's face. Raised and lowered her shoulders less than an inch.

Huxley had pulled out his little notebook and gone back to it.

Mike, alert and ready, armed with a slingshot, inclined his head.

Celia stood, pressed against the window next to Dean. Copied Jane's shrug.

So, it was up to him. His decision-making hadn't been the best thing in the world lately. Best to follow Dean's instincts, since he was so set against continuing in the open.

"All right, Dean, we'll do it your way. Take us under."

Scowling, cheeks dimpled, Dean flipped some switches. Moved a few handles from one position to another. The train rolled and the tunnel approached. Yawning up at them, it invited them into the black.

The dark enfolded them. Only the light inside the train shone. "Got a bad feeling about this, Jack," Celia said.

"There's a light up there, I think." He squinted out the front window, trying to bring the light into focus. "Is there anything on the screen, Dean?"

Leaning his head forward, Dean tapped the screen and squeezed the brake. "I think it's a—"

"Shit. Jack," Jane said. Through the window, the red taillight illuminated her face and the top of the baby's head. Like blood had rained down on them.

He crept to her, gripped her shoulder, and looked out the window.

The end of the tunnel had been blocked by a hundred bodies at least. Though Jack could see only their silhouettes, he recognized their gait. Their shape. Wandering, thin, broken.

Adrenaline pushed itself through his veins so quick his nose got stuffy. Breathing through it, he caught her eye. "Get that bow and arrow prepped."

"Already done." She set her jaw and turned back to the window.

Adrenaline cresting, he returned to the front of the train. "Tell me something good, Dean. We can't go out the way we came." He squinted out the window again. The pinpoint got bigger as they approached the midpoint of the tunnel. Might be an arc-sodium. The only working one they'd seen underground this whole time.

"Uh," Dean said, jerking his chin to the side. "I'd love to do that."

"But."

"But. I can't. Proximity sensors say the opposite end of the tunnel is a bit crowded."

Jack stared at the screen, eyes wide, tendons creaking in his neck. "What do you mean, crowded? With what?"

Shaking his head, Dean stabbed the screen with a pointed finger. "Bodies. Living or dead, I don't know."

"Fuck."

Dean squeezed the brake. "I shouldn't have said we come down here."

Laying a soft hand on Dean's shoulder, Jack shook his head. With a squeeze, he stepped to the front window again. "Try to get us closer to whatever that is," he said, nodding toward the window. "That light."

"Looks like a door or something, Jack. Can't see much else." He tinkered with the screens. "Shit."

"What?"

"The bodies coming from the other end are moving pretty fast. They're gonna be on top of us in no time."

"How quick can we make that door?"

Dean tilted his head. "About the same."

"Fuck, we gotta try," Jane said.

"I'd like to see 'em try and stop us," Celia said, so many weapons drawn Jack wasn't sure how many hands she actually had. Two or twelve.

"The only one who needs protecting is Hux, Dad," Mike said. He'd moved to Huxley's side. "We can all look after ourselves."

Jack glanced at little Katie, wiggling inside the wrap. Mike and Addy both had been in similar situations, and they'd survived. It'd been worse for Michael. The beginning of this mess was so insane.

He exhaled through tight lips. "If we're going, let's go."

The arc-sodium crawled closer. A twenty-foot radius of the tunnel glowed orange. Besides the slight illumination from the train's head and taillights, nothing else held a speck of light. Except, of course, the blocked way out.

As Dean slowed the train to a crawl, Celia slid the window next to him open. She scented the air, tasting with her mouth. "Air tastes like them."

Buzzing echoed off the top and sides of the tunnel, bouncing in the window. No one had to mention the air sounded like them too.

"We've gotten out of a horde a lot bigger than this," Mike said. He held the cup of the slingshot, metal ball presumably resting inside his fingers. "But one of us needs to go make sure the door is open."

"Beat you to it, Cooke boys," Celia said. Pushing off the wall, she headed for the door.

Jane turned the handle before either Jack or Mike could protest. Swinging the door open a crack, she held it as Celia slipped through sideways. "I'll keep it unlocked."

Celia stepped onto the back porch.

* * *

Matt leaned over the bar, speaking in hushed tones with Jim, as Addy and Morgan walked into the next room.

The next room didn't have any couches or old posters on the walls like the room with the bar, that one even had a pool table, but what it did have was a handful of raucous men and women and a chest-high stage.

Their voices were so loud they stretched all the way to the ceiling before they came back to assault her ears, their clothes more deafening than heavy artillery. They dressed like something out of a dream. Lace, plastic, ruffled collars, brocade.

Fascinated, Addy watched as one of the women with her hair tied on top of her head, messy white-blonde tendrils falling around her face, leapt to the stage. Moving about the whole thing, touching her breathless compatriots on the faces and heads, holding their hands, she launched into a speech of some kind.

What more can I ask of you, dear fellows
That thou dost but giveth me freely?
How we could look full into the mirror
Of our own minds and hearts, my loves.
But shall that dark hour sneak through the trees
And visit upon us the things which we seek
Should I reach?
Should I touch
The stardust in thou hearts, and sprinkle it forth
As the long night falls? Or do I but wait
Upon the sun rising beneath your feet?
And ask that thou wouldst do the same for me.
For what is that night but a new favour
The chance for life, for love, for hope?
And as our feet fall bloody across this earth
So they rend from the land, the sea, the sky
That portal through which we doth pass, anon
Onto the journey which asks no end.

Addy stood frozen as the woman sat on the stage with her friends gathered around. Skin so pale it about faded into translucent, red flowers blossomed on her cheeks.

Morgan laughed. "Ah, what an introduction. This is our—"

"Victoria," Matt said, appearing at Addy's elbow, all the wind sucked from his words. "Oh my god." Color flamed in his cheeks, and he grinned with abandon.

Addy hadn't seen such a smile on him in weeks. Probably not since Ella had killed that 'Head.

A twinge of jealousy on Ella's behalf rushed through her, her fingers and face tingling.

And the woman on stage gasped, as if she'd seen a ghost. She squealed into a range only mice and dogs could hear. "Matt?" She leapt from the stage, pushed through her friends as they parted like the sea, and rushed to him.

He caught her, wrapping both arms around her and squeezing. His eyes closed.

"Yes," Morgan went on, "our Victoria."

Releasing Victoria, Matt stepped back. The dimples around his mouth deep in his red cheeks, he flashed a glance at Addy. "Addy. This is Vic. Victoria. We grew up together." Turning to Vic, he raised his shoulders. "What are you doing here?"

"What about you?" She pushed his shoulder. "All grown up. I thought you were out west?"

"Clearly, there's a lot to catch up on," Morgan said, stepping next to Matt. He didn't menace, but he didn't not. "You're one of hers?"

It wasn't Victoria he meant.

And everyone knew it.

Matt scuffed the ground with his foot and readjusted the rifle over his shoulder. "Not anymore, sir."

"That's a story I'd like to hear," Morgan said. "But why don't you catch up with Victoria? Meet the others." He clapped Addy on the shoulder. "I have something to take care of. I'll be back soon to get you." He walked out with a half bow to the others.

"Addy, is it?" Vic asked, hand out.

Addy shook. Not bad. Not great, but not bad. "Adelaide. Or Addy. Um. Whatever," she said, smiling. As she spoke, Vic's bright blue eyes, so blue they were almost white, fixed on hers.

Blinking a tendril of hair out of her eye, Vic smiled. "Addy. You're friends with Matt? How do you know him?"

"That's an even longer story. Some other time," Matt said, hand on Vic's shoulder. "What about you? What are you doing here and not there?"

"A long story, too, Matty. Let's just say I left and didn't go back." She swept her arm at the others. "Let me introduce you to the Wild Bunch. My people."

The five or six people who'd stood beneath her as she gave her monologue gathered around them, introducing themselves at once. Each speaking over the other in such a variety of voices and pitches and tones, Addy fought to keep up.

"Friends! Wait!"

Heart in her throat, Addy spun.

Now on stage, a tall man stood. Cheekbones high, he looked down his wide nose with a smile curving his lips. He could have been hewn from obsidian. Hair in twists around his head, he sat cross-legged on the stage. "We overwhelm our new visitors. Monologue you, I will not, for I am not so good of a writer as our Victoria. But let us come, sit, and speak soft with our new friends."

Victoria gestured at the man sitting on stage. "He talks a fancy game, but he knows as well as I, it's an affectation." She leaned on the stage, cheek pressed to the wood. "Cassius. Relax."

"Join me, Victoria. You too, pretty hazel eyes." Pointing his deep brown eyes at Addy, he smiled and stretched a slender hand out. "And you, my good man," he said to Matt.

Vic grabbed Addy's hand and led her to a small set of stairs around the side of the stage. "Watch your step, Addy. They're uneven and they rock."

And so they did. Addy lost her balance when they tried to go out from under her and threw her arm out.

From behind, Matt grabbed her waist and steadied her. "Legendary, Miss Cooke."

Same thing he'd said to her in the jail. When he took her to visit Dean.

Gritting her teeth, forcing her heart back down her throat, she thanked him and mounted the stage.

He followed, and, along with the others, they sat in a circle.

"So," Vic said, "Cassius you've met. Here we have Rivers"— an olive-skinned brunette woman, no bigger than a two by four, nodded—"Grey, and Talbot—"

"My dear lady!" Talbot leapt to his feet, tipping an imaginary hat and bowing so far at the waist he just about bent in half. "I could not be more pleased to make your acquaintance! I see the good Sir Matt is friends with our Victoria," he said, voice raised to the ceiling, cheeks a lighter brown than Cassius's shining, "and any friend of Victoria's, and their friends, are friends of mine." He bowed again, spiked hair pointing at the floor.

"Sit down, Tal," Cassius said. He laughed. A deep, unrestricted thing. Booming in his chest, his belly tight. "You're such a fool."

"Who better to be Mercutio," Talbot said as he sat. "You know it should be me."

"We know no such thing," the third woman said from her seat next to Matt. She held out a hand to him. "Kendra, if you please." Her grey eyes, set deep in her pink face, inspected him as he shook, narrowed and calculating. "What we all know is *I'd* make the best Mercutio. Why should I have to play the damned servant woman? Because I'm a woman?"

Talbot opened his mouth, a smile teasing the corner.

Kendra stood and paced circles around them, thumping Tal on the head every time she passed. "Did you know, when these plays were written, the parts were *all* played by men? Women weren't allowed on stage."

Grey, with his bright green eyes, white skin, and raven hair, stood and caught Kendra's waist with an arm. He swung her in a circle. "My dear. It would be a crime to hide a beauty such as yours in the dark. Of course we'll allow you on stage."

Prying his arm from her waist, she continued to spin, flowing shirt floating above her waist, caught in the currents of air she created. Her feet approached the edge.

Addy leapt up, legs tensed to grab her before she fell off the side.

With not an inch to spare, Kendra stopped twirling and stood stock-still as her shirt settled. She narrowed her eyes with a sly grin.

Stomach still in knots, Addy sat next to Matt again. "Sorry. I thought you might fall."

Cassius's eyes followed Kendra as she sat again, this time on Addy's side. "And your regard is noted and appreciated." His eyes shifted to Matt, assessing. "So, Victoria, dear. You know this Matt? May I ask?"

She opened her mouth to speak.

Matt inhaled.

Both of their cheeks flamed. A small smile played across Matt's lips.

Rivers gasped. "Wait. Vic. I've heard of this man. But you were just a boy then," she said, wide eyes taking Matt in again. She chuckled.

"It was a long time ago," Matt agreed. "I'd love to go into it, but."

Vic cleared her throat. "But there's no need." She peeped over their shoulders at the door.

Addy sprung to her feet again, machete already half out of its scabbard.

Morgan stood in the doorway. "Fast. Good. There's somewhere else we need to go. Victoria, would you come with us?"

Pulling her knees up to her chest, she rested her chin on them. Round, blue eyes peeked over their tops. "Is it a must, Morgan?"

"I think so."

Matt stood and held a hand out to her.

Taking it, she stood and made a show of straightening her wardrobe. From the back of the stage, she picked up a brocade-and-lace coat, draped it over her shoulders, and settled some kind of oversized floppy hat with a brim over her messy hair. "If we're going to go, let's go."

Sweeping past Addy, she floated down the stairs.

CHAPTER 10

Melinda stared at the map on her wall, eyes crossing from all the new lines on it. The Queen City had grown since she'd left. Exponentially. Of course, that meant more people to cull from when it came time for new test subjects.

Her door rattled with a knock.

Hand on her knife, she opened the door.

Lash stood, arms folded. "Invite me in, woman. Need to talk."

"I'm a little busy, Ilasha."

Lash breezed past her, smelling of soap and fresh skin. "I know. That's why I'm here. What's this I hear about you heading up another raid?"

"We need test subjects." She closed the door and walked back to the map, arms crossed.

Lash spoke to her back. "We stopped doing raids months ago. At some point, these people are going to come for us if we don't stop testing our vaccines and random concoctions on them."

"You'll be happy to know it's not those kinds of tests."

"And besides," Lash went on, as though Melinda hadn't spoken, "you can't lead it yourself. You'll be in danger."

"And that's your primary concern, is it? My safety?"

"You know it is," Lash said, coming to stand next to her. They stared at the map together. "Their defense force has grown."

Melinda tightened her arms. "Sure it has. The city's grown. But they've still got holes in their defenses. I've done my homework."

"Is that where you've been?"

With a sigh, Melinda reached a finger up and swept a lock of hair out of her face. "It's not going to be like it was, Lash. We both know that."

Lash reached for the hand. "Because of Jack?"

Melinda stepped back. The volume of emotions trying to burst through the dam almost toppled her. She curled her fists and shoved them in her elbows again. "Who's heading the defense force these days?"

"Still Morgan. Handsome fucker."

Melinda stepped close enough to touch the map with her nose and examined the perimeter. "Thought you didn't like men."

"Doesn't mean I can't recognize the pretty ones." With a scraping of legs, she pulled out a chair and sat at the table.

Biting her lip, Melinda joined her and cupped her chin in her hand. "I can't believe he's still alive. Seems like he's been in charge of the force over there forever. How long has it been?"

"Seven years, give or take," Lash said. She nudged Melinda's foot with her own. "You're still smarter than him."

Melinda chuckled. "Thanks, Mom."

Lash slapped her shoulder. "I mean it, bitch." She smiled. "What are you getting them for, if it's not for the vaccine or more of your weird cocktails?"

"Immunity research."

"Ain't you off that?"

"Officially, for now, sure. Not for long."

"That's my girl. Always with the plotting and the planning."

Melinda laid her head on the table, the cool wood slick against her cheek. "The last time I went in somewhere without a plan, I died. Would really rather not repeat that mistake." Closing her eyes, she inhaled. The cold, damp, earthen scent of the Molehill filled her nose. "Am I doing the right thing?"

Lash laid a warm hand across Melinda's arm. "What do you mean, baby?"

"Some of the things I've done for this company. For the vaccine. For immunity. They haven't been. Well." She sat up, holding her head. "I question if we're on the right side of this."

"What are sides? There's living, and there's dead." Lash squeezed. "Is my hand warm?"

"Yes."

Lash tugged Melinda's hand free and gripped it. "Is your hand warm?"

Melinda's eyes stung. "Yes."

"You're alive. I'm alive. All the people who've taken the Cure—the one *we* made, by the way—they're alive. This girl you gave the vaccine to. She's alive. Her baby's alive. Melinda, look at me."

She did, a tear falling from each eye.

"Because of you. They're all alive. The work you've done. One bad decision to go into a sporting goods store, and countless people live because of it." She let Melinda's hand go and stroked her cheek. "I wouldn't have it any other way."

More tears slipped down Melinda's cheeks. "Thanks, Lash. I needed to hear that."

"I wish you'd stay here. Let someone else handle the raid. Would you do that for me?"

"I won't go near the city. I'll stay in back. Good enough?"

"It'll have to be, I suppose. Take someone with you. One of your kids."

Melinda scowled. "I don't even know who I can trust anymore."

"A shame, what you told me about Matt," Lash said, standing. She stared at the map. "He was always a good kid."

"He turned on us. I'll kill him if I see him again, the traitor."

Lash shook her head. "Best if you stay in back, like you said. Morgan would kill you himself, you give him the chance."

Melinda laughed. The chair creaked under her. "You're not wrong, my dear. He hates me." She laughed again. "As well he should."

Lash laughed with her. "It's good to have you back, Em. I missed you." She headed for the door. "Be safe."

As Ilasha opened the door, Melinda called her. "When I get back, you want to join me on top of the hill? I was looking forward to dusting off the telescope."

Lash didn't turn. "Sounds like fun. See you later."

* * *

Morgan cleared his throat. "So, Matt."

The uncomfortable smile on Matt's lips strained across his teeth.

Addy's nerves jangled in sympathy.

"So. Sir."

"Just Morgan is fine, really, son."

"Not your son."

"Right. Right." Morgan stopped, thumbs hooked in his pockets. "I need to know the story."

Matt glanced at Vic.

Wisps of her hair flying from under the cap, she frowned with one side of her mouth. "I haven't hidden anything from them. Coming to their side was a choice. I made it. I've stuck to it."

"My story can't be that much different from Vic's," Matt said, crossing his arms.

Morgan walked away. "Possibly. But I want you to tell it anyway."

Throwing Matt a look, brow knitted, Addy followed. She could infer all she needed to from what she'd already seen. But it would be nice to hear it from his own lips.

Those same lips pursed, he caught back up with them.

Victoria between him and Morgan, she hooked an arm through Morgan's. "We grew up together."

"He can tell me, Vicky."

She pressed her mouth into a white line.

"She showed up at the Molehill about eight months after I did. Me and Tim were some of the first."

"How is Tim?" Vic asked, staring at the horizon.

Addy choked on her own spit and coughed.

Patting her on the back, Morgan waited until she was done to ask if she was OK.

"Dead." She scowled. "He's dead, Vic."

"Oh, you knew him? Fine specimen of pretty boy that he was?"

"Another story for another time," Addy said. Would she ever be clear of him?

"One I'd like to hear the rest of, too," Matt said. "Victoria here was pretty feral. She cleaned up nice though."

"Way I hear it, you were too, my dear. Caked in so much dirt, it took two weeks to wash it all off you."

"Nice. Nice. I guess that's true." Matt chuckled and went on. "We had school together, since we're close in age."

"I am ten months older than you, good sir. Don't you forget it."

"How could I? You remind me every freaking chance you get," Matt said. Shaking his head, at least one of the dimples reappearing, he grinned. "We palled around for a while. Then I noted she was a girl." He flushed. "A pretty one."

"So long after I noticed this cute boy I thought he'd forgotten I was female. Or wasn't into girls."

Addy chuckled. She'd never gone through that with anyone. The only boys she really knew at that age were Mike and Dad. And Jane's dad. As they talked about their upbringing, the way they'd flirted and one thing led to another and everyone so young and together, jealousy bubbled up in her brain stem. She'd never, ever been jealous of someone else's childhood.

Maybe she hadn't known what she'd been missing.

Either way, Matt finished the story at the point when Mom sent him away from the Molehill.

"How'd you get here, Victoria?" Addy asked. At least as much to escape the jealousy as to satisfy her curiosity about Vic's arrival here. And how she'd gotten out from under Mom.

Morgan laid a hand on Addy's arm. "I believe this ties in to where we're going."

Victoria sucked a breath over her teeth. "I'll tell the story, if it's all the same, Morgan."

"Be my guest, my dear," he said, guiding her under a branch.

Ahead, some buildings had been partially knocked down, their red bricks reconfigured to make a tunnel of some kind. The dark yawned out at them.

"Are we sure it's safe to go in there?" Addy asked, hand on her machete.

"Pull your weapons if you like, Addy," Morgan said. "You never know what might be lurking in the dark."

Victoria sniffed. "They send people over here, you know. Talus. They send troops. Attack troops."

Matt, rifle raised to the dark ahead, choked. "What? Why?"

"Things changed after you left, baby."

Again, jealousy on Ella's behalf flamed through Addy's gut. Good lord but she was full of jealousy today.

"After you left but before General Thibodeaux did, they started vaccine testing. Did you know about the vaccine?"

He shook his head, eyes still trained on the darkness ahead. "Not until." Pausing, he glanced at Addy. "Not until a few months ago."

From her crown to her toes, a chill ran down Addy's spine like a bucket of cold water had been emptied on her head. These people didn't know who she was. Mom had been going by her maiden name since she died. And Matt stopped before bringing it up.

Why they continued not knowing beyond her, she trusted Matt's instincts to keep it under wraps. If nothing else, it felt right. And it kept things less complicated.

The small voice that'd morphed into Yaz's from Picard tickled at the back of her mind.

But what if they find out, Addy? They'll think you're a liar.

They passed into the first shadows thrown by the top of the tunnel.

Vic lowered her voice as they entered, holding the echoes at bay. "They needed test subjects. Where better to get them than the city closest by?"

Matt stopped and gripped Vic's arm. "Did you come here and take people back?" Voice gruff, he stared at her. Through her.

She dropped her eyes and clung to Morgan. "You know what it was like. She told us to jump…"

"We said how high. Yeah. I know." With a sigh, he released her. "What made you change your mind?"

"What made you change yours?"

He backed up a step, one side of his mouth curled.

Addy found all at once she couldn't hear her name aloud. Not yet. That last moment, as she stood in the wind from the helicopter blades and smiled, it screamed into her head with the force of a train.

Oh god, a train.

You're a mess, Adelaide.

"Something similar. Growing up. Meeting people. Finding out it didn't have to be that way," Matt said. Not her name.

Addy exhaled. Her abs hurt.

Victoria laughed. A small laugh, like a tiny bell, but a laugh. "Yeah, it was a boy for me. He's up ahead." She pointed into the dark.

"Oh, I'd like to meet the man who captured Victoria's heart. That's a hell of a feat."

She snorted, pulling Morgan closer. "You're one to talk, Lyburn. Where is she now?"

The urge to puke washed over Addy so hard, her mouth watered.

"Heads up, you two," Morgan said. "We're essentially safe here, but like I said. You never know. And. Well. You'll see."

Addy gripped her machete, redbrick walls of the tunnel closing in on her shoulders. The stench of stagnant water crawled up her nose. "Give me my knife, Matt. It's too close in here for this thing."

"My knife," he said, holding it out to her.

Without looking, she sheathed the machete and gripped the knife. The bow and arrow would be nice, but they weren't as fast to reload as his gun, and as the darkness enclosed them further, her precision with them would drop. Best to stick to the knife for up close, let Matt handle the range.

The smell of the tunnel became earthier. Wetter.

"Are we going underground?" Addy asked. She peeked over her shoulder at the receding sunlight. Waited for it to be blocked. To be trapped with no way to go but down.

Her breath shortened.

Morgan gripped her shoulder with a warm, firm hand. He shook. Not hard. But enough to get her attention. "Hey. It's all right. I need you to be calm. Can you be calm?"

She shook his hand off. "Of course I can be fucking calm. Made it this far, didn't I?"

"She's good, man," Matt said. "Solid. Someone to have in your corner."

"Stop being so nice to me, Matt," she said, gripping the knife and spinning it behind her hand. "It's making me nervous."

He chuckled. Low, but she caught it.

Addy waited for his retort. It didn't come. She raised her hands into a guard position. "Anybody got any damned flashlights?"

"Don't need 'em," Morgan said. "Look."

Ahead, the tunnel opened again. Although the light streaming in had an artificial feel, it was light. That was good enough.

As they closed in on it, the shadows dissipated. The places for people or 'Heads to hide diminished until they were gone.

Addy let out the breath she'd been holding and stepped out into a large cavern. "What is this?"

Morgan hugged Vic and released. "Long, long ago? A parking garage. What it is now is a holding cell."

"Holding cell," Matt said. "For what? Stinks down here."

Addy sniffed, tasting the air as it passed her tongue. Old, clotted blood. Coppery, new blood. Sweat. Feces. Piss. But underneath that. Underneath it.

She inhaled through her teeth. "It smells like a hospital. Deep down, like a hospital. Are these people. Did you."

And all at once it hit her. It hit her so hard she sat on the ground, teeth clacking together, almost taking a piece of tongue with them.

Andrew, in his paper gown, shouting as he leapt from the roof to the tower. Clutching Mom and Dad in massive arms. Falling to earth without a scream. Blood filling his throat as he lay dying, unable to die.

"You have them here, don't you?" Eyes wet, she stared up at Morgan from beneath her brows.

He knelt before her.

"The ones they experimented on but didn't kill. You have them." She breathed heavily through flared nostrils. The scent hit her again. Wet earth on top, but beneath, the scent of death. Of reanimated corpses. And of hospitals. The same peculiar smell Mom's hospital on Emerald Isle had held.

Kneeling before her, Morgan stretched out a hand. "Look, we didn't do this to them. But we also can't fix it."

Arms wrapped around herself, Victoria stared at the ground. All the bravado, all the brightness, all the life sucked from her face. "They can't help what they are."

Matt shifted on his feet, glaring at Morgan's hand on Addy's knee. "Why don't you back up, all right, man?" He held his own hand out to Addy.

She took it, eyes fixed to his. "I've seen someone like they're talking about. It was awful." Shifting her gaze to Morgan, she swallowed. "One of the worst things I've ever seen." She swallowed again, the vision of Andrew's swollen throat stuck in her mind. Unable to die. Dad's horrified eyes.

That hurt more than the rest of it. Told her what kind of trouble they were really in. Dad's eyes as he watched his friend suffer.

Balling her fist into her midsection, she attempted to grip the hole in her center. To close it somehow. "How many of them are there?"

"More than there should be," Vic said, moving away. She floated, like she was the central character in someone's dream—or nightmare—and disappeared into a shadow, her voice drifting from the dark. "There's a lot of things to love about this city. This is not one of them."

Morgan invited them to follow her. "Please. And have your weapons ready. We've restrained them, but—"

Addy drew her machete again. "But you never know with the dead."

"They're not exactly dead," Morgan said, walking ahead of them. He told them what kind of routine they had them in, that they expected it, that you could still talk to them sometimes.

The words bounced off the insides of Addy's empty heart.

Matt gripped her hand.

Her heart skipped as he uncurled her fingers from the knife.

"My knife, please." The slightest bit of smile raised his lips, and he eased the knife out of her hand. Gun holstered, he tossed the knife from hand to hand. "Where'd you get it?"

"My mom gave it to me as a birthday present when I was a kid." She cleared her throat, trying to cross her arms and cover the hole in her stomach without slicing one of them with the machete.

Matt flushed, mouth flapping.

Morgan looked over his shoulder. "Where's your mom now, Addy?"

She cleared her throat again. "She died a long time ago."

Morgan stopped in front of an empty doorway, a wall and door made with some of those bricks from outside, and extended an arm. "Through here."

With a sideways glance at Addy, Matt went through and joined Victoria.

Addy peeked through the cavernous doorway. "Where are the lights?"

Morgan leaned around the door and hit a switch. Fluorescents flickered to life overhead.

Shaking her head, she lifted her machete and preceded Morgan into the room. The ceiling high, it still crowded down on her. Piles of bricks, old drywall, refuse of any sort, lay in the corners and against the walls. The stench of 'Heads, of unwashed people, of mold, floated around her sinuses. Each scent vying to outdo the others.

She wrinkled her nose. Opening her mouth to make a comment, she inhaled over her tongue. Which amplified the odor a thousand times. Gagging, she closed her mouth and covered it, holding the dry heaves at bay. Saliva built up between her teeth.

"I know," Morgan said. "It stinks. Everything about this stinks."

"You heard what I told Matt, right?" Voice muffled from behind her hand, she swallowed and lowered it. "About seeing one of them?"

Morgan bobbed his head. "Through here," he said, holding his arm up again.

She entered a large room, as big as a banquet hall, which had been partitioned off with blankets and sheets of varying colors, lengths, and fabrics. Each cubby about big enough for one person.

Vic and Matt stopped about halfway down. They stood facing each other, arms crossed over their chests. Matt didn't smile, but he didn't frown.

If Ella had seen this, she would have walked right up next to him and stared at Vic until she melted into an embarrassed puddle. Or she would have huffed at Matt, or rather, *Matthew*, and folded her arm through his, pressed against his side. She certainly wouldn't have let Vic continue to flirt.

But the memories of Ella, alive and strong, had no place here. Not in this room.

The clinking of chains, moans, growls, buzzing, undead death, that's what belonged in this room.

Addy's skin crawled up her scalp, the hair trying to follow.

Pulling her cap farther over her eyes, Victoria looked past the sheet in front of them. "He's awake."

Morgan stepped inside the sheet. It flapped closed behind him. He put on a bright, jovial voice. "Hey, Adam, how's my main man?"

Adam gurgled. "Fix it?"

"No, my friend. We haven't found a way to fix you. Not yet." Morgan sighed. "Got some new people for you to meet."

Gurgle.

The sheet opened. "Come on in, guys. He's receiving visitors today."

Vic pushed through, arms crossed tightly over her chest, eyes red.

"Hm. OK." Matt inclined his head and disappeared behind the sheet.

Addy followed, stomach a mess of slick knots. Her throat worked, fighting a dry heave.

A man, no more than twenty-five or so, sat against the wall. Slack chains hung from a ring on the wall and connected to large metal cuffs on his wrists. Giant forearms rested on his knees.

Addy took a breath and held it. His slack expression that of a Dead Head, his eyes jarred her. They bore consciousness. Intelligence, even. His skin wasn't rotting from his bones, but the stench emanating from his mouth made her wonder what the hell they fed him.

He took her in, eyebrows raising a millimeter. "Who?"

Victoria knelt next to him. "Adam, honey, Matt here is an old friend of mine. And this is his friend, Adelaide." She took in Addy, eyes resting on her drawn machete.

Heartbeat thready in the side of her neck, Addy slipped the blade behind her back. "Hi, Adam. Good to meet you."

He snorted, snarled at Matt, and turned back to Vic. "Play…going?"

"Great," she said, smiling. She lifted the hat away from her eyes. "I wrote a new monologue for you. Would you like to hear it?"

Drool slipped from the side of his mouth and formed a string below his chin.

She repeated the monologue that had introduced her to Addy, without the theatrics. She whispered it to him, like a lover's promise.

Addy's heart broke. A thousand tiny pieces that'd been trying to glue themselves back together shattered into her ribs. Loss was a part of the world she'd grown up in. But this. This was something different. Dead, not dead, here, not here. What the hell could you do with that?

As Vic finished her monologue, a tear slipped down Adam's cheek. Victoria raised her hand to wipe it.

As she did, Morgan spoke her name.

In the same breath, Adam snarled and snapped his teeth at her. His head struck the air with the speed of a rattlesnake.

Addy's machete popped out again as Vic, Matt, and Morgan jumped back.

Arms outstretched, Morgan got between them and Adam, pushing them toward the sheet.

Adam snarled and gurgled. He worked to his feet and took three shuffling steps, chains catching his wrists and pulling his hands behind him. Stretching his arms to their limit, shoulders threatening to pop from their sockets, he snapped at them.

His growls rattled up from deep in his chest, settling into Addy's brain like an ice pick through the ear. She clenched her fist, controlling the need to take his head off at the shoulders.

Snarls sounded around them. The room filled with gurgling growls.

Morgan stepped back. "Once one of them gets going, it usually sets the others off. We should make our exit."

Addy blew past the sheet and down the center of the room. Each compartment she passed growled at her.

Her stomach roiled. A dry heave found its way up, but she stuffed it back down, throat burning.

"Jesus, Vic," Matt said as they all joined Addy in the outer room. "What the hell?"

Morgan laid a hand on his shoulder. "This is exactly why I have so many fine men and women like yourself and Addy on my defense team. Dead Heads, we all know. We know what to do and have a pretty good idea how to plan. But Talus Crest, those assholes." He stopped, jaw working.

Arms slack at her sides, Vic smiled. "You should have seen him. He danced. He lit up everything." She swayed, as though she were dancing with an invisible partner, and twirled about the room. "Everything was more beautiful because he touched it. Even me." She stopped, back to them, and dropped her arms again. "Then they came. This was the last raid, almost a year ago. They came, and they took him. And when he returned to me a few months later, he was."

"He was like the rest of them," Morgan said.

"Are they all like that?" Addy asked. "Can they all talk?"

Morgan stuck a nail between his teeth. "Most of them. There are varying degrees, but they all know what's happened to them. They all have moments of awareness. Some of them have taken matters into their own hands."

Flinching, Addy closed her eyes. The sight of Dad killing Andrew as he begged to die splashed across the inside of her eyelids.

Opening her eyes, she found Matt staring at her. He furrowed his brow, a lock of brown hair resting on his forehead. "And the rest of them ask to stay like this?"

"We're trying to find a way to turn them back. Or to force Talus to."

"You can't," Addy said, swallowing. Her mom's voice floated through her head. "There's no way to reverse the process."

Victoria took two large steps and invaded Addy's bubble. "How do you know that?"

"I heard it somewhere." Staring up into Vic's red eyes, she held her ground. The story of Andrew was hers, and she could choose to do what she liked with it.

Melting, deflating like a balloon with a pinhole, Victoria sank to the ground and laid her head in her hands.

"I could use people like you two on my defense force," Morgan said, glancing between Addy and Matt. "You could both be real assets. As you've seen, this community is vibrant. We have a lot to live for here. And a lot to defend. Will you help us?"

Stomach still gurgling, Addy looked at Matt. Whatever choice she made, she didn't want him to go elsewhere. This thing with the half 'Heads frightened her on a level she hadn't expected. Without admitting it out loud, she needed friends near. People she trusted. And he was at the top of a nonexistent list.

He shrugged.

"I'm in," she said. She hoped he'd follow.

He sat next to Vic and threw an arm around her shoulders. "The general took her from me. My girl. I'd like nothing more than to keep people from feeling what we are right now. We'll help you."

CHAPTER 11

On Dean's proximity screen, one tiny red dot appeared next to the train, making a beeline for the door under the light.

Jack joined Jane in the rear. "There's a lot of them. On either side."

Sliding her arrow back into the quiver, she produced a knife in the same fluid motion. She ran a cool finger down his cheek, gripping the knife with the other three. "We got this. Don't worry about me. You get yourself to that door. I'll be right beside you."

He grabbed her hand. "I know you will. I know. But you let me know if you need me. I'll be right there."

She produced three more knives. Two slipped between the fingers of each hand, ready to be thrown.

Pulling her closer and sinking into a kiss with her rippled through his mind. Playing the film to the end, he saw her pressed against him. He felt himself react to her. He wanted to react to her.

His stomach turned.

He settled for cupping her cheek.

She leaned into his palm, eyes closed, and smiled.

Releasing her, he glanced at Mike.

Slingshot ready, he stared at the ceiling with a studious eye.

Jack cleared his throat, stepping toward him. "You ready, son?"

"Need one more thing," he said, holding the slingshot by the cup. He dug into his pouch and fished out a couple suckers. Raising his eyebrows, he offered Jack one.

He took it. Didn't notice the flavor. Just anticipated the sickly sweet coating it would give the inside of his mouth and sinuses as he fought his way through clotted, stinking blood. "Thanks, Mike."

"No problem," he said, voice bouncing around the sucker already sunk into his cheek. "Stay safe."

Jack grabbed him into a hug. "You too."

Mike squeezed him for all he was worth.

Closing his eyes, blood rushing through him, Jack squeezed him back. Thank god the boy was such a kind, forgiving soul. He didn't deserve such a kid. Yet here they were.

Pushing off, he joined Dean again. "How's she doing?"

"We're cuttin' it close. She's at the door but still outside it. I don't see any indication it's open."

"Our choices are slim. How good of a fortress is this train?"

Dean shook his head. "Most of the weapons are in that locker. We could get to them if we—"

Celia shouted.

Dean brought the train to a dead stop.

"They're coming in fast," Jane said, face pressed to the window. "Now or never, boys."

"Hux, stay in the middle of us," Mike said, dragging him to the door. "I've seen you fight. Don't do it. Just stay with us and get to the door."

"What if she doesn't get it open, Michael?" Huxley asked, peeking out the front window.

No one answered him. Jane stepped out, Mike and Huxley followed, and Jack and Dean pulled up the rear.

"Cee," Mike called, voice pitched low. "How's it coming with the door?"

Her voice floated through the dark between them and the circle of orange light she stood under. "Hurry the fuck up."

Jane charged down the stairs, bright eyes everywhere at once. The buzzing grew louder as the two hordes closed in, and as they bumped and wobbled their way down the tunnel, it rose in pitch. The echo deafened Jack. Threatened to pull his brain out his ears.

Mike pushed the doctor in front of him, hitting a 'Head in the eye with his slingshot as it stepped into the circle of light.

Jack checked the safety of his gun with one finger while pulling his knife from its holster with the other. The gun might not be the best weapon to use down here, it was likely to deafen everyone, but he was most accurate with it. There was no good reason not to use it. It's not like they had to worry about drawing a horde.

It was already here.

One bumped into him, in the dark soup between them and the light circle. Without stopping, he sliced and shoved. It fell away, buzzing modulated as it hit the ground. "Tight in here already. Get to the door, Jane."

"I told you," she said, a knife spinning off into the black. Somewhere, a buzz that'd been part of the cacophony of them stopped. A body hit the ground. "Don't worry about me. Get your own sweet ass to the door." Another knife appeared in her hand. The baby hiccupped. "You spend too much time worried about me, you'll get clipped. Look out."

A whizzing knife flew past his head and buried itself in the temple of a 'Head reaching for him.

Heeding her advice wasn't such a bad idea.

Stepping back, he pulled his knife up and sank it into the forehead of the closest 'Head.

Dean and Mike struggled against their own, puffs of breath escaping their lips as they fought to keep Huxley safe. Far away, Celia pounded on the door.

Narrowing his vision and sinking his knife into the rotted melon of yet another of this stinking horde, Jack quieted all the sounds around him. "Get your own sweet ass to the door," he whispered, jamming his knife through the jaw, soft palate, and brain of another. Yanking it free, he flipped it to release some of the blood it'd claimed. Switching to a backhanded hold, he sliced through the neck of another, the knife dragging through desiccated flesh, half a windpipe, and out past the cartilaginous ear. The sound of the gristle ripping enough to gag him, Jack stepped closer to the door. One foot inside the orange circle.

The next one came out of nowhere. He didn't have time to think. To consider. Reaction all he was made of, he lifted the gun and sent a bullet through its eye. Aim so true, it traveled through to the one behind it. They both dropped.

Ego a thing for young men and fools, he dropped the next one. And the next. Swinging the knife, firing only precisely aimed shots, his brow cool and calm, he kept a feel for the other living bodies around him. Far away, the scent of flowers floated into his brain. Thoughts focused to a laser point, it registered and was catalogued but did nothing to sway him from the task at hand. And when he dropped one clip for the next, the warm bodies around him covered him. Whizzing, flying, cutting. Clotted blood splattered on his skin, and he wiped it away.

"Got it," he said, standing to face his enemy again.

Within the full light of the orange arc-sodium, the faces of each 'Head in front of him swam into focus. The one before him had, at one point, long, brown hair. It'd been tied when she died. Not a lot of difference between this one and Melinda, really.

His mind faltered, but his hand remained true. Taking over for him, the muscles did the work of maintaining the radius of breath between them and the dead. In the rear, that was what you did. Kept the ones in the front from becoming the ones in the back.

The hordes closing in, one 'Head ran into another. Tripping over each other's feet and their own, they fell at Jack's. Snarling, bubbling, buzzing, they clawed and gnashed their way toward the group. As Jack executed every single one in front of him, the pounding on the door behind him ceased.

Celia grunted. "On your feet."

Jack peeked behind him.

Dean had stumbled to his knees. Hands under his arms, Celia hauled him upright.

"Celia, watch it," Dean said, swinging his machete.

Sleeve caught by the 'Head, Celia stumbled. She grabbed a handful of Dean's shirt and tugged. "To the door, jackass."

Teeth clashed next to Jack's ear.

He opened his mouth and cocked his knife-hand.

A small dagger sank into the eye of the 'Head, hilt deep. It dropped like a sack of rocks.

Grinning, he didn't have to look over his shoulder to know from where the knife had sailed. Instead, he raised the gun and continued blasting away. "Is that door open?"

"No," she said, warm shoulder brushing up against his back. "Celia couldn't get anyone to answer. And it won't budge."

"I'll shoot it open if I have to. We've got to get in there."

The door, thick wood, had two twins that had long ago been blocked by piles of detritus. Ornate carvings adorned the one remaining.

"Get it open, Mike," he said, aiming everywhere at once and herding everyone behind him. He reloaded again, Jane covering.

"We don't want to break the door," Mike said, his voice soft yet firm. "We will though. We are here for the books. Please, let us in. I can hear you in there."

Jack shot the next one in the mouth. "Can you?"

"Someone's in there. I hear…a woman." His eyes slipped half-closed.

Huxley backed into the wall between Mike and the door, his tiny notebook clutched in both hands and raised to his chest.

Jack absently ended two more, still focused on Mike's slack face.

"She sounds familiar maybe…she's telling someone to open the door." One side of his mouth turned up. He shook his head. "I can't hear the rest, but it sounded like 'or else.' I think—"

On squealing hinges, the door cracked open. An old man, frail, at least ninety, stood behind it. "In here." He waved at them with a cane. "Get in here." Glancing over their shoulders, his watery eyes widened. He fixed them to Mike. "You should hurry."

Knife whipping through 'Heads like they were butter, gun blasting, Jack covered them all as they retreated.

As Celia half dragged Dean backward, he stumbled again.

"Watch your leg, Dean," Jack said, swinging the other way. "Get the fuck in there."

"Come on, Dad," Mike said. "We're not closing the door without you."

A knife whizzed past him, sinking into the 'Head before him. Her slender hand grabbed his shoulder, the scent of flowers wafting past his nose again. She dragged him with her.

The old man, leaning on his cane, stared at Jane with his mouth open. Everyone else backed through the doorway past him, Jack and Jane with the baby the last ones out.

Hand in the small of Jane's back, Jack propelled them both toward the door. Five large steps carried them through it, and he grabbed it to yank it closed as he passed.

And like in those old movies, hands gripped it from the other side before he got it latched. Scratching and scrabbling and clawing at him.

Teeth gritted, he bobbed away from the hands. One came inches from his cheek.

Jane stepped next to him and hacked at the fingers, separating them at the knuckle joints from their owners. With the other hand, she grabbed the door handle as well and together they yanked it shut.

She leaned her back against it, chest heaving.

The old man pointed. "You may lock it. There are several locks there."

Without looking, she spun lock after lock. Her eyes remained fixed to Jack's.

Leaving the thoughts out before they had time to curdle into fears, he popped his sucker out with one hand and slid the other under her hair.

For the first time in weeks, he kissed her with abandon. Without thought, he let himself slide into the clouds. Her satiny, cool lips. The gripping fist of fear that'd held him let a finger up. One finger.

Breathless, he let her go.

They'd entered a waiting area in the middle of a hallway. Potted plants, leather couches, spindle-legged tables in a circle. The others already sat, Dean with his leg up on one of the tables. Huxley, between he and Mike, still clutched his little notebook. In her own chair, Celia twirled one of Mike's suckers in her fingers.

Jack put away his weapons. He stuck his hand out to the old man. "Jack Cooke. Are you in charge here?"

The man chuckled, switching the cane to his opposite hand to grasp Jack's. A firm shake but nervous. Jittery. Could have just been age.

"Bryce. You can call me Bryce." He nodded at Jane. "Pretty woman you've got there. If I was sixty years younger, little lady," he began.

Jane's lips curved in a grin. "What? You'd what?"

He faltered. "You'll all have to wait here. I cannot let you in from this point."

"Who can?" Jane asked, eyes batting.

Jack's toes curled, but the old man smiled. "You are something, young woman. Something, indeed. Hopefully, the librarian will be here soon."

"Is that who's in charge here?" Jack asked.

Bryce retreated through another ornate door. "You'll see."

* * *

Sun setting behind her, Addy stood outside the bank building and gazed up its glass walls. "Called them skyscrapers, huh?" She squinted and followed the line of it all the way to its peak. Leaning so far she nearly overbalanced and fell backward.

"Yep. They did." Matt stood next to her, arms folded over his chest, and stared up with her.

"What do we call them now?"

"Old dreams, long dead."

She scoffed. "Five minutes with those actors and you're waxing poetic on me. What's that about?"

"Gotta admit. Some of their whatever rubbed off on me."

"Looked like you wanted something else to." She stopped, the words falling out of her mouth catching up with her ears. It wasn't her place to be jealous for Ella. Ella was dead. Clearing her throat, she shuffled her feet. "We get started on this defense force in the morning, huh?"

"Yeah." His Adam's apple bobbed, the parentheses around his mouth pointing down. They did that a lot lately.

Addy supposed hers did too. Dean losing his mind, making foolish mistakes, it'd put a lot of frowns on her face. And besides Matt, she was alone here. Being alone never sat right with her.

The thought that they ought to talk about Ella and Dean sped through her mind. She shook her head to clear it. "Do you think they'll give us the same assignment?"

He headed toward the bank. "Hope so."

The front door opened, Sly leaning on the handle. "Adelaide. Matthew. Welcome back!"

Matt stuck out his hand. "Just Matt, my man." Smile on his mouth but not in his voice.

"You got it," Sly said, giving him a firm up and down pump. He swung an arm around Addy's shoulders and squeezed for a brief moment. "Addy. I hear Morgan talked you into joining our ragtag little gang."

She stepped into the cool lobby. "Are you always on duty, Sly?"

"Feels that way. I guess you're getting barracks assignments in the morning. You guys eat?"

They shook their heads.

Matt's stomach rumbled. He gripped it. "Been a long day."

Addy chuckled. "You didn't—"

Sly's radio blipped twice. The color drained from his face. As his hand fell to it, it emitted a high-pitched squeal.

Eardrums vibrating, Addy covered her ears and glanced at Matt with wide eyes. She couldn't feel her throat.

Sly removed the radio from his belt and it stopped squealing. It blipped again in a rhythmic pattern.

Addy listened to the spaces between the blips. "Who's coming?"

"What?" Matt asked. "What does that mean?"

"It's Morse code," Addy said, head tilted. "Someone is coming." She gripped Sly's shoulder. "Is it 'Heads?"

"No. Here." Clipping the radio to his belt again, he spun around the desk. From under it, he lifted two rifles, flashlights mounted to the ends. "Take these. Welcome to the defense force and your first Talus raid." He dashed across the lobby and threw open the door. "Let's get out there."

Wooden stock of the gun slick under Addy's hand, she headed back out the door. "Raid? I thought those were over?"

"So did we." Dragging a chain with links as big as his hands from the ground, Sly nodded to Matt. Together, they chained the door.

Addy stopped. "What if the people in there need out?"

"You can get around most of the downtown area on third floors alone. This way," he said, leading them the way they'd come. "When people first came back here, they pretty much lived on floor three and up. The first two floors a buffer against the dead. We still have those old bridges, doors, ladders, what have you." He stopped, fingers encircling Addy's wrist. "You saw the people they sent back?"

She nodded, spit dried, tongue stuck to the roof of her mouth. When they'd made this plan to come here and find out about the Molehill, she'd never supposed how bad it'd been. Or planned for how much worse it was than she imagined.

"The people who live here, they're our number one priority. We have to protect them. We can't let Talus take them away from their families. From their city. From their lives. Follow me."

Breath burning in her lungs, she followed Sly through town, heading toward the perimeter. What if Mom was on this raid? What if they saw each other on opposite sides of the fight? Dear god, what if she had to hurt Mom?

Matt followed close behind, flipping on the light mounted to the rifle. His other rifle still hung over his shoulder. "Addy," he said between breaths.

She grunted. Didn't have the air for much else.

"Same deal as before," he panted.

So many things flew through her mind, she couldn't pin one down. Fighting with him and Ella to get to the hospital. Fighting with him and Dean to get into the jail. Discovering he was the spy. "What deal?"

"If she's here, if we see her, I won't hurt her. Not unless you ask me to."

Oh, right. That deal. "OK."

Small arms fire sounded to the south.

Sly stopped, shouting into the radio. "South end, come in. Davin, what's the situation?"

The radio squealed. Shots echoed through it. It clicked off.

Without looking, Addy gripped Matt's arm. Between her fingers, she twisted fabric. "South end? Isn't that where Victoria and the Troupe are?"

A boom echoed through the buildings.

Sly cranked his head that direction, jaw unhinged. "Jesus, was that a grenade or a ficking claymore?"

The radio blipped again.

Matt gripped her back. "We've got to get over there."

Sly pointed the opposite direction. "My perimeter post is this way."

Shifting from foot to foot, Addy shook her head. She caught Matt's eyes.

And read her own thoughts in them.

"We don't have a post yet, Sly," she said. "We're going to the Tree."

One side of Matt's mouth lifted till his smile touched the corner of one eye. "Why are we still standing here?"

"Suit yourselves," Sly called over his shoulder. "I won't be the one answering to Morgan." He disappeared around a corner. "But if you die, don't ficking try to eat me."

As Matt paced her, Addy hopped a curb. "Can we make it in time? It's a long way."

"I don't know, Addy. We have to try. What else are we going to do?" He zigzagged past a pile of bricks. "Wring our hands at some empty perimeter post?"

Running through the sound of small arms fire and more explosions, they approached the fortress-like building she'd seen earlier, its giant bronze cats out front.

A group of people rounded a corner ahead of them.

"Thank god," Matt said, slowing. He called to the group as they sprinted toward the fortress. "Cassius!"

The Troupe slowed.

Cassius, dark skin glistening, held a hand out.

As Addy caught up to them, she gripped it. "Where's Kendra? And Victoria?"

He pointed back the way they'd come. "Taken. They're not far, my friends, but we couldn't hope to…we're not fighters like you."

Jim kept herding them toward the fortress-like building. "We're going to get inside the stadium if it's all the same, guys." Eyes invisible behind the aviator glasses, he raised both arms and waved the Troupe ahead. "The longer we stay out here, the greater chance we'll lose more of you." He glanced at Addy, smoke hanging out the corner of his mouth. "My heart couldn't stand that."

Matt grabbed Addy's arm. "How far, Jim?"

Jim jerked his head, curls flying. "A block or two. Depending on how fast they're going. You know Vic."

Yanking Addy down the sidewalk, Matt took long steps. "I know."

Addy freed her arm and matched his pace. "What do you know?"

"She's a biter," Matt said. The slightest chuckle crossed his lips. "She won't make it easy on whoever's trying to take her."

As gunfire sounded around them, another explosion rocked the air. Punched all the wind out of it for a moment.

Adam's snarling, foamy mouth dripped into Addy's mind.

They couldn't do that to Victoria. When she was on stage, she shone like the sun. Glimmered like an explosion. All light, and heat, and power.

A woman shouted up ahead.

Eyes wide, Matt pushed a breath out through his teeth. Even in the cold of late February, sweat popped out on his forehead.

"I know, Matt. I know," Addy said, kicking into a jog.

He sprinted ahead and stopped at the next corner. As Addy caught up to him, he peeked around the building. "They're right down here," he said, leaning back in. His shoulder rested against hers.

"How many of them did you see?"

"Five." His jaw worked. "Vic is fighting. I didn't see Kendra."

She looked him up and down. "Well you fight like two. So that's three to their five. We can take them."

One side of his mouth raised. "So do you. That makes us four, plus Vic."

No time to deny the compliment. "Let's go."

"I'll take the left. You take the right. Tell her to get down." He stepped away from the building and rounded the corner.

As Addy stepped around the building, taking in the scene on the street, Matt shot one of them in the knee. He went down screaming.

Another lifted his rifle at Matt, while a third did the same to Addy.

The fourth one socked Victoria in the stomach with the stock of his rifle.

She stumbled, mouth wide, gasping.

The fifth bent down, throwing an arm around Vic's knees, and picked her up. Tossing her over his shoulder in a fireman's hold, he limped away.

Oh, good. One who'd already been injured had decided to play the hero. Perfect.

"Close your eyes, Victoria," Matt called, sighting down the rifle.

Addy approached the one who'd socked Vic in the stomach. Rifle raised.

As the other, the one who'd already raised his rifle at Matt, turned it on Addy, Addy suspected maybe they hadn't thought this through.

Matt fired two quick shots in succession. One chipped the sidewalk behind Vic's captor, spraying his calf with speeding chunks of concrete.

He fell, clutching his calf and releasing Vic. Screaming like a trapped cat.

Vic grunted, landing and rolling. Although she tried, she couldn't gain her feet.

Matt's second shot went through the third soldier somewhere in his lower extremities. Blood sprayed into the street, soaking the fallen boy behind him. His rifle clattered to the ground, and he fell.

Which left two.

Matt spun his rifle to the other, but the soldier beat him on the draw.

The sound of the shot and the realization that it'd been wide hit Addy at the same time.

Thank fuck.

Addy squared off against the last one as Matt closed in on the other.

The last one glared, scowling. "I don't want to hurt you, woman. Come with me. We'll leave your boyfriend."

"Otherwise, we'll cut him down like a dog in the street, bitch," the other soldier said, rifle socked into his shoulder and aimed at Matt.

Who laughed. "Sure. Sure you will. I guess the general would really like that, you killing one of her favorites."

Transfixed, Addy took shallow breaths while Matt stepped closer and closer to the black eye of the rifle, the hole in the end of the barrel dark enough to suck the light from around it.

The soldier shifted on his feet. "You don't know the general. Man, I barely know her. She just came back. She's nothing." His eyes darted from side to side.

"You're lying," Addy said. She laughed. "You're terrible at it. Look at him." She cocked her chin at Matt. "Tell me he's not lying."

The stock of a rifle sailed at her head.

The other guard took another shot at Matt.

As Addy ducked, heart stopped, she didn't have time to see if Matt had been hit. But the rifle sailing at her connected. A glancing blow to the top of the head, but enough to send her sprawling on her ass. She kept a grip on her rifle though.

More shots from Matt's direction.

But the one coming at her, charging her, licking his lips as he knelt to snatch her up, forgot to point his weapon.

She snatched at it, grabbing the warm forestock. Yanking, she pulled herself to her knees while forcing him down to her level. One hand full of his rifle and the other full of hers, she couldn't draw her machete. Too bad, it was a hell of an intimidating weapon.

He grabbed the hand holding her rifle and twisted. Pushed her index finger back onto itself.

Clamping her teeth, she screamed through them as her rifle clattered to the ground. She jerked her other hand, throwing off his grip on his own rifle.

He attempted to regain control of his rifle, tugging Addy across the pavement, her knees burning. As she gripped it with both hands, he stopped and screamed.

Victoria had a mouthful of his ankle. Hands hooked into claws, she sank her fingernails into the meaty section of calf above the bare skin her teeth had sunk into. Like she bit into a giant chicken leg.

He screamed again, trying to jerk his leg away.

Instead, Addy yanked at his rifle.

From far away, Matt shouted. Fists slapped skin, slamming into thick muscle. It'd come down to a fistfight.

The one in front of her, still gripping the rifle, swatted at the woman digging into his ankle with her teeth. "Stop it, you bitch. What the hell," he said, falling backward. He released the rifle.

The lack in opposing force sent Addy onto her ass. Rifle in hand.

From nowhere, the soldier pulled a handgun and pointed it at Ella.

Victoria. He's pointing it at Victoria. Ella is dead.

And this time, Addy didn't hesitate. She shot him.

Sent someone else's son across the veil.

Releasing her jaw and working it back and forth, Vic stood on shaky legs. "Thanks, lady."

Matt appeared, mouth and knuckles bloody. Rifle in one hand, he gripped Addy under the armpit and hefted her to her feet. As though she were made of cotton.

She stared at the dead soldier, silent and still, and her stomach crawled up her throat. Crowded itself into the back of her mouth. Acid bubbled behind her teeth. Like the time she poured salt on a slug and watched it writhe, instant regret for the pain and eventual death she'd caused.

Matt didn't release her arm. "We gotta get Vic downtown, Addy."

Eyes wide, acid gurgling in her mouth, she turned to him. A tear dropped from her eye. Trying to speak, she produced only a creak. Like a rusty hinge.

She cleared her throat and tried again but couldn't get above a whisper. "I've never killed a human, Matt." She swallowed the bile. Had no time for puking. Another tear fell, cold as it coursed down her face and dripped from the bottom of her jaw. "What happened?"

Vic threw an arm around her shoulders. "You saved my life, darling. You're bound to me now."

Matt released Addy's arm. He pointed his rifle at one of the soldiers who reached for his own. "No."

They passed the soldier Matt hit in the extremities. The pool of blood beneath him as large as his body. Pale, he didn't breathe.

Vic knelt to check his pulse. "He's gone," she said, standing. "Must have hit him in an artery, Matt."

"Fuck's sake," he murmured.

Addy wobbled. The same thing killed Dean. The wound that'd ultimately stolen him from her.

What a fucking day.

Matt jutted his chin at the one who'd reached for his weapon. "Watch that one." Kneeling next to the soldier who'd bled out, he unsheathed his Bowie knife. He ended the soldier's chance of coming back, cleaned the blade on the boy's shirt, and returned it to its sheath.

Breathing shallow, Addy turned her back on the whole thing and wandered downtown. Vic's arm around her shoulders, she floated on the top of stilts and felt nothing of the ground beneath her as they passed.

THE SPLIT

CHAPTER 12

In the middle of what Vic said used to be a football stadium, Addy sank into the crackling, brown grass. She stared up into the darkening sky. The moon, shrinking back to new, hung high in the west.

Matt stood out of sight but within earshot, murmuring with Vic and Cassius. "Morgan says everything has been mopped up. He wanted us to stay with you guys till it was done. Will you be all right?"

Angry light played behind Addy's eyelids. He was probably gripping Vic's arm, gazing longingly into her bright eyes. Ella would not approve.

Dean would not approve of Addy not approving, even on Ella's behalf.

And the dead man couldn't approve or disapprove of anything.

She closed her eyes, the shadow light of the moon dancing across her retinas, moving every time she tried to catch it.

"The Troupe will stay here until Morgan comes to get us," Victoria said.

"Food, water, and lodgings," Cassius said. "We have it all here."

Matt grunted. "Someone to protect you?"

"Our good man Jim is more than capable for the time being. And the rest of the defense force stationed here. We hear you'll be right down the street at the bank." Cassius cleared his throat. "And you, dear woman. Who saved our Victoria. You won't be far, surely?"

Pressing her lips together, dead grass biting into her arms, Addy sat up on an elbow. "No. Not far."

"Lock up behind us," Matt said. He squeezed Victoria's hand. "I still can't believe you're here."

"Life is a funny game," Cassius said. Sinking his hands into his pockets, he leaned back. Silver light reflected from his face. "The pieces make no sense, and you never know whose turn it is, but you play anyway." He peeked at Addy. "Hoping for your turn to come."

Matt waved to Addy. "Let's get some shut-eye before we have to be on duty in the morning." They made their way out the sides of what Vic said was the playing field, once upon a time, and found the exit. Jim next to it, shifting from foot to foot.

"Sure you guys won't stay? I mean, there's a whole platoon here. But still." He twisted a toe. "We like you two."

Addy flushed, the only good emotions she'd had all evening swimming through a fog to get to her brain. "We'll be close by. If you need us, get Sly on the radio."

Vic's lips tightened. "That guy. Don't tell him we said hi. We didn't."

"OK?" The beginnings of happy wilted out the bottom of Addy's shoes. The way a Dead Head's blood collected in the feet and spilled onto the ground once the skin split. What a stinking pile of offal.

Victoria threw her arms around Addy's neck. "I'll tell you the story some other time. Return to us tomorrow, all right?"

"If Morgan will let us," Matt said, giving her a side hug.

Stepping out into the cool evening, Addy closed her eyes and took the air in, nostrils wide. The humidity made the inside of her nose feel wet.

Silent, Matt walked away.

With a sigh, she caught up to him. "Something wrong?"

His frown lines ran deep. "Where do I start?"

"You almost told those soldiers who you are. Do you think that's a good idea?"

"She's going to find out we're here eventually."

"I thought putting it off till later might be better. I'd rather she not find out at all."

"I guess I get that," he said, giving her the side-eye, frown lines still deep.

She stopped. "You want to see her again, don't you?"

His feet slowed, but he didn't turn. "I miss her. Losing El…her, well, it hurt a lot more than I thought it would. A lot." When Addy didn't catch up to him, he turned. One foot behind the other. "She's your mom, Addy. I know she's done some shit, but she's still your mom."

The wind fell from her gut. Going from dead stop to charging, she blew past him. "I don't want to talk about it."

He jogged to catch her. "You brought it up."

"Welcome back, you two," Sly said, opening the door to the bank building. "I see you didn't get yourselves killed."

Matt stuck out a hand. "Or you, my man."

They shook.

Addy brushed past them both. Tears threatening with the mention of her mom, Matt bringing up Ella, heart heavy over Dean, the dead man she left in the street, it all crowded in. "Thanks for your help, Sly," she said. "Glad you're OK."

The door closed, locks turned.

Matt followed her up the ladder in silence. When they reached the stairwell, he held the door for her. Still without words.

Arms crossed over her stomach, she hunched her shoulders and climbed the stairs to their floor.

"You upset with me for bringing up your mom?"

"I brought her up." Stilts carried her down the hall, feet so far away they could have belonged to someone else. The pain turned her stomach inside out, acid eating it whole. At their door, she turned to him but couldn't meet his eyes. "Do you even know half the shit she's done, or do you just not care?"

"I know, probably more than you do. I know. That doesn't stop me from missing her." He opened the last door. "It's fucked up, I get that. It doesn't change how I feel."

She crossed the threshold and stared at the window, eyes burning. All those years, over a decade, she missed that perfect woman. The betrayal of the woman who'd survived could hardly be borne. Much less missed.

He closed and latched the door. His bedsprings squeaked. "I don't know why you're so upset at me. I didn't do anything to you."

"It's everything. It's everything. And you," she said, facing him, hair sticking to the tear tracks on her cheeks, "you don't get to miss my own mother more than I do."

He stood, brows knit. Eyes blazing. "Don't tell me how to feel, Adelaide."

"I'll say whatever I goddamned well please, Matthew."

"What did you call me?" In two large steps, he crossed the room. Gripping her arm, he pushed her into the wall. His breath came in short, sharp bursts, his mouth inches from hers.

She inhaled. His scent, masculine and strong and not entirely unlike Dean's, rushed up her nose and into her brain. As what she said replayed itself in her mind, his hips pressed against hers, weight slammed into her gut. The shock of betrayal, both to Dean and to Ella's memory, almost greater than the explosion of heat blossoming from her stomach outward.

Almost.

He sucked in a breath. "Say it again."

Before her spread the opportunity to stop. To push him away. To drown in the guilt and the sadness and the emptiness. It could all come crashing in, rushing to fill the vacuum created by loss and death.

Instead, she gripped hold of the heat and let it loose. It raced like wildfire along every sinew, every nerve. Closing the distance to his mouth, she whispered. "Matthew."

Exhaling, he kissed her, and his lips, like every inch of her skin, were on fire. Pressing into her, pinning her to the wall, he kissed her like a drowning man clutching a life raft. Like he'd die if he didn't suck every bit of the heat from her.

Pouring the heat into him, she ripped off her shirt and let the guilt and all the pain fall to the floor with it. As he picked her up and pressed her into the wall again, the feeling of doing something wrong overcame her. Rather than allow it to dampen the flames, she turned it around and fanned them. Ripping his shirt to get it over his muscular shoulders, she helped him get it off and threw it to the floor.

Closing her eyes as his skin slid across hers, the need to have him washing over her like a riptide, unable to stop wishing it was

Dean, she wrapped a leg around him and let the tide take her where it would. Drowned in an ocean of guilt and flames.

* * *

Jack sat on a couch, Jane sinking down next to him. The baby cooed. "Is everyone all right?"

"I think so," Mike said. He bumped the doctor. "Hux?"

Glancing up from his notebook, Huxley's eyebrows raised. "I'm sorry. Were we talking?"

"Just making sure you're OK, doc," Dean said, leaning back with a hand over his eyes. His healing leg, propped on a shining coffee table, trembled.

"Yes. Yes, Mr. Ross. What about yourself? How is your wound?"

"Fine," Dean said, wiping his forehead. "The hell were you doing, Celia?"

She grunted. "What."

"Going into the horde to help me. I was fine."

"Sure, Ross. Sure you were. Don't blame me because you needed help. Fucking take it and be grateful."

He inhaled through his open mouth.

"Dean," Jack said, "enough. You know as well as I do, we put our asses on the line for one another every day. You can't start complaining about it now."

Dean crossed his arms over his chest. "Maybe I should."

"Don't be like that, brother," Mike said. He dug in his pouch, frowning. "Here. Your favorite." He held out a small taffy.

Wherever the hell he'd gotten one of those.

"Candy. Now that *is* a surprise," a voice said. They approached from the hallway facing Jack, the light behind them. Slender at the waist, yet broad-shouldered, with a swinging gait. Their hands clasped behind their back, they stopped in shadow, outside the circular light under which the tables and chairs sat. "I expected we'd see someone soon. It's been so long since this library has welcomed guests. You are here for the library, are you not?"

Squeezing Jane's knee, Jack stood. "We are. Jack Cooke. Are you the librarian?"

They stepped into the light.

Few people made a real impression on Jack. This Librarian made more than an impression. They made a damned mold and broke it. As tall as Jack himself, their long frame wrapped in a wild variety of fabrics from silk to corduroy, large curls rested atop their head in the shape of a Mohawk. The frilled button-up shirt they wore had been unbuttoned to halfway down their smooth, tawny chest.

The librarian extended a long-fingered hand. Rings on every finger. "Pleasure." A light accent tinged the words, speaking of the secrets of every back alley and cobblestone street in the world.

Jack took the extended hand, grasping the cool fingers. The librarian's handshake fell somewhere between a curtsy and a firm greeting. "Likewise."

Smiling, high cheekbones cutting the air, the librarian gestured to the couch where Jack had been sitting. "Please. There is much to discuss."

Jack sat. "What should we call you?"

The librarian chuckled, sitting in a creaking leather chair and tenting their fingers. "Here, now, you can call me Quinn."

"Quinn. This is your library, then?"

Quinn's head shook side to side. "Libraries belong to no one. They belong to everyone. I keep this one tidy. Who are these lovely people you've brought with you?"

Jack angled his head at each person in his party in turn. "Celia, Dean, my son Michael, Dr. Huxley." He smiled at his girls. "My youngest, Katherine, and her mother, Jane."

Quinn sat forward. "Lovely to meet you all. You want in my library, I presume?"

Jack chuckled. "Thought you said it didn't belong to you?"

"It does not belong to me, but it is mine." Quinn leaned back, crossing one booted ankle over a knee. "And in order to enter this library, there must be payment." Staring at Jane, smile lighting curious hazel-blue eyes, Quinn leaned forward again. "I am certain arrangements could be made."

Jack's stomach clenched. He'd no idea what this Quinn was suggesting, but if it involved Jane, the suggestion would need to be rethought. He wasn't about to let her make any sort of "payment." He opened his mouth to say just that.

Mike beat him to it. "What's the payment? Do you mean like, money?"

Quinn's eyes narrowed as they took in Mike from head to toe. "Money is a thing of the past in this world. A thing of the past." Fingers folding, they slipped under Quinn's sculpted jaw. "I am not at all certain you'd be able to provide the requisite payment, but I would be willing to consider it. Your doctor friend there as well." Quinn bowed to him.

Jane cleared her throat. "What's the payment, Librarian?"

"Please. Call me Quinn. You, dear Jane, may be most likely of all to have what I need. Look at you." Glancing between Jack and Jane, the corners of Quinn's mouth raised, teeth peeking out from between their lips. "So young and fresh-faced. And yet. Here you are. Nursling at your breast. This man must be twice your age at least. And those knives on your back," Quinn said, leaning forward to inspect her harness with a twinkling eye, "deadly. Hidden, but deadly. Yes. You'd do nicely."

Jack tensed his legs to stand. The librarian didn't menace, but he wouldn't have Jane spoken about like a slab of meat to be traded on the block.

Slender fingers gripped his knee. One quick squeeze.

He deflated and deferred to her. She could take care of herself. He should know that by now.

She stared the librarian in the eye. "Tell me what the payment is."

Quinn stood and extended a hand to her. "Nothing more than a story. Your story."

Jack closed his eyes. Whatever secrets this library held, it'd continue to do so. He'd learned more about her in the past year than the previous ten combined. And only because he'd pried. Only because she trusted him with her whole heart. Yet, he didn't know everything. Not by a long shot. It hid under her layers and layers, like a wall that'd been painted for decades with a fresh coat and color every couple years. Peeling the layers was messy work, requiring special equipment.

But she was always full of surprises.

She stood, slipping one hand into Quinn's. "Not here."

"I will grant you that, my lovely young lady. If you would, please," Quinn said, looking around at the rest of them, "lay all your weapons here in the center and await our return. If Jane's payment is sufficient, I shall allow those who require access into the library."

"What if we don't 'require access'?" Dean asked, gripping a large hunting knife.

For no reason at all, Addy's face, with her wide, round hazel-brown eyes, popped into Jack's head. He hoped she was doing OK.

"There is a place for those of you who will not be entering the library to stay and relax. Sleep, eat, wait. Unless, of course," Quinn added, eyes on Celia, "you would like to explore the city."

Celia scoffed, unbuckling her gun. "Wait. My favorite thing. Watch yourself, girl. Anybody who puts that much product in their hair cannot be trusted."

Quinn, doubling over, belly laughed. Mouth wide, every tooth showing.

Jack snaked a hand out and grabbed Jane's wrist before she left his reach. "Be careful."

One corner of her mouth turned up. She laid on the fake Scottish accent, something he hadn't heard in months and months. "I'll be fine, dear lad. You watch these animals."

He kissed the baby on the head and laid his cheek against Jane's. "Come back to me, baby."

"I always will. Don't you ever doubt that."

Quinn released her hand and tapped a hair back in place. "I'll have you know, Miss Celia, I hold my hair up with pixie dust and dreams."

Mike snorted.

Laying her own huge knife on the pile forming in the center of the room, Celia slapped him on the shoulder. "Don't you laugh at me, Michael Cooke. I know where you sleep."

He waved a hand in front of his face, still chuckling. "I'll add my story in, if it'll help."

Quinn's lips curled up in a slow twist. "I believe Mrs. Cooke's here will be sufficient. But I will remember your offer, Michael. I will remember."

Jack opened his mouth to tell the librarian they'd never been married. Reconsidered. With the way the world was now, how much did the ceremony matter? She'd agreed to. That was about all they needed.

And as Quinn took her hand again, leading her out of the light and down the hallway, she glanced over her shoulder, her own smile wide. "I'd say something about a honeymoon, but we're in front of all these people." She dropped him a wink.

For the first time in weeks, like the kiss, he floated. Just for a moment, but it was there. The weight had begun to lift.

* * *

Addy woke alone, staring at the ceiling.

She and Matt had gone to sleep eventually, limbs tangled together and clutching each other for dear life. Like two people drowning after a shipwreck.

Now, she didn't have to look around to know she lay alone in the room. The bed, empty and cold, too small for two, held only one. No one breathed in the room but her and her ghosts.

"Great, Addy. Good job," she said, sitting up. Her hip protested. She'd never woken sore after a night like that, but Dean had never been so rough, nor had any night been quite like that. Matt had been every bit as rough as she wanted in the moment, keeping her thoughts clear and empty as they had sex against every surface in the room. And then some.

But now.

"Now you're alone. Again. I repeat. Good job," she muttered, rolling off the bed and falling in the floor. Her shirt was down here somewhere. As she located her clothes, lying wherever they'd been dropped, she berated herself for not stopping him. She'd had that one, slim chance. Instead, she'd gone and complicated everything. And the shady image she'd seen of Ella around every corner had gone silent.

The woman would never forgive her.

"She's dead, Adelaide." She whispered to herself as she dressed, strapping on weapons. "Dean doesn't want you. And now you've made it weird with your only friend."

Finding her machete scabbard empty, she glanced around the room. Matt's pack was gone too.

Tears threatening, she dropped to her knees and looked under the bed. Scored her machete. Her eyes burned as she slipped it into its sheath and opened the door. Swiping at them, she closed it behind her and wandered to the third floor, where Sly had told them there was a cafeteria of sorts.

Exiting the stairwell, she stopped worrying about directions. The bitter scent of coffee pulled her to the room with the food. It took up an entire corner of the building, rows and rows of tables crossing it.

Stomach complaining, she took in the food bar on the far side.

And caught Matt, sitting alone, back to the door.

Stopping, she considered. She could get coffee and a couple slices of bacon and sneak out. He'd never even see her.

Or she could do whatever it was her feet were carrying her toward, undoubtedly commanded by the coffee. She let them lead.

They carried her to the food. She loaded up on eggs and potatoes, snagged a giant mug of coffee, and faced the room again.

Matt dropped his eyes before they met hers.

Downing a searing gulp of coffee, she hesitated.

I mean, what's the protocol here? Forget he exists? Forget the hours of hot animal sex? Just, kinda, pretend it never happened?

All in all, those were terrible choices.

Sliding onto the bench across from him, she cleared her throat. "Coffee's hot. Burned my tongue."

One side of his mouth turned up. A good sign.

He sipped his own. "Cold coffee sucks. I like it hot."

I know.

She shook her head. Probably should put some words here. None came.

They ate in silence, bacon crunching between her teeth. Good, but overdone.

After what was maybe five minutes but could have been hours, he opened his mouth, right as she'd opened her own to confront the silence.

"Addy, I—"

"Listen, Matt—"

They stopped. Addy's cheeks burned.

He extended a hand. "You first."

She cleared her throat. "Not that it wasn't great, amazing even, but last night was. It was…"

"A mistake," he finished for her.

Relief flooded through her. Her head spun, face tingling. "A mistake."

The whites of his eyes red, he met her eyes and held them. "I'm not ready to let her go."

She gripped his hand and squeezed. "I know that. Me neither. Or Dean." She pulled her hand back, balling it into a fist. "You're my only friend here, Matt. I don't want to fuck that up. Good lord. What were we thinking?"

A grin flashed across his face. So quick, she would have missed it if she hadn't been still looking at him. "We weren't." He met her eyes again. "Forgotten?"

"Forgotten." Her stomach gurgled. The bacon sat heavy. "Now what?"

He downed the rest of his coffee and shoved a piece of toast in his mouth. "Let's go find Morgan."

CHAPTER 13

Melinda's little girl backed into a clothing rack, knocking it into the display case. The glass broke, calling the 'Heads outside like a whistling beacon.

"Addy, get behind me," she said, pushing her. They spilled in through the door, dozens upon dozens of them. Some trampling others to get to the two tasty meals in front of them.

Only one, if she could help it. If only she'd let Jack come with her.

She took on as many as she could, but it wasn't enough. It was never enough.

Her little girl was bitten. Again and again, bitten.

She cried, trying to fight her way out of the nightmare. Kicking the covers twisted around her feet, she cried, "No, Adelaide. No, baby, no."

But her baby stood, smiling down. Light framed her head. "I'm immune, Mom. You don't have to worry. I'm immune."

As she lay in the floor, bleeding to death, and her beautiful Jack came like an angel to take her baby to safety, she cried. Immunity. What a miracle.

Opening her eyes, she stared up at the rounded dirt ceiling.

Thank god Jack had been there. She'd been a fool to go without him. And she'd done nothing but drive him away since. Like it was his fault.

She kicked the covers to the floor and stood. The fact was, immunity intruded on her dreams. Although Adelaide wasn't likely immune, to be able to give that gift to another parent was a dream worth having.

She rolled the future of these experiments over in her mind as she dressed and twisted her hair into a knot so tight it gave her a headache. Anthony needed to put her back on the project, and she wasn't about to take no for an answer.

On her way out the door, her thoughts turned to the dream again. And her little girl. A little girl who didn't have the imagination to understand what Melinda was doing with the vaccine and immunity.

"I tried to show her, the ingrate," she whispered, shutting the door behind her.

"Show her what?"

Melinda jumped. "Ilasha, dammit, don't sneak up on me like that." She spun and clacked down the hall, her boot heels echoing off the tiled floor. "It seems like you're everywhere lately. Don't you have paper to push or something?"

Lash fell into step next to her. "Wake up on the wrong side of the bed, sweetie?"

"No." She blew a breath out the side of her mouth. "Is Anthony in today?"

"He's in the office, yeah. Something on your mind?"

"I have incubators. I want to get started."

"Hey," Lash said, gripping Melinda's arm. "I thought he took you off the project. What are you doing?"

"Getting back on it." She stopped and leaned into Lash's ear. "After he puts me back on immunity, I have something I need to talk to you about. Something Burke said about IRF."

Ilasha leaned back, long lashes flapping. "Is it a big secret?"

"I don't know." Lowering her voice to a fierce whisper that scraped against her throat, Melinda glanced up and down the long hallway. "Something isn't right."

Lash hooked her arm in Melinda's and gave her a gentle tug. "Why didn't you bring it up before?"

Melinda cleared her throat. "I didn't know if you wanted to, um. Be my friend again."

"You mean you didn't know if you could trust me?"

Following along in Lash's wake, Melinda shrugged. "I still don't. But I've got to talk to someone about it." She cleared her throat again. "Victoria is in the city, did you know that?"

Lash nodded.

"She's not the only one, is she?"

Lips pressed together, Lash shook her head. "The ones you left here. Some of them didn't do too well with the way Anthony runs things."

"I wish I could've taken all the kids with me." She stopped, brow furrowed. "Some of the men came back, the ones who saw Victoria, and told me she had a man with her who killed or injured several of ours and said he was 'one of my favorites.'"

Lash inhaled across her teeth. "Did they say anything else about him?"

Melinda shook her head, stomach in a twist. Bits of Ella's brain, along with the side of her head flying into his face put Matt near the top of a short list. "I might know who it is. But I don't want to jump to conclusions."

They approached Anthony's office suite. Lash rubbed her arm. "He woke up on the wrong side of the bed too. Tread careful."

Extricating her arm from Lash's, she smoothed her hair down one side and grinned with half her mouth. "I got this."

Chuckling from deep in her throat, Lash opened the door and held out a hand. "After you."

"Don't you be lookin' at my ass."

Lash scoffed. "Do what I want, woman."

Cheeks tingling, Melinda floated into the outer office. It'd been some time since she had anyone on her side. She'd forgotten how nice it was to have adult friends she didn't have to manipulate into liking her. "How are the people we brought back yesterday? What was the final count?"

Lash swept across the room to her desk, picking up a paper from the middle of a pile. Went right to it. "Eleven. Killed nine. Wounded about twenty."

"I need more than that." Rolling the other numbers over, she paused. "Nine dead. What about on our side?"

"Four. Two killed by your boy and his companion." She narrowed her eyes, riffling the paper. "Sixteen wounded. One missing."

"Missing? Who?"

Lash sat at her desk and sorted papers. They rustled against one another like sand on the bottom of shoes. Ghostly. Skeletal.

"You don't know him. He hasn't been with us long. Name's Gian."

"Will he give anything up?"

Lash chuckled again, throat rasping. "He doesn't know anything to give."

Melinda smoothed her shirt. "I'm going in."

"Be my guest. Just remember what I said."

"Dinner?"

"Sure."

"I'll bring the wine this time."

Grinning, Lash continued sorting papers. "Sure."

Giving the heavy door between the outer and inner offices two crisp raps, Melinda pushed it open and stepped inside.

Anthony looked up from his desk. "Ah. General. How did the raid go?" He lowered reading glasses down his nose and glared over the top of them.

"We need more women, but we can begin with these. Get them prepared. There's a couple weeks of hormone therapy first."

His eyes pierced her. "You sound an awful lot like you think you'll be working on this immunity project."

She approached the desk. "I don't think so."

"Well that's good."

"I know it." She sat on the front of the desk, left foot on the floor.

His brow drew together and he glared at her leg. Slowly, his eyes traced up it, all the way to hers. "General. Melinda. We already discussed this. You're working on the vaccine. Not immunity."

"No."

"Considering your missteps with Commander Burke, we think it's best—"

"You think it's best I continue working on immunity. Since I'm the one who created it." She held tight to the thought, the only thing getting her through this, that they wouldn't have immunity without her. "It's because of me, no matter how you slice it. I deserve to be on this project."

Sighing, Anthony laid the paper on the desk and slid his glasses off. Closing his eyes, he rubbed his nose with one hand and twirled the arm of the glasses in the other. "I suppose you're right, my dear. But what happened with Burke. You really must think these things through."

"I already apologized for killing him, sir. I thought—"

"Not killing him. Good lord. Yes, that should have been avoided, but that's not what I'm talking about, Melinda." He sighed. "You let him get too close to you. You slept with the enemy."

She flushed from her toes to the crown of her head. "I didn't let him do anything, sir. I chose to allow him to think he was close. And he was the one giving up information. Not the other way around." She stood. "What do you take me for?"

He considered. "Loyal. To a fault. Smart." Narrowing his eyes, he smiled. "Crafty."

Arms crossed, she sat on the desk again. Caught his eyes and held them. "Do you think I gave him any of our secrets? Anything that really mattered?"

Anthony leaned back in his chair. "I know you didn't. If you had, you wouldn't be sitting here, demanding anything of me. You'd have run away with your tail between your legs long ago." He stared at her thigh, likely thinking about something between her legs. "Fine," he said, sighing, "get started on your damned immunity project. But dammit." He slipped his glasses back on and picked up the paper again.

She tensed. If he was about to tell her who she could and could not sleep with, she'd take his head off at the shoulders. No one had that kind of control over her. Not since Jack left her.

Instead, he cleared his throat. "Don't shoot anyone unless I tell you to."

* * *

Jack arranged the straight of four hearts in his hand and discarded a spade. The other three cards didn't even match each other, much less the straight.

Celia chuckled, reaching for the discard.

"Don't even think about picking that up."

Cutting her heavy-lidded eyes at him, one corner of her mouth turned up. She shuffled the card into her hand, then laid all her cards out and discarded the last. "Kiss my ass, boys. Gin."

Slapping his cards on the table, Dean cursed.

Jack caught at least five face cards. Lot of points he just gave away.

Michael laughed. "Cee, you can kick my ass in this game any day of the week." He laid all his cards out. Nothing above an eight.

"Can and will," she said, looking at his cards. "Remember when we learned to play?"

Jack chuckled, counting his cards. "I used to have to let you guys win." He glanced at Mike's stack. "Not many points there."

Celia lowered her lids and pursed her lips. "Smarter than he looks, Jack."

"Hey!" Mike bumped her shoulder. "The hell is that supposed to mean?" His tone may have been serious, but his smile called him out.

Light splashed into the corner of Jack's eye.

Dropping his cards on the table, he stood, knees creaking, and stared down the hall. One by one, lights came on.

In the circle of light cast by each set, Quinn and Jane walked arm in arm. As they closed the distance, lights overhead illuminating seemingly of their own accord, Quinn's red eyes came into focus.

Jack took a step back. Had the librarian been crying?

Jane grinned at him, the last set of lights coming up. White light glowed on the top of her head like a halo.

He stared at her, breathless, waiting to see if they'd be allowed in the library.

"If everyone would take their weapons, please," Quinn said, sweeping a free arm at the pile, "I will escort you all to the main stacks. Michael, Dr. Huxley, and Jane"—he patted her arm—"will be allowed to enter, and my Librarians will guide you to the information you seek." Releasing Jane, Quinn leaned down into her face. "Please, Ms. Doe. Allow me to apologize for making assumptions. And allow me to pass on a piece of advice I was given by a dear friend."

Jane took Jack's arm, smiling up at him. "Anything."

"Savor every moment you have together. Even the mundane. For it is in those moments life is given meaning."

Through her smile, a tear slipped from the corner of one eye.

Jack's knees trembled. Though Quinn exuded an air of ageless knowledge, Jack could have given that advice himself. Even with a paltry forty-seven years in which to gather it. He wiped her cheek with a thumb. "The relationships we have with others is kinda all I've had in this. It's just so hard not to fuck them all up." He glanced at Mike.

"This is one of those moments, Jack," she said, hand on his cheek.

He refocused on her, letting warmth travel down from the crown of his head.

She cut her eyes at the librarian. "You can't come into the library, but I can. I'm going to get some books, like we talked about." Pulling him close, she whispered in his ear. Breath light on the side of his cheek. "We will get you through this."

He kissed her on the forehead, nose full of the scent of her hair. "You're a miracle." Letting her go, he scooped up his weapons. "So, Quinn. The library?"

Long, slender fingers extended, Quinn stepped to the side of the hallway with a bow. "Please."

"Doc," Mike said, "let's go."

Huxley, nose buried in his notebook, perked up. "To the library?"

Laughing, Mike extended a hand to help him off the couch. "Yes, Hux. We're going to the library."

As the group of them filled the hallway, Quinn paced them with folded hands. "I am afraid I cannot allow the others into the stacks, and this includes you, Mr. Cooke. Perhaps you would like to take in some of the city?"

Jack sighed. "That doesn't sound incredibly fair. We can't even browse?"

Quinn stopped in front of massive double doors, which were carved with a tableau of myths and legends. "I have given you the terms of our deal. If you do not wish to follow them, you may all leave, now."

He shook his head. "No thanks."

"Very well. You accept the terms of our deal?"

Jack shifted from foot to foot, eyes on the others. If he didn't agree, none of them would get past these doors. There was really no question and never had been. "Agreed."

Light fingers gripping the massive door handle, Quinn tugged. It eased open on silent hinges.

Following the librarian through the doors, Jack's lungs froze.

The colossal three-story room held books on all sides. The center of the room vaulted all the way to the top, where skylights filled the entire commodious space with daylight. And the way the stacks upon stacks upon stacks of books smiled down on them made him feel younger than he'd been in decades. Like a child, gazing up at the adult book section from the children's playmat as his mother went in search of new books to read.

Quinn waved a hand. Three people appeared from the stacks, as though they'd been waiting for the signal. Waving two of them over, the librarian directed them to show Michael and Huxley to the section about the Black Death. "Don't leave anything out, young Mr. Cooke."

Mike grinned. "Come on doc, let's get started." He held out a sucker to Quinn. "Thanks."

Quinn smiled, took the sucker, and unwrapped it with delicate fingertips. "Ms. Doe has some exceptional things to say about you, young man."

Blushing, Mike followed the other Librarians. "All lies."

Quinn motioned to Huxley. "If you should find your research leads you to another section, please do not hesitate to ask your guide to take you to it. We are only too happy to oblige you."

Stuffing the little notebook in his pocket, Huxley quick-stepped to Quinn. He grasped the librarian's hand and pumped up and down, smiling, buck teeth protruding over his lower lip. "I cannot thank you enough for this opportunity, Quinn. Your library seems"—he paused, taking in the massive shelves upon shelves of books—"extensive."

"Enjoy, good doctor."

Hux wandered away, vaguely following Mike.

Jane slid her fingers up the back of Jack's neck. "Whatever you choose to do while Katie and I are here, be careful, love." She kissed him beneath the jaw.

The baby wiggled and cooed when he kissed her on top of her warm head. "I'll miss you, ladies." He searched Jane's sparkling eyes. "Don't do anything I wouldn't."

"Likewise."

Stamping down the fear, he kissed her. Not as long as he would have liked, but long enough. "Love you."

"Back atcha, lover boy." She narrowed her eyes at Quinn and the remaining Librarian, a brunette with hair twisted in a bun, long skirts brushing the floor. "Who's taking me where I need to go?"

"If you'll follow my dear Aluria here, she knows what you need." Watching Jane and Aluria fade into the stacks, Quinn bowed to Jack. "And now, if you'll excuse me. The library requires tidying."

Five feet into the stacks, the shadows swallowed Quinn whole. Gone, as though the librarian had never been there.

Pages rustled around them. The hollow sound of books being slid onto and off of shelves echoed. No one spoke above a whisper.

"Well, Jack," Dean said, pulling out a chair. The legs slid across the marble floor without so much as a squeak. "Now what?" He sat, resting an elbow on his knee.

Celia cleared her throat. "I've got an idea."

* * *

"Adelaide, Matt. Welcome to HQ," Morgan said, ushering them inside. "Thank you for escorting them, Sly. You're off shift now?"

Sly curtsied. "About to go get some shut-eye."

Hooking a thumb over his shoulder, Morgan motioned toward the desk. "Thanks for the report too. And the other thing. You did good."

Grinning, Sly pointed finger guns. "See you crazy kids later."

Addy flushed. Did he mean something by that? Flashes, images assaulted her mind. They hadn't exactly been quiet.

She swallowed, gulping down the heat that wanted to rush up her throat and into her cheeks.

Remember to forget it, Adelaide.

Morgan waved them to the chairs in front of his desk. He'd situated his office off downtown, in a small brick building with huge, dusty picture windows. A striped pole hung outside.

Inside, a wall ran the length of the room, broken by a single door. A corkboard hung on another wall, sporting photos of the leaders of the defense force and a map of the city with pins in it. Morgan sat at the desk in the middle of the room and drew a small file box out of a drawer.

He might have taken the medal for the most organized person Addy ever met.

"I need your full names, please." He pulled two blank index cards out of the file box.

They gave them.

"Birthdates? If you know them."

Unsurprised to find out Matt was only a couple months older, Addy gave her birthdate and age as twenty-four. She hadn't remembered to celebrate her birthday in the last year, but she'd noticed when it came and went. Too much had been going on to care. Over half of her birthdays had been that way.

"Favored weapon?"

Speaking of birthdays, Addy paused, glancing at her Bowie knife. Well. Matt's knife. "I use the machete the most. But I'd say the bow and arrow, I guess."

Matt followed. "I'm a good shot with a rifle. This knife is fast climbing the charts though." He patted the holster. "Handy. Multipurpose. Stolen." He grinned sideways at Addy.

Swallowing, she thought of the day he took it. The day they fought side by side with Dean and Paul and Celia. Fighting to get back to Ella. When Dean carried her because of her busted ankle, her head thumping against his chest as he surrounded her in light.

Guilt flooded her throat. It closed, leaving her breathless. She coughed. "What do you need us to do, Morgan?"

"I have something special I'd like from you two. But first, follow me." He crooked a finger and crossed the room to point at a map. "When we're done here, you'll report to the south end guard post. Here." He tapped a red thumbtack. "They can share the rules with you, guard routes, that sort of thing."

Matt hooked his thumbs in his belt. "What's the special thing you need?"

"We can discuss that in a moment. I have something I need to finish up. Through here." He opened the single door. It squealed. Weak light from the dusty windows penetrated the space behind it for about two feet. Morgan extended a hand and waited.

Matt went first.

Heart in her throat, Addy followed. Was this the part where they got branded, tattooed, or initiated into the gang? A toe taken off maybe?

Morgan closed the door, plunging them into dusty midnight. "All the way to the end of the hall, guys. There's lights, but we don't need them."

Another memory from Magnolia surfaced. The morning Matt led her through a dark room to meet Dean. Doing her best to brush away the memories of the five minutes with Dean, she remembered she had no fear being alone with Matt in the dark. Lying about his identity or not, he'd never made her feel uncomfortable.

Instincts were always worth trusting. Something Dad had taught her. Reaching out, she grasped Matt's jacket.

He gripped her wrist and tugged her down the hall with him. Stopping, he shuffled a foot. "Aha." After a squeak, light filtered around the edge of a door. Three white lines.

Addy released him. Instead, she wrapped her fingers around the haft of her machete. Could be a room full of Dead Heads in here for all she knew.

But no, there were chairs. Weird chairs, with high backs and tiny pedestals below. Little footrests.

In one of the chairs, someone sat, strapped down with spindly ropes that cut into their wrists and ankles.

He watched them as they entered, attempting to raise his head. A gag stretched his jaw to an extreme angle as it looped around his head and tied behind the headrest. He twitched, his pale skin red where the ropes and gag dug in.

"You guys, this is my new friend Gian. Gian, say hi to the nice lady and her friend."

A single finger raised. The middle one.

"That's not very polite," Morgan said, standing next to the chair. He laid a foot on a long bar toward the bottom. "You should be nicer to the lady." He winked at Addy and pressed the bar down with his foot. The chair fell with a hiss.

As it clunked down, Gian flinched. Murmured something from behind the gag.

"What was that?" Morgan asked, lowering it.

Gian tongued the roof of his mouth and smacked his lips a couple times. "Fuck off, asshole." He sneered at Addy. "And fuck you too."

Matt stepped in front of her. "No need to say that shit, man."

"I'd spit in your face, if I had spit. Fuck you too. *Man.*" Narrowing his eyes, he glared at Morgan. "Get me some fucking water."

With the speed of a rattlesnake, Morgan grabbed Gian under the chin, his fingers digging into the soft flesh beneath his jaw. "Your men killed nine of mine. Nine. You people never killed so easily before. Why start now? What did you come here to do? What were your orders?"

Gian frowned, lips pinched like a fish. "'S'lot a questions I ain't gonna answer."

Morgan pulled a tiny pocketknife from his back pocket.

Addy had seen such a small knife once. When they'd run into a man who did woodcarving. Otherwise, a knife that small seemed pretty useless.

Morgan flipped it open with one fingernail and laid the blade on Gian's cheek. "It might be small. And it might be dull. And it might be rusty. But you know what?" He scraped it down Gian's cheek, dragging a jagged red hole along behind it.

Gian jerked in the chair, groaning through his pinched lips.

"Had your tetanus shot lately, Gian?" Wiping the blade on the boy's shoulder, Morgan grinned. "Probably not. We'll be sure you get one. Maybe. If you tell me what your orders were."

The bile climbed up Addy's throat. Not over the torture. Not that she'd seen anything like it before, but her brain seized on the mention of tetanus shots. The thing Cameron, Dean's brother, died over. She stumbled.

Matt glanced behind him, brows knit. His face pale and sweaty. "You all right?"

Steadying her feet, she shrugged.

"Me too." He spun back to the drama before them.

"Ain't telling you shit, old man. I already said."

"Maybe there's something else useful you can tell me. Before you die of lockjaw." He clucked and raised the gag again, tightening it until Gian's jaw opened wide enough to about pop it out of place. "Painful way to go. All your muscles seize up. At first, it's your mouth. Then your legs. Eventually, your lungs. Your heart is a muscle, you know." He thumped the kid on the chest. "Seizes up, like an old gasoline engine with no oil. Terrible way to go." Herding Addy and Matt back to the door, he peered over his shoulder. "Let me know when you want my help. If it's not too late, of course."

Addy shoved the door open. She plunged into darkness, the taste of bile behind her teeth.

"Addy, wait." Matt grabbed the back of her jacket like she'd done his.

She stopped, eyes closed.

The dark enfolded them again as Morgan shut the door. "Sorry if that upset you, Addy. Enemies don't deserve the holiday suite." He paused, feet shuffling. Bumping Addy's shoulder, he opened a third door, in the center of the hallway. Dishwater grey light filtered out, casting shadows over his eyes. "Neither do traitors, now I mention it."

Although this was the perfect opportunity to tell him who she really was, all she could see was the gash in Gian's cheek widening as Morgan tightened the gag. The blood soaking into the cloth and dripping down his cheek to pool in his ear. Rather than volunteer the truth, she crossed through the open door.

Comically long and thin, the room held racks of rifles, bows, bladed weapons, and a random variety of strange things. Slingshots, meteor hammers, and the like.

Morgan hit the lights. White neon splashed over everything. "This is where you restock. Take your pick, if you're looking for something new. I notice some of your weapons are worn."

Clenching the haft of the Bowie knife, Matt set his rifle down and wandered to the racks of rifles. He caressed a few until he found one that lit his face like a jack-o'-lantern. He picked it up and looked down its sight line, barrel pointed at the floor.

Still trembling from the display in the other room, Addy sidestepped until she got to the bows. Polished, pretty, and even…

"A compound bow? How is this. Where did you. Can I have it?" Hand out, she stopped short of touching it and stared.

"You can have whatever your pretty little heart desires. As long as you'll do the job I ask of you."

She dropped her hand, slapping herself in the leg with her palm. Eyes on the bow, she arched a brow. "What's the job?"

"I've gotten full reports from all my team leads about last night. And from Jim. I know all about what you did to protect our Victoria and the others."

"No big deal. They needed us. We still lost Kendra."

"They need people like you, it's true. And they've requested you and Matt be their personal guards."

Heart leaping into her throat, Addy goggled. "Their what? Morgan, I've never—"

"We'll do it," Matt said, slinging the new rifle over his shoulder. "When do we start?"

Addy frowned. "Don't speak for me, Matt. I can't—"

He rolled his eyes. "Yes you can. Don't be like that. You'll be fine."

Crossing her arms, she played a few responses through her head. None of them sounded good.

"Fine. I'm in."

CHAPTER 14

"Excuse me," Jack whispered. He waved to one of the wandering Librarians.

A young man approached him, his fingers tented in front of his chin. He pursed his lips and bowed.

Sitting atop the back of a wooden chair, Celia checked her nails. "Need to know where the best exit is."

Jack stood. "Can you tell the redhead we'll call when we can? I'm not sure how long we'll be gone. Could be days. Could be longer."

"You will not be staying while your friends are here?" Brows lifted, he looked between the three of them. "That one seems to require rest," he said, pointing his forehead in Dean's direction.

"I'm fine," Dean growled.

Blinking, the man stepped back. "Someone will show you to the outer door." He guided them out the massive double doors and closed them with a smile.

Jack stared at the door, thumbs hooked in his belt. Caught sight of Orpheus, leading Eurydice from the underworld. The boy had turned to look over his shoulder. The fool.

"I guess we go back the way we came?" Celia leaned on the door. "Sorry, Jack. I thought they'd be. I don't know. Nicer."

Patting her on the shoulder, he smiled. "No need to apologize now." He glanced at Dean. "You sure you're up for this?"

"Going to Celia's old neighborhood? Sounds like a freaking blast. Sure to be tons of fun," he said, looking her up and down, "if Celia's any indication."

Arms crossed, she tried on a frown. It didn't stay planted. She let the smile raise one side of her mouth. "You are almost as much a pain in my ass as Mike."

Someone cleared their throat. "Mr. Cooke. It's a real pleasure."

Jack peered into the dark beyond the doors. "I'm sorry, I can't see you."

A slight woman stepped into the light. Elbows held out at an angle, she clasped her hands before her breastbone. Narrowing her eyes, she looked him over. "Just as she said." The woman clucked her tongue. "She does have a knack for detail."

"What are you talking about?"

"If you would all follow me." Silent feet covered in ballet shoes, with laces drawn around her calves, she started down the hall.

Jack led Dean and Celia after her. "I don't think we can go back the way we came. There's a horde out there."

She chuckled. "Quinn told me about the rest of your party, still in the library. They sound interesting. What can you tell me about this redheaded woman?" She stopped, looking over her shoulder. "Jane?"

He'd never heard her name roll out of someone's mouth that way. As though she savored it. Like it tasted like roses.

And how was he supposed to answer a question like that? "She's one of the bravest women I ever met. She saved my heart and soul without even trying."

Twirling on one toe, the woman laughed. "That's the most beautiful thing you could have said." She began walking again, taking large, dancing steps. "I am glad you weren't a disappointment."

"What's that supposed to mean?"

"I'm afraid we've arrived at your door." She faced them, twirling with such grace, Jack all but heard the music box tinkling. "Please do be careful," she said, curious purple eyes effervescent in the dim light.

"If that horde's still out there," Dean started, stepping close to her. He didn't limp, but he still carried himself with ginger hesitation.

She chuckled. A low, throaty laugh. "You'll find"—she unbolted the door before Jack could stop her—"nothing of the sort." Flinging it wide, she laughed as she retreated. "Please close it behind you. When you return, I suggest you find a different entrance."

Tense, Jack pulled his gun in the time it took his heart to skip a beat. He scanned the area beyond the door. "It's clear."

Celia edged past him, into the tunnel. "What is wrong with these people?"

Dean followed, and Jack took the rear. Pushing the door closed, he laid a hand on the dark wood. "What a strange place."

Libraries held their own magic, with all those books rubbing covers the way they did. But he'd never stood in the midst of crackling electricity and whispering sheaves of paper in the same way he'd just done.

He gazed down the tunnel. The sun had continued its trek across the sky, but it was only a hair past where it'd been when they came in. How could that be? They'd gotten to thirty thousand playing Gin. With the highest card counting for thirteen, that took a while.

A few pieces of Dead Heads still lay in the tunnel, but no bodies. He scooped up a couple of Jane's knives as they passed them lying alone on the ground. "Do you guys feel like you've been awake a whole day?"

"No," Dean answered. "In fact, I feel better than I did when we went in. Like I've been resting."

Jack glanced over his shoulder. "What a strange place," he repeated.

"Look, boys, we can jaw all day, or we can get this over with," Celia said, mounting the train's stairs.

"If you don't want to go, Celia," Jack started.

She paused, hand on the doorknob. "No. We need to. We're here. I should find out if there's anybody left."

"When was the last time you saw them?" Dean asked, climbing up the stairs, babying his leg.

"I was eleven. Don't ask how many years ago." She pulled open the door and disappeared.

"Hey, Dean."

"Yeah, Jack."

"Let me see the key to the weapons locker. I'd like to liberate a few for this trip."

Dean tossed the keys down. "I'll get this bucket started up." He disappeared after Celia.

Jack crossed behind the train. The quiet, especially compared to the cacophony it'd been when they entered the library, set his teeth on edge. He clenched and ground them, the squeaking echoing inside his ear canals. His heart raced as he knelt in front of the locker.

What if this was all a trick? What if he couldn't ever get back to Jane? What had he been thinking, leaving two of his children in the care of these odd strangers? And the doctor. He could really do some good in this world, and Jack left him with these people.

Sweat formed on his upper lip, heart thumping so loud in his chest he swore it hit his ribcage.

Dean called his name from inside the train.

Jumping, he closed his eyes. "About done."

"Ready when you are," Dean answered.

Jack took five measured breaths. "You are not in danger right now. Not in this moment. There is no danger." Over and over, he repeated the things Jane suggested. Threw in a twist or two about how she wasn't in danger either. About how his kids were fine. But for the most part, about how he was free, and not tied up, and not in danger.

His forehead dried. Arms loaded with weapons, he boarded the train, bolted the door, and spread the weapons on the bed. "Let's go."

"If I tell you about where it is," Celia asked, "can you find the place?"

"Sure thing," Dean said, tapping the map in front of him. "Let's get out of this tunnel, and then I'll take you anywhere you want to go."

"Anywhere?"

"Within reason."

Celia chuckled. "Let's get the hell out of here and head north."

* * *

"Is that the building up there? The one Morgan told us to find?" Addy pointed down the block. A twelve-story brick rectangle rose from the ground, casting a long morning shadow on the street.

Squinting, Matt grunted. "Better be. I'm not climbing a bunch of stairs just to find out we're in the wrong place."

"Agreed."

But on the top floor, they found a door that told them they were in the right place.

"Defense Team Red HQ," Addy read aloud. "We're team red?"

"We're team actors, apparently," Matt responded, hand on the doorknob.

"That's a shitty team name, Matt. We can do better."

"Let me go first. Make sure we can trust them." Before she had a chance to respond, he twisted the knob with one hand and knocked with the other. "Hello?"

A chair squeaked. "Yes? Can I help you?"

Stepping through the wide door, Matt dropped one hand to the stock of his rifle. His back straightened. "Matt Lyburn and Adelaide Cooke. Morgan told us to report here."

Somewhere between Morgan's horror room and here, she'd realized she was currently involved in doing the same exact thing Matt had done to her in Magnolia. Hiding her association with her mom. It'd made her insides feel full of worms. Worms that tried to feast on the pink, fleshy insides of her lungs.

Morgan's little speech about enemies and traitors replayed itself. Over and over. What would he do to her when he found out? Because, let's be honest, it was when. Not if.

Despite that, Addy tried to step into the room, but Matt blocked the door.

The chair squeaked again. "Sure, come on in. Morgan radioed, says you're going to the Tree? They haven't had anyone be their personal guard since that thing with Sly."

Now there was some gossip Addy would pay to hear. She ducked past Matt.

The room before her had windows on two sides, one letting all the morning sun in. What would have run the length of the other wall had been divided in half by more drywall. Addy shuddered to think what might be on the other side of it, if Morgan's office was any indication.

"Here, let me get you guys some radios and whatnot," the man at the desk said. In his crisp shirt and tie, he looked like a tidier version of Mike. "I'm your daytime supervisor. Name's Paxton. Report in every eight hours."

"Only every eight?" Matt asked, following him to the next room.

"Your schedule is different from the rest of my guys," he said, plucking two radios from a charging station and handing one to each of them. He opened the cabinet below the charging station. "In fact, take these. Where the hell did I put those things?" Rummaging, he muttered to himself.

Addy glanced at the walls. Photos of Talus Crest's higher-ups plastered one wall.

Mom stared out from one of the photos below a man with piercing blue eyes.

Her mouth went dry. She bumped Matt with her shoulder.

He followed her eyes when she pointed them at the picture of Melinda. He paled, his Adam's apple bobbing, and peeked at Paxton. "Where do we sleep?"

"Aha, here we go," Paxton said, standing. For the first time, he smiled. Elven ears lifted, the corners of his eyes squeezing together, his smile made him look like a fairy of some kind. Mischievous. "The Troupe will have a place for you guys to sleep. I'd prefer if it's in the same building with them. They tend to get…" He trailed off, smiling. "Rebellious."

"I'm sure we'll be fine," Matt said. Taking the small cords Paxton pulled from the cabinet, he dropped one in Addy's palm. "Chargers?"

She curled her fingers around it. "Keep the radios juiced." Brow raised, she motioned at the small green light under the remaining radios on the charger. "How do you guys power this city? Hydro? Did you get the nuclear plant back up?"

Paxton shrugged. "Above my pay grade." He led them back into the other room and leaned over a table filled with maps. "Look. We don't have a lot of rules. Especially for what you'll be doing. Keep them safe. Don't let them wander past the city's boundaries," he said, outlining the boundaries on the map before him. "And no fraternization. With them or any other defense team people. House rules."

Addy tried to bite back the blush creeping up her throat.

"You'll have relief for night watches, so you can all sleep at the same time. Wouldn't do much good to keep one of you up half the night." Sitting back at the desk, he leaned on it. "Everyone loves the Troupe. They're one of the best things about this city. You've met them. Have you seen them perform?"

Addy and Matt shook their heads, though the corner of Matt's mouth turned up. "We did see Victoria deliver a monologue she wrote. It was beautiful."

But Addy's mind shot to Vic, whispering the monologue to her poor, doomed boyfriend.

How useless it all was threatened to wash over her again. She put a hand on the desk. "Why are you using people to do a job like this? Isn't guarding the perimeter against Dead Heads and Talus more important?"

Paxton chuckled. "Guarding people, growing food, all that stuff, that's *how* we live. Art is *why*. Keep them safe, all right?" He crossed his arms. "Losing Adam, and now Kendra. Well. It's been difficult on everyone. I wouldn't be surprised if they give you some trouble. Everyone is feeling on edge since the raid yesterday."

Addy frowned. It hurt her cheeks. She clipped the radio to her belt. "I'm sure I have no idea what I'm doing, but whatever it is, let's get to it. Matt?"

"Every eight hours," Matt said, clipping his own radio.

Paxton pointed at him. "You got it."

CHAPTER 15

A pproaching the Tree, Addy frowned. "These fences need to be updated."

"Didn't bother you yesterday."

"Yesterday I wasn't in charge of their security."

Matt chuckled. "You're not wrong." As they walked through the gate, he grabbed the top of it and pulled. It wiggled off the bottom hinge and listed to the side. "Repairs are definitely in order." Narrowing his eyes, one parenthesis dimpling a cheek, he let go of the gate. "What kind of updates are you thinking?"

"Proximity sensors. An outer perimeter. At the very least, new fencing."

"What are you two whispering about over there," someone called.

They walked into the yard.

Rivers stood outside, attempting to spin some sort of striped ball on one finger.

"Is that what I think it is?" Matt asked, walking to her.

She grinned, tiny teeth dimpling her lip. "A basketball. The court is down the road."

As Matt spoke to her about some kind of game, Addy shuffled to Vic and Cassius. They lounged on the dock not far from Grey and Tal, who were buried nose deep in a book. Stretched out on the cement, Cassius lay with his head in Vic's lap.

Addy leaned against the dock. "Hey, guys. How, um, how are you?"

"We've been better," Cassius said, staring at the overhang above his head. "I don't know if we can recover from this latest loss."

"Kendra was our laughter," Vic said. "What are we supposed to do without our laugh?"

Addy shrugged. "Make more?"

Cassius turned his head, hair scratching against the fabric of Victoria's skirt. "Is it so simple?"

Addy shrugged again. "Sure." She chased her memories, finding a loss that'd had more time to heal than Ella and Dean. "I lost my mom when I was a kid," she said, pausing to let the words sink in. She'd never seen the woman again, though flashes of her appeared every now and again when they lived on Harkers together. Painfully brief though it'd been. "I lost my laughs. My spirit. My heart."

Vic leaned forward. "I don't remember my mother. What I remember of my father is sparse."

Cassius lifted a hand and dropped it. "What did you do, Adelaide?"

"It grew back. My heart. It wasn't the same, but it grew back."

"I guess we all have a story or two like that," Matt said, he and Rivers approaching. He stopped next to Addy. "Here." He bent at the knee. "Use my leg for a step."

Hiking her foot onto his thigh, she put a hand on his shoulder. As she stepped up, he grabbed both sides of her hips and pushed. Grasping the edge of the dock and spinning to sit on it, she smiled down at him.

Eyes round, he met hers. And held them for a beat too long before dropping them and lifting Rivers. With the hand cradle.

Addy and Cassius helped him up, and Victoria knelt behind Tal and Grey.

Grey turned his lamp-like green eyes on her, his pale skin wan. "We can't pick one. The only ones we liked before don't seem right now."

Tal closed the thick book in his lap and tossed it down next to him. *The Complete Works of William Shakespeare* on the cover. "I don't want to do a comedy." He covered his face. "Titus Andronicus seems a good choice."

"Or MacBeth. Out, out damn spot," Grey said, laying back on his elbows.

"I don't know," Cassius said, "I still vote for the Shrew." He snagged Addy's hand and knelt before her. "Be patient, gentlemen. I choose her for myself; If she and I be pleas'd, what's that to you?"

Blushing, hand warm inside Cassius's, Addy laughed along with everyone else. She curtsied. "Thank you, good sir."

Victoria glided to Addy's side. "Wonderful, Cassius. Let's do that one."

Talbot, spiked hair wilted, stood and matched Cassius's height. "It's a comedy, Cassie. Besides. We've got just over a month to curtain-up. I don't know if we can be ready."

Rivers chuckled. "Of course we can. We're good enough. At least we know who'll play Bianca, and who'll play Kate." She cut her eyes to Vic.

Cassius straightened. "Of course. And I," he said, hooking his thumbs into his lapels, "will play Petruchio. I've been waiting for this role, dear Victoria." He bowed to her.

Matt shuffled his feet. "Can someone show us where we're going to be sleeping and stuff? We have some security checks to do. Plans we gotta make."

"We appreciate your help," Vic said, clutching his hand. She kissed the back of it.

Addy found the jealousy on Ella's behalf hadn't dimmed. She shifted from foot to foot and inhaled through flared nostrils. "It's our pleasure. Seems more fun than patrolling the perimeter."

Cassius tweaked her cheek. "Oh, I promise you, my friend. It shall be." Walking backward, he blew her a kiss and disappeared through the large, roll-up door that led to the stage room.

"Jim can guide you through all that," Vic said, squeezing Matt's hand. She dropped it and hugged Addy. "It'll be fun to have you with us." She smirked. "Funny he thinks he's going to play Petruchio. I always wanted to do a gender-bend on this one." Dropping Addy a wink, she disappeared the way Cassius had gone.

Rivers followed, arms wrapped around her basketball. Tal snagged the book, and he and Grey faded into the dark room, arm in arm.

"I guess we go see Jim," Addy said. Closer than she thought he was, she ran into Matt when she turned around.

He caught her. "Whoa." He shifted his feet. "How are you simultaneously clumsy and coordinated? You're an enigma, woman."

She swallowed the smile that wanted to pop up. Instead, she walked down the dock to the door they'd entered with Morgan.

Jim wiped the bar down, smoke hanging out the corner of his mouth. "Oh look, Addy and Matt are back. You guys staying longer this time?"

"Gonna be your personal guards," Matt said.

"No shit?" Dropping the rag, Jim put one hand on the bar and leapt over it. "Let me show you to where we sleep. Give you the nickel tour." Pulling the smoke from his mouth, he favored Addy with a grin that stretched from ear to ear. "This is awesome, you guys. Oh, gods," he said, hand on his chest. "I need to sit down." On unsteady legs, he wobbled to an overstuffed couch and sank down. "It's been a long time since I had someone to help me look after these fools."

"We'll do the best we can," Matt said, sitting on the arm. His brows drew together. "What happened yesterday?"

Jim massaged his forehead. "Nothing out of the ordinary. For them. Sometimes they like to walk over to the theatre where they perform. Prance around the stage, get a feel for the place." He shook his head, curly brown hair bouncing. "Smells a bit musty, but once we get in there, get the air moving, it helps. We've got to freshen up the sets, so about a half dozen more trips before we're ready for curtain-up."

Curtain-up. Addy had heard Tal say that before. "In a month?"

Jim let out a barking laugh and leapt up. "Gods, is it that close already? I've got to get you guys settled in. There's a lot to do."

Addy stopped him. "What else happened? What happened to Kendra?"

Jim sank back to the couch, almost missing the edge. He spoke fast, tripping over his own words. "We were out for a walk, just to stretch our legs. The soldiers came through the city. We came around a corner, and there they were. Shooting men in the street. Had a couple of women thrown over their shoulders already. I tried to get the guys back around the corner quietly, but you know them."

In unison, Addy and Matt shook their heads.

"They were in their own world. Didn't even know they were in danger at first. And by then, we'd been spotted." He leaned back. "I thought we were all goners."

"Hey," Addy said, hand on his shoulder, "you did the best you could. You got them out of there."

"We still lost Kendra."

Matt stood, pacing a circle around the couch. "Look. You know my history. You know Vic and I know where they've been taken. Maybe we can get her back. And you saved everyone else."

"You and Addy did most of the saving," he said, pulling on his smoke. "I don't know what I would've done if we hadn't run into you."

Addy's forehead tight, she stood. If they hadn't chosen to run from Sly… Well, it didn't do to dwell on it. "Show us around, Jim. We need to get security updated around this place."

Matt agreed. "Then we'll go over the route to the theatre and check it out too."

"Sure, sure," Jim said. He stood. "Follow me."

* * *

Celia sat in the front window, gazing out at the tracks before them. "We're getting close, Dean. Slow it down."

"As you wish," he said, hitting the brakes.

Stationed at the back window, Jack watched the city slide by. They stopped in a disused part of town, though a few buildings still had a little shine. These gas pumps and propane tanks they'd parked next to, for instance. They may still be in use in some capacity. But otherwise, it was burned-out 7-Elevens, stripped strip malls, and crumbling city blocks as far as the eye could see. "There might not be any people left around here, Celia. Looks pretty wasted."

She grimaced. "Fine. It'll be a quiet trip."

Jack made his way to her, rocking with the slowing train. He laid a hand on her shoulder. "We'll be right there with you. Whatever we find."

She gave him the side-eye. Opening her mouth, she inhaled, wrinkled her eyebrows, and closed her mouth. She went back to staring out the window.

Train coming to a halt, they all rocked forward. Dean shut it down and stood, leaning on the chair. "We ready?"

Jack waved at the bed. "Need any extra weapons?"

With a grin, Dean wobbled to the back. Checking his machete and handgun were still in place, he plucked a sawed-off shotgun from the umbrella stand by the door. "Just my baby. Come on." He opened the door and stepped onto the porch.

Jack and Celia followed him out. Celia looked around. "I grew up a few blocks from here." Shading her eyes, she pointed over the trees. "Those. Apartments."

Following her gaze, Jack counted three taller buildings close together and another set farther away. "A couple of them look to be in pretty good shape."

Dean joined them. "You think there's still people there?"

Kicking a rock and setting off toward them, Celia spoke over her shoulder. "We came all the way down here. Might as well check."

"Celia," Dean said, struggling to keep up, "slow down, girl."

Stopping, she sighed. "Pick it up. Stop whining." She set out again, a touch slower than before. But not much.

Jack shook his head. "I'll stay with you, Dean. She'll slow down eventually."

"She's in a hurry to get this done, isn't she?"

"I guess."

"Why?"

"I know literally nothing about her real family." Jack shook his head again. "She speaks less than I do. And she never talks about herself. You know what happened with Oren."

"I was there when he died."

"Right. Right. She's never brought it up. Not once." Staring at her back, Jack allowed a moment of heartrending pain to course through him. Fists clenching, he imagined if something happened to Jane before he'd had a chance to tell her how he felt. Before he'd had a chance to be with her. Reminding himself of the way his gut twisted, the night Renzo led him to the cell. He thought Jane was dead. "I guess she wants to connect with these people from her past if she still has a chance. At least to say goodbye."

"Did you ever think—"

"You boys gonna jaw all day, or are we doing this?" Hand on her hip, bow in the other hand, she stepped away from the tracks.

The rail twanged with a zinging high pitch as a bullet bounced off of it. The crack of the gun followed close behind it. The invisible shooter called out. "Stop right there, all of you. Men. Get off the tracks."

Dean lifted both hands. "Want us to stop or get off the tracks? Can't do both, brother."

The voice called again. "Get off the damned tracks."

Jack stepped away and judged the distance to the voice. Sounded like it came from behind a building about twenty feet to their left.

One of Dean's feet got stuck beside the track, and he flailed, falling.

Jack gripped his arm and pulled him back to his feet. "You all right?"

The voice called. "What's wrong with that one?"

"Nothing. He slipped," Jack said. He narrowed his eyes at Dean and dropped his voice. "You all right?"

Dean rebalanced and stood tall. "I'm fine."

"Weapons on the ground, you three."

Celia nocked an arrow and loosed it before Jack had a chance to breathe.

Someone grunted. They hit the ground moaning.

She nocked another.

A bullet splintered the pavement in front of Jack. Shards of asphalt peppered his boots. He flinched, the memory of being shot in the leg popping up like some kind of bloody Jack-in-the-box. Pop goes the bullet wound.

"Drop it, girlie. Or next I shoot one of them."

Crouching, Celia lowered the bow.

A man crept from behind the busted front of the closest building. "How bout we shoot one of them anyway?" He trained a rifle on Dean.

"I wouldn't," Jack said. "It'll be the last thing you ever do."

"Maybe I shoot you," the man said, altering his aim.

"Then it'll be the last thing you'll wish you'd done," Celia said.

"What's that supposed to mean, bitch?"

"Means I'll make you wish you were dead, pendejo." She took one crouching step toward him.

"Celia," Jack said, lowering his weapons to the ground.

She ignored him. Hand hovering over the bow, she glared at the man still pointing his gun at Jack.

Jack glanced at the man. Though he had the upper hand, he wouldn't win a staring contest with Celia. Jack didn't know anyone who ever had.

This man no exception, he lowered his rifle. "Fine. Just all of you drop your weapons. We gotta take you to Emmanuel anyway. He'll figure out what to do with you."

CHAPTER 16

U nlocking the door with her key card, Melinda considered how it was possible Matt turned on her so completely that he'd given his key card to Jack back in Magnolia. He still sat at the top of an exceedingly short list, but she couldn't convince herself it was him out there killing her men.

She relocked the door and faced the room.

Eleven women stared at her, each bound to her own station in the lab.

She checked her clipboard. Two of them were ready. The others would need to wait.

She cleared her throat. "Ladies, welcome to your new home. My name is General Thibodeaux, and I'd like to offer you the chance to live with us unrestrained."

One of them laughed.

Melinda eyed her.

The girl's thin lips lifted in a smirk. "Though the bird may live in a gilded cage, it remains a cage." Her grey eyes flitted about the room. "This is hardly gilded, dear General. I'd really rather return to my cage with pillows. And sky."

Some of the others chuckled.

Checking her clipboard again, Melinda approached the girl. She used an interesting turn of speech. Formal. Showy. "We don't have much on you, Kendra," she said with another look at the clipboard, "but it says here you were with someone we both know."

Pulling at her bonds, Kendra shook her head. "I am certain I have no idea what you mean, my gilded lady." She narrowed her eyes. "Are *you* certain you are not also within the cage?"

Leaning on the table next to her, Melinda smiled. "How is my Victoria? I do miss her."

Kendra worked her jaw. "You destroyed her. She is but a beautiful shell of the woman I met."

"Me?" Melinda leaned back. "I did no such thing."

"Don't fool yourself. By leaving her to these wolves, you might as well have rung the dinner bell yourself." She frowned, thin lips disappearing. "You said yourself you're a general. Surely you must be in charge of these things."

Melinda shook her head. She wouldn't be distracted by trivialities.

Running a finger down the side of Kendra's face, she grinned when Kendra shuddered. "You, my dear, and the rest of you." She stood and walked to the freezer. "You are not here for the same type of experiments we've run in the past. In fact, what you're here for isn't really an experiment at all. It's one of the oldest things humans do."

With a smile, she opened the freezer, breaking the seal and sending ghostly wisps of smoke into the room. She extracted two embryos and set them on the desk. Picking up the phone on the wall, she dialed Lash.

"*Anthony's office.*"

"Ilasha. I need two assistants in the main lab, please."

"*On their way. Are you starting the immunity trials already? Isn't it late? I thought we—*"

"I have two subjects who are in their fertile period. They will be ready for implantation shortly."

Kendra shouted, yanking at her restraints again. "I won't let you experiment on me! You won't implant me with some kind of virus! You can't do this!" Her restraints clanging, she slammed her head against the table, exclaiming with each impact. The metal table resounded like a bell with each one.

"Dammit, Lash. Hang on." She laid the phone on the table and retrieved a vial from a glass cabinet in front of her. Filling a syringe, she crossed the room. "I wouldn't normally do this, but you are a friend of Victoria. I'd like you to be comfortable."

She ignored the screaming in her ear and injected the sedative. "Sleep, beautiful. You'll be fine."

Laying the syringe in the sterilization tray, she picked up the receiver again. "Lash?"

"I'm here."

"Do you have the list of equipment I need?"

"Are you sure about this, Em?"

"Just get me the equipment and two assistants." She hung up the phone, slamming it into the cradle as hard as it'd go.

Resting her chin on the palm of her hand, she swiveled her head and stared at her other fertile subject, a mousy girl with scared eyes. Half these girls didn't deserve to be incubators for what could be the future of the species. If she'd still been able, she would've done it herself.

The lab door opened. Two people in white coats wheeled in three carts. When she got a glimpse of vaccine doses on one of the trays they wheeled in, it pulled her up short. Her work on the vaccine in Magnolia made her think of Burke. How much of what he said was true? She still needed to talk it over with Lash. An uneven feeling, like a wave, rolled through her.

But she looked over her test subjects again. A warm feeling washed over her. She'd grow these babies, give the world immunity, and save everyone. And get the one thing she'd always wanted but had never been able to get.

Control over this damned virus.

* * *

"We have ooo goo inna aooo," Addy said. She closed her eyes and covered them with the palm of her hand.

"Wanna try that again without the yawn in the middle?"

She smiled. "Sorry, Matt. It's been a hell of a long day."

"No kidding," he said. The table creaked.

She opened her eyes.

He sat on the table, a pile of maps behind him. Arms crossed, he hiked one foot into the empty chair. "Our night relief got here an hour ago. We should hit the sack."

"We have to make a plan for tomorrow. The gate needs to be fixed. The fence needs updating." She stood, pushing her chair in. Down a short hallway from the bar, they'd made an empty office their "security room." Chairs stacked in haphazard piles lined one wall. A musty couch slumped against another.

"This is supposed to be our nerve center, and it's a wreck." Crossing her arms, she looked at the map on top of the pile. "And the route these guys take is foolish. Too open. How the hell are we supposed to get them to change it?"

"Why?" He sat in the chair and leaned his elbows on the table.

"Why what?"

"Why get them to change?"

"You can't be serious."

"I dunno. These guys seem about as likely to see the danger as a turtle with its head in its shell."

"Even after the raid? After Kendra was taken?"

"I don't know. I mean we can talk to them."

She sat, chair creaking, and slouched over the table. Her eyes unfocused, and she stared at the map, brain sluggish after touring the Tree, getting set up with her own bunk, walking the route twice, and stopping to discuss potential hiding places multiple times. "We need contingency plans. Safe rooms. Weapons caches."

Leaning back in his chair, Matt interlaced his fingers and put them behind his head. "Tomorrow, Addy. I'm exhausted." His eyes slipped closed.

"We can't let them walk this route again without a plan."

He nodded, eyes still closed. "I've been thinking."

Heart leaping into her throat, Addy froze. She'd tried not to be thinking, but she had been too. The guilt had been crushing, off and on throughout the day. Especially given how fun he had been. "Oh?"

"Yeah." He opened his eyes. "I think we could get Kendra back, instead of doing all this," he said, waving at the map. "We came here to bust into the Molehill, eventually."

And here she'd assumed he was talking about her. Seemed like he was sticking to the "forget about it" better than she was.

Either way, she was in no way ready to go to the Molehill. "It's a good idea, but I don't think now is the time." She glared. "Are you just trying to get in to see Mom?"

"Oh, fuck's sake." He stood, pushing the chair back so fast it wobbled. "I let it slip I miss her, now you think everything is about her." He leaned on the table and loomed over her. "It's not all about her."

"Then what is it all about? Why do you want to go in there so bad?" She stood.

"You know who it's all about, Addy. What kind of question is that?"

She winced. Dean and Ella ran circles around her head all day, and yet she'd gone and asked such a senseless question. Still… "She wouldn't want you to do something so reckless."

"Don't act like you care what she wanted. You knew her less than half as well as I did."

"Just because I didn't know her as long—"

"You got close to her because of who she was, not because you cared."

"Don't accuse me of that. I loved her too." And like that, her eyes stung. A tear dropped before she could stop it.

"Ah shit." He grabbed her in a hug. "I'm sorry. I didn't mean it."

Arms folded between them, she covered her face and rested her hands in the hollow of his shoulder. Tears covered her palms. When her throat no longer hurt and she thought she could speak without a quiver in her voice, she spoke to her hands. "My mom was responsible for it. I don't know why, but I always feel like the things she does are somehow my fault."

He chuckled, pushing her back by the shoulders. "Tell me about it. I supported her for years, even after she sent me away. I probably *am* directly responsible for a lot more shit than I wanna admit." He kissed her forehead. "We'll get through it."

She breathed shallow, trying not to take in his scent. To block the mistakes they'd made the night before. She couldn't stop the mixing of guilt and heat though.

His face reddened. Arresting blue eyes catching hers, he stepped into her.

Grabbing a fistful of his hair, she slogged through the guilt and met his lips with hers. They weren't as soft as Dean's, and, of course, the animal urgency he kissed her with was nothing like Dean's gentle touch, but god, it was touch. It was forgetting, it was engulfing.

Gripping his shirt, she let him push her to the musty couch.

Handle of the Bowie knife digging into her hip, he covered her neck in biting kisses.

She smiled, tilting her chin up. "I thought we were supposed to be forgetting what happened."

His lips made their way up her neck from the base to under her ear, his breath hot on her earlobe. "Forget what? Nothing happened. Nothing's happening right now."

She tingled. "Right," she said. Sighing, she unbuckled his belt. "Can't be breaking the fraternization rule if nothing's happening."

He met her eyes. Returning the favor with her belt, he grinned. "Exactly."

And goddamn if nothing didn't feel good.

CHAPTER 17

Leaning against the wall, one arm resting on a tented knee, Jack waited as Dean and Celia woke.

"Oh hell. Haven't slept that uncomfortable in forever," Dean said. The side of his face flattened by the floor, he shook his head and sat up. "Morning, Jack. Sleep well?"

"Oh yeah. Like a bag of rocks." He grinned with one side of his mouth.

"That doesn't sound good."

"I think what's worse is we spent the night in a jail."

Dean grunted. "Spent what felt like most of last year in jail. You're right."

"Thanks for giving me the bed, guys," Celia said, slapping her hand on the metal slab where she lay. "Comfy." She sat up, hair a mess, heavy eyes red, and cracked her neck. "I know these guys."

"Cee," Dean said, "like, *know* know?"

"Yeah."

Jack started. "Are they your. Did you know them from before?"

"They're not my family. But yeah, I knew them from before. Couple of them, anyway. Didn't realize at first."

Dean sat on the slab with her. "Do you think they recognized you too?"

She shrugged. "I laid awake half the night trying to figure out who they were."

"You sure it wasn't just the metal bed?" Dean asked, popping his back.

"Well that too."

Jack's heart ached for her. These men took them prisoner without so much as a question and threw them in this cell. Given their indifferent attitude while bringing them here, being thrown into a cell was about the best they could have hoped for. "You sure, Celia?"

"I can handle these assholes. Used to wipe their damn noses, little shits."

Dean laughed.

With half a grin, she laughed with him.

A door slammed open, out of sight. "The hell you laughing at down there?"

"How funny your mom looked when I fucked her last night," Celia called. She winked.

Covering his mouth, Jack bit the back of his hand. When Celia decided to do something, she didn't take any time getting it done, did she?

A tall man with hips wider than his shoulders came into view, grey at the temples, frown scrawled across his jaw. "What did you say, bitch?"

"Does your mom know you talk to ladies like that, Jaime Figueroa?"

Forehead wrinkled, he opened his mouth to shout again. "Listen here…you…what?"

Celia stood, arms crossed, and sidled right up next to the bars. "Look at me, Jaime. Look real close."

Mouth open, one hand on his gun, he leaned close to the bars.

She punched him in the nose, slim fist catching the bar on one side. Cursing, she gripped her hand.

Jaime narrowed his eyes, one hand raising to his nose. But slow, as though it traveled through molasses. Wiping his bleeding nostril, he stammered. "What the. What. You." He stopped, glancing at the blood on his hand. "Dios mio. Celia?"

"Thought that might jog your memory."

Eyes wide, hand halfway to his face, Jaime backed away and disappeared down the hall. The door closed with a clang.

"OK," Dean said. "Did that go as planned, or?"

Celia exhaled through her nose. "He'll be back."

"With friends," Jack said.

Celia sat with her back to the bars. "He was always an asshole. Wanted to punch him in the nose since he was a kid. Hurt my hand, but damn, it felt good."

Jack grinned. "Well. I hope we don't—"

The door down the hall opened again. Voices filled the hallway. One speaking in Spanish about a mile a minute.

Back still resting against the bars, Celia tented one leg and laid her arm over her knee. She leaned her head against the bars and closed her eyes.

Jack stared at her. Either her plan was brilliant, and she was incredibly brave, or she was about to get all three of them brutally murdered. He didn't understand enough Spanish to know, but he trusted Celia, so he kept his ass planted and waited.

The footsteps stopped before any of the group came into view. "Wait. Jaime, wait. Are you saying this is Celia? Martin and Fabiana's youngest daughter?"

Eyes still closed, Celia grimaced. "That's what he's saying, Manuel."

A thin, olive-skinned man stepped in front of the bars. Grey beard and mustache, slick hair teased into a pomp. "Celia Barrios," he said, "as I live and breathe. Your mother thought you were dead."

"I am. Let us go."

"Who are these men with you?"

"Let them go. They don't have anything to do with you."

"They intruded on my territory. That makes it my business. You should know that."

She finally stood. With slow precision, she straightened her pants and shirt and turned to face him. "Are you serious? After all this time, and you still talk about territory?"

Drawing a ring of keys from his pocket, he shook one out. "It means more now than it did last time I saw you. I would have thought you'd understand." With a clunk, the cell door unlocked.

Dean struggled to his feet.

Jack watched. "*You OK?*" he mouthed.

Dean stepped up next to him. Slight limp. "Think I twisted my ankle or something. It's not bad."

"Learning Addy's tricks," Jack said.

Dean paled. He opened his mouth, flapped it, and closed it.

Oh, that was smooth, Jack. Like sandpaper. Jesus.

Jack shook his head. "Sorry."

Returning the head shake, Dean watched Celia. "Is this working?"

"Hell if I know. We might all be dead in a couple minutes. Or we might meet her family." He paused, considering the alternatives. "Kinda exciting though. Either way."

"Just when I think I've got you figured out, Jack. You've got a weird sense of humor."

Celia's hands wrapped around the bars of the door, and she braced herself when Emmanuel tried to open it. "Let us go, Manuel. This is nothing to do with you."

Shoving the door, he knocked her in the floor and stepped into the cell. Holding a hand out, he smiled. "I didn't think I'd ever see you again. I thought you were dead too."

Slapping his hand, she scowled. "I didn't come here to see you, Manny." She stood. "Where's my family?"

"Upstairs. I'll take you to them."

Something in the man's smile put Jack off. His eyes shifted to the left. His mouth twitched.

Jack went to follow Celia out of the cell, Dean limping behind them.

One of the others put up a hand. "Not you, hombre."

Jack opened his mouth, but he needn't have worried.

Celia grabbed the man by the pinky finger and squeezed. She dragged him down to her level and stared into his eyes. Gripping his arm with the other hand, she twisted it while folding his pinky over itself.

"OK, OK, they can go," the man whimpered. He dropped to his knees, sweat popping on his upper lip.

Jack stepped past them, Dean following. Stifling a grin as he passed Celia, nonetheless, his heart swelled. Why anyone would want him to stick around sometimes beyond him, it was always nice to be reminded those people existed. Someone like Celia didn't need him, yet she put herself at risk for him time after time.

Manuel stood in the hall, fists balled into his elbows, lips curled into a frown that wanted to be a grin. "She hasn't changed, has she?"

* * *

"Missed you at dinner last night," Lash said from the doorway.

Melinda kept her eyes buried in the microscope. "I got distracted."

A chair squeaked away from one of the lab tables. "I brought the wine."

"For breakfast?"

"You know what they say."

Looking up, Melinda took in Lash, the glasses she'd brought, the bottle of wine. She wanted to apologize. But it got stuck in her mouth. "What do they say?"

"Pour the damn wine."

Melinda chuckled and poured. "Thanks. I needed a break."

"What are you doing down here so early?" Lash narrowed her eyes. "Have you slept?"

Once she downed the wine, Melinda set the glass on the table. Eyes closed, she massaged her temple. "I don't need sleep. I need to know what the fuck is going on."

"Is this what you were talking about? About what Burke said?" Lash poured more wine.

Melinda rolled a sip in her mouth. Swallowing, she leaned closer to Lash. "It's a long story. But the short, short version is he called Talus for extraction. With the push of a button." She leaned back. "I mean, what the hell? Why would a commander for IRF with his credentials have Talus on speed dial?"

Lash chuckled. "Speed dial. Haven't heard that one in a while."

"I'm serious."

"I know you are, Em." Lash leaned farther onto the table. "But what else do you want me to say?"

Melinda turned back to the microscope. Watching the vaccine destroy the virus always had a calming effect. She focused on the molecules of vaccine attacking the virus. Their formations...

"Ilasha," she breathed. "Something isn't right."

Lash stood and hung over her shoulder. "What? What is it?"

"It's. I have to check this." Standing so fast the stool wobbled, Melinda walked with slow precision to the cooler. If she rushed, her heart would race. If her heart raced, she'd get distracted. If she got distracted, she'd make a mistake. Now was not the time to make a mistake.

The cooler squealed as it opened. Pinching the plastic top of a vial, she extracted one, "VACCINE, TEST 26AB" printed in close script on the side. Huxley's hand. She'd seen so much of it over the months in Magnolia. She'd know that cramped, yet neat, handwriting anywhere.

She walked, still calm, to one of the other tables. The microscope here had been attached to a projector.

"Em?" Lash took a step toward her.

Melinda laid the vial of vaccine on the table and turned on the scope. "Ilasha. Get me a sample of the virus, please."

It shocked her how even her voice sounded.

"Melinda? What do you need with th—"

"Just get me the goddamned sample," Melinda said, slapping her hand on the table. The vial of vaccine jumped. She grabbed it and plucked a clean glass slide from a stand next to the scope.

Lash cleared her throat.

Without turning, Melinda held out a hand.

Laying the vial in her palm, Lash cleared her throat again. "I'll go. You seem busy."

"No, Ilasha, stay." She leaned over the scope, vial of vaccine in hand, and laid the slide of virus onto the tray. "I'm sorry I shouted. Please."

Blowing a forceful exhale from her nose, Lash moved a stool.

Allowing her abs to loosen, Melinda thanked her lucky stars she hadn't scared Lash off. She was so good at that sort of thing, lately. Everyone who saw her wanted to run the other direction.

Without taking her eyes from the scope, she introduced the vaccine to the virus and covered the slide with another. Eyes narrowed, she waited.

The vaccine formed up in a specific pattern.

"Goddamn, Lash. This can't be."

Silence.

Melinda glanced up, heart in her throat. Had she left while she'd been concentrating on the scope?

Lash sat, one elbow resting on the table, chin in her palm. "Thought you forgot I was here."

Eyes downcast, Melinda apologized. Again.

"Tell me," Lash said, standing, "what'd you find?"

Brain going back into overdrive, Melinda pointed at the scope. "This vaccine. It came from IRF. It's got Huxley's handwriting on it. It's what he was working on."

"Right. Does it not work right?"

Melinda shook her head. "It's mine. It's my vaccine. The one I was working on when—" She stopped.

Tim radioed ahead when they arrived on Emerald Isle. She took the evening off and went down to the prison to watch. Addy and Mike weren't there, but when Jack walked in, she lost her breath. He looked even more handsome than when she'd last seen him. He wore the years well. Did she still look as good?

From her perch in the shadows, she straightened her hair and crossed her arms. Did he still smell the same? Did she?

As he and his friends walked across the yard, Jack watched the other prisoners. Did she think he'd sense her here? Did she hope he would?

Tim left them and walked into the room with her, but before he hugged her and knocked her off her feet, she saw the way the redhead looked at Jack.

She chuckled. The girl was easily half his age. Of course she looked at him like that. Look at this man. In all the years they'd been apart, she'd never met another like him.

Of course, that moment was after Ilasha had broken her heart.

"I was working on this exact same vaccine before the prison was destroyed." She spun. "Ilasha, this is my vaccine."

"Are you sure? How can you be sure?"

She slapped the table again. The glass slides jumped in their holder. "How did IRF have my vaccine? How?"

"Let's say they did," Lash said, pulling her stool closer and sitting. "Are you sure this batch isn't from after you got there and told them how to do it?"

"I never gave them this formulation. Never. It's the one I injected into." She stopped, again. Fighting a sneer, she spat it out. "Jack's new woman, Jane. It's the last trial I ran. I never gave this to IRF."

"Jane didn't have it in her blood?"

"Of course she did," Melinda said. "But not an unpolluted sample like this. And it cannot be extracted from the blood once injected. It binds to the white blood cells."

"Isn't that strange? I didn't know anything could do that." She scooted closer still.

Melinda flushed. "It is. But there's not a lot normal about this virus."

Lash chuckled, low in her throat. "You can say that again." She touched Melinda's knee. "What do you think it means?"

Melinda crossed her arms over her stomach. "Somehow, they got into my research. Maybe they intercepted my transmission. We should check the records." She tapped her chin. "Or…" Eyes wide, she straightened. "Or they *do* have some kind of connection with Talus, like Burke suggested."

Lash's round, brown eyes widened. "He said what?"

"He told me," she said, eyes rolling half-closed, "there was so much I didn't understand. That he'd called Talus for our exit, not IRF. He was trying to tell me something." Half her mouth curled up. "I guess I should have let him finish before I shot him in the gut."

Ilasha grinned. "Remind me to stay on your good side."

Melinda scoffed. "I'll find out what he was talking about. You mark my words. This vaccine is the tip of the iceberg."

"Oh, shit, speaking of icebergs," Lash said, slapping Melinda's knee, "a communique came across my desk on its way to Anthony's last night."

"Did it?" Melinda sat back. Lash always had the best gossip.

"I know which one of your adopted kids is in town."

* * *

Addy rolled toward the edge of her bed as it depressed under someone's ass.

"You came to bed late," Victoria said.

Opening one eye, the other still glued shut, Addy grinned. "We had a lot of plans to make."

Vic smiled, every tooth visible inside her wide grin. "OK."

Addy glared at her, holding the frown for as long as she could before losing it to a grin. "You guys are terrible at security. We're going to have our hands full."

Blowing her a kiss, Vic sauntered out of the room, pajama shirt hanging off one shoulder.

Wiping the sleep out of her eye, Addy sat up. Her bunk backed up against one wall and two other bunk beds lined the walls.

Curtains hung from the front of Vic's bunk, creating a cozy cocoon inside.

"Do you have a boyfriend somewhere out there, Adelaide?" Rivers, in her own bunk crammed full of pillows and fluffy blankets, stretched.

Funny how she punched Addy in the gut without touching her. "I. No." And the day began so bright.

"I do," she said, flipping the blanket off her head. A sheaf of blonde hair covered her face. "He is a sea captain. So dashing."

"A what what?"

Laughing, Rivers stood. The blanket thought about being displaced, then changed its mind. "A sea captain. You know, boats. Sailing. The sea."

Addy smiled. The ocean, that great living thing. She missed that beauty. Opening her mouth to tell Rivers about it, she stopped.

The first time she'd seen the ocean, it'd been with Dean. He'd taken her there.

Could Rivers stop punching her in the gut?

Storm cloud resting over her head, she dressed and headed to the bar for breakfast.

"There's my girl!"

Before she got her hands up, a dark-skinned blur knocked her off her feet. She flailed, but he cradled her and spun.

Gripping his shoulder, she called up as much command as she could muster. "Put me down, Cassius."

"My lady," he said, setting her on her feet. "Good morrow."

Head spinning, she waited to take a step. "Good whatever. Morning. I guess." She squinted out the open door. "Is it morning?"

Matt sat at the bar, back to her. "Not really. It's not noon, but the sun's been up forever." He faced her, clutching a cup of coffee. "These guys are not exactly morning people."

Taking a stool two down from him, she shook her head. "I usually am. I can't remember the last time I slept this late."

"We had a busy day. And a long night," Matt said. He cleared his throat. "Making plans for these goofballs."

"And what sort of plans have you for us, good sir?" Tal asked, sitting between them. Obstructing their view of each other.

Which was just as well. Addy had no intention of discussing what had not happened the night before.

She pointed a finger at Jim. "Get me one of those coffees, would ya?"

Smiling, ever-present cigarette hanging from the corner of his mouth, he squinted through smoke as he poured.

"We want to make sure there are places for you guys to hide. Fortified. Weapons. Traps. Stuff like that," Matt said, speaking to Tal.

Talbot nodded, his spikes standing on end again. "Do you have the weapons you need?"

"We're going to have to go get more before the day is over."

Talbot popped up from the stool. "Field trip!"

And though Matt and Addy protested, loudly, none of the Troupe listened. They bustled about, gathering coats and hats and scraps of paper. Rivers got the basketball. Helpless, Addy and Matt waited until they were ready, chewing the breakfast Jim brought them in the meantime.

"Hey, Jim," Addy said, facing the bar again. "What is this, on this toast?"

"Currant jelly. Fresh made by a friend." He flicked his ashes and reinserted the smoke in the corner of his mouth. "She helps us with the sets. Brings the jelly when she has it. These guys love it."

"As well they should. It's delicious." The sweet yet tart fruit wasn't like a raspberry. Or a blackberry. But it was. "I've never had anything like it."

"She'll give you some if you ask."

"What would she need in return?"

Jim chuckled, flicking ashes again. "You're on the defense force, Addy. You don't need to do anything in return. You already are. Bartering is a nonissue for you."

"Oh." She stuffed the last of the toast in her mouth. That could either be incredibly useful or incredibly harmful.

Matt moved to the stool next to her, elbows resting on the bar. He leaned close. "Listen. I don't—"

She shook her head, meeting his eyes. "The less words, the better."

The parentheses around his mouth turned down. "Agreed. I think we shouldn't, um."

"No, we shouldn't."

He slid off the stool and tried to round up the others. "Guys, guys. Let's head for the door now, OK? We need to go see Paxton."

Jim chuckled behind her. "It's like herding cats."

Leaning back on the bar, she grinned. "Looks like they got their smiles back."

He grunted. "Don't let them fool you. Every blow takes them lower. So they bounce higher." He tugged her shoulder.

Her heart raced. She identified with bouncing off the bottom. She met his eyes.

"Look after 'em. They ain't the same as everyone else."

Eyeing Matt as he herded them to the door, she nodded. "I know it."

CHAPTER 18

The cacophony the Troupe made as they mounted the stairs to Paxton's office could have woken the dead.

Addy and Matt followed behind. "No wonder Jim had such a hard time getting them to safety," Addy said. She frowned. "They have literally no idea where they are."

Matt's frown matched hers. "We have to be their eyes."

"For how long?" She caught his arm, stopping him mid-stair. "We have other things to do while we're here. You yourself reminded me of that last night."

He flushed. "I know we do." Stepping onto the same stair with her, his fingers danced over her bicep. "But maybe you're right. Maybe we should go with the flow for now. See where the wind takes us." He cleared his throat and climbed the stairs again. "We'll get around to the general. We both know that too."

Forcing herself to not read into his words, she followed him up the stairs.

At the top, the Troupe gathered on the landing, waiting for them.

"Are the two of you always this slow?" Grey's shaggy black hair floated around his head as he shook it. "Perhaps we did not choose our protectors wisely."

Vic backhanded his shoulder. "Watch yourself, sir."

Stepping between them, Matt grinned. "It's all right. We were being slow. Addy?"

Mounting the landing, she followed Matt through the middle of them and down the hall. "We need to see our supervisor. Let him know our plans and get supplies. You guys behave."

Cassius bowed so deep she thought his forehead would touch the floor. "Of course." He took Victoria's hand and laid it on his arm. "Milady. If you would be so kind as to accompany me."

Vic curtsied. "Delighted."

Rivers still hung onto the basketball. She'd settled it over nonexistent hips and crooked an arm over the top of it. "We shall follow your lead, dear Adelaide."

Together, Addy and Matt knocked on Paxton's frosted glass door.

For no reason at all, Mike's knock popped into Addy's head. She chewed her lip and wondered if they were doing all right. And when she'd see them again to find out. Looked like she was going to be in the QC for the foreseeable future.

At least that meant no Dean. No getting punched in the heart every time she saw him.

"Come on in," Paxton called.

Matt opened the door. "After you, Addy."

Stepping in, she found the room empty. "Pax?"

He stood from behind the desk, setting a book on it and tucking a fine gold chain under his shirt collar.

Before the pendant disappeared beneath his shirt, Addy caught sight of a thin, golden cross. The book on the desk bore the same symbol on its front cover.

Catching her eye, he shook his head. "Sometimes when I have quiet time, I like to do some prayer and meditating."

She shrugged as the others flowed through the door like a wave. "I've seen the cross before. My dad never told me much about it. I guess he kinda shied away from anyone wearing it."

"If you're ever curious, my door's open." He laid the book in a drawer. "What can I help you guys with? Matt's last report mentioned something about mapping the route."

Oh, hell. The report. Thank god Matt remembered.

Skin on her forehead tight, she stepped to the map table and sorted through them until she found one that suited her. "Yeah, let me show you the route they take to the theatre."

"The theatre is an oven," Cassius said, opening the door to the other room. "What's in here?"

Paxton took a step. "Please don't—"

"Oh, is this a real fish?" Rivers prodded a fishbowl, sloshing the water. "My boyfriend is a sea captain."

Reversing direction, Paxton reached for her. "Don't touch the—"

Vic squealed from the other room. "Can we have some of these extra radios?" One of the walkies let out a high-pitched tone.

Covering one ear, Matt headed into the other room. "Please, Vic. Put that down." He crossed in front of the door. "Cassius, don't touch those. They're—"

Glass broke.

"Oh, my goodness. I am afraid I have broken your… What is this?" Cassius appeared in the door, holding shards of glass in his palms. Eyebrows raised.

Rivers prodded the fish tank again. "Is this a saltwater fish? Did you know the sea is made of salt water? Except the Black Sea. It is predominantly fresh water." The goldfish swam in circles, bumping into its little castle every time she thumped the tank.

Addy started toward the other room. "Cassius, please be careful. You're going to cut yourself."

"My dear Cassie," Tal exclaimed. Dashing across the room, he landed in a wheeled chair and flew halfway to him. One of the wheels hit a bump in the linoleum and the chair tipped, dumping him in the floor face-first.

Grey laughed from the corner. "We would have to vote about Mercutio after all, Tal. You, my dear, are a mess." Skipping past Rivers, bumping the map table, Grey held a hand out to Tal.

All the maps slid off into the floor.

Hands on the sides of her head, Addy tried to look everywhere at once. "Would everyone please stop moving!"

They all froze. Like statues.

Even Grey, with his hand extended, and Tal, halfway off the floor. Frozen. Like she'd pushed pause.

Only the fish moved, swimming in circles.

She couldn't see him, but Matt spoke from the other room.

"Worse than herding cats, man. Worse."

Paxton started moving again, gathering the maps and returning them to the table. "All right. About your route."

Addy went back to the maps. She didn't unfreeze the Troupe, and they remained in their positions long enough for Matt to come out and eye them all.

"Addy," he whispered, leaning close, "they're stuck."

"Thank goodness. Look. Here, here, and here," she said, pointing to the spots on the map she and Matt picked out last night before they. Um. The spots they picked. "These are places where we'd like to set up weapons caches. And fortify some safe rooms."

"What do you mean fortify?" Paxton rested one hand on the table. "I'm sure we can dig up the materials, but I don't want to step too far over our bounds on getting it done."

"Some locks. Bars for the doors. Things like that. Nothing fancy."

"We don't have time for bulletproof glass and reinforced steel," Matt said, sitting at the table.

Her gut flip-flopped. His mention of bulletproof glass reminded her of Magnolia. The first time they'd met, he'd brought up the bulletproof glass. The walls. The safety of the place that'd been flattened by a horde anyway.

"…and see if he can loan us some weapons. Right, Addy?"

"Sorry, what?"

He narrowed those electric blues at her. "We need to see Morgan and ask if we can get some weapons from him." He touched her hand with light fingertips. "You all right?"

"Sorry. Yeah. Sorry. Just thinking."

"My dear lady," Cassius stage whispered.

Grin turning up one corner of her mouth, she kept her eyes on Matt. "Yes, Cassius?"

"May we move now?"

"If you promise not to touch anything."

"We promise," Tal said, legs shaking. "We are fairly good at this, but this position is not as comfortable as it may seem."

"Your plan sounds good," Paxton said. "I'll get you the materials you need. Some hands if they can be spared."

Addy grinned. "Yes, you guys can move."

As one, they exhaled. Chattering, they put everything back in its place.

She shook her head. "Let's go get weapons."

* * *

"The stairs are a little much, Jack," Dean said, leaning against the wall. He slid down the banister and stumbled onto his bad ankle.

Jack stepped up behind him and blocked his fall. "Are these cuffs necessary, Emmanuel?"

Manuel grunted. "Help him."

The man to his left fell back and gripped Dean under the armpit. "Let's go, amigo."

"Torn between telling you I'm not your amigo, and kicking you down these stairs, Jose."

"Hey, sorry," Jose said, releasing him. "You act like it's my fault you're here, ese."

Jack joined him on the same step and stared into his eyes. "You're the one who pulled a gun on us."

"Only after Celia shot my friend." He jerked his chin. "He had to have six stitches. She could have killed him."

"Tell that Nancy he shouldn't have shot at my friends first, Jose," Celia said. Walking up the stairs ahead of them, uncuffed, she spoke over her shoulder. "If he'd have hit one of them, stitches would have been the least of his worries." She paused. "*Ese.*"

"Leave it, Jose," Manuel said. "We don't need to upset Fabi. Let her see her little girl. After, we can talk more." He motioned to Jack as he spun around a banister. "Tell your friend we are almost there."

Leaving Jose to stew, Jack joined Dean two steps up. "You gonna make it?"

"Ankle hurts. Leg's tired." He huffed out a breath and growled. "I'll make it."

The urge to ask to have the cuffs removed came over Jack again. Addy would never forgive him if he let Dean die in some stairwell.

One look at Manuel's face canceled that idea.

Two more flights up, one of the men finally opened the door to the hallway. Emmanuel reached for Celia's arm.

Snatching it away like his hand had erupted in flames, she stepped through the door. She scowled, waiting for Dean and Jack.

Passing through the door after Dean, Jack hoped they wouldn't have to leave anytime soon. His own knees were about done as well. Twelve flights didn't seem like much until you were looking down from the top.

In the hall, he caught up with Manuel. "Why don't you use the elevators?" He took in the hall lights. "Clearly you have power."

Manny's hand see-sawed. "So-so. One of the things the Triad do is cut our power. Sometimes, you would not like to get stuck in an elevator. We use the stairs. They always work."

"Triad?"

"Did you see four buildings on the way here?"

Jack nodded.

"We are in the eastern one. Uno este. They are in the three."

"Triad. Got it."

Manuel stopped, watching Celia's back. "They take our supplies. We take them back."

Automatic gunfire filled Jack's brain. The smell of gun smoke and blood. He'd been in a scuffle like this once, about four years in. With Addy just a tot, they'd tried to find somewhere to settle.

It didn't work out.

He leaned close to the taller man. "You don't have to live like that anymore, you know. There's plenty for everybody."

"I take care of mine," Manuel said, standing straight. "You don't need to tell me how."

"You're right. It was presumptuous. I'm sorry," Jack said.

Manuel walked away, catching Celia in a few large strides.

"What was that all about?"

He grimaced. "I don't want to stay here any longer than we have to. This could go south at any moment."

"I'm gonna need like a five-minute break. Maybe a snack and a nap." He grinned with one side of his mouth.

"Me too. Let's catch up."

Hurrying, they joined Celia and Manuel at a door. 1204.

Manuel knocked.

The door opened, and a woman with hair greying at the temples and quick, heavy-lidded brown eyes took them in. "Emmanuel. What can we do for you?"

Jack might've been slow on the uptake sometimes, but he couldn't miss her unmistakable resemblance to Celia. This woman had to be her sister. Stomach in knots, he waited for one of them to realize it.

Celia, crossing her arms, narrowed her eyes. "Luisa. You stopped coloring your hair."

The woman, Luisa, touched her hair. "Many years ago. Manny," she said, still staring at Celia, "what is this?"

"Let's go, Jack," Celia said, putting Luisa to her back.

He strained against the cuff, trying to catch her before she ghosted down the hall. "Celia, stop. We didn't come all this way to—"

"Celia?" Luisa stepped into the hallway. "That's a lie."

Celia spun. "I'm sure you wish that were true. Probably glad when I left."

With a shout, Luisa jumped on Celia. Jack didn't even see her move. One moment, she stood in the doorway. The next, her arms engulfed Celia.

"We thought you were dead. Dios mio, Celia! Where have you been? Mama!" Luisa tugged Celia's arm, dragging her into the apartment.

She cast a glance at Jack.

He moved to follow her.

Emmanuel laid a flat hand on his chest. "This family reunion is not for you."

Pushing against his hand, Jack stepped into Manuel's bubble. "Celia is *my* family. I'm not letting her out of my sight." He lowered his voice. "Either let me follow her, or I'm afraid we're going to have to upset Fabi."

Emmanuel removed his hand and slicked his hair. "After you. Do not say I didn't warn you."

"Dean," Jack said, jerking his head, "come on."

Eyes wide, Dean followed him into the apartment.

Celia crossed half the living room, feet silent on the carpet. An old woman slept in a chair in front of a fuzzy TV. It was receiving a signal, but the reception was too poor to make out the picture. The sound was turned down so far it almost didn't exist.

Celia's face creased. Lips tight, she swallowed. Shook her head.

Jack stared at the old woman. Her hair was white, mouth turned down, face slack. He couldn't tell for sure, but this was probably Celia's mother.

He stepped across the living room, footfalls sinking into the worn carpet. "Wake her up. It's what we came here to do, right?"

"I don't know what I came here for, Jack. I want to go home." Her shoulders drooped.

Fighting the iron bands around his wrists, he laid his head against hers. "We will, Cee. We will. Say hi, and then we'll go."

Shrinking, she stepped back. Swallowing again, lips tight across her teeth, she knelt in front of the sleeping woman. "Mama."

The woman didn't move. Drool dripped from her lower lip and stretched out.

Celia laid her hand on the woman's knee. She shook her but didn't raise her voice. "Mama."

She stirred but still didn't wake.

Luisa came around behind her, hands covering her mouth. Eyes wide and eyelashes wet above them.

Celia raised her hand. Hesitating, she stopped and searched the woman's face before gripping her shoulder. "Mama!"

When her eyes fluttered open, it became clear from where Celia got her heavy lids.

Her mama smiled. "My little baby. Am I in heaven? Is it time to go? Are you here to take me?"

"No, Mama," Celia said. "You aren't dead. I'm here. I'm alive, Mama."

Sitting straight up, the woman looked around. "And who are these people?"

"These are my friends. My family."

Caressing Celia's face, her mama gripped her hand and stared in her eyes. "Then why are they wearing the handcuffs?"

CHAPTER 19

L uisa stood over the stove for an hour, cooking tacos for them all. Jack tried to tell her not to go to the trouble, but she insisted it was a special meal they no longer ate.

"It was always one of Celia's favorites too. Let me," she said, pushing him into a chair at the table.

Dean, Celia, and Fabiana gathered around the kitchen table, Celia asking her mama to catch her up, while her mama asked Celia about all that had happened to her. Both spoke at once, and Jack doubted they heard each other.

Before they left, Emmanuel's men unlocked the cuffs, and Manuel explained Celia's father hadn't made it long. His own father looked after the Barrioses after that, and that's how they'd come to be part of his own very large, very extended family. The last thing he said before leaving followed something along the lines of "Hurt Fabi, and I'll kill you."

Jack leaned close to the stove again. A fried tortilla wasn't an aroma he ever expected to smell again. His mouth watered. "Luisa."

Back to him, she nodded.

"How many siblings do you have?"

She stopped stirring. "We have four." Her shoulders drooped. "Forgive me. Two, now. I've called them."

He sat back. Celia was the baby in a family of six siblings. Her independence made sense. A way to differentiate herself from everyone else. The question of why she hadn't been home when the apocalypse happened rolled around and around his head. A question for another time.

"Luisa," Fabiana said, "have you called your sister?"

"Yes, Mama."

"Did you tell her?"

"No, Mama."

"Good. I want her to be surprised. Reynaldo too."

Jack raised a brow at Celia.

"My youngest brother," Celia said. "What about Maria?"

Fabiana covered her face. Luisa's shoulders drooped.

The oil popped.

Celia crossed her arms and lowered her head. "When?"

"With Papa. Many years ago," Luisa said.

"Her kids?"

Fabiana sobbed into her hands.

Luisa's shoulders dipped. "It's a long story, manita."

Releasing a longer string of Spanish than Jack could keep up with, Fabiana spoke to her hands.

"Mama," Celia said, holding her arms tighter, "I don't understand you. I can't speak Spanish very good anymore. You have to slow down."

"We've got time for long stories," Jack said.

Turning off the stove, Luisa lowered another plate full of tacos to the table. "It will take some time to explain."

Fabiana enunciated every syllable. "No quiero hablar de eso."

Taking off half the taco in one bite, Dean lifted his eyebrows. "What'd she say, Cee?"

Jack smiled. Certainly, talking around his food was one of the things Addy loved about him. Because no one else could.

"She doesn't want to talk about it," Luisa answered. "I don't blame her." She laid a hand over her mama's. "But, Mama. We must. Celia has come all this way. She deserves to know."

Fabiana crossed herself.

* * *

"Three weeks!" Cassius shouted, jumping from the sidewalk to the street. "Only three weeks to opening night? My darling woman, you must be joking."

Addy pulled a notebook from her pocket. Keeping track of days so precisely was new, but at least she wasn't as helpless at it as Jane would have been.

She spun it around, showing him the calendar she'd scrawled inside. "Three weeks, Cassie dear. Look." She tapped a line of marked-out squares. "That was last week. You guys didn't do any work on the sets or anything. You," she said, poking him in the chest, "argued for half the week before you agreed to the gender swap. Even though you know Vic makes a better Petruchio than you."

He flipped his coattails. "I know no such thing."

Matt rolled his eyes. "I thought *I* was stubborn."

Stubborn was right. He'd stubbornly avoided being alone with Addy for a week, and she couldn't decide if that was for the best or not.

Vic walked between Matt and Addy. "Oh no, honey. Our dear Cassius will take that award any day of the week." She floated down the sidewalk, snatching Cassius's hand and twirling down the street with him.

Rivers, dribbling her ever-present basketball, walked beside Addy. "When will you allow me to teach you this fine game?" She attempted to spin the ball on her finger. It bounced into the street.

Tal snatched it and ran the opposite direction, smile wide. "You'll have to steal it from me!"

Eyes rolling so hard they could see into next week, Matt backtracked to collect Talbot. "Addy, keep these fools together. I'll—"

Their radios blipped twice, followed by a high-pitched squeal.

Nausea socked Addy in the gut. "Another raid?"

Matt's wide eyes met hers. "How far are we from the next safe room?"

She shook her head. "Too far. We go back. It's only a block." She spun. Cassius and Vic rounded the corner of the next block.

Shit.

"Rivers, go with Matt. Grey," she said, leaping two steps and catching his collar.

He glanced down. "Your radio is being very chatty."

It blipped in a rhythm, Morse code tapping out a message.

She couldn't round them up and listen at the same time. Good lord, why had they gotten so far apart? "There's a raid. Go with Rivers and Matt. I'll be right behind you."

As she sprinted for Vic and Cassius, she checked over her shoulder to make sure Matt had gotten the others together.

Instead, she tripped over her own foot and skidded face-first on the pavement.

Wind knocked out of her, she lay on the sidewalk. It wasn't as cold on her cheek as it would have been a few weeks ago.

Pushing up, she swiped her cheek with her sleeve. It stung and left streaks of blood on her jacket. She ran her tongue over her teeth, checking they were still whole.

Good, Addy. Good. Next time watch which foot you're tripping over instead of anything but.

Nocking an arrow, she sprinted around the corner.

Vic and Cassius continued down the sidewalk, heading toward the theatre, swinging their clasped hands.

"Victoria, Cassius," she called, pitching her voice low.

They spun around each other like two dancing stars. Cassius's deep brown eyes fell on her armed bow. "My dear," he said, ducking, "are we under attack?"

"Come on." Her gaze darted down the street. "We've got to go back about two blocks, get into the safe room."

Victoria grabbed her shoulder and clenched. "And we'll be safe there?"

Addy slowed to turn the corner. Peeking, she found it still clear. "Yes."

Gunfire split the air a block or two away.

Cassius jumped and grabbed Addy's other shoulder. "Can we get there in time?" For the first time, he dropped the affectation he constantly used.

His voice deeper than she'd expected, it jarred her ears. Jangled her nerves. She bit her lip. Why did they have to get separated from Matt and the others?

"Yes, Cassius. We'll get there. You guys stay quiet. No matter what." The calm radiating from her throat and out through her voice shocked her ears. Because her insides were a mess. Jumpy heart, twisted stomach, and she had to pee.

Leading with the armed bow, Addy hurried them down the block. They passed Rivers's basketball lying in the gutter.

Vic stopped and reached for it.

"No time, Victoria," Addy said.

The echo of explosions cracked through the buildings, closer than the gunfire.

Although Addy locked a shout behind her lips, Cassius let a small one fly.

"Sorry, Addy," he said, gripping her shoulder tight. "I've never fired a gun a day in my life."

"I'll do the shooting for both of us. Just come on." Dragging them both, she led them the last half a block to the safe room.

Matt stood in the door, hopping from foot to foot, rifle pointed everywhere at once. When his eyes landed on Addy, the blood rushed to his cheeks. He lowered the rifle. "Thank Christ. Get in here, you guys." Flinging the door wide, he stood back and ushered them in. As Addy passed, he gripped her arm. "Are you OK?" Brow creased, he took in her face.

Oh, right. The fight with the sidewalk.

"Fine. Let's get in here."

* * *

Jim set another full glass in front of Addy. Something he'd called a "Long Island iced tea."

She picked it up. "Another one?"

"The lady drinks free tonight."

"I drink free every night, Jim."

"Tonight's special." He plucked the smoke from his mouth and leaned over the bar. Easier than raising his voice over the deafening music the Troupe had going in the other room. "I couldn't repay you enough for saving them." He stuffed the smoke back in his mouth, taking a puff. "They told me how cool you were. Even with your face all banged up."

The unbusted side of her mouth turned up. She rubbed her bandaged cheek. "My own fault. And I didn't do it alone." Picking up her drink and sipping, she found Matt in the doorway to the next room.

"Addy."

She turned back to the bar.

"Take him this one," Jim said, pushing a glass with something clear in it. Ice cubes clinked against the sides.

"What is it?"

"He'll like it."

With a shrug, she snatched Matt's drink. Joining him in the doorway, music so loud she could hardly hear herself think, she bumped his shoulder with hers.

He started, turning so fast he knocked both drinks with an elbow.

She jumped back, spilling some of her "iced tea" on her shirt.

"Ah hell, Addy. Sorry. Here," he said, reaching for the glasses.

She handed him his and brushed her shirt. Most of the liquor soaked in, but some of it sprayed him as she brushed. "There. No big deal." She stared into the room. "Where'd they get the colored lights?"

"What's that?" He leaned over. "Music's too loud. These guys know how to throw a party."

"Should they be?"

He took a sip. "What is this?"

"Jim said you'd like it." She pointed over her shoulder.

"He's…" The rest of his words floated away on the music.

Stepping closer, she sipped her drink. Jim said there were seven kinds of alcohol in it.

Didn't taste like it.

She took a bigger sip. "What? I couldn't hear you."

He leaned into her ear. "He's not over there."

And whether it was the alcohol, the euphoria of getting the Troupe through the day alive, or the fact that he smelled really, really good, she didn't know. But the fire that licked the inside of her eyelids sprung up unsolicited and immediate.

She stepped away.

Clearing his throat, he leaned on the doorjamb again.

Addy followed his eyes.

Victoria danced in the center of the stage, alone in a lavender spotlight, faded chem lights in both hands. She lifted her face to the light, eyes closed, and flung her arms out.

Soon, Grey joined her, and they danced in circles until they were both breathless and laughing and falling on the stage.

Laughing with them, Addy polished off her drink and stepped closer to Matt again. "She reminds me of her."

Staring at the empty cup in his hands, he rolled it between them. "I could see that."

She covered her mouth. "Shit, Matt. I have no idea where that came from. I'm sorry."

The parenthesis on one side turned up. "You were thinking of her. You don't have to be sorry." He lowered his head. "It's not like I wasn't."

Ghostly shapes danced through the haze of memory and what could have been.

He and Ella spinning, his hand in the small of her back as she flounced about the room.

Next to them, Addy laughing and hanging on Dean's arm. His emerald eyes sparkling as the corners of them crinkled. Picking her up and twirling her all about the room before setting her on dizzy feet.

"Yeah," Matt said, shuffling his feet. "Anyway. Night, Addy."

Something flitted across her mind. "Wait, Matt. Wait. We forgot something. It was something." The alcohol slowed her brain. That warm feeling still floated around her navel.

Ugh, no, Addy. There's something important.

Matt snapped his fingers. "We have to report to Paxton. You're right. Crap I can't believe we almost forgot."

"The night watch is here. We can report and go to bed," she said, starting toward the office. She stumbled.

He caught her. "I agree. These feet are tricky. What was in that drink?"

"Liquor."

Chuckling, he helped her, and she helped him, and together they got to the office. He shut the door and leaned on it. The music quieted by several hundred decibels. "So much better. It's like I can brain again."

She laughed, almost missing the chair she tried to sit in. "You can't ever brain."

Laughing, he sat across from her and pulled out the radio. Wiping a hand down his face, his grin disappeared under it. He held the straight face until she started laughing again. He tried to push the button on the radio, but though he tried and tried, nothing happened. "I can't push the button, Addy. Did I break it?"

Leaning on the table, she rounded it. "Oh my god, Matthew, you're not even hitting the button." She laughed, losing her footing.

Cheeks flushed, he stood and steadied her. "Don't need you to fall over again. Don't, uh. Thing. Don't." He stopped. "I was going to ask you something." Laughing, he shook his head. "I have no idea what it was."

Steadying herself, she stood tall. "I want you to move your hands, sir."

He looked at his hands where they'd landed on her hips. Still looking down, he asked where she'd like him to move them.

"Anywhere," she started. With the full intention of saying anywhere but there. Instead, her mouth carried on without her. "Anywhere you want."

His bright blue eyes half-lidded, he met hers. "Good god, Adelaide. This is bad."

"You're telling me."

"OK. All right." Looking down at his hands again, he stepped back.

Fighting the urge to mirror his step, she planted her feet and waited for his eyes to bob up.

They did, and he spoke before she had the chance. "Maybe, like. One more time. And then. You know. That's—"

"That's it," she said, moving his hands to her back.

Yanking her close, he stopped short of her mouth. "I know what it was. I was going to ask you not to call me Matthew. But I kinda like it when you do." Without giving her a chance to respond, he covered her lips with a kiss she'd come to think of as fire-breathing. Everything about it was hot.

When they knocked over one of the stacks of chairs, someone tapped on the door and asked if they were all right.

"Fine," Addy said, Matt kissing her neck and slowly moving his hips back and forth, back and forth.

"Do you guys need any help in there?"

She stifled a moan with a laugh. "No, it's a huge mess. We'll get it cleaned up. Go back to the party."

And when the radio blipped, asking for their overdue report, Matt strained to get it from the table. When he couldn't reach and they asked again, he picked her up and sat her on the table. Figuring out the button this time, he made his report as she covered his neck in kisses, hooked her heels behind him, and pressed as tightly as she could get against him.

When he finished the report that would never end, he turned the radio off. "No more interruptions. We gotta get this last time right."

And right there, with his use of "we" and a twist in her gut, she realized they'd been saying "we" about each other for weeks now. "We" are on guard duty, and "we" run security for these fools, and "we" are making a mistake.

The slim moment in which she wanted to stop ended abruptly when he bodily carried her to the couch and blew away any concerns about anything that ever existed.

"We" can worry about all that tomorrow.

* * *

Lash followed Melinda down the hallway, taking the flashlight she offered. "Are you sure about this?"

"No."

"What if someone catches you?"

She stopped, gripping Lash's shoulder. "That's what you're for. Keep anyone from catching me. It's this way, right?" She pointed down an offshoot like a mining spur in front of them. It dived deeper underground, sides of the tunnel turning to plain dirt partway down.

Lash turned on the flashlight and sighed. "Yes." She started down the stairs. "How did I let you talk me into this?"

"I need to see the files, Ilasha. I need to know how IRF got my formula."

As they passed the point where the tunnel became all dirt except the wooden stairs beneath their heels, the temperature dropped another five or ten degrees.

Melinda shivered.

"What if it's a spy? These files won't help," Lash said. Her teeth chattered as she spoke. "Em, wait." She stopped, untying a jacket from her waist. Wiggling her shoulders as she threw it on, she smiled. "Mm. All toasty."

Grumbling about how Lash could have told her how chilly it was down here, Melinda continued down the stairs, her footfalls on the wooden stairs flat. Without echo. The question she wanted to ask surfed up to the edge of her lips and stopped. The "what if I find something I can't handle" question.

She flipped her hair over her shoulder and aimed the flashlight at the bottom of the staircase. "What do you think about all this?"

"All what?"

Stopping, Melinda faced her and leaned on the banister, one foot on a step higher than the other. "I don't know. Burke didn't say IRF and Talus were working together, but he didn't not say it. You feel me?"

Lash joined the higher foot on the same step and popped her bubble. "I'd like to."

"I'm serious, Lash. Do you think—"

Before her thought train pulled into the station, Ilasha covered her mouth with lips of silk that teased and fluttered. So unlike all those needy, forceful men, Lash's kiss was patient. Velvety, gentle, and luscious.

And oh, Melinda had forgotten how soft she was. How like leaning into her was like falling into a bed covered in satin sheets and down pillows. Like home must feel, if she had one.

Fingers covering Melinda's hand, Lash leaned back. "Have there been any other women?"

Melinda shook her head. "Just you."

"Good." She took her hand. "Let's go find these damn files." Tugging, Lash pulled her down the stairs. "Can't believe you talked me into going into this basement of a basement. I must be nuts."

"You saw the vaccine."

"I saw what you told me. You know I don't know as much about it as you do."

"Don't try to fool me," Melinda said, squeezing her hand. "You know more about everything than I know about anything."

"Talking in circles will get you everywhere."

Tip of her nose cold, Melinda chuckled. The dark closing in, the walls and floor all dirt at the bottom, Melinda took a moment to be grateful she'd at least brought flashlights for each of them. "Are there lights down here at all?"

"Once we get in the file room, I'll turn some on. It's OK, Em. I know this place like the back of my hand."

Stomach twisting, brow scrunched, Melinda held Lash's hand and tried to catch the writing on the door plates as they passed. "Come down here a lot?"

"It's where we keep the files. Of course I do." She sniffed. "Or did you forget I spend most days up to my tits in paperwork?"

"Right. Right. Hey." She stopped, tugging.

"What?"

"Do you have all the notes about my kids down here?"

"Which kids?"

An ice pick shoved its way through her stomach. "Not my traitorous biological children. My *kids*."

"They're still your kids, Melinda." Gripping her shoulder, she squeezed. "Even if they don't agree with you, they still love you, right? And you love them."

"I wouldn't be so sure." Their faces as she mounted the helicopter flashed through her mind. Addy's heartbreak. Mike's disappointment. Both of them choosing their weak-willed father.

Shaking her head, rock in her gut, she walked past Lash. "Which room?"

"That one. On your left." Voice sad, it carried from where she'd disappeared in the dark.

Doorknob cold in her palm, Melinda pulled the door open and felt for the light.

"Wait till we're inside," Lash said, appearing next to her. "If anyone sees the light, they might come see what we're doing."

Melinda stepped into the room and held the door for Lash. "Wouldn't want that."

Ilasha closed the door and turned off the flashlight. The dark, soupy and impenetrable, enfolded them in its cold arms. "This is a hell of a room, Em. You ready?"

"As I'll ever be."

Turn on the damned lights. It's too dark.

Lash hit the lights.

Blinded, Melinda squinted and waited for her eyes to adjust.

The rounded dirt ceiling of the room extended a football field's length. The room was a cathedral for filing cabinets, and they took up all the available floor space in haphazard rows.

She stood, mouth open, trying to still her heart. Finding what she was looking for in here was like a needle in a haystack.

Lucky for her, Ilasha was like a magnet. Melinda pitched her voice low. "Where do we look?" Stepping in front of the closest cabinet, she checked its label.

Blocky hand lettering read "OCTOBER–DECEMBER 2037. TC."

She shook her head. "How do you find anything down here?"

Lash stepped deeper into the room. "When did you send it again?"

"April, last year."

Mumbling to herself, Lash wove between rows, tapping her teeth with her fingernails.

Melinda wandered the other way, checking every few placards. Most of them displayed months and years, each year separated into quarters. Nearing the middle of the room, she found a few that read "CURE TRIAL. TC." These were followed by the designation of the trial and the month and year in which it was run. When she found the cabinet labeled "CURE

TRIAL 004. TC. JUNE 2032," she slid the top drawer open and fingered the named and numbered files.

And, of course, there was hers. "THIBODEAUX, 28144."

Pulling the file out and laying it open, she leafed through the nearly ten-year-old test results.

"*SUBJECT M. THIBODEAUX. THIRD DOSE OF TRIAL CURE. SUBJECT SHOWS CONTINUED IMPROVEMENT AND RESISTANCE TO VIRUS. VIOLENT TENDENCIES DECREASED FROM PREVIOUS TEST. IRRATIONAL BEHAVIOR INCREASED. PREFRONTAL CORTEX POSSIBLY COMPROMISED. FUTURE TESTS TO DETERMINE LEVEL OF BRAIN DEGENERATION RECOMMENDED.*"

"Holy shit, Lash."

"What is it, baby?" She slid the drawer in front of her open. "You find something interesting?"

"This test says I might have brain damage?"

"Twice now, you've agreed to go out with me. I'd say so."

"You didn't officially ask me out yet. Don't count your chickens." Folding the file, heartbeat in her temples, she closed the drawer and wove through the cabinets. Lash stood in front of one that read "SHANTI STATION. APRIL–APRIL 2041. TC."

"Some interesting stuff here, Em. I remember when it came across my desk." She flipped through the tabs in the second drawer and pulled a file out. Her eyes round, she opened the file and read aloud. "*TIMOTHY AND HECTOR DELIVERED JACKSON COOKE AND COMPANIONS TO SHANTI STATION. TIMOTHY STATES ADELAIDE AND MICHAEL COOKE HAVE FOLLOWED, WHEREABOUTS CURRENTLY ASSUMED TO BE HARKERS ISLAND. WILL GAIN CONFIRMATION. COOKE COMPANIONS SCHEDULED FOR CURE BUILDING AND VACCINE TESTING.*" She closed the file. "Made your plans for him pretty quick, didn't you?"

Melinda waved her hand, swallowing. "They were perfect subjects. Their initial blood analysis showed his friend had been bitten over a year before coming, and the girl never had. They were exactly what I was looking for at the time." She gestured at the cabinet. "That's not what I came down here for. Is what I'm looking for in that cabinet?"

"I—"

Light spilled under the door from the hallway.

Lash grabbed Melinda's arm and dragged her through the cabinets. "Get back here," she whispered.

"What about the lights?"

"No time. They'll see them turn off." Pushing Melinda ahead of her, she crouched behind some cabinets by the wall.

Melinda crouched next to her, sweat popping out on her lip. "It's OK if we're in here, right?"

"Sure. But you want someone to ask what you're doing?"

The door squealed open. "Ilasha?"

Cormac. That meathead.

"Ilasha, are you in here?" He stepped into the room, weapons on his belt clanking. His boot heels ground into the floor. Sighing through his nose, he walked deeper into the room.

Melinda held her breath, leaning out of sight when his leg came into view.

He spun on a heel. "That woman is never around when I freaking need her. What a waste of skin." Slapping at the light switch, he plunged them into darkness before slamming the door behind him.

Remaining crouched, her knees aching, Melinda counted to fifty. Once she got there, she did it again. The worn file folder in her palm warmed, sweat making the paper slick.

When Lash's hand fell on her shoulder, she clamped a shout behind her teeth and stood, holding Lash's hand.

"Let's get out of here. We'll come back later," Lash said, tugging.

Melinda marked the cabinet where she'd found the last few reports from Shanti Station. "I'll come back later, all right."

CHAPTER 20

Jack stared down into the street, arms crossed. "Celia. It's been a week. What are we doing?"

"We should go," she said. Joining him at the window, she leaned on it. "My brother doesn't want to come home."

"Not the one we met. The other one. Right?" Dean leaned on the wall beside her. "The one your mom says doesn't exist?"

Celia sighed. "I don't know why I let this bother me. There's a reason I ran away when I was nine. And ten. And eleven."

Jack tried to imagine hating your life so much at nine you tried to escape from it. He tried superimposing his current desire to run away from the negative things in his life, his ex-wife included, on someone much younger. It didn't help. "Doesn't sound like the best situation."

"It wasn't. My parents were great. But they were always at work. What could they do?" Shaking her head, she leaned against the window. "I was in a gang by the time I was eight."

"All I ever knew about gangs I learned from TV," Jack said. "I have no clue what it was like for you."

She shrugged.

"I am glad, however, you crossed my path. No matter the reason."

"I second that," Dean said.

"This is why I can't trust either of you." She laughed. "You want to head back to the library?"

Jack considered. They still hadn't gotten to a place with cell reception, but he wanted to help Celia straighten out her past. Not everyone got the chance. "What I want is to get a call through to Mike and help you see your brother. What's his name again?"

"Felipe."

Dean shifted, clearing his throat. "And your niece and nephew, your eldest sister's kids?"

The corners of her mouth turned down. "Guess they're only a few years older than Addy. The twins. Lucinda and Ramon. I don't know why they would break Mama's heart like that."

"We've been here this long and still can't get it out of your mom. We could go ask them," Jack said. He looked across the way at the other buildings. "Better than sitting around here any longer. What do you say?"

She laid her forehead on the glass. "I shouldn't have come back here."

Dean gripped her shoulder. "If you really want to leave, we'll leave. But Jack's right. We should find the rest of your family first."

Nodding, hair scratching against the glass, she poked out her lip. "Should we tell Manny we're going?"

"That sounds needlessly complicated," Jack said. "He'd try to stop us."

The corner of her mouth turned up. "Do you think it would piss him off?"

Jack chuckled. If there was one thing she had a nose for, it was trouble. Always had. "I do."

Dean stood straight. "What are we waiting for? Where's our weapons?"

* * *

"Shit. Addy," Matt said, shaking her shoulder.

With a start, she sat halfway up, the furthest she could get with her legs tangled in his. "You OK? What's going on?" Fighting to disentangle her legs, she fell back into the couch. The musty smell had lessened, but it'd always smell a bit like dust.

"What time is it?" Stretching toward the table, he tried to snag the radio. "I forgot to turn this back on. Fuck."

"Nobody's banging on the door yet," she said, tugging her leg again. It'd fallen asleep from the knee down. "So, that's—"

The door rattled with a light knock.

Matt's wide eyes met hers. Running a hand down her thigh, he helped her untangle her leg. Snatching his pants from the floor, he tried to whip them on without banging his weapons together. The Bowie knife clanked against his gun.

The person on the other side knocked again. "Guys? Are you in there?" Jim. Whispering.

As Addy threw Matt's shirt at his face, he tossed hers to her. He turned his right side out, pulled it over his head, flattened his hair with one hand, and pulled the door open an inch. He spoke through the crack. "Yeah, Jim. Everything OK?"

Stomach in knots, mouth clenched shut, Addy tried to cover everything with the shirt alone. If Jim came in, the fraternization rule was busted. No two ways about it.

In addition to having to admit, out loud, what had happened. Three times now.

"It's fine. Just wanted to make sure you were up before the Troupe. To, um. Well, you weren't in the room. I didn't want them to worry about you guys." He cleared his throat.

"Yeah," Matt said. "Sorry. You know, uh. Fell asleep after that drink you made. It was good." He shuffled his feet, speaking about three times faster than normal. "What was in it?"

Smoke wafted through the door. "Liquor. You liked?"

"Never had a drink do that to me," he said, glancing over his shoulder. Two spots of color on his cheeks.

Addy flushed, shrinking farther under the shirt. Her pants were under the table, but there was no way to reach for them without breaking the scant cover the side of the couch afforded. And was he trying to say it'd been the alcohol? Or. Or what?

"Anyway," Jim said, voice receding, "just making sure the drink didn't kill you." A stilted laugh floated into the room. "That old chestnut."

Matt shook his head. "Thanks, Jim." Closing the door, he leaned on it.

"Is the sun up?" Addy asked, reaching for her pants.

He fished them out and handed them off. "Barely. I think we're OK."

"Jim knows."

"Pretty sure he already did." He sat next to her and flipped the radio on. "I also think we should talk about—"

The radio blipped. *"Team Tree, come in, over."*

Matt jumped, radio slipping.

Addy stifled a shout. "Answer him."

"Team Tree here. What's going on, Paxton? Kinda early, isn't it?"

"10-4, Matt. Adelaide with you?"

She shook her head.

"She is."

"Good. Morgan needs to see you both right away."

Mouthing a silent curse, Matt pushed the button and stared at her. "10-4. What about?"

"Not sure. But he said it was important."

"Roger. We'll get right over there, over and out." He rested his head in his hands. "How do you want to handle this?"

Dressed, Addy shook her head. "Maybe it's about something else. Do you think anyone besides Jim knows?"

"Hell if I know, Addy. Looks like we're going to find out." He stood, clipping the radio to his belt. "Let's get this over with."

She took his outstretched hand. Thought about saying it was fun while it lasted. Rethought.

It was confusing while it lasted, is what.

Preceding him into the hallway, she tiptoed out to the bar.

The scent of eggs and coffee, something she'd become accustomed to already, floated through the room. No movement though. Jim must've been in the back, readying breakfast. Drawing the Troupe from their post-party slumber with the promise of food and fuel. If Morgan was about to bust them down for breaking the rules and send them to the farthest corner of the city, she would miss all this. She already felt part of a special group, the air around them electric.

Matt bumped her shoulder.

She followed him outside.

The sun still below the horizon, the sky pink, the dew on the grass smelt of sunrise. Mist rose from the ground, covering it in a shifting curtain of cloud.

Matt shook hands with the night watch. "We gotta go see Morgan. Be back soon."

"We'll wait," a freckled boy said. "He told us you'll be a few."

Swallowing, Addy followed Matt into the street. The misty fog dampened their footfalls on the pavement.

"You ever drive anything, Addy?"

An iron fist punched her in the gut. "My old pickup. And Dean's train."

He stopped. "Sorry. Uh," he said, walking again, "ever ride a motorcycle?"

She shook her head. "No. But I've seen them. Look wild."

"Wild fun."

As they walked the few blocks to Morgan's building with the striped pole out front, Matt told her about learning to drive a motorcycle as a kid, and one of the times he'd ridden away from his gang and a horde on one. "I couldn't have been more than ten."

"I was still sleeping between my parents more often than not at that age."

One parenthesis pointed up. "Lucky."

"I was." She sighed. "I was."

"You'll have to tell me what she was like."

Pressing her lips together, Addy tried to ball up the memories and shove them aside, but they cascaded through her like a waterfall. Her eyes stung.

Morgan's office building appeared from the mist before she got a nail under where to begin.

After knocking on the door, she took four steps away from Matt and stood with her arms crossed.

Shirtless, Morgan answered the door. "Sorry. You guys got here fast. Still waking up. Please," he said, opening the door wide.

They sat in front of his desk while he got them coffee.

Matt gnawed a nail, then dropped his hand to his lap. Crossed his legs. Uncrossed.

For what it was worth, Addy's insides did the same dance. She did marginally better at not showing it.

Setting a small white cup in front of them both, Morgan sat behind his desk. "So."

Addy cleared her throat. "So."

"You guys did a stellar job yesterday. Stellar."

Waiting for the "but," Addy took a sip of the coffee. The full-bodied taste flattened her.

"A couple things."

Matt leaned forward in the chair. "Sir. Listen."

Waving a hand, Morgan picked up a paper. "Twenty wounded. Six dead. Eighteen missing. *Eighteen*." He paused and slipped on a pair of thin glasses. Staring at the paper, he frowned.

Eighteen? Good lord.

Lowering his glasses and the paper to the desk, Morgan interlaced his fingers and leaned on them. "Listen. The fact your guys didn't even see any of this action is a small miracle in itself. At least four were taken a block away from your safe room."

Matt sat forward. "The one we were in? We didn't hear any of that."

Morgan put the paper down and ran a hand along his forehead. "The Troupe is so important to this community. So important. You guys did such a wonderful job. I can't thank you enough."

"It's what you asked of us, Morgan," Addy said, leaning on the desk. "Plus, they deserve it."

He smiled, eyes closed. "They do. And you two"—he pointed between them—"deserve a reward."

Matt shook his head. "That's not necessary, sir."

"Take the day off," Morgan said. "Don't argue. See some of the town. Don't worry about them. I'll keep an eye on them myself." He stood, pulling a button-up shirt off the back of his chair. "I'll walk back with you."

* * *

Holding the machete handle toward Jack, Celia grinned. "Don't ask."

He took it and slid it in its sheath. "Your feminine wiles?"

Dean snorted.

Grinning with her mouth turned down, Celia sheathed her own long-handled blade. "We gotta sneak out the back. It's over here." She pointed and, without waiting, set off down a hall where most of the rooms had been damaged by a long-ago fire.

Jack trotted to catch up to her. "Did you tell your mom we're going?"

"Tried. She wouldn't listen."

He frowned, feeling her disappointment for her. "What about Luisa?"

"Cursed in Spanish and told me to get the hell out."

Dean jangled as he jogged down the hall to catch them. At least their time there afforded him a healed ankle. "Safe to say we're not coming back?"

Celia leaned on the exit door buried at the end of a dark hallway. "I'd like to get Felipe to talk to Mama, but I won't force him. Guess we'll find out." Pushing the door open two inches, she stared into the bright afternoon. "Clear."

"After you," Jack said, gun in hand. "Get in front of me, Dean. I'll take the rear."

As they snuck out the door, Jack considered the fact it opened onto the street. "Shouldn't someone be guarding that door?"

Nodding, Celia nocked an arrow and pointed it everywhere.

"More of your feminine wiles?"

"Jaime likes being hit in the nose."

Dean chuckled again. "He's not the only one."

She straightened her shoulders, stopping. "What's that supposed to mean, Ross?"

"Not a thing, Cee. Not a thing."

"Better be not a thing," she muttered, moving again.

Jack glanced back at the building. Someone had covered their escape well. No faces appeared in the windows on this side. "Let's get to those bushes over there."

In the silent street, Celia angled toward a small greenbelt between buildings.

As they entered the green, Jack's jaw relaxed. The thought of being captured, again, pumped adrenaline through him in a constant singing beat of terror. Not for the first time, nor the last, he reminded himself Melinda and her metal table was far behind him. Closing his eyes, he allowed the memory to float away.

Creeping through the evergreen bushes next to an old, hilly basketball court, Dean gave a low laugh. "Basketball. There's something I haven't seen in forever."

Celia laughed. "I'd kick your ass in one-on-one, white boy."

"Bet you would."

"Guys," Jack hissed. "We're getting close. Banter to a minimum, please."

The first of three buildings loomed, filling the street with its imposing shadow.

Dean blew a breath out his nose. "I hope getting into this one is easier than—"

"Aunt Luisa?"

They stopped, looking around.

Celia shook her head. "No. But I am your aunt. Ramon?"

"I don't know you. Who are you?" The voice came from behind them. He'd let them pass before speaking.

Jack tilted his head and pointed his gun at the ground. "We're not here to hurt you, Ramon. This is your Aunt Celia."

No less than five people stepped out from around them. Crowding the thin greenbelt. They each drew at least one weapon, but though Celia aimed her bow, none of them raised them. A boy emerged from behind Jack.

"Why are you coming from over there?"

"I want to see Felipe. And you and your sister." Celia said. "Mama wouldn't tell me what happened."

"We thought you were dead," Ramon said, brushing past Jack with a glance.

Celia stepped back. "You were wrong. Are you going to take me to your uncle, or do we need to leave?"

"You're free to leave if you wish," a man said, out of sight. "But I would like to hug you first, flaca."

Lowering the bow, she smiled into the bushes. "Mijo."

"Let's get inside," the same man said, stepping from the bushes. Most of his hair still dark, lines crossed so much of his face he looked like a map that had been folded the wrong way too many times. "Manny is a tricky one. I wouldn't trust him any farther than I could toss him."

Emmanuel pushed into the bushes, a dozen men trampling them behind him. "You're not wrong, Felipe." He raised a rifle and took aim.

Before the sound of the shot hit his ears, the air buzzed in front of Jack's face. Celia leapt in front of her eldest brother, shouting.

Blood flew.

CHAPTER 21

"**C**elia!"

Too late, Jack leapt forward.

Celia slumped, her eldest brother stippled in blood. Before Jack could so much as take a breath, the air around him filled with deafening gunfire, flying blood, and gun smoke that crept up his nose and drilled into his brain.

At Felipe's feet, Celia writhed.

Jack crawled to her, covering his head. And though he never dealt much in god, he prayed. As Spanish and bullets flew over his head, he tugged Dean's pants leg.

Dean dropped next to him, grabbing Celia's ankles.

Jack wrapped her in a bear hug and pulled her toward the nearest bushes, Dean doing his best to keep up.

She muttered. "Felipe."

"You first," Jack said, dragging her deeper into the bushes. Sticks raked his arms, reaching out to poke at his eyes and catch in his hair. A couple drew blood across his shoulders, even through the shirt. Not that he noticed it until much later. "Dean," he said, pointing at Celia, "get the bleeding stopped." Drawing his gun, he spun to join the fray.

Felipe backed over him. "Get Celia back to the building. Go, now!" He fired over their heads, shouting to his nephew.

Holstering his gun, Jack hauled Celia off the ground. "Can you walk? Where were you hit?"

"Yes." She sucked a sharp breath over her teeth. "I don't know." Stumbling, she headed toward the building.

Covering their side, Dean drew and aimed toward Emmanuel and his men. He never fired, but his eyes took in everything at once. "Are we taking sides in this?"

"I'm on the side of don't get shot, Dean," Jack said. "And right now, that means getting into this building." Its shadow cooling the air above them, he pushed Celia toward it.

Muzzle flashes lit several windows on the second and third floors. A door on the ground floor opened, a boy no older than twelve standing in it and waving them inside. His hair bleached white, the dark brown eyes peeking from beneath his bangs put Jack in mind of those boy bands from the old days and their frosted tips.

What a strange memory to have while he ran inside the building, pushing Celia before him and pulling Dean behind.

Celia tried to stop once they'd entered the building, but a quick look behind them told Jack she couldn't stop in the door like she wanted. "Just a little farther, Celia." With one arm around her waist, he picked her up and propelled her deeper into the hallway.

She curled one arm around his neck and leaned.

"Jack, here," Dean said, shoving a chair out of an open doorway. "Set her here."

Helping as much as she could, Celia sat in the doorway as the rest of the eight or ten men sprinted into the building and the kid shut the door after them. Her hair stuck to her pale forehead, she glanced down. "Can't feel my arm too good, Jack." Leaning on him, she gazed up, trying to meet his eyes. "Doesn't hurt, at least."

"Dean, can you get me some light?" Jack asked, ginger hands lifting her arm. Her bloody coat made it impossible to see where she'd been hit or how bad the damage was. "I'm gonna have to take off your jacket, Celia."

"Can I help?" Felipe knelt next to him. The lines crisscrossing his face etched deep.

Jack helped Celia shrug the good shoulder out of its sleeve. "You got an infirmary or something?"

"Not in this building. But there's a first aid station."

"Close?"

"Yes."

"Good. Bring me some gauze. Alcohol. Anything to clean this with. We're going to need a real infirmary or medic or something. I don't know if the bullet's still in, or where it hit her or anything." He tugged the jacket with light fingers.

Celia winced but didn't cry out as her injured arm slid from the sleeve. At least she liked to wear jackets two sizes too big. Always said it gave her something to slip out of if she got grabbed.

Knees crackling as he stood, Felipe hurried down the hall.

The young man who'd first greeted them leaned against the wall. "She looks just like my Aunt Luisa."

"I ought to," Celia said, shifting against the doorjamb. She winced, clutching her injured arm.

Jack lowered her hand, looking down the hallway for Felipe. The bleeding had slowed, so she wasn't going to bleed to death. But he preferred to get her wrapped up before they moved her again.

Celia struggled to sit up straighter. "Where's your sister?"

Ramon shook his head. "Upstairs. She runs the daycare."

"Just like Maria."

He slid down the wall. "Tell me about my mama. We were three when she died. Did she look like you, too?"

Nodding, Celia began a slow fall sideways, pasty forehead trapping more hair.

Jack caught her, letting her lean into his lap. "Don't fall asleep, Cee."

Still nodding, half a smile curved her mouth. "Felipe is the only one who looks like Papa. The rest of us all take after Mama. You, too, Ramon."

Lights dimmed as Felipe came back down the hallway. Behind him, two men carried a stretcher.

Jack chuckled.

Good luck getting her on that, Felipe.

He shook her shoulder. The uninjured one. "Cee. Sit up, honey. Let's get that wound dressed so we can get to the infirmary."

She sat up, still leaning on him. "I'm fine, Jack. You don't have to baby me."

He took the gauze from Felipe and dabbed at her arm.

She locked a scream behind her lips and paled, even in the low light. "Felt that."

"I know you did. Dean," he said, holding his hand out, "take her hand. I need to clean this." He rubbed her shoulder. "Keep it as steady as you can, Celia."

She pressed her lips together.

As he cleaned, Jack spoke with Felipe and learned about the Triad.

* * *

Addy ducked under a branch and stepped around the corner of the building the tree had grown through.

Back to her, Matt loaded something into a saddle bag strapped to the side of a motorcycle. Pack on his back, he fussed around the bike.

Stopping, Addy held her breath. Something about the way he bustled called Ella to mind.

She backed up, running into the building. Whatever it was he wanted to show her, maybe it wasn't worth the guilt that still floated around her insides, clenching her stomach in an iron fist.

Kneeling, he faced the bike. "If you don't want to go, I get it."

She took a step toward him. "I don't know, Matt. I don't know."

He stood, removing the pack from his shoulders, and leaned on the bike. "Well. Why don't you come with me? I want to talk to you, and we shouldn't do it where people can hear. Don't you think?"

He wasn't wrong.

She took the pack and flipped it onto her back. It sat heavy, and something inside shifted and clinked.

"Careful. Don't want to break it." He sat on the bike. "You said you've never been on a motorcycle?"

Throwing a leg over the side, she shook her head. "No. What do I do?"

Twisted at the waist, he showed her where to put her feet. "You can hold the back of the bike. Or the bottom of the seat.

Or, um"—he cleared his throat—"you can hold me. Um. My waist. Here." He tapped the side of his hip. Red rushing up his cheeks, he hurried on. "When we go around corners, don't fight it. Lean with me. If you can't do that, sit as still as you can and let me drive. OK?"

"Is this dangerous?"

The parentheses turned up. "Yes." He raised the kickstand.

Under the roar of the engine, she couldn't hear herself say "good." Holding the seat, she leaned back. As they rode out of town, the wind sighed in her face.

Not unlike the time Dean rolled her through Magnolia in a wheelbarrow. When she'd busted up her ankle.

Tears whipped away in the wind, and she closed her eyes. The machine beneath her grumbled and growled and vibrated. The metal cold where she gripped it, her fingers soon became slivers of ice. Her nose disappeared into the "too cold to feel it" zone.

Once, when they slowed to slalom around some piles of debris, Matt cocked an eye over his shoulder. Grinned at her red face. "You cold?"

She raised her voice above the engine. "Can't feel my fingers."

Grasping her right hand, he faced the road again and tugged her forward.

She almost resisted, but his hands were as cold as hers. At least they were in it together.

He folded her hand around his waist and accelerated.

Gripping his abs, fine abs that they were, she slid the other hand around him and leaned into him.

Leaning like this did make going around corners that much easier. And he made a good wind block.

Eyes closed, she let him lead her around the corners as the wind kept whipping away the tears. When he slowed and turned off the roaring thing, she could hardly move her frozen arms.

Chuckling as he helped her extricate herself from the bike, he steadied her when her legs decided they'd had enough. He took the pack from her.

"Oh, don't break the pack, Addy." She mimicked him, head shaking.

"You can heal," he said, looking her up and down. "I've seen it. But this," he said, jiggling the pack, "took some searching. We'd be hard-pressed to replace it." Glancing at a skeletal structure climbing into the sky, then swooping back down behind the wall before them, he held out a hand.

She gave him her freezing fingers. So cold they hurt. "What is this place?"

"It used to be called an amusement park."

"What's funny about it?"

He laughed. "Not amusing. Amusement. Like you come here to have a good time."

"Oh. Is it clean?"

"Probably not. That OK?"

"You've got my trusty Bowie knife you won't give back. And I've got my machete." She unsheathed said machete. "I guess we'll be all right."

"My knife."

"Whatever."

Tugging her into the park, he guided her under the structure. Made of metal, flaking and chipped paint covered parts of it. Whole swaths of rust had eaten through the other parts, and some of it lay on the ground. The rest hung precariously from the sky, waiting to fall on their heads.

"It looks like track or something," she said.

"Came here once with your mom. She says this was called a roller coaster."

Stopping, she stared up and up and left his mention of Mom on the ground. "A what what?"

"I don't know. Let's go farther in." He tugged.

Freeing her hand, she tucked her machete under her arm and rubbed her hands together. "Is it warmer?"

He laughed, leading her deeper into the park. Unsnapped his knife but didn't draw.

She kept an ear out, but the park remained silent. They had it to themselves. Just them and the skeletal roller coasters. After they'd gone through the whole park, he pointed to a coaster. "Here, that one. It's tall."

Craning her neck, she shaded her eyes and took it in. "It is. Is it intact?"

"It was last time I was here. There's a way up, look." He pointed, angling off through some bushes. He disappeared, the bushes snapping back behind him.

"Matt, wait," she said, hacking at the branches. A stench caught her nose. Stagnant water. Flat, rotten mold. And.

She broke through the bushes.

He stood under the coaster, pulling the knife from the side of a 'Head's skull. "So, it's not completely abandoned."

Grinning with the sides of her mouth turned down, she passed him. "Is this the ladder?" Without waiting for his answer, she climbed.

"Shit, Addy. Let me go first."

Ignoring him, she continued up. "Seems all right. Come on." Climbing higher and higher, she eventually found herself standing on the tracks. Once he joined her, she pointed to the top of the track. "We going up there?"

He nodded, pushing to get in front of her. Grabbing the handrail, he shook it back and forth, testing it. It held. "Watch for holes. Stay on the path here," he said, pointing at his feet.

An old walkway stretched between the track and the side. Mainly complete, a few holes had rusted through the lattice of metal.

She followed him to the top and waited, clutching her waist, as he set the pack down and pulled out a blanket. "Not much, but all I could fit in there. Here, sit." Laying the blanket on the walkway, he pointed.

Averting her eyes from the ground, she sat. "Thanks for introducing a new, stomach-wrenching fear."

He rummaged in the bag. "What?"

"Heights. This is terrifying."

Laughing, he pulled two glasses from the bag. "Hold this. Don't look down."

She took the glasses and didn't know whether to laugh or cry when he pulled out two bottles. Orange juice in one, what had to be champagne in the other.

When he poured for them both, she laughed, a tear slipping down her cheek.

He strapped the bag to the rail and rested the bottles back inside. He clinked her glass. "To lost loves."

Fighting a laughing sob and losing, she drank. The bitter juice mixed with the sweet champagne. "You don't make them as strong as she did."

He gazed across the park, cheeks ruddy. "Ella liked them strong. It's true."

Addy caught her breath. He hadn't said her name aloud since the one time he'd done it by accident before they left the island. She sipped. "What are we doing up here?"

Sighing, he side-eyed her. "I miss the fuck out of her, Addy."

"Me too. Not as much as you do, I'm sure."

He shook his head. "Do you want to stop what we're doing?"

She opened her mouth to answer but found she couldn't spit it out. Either yes or no. Whatever the right answer was.

Looking off across the park again, he took a drink. "Me neither."

Bumping his knee with hers, she frowned. "We should talk about it though." She cleared her throat. "I thought about Dean almost all the way out here."

Parentheses pointing down, he exhaled through his nose. "I kept thinking about the damn champagne bottle and hoping it didn't break. Ella would have cried over spilt champagne." He glanced at Addy. "I hated it when she cried."

Addy goggled. "She cried?"

Laughing, Matt finished his drink and poured them both another. "Not much." Grinning, he caught her eyes with his. "Is it OK to do whatever it is we're doing and still talk to you about her?"

"Can I talk to you about Dean?"

"Of course."

She downed the rest of the drink. "I like you, Matt. I do. You're a good friend. And a good. Um. Yeah."

He turned an alarming shade of red. "What you said." Clearing his throat, he spun his empty glass between his hands. "I love her though. I don't think that'll ever change."

She gripped his knee. "It doesn't have to." She sighed. "Sometimes I think once we leave here and go back to Harkers, Dean will have come to his senses."

"You'd be all right with that?"

She shrugged. "I'd be fucking ecstatic with that. I love him." Half a smile touched her mouth. It was the best she could do.

"God, Addy. We're a wreck."

Laughing, she held out her glass. "Get me a refill. Tell me about how you met Ella."

* * *

Arm in a sling, Celia grinned when Jack stepped into the infirmary. Four of the beds occupied, she lay farthest from the door.

Walking down the row of beds, Jack took in each of the other three. Flashing on Andrew whether he liked it or not. But none of these people were hooked up to mystery substances. For the most part, they were recovering from the same thing Celia was.

"How's your arm?" He slid a chair closer to the bed and sat.

She shrugged, wincing when her arm moved. "They got the bullet out. Lucky it was a metal slug and not one of those hollow points. Broke the bone but didn't shatter. I'll heal." Her eyes slipped past him.

Dean shifted from foot to foot in the door, sweat on his forehead. His eyes jumped about the room, both looking and not looking at the beds.

"What's his problem?" she asked, jerking her chin at him.

"Don't know. Probably something to do with last time he was in a hospital. Or something."

Brows creased, she stared. "He say anything about Addy?"

"No. But I haven't asked."

Still looking past Jack, Celia frowned. "He doesn't talk about her at all?" She blew a breath out her nostrils. "Dick."

Jack's stomach slipped sideways. He'd been so concerned with himself lately, he hadn't considered what he might do to fix things between Addy and Dean. Maybe he could talk a little sense into the man like Paul did to him. Worth a shot.

But in the meantime. "Your brother told me all about the Triad here and what happened between him and your mom." He grimaced. "If you're interested, I'll tell you."

Laying back on the pillow, she punched it into submission and stared at the ceiling.

Taking her silence as assent, Jack explained what Felipe told him. How in the beginning, it had solely been about surviving. As the urban area became overrun, they blocked off the ground floors and holed up. If they didn't, the old people and children, and anyone who couldn't move fast enough, would get eaten alive. They'd seen it with their own eyes.

Then the power went. More people left. Got devoured. Right out in the streets.

Some of the diabetics in the complex began falling into comas and dying. Celia's sister Maria and their father, Martin, went for medical supplies. Felipe went with them.

Only Felipe made it back.

Manny's father started to come around. Felipe, in his twenties, now the man of the house, did not take kindly to another man trying to care for his mama. Especially when the man still had his own family. His own woman.

"He wouldn't stand for your mother being a side piece," Jack said. "His words."

Eyes closed, Celia chuckled through her nose. "I wouldn't either, Jack."

Grasping through the fog of memory, he pictured his own mom. Caught a memory of an eleven-year-old Jack standing on his mom's feet as she taught him to dance. To the very same song he'd taught Jane to dance to.

Even at that age, another man would have had to come through him if he tried to treat his mom like a disposable piece of meat.

"Anyhow," he said, coming out of his reverie, "in the years that followed, the rift only widened. Felipe raised Maria's kids with his girlfriend, had his own kids, and rose to lead what's become the Triad. When the first apartment building fell, he pooled his resources and got an engineer in to look at the rest of them." He pressed his lips together. "They lost almost a thousand people when that one went."

"Funny he got an engineer. He always wanted to be one." A tear slipped from the side of her eye. She shifted her broken arm. "The building they're in is unsafe, isn't it?"

Jack nodded. "The fight that followed split your family. Manuel accused Felipe of being jealous and wanting to take over his territory. Felipe started trying to force them out by cutting their power and stealing their supplies."

"And here we are."

"And here we are." He laid a hand on Celia's shoulder. "He wants to see you when you're ready. Let you meet your great-nephew."

She grinned. "Great-nephew? Am I old enough for that, Jack?"

Chuckling, he shook his head. "What is age anymore? Think about who you're asking."

She narrowed her eyes and sat up. "All right. Let's go see mi hermano and this great-nephew of mine."

CHAPTER 22

As he played with the babies in the daycare and watched over Celia, getting to know her family again, Jack found himself missing his own baby more than he could stand. When Dean suggested they go up on the roof, he jumped at the chance.

Climbing the stairs, Dean spoke over his shoulder. "Took note of what you said about calling Mike and them."

Baby smell still deep in his nose, Jack smiled. "It would be nice to talk to them. Make sure they're doing OK."

Dean stopped. "What about you? How are you doing?"

"I've been better. And worse." He continued up the stairs, eyes on the set of Dean's shoulders. "And you, Dean? You've been pretty quiet."

Dean pushed the door to the roof open, coughed, and spit out a chunk of bloody mucus. "Still getting past the virus." Fists on his hips, he spun a circle. "Ah. Here we go." He made a beeline for a satellite dish. Fiddling with the base, checking the wires, he cursed when a spark of electricity jumped.

Jack sat next to the dish and considered what Paul would have said to him. The guy had been so good at no-nonsense straight talk. He opened his mouth to ask about his daughter and found the words stuck. He asked about the dish instead. "Think you can get it working?"

Dean sat and toyed with the junction box on the back side of the dish. "I think so. Gonna be a sloppy job, but it should do for a few phone calls." Glancing up, he stopped. "What?"

"What?"

"You're lookin' at me funny. Something on your mind?"

Caught out, Jack had no choice but to nod. "Tell me why you broke my little girl's heart, Dean."

Dean inhaled. But the corner of his eye crinkled. "Thought you said you wouldn't bring it up."

"Sorry."

Going back to the satellite, Dean slid a multi-tool from his belt and flipped a small Phillips-head out. He started unscrewing a panel. "Tough to explain." His eyes reddened, and he met Jack's with them. "You saw what she tried to do."

"Yeah. And I get why she did. It was wrong, but I get it."

"Me too. Too well." He worked in the box, cursing again when sparks flew. "Do me a favor. Reach over there and pull that plug out," he said, pointing to the opposite side of the dish.

Jack did. "Then why?"

"It was an unreasonable risk, Jack. All of it. Carrying me through the horde. Patching me up. Sitting with me while…" He began working inside the box again. "If being close to me makes her take those kinds of chances. Ow! Shit." Removing his hand from the box, he stuck a bleeding finger in his mouth. Round eyes met Jack's. He took the finger out of his mouth, checking the bleeding. "I can't be responsible for that. I can't."

"She's a big girl. She makes her own decisions. We don't have to agree with them." He grimaced. "We can't save her from the bad ones."

"You did. I saw you tackle her to keep me from biting her. Clear as day."

Mouth open, Jack didn't answer. Couldn't deny what he'd said.

Meeting his eyes before going back to the box, Dean sighed. "She's a hell of a woman, your daughter. Gonna make someone very happy." He pointed at the plug. "Plug it back in. Think that's got it."

Reaching for the plug, listing to one side, Jack about fell over when the door to the roof banged open.

He leapt to his feet, Dean next to him.

Celia stood in the door, eyes alight and panting, her broken arm bouncing up and down in the sling. She didn't seem to notice.

Jack took a step toward her, hand out. "Celia? You all right?"

"You're not going to believe this."

* * *

The countryside slipped by, Matt's motorcycle growling. Leaning into him, Addy raised up into his ear, his hair tickling her lips. "Where are we going?"

He gripped one of her hands circling his waist and squeezed. "Molehill," he shouted over his shoulder.

Hands popping open, she leaned back. Raised her voice well above the singing of the road and the growling of the engine. "Stop."

Downshifting, he rolled the bike to a halt.

She leapt off, dropping the pack, and started walking back the way they'd come. Her fists and teeth clenched.

Cutting the engine, he lowered the kickstand with a clink. His feet pounded the ground as he jogged to catch her. "Addy, wait."

She didn't stop walking. "The hell, Matt? Just gonna take me there and turn me over to my mom? Was that your plan all along?" Shoving her hands into her elbows, she exhaled through clenched teeth. "I swear, fucking men."

"No, Addy, wait. No." He gripped her shoulder. "Stop."

Stomach in knots, she shook his hand off and kept walking.

"If I was going to do that, I wouldn't have stopped the bike. Would you just wait for a second?" He sighed, an eye roll in his voice. "Please?"

She stopped, staring at the rolling foothills through a break in the trees.

He rounded in front of her. Tugging one of her hands loose, he gripped it. "Your hands are still freezing."

"No shit."

Cupping his own hands around it, he breathed into the knot of them and rubbed her fingers. "I thought you'd like to know where it is. Look at it. From a distance. That's all."

"Could've asked. I don't much like surprises." Tugging her hand free, she stuffed it back in her elbow.

"I'm sorry. I didn't mean anything by it."

She kicked at a rock. Nervous laugh escaping her lips, she frowned. "I don't think I'm ready to see her yet. I don't know why I'm telling you that."

"Who else are you gonna tell?"

"Good point." She sat in the road.

He sat next to her. "You remind me a lot of her sometimes, you know?"

"My mom? Yeah. You said that."

"No. Ella."

She jumped. "What? No? Why?"

Chuckling, he nodded. "I told you about when we met. What I didn't tell you was how she was. Her dad had gone to make a phone call. By the time he'd finished, I was hers." He stared down the road. "She was like a force of nature. Pulled me along in her wake without even asking. You're a lot like that too." Catching her eyes, he smiled. "I guess I just wanted to give you something you wanted. Not to see your mom. But at least to know where she is. Know where they are."

"Do you miss it?"

"Sometimes." Drawing his knees up, he rested his chin on them and stared into space. Probably into the past as well. "I had a lot of fun after I got there. Tim was always kind of an ass, but he was like that one friend you have that's just an ass."

"I don't know what that means."

He chuckled. "That's all right. But you know, Vic was there, and lots of other kids. They made us do school, which was weird after thirteen years of nothing. But I liked learning to read." He cut his eyes at her. "Do you read?"

"I'm literate, if that's what you mean."

"No, I mean for fun."

She grinned. "Not much. My dad and Jane do." Jane flitted through her mind, sitting on the couch with the pages of her book feathering, Addy having just walked in from Tim asking her out. Wasn't that the night she met Dean? Or was it the next night?

She sucked a breath through her nose. "Dean does too."

"I found it educational. But practicing with weapons was more fun." Unsheathing his Bowie knife, he twirled it around his hand and juggled it a few times. "Ella didn't read much, but she always encouraged me to read more." He gouged the ground between his feet with the tip of the knife. "Melinda always put a weapon in my hands. Ella always put a book."

Addy narrowed her eyes. "Which one do you think is more important?"

"Does one have to be more important than the other?"

She stood and offered him her hand. "I guess not."

Sheathing the knife, he took it and stood. Holding her hand a moment longer than strictly necessary, he squeezed and dropped it. "Let's get back to town," he said, heading for the bike.

Arms crossed, eyes closed, Addy called him. "Matt."

He raised the kickstand, cocking a brow.

"Let's go see the Molehill."

* * *

Lying flat on the bed, Melinda raised her test results to her eyes. Arm across her forehead, she read through them again and again. Lips moving over the words, "prefrontal cortex." And over, "further testing."

And no one, not even Lash, had taken the time to mention this to her. Had never brought up her own results.

She laid the paper over her face, closing her eyes and breathing into it. Her breath warmed the paper and circulated back around to her eyelashes.

Wasn't the prefrontal cortex in charge of decision-making?

What did that mean about the decisions she'd made over the last ten years?

Pursuing the perfection of the Cure, and the creation of the vaccine, with dogged enthusiasm.

Using all those people to incubate the virus and then trying to heal them. Failing miserably.

The experiments with awful side effects.

Doing it anyway.

Then there was what she'd done to Jack. Kidnapping his woman. Forcing her to undergo the vaccine trial against her will.

Against the will of all of them. She knew, even then, what she was doing to him.

And before she could revel in the outcome—a successful vaccine, an immune baby—her mind sped on to Adelaide.

In the snow. Pleading with her to think. Trying to slow her down long enough to talk about it.

Addy's blood spilling on the snow, red mixed with white. The shape of her own knuckles imprinted on the lab coat.

Snatching the paper from her face before she thought about Jack again, and all the rest of the spectacular failures she'd had with him, she sat up and crumpled it into a ball.

"I'll just have to find those test results. See what the conclusion was about my head." She swiped at her eye, knocking a tear off the side before it took hold. "Besides. I created immunity. Brain damage aside, I did that."

Pulling out her pajamas, something she hadn't had during all those years out there with the Cookes, she changed clothes still thinking about Addy's nose spurting blood into the snow. Her wounded eyes as she fell next to her father.

Melinda's gut tried to crawl inside her lungs and choke her.

And for the barest of moments, before her phone rang, she looked sideways at that decision. Maybe it could be explained by damage to her mind. The virus did it. Broke her little girl's heart.

Broke her father's spirit.

But the phone did ring, and when Ilasha spoke on the other end, she jumped at the distraction.

"*Em, sweetie. Are you all right? You sound down.*"

"I didn't find what I was looking for down there." She stared at the crumpled ball of paper in the middle of the bed. "And I need to know more about the tests they did on me."

Lash blew across the mouthpiece. "*You're fine. You know you are.*"

"Not good enough. I need to see it."

"*All right, well, look,*" Lash said. She whispered into the phone, voice almost disappearing under the hiss of static. "*I've been thinking. There's somewhere else we should look.*"

Melinda stopped rubbing her forehead. "Where?"

"*His office. He keeps all the sensitive stuff in there.*" She blew across the mouthpiece again. "*I should've thought about it.*"

"You think my test results will be in there?"

"*I'll dig those up for you. Promise you that. But no,*" she said, lowering her voice again. "*This business with IRF having your vaccine, I think that might be in his files.*"

Leaning into the phone, pressing it so hard against her ear it ached, Melinda lowered her own voice. "Why do you say that?"

"*You know I see a lot of stuff come across my desk.*"

"Ilasha," Melinda said. Her heart skipped. "Did you see this?"

"*No. That's what I'm trying to tell you. There was something, about a year ago, I guess. But.*" She lowered her voice again, and Melinda pictured her looking left and right before continuing. Deep brown eyes round, phone pressed right up against her lips. "*There was a message Anthony came and snatched off my desk before I even worked out what language it was in. He was that quick.*"

"Didn't want you to see it. That is odd, Lash."

She chuckled. "*Don't I know it.*"

Breathing into the phone, plastic still slippery and warm, Melinda opened her mouth. To invite her over? To have someone to hold on to and tell her she was all right? Tell her brain damage could explain what she'd done to her family?

"*Come see me in the morning, Em.*" The phone went dead with a soft click.

Staring into the receiver, Melinda considered crying. Or screaming. Or feeling something, anything other than the guilt that wanted to eat into her spine.

Instead, she finished dressing for bed and laid on top of the cold covers until the night took her.

* * *

With Celia tugging him down the hallway, sweaty hand clutching his, Jack hardly had time to notice the line of people.

But he did.

Adults and children, in every size, shape, gender, and race. They followed them with their eyes as they passed.

"Celia, are we cutting in line or something? What's going on?"

"You give this to him," a woman said behind him. "You give this to him and tell him to be strong. That we are here, and when he is ready to lead us, we will follow."

Jack slowed and checked over his shoulder.

Dean had been stopped by an older white woman, who pushed a blanket at him with force. Picking up his hands, she put it in them and shoved it toward his body.

"Give it to him. Give it to him. Give it to him."

Eyes wide, Dean glanced up. "Jack?"

Some of the people in the hall picked up the woman's chant. "Give it to him. Give it to him. Give it to him."

More joined.

Some stood, pressing toward Dean, surrounding him with their insistence in the cramped hallway.

He stepped back. "I don't. Cee? Could one of you guys help?"

Jack laid a hand on his gun. Not that shooting people would help, it certainly hadn't in that godforsaken hospital.

Shuffling his feet, he leaned toward Celia. "Suggestions?"

"Step aside. Stand aside," Felipe said, pushing down the hallway. He hooked a hand under one of Dean's arms and tugged, taking the blanket from him and returning it to the woman. "You'll get to see him. You can give this to him yourself. Be patient, please." Pushing Dean in front of him, he waved off the people, who fell back. "You will all get to see him. If not today, then tomorrow or the next day."

A voice called. "What's the holdup?"

Without turning, Felipe continued to push Dean. "He's a baby, Val. He needs his rest. You'll get your turn."

"Gonna be an old man before I get to see him," Val grumbled.

Ignoring him, Felipe continued to push through the crowd, who backed to the walls again. When he got to Celia, he released Dean and grabbed her. "Let's get inside," he said, pulling her down the hall by her unbroken arm. "These people mean well, but they can be...impatient."

At the end of the hall, they met another in a T junction. Felipe turned right and knocked on the first door on the left. "It's uncle. Let me in, Ramon."

The sound of no less than five dead bolts echoed through the door. And at least two chains. A bar slid, and the door opened.

Ramon stood behind it, peeking out. "Uncle Felipe. They're pushy today. Lucinda just got him down." He glanced at Celia, Jack, and Dean in turn. "He's sleeping. Don't wake him."

Felipe motioned them all inside. "Please."

Narrowing her eyes at him, Celia crossed the threshold. Dean and Jack followed. Felipe locked all the locks behind them. Chains. Security bar.

"My kind of man," Jack said.

Felipe laughed without humor. "We don't have to worry about the 'Heads too much up here. But it pays to be cautious. Especially after—"

"Mijo, tell them." Leaning against the wall, Celia rested her head on it. Eyed Felipe from under heavy lids.

Felipe motioned to the living room. "Por favor. Have a seat. Ramon, water, please."

"Yes, Uncle. Ice?"

In the middle of sitting, Jack steeled his abs and gave Ramon one slight nod. He lowered into the seat and turned to Felipe. "What's up?"

Elbows on his knees, Felipe leaned toward him. He glanced at Dean, who'd sat on the couch next to Jack. Celia still stood against the wall. "I'll try to make this a short story. A week ago, Ramon and I had a fight with his sister. She wanted to take her infant son, Daniel, to see his great grandmama."

Dean pulled a breath through his teeth.

Felipe nodded. "Yes. Ramon and I could not allow her to take such a risk. We could have lost them both to Emmanuel and his people. In that building that is ready to collapse."

Ramon came in, juggling five water glasses. He handed one to Jack, ice tinkling against the side.

Such a lovely sound. There'd been a time Jack wasn't sure he'd ever enjoy ice—or anything else for that matter—again. He fished a piece out and crunched it between his teeth. It squealed as it broke and coated his mouth in frost.

Felipe took a swallow of water. "She's just like you, flaca." He smiled at Celia.

"Went anyway," Dean said, half his mouth turned up.

"In the middle of the damn night," Ramon said. "Alone."

Jack swallowed the melted ice and fished out another cube. "How'd you get them back?"

"She came back. After the baby was bitten."

"Did she give him the Cure?"

Ramon shook his head. "She had to wait outside for hours. Between Emmanuel's men and the horde that attacked her, she was pinned until morning, and she had no dose."

Though the idea she could have been attacked by the same horde that attacked them at the library flitted through his thoughts, it didn't pause on its way past. What stopped and settled into the middle of Jack's forehead was the baby hadn't been given the Cure.

Dropping the ice cube in the glass, he sat back. His breath poofed out in a woof. "The baby's immune."

Celia smiled, uninjured arm crossed in front of the broken one in its sling, and nodded. "They've never seen it before, Jack."

Dean chuckled. "They think the baby is some kind of savior, don't they?" he asked, jerking his head toward the door. "They're waiting to lay their gold, frankincense, and myrrh at his feet."

Felipe's brows drew in. "You don't seem surprised?" He stared at his little sister. "And what do you mean, 'they'? Have you?"

Jack sat forward. "We have. My son is investigating the reasons now. Along with a doctor friend." He tapped Dean. "Think you should get him on the phone. He's going to want to know about this."

Sliding to the edge of his chair, Felipe gripped Jack's wrist. "Daniel isn't the only one? Those people"—he pointed at the door—"they think it's some kind of miracle from God."

"It is a miracle," Jack said, "but I don't know how much God has to do with it."

CHAPTER 23

Coffee in hand, Melinda wandered down the hallway. Not that she chose to drink coffee all that often, because when she did, Jack's smiling blue eyes popped into her mind, but today it was life. She'd woken no less than eight times in the night, shivering and fighting with the sheets. A vise squeezed her temples.

She knocked on Lash's door.

Lash opened it, satin kerchief knotted around her hair. Without a word, she widened the gap and waited for Melinda to come in.

"Forgot about your sleeping regimen. That thing is as cute on you now as it used to be."

Lash flopped on the couch. "Bring me any of that coffee?"

Melinda shook her head, taking the other end of the couch. "I'll make some for you if you have the stuff."

"Get to it. It's your fault I got two hours sleep."

"I was in my own bed, thank you."

"Yeah, but you did circles around my head until I got up and found the file you were after."

"Which?"

"Make me the damned coffee, woman. I'll get it." She stood, flapping a hand at the kitchen. "You know how I take it." Disappearing into the bedroom, she left the door cracked and changed clothes in front of it.

Shaking her head, uninvited smile on her lips, Melinda shuffled into the kitchen. She stared at the cabinets. "I can't remember where you keep everything."

"Don't give me that."

Melinda closed her eyes. Thoughts clear, she opened her eyes and went right to everything. Relying on muscle memory more than anything, she found the filters, coffee, and measuring spoon. Lash had a new pot, but it was automatic, just like her old one. How she managed to find such fancy things a constant puzzle, Melinda shook it off and dropped back on the couch.

"You better not be watching me dress," Lash said, crossing in front of the door again.

"You shouldn't have left the door open."

Hair and clothes put together, Lash stepped into the living room. Thick file in hand. "Here. This is what my lack of sleep found you."

Heart beating in her ears, Melinda restrained the hand that wanted to snatch at it. Instead, she took it with a lazy grab, exhaling with slow precision. Telegraphing "no big deal." And as the coffee pot bubbled and belched steam, she leafed through her test results.

Here, a typed report about her brain. Signed by Anthony.

Here, a black-and-white reproduction of a CT scan.

Here, an x-ray to be held up to the light.

An MRI.

Physical pictures.

Genetic analysis.

Lab results.

And finally, volumes of psychiatric evaluations. Stapled together, with a cover page and everything. As though they'd been presented to someone, or several someones.

She leafed through the eval. "Did you read this?"

Arm leaned on the back of the couch, Lash rested her cheek on her hand. She shook her head.

Melinda flipped back to the CT scan and MRI. "The radiologist noted some issues here"—she pointed to the MRI—"in my prefrontal cortex. And," she said, holding the report up, "here. In my"—she checked the paper again—"Amygdala." She stared at the couch. "I guess that's why people have a hard time remembering being turned. It damages the short-term memory processing. And god knows what else."

"That coffee is done," Lash said.

Still staring into space, Melinda laid the papers on the couch and got up to make Lash's coffee. She blinked. "Still mostly cream and sugar?"

"Unlike you. Do you even put anything in there? Ever?"

Melinda winked. "I like my coffee like my women." Light on her feet, she let the moment carry her through making the coffee. Let the test results go.

But when she handed Lash the cup, she fell back into them. "Do you think it's still damaged? Of course it is. I wonder how I was able to remember anything?" She tapped the MRI photos. "Did you know the prefrontal cortex is in charge of decision-making?" Swallowing, she whispered, "Have I been making the right decisions, Ilasha?"

"I'd give you the same answer I gave you yesterday, but I won't." She slid closer, setting her coffee on the table. "It seems like this is saying there was some permanent damage."

Melinda nodded, eyes hot.

Lash took one of her hands and held it in her warm fingers. "This is no shit. You are one of the strongest, bravest, and smartest women I ever met. And that you've been able to do the things you've done, even with brain damage, is nothing short of astounding."

Blinking back tears, Melinda looked up. She gave Lash a crooked smile as her stomach somersaulted over itself. "It hasn't all been good."

"Pfft. It hasn't all been bad." She cupped Melinda's jaw. "You're amazing. I love you."

"Even if I'm broken?"

"Shit. *Because* you're broken. Nobody said you gotta be perfect." She swiped at a tear as it rolled down Melinda's cheek. Kissing the spot, she washed the tears away with her lips. "You've done some of the most important work that's been done on this virus. Your ambition to beat it knows no bounds." Pushing the papers aside, she leaned in and rested her forehead against Melinda's. "You're incredible."

Something inside Melinda uncoiled. Not only was Ilasha right, but also the terrible things she'd done to Adelaide, and Jack, and even her dear, sweet Michael, could be explained by the equally terrible trauma her brain had gone through. She hadn't been herself.

"Before we get into this," Melinda said, pointing between them, "I need to tell you what happened in the last year."

"Is that your prefrontal cortex talking?"

Chuckling, she shook her head. "I love you too, Lash. But there's some things you need to know."

* * *

"How was your day off, Addy?"

Facedown on the bar, she shook her head back and forth. "Good, Jim. Thanks for asking."

A cup thunked down next to her. "Coffee up, honey. We got a long day ahead of us."

She sat up and took a swig. "God. What now?"

"Not long till curtain-up, remember. Sets need to be freshened. Security checks on the theatre. Stuff you were going to do two days ago."

"But then the raid happened." She took another swig, burning her throat. "Right. Right."

"What'd you spend your day off doing?"

"I taught Miss Cooke to ride a motorcycle," Matt said, taking a seat next to her. One parenthesis dimpled his cheek. "She's not too bad at it. Could use some work though."

Which was true. She'd about spilled them on the ground when the Molehill came into view. Matt had cursed under his breath but kept them upright.

The massive hill, surrounded in chain-link and razor wire, sat just as he'd described it. A helicopter parked on top, looking like the same one from which a grenade had been thrown. The one that took Dean away.

Beside the helicopter pad, a telescope. A huge one. Far nicer than anything they ever had when she was a kid.

For a bare moment, she'd wished she could look through it. Then reality reasserted itself, and she'd cried on Matt until her head hurt.

Shrugging, she took another sip of coffee. "I try, I really do. The klutz thing just comes so natural."

Matt grinned, looking around Jim. "You got some food back there? I'm famished."

Addy smiled. "That's a fancy word. Thought you said you didn't read much."

"That's not what I said." He bumped her shoulder. As Jim walked away, Matt leaned close and lowered his voice. "I am both hungry and exhausted. What about you?"

Her cheeks tingled. They'd gotten back to town late. The building they'd parked next to turned out to be a two-story derelict, but someone had set up the top floor as an apartment and never moved in. Down here in the old business district, the Tree was the only residence for blocks, which meant Addy and Matt had the derelict and the surrounding blocks to themselves. So they'd claimed it, loudly. And for hours. The sun hadn't been up when they got back to the Tree, but it was close. The stars at their brightest point before the dawn. At least Morgan hadn't been in. The night watch opened the newly fixed gate for them, no questions about where they'd been.

She gulped cooling coffee. "Regrets?"

"None."

"Good. Me neither."

A hand encircled each of their shoulders, and before either of them turned around, Cassius squeezed them together in a bone-crushing hug. Addy's cheek pressed into Matt's, grinding her teeth into it.

"Cassie, you're killing them," Jim said, returning from the kitchen with two plates. "Let them eat their breakfast before they die."

"We missed you two," Cassius said, letting them go.

Addy spun. "Did Morgan treat you all right?"

Victoria blew in, pajama shirt hanging off her shoulder again. "Morgan is perfectly lovely. He just can't be here all the time."

Cassius nodded. "If the lady says he's good, he's good." He dropped Addy a wink. "He's not as pretty or as nice."

Bouncing her basketball from hand to hand, Rivers sat next to Addy. "If we have time after the theatre, we can stop by the basketball court. I shall teach you how to play."

Chuckling, Addy stuffed food in her face. "Let's not waste time, then," she said, speaking around it.

Matt rolled his eyes and paused with his fork halfway to his mouth. "That something you learn from Dean, talking with your mouth full? Or just something you have in common?"

Shoving her plate halfway across the bar, Addy stood. Her forehead tightened. "I'm not hungry anymore. Let's get the fuck out of here. We've got work to do." Without waiting for any of the others, she charged across the room and out onto the dock, stopping only when she hit the ledge.

As she considered the drop, wondering if she would break an ankle if she jumped and whether that might be a good thing, a basketball bounced behind her. Airy plastic thunks echoed off the dock.

Rivers stopped beside her and stared off into the yard. "Who's Dean?"

Peeking at her, Addy frowned. "Someone I used to know."

"Did he die?"

"Yes."

Rivers tucked the ball under one arm and threw the other around Addy. She wasn't tall enough to throw it over her shoulders, so she hugged Addy somewhere around the elbows, pinning her arms to her sides. "It is difficult to lose someone we regard. Especially if they open their eyes once more, changed. Reborn, but not unto this."

How did this woman keep socking her in the gut without using a fist?

Addy sat on the dock, crossing her legs. She rested her elbow and tucked her chin into her palm. "What about your boat captain? Did he die?"

Rivers floated away and back, washing back and forth like the tide. "He is with the sea. And she is with he. There is room in his heart for me, but never together shall we be."

Staring up at Rivers, Addy let one side of her mouth turn up. "I don't know what that means."

She floated down next to Addy and sat on the ball. "He is not dead. And yet, he is gone."

"Well that's as clear as mud."

A laugh bubbled up from inside Rivers's chest, careened from her mouth, and knocked her from the ball. Drawing her knees up and clutching them, she laughed until tears sprang from her eyes.

The kind of laugh you had to laugh with. Impossible not to.

The rest of the Troupe, followed by Matt, walked through the door and onto the dock.

"We learn to laugh again," Vic said, tugging Addy to her feet. Wrapping her in a hug, she rubbed her back and released her. "Thank you for bringing a real smile to Rivers. It's been a while."

Addy glanced at Rivers, wiping a tear from the corner of her eye. "We've got each other to thank." She looked around. "Are we ready?"

Cassius held out her bow. "Your weapon, milady."

"Addy," Matt began.

Addy took the bow. "Let's go."

* * *

"Three hours, two useful set pieces, six 'completely unacceptable' ones, and an airtight theatre. Seems like a good morning," Matt said.

Walking behind the Troupe, making them stick together a little better than they had two days ago, Addy smiled. "They do a lot of prancing. Jim wasn't wrong about that."

Matt chuckled. "Listen, Addy. I didn't mean to hurt you earlier." He touched the small of her back. "I'm sorry."

She smiled sideways. "It's forgiven. But you can't just say sorry."

"Oh?"

"You have to try not to do it again. Otherwise, it's not a real amends."

One parenthesis showed for the first time since the Tree. "You got it. What do you say we—"

Rivers squealed, running around the next corner and out of sight.

"Shit. Rivers!" Addy jogged, pushing through the others and rounding the corner.

Past it, a large rectangular area between two buildings had been fenced with chain-link at least twelve feet high. Three guards stood on each side of the area, and one gate led in and out. A couple sets of half-rusty bleachers cozied up against the chain-link.

About twenty or so people played with basketballs inside.

Addy stopped, mouth open.

Matt stopped next to her as the rest of the Troupe chattered and entered the court. "You said you never played basketball, right?"

She nodded.

Someone threw the ball with some kind of jumping motion. It sailed through the air and went through a suspended hoop, clinking against the metal chains hanging beneath. A few of the people on the bleachers cheered.

"It's fun. We'll teach you. Look." He pointed. "Rivers is already making baskets."

And so she was. Throwing her ball through the hoop, rounding it up, and doing it again. Someone called her to join their team, and she let the ball drop, running to play with them. Sweaty and smiling.

"Come on, you two," Vic called. Laying her brocade-and-lace coat over a bleacher, she waved them in. "Come play."

Addy let Matt tug her toward the court. "Should we? What if something happens?"

"They're right here with us. And look," he said, pointing, "look at all these guards. We've got plenty of backup." He smiled. "Let's play."

For the next hour or so, she let them all teach her about the game. What one of them didn't know about shooting, another did. What one of them didn't know about defense, another explained. After a while, she got the hang of it. And removed layer after layer of winter clothing, the spring wind warm on her skin. Although only mid-March, the warmth and humidity announced summer right around the corner.

Flushed, sweating, and breathing hard, she flopped on a bench. A cooler full of water and some cups sat at the end of the row.

Matt, who had ditched his shirt at some point, brought her a cup and flopped next to her. Drinking his in one gulp, he grinned. "Takes it out of you, this game," he panted. "Forgot how much fun it is."

Sipping her own water, the way her dad taught her to avoid cramps, she looked for the others.

Vic and Cassius fell out long ago, retreating to one corner and watching the others with bright eyes and big smiles. Grey and Tal still played, now down to one-on-one, being more physical with defense than strictly necessary. Rivers was.

Rivers…was… Where was Rivers?

Addy stood, eyes narrowed. She checked under the bleachers, then walked out onto the playing court and spun in a circle.

Matt sat up. "What's wrong?"

"Where's Rivers?" she asked, walking back to him.

"There's only one way out. Those guys must've seen her." He stood and wiped his forehead with a sweaty arm. "I'll go ask."

Addy gripped his bare waist. "Sit. I'll find her."

Catching her wrist before she walked off, he picked up his knife from their pile of weapons on the bench and laid it in her hand. "Take this. Just in case."

Flipping the blade so it lay up her arm, she walked over to the gate. "Hey, man, did you see Rivers come through here?"

His flat eyes took her in. "Who?"

"Skinny woman. Yay high," she said, holding her hand at shoulder level. "Messy hair. Tiny nose."

"Yeah. She walked out about fifteen minutes ago."

Addy put her hands on her hips. "Shit. Did you see which way she went?"

Pointing over his shoulder, the guard shook his head. "That way."

"Thanks," Addy said, walking through the gate and into the street.

If I were Rivers, where would I go?

Closing her eyes, Addy Listened.

Water. She heard water.

Setting off in that direction, she walked around a corner and lost the sound of the court. But the trickling water grew louder. About a block away, she found a fountain, statues of children playing all around it.

Mouth open, she approached. That it worked meant the people who lived here had, at some point, put effort into making it do so. And given it water they could have been drinking instead.

But though Rivers should have been there, the fountain burbled to itself.

Shadows moved down an alley, and something fell.

Holding the knife ready, Addy snuck toward the alley. Could be 'Heads, could be Talus. Could be anything.

Stopping next to the alley's entrance, she Listened again.

"Come on, Riv. You owe me. I am going to get my payment, one way or another."

"I refuse payment. My boyfriend, the sea captain—"

"Don't give me that bullshit. Your boyfriend doesn't exist. And I take my payment for services rendered however I ficking want to."

Rounding the corner, Addy narrowed her eyes. "Sly. What the fuck are you doing?"

Pressing Rivers into the wall, arm across her throat, Sly didn't look up. His mustache tickled Rivers's lip. "Taking my payment. None of your business, Addy."

Rivers stood, crushed into the wall, eyes closed. Face wet. Her lips pressed together so tightly they disappeared.

"Let her go, Sly. She's got no payment to make you."

He glanced at her.

The man she'd met at the bank had been jovial, congenial, and overall funny and open. This face was one of the ones she'd seen out of Tim, there at the end. Lupine, predatory, with narrow eyes and a cocky smile stretched across his wolfish mouth.

In two large steps, she caught up to him, the knife hidden along her arm lashing out. It nicked him in the ear. A rock sat in Addy's gut, but she straightened her shoulders and flared her nostrils. "Let her go."

Moving back with slow, calculated steps, Sly touched his ear. Lowering his fingertips, he sniffed and tasted the blood there. "The fick are you doing?"

"Rivers, go back to the court. Stay with Matt. Wait for me."

Ducking her head, Rivers dashed out of the alley.

Addy glared at the man before her. "I suggest you get the hell out of here, Sly. Before I do something I won't regret." His face shifted, became Tim, and resolved back into Sly.

"Look," he said, hand falling to his sidearm, "I don't know if anyone's explained to you. We're on the defense force. We take what we need. We don't ask for it."

"Bullshit. You can't act that way."

He snorted, taking a silent step toward her. "We don't need to pay for the things we get. We already have. And we take what we want, when we want it." He pointed his forehead toward the end of the alley. "And I want my payment from the girl."

"Not as long as I'm standing between you, you don't."

Grinning, he lunged at her.

Slashing with the knife again, she caught him across the chest, opening a line through his jacket and the shirt beneath. "I didn't have to miss. That was your warning."

Knocking her hand aside with surprising alacrity, he grabbed her wrist and pulled. Chucking her over his hips, he pinned her to the ground.

As she sailed through the air, sky and land swapping positions, a vision of Tim clutching his pants and bleeding from the mouth and nose flashed through her head.

Landing on the ground with a woof, she coughed and smirked at him. "That all you got, pansy boy?"

He kicked her in the gut.

She rolled to her knees, forehead down.

When he dropped, knee on the ground behind her, she rolled to her shoulder, hooked a leg behind his knee, and pulled him over.

All that sparring time with Michael had to come in handy eventually.

On her back, she hooked her ankles in his crotch and yanked his foot up next to her head. Both arms wrapped around his ankle, she twisted. His knee hyper-extended and popped.

He squealed like a baby rabbit.

She laughed, twisting harder. Adrenaline lit her up like the night sky, her fingertips tingling. "Bitch." Releasing his leg, she kicked him in the thigh of the other.

Disentangling her legs, she snatched up the knife. She stood and swiped at the hair that'd fallen in her face. "Touch her again," she said, leaning over her knees, "and I'll stick this knife where the sun don't shine. And castrate your ass while I'm up there."

He cradled his knee and whimpered.

She made her way out of the alley, fighting a limp. At the end of it, she turned back to the sniveling heap. "*Fick* with any of my friends, and that's what you'll get. Jackass."

CHAPTER 24

"**M**ike wants to talk to you, Jack." Dean held the phone out.

Settling down on the crunching roof, eyes drifting across the setting sun, Jack took the phone. "What's up, Mike?"

Static crackled. "*I'd love to stay in this library forever, but I think we're about done.*"

"Did the info about Celia's nephew help?"

Mike blew across the mouthpiece. A chuckle. "*It did. Really helped us focus our research. Before that, it kinda felt like looking for pieces to one of those old puzzles.*"

"A jigsaw?"

"*Yeah, without the picture. But—*" static crackled, slashing across his next words.

"Say again, Mike. Didn't catch that."

"*Jane says hi.*"

The background mumbled, Jane's voice rising in pitch as she shouted across a room.

"*She says 'hi' isn't what she said.*" He laughed. "*She said, ouch, Jane, I'm telling him! She said time to get your ass back here. How long has it been?*"

Jack grinned at the phone. "Two weeks. We'll head back in the morning." Though he'd go right this minute if he could.

"*It'll be nice to see you guys.*" Mike paused, static rising and lowering. "*How's Celia?*"

Shrugging, Jack glanced at Dean. Like always, Dean fiddled with something while pretending not to listen. Hearing every word. "All right, I guess. Seems like her brother is her favorite, but she wants her family healed. She's been working her ass off these last two weeks to try and do that. They're as stubborn as she is."

Mike laughed, voice fading in and out. *"She's got her work cut out for her. Will she be OK leaving them like that?"*

Opening his mouth to answer, Jack stopped. His cheeks flamed. He'd been absorbed in the immunity mystery, missing Jane, concentrating on not asking Dean about Addy again, and forgetting Melinda existed sixteen times a day. He hadn't stopped to consider how Celia would feel about leaving.

"Shit, Mike. I guess I'll have to ask her."

"See you tomorrow, Dad."

"Watch yourself." Jack closed the phone, holding it out to Dean without looking. Staring into the air, he let the feeling of having been so self-absorbed he hadn't considered Celia's feelings worm around his stomach.

Dean took it. "Everything all right?"

"Yeah. Yeah. They're fine. Dean?"

Dean leaned over a knee.

"I forgot to worry about how Celia's feeling." He grimaced. "Especially about leaving."

Dean leaned farther, eyebrows raised. "Can I tell you something, Jack?"

He nodded.

"You can't worry about everything all the time. It's too much." He tented his knees. "You gotta let the rest of us take care of ourselves. I know you want to, but you can't do it all."

"You're right." He stood, brushing the gravel off his ass, and stuck a hand out. "You're right."

Dean took his hand and stood. "Even your kids." He cleared his throat. "Except that tiny one. You can worry about that one." He winked.

With a chuckle, Jack preceded him into the stairwell. "Mike and Jane want us to get back to the library. I'm sure you heard that. They think they're done, and it's time to get our asses out of here."

"Think Cee'll come with us?"

Jack stopped, his foot stuck out in the air. "What?"

Dean joined him on the step. "Do you think she'll come? Or do you think she'll stay?"

"I." He stopped, swallowing. "I hadn't considered it." Brow wrinkled, he stared at Dean. "Do you think she'll stay?"

He started down the stairs, limp almost not noticeable anymore. "One way to find out."

* * *

Clutching Luisa's arm, Fabiana picked her way across the hilly courtyard outside the building Jack had come to think of as Felipe's number one.

Manuel walked behind them, twitching at every step.

Celia flanked her mother. Clearly the talking she went to do with Manuel and her mother succeeded. Jack hadn't known her to be silver-tongued before, but she told him she'd picked up some tricks from watching Addy talk with Mann.

And the night before, as they turned in, Jack put the question to her. Stay or go?

Now, as she approached, uninjured arm linked with her mama's, his forehead tightened. Saying goodbye to her had never crossed his mind. He always figured either one of them would die fighting, or one day she'd just slip away and never come back.

Fabi's entourage stopped in front of Jack, where he stood with Felipe, Dean, Ramon, and about a half dozen other people. Fabiana extricated her arms from her daughters and covered her mouth. "Dios mio, Ramon. You've grown so tall." She spread her arms.

He fell into them, cheeks wet. "Nana," he whispered, hugging her hard enough to make Jack worried about her shoulders.

Jack smiled. After everything that'd happened, this world could use all the love it could get. If leaving Celia here meant she'd be happy, it would be worth it. As much as it opened a hole in his own heart.

Felipe and Manuel eyed each other, their backs stiff and faces stretched. But no one went for weapons, and when Lucinda stepped out of the building, cradling baby Daniel, Luisa and Fabiana both cried aloud. They passed the baby back and forth, exchanging hugs with everyone nearby. Even Jack and Dean.

After a few minutes, and Felipe and Manuel hadn't killed each other, Jack stepped away from the crowd and looked toward the south, where they'd left the train. He motioned to Dean. "Ready to get back?"

Dean glanced at the crowd. "You think they'll be OK?"

Jack followed his gaze. Felipe and Manuel had gotten close enough to exchange a few pleasantries. And Manuel's shoulders had loosened.

"Yeah, Dean. I think they will be." He turned to leave.

A hand caught his shoulder.

He turned, eyes falling on Celia's. They were soft around the edges in a way he rarely saw.

"Gonna miss you," he said.

"You're about the only one."

Dean cleared his throat. "That's not true, Cee."

She looked him up and down. "You fit in this family, Ross. You're as odd as they are."

Smiling, he pulled her into a hug. "Take care of these guys. They don't know how lucky they are."

Felipe joined them and smiled at his sister. "Got a pretty good idea, amigo. Flaca is irreplaceable."

"I wish you wouldn't call me skinny, mijo," Celia said. She stared at Jack.

Who took a breath. His stomach tightened into a fist, crammed into his ribs. "You sure you'll be all right?" He glanced over her shoulder, where the family reunion had taken a jovial turn. Even the baby was laughing. When his eyes landed back on Celia, she stared, heavy lids low.

"Right." He chuckled. "I know it's a silly question. You know I have to ask it."

"I'm all growed up, Jack."

He cleared his throat, eyes hot. "I know that. I know it."

She moved so quick from where she was to hugging him, he almost didn't see her move. Having done away with the sling, she threw her broken arm around him, too, crushing him with the cast.

Eyes closed, he hugged her back. Tight enough to crack ribs. He kissed the top of her head. "Keep your nose up."

She hugged him like she never had, tight and long. With a sniff and a swipe at her nose, she let him go and stepped back. "You going back to Harkers after all this?"

"Gotta talk to the doc. Probably go to this city Addy went to. Try and meet up with her first."

She cast her eyes down and crossed her arm over the cast. "One of these days, you get back to Harkers, maybe I'll be there. We can run into each other."

"Sure. I'm sure." Before the waterworks really got going, he glanced at Felipe. "Thanks for the extra weapons." He patted the gun sticking in his waistband and unsheathed his newly sharpened machete. "I'm sure they'll come in handy."

Felipe opened his mouth to answer and stopped.

That smell, the one that seeped into your sinuses and made its way directly to your gag reflex, the scent of coppery, old blood and roadkill rotting by the side of the road, it crept around the side of the building behind them and slapped Jack in the face.

The others smelled it too. Luisa gasped and clutched her mother. "Mama, we must go."

Felipe held out his arm. "Everyone get inside." He frowned. "Even you, Manny. Now." He waved.

The group broke away from Jack, including Manuel and his men, and scurried toward Felipe's building as a few 'Heads from what had to be a horde cleared the building and shambled toward them. Fabiana aimed an emphatic pointing finger at Jack and Dean, speaking quickly in Spanish. Jack couldn't translate, but her concern for them was evident.

Backing away, Jack kept his machete aimed at the smell. "Be seeing you, Cee."

She sketched a salute with a pistol in her hand.

The group disappeared into the building, Celia, Felipe, and Manuel bringing up the rear. Celia glanced toward Jack and waved him away, mouthing, "*We got this.*"

He bumped Dean. "Let's get out of here."

Scowling, Dean followed as he ducked and ran toward the direction of the train. "You sure about leaving her?" He pulled his gun.

"No."

"Makes two of us."

"She made her choice," Jack said. Gunfire echoed down the block, fading as they jogged.

He scented the air, keeping his nose up.

The stench remained.

"Nine o'clock, Jack."

And indeed, there they were, coming between them and the train. Through the trees.

Like the tunnel, coming from two directions. Were they being herded in some way? Were they involved in their own inexplicable war?

Without patience or time to answer those questions, Jack angled for a clear area left of the road. Dean followed, and they covered each other's backs.

A few 'Heads came their way, and they cut them down. The rest funneled toward the apartment buildings, no doubt drawn by the gunfire as it continued.

Jack separated a 'Head from its skull with one hand and shot another in the ear with the other. "How quick can you get the train going?"

"It's pretty quick. She's fast."

"You get there first and then—"

One of them jumped Dean, and he shouted, grabbing at his ankle again as he went down. More closed in between them and the train. Dean killed the one on top of him and struggled to get to his feet.

And, not that Jack would ever claim to be the smartest man alive, but he made a hell of a mistake at that moment. One that would keep him up for too many nights to count.

He needed to clear a path between them and the train. Most of the horde had gone around to the apartments. If he could get this handful in front of them clear, they could probably make the train before he had to reload. But what was behind those 'Heads was what he should have worried about.

He emptied his gun, some of the bullets ricocheting off the ground in a hail of sparks when a 'Head pounced on his back.

Thank fuck they were far enough away when the propane tanks went up, one right after the other, with booms that like to have deafened him.

As it was, they were picking themselves up from the pavement, the 'Heads around them flopping like beached whales, before it fully set in that the train had been engulfed in hungry flames.

"No! Cameron!" Dean shouted, running for the train. Limp pronounced again.

Sprinting toward the fire the last thing Jack expected him to do, he almost didn't catch his arm. And even with an injured ankle, he nearly pulled Jack over as he charged for the train, calling his brother all the while.

"Dean, stop, dammit, stop," Jack said, tugging on him and looking everywhere at once. "We need to get out of the open."

"No, it's all I've got. Just that one picture. Cam!"

"Dean, please, listen to me, we have to go." But no matter how hard he pulled, Dean pulled harder. Dragging them both closer to the inferno.

"Ross, you have to be one of the most stubborn people I've ever met," Celia said, latching on to his other arm.

Warmth rushed through Jack, his fingertips tingling. Heart pounding against his ribs while simultaneously stuck in his throat, his mouth flapped as Celia helped him drag Dean away from the train and to an area free of 'Heads behind one of the buildings.

Once they pulled him out of sight of the train, Dean sagged.

Jack looked over his head at her. "Thought you were staying with your family."

"I am. Let's go."

CHAPTER 25

The remaining weeks before curtain-up passed like a whirlwind. Addy could hardly keep up with the days. Were it not for the notebook in which she'd scrawled the calendar, she probably wouldn't have.

In the notebook, she also wrote down some of the books Ella had gotten Matt to read. Made note of the passages in the play she liked the best. Recorded the best places to find both sun and shade in the city.

She and Matt spent time together where they could squeeze it. Often after the Troupe had gone to sleep, they slipped away to their derelict apartment and kept each other awake for too long.

And the flowers bloomed.

This place, with these people, was undeniably beautiful. With a few exceptions—Sly being one—the community worked together with effortless ease. She convinced herself it was some kind of impossible utopia. Like the place Picard and the others lived.

And for a while, it was.

When opening night came, the Troupe dressed in their best and made their way to the theatre. Loudly reminding all they passed about the play.

Grinning as they followed, Matt and Addy kept them together as best they could. When they got this excited, it was impossible to keep them in a tight group. They had too much prancing and singing to do.

Leaving them in the locked lobby, Addy and Matt checked the hall and went up to the balcony. It was safe for a small group of people, but Morgan said one of the few engineers the town guarded like gold came in to look at it and deemed it unsafe for more than twenty.

Matt walked to the edge and peeked down. "Great view though."

Addy stood near the back. "I'm sure it is. Are we secure?"

"Come look, Addy." He held out a hand.

She backed up a step. "Just because I've slept in a tree and climbed that damn roller coaster with you doesn't mean I liked it."

He gripped the rail and leaned out. "And climbed the wall in Magnolia. That thing was twenty feet high."

"Can we go back down? They need to get ready." She held her breath and fought asking him to come away from the edge. "Jim's working the lights. Aren't there people coming to work the doors?"

"Morgan's sending down some guys for security. And I guess the lady who makes the jelly is bringing a group to help with seating and stuff." He met her at the top of the stairs and narrowed his eyes. "You all right? You look pale."

Head shaking, she left the balcony. "Fine. Stuffy up here." Her feet slowed. "Sly's not coming, right?"

"He better not. Morgan knows he's not welcome around these guys."

She started walking again, descending the side stairs to the ground floor. "Do you think he knows why?"

Matt matched her step for step. "Who knows? Do you think he needs to?"

With the sounds of the Troupe's voices echoing from the lobby, she stopped. "I mean, I get we're doing a job here, so we don't have to grow food and make things. But he acts like he owns the place, Matt. Like they all owe him something."

He gripped her shoulder, thumb moving in a circle, and jerked his head toward the lobby below. "We won't let him, or anyone else, hurt them."

She let his warm hand center her, bringing her back to the moment, his fingers pressing her skin but not clenching. "Let's get these guys into costume."

The next couple hours passed in the same whirlwind Addy had been caught up in since she'd met them. Costuming, setting up the stage, getting all the security in place, making sure all the people found a seat.

Not long before curtain-up, she found herself helping two old women down to the front where they'd be close enough to see and hear. She didn't think she'd ever seen someone as elderly as these two, not even Paul. And they bickered all the way to their seats.

"I told you, Judith, they'd get us good seats."

"Mandy, you know I worry about getting the right seats. Young lady," Judith said, tugging Addy's arm, "where are you putting us frail little old ladies?"

"I doubt you got this far being frail," Addy said, pointing down the row. "In the middle, there. Saved a seat just for you and the other old ladies."

"Don't get lippy with me, girl."

"Sorry, Judith."

"Judy, be nice to her. She was meanin' to give you a compliment."

"She called me old, Amanda."

Mandy patted Addy's hand. "She didn't mean nothing by it. She's always been cranky. Ever since the thing with the cat."

Addy didn't know whether to grin or not. "What thing with the cat?"

"There was no thing with the cat," Judith said, making her way down the row, easing past everyone without touching.

Might have been old and frail and cranky, but she knew how to maneuver in such a space, even still. No, she didn't get this far by letting others take care of her.

"It was a thing, don't let my sister lie to you," Mandy said, following her down the row.

Addy shook her head. Two sisters, still together after all this time. No doubt having killed their fair share of 'Heads.

Utopia.

The feeling that'd been waiting to bubble up finally spilled over the sides, threatening to knock her over as she made her way up the aisle and into the lobby. Effervescent joy. In such a world, where she'd had to kill a man, where getting her dead mother back had only made things worse, a glimmer of beauty had eked out a sliver of land. Sprung up to smile at the sky, proclaiming as the Troupe took the stage that it was here, and it was real, and she could even have a piece of it.

Floating to the lobby, she walked into the scent of cool night air. The open doors let the evening in, threatening to bring mosquitoes with it. "Close the doors now, guys," she said, searching the room for Matt. "Theatre's full, curtain's up."

The security guards closed and locked the doors. Some sat near their doors, some grouped up and brought out packs of cards and such. They chattered, and Addy heard nothing of the Troupe on stage.

Matt came in from the auditorium. "Addy! You're missing it." Legs extended, he crossed the lobby in three large steps and took her hand before she had the chance to argue. Tugging her along, he mounted the stairs.

"I don't know, Matt, shouldn't we watch the doors?"

"They've got it. We should make sure no one tries to get in the balcony."

She stopped, feet on two different stairs. "Are you going to try and get me to look down?"

He joined her on the lower step and leaned into her space. "Not unless you ask me to."

"I have no intention of doing any such thing." But that bubbly feeling still floated around her middle. Like the taste of champagne in her nose. She let him take her to the second-lowest row, where he leaned his rifle and she leaned her bow and they watched the play unfold with breathless glee.

The Troupe shone like diamonds, even all the way up in the balcony. Their light reflected onto the entire theatre, covering everyone in life and air.

When Matt snuck an arm around her shoulders, she didn't stop him. When he leaned over and breathed into her hair, kissing her neck and scooting as close as the arm of the chairs would let him, she did her level best to shove Dean and Ella aside. She'd hardly had time to think of their names in the last couple weeks, which made it that much worse when she did, but they moved aside as best they could. Crowding the edges of her thoughts.

But just the edges.

The only thing that brought her out of her reverie and up for air came at the beginning of the fifth act.

Talbot had taken the role of the Shrew's younger brother, with Grey cast as his suitor.

"Before we exit this stage, I must, my lord, but speak with thee," Grey said.

Addy stopped, hand on Matt's chest. Fist full of his shirt. "That's not the line."

He glanced at the stage. "Weird."

Leaning forward, Addy let him go and stared down at the stage. "He's kneeling. What's he doing? That's not in the script."

Grey didn't leave her wondering for long. He held out one arm, the other hand over his heart. "I must ask, my dear Talbot, for thine hand in wedlock. For I have adored thee as the planets do the sun, from the day first we met."

Addy, and the entire crowd, gasped.

Talbot, one hand in the air, stopped in the middle of rattling off his next line. Running down like a record player that had been switched off, the table turning slower and slower on each revolution.

The crowd whispered as the two actors and Victoria, Cassius, and Rivers off to the side, stood stock-still onstage. Victoria with her hands over her mouth.

Matt chuckled. "I'll be damned. I didn't think he'd go through with it."

Addy bumped him. "You knew?"

"I do sleep in the bunks sometimes. Grey stays up later than everyone. He gets chatty."

Someone in the crowd shouted from below. "Say something!"

Tal smiled so wide, Addy could see it from up here.

"My good man," he said, hand still suspended in the air, "I thought you'd never ask."

The crowd erupted.

* * *

The after-party for the play put the raid's after-party to shame. The Troupe brought half the city to the Tree with them, and the place rocked and rolled for hours and hours.

Addy narrowed her eyes as Cassius tracked Victoria down for the seventh time in five minutes.

"Victoria, my dear!" Hooking his arm into hers, he spun her in a circle. "I will give you this," he said, plucking a flower from the bouquet he'd carried for hours, "my dear star. For you were a better Petruchio than ever I could aspire to be."

She handed him the one he'd given her last time. "And you, lovely Cassius. The best shrew one could ask for." With a grin, she curtsied.

From her perch at the bar, Addy watched them do this four or five more times.

In the other room, Rivers danced on stage, twirling in circles until Addy got dizzy.

Matt bumped Addy's elbow. He'd been planted at it since they got back. "She did good. Who was she again?"

"Hortensio. They changed the name though."

He snapped his fingers. "That's right. It was interesting, the way they did the love triangle between her and Grey and Tal's characters."

She grinned. "I didn't know you paid that close of attention."

He took the drink Jim slid across the bar at him. "I may as well figure out what's going on. We're going to have to watch this play, what, six more times?"

"They're running it for a week, yeah," Addy said. She bit into a nail. "I was so nervous tonight. Do you think it'll get better?"

He leaned closer, lips tickling her ear. "If it doesn't, I'll keep you distracted."

"Adelaide, Matt," Morgan said, materializing from nowhere.

Matt leaned away, sipping his drink.

Addy's cheeks had to have flamed into magenta, at least. She started talking before Morgan had a chance to focus on how close she and Matt had been. "Morgan. Did you see the show?"

He shook his head. "I never watch opening night. I usually go on the fourth night." Reaching between them, eyes catching

Addy's, he took the drink Jim brought. "Thanks, Jim," he said, eyes still hooked to Addy's. "I hear tonight's was extra special."

Fighting the itching desire sweeping through her to reclaim her bubble, she maintained eye contact. "It was even more exciting than we thought it would be."

Morgan made a show of looking around. "Where is the happy couple? I'd like to congratulate them."

Matt shrugged. "Somewhere private."

Staring over the top of his glass, Morgan copied Matt's shrug and smiled. "Anyway, look, I came here for a reason." He glanced at each of them, eyes lingering on the space between them.

Again, Addy fought the urge to scoot away. To create distance from Matt but also to get out from under that gaze. It showed friendly on top, but underneath, he wanted something.

His ice clinked against the side of his glass as he jiggled the drink. He stuck one hand in a pocket. "I've got some guys on the inside at the Molehill."

Addy almost fell off her stool.

Matt moved to catch her, stopped, and picked up his drink.

She righted herself. "What? Have you heard something?"

"I've heard a lot of things, Addy." He stared, brown eyes piercing. Jaw pulled into a frown.

Her heart leapt into her throat, galloping at least two hundred beats per minute. Her eyeballs pounded, and a ringing started in one ear.

"I don't want to discuss it here. But listen," he leaned closer, and Addy and Matt both leaned in to catch his quiet words, "I need you to take me to the Molehill, Matt."

Matt fell against the bar, all the breath pushed out of his lungs. "Now?"

Smiling, finishing his drink, Morgan shook his head. "Let's wait until the week is over. Let these guys get through their shows. Then, we'll go." Tipping back the glass, he opened his lips and let a piece of ice slide into his mouth. "You too, Addy," he said, setting the glass on the bar next to her. He leaned close. "Need you to come too." Stepping back, he grinned. "Need some capable hands to watch my ass."

"Yes, sir. I'll be there," Matt said.

"We," Addy said. Not much more than a croak. She cleared her throat. "We. We'll be there."

* * *

Outside the front entrance to the library, Dean slouched before the steps. All hundred of them, minimum. He grunted. "Let's get this over with."

As Jack and Celia helped him limp up the stairs, Celia chuckled. "Better get used to it, Ross. How do you think we're traveling from now on?"

Sagging, he stopped. "Shit."

"We'll get you some crutches or something," Jack said. "Let's get inside."

Insides light as air, Jack floated up the stairs, even with Dean in tow. Celia's desire to stay with them, admitting she thought of them as family, buoyed him in a way he hadn't felt in weeks. And Jane and Katie and Michael were right on the other side of this door. With every step toward the library, his heart lifted higher and higher. Like a hot air balloon, its tethers released.

When they mounted the last stair, Dean panting and drenched in sweat, thick doors before them, Jack stepped out from under his arm and raised a fist to knock. "You think they'll hear?"

"I feel like there's Librarians in every corner of this place," Dean said. With Celia's help, he sat on the top step. "Sure is quiet out here. Compared to last time."

Jack did his best cop knock on the door. "Indeed. Thankfully."

Celia sat sideways next to Dean, one foot on the stairs. "I kinda feel like your train is my fault, Dean. Sort of a wasted trip."

He side-eyed her, blinking fast. "It wasn't. It was important to you. That's not wasted time."

She shrugged.

Jack joined them, sitting next to Celia and looking out at the street. "I have to admit, I'm glad we went. Not only did we find out about your nephew, you figured some things out about yourself." He bumped her shoulder. "Didn't you?"

She hid a grin and watched the street with them. "Thanks, men."

The door creaked open.

The three of them spun.

Quinn stood in the door, framed in sunlight. Fingers interlaced in the back, the mysterious Librarian joined them on the step.

Another twenty-something Librarian stood inside the door. "Will you be needing me anymore right now, Quinn?"

Waving a hand, Quinn glanced at the street. "That will be all, Mr. Collins. Please tell the kitchen to prepare their meals. And some rations they may take on their travels."

Collins bowed, smiling at the four of them.

Something about the sparkle in his eye caught Jack. He threw his mind at it, but it was all he got. Just something about the sparkle.

Shaking his head, he turned back to Quinn. "How are things in your library?"

"Tidy. Your Jane's story has been recorded and placed in my personal library. Please," Quinn said, holding out a hand, "tell me the story of your travels, Jack."

Jack hesitated. If it wasn't good enough, were they going to be left out here to rot? Stomach churning, he turned to Celia. "It's hers to tell."

Leaning around him, Quinn's curious blue-hazel eyes landed on her. "Proceed, dear Celia."

Narrowing his eyes, Jack held his breath. He'd tell the story if she refused but doubted it'd have the emotional impact the librarian was looking for.

Pushing a sigh through her nose, she nodded, angling her forehead at Jack. "The first thing you have to understand, Librarian, is this man has been family to me for many years. And home is on the ocean. But the people we went to see, I started out with them."

CHAPTER 26

After a week of performances, each special in their own way but none as spectacular as the first, Morgan reminded Addy and Matt of the trip he wanted to take to the Molehill.

As his building came into view, striped pole out front, Matt grabbed Addy's arm. "Addy, wait." He eyed the street and tugged her into a nook between one half-demolished building and a block wall.

She followed, flashing on him pulling her out of sight of the jail in Magnolia so they could talk about Dean.

Funny how that stung less than it did last week. Instead, butterflies flew around the memory. Just on the edges of it. Dark, flappy shadows.

Once in the nook, he let her go and rubbed the side of her arm. "I just. I don't know what's going to happen today. And I know we kinda pulled out all the stops last night, but…" He flushed, dropping his eyes.

A single butterfly flapped its wings in her stomach. She told it to fuck off. Waited for him to finish his thought. Willed him not to be trying to tell her he loved her or something.

He rubbed the cheek where Ella had once slapped him over a misunderstanding. "The last month or so has, um. I've had a lot of fun with you, Addy. Both," he cleared his throat, looking at his shoes, "with and without clothes."

She grinned, leaning against the wall behind her. "Me too. If Morgan knows, and we get in trouble, was it worth it?"

Color rising in his cheeks again, he caught her eyes. "I still, uh, with Ella and everything, it feels…" He trailed off and shrugged. "But yeah. Totally worth it."

She jutted her chin out, staring at a point on his chest. "Agreed."

"Hey." Two fingers under her chin lifted her head.

Raising her eyes to his striking blues, she waited.

"I know sometimes it feels like we're doing something wrong. And strictly speaking, we are. And," he smiled, parentheses framing his mouth, "I know that's part of the fun." He shook his head, smile fading. "But it's not wrong. OK?"

She nodded, eyes hot. Why she should be on the edge of tears baffled her, but she let it be what it was. "OK."

While the kiss he laid on her couldn't be called tender, it couldn't not. She let that be what it was too.

* * *

Clearing the inner circle of guard towers at the city the guards called the QC, Jack stopped. "Where to now?"

"Here, let me ask these guys," Mike said. Before Jack could object, Mike backtracked and spoke with the guards. He laughed, clapping one guard on the shoulder. The guard laughed along with him.

The boy pointed south, slinging his rifle over his shoulder and gesturing with his free hand. He laughed again.

Mike did too, crossing his arms and leaning toward him. He spoke under his breath.

As the guard laughed harder, Mike walked away with a wave.

"Good news. This guy knew exactly where she is. Turns out she's on the defense force too, but she's got some kind of special job. Something to do with actors."

Jack smiled. Of course she was out here helping people. Protecting them. She was his daughter, after all. "Did he tell you how to get there?"

"Yeah. It's about twenty minutes south of here."

Dean groaned. "When are we going to sit down?"

Jane chuckled. She leaned into Jack's ear. "It's like they're a matched set."

He nodded, ear warm from her breath. In the week that it'd taken them to get here, each night they'd worked on a new therapy technique she'd learned in one of the library books. She called it EMDR, and combined with what they were already doing, his mind and emotions had begun to flow along a significantly more even keel. When his skin wanted to tingle from her breath in his ear, he let it.

It was like the miracle of finding her, all over again.

One side of his mouth lifted. "Don't tell him that."

She narrowed her eyes and shot daggers at Dean.

As they crossed town, Mike and Celia on either side of Dean, Hux walking alone with his nose buried in his notebook, Jack caught Jane's hand and laced his fingers between hers.

She rubbed the side of his hand with her thumb. "You seem to be feeling better."

"I think so. You're a good doctor."

"Ha. Flattery will get you everywhere." She wrinkled her nose, rubbing the baby's back through the sling. "Oh my god. We need to change this child."

"Want me to carry her?"

She stopped. "Yes. Yes, I do."

Settling the stinky baby into the crook of his arm, he rubbed her nose with his. "Hey, little Katie. Have a good nap?"

She gurgled and cooed, wiggling. Blue eyes the same color as his, she stared at his face.

The other shoe hung in the air over Jack's head. Waiting to fall directly on top of it.

He took Jane's hand again and they walked through town. People starting to get out and about for the day, some watched them as they passed. All sorts of people, from the very young to the very old. Jack hadn't seen such a city since the virus had come.

"Mr. Cooke," Huxley said at his shoulder.

"Yeah, Hux."

"I wonder if any of these children are also immune? How populated do you think this city is?"

Considering the number of skyscrapers, and how many people they'd passed as they crossed town, it had to be large. "Ten, twenty thousand."

Huxley scribbled in his notebook with a stubby pencil. "Big city. Yes. Yes. There must be some. Must be." He tapped Jack's shoulder, stopping. "Do you think we'll be staying here a while?" Eyebrows lifted, teeth hanging over his bottom lip, he waited.

Jack stopped. "I honestly have no idea."

"Well. It's. Hm." Going back to his notebook, he began walking again, vaguely following Mike and the others.

They made their way across town, following the directions the guard gave them.

Approaching a blocky building with new fences, Jack considered. This had to be the one. One guard stood by the gate.

Switching Katie to the other arm, Jack waved to the guard. "Hi. We're looking for the Tree?"

"Found it."

"Is Adelaide Cooke here?"

"Not right now. Who's asking?"

Jack's stomach fell. "Where is she?"

The guard repeated his question.

With Celia on his heels, her hand hovering over her blade, Mike approached. A thousand-watt smile lit his face. "Mike Cooke. How are you?"

The guard's eyes flitted between Mike and Jack. "Oh wait. Are you...are you guys related to her?"

Jack grinned. "What gave us away?"

Laughing, the guard swung the gate wide. "Addy's good people. This isn't my usual gig, but she had to go out of town today."

Stepping through, Jack took in the yard. "Where is she?"

He closed the gate with a shrug. "You can ask inside."

When they rounded the corner and the loading dock came into view, Dean chuckled. "No way, Jack. Not gonna happen."

Jane gripped the side of the dock and pulled herself up. "Hand me the baby, Jack."

Someone squealed from inside as Jane knelt to change Katie. "A baby! Guys, come look!"

A waif of a woman with brown hair and a black jacket three sizes too large dashed out onto the dock. She knelt beside Jane and stared at the baby with wide eyes. "She is beautiful. What a queen."

Jane smiled. "That she is."

"Dad, here," Mike said, lacing his hands for a step.

With a grunt, Jack stuck his foot in the cradle and mounted the dock. "Dean, you stay out here. I'll go inside and see if—"

The woman's mouth dropped open. "Your name is Dean?" She sat on the dock, legs dangling over, and leaned her elbows on her knees. "She said you were dead."

Dean closed his eyes. "She did, did she?" He slid down the wall. "I guess that's true."

Another woman floated out onto the dock as Jane picked the baby up. She tossed her white-blonde hair, reminding Jack of Matt's girl for a fleeting moment. She took one look at him and smiled. "She doesn't have your eyes, but you cross your arms the same way she does. You must be Addy's father."

He grinned, sticking out a hand. "I am. Jack Cooke. You are?"

"Victoria," she said with a curtsy. "She's not here. Morgan left us with animals and took her." Her brows creased.

"Where'd they go, Victoria?" Mike asked, leaning on the dock.

A dark-skinned man glided onto the dock from another door. "Deep underground, they went. Deep underground."

Victoria faced him, hands on her hips. "How do you know that, Cassius?"

He approached, shaking hands with Jack. "Overheard she and the dear fellow speaking about some molehill." He bowed to Jane. "You are as beautiful as our Victoria. Breathtaking eyes, my dear." He took her hand and kissed the back of it.

But Jack had gotten stuck on what this Cassius had said. "They went to the Molehill?" Heart beating in his ears, he struggled to hear his own voice over its cacophony.

The color drained from Victoria's face. "My god, Cassius. Why didn't you tell me this earlier?"

"What business is it of ours if they are going to kill a few pests?"

Victoria dropped the fancy speech she'd been using. "Not *a* molehill, Cassius. *The* Molehill." She spoke to Jack, eyes aflame. "If you take me with you, I can guide you there. We must go now."

Dean stood, wobbling. "You got transpo?"

Jack spoke at the same time. "Is Matt with her?"

A man stood in the other door, aviator glasses hiding his eyes. "He's with her, all right. Here." He tossed keys.

Jack caught them. "What are we waiting for?" He glanced at the doctor. "You stay here."

Mike helped Hux onto the dock.

Victoria turned to Cassius. "You and Jim watch these guys. If anything happens, close this place up and hunker down like Matt and Addy showed us, all right?"

Cassius grabbed her hand. "Are you sure?"

She shook her head. Tugging him down, she kissed his forehead. "We'll be back before you know it."

CHAPTER 27

A ddy fidgeted in the front seat of Morgan's truck, unraveling her sleeve at the seam.

Matt rode in the bed, back pressed against the window.

Yasuo once complimented her on learning to share silence. This one was hard though. Her lungs burned from it.

"What did your guys on the inside tell you?"

One hand draped over the wheel, Morgan grunted. "Addy, no offense, but I don't think I want to share that with you. Needless to say, it's bad going to worse."

"Do you not trust me, or do you think I can't handle it?"

Laughing, Morgan shook his head. "I know you can handle it. I have no doubt about that." He jerked his free thumb over his shoulder. "How much do you think you can trust that boy?"

Addy narrowed her eyes. "Completely. Why?"

"Are you sure? He used to work for these people." He angled his chin. "How do you know he isn't still?"

Her heart tried to speed up. She swallowed it down, breathing deep. Cooling her head. "It's a long story." *Which involves my mother, but you don't know that.*

Morgan shook his head. "It's another little bit before we get there. Why don't you tell me this"—he raised his hand, hooking his fingers in the air—"'long story' of yours, and let me decide."

Staring out the window at the newly green trees as they flew past, she frowned. Speaking with slow precision, she told him how she and Matt met. The train. The interrogation room. Leaving out any detail that could give away her identity, she explained the bare-bones version of Magnolia. And Ella.

She lingered on how Matt helped them get into the hospital, the way he put himself in danger for them when they fought together, and even how the general escaped.

"Mmm. Yeah. The general. She's a piece of work, that woman." Morgan shook his head. "Damn shame she's so pretty."

Addy's heart settled somewhere in her throat. Her jugular popped out with each beat. "Why is that a shame?"

"Hate to kill pretty women. Seems a waste."

Practicing aloof and uninterested in her head before she opened her mouth, she resisted swiping the sweat from her forehead. "Why would you want to kill her? Don't you think you could talk to her?"

He did more than glance. He looked at her so long, she became concerned about staying on the road.

"Adelaide, we are so far past talking. So far."

Addy stared out the window again. As a tear rolled down her cheek, she pretended to cough so she could wipe it with the back of her fist. "Matt had plenty of chances to turn on us. He's had so many more since. And besides." She stopped, leaning around the seat to look at him.

His hair, brushing his neck, riffled in the breeze. Arms wrapped around his knees, he'd buried his face in the space between his body and drawn-up legs.

She considered all the times he could have hurt her. Could have turned her over to Mom. Could have killed her, if he wanted.

Morgan shifted his eyes to the rearview. "Besides?"

"Besides. He's been more than solid in a lot of close situations. If he was still working for them, his instinct when things get tight wouldn't be to save me. It'd be to destroy me."

Chuckling, Morgan side-eyed her. "Don't get me wrong, Addy, please, but why would you even be on the radar for these people? No. If he's working for them, he's looking for a bigger fish." He thumped his chest.

Addy opened her mouth to laugh and tell him she was the biggest fish Talus could find. The words stuck in her throat.

Right. He didn't know who she was. And here she almost told him.

The Talus soldier, Gian, bleeding into his gag from the rusty gash on his cheek, filled her vision. Morgan hid worse up his sleeve for liars and traitors.

Clenching her teeth, she said nothing more until the truck slowed.

Morgan pulled to the side of the road and shut it off. Leaning on the armrest between them, he lowered his voice. "I'll trust him for now. But if he gives me one reason, any at all, he'll wish for death before it's over."

Eyes wide, Addy breathed shallowly.

He smiled. "You might not be a big fish, but I won't let him hurt a hair on your pretty head either. You're one of mine now. I take care of my own." He opened the door.

Grabbing his sleeve before he slid out of the truck, she cleared her throat. "Morgan, to use your words, no offense, but I can take care of my damn self. Thank you."

Staring at her hand, his smile widened. "Of course."

She slid out the door and slammed it as Matt jumped down from the bed.

Cheeks ruddy, forehead creased, he checked her over. "You all right?"

She glared as Morgan came around the truck. "Sure. Interesting ride." She lowered her voice. "Tell you about it later."

Hands on his hips, Morgan stood in front of the truck and stared at the horizon. "You two ready?"

Matt wrapped a light hand around her arm and tugged.

She followed them into the woods, curious what Morgan would do when he found out the truth.

* * *

Standing in roughly the same spot Addy and Matt had a month ago, Morgan gazed down onto the Molehill with a pair of binoculars. "Addy, take a look at this," he said, holding them out.

Squinting through them, she adjusted the focus. "What am I looking at?"

"There's a group of people down there near the fence."

Lifting her eyes, she found the people. Pointing the binoculars at them again, she searched each face until she saw what Morgan had seen. "Shit. Here." Without taking her eyes from the group, she held the binocs out for Matt.

He stepped closer and took them. "Where?"

Grabbing his shoulder, she pointed.

After finding them and focusing, he swore. "Kendra. What are they doing with her down there?"

"Morgan," Addy said, "do you have bolt cutters?"

"Matter of fact, there's some in the truck."

"Can we get her out of there? Cut the fence?"

He scratched his chin, staring down at the compound. "Maybe. Maybe. My guy says there's a blind spot. Have a look at that quadrant," he said, pointing north.

Taking the spyglasses from Matt, she aimed them at the north corner. "Yeah. What about it?"

"He says there's a spot there between the trees neither of the surrounding guard towers can see. They can see it from across the hill, but they hardly ever take a peek that direction. Guess it's hard to see but can be done. It's only about four feet wide, so they don't worry too much about it."

Matt grunted. "Aren't there foot patrols?"

"Every hour."

Addy lowered the binocs. "It's not much room. Or time. But if we can get her over there, I think we can get her out."

"There's a lot of people in there against their will, Addy," Matt said. Shoulder warm against hers. "I don't think we can get all of them."

Rubbing against his shoulder, hers moved up and down. "We can at least try to get the Troupe's smile back."

Morgan tapped her, holding out his hand for the binoculars. "I'll go get the bolt cutters. You guys get down to the fence and see if you can get Kendra to go that way. I'll meet you there in five minutes."

Addy handed him the binoculars, and he walked off.

Knees bent, she and Matt descended the steep hill. Crawling at some points to keep from sliding.

"Don't look down, Addy."

"I'm not. I'm not."

"Hey, Addy."

She stopped, grabbing onto a bush. "Yeah."

"I saw your mom down there too."

She glanced at the compound. "Did you really? Shit. Shit. Fucking shit."

"Did you tell Morgan who she is to you? On the way here?"

She exhaled a humorless laugh. "It was close, but no. He questioned your loyalty."

Matt matched her humorless chuckle. "What'd you tell him?"

"What do you think? I trust you." She turned away from the compound and met his eyes. "Completely."

He swallowed. "I appreciate that. Really."

"Good. Because you earned it."

Flushed and smiling, he started down the hill again. "If we see your mom. I mean, if she sees us."

"It could go really bad, really fast. You don't have to tell me that." She knelt, sliding on flat feet down about three feet of hill.

"That's not what I was going to say." He stood, gripping a sapling. "Our usual deal applies. I'm not going to hurt her. Unless I have to."

She joined him, gripping the sapling. The loose dirt around it wanted to rip her feet from under her. "Even after Ella? She could have stopped him, you know. She could have said freaking something."

"Wait. Did you change your mind? You never—"

Letting go of the sapling, she took a step away. "Ah hell, Matt. Let's play it by ear, why don't we?"

The ground beneath her leading foot shifted. Trying to slide her back foot forward before the ground pulled her into an impossible split, she lost her balance.

Of course.

Sliding, she tried to get low, force her center of gravity close to the ground. Slow her rate of descent. The hill was too steep, the dirt too loose from recent drought. She kept sliding, flinging her arms out to try to catch something.

"Dammit, Addy," Matt said, throwing himself low to slide after her. Pushing down the hill, he caught up to her and snagged one of her flailing hands.

Before he hooked his arm around a tree, containing the shout behind his teeth as the weight of both of them pulled through his elbow, she figured they'd go careening down the hill and finish up at Mom's feet. Likely as not.

But he did catch them, and they didn't slide down the hill.

In silence, they finished their descent. Addy took her steps much more deliberately. When they reached the bottom, she gripped his shoulder. "Thanks for stopping me."

"What's that Vic said? You're bound to me now?"

She flushed. "Stuff it." Unsheathing her machete, she looked at the fence. "Which way to Kendra?"

Grinning, he pointed ahead. "Up there. But Addy—"

She crept off through the undergrowth, walking in a half crouch.

He joined her, Bowie knife in hand, his rifle still firmly slung in place over his shoulder. It was like he glued the thing on. "If we get too close to the fence, someone will see us."

"Yeah, Kendra, hopefully."

"Or your mom."

"Did you see Ricardo?"

Matt stopped. "You mean Hector? No. If I had, I would have shot him already. And damn Morgan, Kendra, and your mom. He's mine, Addy. I ever see his face again, I'll put a bullet through it so fast the only thing he'll know is it was me. I want him to look in my eyes first."

She backtracked, standing up next to him a good thirty feet away from the fence. "I've got no problem with that, Matt. But look."

He stared through the trees, eyes narrowed.

Cupping his jaw, she forced his head to turn. Once she'd caught his eyes, she went on. "Look. Don't get yourself killed to get revenge. Ella wouldn't have wanted that."

He frowned, mouth pointed down at such a severe angle his jaw might fall off and roll away on the forest floor. He sniffed. "Yeah. All right."

She kissed him on the cheek. "I mean it. Protect yourself. *I* don't want you to kill yourself getting revenge. All right?"

One side of his mouth turned up. He pulled her into a hug. "All right."

* * *

"Pull in behind this truck, Jack," Victoria said. "That's Morgan's. Oh. He's here."

Before the van rolled to a stop, Victoria opened the door and jumped out. Jogging kept her inertia going, and she flew toward the man she'd called Morgan.

He caught her, spinning and setting her on her feet. He dipped into the cab of the truck for something. She pointed at the van, chattering.

Shutting the van down, Jack glanced at Jane. Katie had gone to sleep nursing on the way. He cleared his throat, opened his mouth to ask if she wanted to stay here, and snapped it closed. She'd tell him what she wanted.

She caught him staring. "You want to carry her through the woods? Was nice to have that sling off earlier."

Melinda had so rarely let him carry the kids. It was too much out of her control to allow it. "Yeah. Show me how to use the sling."

"You got it, lover boy. Here." She handed Katherine to him, fixed her shirt, and crawled out the side door.

Settling the warm baby into the crook of his arm, he slid out the driver's side door and took in this Morgan. They were similar in age, and he seemed a solid type of guy, just from the set of his shoulders. But time would tell if that suited him or not.

Jack approached, sticking out the wrong hand to shake. "Jack Cooke. You're Morgan?"

"You got it." Morgan took his left hand with his own left and shook.

Firm. No hesitation. Adaptable, like Hux. The doc was a little driven, focused on the virus, and sometimes flighty, but adaptability was an important trait in what the world had become.

Jack smiled, eyes narrowed. "Good to meet you."

"And you. You're Addy's dad?" He grinned down at the little one. "What about this one?"

"Her too, and me," Mike said, approaching with his hand out. "Glad we ran into you. I'm pretty eager to see my sister, to tell you the truth."

Pulling a pair of bolt cutters from the truck, Morgan shut the door. "I can take you all to her."

Mike freed his phone from his pocket. "I'll call her."

"No, son, don't do that," Morgan said, hand over the phone. "She should be right down next to the fence by now." He jerked a thumb over his shoulder.

Dean stepped up next to Jack. "Fence? To what?"

"The Molehill."

Victoria cursed. "Morgan, you didn't. You didn't leave her and Matt alone to have a go at the Molehill by themselves?"

"They'll wait for me. I've got the cutters, after all."

Celia chuckled. "You sure you've met Adelaide Cooke? Cause it doesn't sound like you know her."

Jane approached and started wrapping Jack in the sling. She looked over her shoulder. "We better get down there before she gets herself into trouble."

"I think you underestimate her," Morgan said, looking around at the group. "Obviously I don't know her as well as you people do, but she's gotten herself out of some pretty tight spots in the last month."

"We didn't say she couldn't," Dean said, setting off toward the direction Morgan indicated. Wobbling so much over his ankle, each step put him in danger of falling over.

"Mike," Jack said, jerking his chin.

Mike set off after him.

Jane finished wrapping and helped Jack settle the baby into a fold, tucking her feet into it. "There. Now she won't get cold, or bounce out." She winked. "Thanks."

He ran the back of his hand down her cheek. "No. Thank you." He glanced at Morgan, the man's eyes calculating but warm. Didn't seem like a bad sort, not at all. Had more than one secret though. "Let's get down there."

Victoria hooked her arm into Morgan's and pulled. "I know the quickest way down." She gestured in the direction Jack assumed to be the Molehill. "I used to live there too. Grew up with Matt. Long story."

"With the general, everything is a long story," Jane said.

"I see you've met her as well," Morgan said.

"Oh. We've met."

Jack figured he was the only one who saw her finger her knives. Not for the first time since they'd left the city, he considered how the end of this day would look if Melinda were no longer of this earth. The soup of emotions too much to take in, he shut it down like the other times. He shouldn't have come.

One hand around the baby, covering pretty much her whole back, he took Jane's hand in the other. Her fingers thrummed.

She closed her eyes for a beat and breathed deep through her nose.

Her fingers relaxed in his hand. But one of them had sweaty palms, and at this point, he wasn't sure which.

"Listen, Vic," Morgan said, "we saw Kendra. That's what these are for." He raised the bolt cutters.

Vic goggled. "What, you're going to break her out in broad daylight?"

"My guy on the inside says there's a blind spot. We can make it work if we're fast, and lucky."

Stopping, Vic dropped his arm. "No, Morgan. That's—"

A shot cracked through the forest.

Jack ducked, pulling Jane down with him, heart racing. Katie whimpered but didn't cry. She had to be the quietest baby he'd ever met. His mind tried to distract him from the danger Addy was in with wondering how Jane got the baby to be so quiet. Maybe she'd—

Stop woolgathering, Jack. Your baby needs you.

He stood. Dean, Mike, and Celia had already disappeared through the trees. "Lead the way, Victoria. Get me to my little girl."

* * *

Creeping through the trees, northern corner in sight, Addy spoke over her shoulder. "I can't believe that worked."

"Pfft. About five percent of the plan worked. Get Kendra to notice us. There's still ninety-five percent of this that can go horribly sideways."

At the northern corner, Kendra shuffled her feet and approached the inner fence. Two layers of fence, both girded in razor wire, stood between them. She pitched her voice low and used her actor's magic to make it carry. "What are you guys doing here?"

"Busting you out," Addy said, approaching the fence in a crouch. "Are you all right?"

Shaking her head, Kendra rubbed her stomach and twisted her lips. "Less so than I was last time we spoke."

Matt slunk toward the fence. "What are they doing to you in there? Have you seen anyone else from town?"

"Your general is not a kind woman, Matt. I see why you and Victoria left her. She—"

A guard shouted from the yard. "You there! Time to get back in!"

Kendra stepped closer and clutched the fence. "Whatever they did to Adam is different from what they're doing to us. It's all women, and we." She stopped, swallowing. Her eyes darted back and forth. She licked her lips and leaned close to the fence, razor wire catching her shin and cutting through the leg of her jumpsuit. Blood stippled the cut. "When they took me, I could not have imagined I would be both given a vaccine and also implanted with something more terrible than a virus."

Addy glanced at Matt, and his slack jaw and wide eyes matched her own.

"Kendra," he said, gripping Addy's arm, "what do you mean?"

"She means she's growing what some would call a parasite. What others would call a baby."

Addy's blood ran cold, her joints freezing. Matt's grip on her arm tightened like a vise.

"Jesus, Addy, come on," he said, tugging.

"I wouldn't." Melinda walked along the outside of the fence, closing the distance with long, purposeful strides. Hands behind her back, she smiled. "My guards are thick, but they are not slow. And they are all dead shots." She stopped before them, smiling down her nose. "As you well know. My darling boy."

Color rising in his cheeks, he released Addy and stood. "Good to see you again, General. Where is Hector, anyway? Got a little something for him."

Addy stood, laying one hand on his arm. "Mom. Why are your men killing people in town? And what the hell do you mean, a baby?"

Melinda shook her head. "You refused me before, little one. Why should I tell you anything?"

Against her own logic, Addy took a step toward her. Matt reached for her, fingers slipping off her sleeve. "We can't let you keep hurting all these people. I've seen how you leave them. More than once. There's dozens in town you left just like Andrew."

Matt shifted on his feet. Face pale, brow sweaty, his eyes flew between them. He shook his head.

With a frown, she turned back to her mom. Well. The woman who looked like her. "Why don't you explain it to me?"

With a quickness Addy had only seen in snakes and the newly dead, Melinda lashed out and grabbed her shoulder. Pulling her in, she wrapped one arm around her throat.

"No!" Matt yanked the rifle off his shoulder, aimed, and fired at Melinda's feet all in one motion. "Let her go."

Melinda chuckled, tightening her grip. Grabbing Addy's arm, she twisted it behind her and shoved her wrist into her shoulder blades.

Addy locked a cry behind her lips, her arm and shoulder burning.

Melinda turned Addy's body so it blocked her own from Matt. "Considering her half sister is immune, Adelaide here would make an excellent test subject. The current run would be inappropriate, but for a new group."

"I don't know what that means, Mom, but—"

Melinda tightened her grip. "Shut up."

Struggling to pull a breath down, Addy kicked backward.

Matt, panting, stepped sideways. Every time her mom positioned Addy in front of the gun, he wavered. "Please. Melinda, stop."

"I don't know what I did to you to make you turn on me so fully, but here we are, traitorous boy."

"If you let her go, we can talk about it."

"If I'll take you instead?"

He shook his head. "I'll never step foot in the Molehill again. Let. Her. Go." His finger caressed the trigger. "Give me an opening, General."

Addy went to pull down a breath, tell them to stop for a second before someone really got hurt, and found the way in for air had been closed. She bucked, her free hand scratching at Mom's arm.

Melinda torqued her captive arm again, yanking it higher. "Stop fighting me. You'll understand soon."

But Addy couldn't breathe. Couldn't inhale or exhale or anything. Her body fought on her behalf as her head swam. She kicked and scratched, yanking at Mom's arm and sucking in a bare trickle of air.

Fear clouded in. The edges of her vision black, her ears ringing, she caught snatches of Matt's high eyebrows and wide eyes, the dark eye of the gun. The trees. It all faded. Her struggles weakened. She couldn't pull down that damn breath.

Oh god, please let me breathe.

Her feet slid from under her.

Melinda screamed, a throaty grunt, her arm popping free.

Addy stumbled, rushing face-first at the ground, lungs singing as they took in cold air.

Somewhere far away, a rifle clattered to the ground. Hands gripped her before her face bounced off the ground and went with her as her inertia carried them both down.

One arm under both of hers, encircling her chest, Matt flipped her around, pulled her close against his body, and brandished his knife with the other hand.

Through blurry eyes, Addy stared up at her mom.

The side of Mom's chest had grown a knife handle. Weird place for one.

Melinda sucked in short, sharp breaths. One hand wrapped around the knife handle, and she stopped. She dropped her hand and backed into the fence, knife still protruding from what had to be a lung.

"More where that came from, bitch. Now I got a clean shot at your heart, like I promised." Jane stepped out of the trees, drawn knife in one hand, ready to throw. The other pointing at Melinda, aiming with it.

Addy pulled more air down her aching throat, vision clearing. She reached back and took a handful of Matt's shoulder.

Dragging her with him, he stood. He held the knife in front of them both, wrapping a tight arm around her waist.

Half a dozen armed men came from the direction Melinda had.

Dad, Dean, Celia, Mike, Morgan, and wouldn't you know it, Victoria, cleared the trees.

Mom's eyes narrowed, flitting across all of them. She tried to inhale, got halfway there, and screwed up her face. Still breathing in short, sharp gasps, she waved the men off. "You…see…what you've…gotten our children…involved in…Jackson?"

Matt cursed.

Morgan's mouth fell open.

She forked two fingers at Victoria and Matt. "Deal…with traitors…later." Falling against the fence again, she waved one of the men over. "Mind the…knife."

Jane continued to hold up her knife, aimed to deliver the killing blow.

And looking back on it in the coming weeks, Addy believed she would have, if Dad hadn't laid a hand on her shoulder.

She lowered her arms, backing up, and glanced at Addy and Matt.

Matt's arm tightened on her waist, and he spoke in her ear. "Can you walk? Are you OK?"

Ignoring them both, Addy watched as Mom staggered away down the fence, wheezing orders. Inside the fence, Kendra lowered her head and wobbled toward the Molehill.

Outside the door, a Black woman stood, arms crossed, and watched them all.

"We're lucky she didn't kill us all yet," Matt said, still gripping her.

She let his shoulder go, flexing her fingers. "'M'ok. You can let me go." She cleared her throat.

Breath catching, he did, and picked up his rifle.

"Maybe once we get the fuck out of here, you can explain to me what just happened," Morgan said.

Addy cleared her throat again, sandpaper scratching the inside, and nodded.

Dean stood there, wobbling with a brace on one ankle, and her throat thickened, eyes burning. He took a cautious step. "Addy, are you all right?"

Ignoring his question, she smiled at her sister strapped to Dad's chest and threw an arm around Mike's shoulders. "I think it's time to go."

Reunification

CHAPTER 28

Ilasha closed the door to Melinda's recovery room. Crossing her arms, shoulders hunched, she moved a chair next to the bed and hovered beside it.

"This hospital wing is nicer than I remember," Melinda said, gazing at the ceiling. Oxygen tube stuffed up her nose, she pulled down a breath and winced when it hit her punctured lung. After removing the knife, which now sat on her bedside tray, and stitching her up, the doc told her the lung would heal on its own with some oxygen and rest. Still hurt like a son of a bitch.

"How's it feel?" Lash asked, perching on the edge of the chair.

"Hurts. How do you think."

"Not your lung, woman."

"Not what I meant."

"What were you doing? Why did you go out there?"

"One of the guards watches that blind spot." She stopped, taking a cautious breath. Lifting the knife by the bloody handle, she spun it on its tip. "Radio said one of the test subjects had gone over there and there was movement in the woods." She lifted the corners of her mouth, not reaching her eyes with the smile. "You told me three hours ago Addy was in town. I didn't even know if she was alive, Lash. I." Shifting again, she held her side.

Lash took her free hand. "You were hoping she'd come looking for you."

Blinking, a tear wetting the side of her face and soaking into the pillow, Melinda nodded. "I thought it was a hell of a coincidence. I knew it had to be her." She closed her eyes, sucking oxygen through her nose. "I wasn't wrong."

Lash squeezed her hand. "What happened?"

Eyes still closed, inside of her nose filled with the faint scent of plastic, she shook her head. "She didn't come here to find me. She came here to undermine me. Again." Picking her head up, she pulled the tube from her nose. "She doesn't understand anything, Ilasha. Nothing. She's an ungrateful brat, and she always will be."

Lash stuck the tube back in her nose and pressed her forehead with a firm, warm hand, until she laid on the pillow again. "You still love her."

"Of course I do. You don't stop loving your children just because they're idiots."

"But."

"But. I don't know. I feel like I can't think straight. Must be the damage my brain sustained during the Cure trials."

Her chin resting on the side rail, Lash smiled. "I still love you. Brain damage and all. Promise me you won't leave these fences without backup like that again."

Pressing her lips together, Melinda shook her head. "You—"

The door opened.

Cormac stood in the threshold, arms crossed. "General."

"Get out of here, boy," Melinda said.

Leer stretching his lips across his teeth, he shook his head and stepped back.

Anthony eased past him into the room. "He's here with me, General. How are you feeling?"

Melinda stared at the knife. "Like I got run over by a pointy truck." Pulling oxygen as deep as it would go before she ached, she set her mouth and narrowed her eyes at Cormac, who'd followed Anthony in and closed the door. She pointed her forehead at him. "He can leave."

"I'm afraid he can't," Anthony said. He waved at the chair. "Ilasha, please."

She stood.

He sat, crossing one knee over the other and leaning on his elbow. He cupped his chin and smiled. "The doctor says you will be here for a few days."

"Not many. I have to sleep upright for a couple of days. Then I should be good as new."

"You took an ill-advised risk today. It almost cost me you and one of our best test subjects. Care to explain yourself?"

Lips pressed together, she shook her head. "A slight error in judgment."

"You might not believe this, General"—Anthony snaked a hand under the rail and grasped the top of hers—"you are incredibly important to this project, and to this organization." He squeezed. "Nearly as important as the Cure. Your tireless dedication is an inspiration to us all."

Cormac smiled, leaning on the end of the bed.

She glared at the fool. "I still don't understand what the hell he's doing here." Though she was beginning to. Anthony was nothing if not a dependable asshole.

"He's going to be taking over the immunity project. You are not to disrupt or disturb the research in any way."

Melinda sat up, fire screaming through her side. She clenched her teeth against it. "The fuck I will. I won't—" Sweat drenching her forehead, she flopped onto the pillow. "I won't just let him have it."

Anthony glanced at Lash. "Honestly, I have no choice. You endangered yourself and our tests today. You're off immunity." He stood. "It's McNamara's project now. Ilasha," he said, crooking a bony finger, "see to it all the paperwork properly reflects the transfer. Send a memo to everyone, immediately. General." He gripped her hand again. "Heal fast. There's still plenty for you to do, and I need you on your feet as soon as possible."

Mouth open, catching flies as her grandmom would have said, she fought to breathe as Anthony left the room.

Cormac, that pinch-faced little dick, stood at the end of the bed, grinning. Gloating. "You'll be sure to show me all your notes, Melinda. And I'll need access to all your test results, test subjects, and equipment."

"Piss off," Ilasha said, stepping away from the wall. She flapped a hand. "Shoo."

Lips twisted in a sour frown, like he'd eaten a whole lemon, he spun on a heel and stalked out of the room. Once in the hall, he spoke over his shoulder. "Get me those notes, secretary."

Lash sighed. "I have to go. Anthony needs that memo."

"Immediately. I know. Don't keep him waiting." Melinda crossed her arms over her lungs. Her side burned like fire, but she'd sooner die than ask for painkillers. Look what morphine had gotten Jack.

Oh hell, where did that come from?

He couldn't even maintain eye contact with her out there in the woods. He'd saved her life, but he couldn't look at her.

Guts full of worms, she shoved it aside. But not before she remembered her behavior. Something someone with severe brain trauma would do. Not the Melinda she used to know.

Lips warm on her cheek, Lash kissed her and walked out.

* * *

Packed into the van with everyone except Morgan and Vic, Addy curled up under her dad's arm and wept.

He stroked her hair and stayed silent, doing one of the things he was best at, making her feel better without saying a word.

She sniffled, whispering at one point. "She's not going to change, is she?"

Patting her shoulder, he said nothing.

She wiped an eye, looking up at him.

He frowned and met her gaze with dull blue eyes. "I think she's too far gone, kiddo."

Addy buried her face in his shoulder again.

With Mike driving like someone's grandma, Celia sitting up front with him, it took longer than it should have. Dean and Matt sat in the back, sharing an uncomfortable silence. Addy could only imagine what was going through Matt's head.

On her other side, Jane wrapped the baby to herself, the little angel sleeping away.

Jane squeezed her knee.

Addy peeked at her.

"Sorry."

Addy shook her head. "About what?"

Jane's cheek twitched. "Knifing your mom." Her eyes shifted over Addy's head.

Burying her face again, uninterested in whatever silent message Jane and Dad passed, she closed her eyes. Dad continued to do what he did best, and before she knew it, he shook her shoulder.

"We're here."

Sleep crowding the corner of one eye, she wiped them both and sat up. Inhaling through her nose, she looked in the back.

Dean and Matt. Sharing the back seat. Dean couldn't look her in the eyes, but Matt caught and held them.

"We're in some deep shit, Addy."

Right. Morgan.

Ducking from under Dad's arm, she opened her mouth to explain.

The side door flew open. "You two. The fuck out here. Now."

Jack stiffened. "Who does he think he's talking to?"

"Let me handle it, Dad," Addy said.

Matt slid up, beating her to the door. "I'll go first."

Before Addy's feet hit the ground, Morgan grabbed Matt by the collar and slammed him into the side of the van. It rocked, and she almost lost her balance as she exited.

"One reason, I said. Give me one." Slapping his gun from his holster, he held it to Matt's temple.

Heart going from asleep to hummingbird speed fast enough to make Addy dizzy, she jumped and caught Morgan's wrist. Gripped it in her fingers and dug what nails she'd been able to grow into the soft skin beneath the tendon in his wrist. She wanted to shout and plead, but Morgan wasn't the type to hear pleading. So she communicated in a way he'd understand.

Squeezing the tendon harder, she twisted his wrist.

With a grunt, he kept his grip on the gun but couldn't keep it aimed. The shot went wild.

Matt shouted, arms above his head, ducking as best he could while Morgan still held a handful of his shirt.

Before he could speak, everyone piled out of the van.

Someone grabbed Morgan, yanking him away from Matt. Someone else took his gun and his other hand and held his arms in place.

Addy couldn't count who did what and who was where. All she could count was one Matt, still standing. She locked her eyes on his, both of them breathing hard.

He backed into the van, brow furrowed, and reached toward her. He glanced at his hand, then Morgan, and Dean holding him, and dropped it. Eyes slipping shut, he leaned his head against the van and slid down it.

Urge to grab him and hold him while he was still whole falling to something manageable, but by no means dissipating, she took in the rest of them.

And Morgan, who stood and let Dean hold him. With Dean's ankle all busted, Morgan could've easily overpowered him. But he didn't. He glared at her, eyes narrow. "You got something you want to tell me, Adelaide?"

"You pretty much heard what you needed to," she said, crossing her arms. "She's my mom."

Ripping his hands free, Morgan exhaled something like a laugh.

And Dad. He couldn't help but react. "Touch my daughter, you'll be dead before you hit the ground."

Morgan held up both hands. "She lied to me." He chuckled, cheek dimpling. His smile warm. "Here she let me go on about big fish. Made me look like an idiot, girl."

"Till just now, we were the only ones who knew about that."

Eyes ablaze, Morgan stared with his mouth half-open. He threw back his head and laughed. "Right you are. Right you are." He looked around the group, taking in each of them in turn. "Anything else I should know?"

"A few things," Jack said. "Is there somewhere we can talk?"

Morgan pointed to his building with the striped pole out front. "Down here, in the barbershop. My office." He held out a hand.

Jack gripped Addy's shoulder. "You coming with?"

She sat in the open door of the van and shook her head. "We've got to get back to the Tree." She lowered her voice, peeking at him from under her brows. "Don't go in his back room unarmed."

Jane settled her knives. "Like we ever go anywhere unarmed." She winked.

"It's good to see you guys," Addy said, smiling. "I didn't know when I would."

Mike slid a crowbar through his belt. "Hey. Can I come with you? Need to pick up Hux."

Matt helped Addy up, holding her hand longer than necessary. "Where is he?"

"We left him with those people of hers," Celia said, jerking her head at Vic. "Interesting group, there."

Addy laughed. "That they are. We better go rescue him."

Jane walked backward, heading off with Jack and Morgan. "Save some fun for me, you guys."

Spinning, Addy ran face-first into Dean.

"Whoa," he said, holding his hands out.

She cursed, walking around him. Balling up every bit of joy at seeing him and every bit of anger at seeing him and stuffing it deep, deep down under her stomach. Down, into her feet.

Limping, he caught up to her. "All right if I come along? It's OK if you say no."

"No."

Vic chuckled, falling in step beside her. "We thought he was dead."

"He is."

"But he's not."

Addy gave her a glaring side-eye. "He is. I don't know that man."

Vic picked up her affectation from wherever she'd left it. A pocket, maybe. "Ah. Changed but not changed, we return from the veil but shadows of who we once were."

"Something like that."

"I shall speak on it no more." She leaned close. "But you know everyone else is going to question you endlessly. Especially Cassie."

Fighting the half a smile trying to curve her lip, Addy nodded. "Run interference for me then."

Vic's brow wrinkled. "Do what now?"

"He's coming anyway, Addy," Celia said, appearing at her other side.

Addy stopped, throwing both arms around her.

Celia hugged her back. Didn't try to make herself small. Didn't try to pull away too soon. Just hugged her back. Her eyes were probably even closed.

"I missed you, you wild woman. How was your trip?"

Heavy lids curved up. "Enlightening." She glanced behind Addy.

"Oh, sister, you should have seen the library," Mike said, sweeping his arm across the sky. "I've never seen anything like it."

Grinning, he started walking, telling her every last detail.

* * *

Morgan jerked a ring of keys the size of Montana from his pocket and picked the right one on the first try.

Jack stared at the picture window out front, the lettering that once identified it as a barbershop long gone. The striped pole didn't have dust inside, but it also no longer spun. Walking in after Morgan, he noted that was just as well. Nothing in this room suggested haircuts.

The military precision with which Morgan organized the maps on the walls, photos, and files called to Jack in a specific sort of way. The order of it all. The straight edges.

"Please," Morgan said, motioning to the chairs before the large metal desk. "Miss. You can use the couch if you like." He pointed across the room, where a plastic couch squeezed up against the wall.

Katie squirmed in the wrap, whimpering.

"She's hungry. Again. Think she's growing." She caught Jack's hand, tightened her fingers around his, and raised her brow.

"Yeah. She must be." He nodded.

Glaring at Morgan's back as the man loaded a coffee pot, she shot a look at Jack.

He leaned into her ear. "I know. Me neither."

"As long as we're clear, love," she said, unwrapping the baby and sitting on the couch with her.

"Clear about what?" Morgan asked, sitting.

Jack sat across from him and leaned back. "We don't trust you."

Losing his balance, Morgan overcorrected and fell forward. His arm slammed into the desk. Eyes wide, he glanced between Jack and Jane, but when he looked back to Jack again, his face broke, and he laughed till he was hoarse.

Undecided whether to laugh with him or to get up and leave, Jack settled for a look of bemused curiosity and waited.

Wiping his eyes, guffawing laughter tapering to giggles, Morgan sat straight in the chair and folded his arms on the desk. "That is most honest anyone has been with me in…" He trailed off, looking at the ceiling. Shaking his head, he smiled again. "Years."

"I'm not sure how to feel about that," Jack said.

Morgan stood. "Cream? Sugar?"

"Sugar only, please."

"Miss?"

"No, thank you. Some of those books I read said too much caffeine might not be good for the baby." She shrugged. "I've had mine for today."

That night in the prison was not the night for it, but if he'd stopped to consider what kind of mother Jane would be, Jack wasn't sure he could've guessed. But she was perfect. Not in a perfection sort of way, because if he'd designed the perfect woman, she wouldn't have come out like Jane. Thank god he didn't have access to that kind of equipment. She was better.

"Here you go, Jack," Morgan said, setting a cup before him. "I give the kids Styrofoam, but I'll share the ceramic with you. If nothing else, for that straight answer."

Picking up the cup, Jack sniffed the steam. Bitter yet fragrant coffee. Oils swirled on the top. "This smells fresh. Where'd you get it?"

Morgan sipped his. "I know a guy. They started growing down in South America again. He drives a boat down every few months, picks up all kinds of things."

Sipping the coffee, easily the freshest he'd had in years, Jack grinned at the full flavor resting on the back of his tongue. And the possibilities swirling about with the oils. Commerce? Trade with other continents? Could this shitstorm become whole again? "What does it cost him?"

"What, money?"

Jack nodded.

"No. No money. That's us." He pointed a finger between him and Jack. "That's old world. These people, they don't do money anymore. And I say good riddance."

Smiling, Jack took another sip. Didn't have to wonder where the catch was though. The man threatened his daughter right in front of him, and if Addy hadn't stopped him, he would have executed Matt without a moment's hesitation.

"But we're not here to talk about coffee," Morgan said, setting his cup down. "You have a story to tell me." He interlaced his fingers.

"But I'd like to know some things as well."

"Sure you would. Wouldn't expect anything less from a man like you."

"Where do we start?"

Morgan sat back, coffee in hand. "Why don't we start with the general, work our way out from there?"

"What do you know about her? How long have you been here?"

Morgan shook his head. "You first."

He'd expected as much, but it had been worth a shot. He bit his cheek, forgetting her face. Pushing it behind the frosted glass that had hidden it for so long. "We met when I was seventeen. Got married and had our first, my son, Mike, by the time I was eighteen. The virus hit when he was four, and Addy came a little less than two years later." He grinned, vision cast into the fog of the past. "All that work I did to impress her dad, finish high school online, guess none of it matters so much now." He raised his eyebrows. "Who knew?"

"The dedication to finish school though, young wife like that, says something about the man you became."

One side of Jack's mouth turned up. "Hadn't ever thought about it that way."

Jane chuckled. "I did."

Morgan dropped her a wink. "Considering Jane here sank a knife into the general, seems like you guys aren't on the best of terms anymore. Tell me about that."

Now that he'd started, he'd have to finish. "I thought she was dead. We all did. She went into a sporting goods store with our daughter, only our daughter came out." He took a long, deep swallow of cool coffee. "I saw her bitten. Over and over. Morgan"—he leaned forward—"this was twelve years ago."

Slopping coffee onto his hand, Morgan set the cup down and shook his hand. "That's years before the Cure. Years. You're telling me Talus had the Cure, even then?"

"Some kind of prototype, I guess. Melinda said it wasn't perfect. But I didn't know she was even still alive." He glanced at Jane and Katie. "Not until last year."

Narrowing his eyes, Morgan took in Jane and the baby again. "Now I'll bet that's an interesting story indeed. But it's not what I need to know."

Jack nodded. "What you need to know is, she came to the Molehill after they Cured her. She recovered. She rose in the ranks. I don't know the timeline for all this, I only know that by the time I saw her again, she was operating some kind of experimental hospital-slash-prison on the coast."

"And she trained up some kids to help her. I know that much. I could tell you things about the Molehill that'll curl your nose hairs," Morgan said. "Victoria, the girl who brought you out there, she used to be one of the general's kids. Matt too."

"I know about Matt. He's solid, Morgan. I trust him. Obviously, my daughter does too."

"She doesn't trust me. I see that now. I scared her."

Finishing off his coffee, Jack set the cup on the desk. "Does it have to do with your back room?"

Morgan stood. "Let me give you the nickel tour."

CHAPTER 29

"So, Hux, he says to this Librarian, 'Where can I find books about the genomes sequenced on Roma Europeans?' And the librarian, I swear to you, Addy, he gives him this flat stare and points right over his left shoulder." Mike laughed with his whole body. "I've never seen Hux look so embarrassed. You should've seen it."

The replacement guards opened the gate. Addy walked through and into the yard.

None of the Troupe sat out on the dock.

She chewed her lip and considered who was going to tell them about Kendra.

Matt walked through the gate, latching it behind them. She was honestly still in disbelief that he was whole and alive. The shot had been so close, it'd ruffled his hair.

He glanced up, catching her staring.

Mouth set, lips tight, he stared back with round eyes.

What she wouldn't give to hold him and make sure he was all right.

Celia bumped her shoulder. "This is what you do without us? Play with actors?"

She grinned. "Did you meet them?"

"Not officially." She shrugged. "They seem nice."

Vic breezed by, holding Matt by the arm. "They're animals. Don't let them fool you."

Jealousy, her own, not on Ella's behalf at all, flashed through her like a bolt of lightning. Fighting it, she smiled at Celia. "Come and meet them. Tell me about your trip."

Mike joined them. He slung an arm around Celia's shoulders. Pulling her close, he raised his voice to a falsetto as sickly sweet as one of his suckers. "She likes us, bean. She really likes us."

And then Celia did something Celia never did. Like, ever.

She blushed.

Spiking an elbow in his ribs, she smiled. "Not you. The rest of you." She jerked her chin toward the building. "Even you, Ross."

Dean leaned against the dock. "They do grow on you." He made eye contact with Addy for a millisecond before dropping it. "Guess I'll stay out here."

After living here for more than a month, Addy could get up onto the dock unassisted. "Don't be silly," she said. "Here." Gripping the edge, she scrambled to pull herself up.

A pair of hands gripped her waist and pushed. Mouth open, she stopped. She'd kick him in the face if he thought he could touch her like that. After the shit he put her through.

But it was Matt, still frowning. Thumbs in her back, fingers wrapped around her hip bones.

Even as her stomach lit up, the cork she'd been plugging her heart with popped out and spilled hot blood all over the inside of her chest. She finished her ascent onto the dock and stuck out a hand for him.

He joined her at the top and leaned down with her to catch Dean.

Mike formed the hand cradle for Dean's good foot. "Here, brother. We'll get you inside."

Grumbling about his ankle taking too long to heal, he let Mike push him most of the way and threw one arm to Addy and one to Matt. They pulled him up, and he ended up on his knees on top of the dock. Panting, he sat. "Thanks, y'all. That was probably more trouble than it was worth."

"Here, Cee, let me help you," Mike said.

Although she sassed him and complained, she let him help her up. She gave him a hand up, but as he cleared the top, he overbalanced.

"Crap. Sorry, Cee. Trying to run you over." He righted her.

Crossing her arms, she tried to frown but missed. "Addy," she said, still looking up at Mike, "you wanted to introduce us to these people?"

"Victoria, you know. Come on inside."

Dean wobbled toward the door.

She chewed her lip. May as well try to be an adult about it. And it was a long drop. "Watch the edge, Dean."

Pressing his lips together, he stuck his hand out to hold the wall. "Yeah, knowing the way my last couple weeks have gone, I'd break my neck if I fell."

Waiting in the door, Matt shook his head. "What happened?" He pointed. "Besides your ankle, I mean."

"Lost the train."

Air sucked from her lungs, Addy spun, mouth open and brows knit. "You what? What happened?"

"Blown up. Gone." He grimaced, watching his feet. "Long story."

A thousand questions snuck up behind her lips. What about his things? The tech? The weapons? His picture of Cameron? All the trips they were going to take in that damned train?

Blown away in the smoke from a fire.

Victoria walked down the wall and stuck out her arm. "Come and meet these guys. They'll help you forget about what you lost."

He hooked his arm through hers. "Sure."

Inside, the Troupe lounged in the barroom. Grey and Tal tangled on a couch together, both asleep, and Cassius lay with his legs over the back of another. His head upside-down and inches from the floor, he held a glass cube up to the light, peering through it. Rivers sat at the bar, chatting with Jim.

Cassius held the cube in front of an eye and smiled, the corners of his mouth pointing at the floor. "Addy! Matt! And I see you've brought guests!" Flinging his legs down, he sat. "Your friend Huxley is in the bunks. He wanted some quiet." He laughed. "We can be quite distracting."

Flopping down next to him, Victoria threw her legs in his lap and rested her arm on the back of the couch. "Addy. Dear. I think you should tell them. Before Morgan does."

Matt pulled out the stool next to Rivers and took the drink Jim handed him. "Here. You need this more than me." He held it out.

Addy took a sip. Choking back a cough, she looked at him with wide eyes.

He winked. "Martini. Without the vermouth."

She took another swig of the foul thing. "Grey," she called, "Tal. Need to talk at you, guys."

"We're awake," Grey said. He kissed Tal's forehead.

"Speak for yourself, my dear sir," Tal said, eyes closed.

Grinning, she took the stool Matt had pulled out and sat next to Rivers. "Listen, guys. I haven't been entirely straight with you."

Dean sat on the arm of Cassius's couch.

Mike and Cee leaned against the pool table, behind everyone, Celia gripping a cue.

Even Matt stood ready, without standing ready. The air around them crackled as they prepared to leap into action if she needed defending.

Meeting the eyes of the Troupe, she steeled her abs. "The general is my. Um. My mother."

The silence deafened her. The Troupe had never been this quiet. Not while they were awake.

Rivers leaned into her and laid her head on her shoulder. "Are you expecting us to say something?"

Cassius patted Vic's leg. "Perhaps she expects us to ostracize her and our gentleman who most definitely knew this already."

"I have no doubt that's what the lady expects," Tal said, eyes still closed. "But that is because we were too busy getting ready for the Shrew to tell her."

Throat burning, she glanced at Matt.

"Tell us what?"

Vic gave him a sad grin. "We are all of us outcasts with our own complicated story. Mine, you know. But these fine gentlemen, and lady, have their own to tell."

"As does our Kendra," Grey said, fingers still stroking Tal's hair. "The only thing we care about, my dear Adelaide—"

"We think you know," Tal interrupted.

Addy sipped the gin. It swirled in her head. She leaned against the bar and set the drink down.

Dean stood. "Sorry. What do we know? Somebody want to fill us in?"

Jim leaned over the bar. "Here. Take this." He slid a beer onto the bar.

Limping over, Dean leaned between Addy and Rivers to take it, making eye contact with Addy for as brief a time as he could get away with. But he leaned too close. Close enough for the heat from his body to warm her skin and to catch a whiff of his scent.

"Her allegiance is to us. And ours to her. No matter her past," Cassius said. He laid his head in Vic's lap.

Clearing his throat, Matt snagged the gin from the bar and left the room.

The air in the room relaxed as Celia, Mike, and Dean exhaled. Hands subtly moved away from their weapons. Mike started racking pool balls.

"When was the last time we shot pool, Cee?"

"Had to be on that run to Tucson."

Mike chuckled. "I remember that run."

"Hard to forget. I'll break."

Laughing again, Mike pulled out a sucker and unwrapped it.

Addy grinned at him as he went around the room, offering candy to everyone else. They all took a piece, and he wandered back to the pool table.

Mouth hanging open, Dean stood while they settled in. He crossed his arms, looked like he wanted to speak, and walked away.

Addy faced Jim. It was probably her imagination, but she swore eyes bored into her back. Her neck hairs raised. Decidedly not turning around to face the room again, she asked Jim what he had to eat back there.

Jim walked off to rummage through the cupboards at the end of the bar.

Rivers leaned over. "Is she nice?"

Addy's hand snuck to her neck, rubbing. Replaying the feeling of her throat closing, the air stopping its constant cycle. She stared into space, trying not to eavesdrop as Dean sat down to talk with Grey and Tal.

Rivers bumped her. "Is she?"

"Sorry. Sorry. No. She's not."

She sniffed. "I thought not. But, I had hoped Kendra was doing well."

"We—"

"Miss Cooke, I need you."

Addy spun, heart in her throat.

Matt stood in the door of the hallway, arms crossed.

* * *

Closing the door to their office, with its stacks of chairs and musty couch, Matt spun the lock. He turned to face her, cheeks ruddy once again.

Standing close enough to breathe down his neck, things went through her brain but none of them stopped to settle and become thoughts.

As he gathered her into his arms, shaking, she closed her eyes and hugged him back. So tight, she popped his shoulder. She buried her face in his neck. He was whole and alive, and so was she.

He cupped both sides of her face in his hands. The color that'd risen in his cheeks was even more red in contrast to his incredible blue eyes. She stared into them and flashed on Morgan holding the gun to his temple. The memory racing through her like a painful jolt of electricity, Ella's brains blowing out the side of her head followed on its heels. In such rapid-fire succession it left her weak, Dean taking his last breaths in her arms rushed after that.

Shoving it aside as much as living with it, she let the heat race through her the way fire rushed across a field of dry summer grass. Matt was as much her life raft as she was his, and, like the first time they'd been together, they clutched each other rather than drown.

Grabbing a double fistful of his shirt, she pulled him into a kiss that lit her up like the dawn sky. They never got around to taking their shirts off, and tears wet his shoulder as she pressed into him, clinging to her life raft. Pushing him down onto the couch, his skin so warm on hers, so alive, she put her hands on her hips and let him guide her. Falling into each other and losing the terror of the morning to the past, they at least kept it quiet.

And for the first time, she saw the fire inside as something good. Something pure. Together, their bodies transmuted the fear from raw pain to smoke that could escape into the atmosphere.

When he threw his head back, squeezing his eyes closed and biting the insides of both lips to trap the shout inside, she could hardly contain her own scream of ecstasy. She gripped the underside of his thigh and held on for dear life until she descended to earth again.

Leaning onto his chest, she closed her eyes. "Is that you trembling, or me?"

He put a hand on her back. "No idea."

She breathed into his neck, taking in the scent of sweat mixed with musty couch. It shouldn't have been pleasant, but somehow it was. "I thought he was going to kill you."

His arm tightened around her. "I thought she was. I. I thought I might have to hurt her to keep her from taking you."

Snaking both arms around him, she dug further in. "You said you wouldn't hurt her."

"I'm not going to let her take you, Addy." He wrapped the other arm around her. "Not without a fight."

Mind drifting, she squeezed him. "We should get back out there."

He let her go. "Before you fall asleep."

Standing, stretching her arms, she grinned from under half-open lids. "I do not fall asleep first. I'm always waking you up, telling you it's time to get to our beds." Snagging her pants, she tried to disentangle the legs from the weapons. One of these days, she was going to catch a leg on her machete and get a big rip in the ass or something. That'd be fun to explain.

"What are you going to do about Dean?"

She stopped, one leg on, the other in the air. "What do you mean?"

"What if he's changed his mind? He keeps looking at you."

Good thing she'd practiced all that yoga with Yaz. Otherwise she'd have fallen over. She finished putting on the leg and stood. "He won't. He's not changing his mind."

"I wouldn't be so sure." He stood, buttoning his own pants. "Have you looked at yourself lately?"

Of course now she would lose her balance.

He caught her by the arm, smiling. "He'd be a fool not to change his mind."

"Well, he won't." She chewed her lip, a rock settling into her gut. "And we have to tell these guys about Kendra."

"We should tell them about your sister too. Speaking of babies."

She headed for the door.

Before she got to it, he reached over her shoulder and laid his hand flat against it. "Listen. I know how you feel about him. You're free to do whatever you want. You don't have to feel bad about me, or anything." He leaned close, lips touching her ear. "There's nothing going on here, after all."

The rock in her gut shifted, crawling up her throat. She turned her face to him. "Would you really have hurt her?"

"One thing I can tell you for sure. I'd choose you over her."

She unlocked the door and pulled it open. "I know that's supposed to make me feel better, but—"

"Oh, hey guys," Jim said.

Addy spun.

Hand raised to knock, his eyes flickered behind his aviator glasses.

Matt leaned over her shoulder. "Been there long, Jim?"

He shook his head. "No. Not long. At all. Just walked down here to see if you guys had straightened out your um. Security concerns. Or whatever."

Addy ducked past him. "There's still more to discuss."

* * *

After taking a tour of Morgan's building, the city, and damn near everything this side of the Mississippi, Jack laid his head on the pillow behind him.

The house, a few blocks from the Tree and Morgan's office, stood alone on its own block. Just as Jack liked, surrounded by fences. Morgan said he'd send someone by in the morning to install a proximity alarm.

"I gotta admit," Jane said, perching on the edge of the bed and peeking into the bassinet next to it, "this night of sleep is going to be almost as good as the library." She laid back and threw an arm behind her head. "Better," she said, turning to him, "because you're here with me."

He rolled onto his side, taking in her face. He scooted his hips closer. "We gonna do a session tonight?"

She shook her head. "We've been working really hard, Jack. You're doing amazing." She ran her fingers down his jaw. "When you put your mind to something, you sink your teeth into getting it done. You deserve a break."

Closing his eyes, he focused on her fingers. Delicate bird feet dancing down his jaw. "I couldn't do it without you. You rescue me every day."

Hips shifting, she laid on her side and slid closer. "Just paying you back. I thought I was broken until we ended up on that truck together."

The other side of his mouth lifting, he opened his eyes. Those long lashes, her green eyes like jewels, red hair splayed on the pillow behind her like fire, it couldn't be possible she was still here. What a year.

She lifted her brows. "Jack."

"Jane."

"I need you to kiss me."

Sliding a hand under her hair and cupping the back of her head, he pulled her close and kissed her. When his fist clenched, he relaxed his fingers. When his stomach wanted to fight the tingling running down his backbone, he breathed deep and took in her flowery scent. Her taste. Let the fear be what it was and reminded himself she wasn't going to hurt him.

She threw her leg over him and pulled herself closer, sliding her hand around his waist.

He broke away, closing his eyes.

"You're all right, honey. We can stop."

He nodded, eyes still closed. "I know. Give me a minute."

"I'll give you anything."

Eyes fluttering open, chest full of light, he smiled at her. "Whatever I did to deserve that." Hand resting on her thigh, he frowned. "What do you think we should do here?"

She pushed his hair behind his ear. "Hux seemed excited about the prospect of such a large population. We should give him a chance to do his research. Maybe he can figure out how to fix those people." Her eyes clouded, and the line appeared between her brows. "Those people are like Andrew was."

"She said it was irreversible."

"Maybe she didn't try hard enough."

"Maybe."

"I talked to Hux while we were at the library some. He's a smart guy. Knows a ton about the virus." Grinning, she rested her hand on the side of his neck. "He thinks Mike is the cat's pajamas."

Jack shrugged, her light fingers on his neck sending pleasant chills down his spine. "He is."

"I know. Anyhow. Hux has all kinds of ideas about immunity, and about the vaccine. He knows how Talus and IRF are doing it." She gripped the back of his neck and lowered her voice. "He says they're doing it wrong."

The chills raised goose bumps. "What do you mean?"

"I don't know, exactly. He's hard to follow sometimes. Something about methodology. But we should get Morgan to find him a lab, or something."

"I'd like to find out more about Morgan and how things run around here."

She smiled, eyes lighting up again. "That'd be good for you."

For the first time since the village, he considered what it would be like. Getting involved again. It hadn't worked out so well before.

Well, he'd gotten Jane out of the deal. So it hadn't been all bad.

Still.

"I'm just gonna hang around. See how it goes."

Exhaling through her nose, she dropped her eyes to a spot on his chest. "Not that I want to bring this up, but."

"But." The pit in his stomach came out of nowhere, pressing into his lower intestines.

"Why did you stop me? I had a shot."

"You know why, Jane."

She traced her finger over the spot on his chest where her eyes remained. "I guess." Meeting his eyes again, she cupped his jaw. "Remember that dream I had?"

He blinked. Dream?

"In Magnolia. About her taking you away."

Glancing at the window, he found the sunset had given way to dark. Casting his memory back to a night when she'd woken him fighting with the covers, he pulled in a deep breath. "You said I was bleeding from the ear. I remember."

"She almost did. I won't let her finish the job, Jack. I won't. And Addy." The frown pulled her whole face into a grimace, lines deep around her mouth. "She couldn't breathe. Did you see that? Was she trying to take her, or kill her?"

Swallowing around the lump in his throat, heart racing along without him, he considered the scene they'd come upon. Matt, trying to get a good line of fire, unable to aim with Addy in the way. Addy, struggling but sagging. Gagging from deep in her throat.

Cold nothingness on Melinda's face.

He sighed. "I have no idea. I don't know the woman she's become."

"But you still don't want me to kill her. Why?"

"You're not going to take I don't know for an answer, are you?"

Silence.

"She's still their mom. She's still the woman I spent twenty years with. Even if she's not, she is." His eyes stung. "Even after what she did to me. I can't forgive her, but I can't wish her dead either."

"And after what she's done to countless others? To Andrew? To me?"

Leaning his forehead into hers, he closed his eyes. "I can't make any more sense of it for you than that. I wish I knew."

"You can ask me not to kill her. But don't get me in front of her again. I'll give you anything. Anything."

He opened his eyes and tried to focus on hers. They were too close, and green filled his vision. "But?"

"But don't make me make promises I won't be able to keep."

"I—"

Katherine shifted, giving a small cry.

Jane stiffened, turning away from him and looking over her shoulder.

The baby kicked her legs, bassinet wobbling an inch or two, and stilled. She inhaled and exhaled what had to be more air than her tiny lungs could hold, and stilled again.

Leg still draped over him, Jane twisted and sat up on her elbow. After staring into the bassinet, she whispered over her shoulder. "She's asleep." She laid back down. "That was close."

In an effort to desert their previous conversation, he grinned. Sneaking his hand down her leg, he brushed his fingertips along the back side of her knee.

She giggled. "Stop. You know I'm ticklish."

Still grinning, he brushed the back of her knee again. "I know."

She laughed and squirmed. Giggling, she told him to stop.

"Ssshh. You're going to wake the baby," he said, tickling harder.

Sliding her leg farther around him, she gripped his hand and pulled it around her waist. Flattening her mouth to a straight line, she stared at him with dancing eyes. "Stop."

Before he had a chance to think about it, he rushed through the nervous butterflies dancing in his stomach and kissed her, drawing her as close as he could get her.

She lit up like a Christmas tree, turning everything up to eleven, and kissed him back like she never had.

But she didn't make him do anything he didn't suggest, anything he didn't ask for, and in the end, they went to sleep holding each other, still mostly dressed. Mostly.

CHAPTER 30

"One week closer to curtain-up for *The Tempest*," Cassius said, sweeping across the Tree's small stage.

The Troupe bounced around the room, settling into their morning rehearsal. They'd set opening night for the first week in June, giving them about five more weeks to get prepped.

In the dark, against the back wall, Addy and Matt sat shoulder to shoulder.

Matt leaned over. "Did he ask you again today if you wanted to be in it?"

She grinned. "Like every day. 'You'd make a great Miranda,' he says." Head leaned against the wall, she rolled it back and forth. "But makes no mention of the fact I have no idea how to act. I can't even lie properly."

"That's true. You're an awful liar." He chuckled.

"You're supposed to compliment me, jackass," she said, elbow snaking into his ribs.

She glanced out the open bay door. Outside, the clouds billowed, the humidity stifling. Every day this week, it built and built and built until the afternoon when it…just…stopped. Maybe a sprinkle, but usually nothing at all. She hoped it would eventually break into rain and cool down the air.

She swiped at her forehead. "This heat is something else."

"Easier to handle with less clothes on."

Over here where the stage lights didn't reach, Addy didn't think he could see her blush. "While that is strictly true, now is probably not the time."

"You never told me what Tim did to make you so upset at me."

Lifting her head off the wall, forehead tight, she gaped. "Why bring that up?"

He drew his knees up and rested his forearm on his knee. "You almost took my head off for stuff he did. And something tells me it's relevant to your mom. Thought I'd bring it up before we see her again."

Addy leaned back again. "Makes you think we're going to see her again?"

"Gut feeling."

"Me too." She gave him the quick and dirty version of how they got to the East Coast. Breezing over her time on the train with Dean without pretending it didn't happen, she focused on her missteps with both Tim and Dean.

"It was silly of me to trust Tim. Especially because Dean. Well."

"He lied for the right reasons."

She rolled her head to look at him. "You know something about that."

"I do." He met her eyes. "I do. Look. I'm sorry. I spent a lot of time lying. The whole time I was with Ella, I lied to everyone. There was a lot of time I was the good little soldier the general wanted me to be."

"What changed?"

"I met you." He lifted his eyes again. "The first time I came clean with anyone was in your kitchen. When you forced me to tell the truth, and I finally did." He smiled at the ceiling. "Do you have any idea what that felt like? Letting the lies go?"

Although he wasn't looking at her, she shook her head. "No. I don't. I don't know what it's like to live like that. I don't understand why you'd choose to."

He shrugged. "It's hard to say." Half his mouth turned up, one tiny dimple in his cheek. "I lied to Ella all the time. All the fucking time."

"Why?" She cleared her throat. "Didn't you love her?"

Hand still draped over his knee, he clenched his fist and forced a breath out through his nostrils. "More than I can explain." The edge of his eye glistened in the dim light.

She stared at the wall and conjured Yasuo. "Here's an idea then."

"Shoot."

"What Yaz told me is called a living amends. You can't apologize to her. She's gone."

He loosened and clenched his fist, working his jaw.

"You can't undo all the lies you told her, or Burke, or any of them. But"—she laid a hand on his arm—"you can stop now. You don't have to do it anymore. Right here and now, you never tell another lie. That's how you make it up to them."

The dimple in his cheek appeared again, and a tear escaped, rolling down the side of his face. "What do they care? They're not here to give a shit."

"*I* give a shit. Remember?" She slid her hand over his arm and touched his chest. "And you care. Right in here. You care."

With the other hand, he wiped the side of his face. "Jesus, woman. What are you trying to do to me?" He stood, holding a hand out for her.

She took it and stood, rocking on her toes. "You chose to be in that kitchen, you know."

He laughed. "How do you figure?"

"You thought you could follow us and get away with it, and when we found you out like you knew we would, you tried to escape by going through me." She put a hand on her hip, the memory of a fistful of hair in her hand as he tried to run overcoming her. She smiled. "I'm no pushover, Matthew Lyburn. You knew that."

He glanced at the stage and slid one arm around her waist. "Watch what you call me, Houlihan."

"Houlihan?" Her brow wrinkled. "What's that?"

He glanced at the stage again and tugged her closer. "Buddy of mine used to be obsessed with old pop culture. Talked endlessly about this army show. Lady named Hot Lips Houlihan." He fixed his eyes to her mouth. "You say my name with those hot lips of yours, drives a man crazy."

She stepped into him. "Oh, I know it does."

The arm around her tightened.

The radio blipped. "*Team Tree, come in.*"

He released her and stepped back. With a grin, he spoke into it. "Yeah, this is us. What do you got, Pax?"

"*Looks like you're getting new neighbors.*"

Matt asked him what he meant.

"I'll walk 'em down, here in a few. Meet you at the gate."

* * *

Jack stood before the rack of unique weapons in Morgan's armory. "It's been at least a decade since I've seen someone use nunchucks."

"Nunchaku."

He ran a finger along the shaft of a spear. "Those." He picked up a short sword, built for someone like a gladiator.

"Pretty impractical against a gun," Morgan said, back to him.

"Not great against 'Heads either," Jack said, settling the sword back in place. It'd get the job done, but he'd also look ridiculous with a short sword stuck in his belt. The machete had always done well for him, and it was multipurpose. He picked a new one from the rack of them and checked the cutting edge.

"Be surprised what some people pick up." Kneeling in front of an ammo box, Morgan spun on a heel. "Your daughter, for example, fell in love with a compound bow I had."

"She's always liked bows. She prefers ranged fighting to melee."

Morgan snorted. "Played D&D, didn't you?"

"Shit yes. Damn," Jack said, joining Morgan, "I miss that game. You?"

Closing and latching the box, Morgan slid it under the rack of handguns. Sliding two speed loaders for his revolver into pouches on his belt, he nodded. "I do. Chess is more my game these days though."

"With Melinda right next door, you'd need to be pretty good at it."

"Read your Sun Tzu?"

"Not in a lot of years."

They left the armory. Morgan latched the door behind them and turned left. "I'll let you borrow my copy. If you're gonna be my right hand, you should sharpen up on it."

"About that," Jack said, following him down the dark hall, "I hope you don't expect me to talk to the council for you."

Morgan chuckled. "No. That's what Paxton is for. He goes to church with a bunch of those people. He's a good diplomat. And they like him." He paused, one hand on the doorknob. "You don't look any better at diplomacy than I am."

One side of Jack's mouth lifted, and he thought back to Wade and that classroom. So very, very long ago. He thought he'd won that one, that he had the upper hand. He'd thought he was being smart, not trusting Wade. "It's not my forte." Taking in the old, black barber chairs in the room at the end of the hall, the plastic on some cracking, he put his hands on his hips. "This is where you scared Addy, right?"

"Yeah." Morgan met his eyes. "I meant to intimidate her. And that kid. I don't believe in keeping people in line with fear, but they also need to know who not to fuck with."

"Can't argue that."

Well I could. But I won't.

"I had one of Talus's guys here. Trying to get some info out of him. But he either wouldn't or couldn't talk."

Jack sat in one of the barber chairs, a rusty stain underneath it. So light, you could miss it, and the smell of pine disinfectant hung thick in the air, but it was there. Old blood, long scrubbed away. "What happened to him?"

Morgan shrugged. "So this doctor of yours."

"Huxley."

"He worked for IRF? I have to admit, I haven't dealt much with them. Are they like Talus?" He sat, leaning on an arm.

"I think so. At first, they seemed kinda like the good guys, but at this point, I don't think there are any."

Morgan stroked his short beard. "What about us?"

"What, good guys?"

He nodded.

With a smile, Jack shook his head. "I don't think there are good guys, Morgan. There's right, and there's wrong, but we all do a little of both, don't we?"

Morgan laughed, mouth wide. "You're a sharp one, Jack Cooke. I'll give you that. But, we were talking about your doctor."

"Well, he's not my doctor—"

"You said he wanted a lab and to run some tests. On the children. Given that these are noninvasive blood tests he'd like to run, I see no problem with it." He stuck a finger in the air. "As a bonus, I found him a lab not far from the Tree."

"So everyone is here, on this side of town? That's nice. I like that." Jack leaned back. Not that he wanted to have a showdown with this man, they could work well together, but there were things needing to be said. "We ought to have an understanding before we move forward though."

Morgan dipped his chin, a signal to go on.

"If you ever threaten any of my people again, it'll be the last thing you do."

Leaning forward so fast the chair rocked, Morgan's brow drew over his eyes. "If they threaten this city, I'll kill them and then you."

Jack copied Morgan's laugh. "As long as we have that understanding, I think we're good."

Morgan stood. "Here. Let me take you up front, explain the quadrants, get you up to speed on the staff. And what I expect of them all." He stopped, hand on the doorknob. "Tell me something."

"If I can."

"Given your history with the general, what do you hope to accomplish here? Why did you come to my city?"

Brow creased, Jack opened his mouth.

"I gave you a week to think about this answer. I hope you were considering it while you settled in here."

Eyes glazed, he wandered back to the barber chairs and sat. "I have. I've wondered why I'd choose to be this close to that woman."

"Your breakup wasn't amicable, I assume."

Jack exhaled a humorless laugh. "Understatement." He stared at the wall, looking into the distance beyond it. "We came here for Huxley, so he could do these tests. Immunity is something we should all concern ourselves with."

Morgan leaned against the door and crossed his arms and ankles. "It does concern all of us."

"More than that." Jack stopped. He didn't want to lie to the man, not when they were just starting out. But at the same time, what did he need to know? Before Morgan prodded him, he went on. "We lost Melinda when the kids were young. After that, we stayed together. All of us. Me and the kids, Jane and her parents. Usually Celia." He shrugged. "I don't like being away from them, if I'm telling the truth." He stood. "So yeah. It's about the virus. Isn't fucking everything? But it's also about my family." He crossed the room again, folding his arms over his chest. "They're my weakness. But they're also my strength."

Morgan stroked his beard again. "I guess the better question is, what is Addy doing here?"

* * *

Leaning against the fence on opposite sides of the gate, waiting for the morning shower that wouldn't come, Addy and Matt stood silent as Pax approached with a group of people. As they neared, they resolved into most of Addy's family, save her dad.

And, of course, Dean was with them.

Clenching her teeth, she exhaled through them.

Matt dropped his voice to a whisper. "You all right?"

"I think it was always going to be too soon to see him," she said, watching the group approach. "But it's too soon."

"Want me to punch him?"

"If he needs punching, I can handle it."

He stepped closer, leaning on the gate with a smile. "Don't punch him, Addy."

The group approached, almost within earshot. She leaned in. "Why not?"

"It won't make you feel any better. I may. But you won't."

Crossing her arms, she jerked her chin. "Open the gate. Don't be so sure."

He opened the gate. "Paxton. People. What's up?"

Pax shook. "Can one of you come with me? I know it's an unusual ask, but it won't take long. And I want you to know where your people will be." He nodded at Addy. "Also your dad asked I show one of you to the lab. It's about a block away."

Raising a brow, Addy stepped through the gate. "Stay here with these guys, Matthew. I'll be back in two shakes."

He coughed, color rising in his cheeks. "Whatever that means." He closed the gate and leaned on it. "Be safe."

Throwing a wink at him, she fell into step next to Jane. "Are you gonna hang in the lab with these guys?"

Jane rubbed the baby's back. "With my shoulder, I'm not as mobile a fighter as I used to be. And Huxley says he'll teach me to draw blood." She grinned, showing all her teeth. "Sounds like a blast."

Hux cleared his throat. "Blood is. Ahem. Well."

Addy stopped. "Huxley. You're afraid of blood?"

"Not when it is. Ah. In vials in my lab, no. But I'm afraid it. Ah." Over and over, he flattened the front of his shirt, running his hand down the buttons.

A warm wave rode down from the crown of Addy's head and washed through her chest. Before she thought about it, she wrapped Hux in a hug. "You mean to tell me you stitched Dean up, even though you're afraid of blood?" She glanced at Dean and grimaced. "Even I hadn't seen that much blood before."

Hux ran a hand over his neck. "You did threaten to slit my throat if I did not comply. You are a difficult woman to say no to."

Dean let out a barking laugh. "You did what?"

"I did. I threatened to slit his throat and leave him for the 'Heads if he didn't stitch you up." She crossed her arms and her jaw creaked inside her head. "I was desperate."

"So yeah. I'm gonna learn lab assisting," Jane said, one hand on Addy's crossed arm.

Celia joined her on her other side. "They roped me into security." Laughing, she waved her broken arm. "Can't let anything happen to the little bunnies."

"I am not a bunny," Mike said, one hand on his hip. "I hate carrots."

"You guys are more fun than a tennis match," Paxton said, eyes flicking between them all.

Addy frowned. "Where's this lab, Pax? I didn't know there was much down here."

The derelict apartment crossed her mind.

Dad's voice tried to pop up and remind her a lie of omission was still a lie, but she told him to stuff it. She could either stop lying or keep sleeping with Matt, but she couldn't do both.

She started walking again. "But Jane. Are you sure? I thought you hated all this stuff."

"I do. But if we're going to be doing it, I'm gonna make sure we're doing it right. Besides"—she smiled, showing all her teeth again—"I like learning new things. And it seems easier than cooking."

And the silent man walking at the end, arms crossed. Did she ask him what he was doing? Pretend she didn't feel his eyes on her? Bonus reason to never date people. Breakups had to be the worst torture ever devised by man.

"Addy," he said, leaning around Celia. "Morgan asked me to come by the Tree later. He's got me working with the cell team. Says their communications are a bit of a mess."

She shook her head. "I've never understood that. They've got everything here, but they can't get phones working? It can't be that hard if you can—" She stopped, sucking a breath through her teeth. "Um. Sorry. I mean."

He shuffled a foot. "It's cool."

Jesus, Addy. Want some salt to go with that foot in your mouth?

Mouth shut, she walked between Celia and Jane and followed Paxton down the block. He stopped after they rounded the corner, out of sight of the Tree.

"Ladies, gentlemen, welcome to our lab facilities." He unlocked and opened the door to a building that, in truth, didn't look much different from the rest of them. Run-down, dirty glass, some of the bricks lying in the street.

Mike waved everyone in. "Looks like we've got our work cut out for us."

Celia stayed behind, ushering everyone in with him and checking the street. "At least it's quiet."

Addy walked in and waited in the shadows behind the door. Neither of them noticed her waiting there.

Grinning, Celia met Mike's eyes. "Get your ass in there too, pretty boy."

Backing through the door, he stopped. "You keep calling me that, it's gonna go to my head, Cee."

"Maybe it should." She looked out at the street again, poking him in the chest with one finger and pushing him through the door.

He held a sucker up between them. "Got your favorite flavor."

She took it, never breaking eye contact from under her heavy lids. "Thanks. You're OK, Michael Cooke."

"I'll remember you said that."

She gripped his shoulder, spun him around, and pushed him down the hall.

Standing behind the door, Addy considered how she'd escape without being found out. Given that the hallway was a straight shot with thin light and no doors, a clean getaway was unlikely.

Rather than delay the inevitable, she closed the door behind them as Mike ambled after everyone else.

Celia's hand flew to her knife. Eyes wide, she popped the sucker from her mouth. "What."

Addy lifted both hands. "Didn't say a word." But she grinned and pointed a finger. "What was that?"

"Nothing." Celia jammed the sucker back into her mouth and stalked down the hallway.

Catching up to her, Addy leaned over. "I've seen a lot of nothing lately. I know what it looks like."

Celia stopped and put a hand on her hip. "Bet you have, Adelaide Cooke. Bet you have." Slow grin crossing her lips, she leaned in. "Pretty sure I'm the only one who noticed. But Dean won't be far behind, you don't tone it down a little."

Crossing her arms, Addy started down the hall again. "I'm sure I have no idea what you mean."

"So this conversation never happened."

"What conversation."

Celia laughed under her breath. "I would have missed you people."

They walked into a room filled with equipment under plastic sheeting, and Addy stopped. "Were you going to leave us?"

She shrugged. "We found my family. I thought about it."

"Dad mentioned that. Why didn't you?"

She glanced at Mike. "Sometimes the family you choose is better than the family you were born with." One side of her mouth turned up. "Not that that's true in this case, but sometimes."

Laughing, Addy bumped her shoulder and wandered farther into the room. "Paxton? Where did this stuff come from?"

Pulling the golden cross from under his collar and fingering it, he looked around the room. "We had some people before. Researchers, like Huxley. There was an accident."

Hux lifted one of the plastic sheets and folded it away from a bank of microscopes. "Exposure?"

Kissing the cross, Pax hid it under his shirt again. "Yeah. It was a rough time. Let me know if the computers still work."

"I'll have some specifications for programs," Hux said, pointing to computers hiding under more translucent plastic. "Michael can help you."

Addy shuffled to Jane and squeezed her arm. "I gotta get back."

"Matt's got them, right?"

Addy smiled. "They're like a herd of cats. You can't watch them all by yourself. Not for more than a few minutes. Come see me though."

Jane pointed a finger gun and clicked her tongue. "Don't do anything I wouldn't."

"So, pretty much everything."

Scoffing, Jane sat and unwrapped the baby.

"Addy?"

Stomach in her toes, Addy faced him. "Yeah, Dean."

"Let me walk you back."

"I can watch after myself for a block," she said, headed for the door.

"Please?"

Stopping, she closed her eyes. "Fine."

CHAPTER 31

"Addy, wait."

For whatever reason, she stopped in the middle of the street and waited for Dean to catch up. When he did, she set off toward the Tree again. He hadn't said why he wanted to walk with her, she hadn't asked, and as far as she was concerned, they didn't have to speak the whole way.

But he apparently had different ideas.

"Hey, slow down. Can I. Addy." He touched her elbow.

She stopped again, arms crossed over her belly so tight, her midsection had gone numb. She lifted a brow.

"I think we got off on the wrong foot."

"How's that?"

He reached out to touch her arm, glanced at his hand, and lowered it. "I'm sorry. I know I hurt you. I'm—"

"You're sorry. Got it." She took a step.

He did touch her arm. "It looks like we have to work together some, with what Morgan needs on the phones. I'll be out of your hair as quick as I can, OK?"

"Good. Sounds good." She took another step and stopped. Matt said not to punch him, but she didn't see how she wouldn't feel better if she did. Balling a fist inside her elbow, she frowned. "I hope you don't expect me to apologize. I didn't do anything wrong."

"That's a matter of debate."

"I fail to understand how saving your life was a mistake. I'm a little sorry I did, but still."

He laughed without humor. "We have to see each other. I'll make it as brief as I can. Is that all right? Can we do that?"

Continuing to hold on to the anger was not something Yaz would have advised, if he'd had advice to offer about this. She reminded herself, again, Matt told her not to punch him.

She bobbed her head once, eyes narrowed. "We can do that."

He smiled, but it didn't make it to his eyes.

They started walking again. In an effort to avoid silence, she looked up at the clear sky. "Seems like the rain has been thin lately."

"I heard some of the guys talking about that. They're talking about having to haul water in if it doesn't get better."

Considering the logistics of getting water to the entire community without rain, Addy fell into introspection. As the Tree inched closer, she fought her slowing feet, stomach roiling. "I'm sorry about your train. Did you lose everything?"

"I've still got my boots. So, not everything, I guess."

She chuckled. "Good thing. I'd hardly know you without your boots."

"What's this city like?"

"Big. Smelly. But interesting. Some of the people are really cool."

"This Troupe? They good people?"

"Oh, Dean, they're the best people," she said, her smile so wide it stretched her cheeks to both ears.

"Anything I should know?"

Brow wrinkled, her smile faded. She stopped again and put a hand on his arm. "Some of the defense people are entitled assholes. Be careful who you trust."

Dean folded his arms. "Did someone hurt you? Do I need to have a talk with anyone?"

Her inane stomach fluttered at his concern. The way he puffed up trying to protect her honor.

Shoving the butterflies down with a swallow, she shook her head. "It's more complicated than that." She glanced at the Tree.

Matt stood at the gate, hand on it, watching them through the fence.

Her cheeks tingled. "I don't need you to protect me." She stepped back. "I can do it myself. And you don't want the job anyway. Remember?"

"Sorry. You're right. Habit. I'm sorry."

"If I have to hear you say you're sorry one more time, I'll. I just." She cleared her throat. "Stop." She tried to cover the last half block to the Tree in as few steps as possible.

And though she again felt his eyes on her back, he didn't follow, or call her. Or try to get her to come back.

He most certainly did not try to change his mind.

Matt opened the gate for her, staring over her shoulder. "Everything OK?"

Laughing without humor, she blinked six or seven times. "No. Yes. Whatever." Matt closed the gate and peeked through it.

Dean headed back the way they came.

Matt's mouth hung half-open like he wanted to ask her about it. But he didn't.

She folded her arms. "I'll tell you later."

* * *

Side still sore, Melinda sat on her couch and stared at the ceiling.

The clock on the wall ticked.

2 a.m.

It had been a week since she'd been kicked off immunity. Again.

That fool Cormac was probably screwing up her timeline. It was time to give the live virus to the first two, to make sure the vaccine did its job. They were ahead of the schedule on which Jane had been bitten, but she wanted to accelerate it a touch. That way, if she had to start over, it would be less time wasted.

And there were four from the next group ready for implantation. It had to be done in the next forty-eight hours, or they'd have to wait another damn month.

Her side twinged.

Looking down at her hands, she found they'd balled themselves into tight fists.

She loosened her fingers and pried her nails from her palms. She'd drawn blood in one spot, and the rest would be discolored for a few minutes as the blood rushed into the half-moons crossing her life lines.

With a loud sigh, she laid her head back and looked at the ceiling again. It would have been nice if she were lying, warm and cuddly, in Ilasha's bed. Staring up at her ceiling. Maybe even worn out and sweating. At least then she'd have some kind of brief satisfaction. And Lash could tell her she was all right.

Tell her it didn't matter her whole family thought she was a monster. Tell her it didn't matter her own daughter couldn't speak to her. Tell her none of it mattered.

She cracked her neck and stepped into the kitchen to dig her flashlight out of the junk drawer, one of those giant old flashlights that took three D cell batteries and doubled as a nightstick if need be. She snagged her hoodie from next to the door and pulled it over her head. Her side protested. She used the pain to focus her anger and yanked the door open.

Listening, as she'd taught her little girl to do all those years ago, she stood in the doorjamb. No feet shuffled. No voices bounced down the hall. Only every other light shone, dimmed for night hours. She clicked on the flashlight and crept next to the wall.

When she reached Lash's door, she stood in a shadow, flashlight off.

Lash had said there were things Anthony kept from even her. Did Melinda want to get her involved? What if Anthony caught them in his office, snooping around? Melinda could handle herself, and no doubt Lash could too, but if something happened to her, it'd be Melinda's own fault for bringing her into it.

She tiptoed away, leaving the light off. "I won't be responsible for someone I love getting hurt. Not again," she whispered, flashlight pressed into her abdomen. Her lung screamed.

Once she turned a corner, she clicked the light on and made her way to Anthony's office.

The outer office wasn't locked, but when she squeezed through the door and closed it, she turned the lock. It made a small squeak, nothing more. On tenterhooks, she crossed the office to Anthony's door.

Closed, latched, and locked tight.

"Damn." She shone the light around the room. Would Lash have a key? And if so, would she keep it in here? Or on her?

She crossed to Lash's desk and leaned the flashlight against her "in" tray. She sat, chair squeaking, and started opening drawers.

The middle top drawer gave her nothing but pens and notepaper and paper clips. A few random pieces of broken-off stapler reloads. The side top drawer was all papers, none of which said anything interesting, and some candy buried in the back.

Mike crossed her mind, wandering through as he would, his eight-year-old self offering her chocolate. He gave his sister suckers, but he always offered his mom chocolate. Her blue-eyed boy.

Traitor.

Digging through the second drawer, she found a few index cards that could be of interest, but her lung hurt and her eyelids drooped. At this point, it had to be approaching three.

No key.

The third drawer—

Was locked. Dammit.

She snagged one of the paper clips out of the top drawer and contorted it until she could fit it into the bottom drawer lock. She hadn't practiced picking a lock in years, hadn't even learned until about a year into the apocalypse, but it was like riding a bike. She worked the clip until the lock clicked open.

In the drawer, she found several files. Pushing past them, she swiped at the bottom. Metal clinked. She grabbed for the key, but it squirted from her fingers.

"Damn."

She aimed the flashlight beam in the drawer and tried to spot the shiny.

Wait.

The tab of each file showed a neatly typed name. Four tabs held the last name "Cooke," one of them crisp, new manila. Slim.

Below that, one marked "Doe" and one marked "Known Associates." In that file, she'd no doubt find Dean and Celia. And dead Andrew.

The face of Jack's friend as he swept them across the roof filling her mind, she plucked the file from under the rest. She considered reading it, seeing what she could discover about the man who'd saved her life. Even though she'd effectively killed him when she injected him with the mutated virus. On the island, she'd always done each one herself. At least no one else would have to—

But before she opened it, she glanced into the drawer again. Beneath the file of the "known associates" hid another. The paper worn and tattered. "M. Thibodeaux," it read.

Breath caught in her throat, she fingered the name tab. What could be hidden in here? What were any of these files? Why did Lash keep them in a locked drawer? What did she know that Melinda didn't?

Should she ask her about it?

Stuffing the "known associates" file back where she'd gotten it, she plucked the key ring from the drawer, closed it, and snagged the light. Marching to Anthony's door, she buried the files deep in her brain and let it simmer. If she ought to confront Lash about it, she'd figure it out later. Right now, the important thing was getting in Anthony's office.

Fitting the key in the door, she turned.

The lock tumbled with an easy click. Sucking her stomach in, she slipped through the inch of space she gave herself.

Even empty and in the dead of night, the office held an air of intimidating breath. The smell of Anthony, aftershave mixed with vodka sweat, hung in the room.

Slinking to the file cabinets, she tried all the drawers. Locked, all the way down.

She tried the small key on the key ring with the door key. The lock squealed as it turned.

Eyes closed, she finished the turn and stopped. Listening, she waited for someone to come through the door and ask what she was doing, dead of night, with a flashlight, in a locked office? Saying she was looking for the bathroom wouldn't fly.

But no one came.

Yanking open the drawers one by one, she skimmed file tabs. Uncertain what she was looking for, she stopped when she found one labeled "December '41." It didn't have the same markings so many of them had downstairs. The "TC" she'd seen all over the file room indicating Talus Crest files. The date was handwritten, in Anthony's childish scrawl. Its label held nothing to indicate what it was, but looking at the date set Melinda's heart racing. December was six months ago and she was in Magnolia. With Burke.

Sitting in the floor, she opened the file and spilled light onto the pages.

A transcript of a conversation.

Between Anthony.

And Burke.

Wind knocked out of her, like a hard punch to the diaphragm, she leaned over the paper.

Burke: Look, the vaccine research is going well. She's making headway.
Anthony: What has she told you?
Burke: Surprisingly little. Your little bitch is crafty.
Anthony: I warned you. Don't say I didn't. But she goes after this virus like a rabid dog. Let her keep using your facilities.
Burke: When should I give you another update?
Anthony: Enjoy the holiday with Ella. Call me if Melinda tells you anything. Otherwise, I'll talk to you again in January after the baby's born.

Heart hammering her ribs, she read over the rest of the file. More conversations, much like this one. Sometimes, they talked about the vaccine. Sometimes, Anthony asked about Ella, sometimes he didn't.

What he asked most about was Melinda. What she was doing. What she was telling him. How much she knew. The work she was doing. And questions about her family that, even though she hated the treacherous bunch of them, made her blood boil. Anthony wondering if her ties to them could be exploited.

That son of a bitch. Anthony was no surprise. Dependable dick, after all.

But Burke had, at one point, said he loved her. Yeah, it'd been after sex. Most men felt all lovey after sex. But still.

Slick knots working their way into her stomach, she closed the file and replaced it in the drawer. Her eyes had fallen out of focus, and getting them to settle back in wasn't working. She closed up the drawers, locked everything, and left.

* * *

Arms crossed, elbow resting atop one of them, Jack cradled his chin in his hand and stared at the map on Morgan's wall. "Tell me again about the security around the Molehill."

"We're not going to break in there, Jack. Not with the resources we have."

He joined Morgan at the desk. His coffee had gone cold. Swallowing a tepid mouthful, he grimaced. "Why not? Don't we have the armament?"

"Guns, ammo. Yeah. Need more explosives." He shook his head. "No, Jack, it's the men. The defense force is sound. Robust, even. But I can't take them all and go fight a war." He lifted his hands. "Who would defend the city? We don't have to worry about 'Heads the way we did three, five, ten years ago, but it's not like they've disappeared. What if a horde came while we were gone?"

Jack frowned. "Yeah. And you can't guarantee Talus or IRF or even someone we don't know about wouldn't see an opening and exploit it. You're right."

Sitting back in their chairs, they shared a silence. Interesting how he'd just met Morgan and already it was like they'd known each other for years. Once Jack resigned himself to becoming part of all this again, working with Morgan came as easy as greased ball bearings on a hot tin rail. He found the man smart, crafty, and personable.

"Jack," Morgan said, taking his cup to refill it, "tell me about the general. What is she doing up there?"

He lifted his lip. "That's two different questions."

"You spent a lot of time with the woman. What can you tell me about her I don't already know?"

Jack's mind stuttered. With alarming clarity, he saw her face as she raped him. A grotesque parody of itself from all their years together and the love that'd passed between them.

Palms sweaty, he cleared his throat and took the full cup as Morgan sat. Lowering it to the desk before his hand shook, he wiped his hand on his leg and took a breath. Tried to let the memory pass through. But it was more like trying to breathe underwater.

Morgan sat forward. "What? Did I say something wrong?"

"No. She's, uh. You know, I've thought a lot about this in the last year." He shook his head. "The girl I met, she was confident. Knew what she wanted. She was kind, and beautiful, and driven. But, and this is one thing that's always been true about her, when she didn't get what she wanted, she was a sight to behold." Grinning, he took a drink of the coffee. Burned off a layer of tongue. "I wouldn't have said this before. Blinded by love and all that."

Morgan blew across the top of his own steaming cup.

"But she was scary. Her ability to seek out and conquer what she wants is eclipsed only by her ability to be a ruthless bitch in order to get it." His lips turned up in a real smile, one that reached his eyes. "Let me tell you, that was incredibly helpful once the world went to shit. She kept me and the kids alive with that attitude."

Morgan stroked his chin, smoothing his beard. He sipped his coffee. "What's she after now?"

"Immunity."

"Like your daughter? The little one?"

He nodded. "She thinks she created it. Immunity. She experimented on Jane, before we knew she was pregnant. Gave her the vaccine."

"I'd heard they developed a vaccine." Morgan's eyes flashed. "Is it effective?"

"Worked for Jane. She was bitten, when she was about six months pregnant or so. Obviously she and the baby survived."

"That must've been scary for you."

"Fucking terrifying, yeah."

"Not to get sidetracked, but I feel like I should ask you about her."

Jack replaced the terror that'd tried to take over his heart with a warm rush of endorphins. "Ah, hell, Morgan. You and I both know in the old world, the way it used to be, she would've been too young for me. But she's not only a lot older than she looks, she's my everything. I can't tell you how many times she's saved me. Still is." He laughed. "And we've got a lot more in common than you might think."

"If you don't mind me saying, I think you're pretty lucky. She seems one of a kind." He smiled, lines beside his mouth running deep.

"What can I say. I have a knack."

Morgan barked a laugh. "I hear Jane's going to work in the lab? What is it your doctor hopes to accomplish that the general has missed?"

"Melinda wants to Cure the world. She thinks she created immunity, and the depths to which she'll sink to continue that research are"—he swallowed—"low. Lower than I can go into."

"Like forcing women to carry babies they didn't ask for."

Jack took a sip of coffee instead of puking. Its bitter taste matched the acid crawling up from his stomach, burning the inside of his esophagus. He considered telling Morgan those babies were likely his.

One of the way stations on that road was covering how Melinda got the samples in the first place. He could gloss it over, but even bringing it up was so unpleasant, his stomach still clenched. He wasn't there yet.

"Yeah, that. Also, whatever it is she does with the people she mutates into half 'Head. Huxley seems to think they're incubating the virus. Using a mutated version to create the vaccine."

Morgan flinched. "I'm gonna be sick. That's awful." He wiped his mouth. "Good god. These people." Lips pinched, he opened a drawer in his desk and pulled out an old-fashioned Rolodex. He flicked through the cards and shook his head. "We should get a plan together. I know a few guys in Florida who can send some men." He glanced at Jack. "Might send you out to Tennessee. One of my friends out there has a cannon. And more men."

Jack's brow creased. He wanted to help, but he'd never take Jane and the baby on an errand like that.

But Morgan beat him to the punch. "They'll need finessing. May be able to get some explosives from them, too, if your tongue is silver enough." He grunted. "May need to go myself..." He trailed off and muttered to himself, standing and pacing over to the map.

The glass in the front door rattled with a light knock.

Jack tensed to stand.

"Sit," Morgan said, hand held out, "I got it." Crossing to the door, hand on his gun, he stood behind it as he opened it.

Addy slouched on the other side, mouth pulled into a scowl.

Jack watched this man frown at his daughter and weighed killing him. Funny how they could go from best of friends to enemies so quickly.

Addy crossed her arms. "Morgan. Dad. Need to talk to you guys."

CHAPTER 32

Slamming the gate outside the Tree, Addy stood in the yard. Inhaling through her nose and exhaling through her mouth, she calmed her mind before walking in. The Troupe were like dowsing rods. If someone was feeling low, they'd pick up on it faster than a magnet picked up iron filings.

Then, god love them, they'd try to help.

Hoisting herself up onto the dock, she peeked through the rolled-up door. None of them were onstage, but raised voices floated out into the afternoon.

Chewing her lip, she walked through the barroom door.

Jim futzed around behind the bar, peeking into the stage room every so often. "Hey, Addy, welcome back. Listen—"

Leaning into the hallway, she caught light spilling from their office. She pointed. "Is Matt down there?"

Jim opened his mouth and inhaled.

Before he spoke again, she thanked him and walked down the hall. Whatever it was, it would wait. She needed to vent.

Approaching the open door, all the switches inside her turned on. She walked in and closed the door. Tugging her shirttail up, she frowned. "I swear to god, the next time that man treats me like a child, I'll—"

"I would not like to have seen what you told him," Dean said.

The hot flame inside wilted and guttering, she yanked her shirt down and faced him. The cork popped out of the hole in her heart, spilling hot blood all over her insides again. She leaned against the door. "Dean."

"Addy." He rummaged in a pack on the floor next to where he sat and brought out a white paper bag. "Brought you this." Not looking up from the papers in his hand, he held it out.

Smoothing the front of her shirt, she tried to form her lips around the words "what are you doing here," but she couldn't figure out the answer and so the question wouldn't come. It sat on the edge of her mute tongue, waiting to be asked.

Matt burst through the door, almost knocking her down. "Shit, Addy, sorry."

She spun, eyes wide.

He looked over her shoulder, brow furrowed, and widened his eyes at her.

She shrugged.

Stepping around her, he walked to the table where Dean sat. "When did you get here?"

Finally looking up, Dean wrinkled his brow. "I don't know. Ten, fifteen minutes ago?"

Matt crossed his arms. "Why didn't I know this? I didn't let you in."

"Paxton walked me down." He shuffled the papers in front of him and stood.

Matt pointed between himself and Addy. "We. We are in charge here. You don't come through that gate unless it's past one of us."

Dean raised both hands. "Whoa, hey man. It's cool. I didn't know. I'll make sure to talk to one of you next time."

Matt rolled his eyes.

"What are you here for, Dean?" Addy asked, breath catching up to her thoughts.

He picked up the white paper bag. "Here. Peace offering. Need to work on the phones."

Addy took it and squeezed. Something small and tightly packed moved inside. Rolling it open, the aromatic scent of fresh coffee beans hit her. Her knees buckled.

"You all right?" Matt asked.

"Tell you about my conversation with Dad and Morgan later. Where were you when he got here?" She raised a finger at Dean.

He turned his back to Dean. "These idiots. Got into a fight because some of them think we're getting Kendra back, like, tomorrow. And some of them know that's bullshit."

Dean scoffed. "They fought over that?"

One side of Matt's mouth turned up, eyes fixed on Addy. "You know how they are. They fought over a part. Couple of them want to save a part for her, and have one of us"—he pointed between himself and Addy again—"be a stand-in."

Addy laughed. "Unlikely. I swear to god. Was it Cassius?"

Matt smiled and dropped his eyes. "I thought Vic was actually going to hit him." He glanced over his shoulder at Dean, whose eyes jumped between the two of them. "He keeps trying to get Addy into the play, but she's—"

"She's absolutely not going to do it."

Matt grinned. "I was trying to keep them from going all-out brawl. Guess that's when Dean got here."

"Sorry, man. I didn't know. I'll be more careful about coming in next time," Dean said, eyes flitting between them. "In the meantime, I've got to get these phones working. I'd like to start on the roof, see what we've got going on up there. Can one of you help me?"

Addy opened her mouth, but Matt beat her to it.

"Addy can. She loves heights."

Red crawling up her neck, she flashed on climbing that damn roller coaster with him.

Arms crossed, parenthesis deep, he smiled at her. His eyes twinkled before he dropped them again.

Stymied, unable to say no, she agreed.

* * *

Climbing the ladder ahead of Dean, Addy spoke over her shoulder. "How's that ankle?" At the top, she helped him up.

He hopped onto the roof and grimaced. "Better. Finally."

"I know a bit about that."

"I know. I thought of that."

He could have stuck his actual fist through her diaphragm. He'd thought of her? Swallowing, she looked around the roof. "What are we looking for?"

He pointed. "That dish will do." Starting off in that direction, he took the pack off his shoulder. "I thought about what you said. I can't understand why their communications are such a mess. They seem to have their shit together."

Her feet stuttered. And now he was thinking about what she said? Her mind tried to slip sideways and focus on things it had no business thinking about. Such as the fact that for someone who wanted to be broken up, he sure did think about her a lot.

She joined him at the dish as he looked it over. "What do you need me to do?"

He met her eyes and inhaled. But he closed his mouth with a snap and shook his head instead of speaking.

What was going on behind those emerald eyes?

Pointing, he flicked his wrist. "Can you tell me where this cable goes?"

Following the cable across the roof, she wound up in the western corner. "Here. It goes down next to the wall."

"Where does it end up? Is it whole?"

"I can't tell."

"Lean over the side of the roof and look." Tools clinked.

Gripping the edge, she leaned an inch. Her sweaty palms threatened to slip off the side. She shook her head. "I can't see anything."

His sigh audible even all the way over here, he told her to look again.

She forced an exhale through her nose, her forehead tight. "Don't fucking talk down to me, Dean. I've had enough of that for one day, thanks." Crossing her arms, she stalked across the roof and loomed over him. "First, Morgan tells me my ideas are stupid, and Dad didn't stick up for me, and now you're trying to force me to do something I'm not comfortable with. Stop." Sighing, she flung her hands out and stomped toward the ladder.

"Addy, wait." Crunching unevenly across the roof, he caught up to her and snagged her hand. "Wait. I'm sorry. What's the problem?"

Stomach churning, she tried to pull her hand back. But to have him touch her again, it sent the blood rushing to her brain, and she did no more than twitch. Her chin trembled. "I don't like heights, all right? I can't lean over the damn roof."

"You didn't have a problem in the lighthouse?"

Ripping her hand free, she crossed her arms. "That was a long time ago. That was different. You know what? I'm sending Matt up. I can't do this."

"No, here, I'll do it. Wait. Tell me what happened with your dad."

She took a breath. And another. "Yeah, OK."

With a grin, the corner of one eye crinkled, he walked across the roof, favoring the injured ankle.

She picked at a cuticle. "I went to talk to them about Kendra. About what Mom said. We need to get her out of there, Dean. We need to get them all out."

His voice coming from far away as he leaned over the side of the roof, he agreed. "Can't argue that."

Closing her eyes, stomach turning over, she tried not to envision him losing his balance and cartwheeling off the side of the roof. "Me and Matt even came up with some strategies. He knows the place pretty well, you know."

Crunching back over, Dean joined her next to the dish. He pulled a cable off the back. "I think we're good. It runs down into the junction box on the side. Looks whole. Dishes like this aren't a hundred percent necessary, but I can use it to boost the signal." His brow drew into a V and he shook his head. "I'll bet he does. Addy, how sure are you he's on our side?"

Her mightiest effort kept the visions of all the times she'd been at her most vulnerable to him under the surface. She couldn't keep the color out of her cheeks though. "Positive. A thousand percent."

He grunted, leaning in to inspect the innards of the dish. "I guess. I just think it's funny how the first chance he got, he wanted to come here. And get you so close to your mom."

"What's your problem with him? I thought you guys got along."

His eyes narrowed. "We do. But I don't know if I trust him around you. Being honest."

"That's not a call you get to make." But she floated inches off the roof. That he still cared enough about her to be this protective had to mean something, didn't it?

"You're right. You're right." He went back to work on the dish. "Your dad helped me with something similar to this in DC."

"How is he?"

"What do you mean?"

"He let Morgan shut me down and didn't even try to make him listen. I have good ideas, dammit." She punched her own leg. "It seems like he's. I don't know. Not the same."

He peeked at her. "You know he doesn't talk much."

"Yeah, well, you knew about Jane before anyone else. What do you know now?"

He flushed. "I guess I did, huh." He dropped his arms and shifted his eyes to the sky. The light shone through them, turning the deep emerald into bright green. "If I had to guess, I'd say something happened to him he doesn't want to talk about. I've seen him getting better, but it's taking a long time." He tapped her on the knee. "I'd guess it has to do with your mom. I know if something like that happened to you, what's happened to her, I wouldn't do too well."

Butterflies crawled up her windpipe, clogging her throat. Trying to swallow around them, she dragged a breath all the way to the bottom of her lungs. Closing her eyes, she tried to ignore his hand lingering on her knee but found it impossible.

When she opened them, she caught him staring into them.

He dropped his eyes and moved his hand. Back to the dish. Clearing his throat, he worked on the dish.

"Dean."

"Yeah, Addy," he said, face buried in a mess of cables.

"I'm gonna need you to not say stuff like that. I'm serious."

He continued to work. "I know. It was foolish of me. I was trying to find something to relate it to."

She stood. "I'll send Matt up."

* * *

Jane's needles clicked.

Sitting next to the baby bouncer she'd dug up, Jack rocked the baby with a finger.

Her eyes fought to stay open. She stared at him, trying to smile.

He melted, smiling back. "I think the EMDR is working."

"Yeah?"

"Yeah. My teeth don't hurt from being clenched all day." He clicked them together. "Thanks."

"Thank yourself. I told you. You're doing amazing."

He went back to rocking the baby, the bouncing hypnotizing.

"We should get a dog or something," Jane said.

"Except for a few times here and there, I've never had one. They didn't last long."

Her needles kept going. "What happened to them?"

"Ran away. Got eaten. Died. We gave up trying after a while."

"I take it they were her idea."

"Yeah," he said, nodding, "mostly. But they were nice to have."

"Probably at least as useful as you and your proximity alarms." She cut her eyes at the kitchen. "Though I'm glad we have one again."

"Me too. Feels good to know. So weird this place has no walls."

Jane chuckled. "It has walls, all right. Just not the kind you're used to."

"I guess. But if Melinda and those Talus people want to come in, it's a lot easier than it'd be with walls."

The baby finally closed her eyes, breathing deep.

He kept rocking so she'd stay asleep. "Of course any wall that would surround a city this big would be about indefensible."

Needles stopping, Jane patted the couch. "She's out. Come sit with me."

He did, leaning on her shoulder as she continued on whatever it was she was making. He'd learned not to ask and wait to be surprised. "She's mad at me."

"Who? Melinda? That's a foregone conclusion."

He pictured his middle child. Her brow drawn over dark eyes. "Adelaide."

"Shit. What'd you do?"

"Why's it have to be my fault?" He lifted his head, peeking at her.

She side-eyed him. "It doesn't have to be. You're right."

Laying his head on her shoulder again, he lifted and dropped one hand. "It is though. She came to me and Morgan earlier. Wanted to talk about getting their people back from the Molehill."

"You said no."

"I didn't say anything. Let Morgan say no for both of us." He drew one foot onto the couch. "I should have explained it to her instead of him. She might've taken it better."

"Explain it to me then. Help me understand. Because frankly, I don't get it either." She lowered the needles. "You and Morgan sure hit it off."

"We did. I like him. I haven't connected with someone like that in a long time."

"What about Paul?"

He sucked in a breath.

"Sorry. Just a question, honey."

He frowned. "He was more like a dad. Morgan is like a brother. Not that I ever had one. But you know."

She shrugged. "Neither did I. But tell me about this thing with Addy."

Backing the tape up in his head, he replayed what happened in Morgan's office. "She came to us with a plan, not half bad really, that involved breaking into the Molehill at night and getting the QC people out before Melinda even knew what was happening."

"Sounds good so far."

"Sure. It does. But she wanted to go, and she wanted to take Matt, and considering they didn't tell Morgan who she was until it was almost too late, he wasn't too keen on the idea." He glanced at the baby. Addy had been that small one time too. "I didn't like it either. After what happened in the hospital in Magnolia, I can't put Addy in that kind of danger. I have no idea what her mother will do to her."

Jane put her needles and yarn down on the side table and turned to face him. "Can't say I disagree with that. What about her taking Matt? Do you still trust him?"

"Addy does. She's spent more time with him than me. And he kept her secret all this time. You know how much he did to get us in that hospital." Cupping her jaw, he stroked her cheek. "What he lost."

Face contorting into half frown, half smile, she slid closer. "I can't imagine." She laughed. "All right. I can imagine. I don't want to. Other than that, what's the problem with her plan?"

He stroked her cheek again and gripped her thigh with the other hand. "Morgan and I are working on it. We're talking about destroying the whole facility. Putting Talus out of commission. Hopefully for good." He tugged her leg.

She unfolded it and slid it between him and the couch. "That'd be wonderful. What do you know about the higher-ups?"

"Gonna have to find out more. There's a few people in town who know about the company. Not only Matt."

Hooking the other leg around him, she nodded. "Good. Addy seems to like him."

"She does?"

Laughing, Jane took the hand on her cheek and wrapped it around her waist. "I love you."

Wrapping the other arm around her, he tugged her hips and pulled her closer. "I love you back."

Curling both arms under his and sliding as close as she could get, she kissed him on the neck and whispered in his ear. "I want you, Jack. Is that all right?"

Closing his eyes, he let her warm breath on his ear tingle its way down his spine. It settled in his stomach and turned pink, easing its way along his nerve endings and setting them alight. He reached under her shirt, her skin like bottled light, and wrapped his arms around her waist. Tugging, he moved his own hips back at the same time.

She ended up on her back under him, smiling. Eyes shining, teeth peeking from behind her lips, she twisted some of his hair in her fingers.

Hand under her neck, he cradled her head, lifted her up, and met her in the middle, kissing her like it was the first time.

Returning the kiss, she hooked her ankles behind him. Quiet, so she wouldn't wake the baby, she still couldn't resist giving him vocal cues and soft moans.

He pressed her into the couch and let the desire to be enfolded within her course through him. Knowing, trusting, she'd let him stop if he got scared or changed his mind freed him to enjoy her in a way he hadn't been able to since before the baby was born. And while he'd planned to savor every second of their first time together again, taste every inch of her, they quickly found themselves in a place where they couldn't get undressed fast enough.

His body reacted to her because his soul was on fire, and he needed to be with her because he loved her more than the air he sucked into his lungs. And finally, finally, there was nothing wrong with that.

CHAPTER 33

"Missed you last night," Matt said, straddling the barstool next to Addy.

She flushed, stomach uneasy. "Sorry. I was so tired. I think all that talking to Dean and everything, being on the roof, really tired me out. I passed out as soon as my head hit the pillow."

He took the coffee Jim brought. "It's all right. I can always use the sleep." Sipping, he leaned over. "You hardly let me sleep at all anymore. I'm exhausted."

Half her mouth turned down in a reluctant smile. "That's as much your fault as mine." Looking him up and down, she made no effort to disguise what she thought of the body hiding under those clothes.

Blood crawling up his neck, he sipped the coffee again. "This is good. Is this the fresh stuff Dean brought you?"

Her lip curled. "Tastes like shit."

"Is that your attitude talking?"

"It makes me sad. I thought fresh coffee would be so good. I guess I'm used to the old, stale stuff we usually have." She rubbed a spot on the bar. "I don't have an attitude."

Scoffing, he waved Jim over. "Got some of that bacon for me?"

Jim popped the smoke from his mouth. "Sure thing, man. Addy?"

Shaking her head, she rested the side of it on her hand. "No, thanks. It just doesn't smell good today. You got some toast back there or something?"

Eyes flickering behind his glasses, he stuffed the cigarette back in the corner of his mouth, nodded, and walked away.

After a moment of silence, she glanced at Matt.

He leaned away from her, eyes wide, and stared.

"What?"

"No coffee? No bacon?" Leaning closer, he lowered his voice. "Who are you, and what have you done with my Addy?"

She shrugged. Her head swam. "I don't know. It's like Dean coming to town has got me all messed up. Out of sorts. I don't feel like myself."

"Here," he said, smiling at Jim, "eat this toast. Currant jelly?" He jutted his chin behind the bar.

"Sounds perfect." Laying her head on the bar, she gazed sideways at Matt from under heavy lids. "Ugh. I feel like I drank too much. But I didn't drink anything."

Jim pushed the plate in front of her. "Milady, your toast is served."

She sat up. Jim had spread the jelly for her. "Aw. Thanks, Jim. You didn't have to do that."

"I know. But you're one of my people now, Addy. Gotta take care of my people."

She took a bite. What began as sweet, tart, delicious jelly flooded her nose and overpowered her sinuses with sugary thickness. Dropping the toast back on the plate, she pushed it aside with a grunt.

Jim tapped ashes into one of the many ashtrays behind the bar. "It's no good?"

"It's great." She sighed. "I'm not hungry."

Matt finished a piece of bacon and wiped his mouth. "You never told me what Morgan said."

Facing outside and leaning against the bar, she wiped her face with her hands. The fuzzy feeling in her head wouldn't subside. "They don't give a shit what we want. They want to do things their way."

He looked out the side door with her. "Their way includes blowing up the general, doesn't it?"

"I'm afraid it does."

"Hell, Addy. What are we going to do?"

Her eyes stung. "Their plan has some merit. We can't let Talus keep doing what they're doing." Facing him, she let one of the threatening tears fall and lowered her voice. "I couldn't breathe, Matt. You have to tell me if she's worth saving. Because between that and Kendra and everything else, I don't know anymore."

Gripping her shoulder, lighting her up with those electric blues, he opened his mouth. When nothing came out, he pulled her into a hug. "I can't say yes. And I can't say no. You know as well as I do, she's worth saving. I saw it a hundred times if it was one. But she could have hurt you. And she's done so much damage." He pushed her back, hand still gripping her shoulder, thumb working a circle. "It—"

A crack of thunder so loud it split the very air in the room rattled through everything. Something exploded, and the lights went out.

Someone screamed bloody murder. Over and over.

Heart in her throat, a vacuum in her lungs, Addy leapt from the stool. Eyes wide, she grabbed Matt's shoulder and tugged him toward the bunks. "Where's your flashlight?"

The screaming continued.

He clicked on a small LED light and gripped her arm. "Is that Rivers, or Vic?"

"Can't tell."

They tugged each other deeper into the darkened building. The flashlight beam wobbled. "That was fucking close. Jesus. I feel like my nose hairs are singed."

"All the hair on my head is still standing up," Addy said, reaching up to smooth it down. In doing so, she almost slapped herself in the face with her machete, whenever it was she'd drawn it.

They burst into the girls' room.

Vic lay in a ball on the floor, screaming. Rivers huddled on top of her, stroking her hair and singing.

The rain began, pounding the roof with enough force to be solid. So loud, it all but drowned out the screaming woman in the floor before them.

Rivers rocked and sang, squinting into the flashlight beam.

Heart still pounding out a rhythm somewhere near her back teeth, Addy knelt next to them as Matt illuminated the spot in the floor where Vic lay. "Rivers, is she OK? Is she hurt?"

Still singing, a light melody with few words and an Irish lilt in her voice, Rivers shook her head. Between screams, gut-wrenching shouts that must have been tearing into the soft tissue of Vic's throat, Rivers told them this happened during every storm. "It's something about what Talus made her do. She won't say much."

Vic screamed, but it had less force, less urgency. She covered her ears and cried.

Rivers sang.

Matt sank down in the floor next to Addy, his knee touching hers. "The general?"

Stroking Vic's hair, Rivers whispered to them. "I don't know. But she'll be fine." She looked up, round eyes pointed at the ceiling. "You guys go enjoy the rain. It might be all we get."

Addy reached out for Vic but didn't touch her. "Are you sure?"

Rivers nodded, still singing and stroking.

Victoria sobbed, her ears covered. But at least she'd stopped screaming.

Matt stood, offering Addy a hand up. "Let's leave them."

The guys crowded the doorway, coming in with flashlights as Addy and Matt passed them.

Addy took Matt's hand, following him into the dark hallway. "Should we stay with them?"

"I can't hear you over the rain. What?" He tugged her closer.

She spoke into his ear. "Should we stay with them?"

He tickled her ear with his lips. "Let's do what Rivers asked."

Passing the bar, candles burning bright down the length of it, they walked out onto the dock. Under the outer tin roof, Addy couldn't even hear herself think over the rain. The scent of fresh ozone and wet dirt filled her nose.

Matt tugged. "Come on," he said, pocketing the flashlight.

Head shaking, she lifted her shoulders. Where did he mean, come on?

He leapt from the dock and stretched out a hand.

The butterflies picked an interesting time to make themselves known. But she wrote it off as whatever had been going on with her stomach.

She sat and slid to the edge of the dock. He helped her down, his strong hands holding her hips as she floated to the ground.

Taking her hand again, he pulled her into the rain and spun her in a circle.

Out here, in the open, the gigantic raindrops didn't feel as hard as they sounded. The worry of yesterday with Dad and then with Dean, the sour taste in her mouth, Vic's screaming, it all melted like cotton candy. Thunder crashed, farther away, and she grasped Matt's hand and spun with him when he threw his arm behind her and twirled her like a dancer.

She laughed. "I didn't know you knew how to dance."

"I don't." He joined her laugh, twirling her again. Almost losing his footing.

She gripped his shoulder before they tumbled into a pile. "Don't knock me over, man. If you're gonna fall, do it on your own."

"Oh hell no. I fall, I'm taking you with me."

Laughing, she tried to pull away.

Catching her hand, he spun her in another circle, then stopped and tugged her in. Wrapping both arms around her, he paused short of her mouth. As he did so often.

The cold rain showered them, his breath warming her lips.

She leaned closer, touching the barest hint of warm skin through the cold rain. And when she couldn't stretch the moment any longer, he swept her into a kiss that warmed her from the crown of her head down. One hand on the back of his neck, one full of his shirt, she pushed him to the old shed full of half-used paint buckets on the far side of the lot. Still kissing him, she tripped over her feet, but his arm firm around her waist kept her from going down as they left the rain outside with the rest of the world.

They struggled with their sopping wet clothes, giving up once they had enough stripped off. One of her pants legs hung around her ankle. It didn't make a difference.

Everything, the pounding rain, the upset stomach, the pain Dean's reappearance brought with it, floated off into the ether.

* * *

Standing outside the door to Lash's office, Melinda found the few hours' sleep she'd gotten hadn't eased her fears about the files she'd uncovered. Both the ones in Lash's desk and the phone transcripts. If Burke had been a Talus spy, what else would she find? What else did they know?

Insides jittering, she pushed the door to Lash's office open.

The office sat empty, papers scattered about the desk. A low murmur came from the ajar door to Anthony's office.

She crept across the office and stood outside the door.

Anthony spoke. "Yes, ma'am. No, I understand."

Melinda's brow furrowed. She'd never heard such a tone on him. Scared. Afraid, even. Who could he be talking to?

"No, don't do that. I can get her to listen. Just—"

Papers rustled.

"Are you sure? The immunity project—"

Someone shifted in their chair.

Melinda leaned closer to the door. No one responded to him. Maybe he was on the phone? His voice continued to rise in pitch.

"McNamara is an idiot. He's going to fuck up the whole thing. What do you—"

A heavy sigh.

"Yes, ma'am. Yes. If that's what you. Yes."

A chair scraped across the floor.

"I'll get this typed up right away, Anthony," Lash said, approaching the door.

Melinda's eyes flitted to the other door. No time to get to the hallway. She'd be caught. Her options were either let Lash open this door in her face, which would announce to Anthony she'd been eavesdropping, or to pretend she just arrived.

Straightening her shirt, she rapped on the door and pulled it open. She stepped into the office, face-to-face with a widemouthed Ilasha.

Anthony sat behind the desk, head in his hands.

Lash grabbed her arm. "Em, what's going on? Are you all right?"

Head snapping up, brow knitted, Anthony glared at her.

His expression inscrutable, Melinda caught something like sadness. Desperation in his eyes.

"General. Do you need something?"

She freed her arm from Lash's grip. "I had come to speak with Ilasha, but since you're available—"

"Come with me, Melinda. Anthony is busy right now."

Following her out of the office, Melinda threw a glance over her shoulder.

With hooded eyes, he watched them leave.

Once Lash shut the office door behind them, Melinda rounded on her. "Who was he talking to? Was he on the phone?"

Eyes wide, Lash leaned in, voice low. "You heard that?"

Melinda crossed her arms. "Some of it. He sounded scared. What the hell? What aren't you telling me?"

Glancing at Anthony's door, Lash bit her lip. She pulled Melinda across the office and opened the outer door. Without checking the hall, she jerked Melinda into the hallway and marched until they came to an alcove with a recessed door. She shoved Melinda into the hole in the wall and joined her in the lightless depression. "The fuck were you doing, eavesdropping on him? Don't you know what could happen if his boss finds out?"

"His boss? You're kidding me." She crossed her arms. "Since when does he have a boss?"

"Since when does he not? What, you think he runs this whole damn thing on his own? The man can barely scratch his own ass without asking me where to find it."

Melinda shook her head. "He always seemed like a competent scientist."

"That doesn't mean he knows shit. Or can think for himself. But if his higher-ups find out you've been spying on them. Jesus, Melinda." Her back hit the wall behind her. "Do you know how fast they could have you killed?" Voice shaking, she covered her breasts with crossed arms.

Words failing, Melinda let her mouth fall open. Lash had clearly been shaken to her core by the implication that Anthony's bosses, whoever these mysterious people were, might find out she knew about them. She pulled down a breath, smoothing her own nerves like the raised hair on a dog's back. "I found a bunch of files in your desk, Lash."

"Snooping through my locked drawers, I see." Half her mouth curved up. "Should have guessed you would." In the dark, her eyes shone like diamonds. "Find anything interesting?"

"I expected the files about my family. Or would have, if I'd thought about it. But." She stopped, leaning against the opposite wall. "There was a file in there, all worn at the edges, with my name on it. Why do you have it? What does it say?"

Lash shrugged. "Nothing, really."

"If it's nothing, why keep it?"

She faced the hallway, one shoulder raising so high it almost met her ear. "It's about you. It's got your picture. After you left, it was all I had."

Her blood pressure had been dropping, but now it sped through her brain as her heart leapt into a gallop. "I wish I'd known you were still on my side. It would have meant a lot."

"I wish you had, too, Em." Uncrossing her arms, Lash dropped a hand against her leg.

Melinda took it. "I noticed the paper was all worn out on my file. Looked at the picture a lot?"

Lash gave her the side-eye. "Every day."

Cupping her opposite cheek, Melinda turned Lash's face toward hers. "I wish I'd had a picture of you. I missed you so much." Without giving her time to respond, she kissed her. Savoring her soft lips, the smile that tried to stretch them as she kissed her back. Even after admitting all the foul things she'd done, all the terrible decisions her damaged brain led her to, that this woman still loved her had to be some kind of miracle. Damn near unbelievable.

Leaning away, Lash frowned. "Working for this man is a nightmare sometimes. The things I wish I could tell you."

"I told you all my awful stuff from the last few years. Why can't you tell me this?"

"It's for your own good. Also, you do not want to know."

Melinda released her. She kept one hand though. "Come see me tonight, OK?"

Lash's hand tightened. "Shit. I can't. You have to— Dammit."

Heart in her throat, Melinda checked the hall. They still had it to themselves. "What?"

"Anthony's boss has something they need you to do."

Stomach joining her heart, Melinda leaned over. "What?"

"They need you to lead a raid. Tonight."

* * *

Sitting on the dock, watching the Troupe practice outside while the power was out, Addy leaned on her hands. "Afternoons like this about make me think everything is OK."

Matt leaned back on his own hands. His arm crossed hers. "Feeling better?"

"A bit. Still tired as all hell."

He peeked at her with the side of his eye. "Sorry. Maybe I'll let you rest tonight."

She chuckled. "Not likely."

"You're right it's— Oh, check it out," he said, pointing. "Looks like we may get power back today after all."

A truck loaded with men and equipment rumbled down the street.

Matt hopped down, helping her down the way he had that morning. He nuzzled under her ear and kissed her on the neck before letting her go.

Cheeks tingling, she let him go and walked toward the car gate. As she swung it open, she glanced at the driver.

Dean.

Great.

Her stomach took a trip to her toes and her nausea returned. She swallowed, telling her stomach to cool it. He wouldn't even have time to talk to her if he was here with the electrical crew to work on the power.

"Like, I know Burke was a smart guy, but how the hell did Dean learn all this stuff in five years?" Matt gripped the gate as the truck rumbled through, pointing her to the other side so they could close it together.

"All what stuff?"

"Phones, power, welding, driving that fancy train. All of it. Seems like a lot."

"He's a fast learner."

"Yeah, I bet."

"What's that supposed to mean?"

Shaking his head, he hooked his thumbs in his front pockets. "Nothing. Another one of my silly questions. Forget it."

She forced a sigh and followed the truck to where Dean parked.

He swung down. "Morgan asked me to check in with you guys, and Paxton said you're out of power?" Without making eye contact, he rooted behind the seat and brought out a tool bag.

Addy pointed at the building. "We heard something explode during a lightning strike this morning, and it went out." Not that he saw her point. He still hadn't looked at her except for when he'd driven through the gate.

"We'll check out the roof, see what's what."

"Do you need us to turn anything off inside? Circuit breakers, whatever?"

"We got it," he said, closing the door. By now, pointedly not looking at her.

Rubbing her forehead, she cut her eyes at Matt.

"Sure you don't need a hand, man?"

Finally, Dean looked up. Two spots of color high on his cheeks. "Oh, I'm sure. I don't need your help. Man."

Matt lifted and dropped his shoulders at Addy.

She cleared her throat, heart slamming her ribs. He hadn't taken a tone like that in the entire time she'd known him. "Dean, are you all right?"

His shoulders drooped. "Sorry. It's, uh. With the storm and everything, it's been a long morning, I guess. I didn't mean to take it out on you." He met Addy's eyes and angled his forehead at the Tree. "Could you show me where the breaker box is inside?"

"Here," Matt said, "take my flashlight. It's dark in there. I think the candles are out." He laid it in her palm, squeezing her fingers before dropping his hand. "I'll keep an eye on these animals. Make sure they stay out of the way." He backed up and walked toward the Troupe.

Eyes narrowed, Dean watched him go. "Which way, Addy?"

Hearing her name roll off his tongue made her knees wobble. "Down the hall with the bunks. Past the bar. Come on." Stuffing Matt's light in her pocket, she tried to scramble to the top of the dock. Something she did at least four times a day or more.

This time, she lost her grip and fell.

Dean caught her.

Once she was back on her feet, he let her go. "Sorry. I didn't mean to, um. Force of habit."

Flushing from her forehead down, she shook her head. "It's all right. I'm usually at least somewhat coordinated getting up this thing. Having some trouble the last few days. Like my footing is off."

His emerald eyes met hers. "Need a hand?"

She eyed the Troupe. And Matt. They all had their backs to them. "Sure."

"Here. Let's do the hand cradle thing. My ankle is still." He see-sawed his hand.

Hand on his shoulder, she settled her foot into the cradle he made with his fingers. "How'd you do that, anyway?"

"Happened in DC. Ready?"

"Go."

He pushed her up, and she grabbed the lip of the loading dock, pulling herself all the way up. At the top, she stuck her hand out for him.

After tossing his tools up, he scrambled after them, keeping most of his weight on his hands and feet. With his long legs and long frame, he didn't have to struggle as much to get up the thing as she did.

He stood next to her, panting. "You do that all the time? And you haven't broken yourself yet?"

She grinned and led him inside. "Shut up. It's this way. Watch out for the couches."

"He's right, the candles are out."

Not only that, Jim had disappeared from behind the bar. They were alone.

Leading Dean through the barroom, she tried to think of something to chatter about. Ease the tension in her neck. But Yasuo popped up in her head. Talking about appreciating the moment.

Boy, it seemed such a long time ago he told her that. Only about six or seven months though.

Heading down the hallway, past the doors to the bunks, she shook her head. "That lightning scared the piss out of us. Victoria, especially." Vic was out there in the yard right now, practicing for the play like nothing happened.

"Me too," he said, voice pitched low in the small space.

She stopped. "What do you mean, you too?"

"I was down at the lab. Only Mike and Celia were there, but I couldn't sleep, so I went over early." The shadows on his face deepened. "Scared the hell out of us too."

"You're gonna have to tell me about Celia's arm sometime," she said, shaking her head and continuing down the hall. "I'm afraid she'll hit me with that cast if I ask her."

"Sure. Here, is that the box?"

She aimed the flashlight. "Yeah. Only reason I know it's here is we've had to flip a couple. Sometimes they need to change the stage lights, and the easiest way is cutting the breaker."

Turning to face her, he passed her in the tight space. Close enough for the heat of him to seep into her pores. For his scent to enter her nose and burrow into her brain.

On his way past, he paused in front of her. When she made eye contact, he dropped his eyes and finished passing her. He set his tools in front of the box and opened it. "You like it here?"

"It's all right. Miss the island, to tell you the truth. I miss." She cleared her throat. "You" was the next thing on her tongue, but she found she couldn't spit it out. The truth was, she'd thought less and less about him until he'd shown up here and ripped the scab off the healing wound.

"If you don't need anything else, I'll leave you with the flashlight. I need some air." She held the light out for him.

He took it from her with both hands. While one held the flashlight, the other kept her hand. Taking a step, he raised it.

For a breathless beat, Addy thought he was going to kiss her palm. Actually felt his lips soft against her skin.

He lowered her hand. "Addy, listen."

The urge to puke on his shoes overwhelmed her.

Taking huge, deep breaths, her stomach and cheeks tingling, she tried to pull her hand back. She lacked the strength. Or will.

He cleared his throat. "I knew as soon as you left the island I made a mistake. I kept trying, though, to convince myself it was the right thing. I couldn't let you hurt yourself because of me, but you didn't deserve to be pushed away because of it. Because I was scared."

Not unkindly, she pulled her hand free. "And you're saying this now, why?"

He shrugged, the light bouncing. "Seeing you has made it pretty much impossible not to. I can't...I miss you."

Her stomach roiled. The nausea from the morning nothing compared to the complete freak-out it was doing now. At the same time, the blood rushed to her head, tightening the skin on her face. "What, you think you can... What is this?" She spun. "I don't want to talk about this."

He spoke to her back. "Do you love him?"

She stopped, face on fire. Jaw aching. She turned back around, ready to tell this idiot it was *him* she loved, not Matt.

Instead, she hesitated.

And answered his question with a question. "How do you know about that?"

"I heard the explosion you talked about. I came down here to check on you. Make sure you were OK." He crossed his arms, light aimed at the wall. "You were OK. You were more than OK."

Goose bumps raced down her arms. "You saw us?" She cleared her throat. "That's. Um. I don't." Stopping, she folded her arms. "I don't have a good answer for you, Dean. You dropped me on my ass. What do you want from me?"

"I don't know, I just—"

"You just what?" she asked, voice rising. "You saw me with him and you thought you didn't want someone else playing with your toys?"

"No, that's not—"

"You don't get to make that call."

"Dammit, Addy, I'm not trying to. I just wanted to say I'm sorry."

"Oh for fuck's sake." She put him to her back and walked off into the dark.

CHAPTER 34

After the power came back on and Dean took his men and left, refusing eye contact with either Matt or Addy, the Troupe wandered inside and spent a lazy evening on the couches. As the sun set, Jim lit the candles again and directed Addy to pull out the ice cream. They all sat on the couches, eating ice cream and swapping sad stories from their childhoods. Laughing over the obvious mistakes they all made when they found their thread of commonality.

Hiding from 'Heads behind a window by accident.

Slipping in mud and having a 'Head follow them, slipping as well.

Learning to kill them and whiffing the first shot every time.

The unspoken undercurrent being some kid, somewhere, wasn't lucky enough to be swapping these stories in adulthood.

As the stars peeked out, Vic grew more and more sullen and quiet until she slunk off to bed. Rivers went not long after her, as did Cassius. Grey and Tal found a dark corner of the room and forgot the rest of them were in it.

Eventually even Jim's head nodded. He smiled at Matt and Addy with half-open eyes.

Matt, in the floor in front of the couch Addy currently stretched out on, reached over and touched his knee with a finger. "You should hit the sack, man."

Blinking at them with owl eyes, Jim stood, wobbled his way to the hall, and disappeared.

Addy breathed deep, eyes falling closed.

"You should too."

With a start, she opened her eyes.

He still sat in the floor in front of her, face-to-face, eyes wide. Forehead wrinkled, lips curved in half a smile and one parenthesis deep.

Inhaling through her nose, she sat up and rubbed her face. "No. No. I need to talk to you."

He lifted up to the couch and sat next to her. "What's up?"

And the butterflies made their reappearance. As if she didn't have enough on her mind.

She glanced at the dark corner where Grey and Tal had disappeared. They could have been looking, for all she knew. And no one in the Troupe could keep a secret to save their lives.

"Not here." Without waiting, she slid off the couch and walked out onto the dock.

The late spring night, humid but with a cool edge, welcomed her with open arms. The anticipation of summer on the breath of every breeze.

Night watch on the dock, the boys waved as she walked out. One of them stood. "Out for a walk, Addy?"

"Around the block. Hold down the fort."

He sat. "You got it."

Not for the first time, she wondered what Matt told them when he slipped out after her. They went down to their secret apartment at least three or four times a week. If not more. But the guards never seemed suspicious.

Clinking through the front gate, she peeked up at the moon. It was waning now, under a quarter of it left until it was new again. Something about the new moon always called up images of flowers and snow. Rebirth and death, all in one. The end of one cycle and the beginning of a new, colliding in one night of darkness every twenty-eight days.

As she waited on the sidewalk, the moon crawled across the sky. The few intact windows around her glowed pale silver.

"You all right?" Matt asked, sneaking up on her.

She jumped and hit him. "How are you always so quiet?"

He sat next to her on the curb and grinned, both parentheses framing his lips. "What can I say. If I wasn't good at being quiet, I'd be dead." He leaned in to kiss her.

She stood. "Not out here. Inside." She jiggled the broken door, and it popped open.

He followed, wedging the door closed again. They'd discussed fixing it, and installing locks and a bar, but decided if anyone found their nest, they might not take it for what it was if the door was broken and unbarred.

Upstairs, she flopped on the bed and laid back, feet hanging off.

He flicked on the small lamp lying on its side in the floor. The mattress next to her depressed. "So? What's up, Houlihan?"

Sitting up, she rested on her arms. "Dean saw us this morning."

"This…" He trailed off, no doubt gazing back in his memory. His eyes widened. "You mean in the rain?" Brow knitted, he stuck a nail between his teeth. "How much did he see? What happened? How did you find this out?"

"He told me." With a sigh, she leaned forward and rested her elbows on her knees. "When we went back to the breaker box."

"So, is he… What does he… All right." He stood to pace. "I'm trying to ask you a question."

"What?"

"I don't know." Stopping at the window, he leaned on it. He lifted and dropped one hand. The crooked drapes fluttered. "Did he say anything else?"

"He told me he misses me. And he admitted he made a mistake."

Matt's breath fogged the window in front of his mouth. "Did he?"

She considered asking him to turn around, show her that infectious smile. Nerves bound the question inside her chest. Instead, she crossed to him and leaned a shoulder against the wall. "He asked me if I love you."

Rolling his forehead, breath shallow, his wide eyes landed on hers. "What did you tell him?"

Captivated, she couldn't turn away to answer. "I didn't tell him anything. I." She cleared her throat. "I didn't know what to say."

He slid his left hand up the side of her neck and gave her a gentle tug.

As he kissed her, his thumb caught under her ear, she stamped on the butterflies. They had no business here.

But he'd never kissed her with something so close to tenderness. With such soft, emotive lips. The bonfire he normally was had instead been fed green wood and allowed to smolder. Smoking with a building intensity that would lead to hot coals rather than leaping flames.

She let him tug her to the bed, and he undressed her with easy, slow hands. The distance between them erased, he became part of her so gently it was as if he'd always been. The rush, the urgency she always felt with him melted into water she couldn't hold between her fingers. An ocean of unwieldy depth and imperfect edges. Impossible to cork or hem. And on this ocean, she held him and sailed, floating along the tops of the waves as they crested and rolled. His eyes her anchor when the fear of being too far out rose in her.

As they floated to shore, surfing the breakers in, he lay behind her, pressed against her back, and held her hand.

Sleep came for her, with its warm arms and pillows.

"Adelaide," he whispered.

"Matthew."

"I have to ask you something."

Eyelids at half-mast, she rolled partway over and caught his eyes. Even in the partial dark, electric blue against his ruddy cheeks. "Ask."

He stroked the back of her hand with a thumb. "Are you all right? You feel different."

Not the question she expected, she rolled farther and wrinkled her brow. "What do you mean?"

"I don't know. You didn't want bacon or coffee, which is weird. And you've been so tired recently." One parenthesis reappeared. "And cranky…er than usual."

Slapping him on the shoulder with light fingers, she smiled. "I am not cranky."

He laughed. Smile fading, he glanced at her breasts. "And. Well. You. I don't know. You taste different. Sweeter." He shrugged.

Grinning, she squeezed his hand. "Are you trying to call me sweet and salty?"

Laughing again, he let her hand go and cupped a breast. He leaned in to kiss her.

"Ouch. Not so tight," she said, pulling his hand down.

Brow wrinkled, he looked down again. "And that." He sat halfway up. "Addy. Are you. You're not pregnant, are you?"

She opened her mouth to say no.

Realized the full moon had come and gone going on two weeks ago, but her cycle, which was supposed to come with it, had not. She hadn't considered it till that moment.

She felt the blood drain from her face, her skin tightening as it went. She tried to swallow but couldn't.

Eyes wide, Matt waited. As the blood drained from her face, it rose in his.

Exhaling, he laid back. Grasping her hand with one of his, he covered his eyes with the other. His chest rose and fell.

She laid down next to him, shoulder touching his, and sent silent tendrils throughout her body. Feeling the insides of it. Demanding it tell her if it was true or if she was just randomly late.

Sometimes it goofs around when there's other women around. That's all it is.

One of the tendrils reminded her she'd felt sick for the last three days. But she didn't like being sick, or admitting to illness, so she pushed it off. Another reminded her she was more tired than she ought to be. Almost all the time.

Yet another said, "How else do you explain all this?"

Lacing her fingers between Matt's, she rolled her head. "It's not impossible." She squeezed his hand. "What even made you think to ask?"

Shifting to his shoulder to face her, he swallowed. Brow knitted, like it was painful. "Ella had four miscarriages. We wanted every single one of them. It wasn't in the cards." His eyes red, he tried on half a smile. It didn't quite make it. "We were gonna try again, since the hospital in Magnolia was so good. She wasn't ready yet."

Rolling to her own shoulder, she kept his hand with her right and used her left to stroke his cheek. When he closed his eyes, she tugged him as he had her and pulled his head in to her chest.

His breath came in short, sharp bursts.

She snuck the hand down to her abdomen and felt around. Pushed with her fingertips.

A tendril told her she felt heavier, and her fingertips told her there was a stiffness there. Not hard, but not not.

Sliding one hand around her, he held her close and breathed into her chest.

Silent, they fell asleep.

* * *

Bouncing in the passenger seat of an Army-style truck, crammed in with Hector and the driver on his other side, Melinda flipped pages inside the file on her lap. "Can you hold this flashlight?" she asked, digging one from her pocket.

Hector took it. "Of course, Mama. How are your ribs?"

She gave him a tight smile. "Would be better if we weren't crammed in here like sardines. But I appreciate the company."

Hector hooked a thumb behind him. "We've got twenty guys back there. And twenty in the next truck. And another. Do you think we'll be able to complete the file?"

She flipped to the first page again. The one with the names of her wayward children on it. All of them, not just the traitors she gave birth to. "All these kids left the Molehill?"

The light bounced. "I talked to some of them that stayed," Hector said. "The ones that left mostly did because Anthony didn't do well when he took over for you."

"So I've heard. Do you know anything about what he did?"

"Some of them had to work in the lab. He told them all of them together couldn't make up for the hole you left." He rocked into her shoulder. "He tried to come up with a new method of extracting the virus that didn't damage the subjects."

"And?"

Hector shrugged, moving Melinda's shoulder up and down with his. "It didn't work."

Melinda turned the page. A paper-white girl with wide blue eyes stared out of the picture stapled to the paper. "Victoria was a surprise, I'll admit. And her boyfriend was later captured and used to incubate the virus?"

Shrugging again, Hector grunted. "She was the pretty girl with the white hair, wasn't she?"

Melinda nodded, staring at the picture. She'd always had an air about her that said "look at me." Now, according to this file, she was acting. How suitable.

Riffling through the pages, she doubted many of these children had ever been loyal. Hector clearly was, and some of the others who'd stayed back, but this file was at least three times thicker than it should have been.

Maybe they hadn't loved her as much as they'd claimed. Look at what Matt had gone and done.

"We'll get them back, Mama. You'll see." He laid his head on her shoulder.

She took the flashlight back, pocketed it, and closed the file. Leaning around the boy curling against her shoulder, she spoke to the driver. "How long?"

"About twenty minutes, ma'am."

"What's your name?"

"Gian."

She leaned around Hector. "I thought you were captured?"

He stroked his cheek. "I was. They let me go. Eventually."

She scoffed. "Unlikely. I've met Morgan. You're going to need to tell me more."

"Happy to, General. If you'll let me settle a score today." He rubbed his cheek again. The dash lights turned his face green, and a scar on his cheek stood out in sharp relief against his skin.

"I tell you what, boy. You take me to where these actors are, and I'll get you to Morgan. Deal?"

"Deal."

CHAPTER 35

The candles on the bar flared, their flames leaping toward the ceiling. Addy stopped halfway through the room, Dean behind her, and stared. "Did you see that?"

"See what? All I see is you, sweetheart."

She floated. He loved her. Took her back. Flying on a cloud of impossible height, she looked down.

Below her, he smiled, the corners of his eyes crinkled. "Don't go too far. I won't be able to reach you."

She turned around just in time to hit the ceiling. She bounced off and floated toward the floor. Dean stretched out his hand.

Matt came out of the hallway. His eyes red. "Addy, don't fall."

Still above both their heads, she floated over to him. The bubbly feeling in her stomach returned, and she rose to the ceiling again. "Come up here with me."

He opened his mouth to speak, and the candles flared again. The wicks crackled, making popping sounds.

She stared. "Do you hear that?"

"Addy."

The candles flared, and she dropped closer.

"Addy, wake up."

Warning sirens wailed. Something she'd heard only once.

Light flared outside the window again. Gunfire sounded far off.

Popping up like a board, she gripped Matt's arm. "Is it a raid? How do they keep getting past the perimeter?"

"Yes. I don't know." He jumped out of bed. "Here." He tossed her clothes to her. While she pulled her shirt on, he jerked on his pants and sat to lace his boots. "We need to get back to the Tree. Like, yesterday."

"Don't have to tell me twice."

They dressed. She tried not to jump each time a grenade landed.

On the stairs, he stopped in front of her. "I'm not going to ask you to stay here. But I want you to know, it goes against every instinct I have to let you run out there right now." Joining her on her stair, he hooked one arm behind her and gripped her waist with the other. "Considering."

She opened her mouth. To say what?

Another grenade landed. Could have been a claymore. Something exploded, either way, and the windows lit up orange.

Her ears rang. "There's no time to discuss this. We have to get back to the Troupe. Go," she said, clutching his shoulder and turning him around. Worry sat tight in her throat. They should never have left.

Yanking the broken door open, he left it off its hinges and stuck his head out. "Clear."

Weapons drawn, they crept down the cracked sidewalk.

"I wish we'd brought our guns," she whispered, eyes everywhere.

"Me too." Settling his knife in one hand, he took her hand with the other. "Keep an eye out for 'Heads too."

They were here, all right. The air hung heavy with the coppery, corroded scent of them. Both fresh and not so fresh.

Stomach a hard knot, she followed Matt to the Tree.

They rounded the corner and stopped in a shadow.

Mobile floodlights washed the yard in daylight. Their light screamed from the heavens.

For a moment, her mind superimposed Gerald's garage the night they took Dad and Jane away, in the glare of headlights.

This glare was ten times worse. There, where that morning she danced in the rain with Matt, a dozen soldiers trained guns on a group of people.

She searched their faces. None of the Troupe knelt in the circle. Which could be good, but also. Not so good.

Still hidden in shadow, as she and Dean had done so long ago, she and Matt crouched across the street.

"I don't care, get her out here," Mom shouted, walking into the light.

Matt inhaled. "Fuck."

Lips pressed together, Addy leaned into him. "What is she doing here?"

He shook his head.

"Cassius!" Thrown into the light by a uniformed boy, Vic fell to the ground and stared up at Melinda. "What do you want with me?"

Melinda leaned down into her face and whispered.

"The hell is she doing, Addy?"

"How the fuck am I supposed to know?"

He rubbed her shoulder. "Sorry. Sorry. I'm—"

Ricardo walked into the light.

Hector.

Whatever his name was.

Ella's murderer.

Against her, every muscle in Matt's leg tensed. He gripped her shoulder, fingers digging in to the first knuckle.

Eyes stinging, her throat worked. She tried to speak, but no words came.

And before she had the chance to stop him, Matt sprang up and sprinted across the road. Making a beeline for Ricardo, knife by his side.

As he charged into the light, eliminating the possibility of surprise and also blowing every inch of his cover, Addy leapt into motion. Taking a more cautious approach, she crept across the street and pressed against the building, staying in the shadows up next to the Tree.

A shot fired, chipping brick ahead of her.

"Hector, I'll fucking kill you!"

Heart pounding, she ducked. Cover be damned, he needed her. She sprinted to the corner of the building and took in the scene.

Mom, holding a still-crouching Victoria by the collar.

Guards standing around a group of people no older than she and Matt. Watching the men in front of them, they'd pushed the people to the side of the yard, against the fence.

Grimacing, she followed their eyes.

Matt, knife held along his arm, eyes ablaze, circled Ella's killer.

The boy trained his gun on Matt but took a lazy stance. "What are you waiting for? You missed your first try. Wanna take another?"

The side of Matt's mouth curled. "My face is gonna be the last thing you see."

Someone made a sound in their throat.

Addy glanced to the side and caught her mom staring at her with her mouth wide.

Victoria caught her eye. "Addy! Cassius is hurt. You have to help him!"

Mom backhanded Vic with her free hand. "My darling daughter, would you like to come with us?" She leered, cutting her eyes to Matt and Ricardo. Uh. Hector. "This is the nicest offer you'll get."

"You take her and I'll kill you, too, General," Matt said, eyes on Hector.

Half a smile lit Mom's eyes. "I don't know how you do it."

Addy's free hand snuck to her stomach. "Do what?"

"Inspire such loyalty." She shook Victoria again. "This girl, Matt there, your father. All this time I've been thinking it was you who was loyal to him. But it's the other way around, isn't it?"

Head swimming, Addy backed toward the Tree. "Matt, you got this?"

He narrowed his eyes. "Oh, I got this. Been waiting for this."

Hector hardly got his gun back up in time to block Matt. As it was, Matt caught him across the bicep of the arm holding the gun.

Blood flew.

The boy cursed and dropped the gun.

A few drops of blood on his cheek, Matt lowered his brow and smirked from under it. "Come on, Hector. Let's do this. I'll put down the knife and we'll have a good, old-fashioned, kill each other bare-handed. What do you say?"

His eyes flitted between Melinda and Matt, landing on Addy for a second. "Sounds good to me. Put down the knife."

Fist balled in her diaphragm, Addy waited. More than any other time, she willed him to be telling the truth. This would be the time it'd be easiest to lie.

True to his word, he leaned to drop it on the ground.

Hector kicked his hand and took off into the dark.

The knife skidding away, Matt chased after.

Addy fought the urge to follow with every cell of her being. She leapt to his knife and picked it up. Stomach now sinking backward into her spine, she held the knife and machete in front of her. "Let Victoria go, Mom. Go back to your hole. We don't want you here."

Mom's chin trembled. Shoving Vic, she let her go and lifted both hands. She spoke to the soldiers without taking her eyes from Addy's. "Load 'em up, we're leaving." Hands up, she rounded Addy on shaky legs. Her voice trembled. "If you change your mind, you know where I am."

Backing out of the circle of lights, she disappeared into the dark.

Vic gripped Addy's arm. "Cassius."

"Take me to him. I'll call a medic."

The floodlights turned off.

Plunged into darkness, Vic shoved her toward the building. "He needs more than a medic, Addy."

* * *

Sharp, new machete in one hand and handgun in the other, Jack sprinted with Morgan toward the lab.

Morgan panted. "Do you think they'll try and take Huxley?"

"I do," Jack said, between breaths. "Since he's camped out upstairs from the lab, they could get their hands on the research too."

Lab coming into view, Morgan slowed to a jog. "Do you see all that light?" He pointed in the direction of the Tree, out of sight. "We ought to get down there."

Addy.

Jack took in the lab building. Dark inside, the outer door was shut tight. He wanted to get to Adelaide, but. "We need to make sure Hux and the research are safe."

Rattling the knob on the front door, Morgan jerked his radio from his belt. "Red team leader, come in. Paxton. I need you."

The radio crackled. "*Yeah, boss. Where are you?*"

"Huxley's lab. Get your ass down here and make sure he's safe."

"*Boss, I'm—*"

"I don't give a rat's ass what you're doing. Get down here. Priority number one."

"*On my way.*"

Hooking the radio on his belt, Morgan turned. Hands on his hips, he gazed down the block. "What now? Do we wait for Paxton or get down there?"

Celia and Mike appeared from the dark, weapons drawn.

"Dad," Mike called.

"Mike. You guys stay here with Hux. I've got to get to Addy."

Celia unlocked the front door. "You got it."

Without waiting for Morgan, Jack took off at a sprint. His knees screamed all this running was ridiculous and it was time for a break. His lungs ached. He rounded the corner.

The yard of the Tree lit with giant floodlights, a group of people surrounded by armed guards took up one corner.

A shot echoed from up ahead. Addy dashed into the lights.

Jack put on speed, and Morgan paced him.

A shadow leapt from beside a crumbling old cafe and blindsided Morgan with a shoulder shove.

He fell, breath whooshing out.

Jack stopped, gun aimed. "Stop. Back off."

The young man looked up. In the glow from the floodlights, a jagged scar crossing his cheek caught Jack's eye. "How bout you back off. I owe this guy."

Morgan swept his legs, catching the boy at the ankles and knocking him off his feet. With the speed of a rattlesnake, he leapt and landed on top of him, ripping a knife out of his hand. "I've got him, Jack. Get to your kid."

With a nod neither of them saw, Jack picked up the sprint again.

Ahead of him, two men circled each other in the yard. One of them ran and the other followed.

Slowing, swallowing breath after breath, Jack missed who was being chased, but Matt was doing the chasing. He took a split second to consider helping him.

But he glanced into the yard again and found Addy facing her mother.

Son of a bitch.

Aiming for Melinda, he gazed down the sight of his gun.

The group of people by the fence crossed between them, and he lowered the barrel. He didn't know who was being taken, but they had a dozen soldiers on them. He couldn't take them all on. If Mike and Celia were here, different story. But with Matt disappeared off to the dark, it was just him and Addy. And, creeping closer, he saw she didn't have a gun. Only her machete and the Bowie knife she'd given Matt.

Melinda released the woman he recognized as Victoria, giving Addy a wide berth, and followed the soldiers with their hostages. As they loaded them into the truck, someone flipped the switch on the floodlights. The world went dark.

Jack unclenched his teeth and worked his jaw back and forth. He approached the truck and re-aimed the gun as his eyes adjusted. "Melinda, stop. Let these people go."

Hand on her hip, she spun. "You leave me to my business. Where are you?"

"Can't do that."

Her voice trembled. "Keep loading. We're only missing two. It'll have to do." Her feet crunched on gravel. "I could take you with me, Jackson. Would you like that?"

Her low laugh traveled up his backbone like cat claws. He shivered. Tried to get his brain to move through the molasses and come up with some sharp response. None came. "Just get the fuck out of here." Creeping backward, he found deeper shadows and crouched. He could still see her, outlined in the silver light of the moon, but he was fairly sure she couldn't see him. "We're not leaving you to keep doing this though. Believe me, we will stop you."

"You have no idea what you're stepping in. Why don't you go back to your island. Take the kids with you."

He lowered the gun, his mouth dry.

Eyes wide, she holstered her gun. "I'm serious, Jack. Take the kids and leave. Please." Creeping closer, looking over her shoulder, she lowered her voice. "Don't let them come near me again."

"Mama!"

That bastard Ricardo ran through the headlights on the other end of the truck and skidded to a halt next to her. He held a bleeding bicep. One eye was swollen shut. "We should go."

Without another word, she let him lead her to the truck. As she stepped into the cab, she peeked into the dark again. "Hector, get this thing started. Looks like we have to leave without our driver."

The truck started, belching exhaust behind it.

Jack covered his nose with his arm. He'd not noticed the stench of gasoline engines as a young man, but now he wished none of them survived the apocalypse.

As the truck rolled, a voice cried out for it to wait.

Running up from the dark street, the boy with the scar on his cheek jumped onto the back of the truck. Foot planted on the bumper, he grabbed a handhold. "Go!"

With the truck rumbling off down the street, Jack stood. Now the question. Back to Morgan, make sure he was all right? The boy had escaped him, which couldn't bode well. Or ahead to Addy? Was she OK? Was she hurt? Had Melinda ripped out her heart again?

In the fading exhaust stench, he backed away from Morgan and spun toward the Tree. His little girl still needed him. Morgan was a big boy.

He dashed through the fence, stopping long enough to push it closed. Once in the yard, he took a running start at the dock and scrambled up the side.

Addy's shrill, high voice floated through the empty front room. "Please, get the ambulance down here. Now."

A radio crackled with static. *"We're halfway across town. We'll be there as soon as we can. Can you stop the bleeding?"*

He couldn't make out her response. Following her voice, he crossed the barroom and passed through a short hallway. Down another hallway, light spilled from a room on the left.

"Hurry. Over and out." Addy cleared her throat.

Rounding the corner, Jack lowered his gun. His heart stopped and started again at a gallop.

Blood. There was blood everywhere.

"Addy, are you all right?"

"Oh, Dad, thank god. I'm fine. It's Cassius. He's." She rubbed the bottom of her jaw, smearing blood all over her face. "Well we got the bleeding stopped." Kneeling next to the ashen man on the floor, she glanced up. "Did you see Matt?"

Jack shook his head. "I saw him run off. He was chasing someone, didn't get a look at them."

"Hector, that fucker," she said, wrapping her fingers around Cassius's wrist. Using two fingers on the other hand, she felt for his pulse. She nodded at Victoria, whose white-blonde hair was highlighted with streaks of blood.

"Addy," he said, crouching next to her, "I saw Ric. Uh. Hector. He got on the truck with your mother and left."

Eyes darting to the door, Addy stiffened. "He. Shit."

Cassius moaned.

She looked back down. "Matt better be OK."

* * *

Melinda hopped from the cab and helped push the gate open. Dust crowding her nose, she sneezed and walked the gate closed once the truck passed. She followed the truck up the drive, where it parked next to the others, already empty and dark.

As the guards unloaded the prisoners, Hector stepped away from the truck and opened the recessed door into the Molehill. "Welcome home, traitors." When he glanced in Melinda's direction, he grinned. "Mama, want to welcome them back? We've missed them, yeah?"

Waving, wiping the dust out of her watery eyes, she changed directions. "I'll be right in. You get them settled." Stomach in a twist, oily acid gurgling up her throat, she trudged to the top of the hill. Flopping down in the grass next to her telescope, she folded her arms across her stomach and stared into the sky. The sliver of moon sat at the western horizon, and the cloudless night showed her the Milky Way in sharp detail.

The grass beneath her chilled her back and head, cold settling into the base of her neck.

"Count was a little short," Lash said, wicking through the grass. She sat next to her, laying a warm hand on her arm. "Missing two. Do I need to guess which ones?"

Melinda shook her head. "You know there's at least another dozen of them, out there in other cities."

"Don't give me that shit, woman. Why didn't you bring them in?"

"Complications."

"Anthony and his bosses aren't going to be happy." She tightened her grip. "What do you think they're going to do?"

Jerking her arm away, Melinda shook her head. The stars doubled. "They can't do anything worse to me." Cold tears tracked down the sides of her face. "Nothing worse than I've already done to myself."

"Em." Lash laid down next to her, their shoulders touching. "What's really going on?"

Melinda tried to catch one of the defunct satellites still circling the Earth. She couldn't focus. "They all hate me." Lips tight, she pulled air over her teeth. It chilled her front teeth, making them ache. "They refuse to see the benefit in what I'm doing. What we're doing. It's as if they blame me for the virus and forget that I'm trying to fucking fix it."

"Ah."

Melinda turned her head, staring at the side of Lash's face. "What?"

"What what? I didn't say anything."

Half Melinda's mouth turned up. "It was in your tone."

"You saw them, didn't you? Can't send you to town without you running into them. It's like they have you on radar."

Melinda eyed the stars again. Saturn shone back, without a twinkle, at the height of its arc. "It's not just them, Lash. Jack hates me, which"—she chuckled—"honestly, I get. He's hated me from the moment he found out I was still alive."

"You told me what happened. I get why he hates you now. Why would he hate you all this time?"

"I don't know. You'd have to ask him. But Addy hates me too." She rolled onto her shoulder. "I could see it in her eyes tonight. If she doesn't understand what I'm doing, doesn't have the imagination to get it, fine. But she hates me. Did you know Matt threatened to kill me?"

Eyes wide, Lash spun her head. "He didn't."

"When I asked Addy to come with me. He told me he'd kill me if I took her." She wrinkled her forehead. Considered his motives. "I don't know. People follow that girl like they follow me."

"She *is* your kid." Lash stroked the side of her cheek with one finger. "Can't say I blame them, if she's anything like you."

Laughing, Lash's finger on her cheek sending a pleasant chill down her spine, she rolled onto her back again. "There's a meteor shower in a couple days. Want to watch it with me? It's supposed to peak this year."

"Sure thing." She took Melinda's hand. "My fingers are getting cold. What do you say we go inside?"

"What do I tell Anthony?"

"You let me worry about Anthony. I'll tell him you gave me your report. Smooth it over." She kissed her hand. "I'm sorry they hate you, Melinda. You shine brighter than those stars up there. The things you've done can't be rivaled. It kills me the people you love most can't see that."

Rising onto her elbow, Melinda curled her free hand around Lash's waist and leaned over her. The starlight played in her eyes, bouncing bright specks of light into Melinda's own. She lowered her voice to a whisper, heart beating in her throat. "Not all of them."

Ilasha smiled, one hand sneaking to the back of Melinda's neck. "Come here."

CHAPTER 36

A serious-faced doctor in splotched scrubs closed the partition sheet around Cassius's bed. "Please. He needs some rest now. He's had a difficult night."

Addy stuck both arms out and tried to sweep the rest of the Troupe into them, herding them toward the door.

Victoria doubled over, face covered with her hands. Before Addy said anything, Rivers took one side and Grey the other. They hugged her and helped her shuffle toward the door. Tal hung back, both arms wrapped around himself.

Jim scowled and stepped close to Addy. "Where were you?"

She shuffled her foot, trying to direct Tal to the waiting area. "I. Uh."

Gripping her arm, Jim stepped closer and spoke into her ear. "We all know about you two. You didn't have to leave."

She stepped back. "You. We. What do you mean?"

"Adelaide, my dear," Tal said, "we of all people understand love does not pick an opportune time. It comes as it will and stays as long as it likes. You did not have to hide anything from us."

She glanced between the two of them, temples pounding. "First of all, it's not. We're not in lo—" She stopped. "Second of all, there's rules, you guys."

Jim removed his glasses. Large, round green eyes rested above deep circles. "We're not about to tell secrets outside the family. Your secrets are ours, my dear. We thought you knew that."

Eyes stinging, she shook her head and moved toward the hallway again. A tear rolled down her cheek. "I'm sorry. We... I guess we didn't want you to get in trouble for our bad decisions."

Victoria stopped. "And now Cassius has lost his leg because you couldn't trust us to keep your secrets. Shame on you, Adelaide Cooke. You are one of us. We would have done anything for you." Sobbing, she sank to the floor. "He was trying to protect me," she said into the tile. "This is my fault."

Addy reached for her. Chest tight, guilt laying over her in a red patina, all she could think was to hug Vic.

Sliding his glasses back on, Jim held out a hand. "Go. I'll handle her."

Tal kissed her on the cheek and released her.

On stilted legs, Addy walked out into the hallway. The lobby down the hall but out of sight, she caught the sound of Dad and Jane, Mike and Celia, and oh. A deep tenor.

Hell.

Waving down a nurse with at least as much baggage as Jim, she crossed her arms over her stomach. "Excuse me, nurse. Where might one go to take a, um." She lowered her voice and stepped farther from the lobby. "A, um, pregnancy test?"

Walking off, he waved a hand over his shoulder. "Follow me. I'm going right by the lab."

Settling a nail between her teeth, she gnawed on it as they flew down hallways and around corners. Leaving everyone else behind, she tried to remember every turn they took.

Eventually the nurse slowed and pointed down a short hallway. "It's right down there. Good luck." Throwing half a smile her direction, he took off down the hall.

One hand dropping to her machete, she ripped the nail off down to the quick.

She shoved the bleeding finger in her mouth and pushed a door labeled "laboratory" open with her shoulder.

A row of chairs with raised arms sat silent. On the other end of the shining room, someone sat at a desk with their head down.

Addy cleared her throat.

A young woman with hair shorn to half an inch looked up and smiled. "Can I help you?" From under her blue-framed glasses, her wide smile crinkled her eyes.

Clearing her throat again, Addy walked down the row of chairs. The room chilled her to the bone, and she crossed her arms. "Um. Someone brought me here and said I could, uh."

"Here," the woman said, holding her hand out to the last chair. "Have a seat. What do you need, hon?"

Sitting, Addy tried on a smile. It kinda worked. "I need a pregnancy test, please."

"No problem." She pointed at her name tag. "I'm Julia. Pleased to meet you. Here." She pulled up a clipboard from the back of her desk and attached a sheet of paper to it. "Fill this out, please. What was your name?"

Addy cleared her throat. Again. "Adelaide. Um. Addy."

Julia patted her on the arm. "Here, sit back. Don't be nervous. It's just a little poke." She arched an eyebrow. "Have you taken the Cure?"

The scene on the beach came to her with such clarity, she would have staggered if she were standing. Dean, giving her his Cure after hers had been lost. Almost dying because he'd rather save her.

Had she judged him too harshly? When he broke up with her, he was only trying to protect her. Misguided though it was.

She shook her head. "Yeah, sorry. Yes."

Julia turned to the cabinets lining the opposite wall. "It'll hurt less than that. By a lot."

"Oh. Good." She frowned. "Do you have a pen?"

"Duh. Yes." She unclipped a pen from the front pocket of her neon pink scrubs. "Here. Catch."

Looking up in time to catch the pen in the middle of its arc, Addy stuck out a hand and caught it.

Bobbled.

It clattered to the floor.

"Damn." Leaning, she overbalanced and about fell from the chair.

Julia chuckled. "Are you always this coordinated?"

Addy laughed, snagging the pen to fill out the nosy form. Name, age, height, weight, reason for visit. City quadrant. "No. Sometimes I fall over."

Julia laughed again, pulling her rolling stool in front of Addy's chair. She sat a tube and some kind of plastic sleeve with a needle sticking out on the chair next to them. "Here. Right arm, Addy. Have you ever cut yourself with that?"

Addy looked at her machete. Stuffed into her belt next to it, Matt's Bowie knife.

Her stomach dropped. Where the fuck was he? Was he OK? Had Hector killed him? Why wasn't he here?

Brow furrowed, she finished the form. "Plenty of times."

As Julia went about finding a vein and putting on gloves, Addy took in the room. It wasn't much, but a few drawings hung up over the desk. Colored with crayon, one thing Mom always made sure Addy had. That and paper to draw on. Learning to write had been as important as weapons training.

"Are those your drawings?"

"My kiddos." She paused. "Little stick." She sunk the needle beneath her skin, the edge of it bowing the skin as it sought the vein.

Addy's stomach thought about revolting, so she kept talking to quiet it. "How old are they?"

"Eight and two."

"Hey, my brother and I are the same years apart."

Sticking the tube inside the plastic sleeve, Julia pushed it into the needle. Hot blood spurted out so fast, it sprayed the back of the tube and fogged the dry side.

Dean's blood, as it spurted from his artery, had steamed. She hadn't taken time to care at that moment, but when she took the memory out with decreasing frequency, the steam hit her in the face. Warm blood, drying on the cold ground.

Julia removed the tube and the needle. "You did great. Hey, question." She peeped at the form. "You live on the south end, and you have some pretty well-used weapons there. Are you on the defense force?"

Addy nodded.

She leaned close. "OK, listen. This is supposed to take a couple of days, but I can get it done in like five minutes, if you can wait."

"Why?"

"My thanks to you and your friends. If it weren't for the defense force, this place wouldn't be worth living in. Even with everything lately, it's the best home I've ever had."

After she left the room, Addy hid her face in her hands.

If the test came back positive, what was she supposed to do? If she and Matt chose to stick it out, at least one of them would have to quit the force. Quit the Troupe.

If they'd have either of them back.

And if she didn't stay with Matt, then what? Dean acted interested in something, she wasn't sure what, but how would it change things if she was pregnant with another man's child? Should she even tell him?

And what about Ella?

Ella, who'd tried four times to have Matt's children.

Ella, who belonged to Matt as much as he belonged to her.

Who'd lost her daddy so suddenly she could hardly say goodbye. Had she even known her mother? Addy never asked.

And who'd been murdered by the hand of a puppet. A puppet whose strings were pulled by Addy's own mother.

How could she possibly take Ella's place in any of that?

Julia walked back in, clearing her throat.

Hands covering her mouth, Addy held her breath.

Holding out a paper, Julia smiled. "Congratulations, Mom."

* * *

Jane nudged Jack's shoulder. "Addy."

Jack looked around.

Addy walked between him and the window showing less of a black sky and more of a grey one. Sunrise wasn't far off. They'd been in this hospital for hours.

Celia and Mike had gone to sleep on a short, uncomfortable couch, leaned against each other. Seemed Celia's choice to stay with them had made her and Mike even more chummy than before.

The back of his mind tickled.

But here was Addy. Deep, blue-and-yellow circles under her eyes. And her eyes sunken, wide, and staring.

"Addy," Dean said, standing. "Are you all right? Is everything OK?"

"Those are two different questions," she said, sitting next to Jack.

Dean took the seat on the other side of her.

"Hey, Dad. Jane. You guys all right?"

Jane rocked the sleeping baby. "She usually wakes me at this time of night anyway." She shrugged. "We're all right. Are you?"

Addy stared at the wall.

It took a lot to rattle his little girl, but when it sunk in this deep, pulling her out of it was damn near impossible. "We heard about your friend."

She leaned her elbows on her knees and rested her chin in her hands, back bowed and shoulders hunched. "Jesus Christ. How's he going to act without his leg?"

Dean rubbed her shoulders. "At least he's alive. Could be worse?"

She buried her face in her hands. "I hate he's in pain."

Staring at the back of her head, Jack considered her. Something more than what happened to her friend weighed on her shoulders. "Baby girl. If you need to talk, I'm always here. About, um. Anything. Your mom, or." He cleared his throat. "Whatever."

She peeked from between her fingers. "Thanks."

He let one side of his mouth turn up and looked over her again. "We're all here for you. Whatever you need, all right?"

"He's right," Dean echoed. "All you gotta do is ask."

She spun her head his direction, and her shoulders loosened a micrometer as he rubbed them.

"Jack." Ragged and wilting, Morgan stood in the door to the waiting room.

Jack stood, leaving Addy to Dean for a bit. Arms crossed, he met Morgan in the door. "So? What's the damage?"

Morgan hung his head. "Paxton's dead. All the kids from the Molehill except Victoria are unaccounted for. I have to assume they've been taken back." Red-rimmed eyes met Jack's.

"Shit. Paxton's dead? What happened?"

"He saw me struggling with that Talus guy in the street. He came to help, but…" He shrugged, eyes red.

Jack closed his eyes. He hadn't known the boy well, but he'd seen the gold cross hiding under his shirt. Knowing Pax believed he'd have eternal life gave Jack some small comfort. Hopefully he hadn't been scared as the end approached.

He met Morgan's piercing brown eyes again. "You said all except Victoria? No one's seen Matt?"

Morgan stepped close, narrowing his eyes. "Jack. We have to consider the possibility he was never on our side. That none of them were. He might have gone home."

Stomach twisting, Jack glanced at his daughter. She'd trusted Matt so completely. The thought of him being Melinda's, like Hector, like Tim, socked him in the gut. Nausea threatened.

He grimaced. "The actor, the tall man, what's his name? Cassius?"

Morgan gripped his shoulder. "What about him?"

"He lost his leg. The whole Troupe is sleeping in a room down the hall. They refuse to leave without him."

"Of course they do. I don't expect them to leave without him. But he. Ah, god." He took a few steps into the room. "We have to do something about Talus. This cannot continue." Turning, he stopped halfway around, eyes wide and staring over Jack's shoulder. "I'll be damned."

With a pat on Jack's shoulder as he passed, Matt limped around him and into the waiting room. Eyes fixed to Addy, he sat next to her.

When she crushed him in a hug, Jack watched Dean's face. The color drained from it as he sat back.

And when Addy gripped Matt by the shoulders and looked him over, asking, in a rush of words, if he was OK and demanding he tell her where the hell he'd been, Jack's eyebrows met his hairline. "Oh boy."

Morgan looked between them and Jack. "Oh boy what?"

He shook his head.

Another man, shaggy brown hair almost to his shoulders and a manicured mustache hanging around the corners of his mouth brushed past Jack. "Morgan, a moment, please."

"Sure, Sly." They stepped away.

The man sneered at Addy.

Who'd stopped everything to watch him cross the room. Her chest rose and fell, and her eyes narrowed.

Jack would not like to be on the receiving end of that stare. Blood pressure rising, he moved a few inches toward Addy. So he could be between her and whatever she might be about to do.

Sly whispered in Morgan's ear, eyes on Addy.

Addy stood, jerking the Bowie knife from her belt. She brandished it. "About time to use this on you, Sly? Or are you going to get the *fick* out of here? Huh?"

Eyes darting between Addy and Sly, Matt stood to one side of her and pulled her machete from its scabbard.

Dean stood on her other side, one hand on her shoulder. "Addy. Breathe."

Sly crossed his arms and smiled.

Jack moved closer to his little girl. He hadn't seen her so unhinged in a long time, and now was not the time for this kid to try to intimidate her. It was good for him they were already in a hospital.

"Oh, that's it," Addy said, stepping toward him.

Matt matched her step.

Dean threw an arm across her chest. "Addy, don't. Not here."

Morgan took several small steps and stopped in front of her, looming.

Jack's blood pressure climbed. Maybe it was him who should be glad they were in a hospital. He was about to have a heart attack. Still, he dropped his hand to his gun.

"Is what Sly says true?" Morgan glared from Addy to Matt, voice rising as he spoke until it echoed off the ceiling tiles. "Were you not there? Is that why the heartbeat of this town is lying in there with half his goddamn leg blown off?"

Jack held his hand up. "Wait, Morgan. What are you saying?"

Deflating, Addy lowered the knife. "We weren't."

Jack's heart dropped to his toes. He could see his little girl drowning, over her head, and there wasn't a damn thing he could do about it. He shifted from foot to foot, one eye on Sly.

"You know why they weren't there, Morgan?" Sly chuckled and bounced on his toes. "You gonna tell him, or should I?"

Addy jumped forward again, raising the knife. "What do you fucking know about it?"

As Dean held her back, someone tugged Jack's belt.

He glanced down.

From her seat, Jane stared up at him. "Jack, don't. Let her handle it."

Relaxing the tight fist at his side, he left his other hand on the gun. "He's not gonna—"

"The first night you two got here," Sly began, "I told you. I don't like it when people shirk their duties to get their fuck on. That's what you wanna do, don't abandon your responsibilities." He smoothed his mustache. "Also, isn't there a rule against fraternization, Morgan?"

Morgan glared at Addy and Matt. "Is this true? Is that where you were?"

Addy didn't meet his eyes.

Matt exhaled a breath so long it could have come from his toes. "It's true."

Dean closed his eyes but didn't drop his arm. He remained ready to hold Addy back if needed.

Morgan snatched Matt by the collar. Addy's machete clattered to the floor. "I can't believe I trusted you, either of you"—he pointed at Addy—"with them." Throwing Matt backward, he sighed. "Get the fuck out of my sight."

Sly stepped up, mouth open. "Morgan, don't you wanna—"

"You'll shut up now, if you know what's good for you," Jack said. "Morgan has said his piece. I think we all need some air." He held a hand out to Sly. "Why don't you come with me. I could use a trip outside."

Sly grinned, a shark showing all its teeth. "I've got a stop to make."

Addy charged, raising the knife again. "Don't you come near Rivers or any of them. I keep my promises, you piece of—"

Dean grabbed her wrist. "He's not worth it, Addy."

Ripping her arm free, she brandished the knife at Sly again and stalked out of the room.

"Morgan, sir," Sly wheedled.

Without looking, Morgan waved a hand and sat in the closest chair. "About that, she's right. You're not to go near the Troupe. You know that." He covered his eyes. "Get the fuck out of here. I've had enough for one night."

As Sly cowered and fled from the room, Matt and Dean shared an uncomfortable moment where Dean picked up Addy's machete and handed it back to Matt. Without a word, Dean left the waiting area.

Heart slowing to something approaching normal, Jack's forehead tightened, and vertigo gripped him.

He sat next to Jane and pulled in a few deep breaths.

As Morgan's right hand but also as Adelaide's father, Jack's next few hours were about to get…interesting.

* * *

Crouching on her heels, leaned against the hospital wall, Addy dozed. Someone had to come out eventually. Tell her where she could go sleep. Dad could come lie to her about it all being OK.

A door crashed open, and Matt charged down the sidewalk.

She jumped, heart racing. Adrenaline dumping into her system, she bolted up. "Matt, wait."

He tripped. "Jesus, Addy. There you are. I didn't know where you went. I gave your machete to your dad. Did you talk to Morgan?"

They put the hospital to their backs. "Not since the waiting room. Why? Did you?"

"Yeah." He squinted at the sun. "Did Cassius really lose his leg?"

Rubbing the back of her neck, Addy nodded. Should have found somewhere to lay down. But her mind raced so fast from one subject to the next, she couldn't stop long enough to think. "I'm dead on my feet. I don't know where to go."

"I do." He stopped.

Stopping with him, she frowned.

His brow wrinkled, eyes bloodshot, his parentheses pointed at the ground. "I have to leave." He started walking again. "Gonna go get my bike. Then I'll be out of here."

"Wait," she said, jogging to him. She grabbed his hand. "You're leaving?"

"Morgan's sending me to the perimeter. I guess we're lucky he didn't kill me." Still walking, he stroked the back of her hand with his thumb.

"You can't. I mean, you don't have to. Can we just leave? We're not even supposed to be doing this. This isn't what we came here for."

He stopped. "A lot has happened that we didn't come here for. And I—"

Tugging the paper in her back pocket, Addy held her breath. The corner of the paper caught on the inside of her pocket. "I got a test done while I was here." Struggling, she freed the damn test results. "It's, um. Well it should be about a year younger than Jane's baby, I guess." She held the paper out.

Hand on hers, he lowered the paper. "I don't need to see it, Addy. We already knew." He stared at her chin. "It's good you'll be here. So you can see doctors and all that like you need to."

Stuffing the paper back in her pocket sideways, she let his hand go with the other and lifted his chin. "You don't have to leave. He doesn't own you. Or me."

Gripping her hand, he lowered it but didn't let it go. "I know. But listen. I want to go."

She pulled her hand loose. "Fuck me. What does that mean?" She blew a breath out. "You're choosing to leave?"

He crossed his arms. "Yes. No. It's." He stopped and closed his eyes.

When he opened them and pinned her with them, tears lining the corners, she plugged her smart comments, her anger, and waited for him to explain.

"It's been three months since Ella died. We were together for so long, I forgot what life was like without her. I don't know if I. I haven't let go of her yet, Addy. I'm trying, but it's not fair to you if I don't get through this first. It's just." He sighed, glancing at his feet.

"I get it. I sat there waiting for these test results and all I could think about was her. How she." Her voice trembling, she swallowed and swiped at her eyes. "How it should be her."

Head snapping up, one parenthesis reappeared. "No, Addy. Don't do that. This is you, and this is me, and this," he said, hand covering her abdomen, "is ours. And that's how it is. Don't think you don't deserve something good."

That did it. Tears streamed down her face.

"Besides. I've seen the way Dean looks at you. You've got a shot to get him back, you know."

Unable to focus, she wiped her cheeks and dried her hand on her pants. "I know. I don't know how to feel. You. You make what I thought was easy very complicated."

"Look, after I kicked the shit out of Hector, he left me pinned behind some 'Heads and my dense ass didn't have any weapons. I had to wait for the cleanup crew to come through. I had some time to think." He crossed his arms. "I think Morgan's suggestion of going out to the perimeter is a good one. I need to sort through my feelings about Ella. Get away from the guilt about, um, about us. Me and you."

The spring inside her coiled. "You're right. You're right. And Dean."

"And Dean. Figure him out, Addy. I don't think just because we didn't stop and think, just because we created a life together, that we need to make a life together." He stepped closer again. "It doesn't have to be *the* reason. If we sort through this shit, then—"

"Then if we want to, we can figure out what to do."

"I know he makes you happy."

So do you.

She crossed her arms over her stomach and wobbled on her legs.

"You find a place to lie down. I'll get out of here."

Adrenaline wearing off, sleep threatened to take her while she was still on her feet. "When will you be back?"

"I don't know."

She pulled the knife from her belt and held it out to him. "Take your knife."

Curling her fingers around it, he shook his head. "You keep it. Give it back to me when I come back, if you want to."

Before she could respond, he took two quick steps and filled her space. Cupping the back of her neck and her waist, he pulled her in and kissed her without hesitating. This time, it was definitely more tender. And the saddest kiss he'd ever given her, saliva mixed with salty tears.

Without looking, he let her go and hurried down the block. He rounded the corner and disappeared.

Though what she really wanted in this moment was to sink onto the sidewalk and sleep, she let her feet carry her home.

She tried to think about what he'd said, and how he'd said the most beautiful things she'd ever heard, and how she didn't know if it was her heart breaking or if it was just nausea. But she'd only slept those couple hours in the bed with him until everything had blown wide open. It was all she could do to string two thoughts together.

Stopping in front of the Tree, she considered going in. They'd gotten all the gates closed and everything secure before she escorted the Troupe to the hospital. They'd be safe when they came back.

There'd be blood to clean up though. There would be that.

Scowling, she walked past the Tree. There was no way they'd want to find Goldilocks in their beds.

As she approached the derelict apartment she shared with Matt, the switches in her mind went from "neutral" to "off" with a quickness. She pushed the broken door aside, wedging it closed after her.

And immediately recognized her mistake.

The 'Head stumbled out of the shadows.

She sniffed the air as she reached for her machete. The thing was still new but too old to save. Past its sixteen-hour expiration date. Curdled, coppery blood and rotten organs stank up the room. She would close the door at the top of the stairs once she cleaned this up and crawled upstairs.

But her machete had gone missing. She groped at the scabbard.

Empty.

Eyes wide, she looked up.

The 'Head less than three feet away reached, gurgling. Trying to kill and eat her and the tiny life inside her.

Speaking of that little life, she couldn't take the Cure if she was bitten. She could, but Mom said it would threaten the baby. Possibly fatal.

Ducking, she dashed across the room and heard another. Like a cicada looking for a mate, it creaked and croaked. Old, old thing. It stumbled from the back.

She'd have to search every inch of the place before she could pass out.

Of course, there was the matter of the missing machete.

With a sock in the gut, she remembered Matt left her the knife.

Grinning, she jerked it from her belt. It sliced the belt in two, and her pants sagged. "Son of a bitch," she murmured, one hand clenched on a belt loop. "Need a damn holster for this thing."

The fresh one's buzzing rose at the sound of her voice.

Slashing at it, she cut the tendon in its upper arm.

Its arm flopped to its side, and before the other one grabbed her, she gave it the same treatment.

Adrenaline rushed through her once again. Surprising she had any left, but it powered her. That and the anger.

Punching the 'Head in the face with her left hand, she kicked straight with her right foot and spun the thing. Stabbing it in the back, she gripped the shoulder. When the knife slowed, crunching through the bone and gristle of the spine, she twisted. The 'Head dropped, communication cut off from whatever passed as a brain to whatever passed as a body.

Not that Matt was wrong about Ella and Dean, he was a hundred percent right, but was now the time to bring that up? He could have brought it up sooner.

Relishing the short, sharp, precise cuts she made with his knife, she kicked the 'Head to the floor and ended it.

There was still another, after all.

It stumbled up the hall at her. Its cicada buzzing preceding it.

Of course, he did bring it up. Forever ago. On top of that roller coaster as they drank mimosas. It's not like either of them had gone in with their eyes closed.

They were both broken. So then they were broken together.

And now they were broken apart again.

The spirit to play with the 'Head departed as quickly as it'd come. Grabbing at her belt loop, she ended the 'Head with one swing and jerked the knife free as it fell. Hitching her pants up, she stalked through the rest of the building. Checking all the corners and closets, bouncing off walls and tripping over random junk in the floor they'd just let lie.

Satisfied, she climbed the stairs. She stumbled over every other one, forgetting the number of times he'd followed her up them, hands all over her before they even got to the top, lips breathing fire, and eventually dragged her feet to the top.

She closed the door behind her, wedging a chair under the handle. Not that it'd keep the door closed, but the noise it'd make falling over would give her time to react, if she needed.

As she crawled into the bed, brain on autopilot, she smelled him on the sheets.

She laid the knife on his side of the bed and fell asleep so fast she forgot to cry.

CHAPTER 37

Dropping a duffel bag on the floor by the front door, Morgan put his hands on his hips. "Are you sure you can handle the council, Jack?"

Jack paused while reading one of Morgan's substantial files on the council members. "No." He shrugged. "I had a bit of trouble with a thing like this. A while back."

Morgan shook his head. "We can't let Talus do this to us again. We have to take this fight to them."

Jack leaned on the desk. Morgan's fancy chair creaked. "I agree. It was a mistake to sit on our hands when we got here. I should have told you everything I knew about her as soon as we met."

Morgan grinned. "I'm gonna bet there's a lot of things you know about her you're not about to share."

Jack got through the next few seconds without clenching his teeth. "While that's strictly true, you know what I mean. Question," he said, picking the file up again. The words blurred on the page, Melinda's face flowing through his memories. He didn't know if he could ever let it go, but at least he could live with it now.

"Shoot."

"Why leave me in charge? You barely know me. And I suck at this." These council members looked so fresh-faced and eager. Almost as bad as Wade was. The snake.

What a simple problem he'd been.

Morgan sat across from him. "I know we just met. But I like you, Jack. Your kid could make better decisions, but she's not a bad kid."

"She's a great woman. We all make mistakes."

Crow's-feet deep beside his eyes, he laughed. "That, we do." He leaned on the desk. "The thing is, of all the people I've ever met in this town, and of all the people who've ever worked for me, or I've worked with, you're the only one who truly, deeply understands what we're up against." Leaning forward, he dropped his voice. "Why she's so dangerous."

"That, I get," Jack said. "In intimate detail."

"God save me from idealists and assholes," Morgan said, standing and popping his back. "All right. I'm gonna round up some troops. The first ones, the ones from Florida, should be here next week. Probably take a few weeks to get enough for this plan. Hopefully we can avoid Talus raids until then."

"If not, we'll have extra hands to help. That'll be good." Someone to stand between him and Melinda, at the least.

"Come take a look at the map. Then I'll get outta here. Go get us a cannon." Morgan frowned. "You know, you got a family here too. All of them, it seems like. You're the kind of man who'd do anything to protect them."

Joining him at the map, Jack folded his arms. "How do you know that?"

"They're all still alive."

Corners of his mouth turned down, he smiled.

Morgan clapped him on the shoulder. "Just the kind of man I can trust with my city. Now, look here." He pointed to the map. "I want the troops to filter in here, here, and here," he said, pointing to three buildings downtown. "They've got room, supplies, and people to feed and house them. They won't need to do anything while they're here, but if they want to help out with the animals or the farming, their hands would be appreciated."

Jack grimaced. It had to be asked. "What about Addy?"

Morgan's frown went so deep, his jaw about hit his chest. "I sent Matt to the perimeter. I can't send her back to the Troupe. Even if they want her." He sighed. "I'm not sure they do." He shook his head and took up pacing again. "I really thought I had the Troupe licked. They're so finicky. And easy to exploit. It's hard to find good security for them."

"What do you mean, easy to exploit?"

Crossing his arms over his chest, Morgan stopped. "Take Sly, for instance. When he was their guard, he felt like they were his personal property. He's a great soldier, but he's got a sense of entitlement as wide as the Atlantic."

"Ah. I've met guys like that. Why do you keep him on?"

Morgan came back to the map. "Lots of reasons. The guys look up to him, he's a good leader, and like I said, he's a good soldier. But I'm surprised he can fit in the room with his own ego sometimes."

"So keep him away from the Troupe. And Addy. She's likely to kill him."

Barking a laugh, Morgan glanced at the map again. "I don't know what to do with her. I appreciate what they did do. But I guess Jim will have to do until I can find someone else." He headed for the door. "You decide what to do with Addy. I trust your judgment. Pax can tell you—" He stopped, back to Jack. His shoulders fell. "Shit. Davin. He was second for Red Team. Davin is your man for that quadrant now. He can tell you the finer points of policy. You, my friend"—he spun, finger pointed—"have to speak to the council about taking action against Talus. They'll go for it. But you have to get them there."

Jack bit his lip. "Time to polish up my silver tongue."

* * *

Addy woke alone, staring at the ceiling.

She didn't have to look around to know she lay alone in the room. The bed, empty and cold, where there should have been two, held only one. No one breathed in the room but her. There were no ghosts. They'd all fled.

Scooping up the knife, she shoved it down the inside of one boot.

The dresser with two of its four drawers gaped at her. The drapes hung sideways. The lamp accused her of not caring enough to set it upright and make this into a real home.

Arms crossed over her stomach, she rushed down the stairs and out the door before the tears caught her. She'd had enough of them.

Pants sagging, she trudged up the block and passed the Tree. She had an extra belt in there. Clean shirts. Angry friends.

She continued past without slowing and on to Morgan's office. Evening wasn't far off, the sun well past the height of its arc. She'd never slept so late. Not ever. Her brain fuzzy, she approached Morgan's door.

Thought about not knocking. About turning around and walking out the way Matt had gone.

She knocked.

"Come," Dad called.

She opened it and hung on the door handle. "Hey, Dad. Where's Morgan?"

"Come on in, little girl. Shut the door."

She did, joining him at the desk. "Is he in the back? Does he not want to see me?"

Dad held up a finger, finished reading something on the paper in front of him, and put it on the desk. "One, no he's not in the back. Two, no he doesn't want to see you."

Her gut crawled up her throat. "Does he want me to leave? He already pushed Matt out."

Dad frowned. "I don't blame you for what happened, Addy. They had guards. The night watch was there. You were on your own time."

Tears stung her eyes, and her stomach growled.

Smile touching his lips, he glanced at her midsection. "Hungry?"

"Kinda."

"Let me take you home. We'll get you fixed up. It's about time to head there anyway." He stood. "There's a dribble of coffee left. Want it?"

"No, thanks. Where's Morgan?"

"You don't want any? Who are you and what have you done with my daughter?"

Matt's words sprang to mind with force. He'd asked her that just yesterday. Yesterday? How had her life changed so completely since yesterday?

She buried her face in her hands. Fingers wet, she swallowed the rest of the tears down her burning throat.

"Hey, little girl, hey. You all right?" He came around the desk, pulling her up and into a hug.

She shook her head against his shoulder.

Smoothing her hair, he led her to the door. "Let's get home. Here. Let me turn off the pot."

She dried her face and straightened her hair and shirt. Her pants sagging again, she hitched them up.

"Morgan's gone. He's rounding up soldiers, a cannon, some other equipment. All we need for a full assault on the Molehill."

Her breath hitched. "A what?"

He ushered her out the door and locked it behind them. "Addy, we can't let them keep doing this. Not after what happened to your friend, the others. After they kidnapped all the kids like Matt and took them back to the Molehill."

Staggering, her gut wrenching, she grabbed at his shoulder.

He took her hand.

"They did? Is that who all those people were?"

"All except Matt and your friend Victoria. They're the only ones left in the whole city."

Leaning on his shoulder, she let him lead her to his house. "I guess you're right."

"But Mom" stuck on her tongue and wouldn't pop out. It's not like she deserved to be defended. But a full-scale assault might leave her dead.

And Addy still wasn't ready to go there again. It was almost more difficult to have her alive than it was to have her dead, but did they have to kill her again?

He unlocked the gate to his yard, because of course he had a fence, and led her up the walk. "Do you have somewhere to stay?"

She shook her head.

Inside, he reset the proximity alarm with a button by the door. Because of course he had an alarm. He ushered her in and relocked the door. "You can stay with us, if you want. We've got an extra room, the couch, whatever."

She flopped on the couch and covered her eyes with her arm. "Is there somewhere Morgan wants me to go?"

The couch depressed next to her. "He left it up to me."

She chuckled. "OK then. What torture have you cooked up?"

"I haven't. I'll let you decide. You know Paxton is dead?"

Covering her face with her hands, she closed her eyes and saw his golden cross. "Yeah. Fucking sucks."

"A guy named Davin is in charge of this quadrant now. But he needs a second and administrative help. Want to check it out?"

Wiping her face, she stood. "Considering my failure with the Troupe, it's a bad idea for me to be a lieutenant again. But I'll see if he needs help filing papers or shooting 'Heads or something."

The baby cooing, Jane walked in and laid her on a blanket in the middle of the floor. "Hey, Addy. Going somewhere?"

Katherine lay on the blanket, her fists flying as she bicycle-kicked her legs. She gurgled and smiled at her mother.

Clutching her stomach, Addy knelt next to her sister. Seeing the baby reminded her of her own and of all the complicated shit that sprang from its very existence. Dean, Matt, the fact she was somebody's mom now. Now and forever. Her thoughts twisted around themselves. "It's getting late. Maybe I should stay here."

"Sure," Dad said. "Let me get the room ready, then I'll get some food on."

* * *

"Jane," Jack said, setting the plates in the sink.

"Jack." She leaned against the counter, baby in the crook of one arm.

"Here," he said, sliding his hand under little Katie's head, her baby hair soft against the rough palm of his hand.

Jane slid her into his arms and stretched. Skin of her stomach peeking from under the raised hem of her shirt.

"Do you think Addy's OK? She hardly ate anything. And now she's in bed." He glanced at the window. "The sun hasn't even finished setting."

"No. Her friend lost his leg. Dean came. Matt left."

Rocking the baby, whose eyes rolled around, trying not to close, he walked into the living room and perched on the couch. "What's Matt leaving got to do with it?"

With a laugh, Jane reclined in the high-armed chair she'd chosen as her own. "Don't be thick, honey."

He slid back. "What's—" Something poked him in the hip.

Scooting forward again, he checked the couch. Protruding from between the cushion and the back of the couch, a folded paper stuck a corner out. With his free hand, he teased it loose. "What's this?"

"Maybe it was there all along and we didn't notice it?"

He unfolded it.

A lab report of some kind.

Addy's name under the words "TEST RESULTS FOR."

Her age, height, weight, and all below it.

Below that, boxes to check for the type of test.

The box for pregnancy test was checked.

Jack's breath caught. His temples pounded. Of their own will, his eyes traveled to the "results" block.

A check mark next to "positive" and scrawled below that, a due date in late December.

"Jack? You all right? You look like you've seen a ghost."

Eyes wide, his arm rocking the baby, he stared up at Jane. The spit had dried in his mouth. It was the goddamned Sahara in there. "I." Without words to continue, he handed the paper to Jane.

Fine line between her brows, she read it, eyes flying over the paper faster than his own had.

A smile touched her lips. She looked up at him, eyes alight.

She looked back at the paper. Her mouth moved. "Shit. Oh. Dammit, Jack."

Swallowing, manufacturing saliva, and swallowing again, he found at least a couple words. "What? What's wrong?"

"It's not Dean's. She's not far enough along. We were in DC when…"

Jack waved his hand in the air. "Stop. I surrender. It's enough that my little girl is pregnant. I don't need to think about the complications of her love life."

Folding the paper up, Jane traded him for the baby.

He flipped the test results around in his fingers. "What are we gonna do?"

"What do you mean?"

"Do we tell her we know? Does she need our help, or. Or what?"

She pulled her new nursing top down to feed the baby. "If she wants our help, she'll let us know. The question is whether or not to tell her we know." Chuckling, she narrowed her eyes. "You're not usually this indecisive."

"I. I guess I didn't expect to. I don't know." He stood, crossing his arms over his suddenly too-full stomach. "Whose is it?"

Jane scoffed. "You know the answer to that."

"Yeah. I guess I do." Stopping, he stared off into the past. "Did you know Melinda and I broke up for a few weeks?"

"When?"

"Before she got pregnant with Michael. I don't remember why. I think she was mad at me for something." Narrowing his eyes, he gazed harder. The memory fuzzy, he had a difficult time sharpening the focus. "I think she thought I'd had my eye on another girl or something. Whatever teenagers get mad about."

Jane laughed. "I guess. My teen years were a little different."

He sat on the couch again. "Why did I tell you this?"

"Why did you?"

He glanced up at her, that fine line between her brows, the way her nose reddened as he looked her over, her hair spilling onto her shoulder. It grew so fast. "Oh, right. The rebound."

"And this is the story of why it took you ten years to get into another relationship after she died, isn't it?"

"Dating was different then."

"Ha. True."

"But I did see someone else while we were broken up. I was so hurt. She killed me, breaking up with me like that. It was so sudden." He frowned. "I guess breakups often seem sudden to the one getting dumped."

She leaned forward and squeezed his knee. "Sorry."

He met her eyes. Round and soft. "For what?"

"Dumping you that one time."

"Thanks. It worked out." Smiling, he lifted up and leaned into her space. Kissed her on the side of the mouth. "I don't even remember the girl's name. It meant that little to me."

"I see what you're getting at." She sat back. "Matt and Addy were each other's rebounds."

"Ella just died, Jane. He was using my little girl to make himself feel better." His temples pounded again.

"Addy's a grown-up, Jack. And it's not like she wasn't doing the same thing."

"That doesn't make it any better."

"I don't know. Why don't you talk to her about it?"

He glanced at the test results. "I don't want to intrude. I already have. I'll leave it up to her."

She stood. "This baby is asleep. Let's put her down," she said, holding her free hand out to him, "and I can make it up to you for breaking your heart."

He took her hand and stood. "Ah, Jane. You don't owe me for that."

Standing on tiptoes, she kissed him on the temple. "If you say so, love." Taking his hand, she pulled him through the house.

Once in their room, Jane laid Katie in her bassinet. "Gonna have to get her a bigger bed soon. Or bring her back in the bed with us."

"Hey, Jane, question."

"Shoot." She laid back, arm behind her head.

"How's things going in the lab? You guys making progress?"

She shrugged. "I still don't understand a lot of it. But Huxley says there's another way to manufacture the vaccine. He says he doesn't have the facilities here, but he's ninety-eight percent sure he can do it."

He faced her. "That's good. We're going to launch a real assault against the Molehill when Morgan gets back, and I'd like us to be able to replicate the Cure and the vaccine. And if we need their research on immunity, we need to know that before we go in. We'll need to raid their labs before we blow the place up."

Lips pressed together, she turned her head and stared at the bassinet. "Tell me something, Jack."

"Anything."

Flushed, she wiggled her feet but didn't face him. "Why didn't you take Melinda back? When we were split up?"

Melinda's face tried to intrude. Not the one he had loved. The other one.

He pushed it aside. It fell away. Opening his mouth to answer, he stared at the side of Jane's face.

Her jaw worked. "We can change the subject if you want to."

Swallowing, he slid closer and cupped the opposite side of her jaw, though he didn't tug. If she wanted to hide her face, he'd let her.

But she didn't. She turned back to him, eyes wide and naked.

"I don't know if I could have told you this before. I didn't know before." He nuzzled her nose. "And the answer scares the shit out of me, because it could happen to anyone." Swallowing, he met her eyes again. "To you, even."

The line appeared between her eyes. Deeper than it'd been a year ago, but still fine and thin. "What?"

"I resent her."

"Even then?"

He rolled to his shoulder. "Even then. It was, it was awkward at first. Because she'd been gone so long. It still might have been OK. But then she took us to the hospital and. She. Well." Gazing into Jane's eyes, he grimaced. "She was dead for over a decade. It took me a long time to accept she was gone. And even longer to be all right with that. And while I worked on those things, I remembered how beautiful and perfect she was. It kept me going on so many of those cold, lonely nights."

Jane sighed. "She's not perfect. And you resent her for that."

"When you put it that way, it sounds silly."

"It is, Jack. No one's perfect." She laughed. "Not even me."

Scooting close again, he kissed her under the ear. "No kidding."

"Oh, what the hell," she said, leaning away and punching him in the shoulder.

He grabbed her wrist, preventing her from hitting him again. He tried to pull her in for a kiss.

Resisting, she laughed and squirmed. Without freeing her wrist, she scooted around and threw a leg over him. Pushing with her hips, she avoided his other hand and vaulted herself on top of him. "You better enjoy this perfection while it lasts then."

And oh, he did.

CHAPTER 38

Addy's eyes opened. With the shades in the room drawn, hooks under them like Dad's house back in Arizona, the weak morning sun could have been sunset. God knew she was tired enough for it to still be the same night.

She sat up and threw her legs over the side of the bed. One of her feet was asleep. Rubbing her leg, she kicked it until the pins and needles started, waiting for them to pass. The worst thing in the world was bumping a waking limb. It hurt worse than whatever grey lump had taken up residence inside her chest instead of a heart.

OK, maybe not that much.

Either way, once the pins and needles stopped, she stood on the foot and tested it. Her ankle held, so she dragged the blanket off the bed, wrapped it around her shoulders, and limped down the hall. The ghosts of coffee past floated toward her.

"Dad? Jane?"

Red hair flying, Jane popped her head out of the kitchen. "I'm in here. Hey, you dropped something last night. It's on the coffee table."

Feeling for her belt, her questing hand found the pajama pants she'd borrowed from Jane that were two sizes too small. "Right," she mumbled, shuffling toward the coffee table.

On it lay a folded piece of paper.

Sleep brain still fuzzy, she leaned over to pick it up. What it was hit her when her hand was halfway down.

"It doesn't look better today," she whispered. "I thought it would."

Jane called from the kitchen. "What's that?"

"I said did you read it?" Leaving the test results on the table, she shuffled to the kitchen.

Jane bustled about, washing up breakfast dishes. "Look at me, all Janie housekeeper. Weird, right?"

"Very. What's wrong with you?" Addy sat at the table, chair creaking. Had she started to gain weight already? She knew next to nothing about having babies.

"Yes, we read it. Coffee?"

"A splash, please. With some milk."

Jane chuckled. "The test results didn't lie. Though," she said, handing her the cup, "you seem less sick than I was." She got the milk from the fridge and took the chair next to Addy. "How are you feeling?"

Addy poured in a dash of milk and sipped the cooled coffee. "He likes sugar in his coffee."

"Matt?"

Pressing her lips together, she nodded. "He's the father, you know."

"I do."

"What did Dad say? Where is he?"

"Oh, that's why I'm doing the damn dishes. He had to go diplomat some people. He showed me how to tie a tie. It was interesting."

"He wore a tie? I don't think I've ever seen that," Addy said, taking another sip. The coffee cooled so fast with milk in it, but the thought of black coffee made her sick. "He owns one?"

"No. He and Morgan got it from Paxton's things. I'm shocked he knew how to tie it, honestly." Frowning, she rubbed a spot on the table. "He was pretty upset at Matt. Accused him of using you."

"That's—" Addy started. Trailing off, she tried to stop the assault her memory wanted to hit her with. It didn't work, and she pictured the first time they'd been together. The way he breathed on her mouth, all hot and forceful, when he'd told her not to call him by his full name. And the way she had a moment to stop him, but the hurt and the anger and the fear were too much. She needed him to make it go away. "That's ridiculous. If anything, I used him."

Jane stood and made herself a small cup. "What's going on with you two now?" She sat and laid a hand over Addy's. "What about Dean?"

"That's. It's. Can we change the subject?"

"Sure. To what? Want some eggs?"

"I don't think so. I don't feel sick, but my stomach also doesn't seem to like me. Got some toast or something?"

"I'll do you one better," Jane said, standing. She opened a cupboard above the coffee pot. "Mike got me a bunch of these while I was pregnant with Katie. My morning sickness was pretty awful, but these helped. Sometimes." She offered Addy a red-and-white striped candy shaped like a hook.

Unwrapping one corner, Addy licked it with the tip of her tongue. It stung but also soothed. Made the inside of her mouth feel like the middle of a strong breeze. "What is it?"

"Peppermint. He called these candy canes. But everything is candy something to him."

Addy laughed. "True." Unwrapping more of it, she stuck the end in her mouth. Her stomach decided it felt better and stopped being so fuzzy around the edges. "Tell me about the lab. What are you guys doing, exactly? Do you need help?"

Not that she necessarily wanted to help out there. But where the hell else was she going to go?

"You're always welcome, you know that. As for what we're doing, it's funny you should ask. Jack asked me about it last night."

"I guess that makes sense. After seeing Mom again." She tongued the candy cane. "It did get me thinking about what she's been doing. About all that talk about the vaccine and immunity and all."

Jane shrugged. "Hux is pretty convinced immunity is biological. He's tested a handful of babies. And you know about Celia's nephew?"

"Celia's what now?"

"Her nephew. Great-nephew, I guess. Long story, but the bottom line is, he's immune. Like Katie. And about half a dozen other babies Hux has tested."

"You mean they...these people never even saw my mom? Or Talus? Haven't had the vaccine or anything?"

She shook her head. "No. The only one who's ever been touched by Talus is me. Even if the ones here in town were lying, and I don't think they are, Celia's nephew couldn't possibly have been tainted by them." She knocked back the rest of her coffee. "The way I was."

"I ran into some 'Heads the other night. When I remembered what Mom said about the Cure and how it might affect the baby, I almost lost it. It terrified me to think what a bite could do." Swallowing, she glanced up at Jane, her eyes wet. "I've known this baby for a day. I don't want it to die."

Laying her hand over Addy's again, she squeezed. "I know."

Addy set the cup down and grabbed her hand with the other one. "I'm glad you got the vaccine before you were bitten. What if something happened to the baby? Or"—she swallowed, a tear dropping to the table—"or to you?"

Jane's chin trembled. "We're all right. And you will be too." Sniffing, she swiped at the corner of her eye and punched Addy in the shoulder. "Just don't get bit."

Addy stood. "Grab the baby. Let's go down to the lab. You can show me all the fancy stuff."

Jane set their cups in the sink. "Sounds fun."

* * *

Jack sat in a vaulted-ceilinged lobby, smoothing the ridiculous tie. He hadn't worn one since some honor roll presentation in high school. Before he'd met Melinda. To say he felt like he couldn't breathe was an understatement.

The giant wooden door behind him creaked open. "Mr. Cooke?"

Wiping his sweaty palms on his pants, he stood. Flattened the tie. "Yes? Mr. Knapp, right?"

The thin man stepped away from the door, hand extended. Long, slender, piano player fingers gripped Jack's hand, giving him a good, if young, handshake. "Thank you for coming down today, Mr. Cooke. We understand Morgan has entrusted you with the defense force. We appreciate being able to put a face to a name."

"What about Morgan's plan?"

"The assault?" He crossed his arms.

Watching his face wrinkle, Jack frowned. His fight here was only beginning.

"We're split. A little less than half of us, myself included, agree with Morgan and yourself." He swallowed.

Scowling, Jack paced. "What about all the people they've kidnapped or killed? The people who've been turned into monsters and sent back to live some kind of bullshit half-life, tied up underground?" Stopping, he slapped his leg with his hand. "Do those people not matter? Do they not get a vote?"

Knapp swallowed again, green around the gills. "There are those on the council who think it's an acceptable risk. That our population is safe, by and large." He cleared his throat. "That the percentage of those kidnapped or killed is slight, compared to the rest of the city."

"Acceptable…you know Melinda talks like that?" He stepped in and filled Knapp's bubble. "There is no acceptable risk. Every single person in this city matters."

"There are those," Knapp said, crossing his arms, "stuck in the middle. Now that you bring up General Thibodeaux, I have to tell you, it's your personal experience with her that is keeping some of those in the middle from agreeing with you. They think you're biased."

Jack's heart beat faster. Clenching his sweaty hands, he backed up a step. "I'd think that'd convince them. I know her, Knapp. She won't rest until she gets what she wants."

"And do you know what she wants?"

"Immunity. She wants to prove she can create immunity."

"Do you think she can?"

Jack shook his head. "I think she's delusional. Our doctor thinks it's biological. Nothing more."

"See, that's the problem. You think she's delusional, but she's your ex-wife. There are some who think you're prone to exaggerate when it comes to her."

Heart jumping into his throat, he put his hands on his hips. "You're kidding. This isn't about me and her."

"I know that," Knapp said, hand out, palm down. "I know. But some of them don't. Listen. Let's walk outside."

Jack followed him out the front doors and onto the steps. Giant pillars held up the marble front. The building looked at least a hundred years old or more.

Knapp stopped at the top of the stairs. "Some of them can be swayed."

Shoulder against a sun-warmed pillar, Jack crossed his arms. "What do you think it'll take?"

"You didn't hear this from me," Knapp said, leaning in close, his breath hot. "If your daughter could get her actor friends in here, especially Cassius, it would help. They mean a lot to everyone. Some think of them almost as royalty." He backed up. "If they see what has happened to them, hear their story, it may help sway them. We only need to convince three others and you'll have your war."

Jack stepped away from the pillar, stomach churning. "I don't want a war, Knapp. I want to end this."

CHAPTER 39

"Haven't seen you around enough lately, woman," Lash said, climbing the hill. "You been keeping busy?"

Melinda frowned, staring through the telescope at Saturn. Although she'd visited the basement file room and Anthony's office several times over the last few days, nothing she found assuaged her doubts. Nor had she learned anything more substantial. "Not busy enough. I need back on immunity."

One of the folding camp chairs Melinda had set up creaked. "You know that's not gonna happen."

Exhaling through her nose, Melinda bumped the telescope and lost Saturn. She stood, cracking her back. "Fuck's sake. Why not?"

"Anthony's not happy about that risk you took with Addy. Neither am I, to tell the truth. We worry about you, Em."

Teeth clenched, she leaned back into the scope. "Maybe *you* do. Anthony only worries about what I can give the company."

"If you say so."

Melinda adjusted the focus. "Want to see Saturn's rings? Pretty spectacular." She stepped back, lifting her face to the sky. "The last time this meteor shower peaked was 1982."

Standing next to her, Lash looked up. "I don't see any."

"It usually gets going after midnight. Here, take a look at Saturn."

Leaning down into the scope, Lash raised her hand. "Where's the focus?"

Laying her hand over Lash's, she guided it toward the focus. "Here."

"Need to get your eyes checked."

"Whatever. You—"

Behind and above them, the sky lit up.

Melinda spun, eyes drawn skyward. White light filled the sky. Several thoughts blasted through in quick succession.

A camera flash?

Not from the sky.

The sun? At this hour?

No, it's the wrong angle.

A missile. We're under attack.

In the middle of the white, a spot turned purple.

Her rising blood pressure bloomed into adrenaline and dopamine. Elated, she stared as the purple spot resolved into a revolving hunk of rock.

"Holy shit," Lash breathed.

The flaming rock skidded right and exploded into blue and green fragments as it crossed the sky, leaving a trail of dust that could have been a mile wide.

Smile almost touching her ears, Melinda turned to Lash. "Did you see that?"

Lacing her fingers between Melinda's, Lash cozied up next to her. "I did. Did you make a wish?"

Melinda scoffed. "I haven't wished on a shooting star since I was six. But if I did, I would have wished for Anthony to fly off a cliff in a fast-moving car. Preferably while in flames."

Lash laughed from deep in her throat. "I'll light the match."

Chuckling, Melinda leaned into her shoulder. A cluster of meteors streaked across the sky. "How are my subjects doing?"

"Good. The first group has been exposed to the active virus."

"And?"

"One hundred percent survival rate. Your vaccine is a success."

Melinda found the chairs before her knees gave. "Thank god."

Lash sat next to her, pointing out another bright meteor. "You glad they made it? Or are you happier your vaccine works?"

"I'm glad they made it."

"Mmmm-hmmm."

"If they hadn't, we wouldn't be able to test my immunity theory. We'd have to wait for the next group."

With a chuckle, Lash sat back and grabbed her hand again. "You got a black little heart, my love."

Ignoring the sky, Melinda turned to her. "I do not. Do you know how many people we could save if we give them immunity? We could save the whole planet. Isn't it worth that? A few women?"

"I thought the vaccine would be enough for you." Lash continued to search the sky for meteors, eyes darting everywhere.

"I'm thrilled it works, don't get me wrong." Melinda stopped, the image of Jane in that testing room coming back to her. The sheaves of her hair in the trash after they'd shaved the side of her head. She assumed the girl wouldn't survive the trial.

Of course, the results had been serendipitous. It was lucky she'd been impregnated prior to the trial. What a wonderful accident.

"Where'd you go?"

Melinda shook her head. "Sorry. Sorry. I was thinking about the mistake that started all this."

"I'm sorry Anthony keeps coming between you and your project," Lash said, squeezing her hand. "Don't tell him I said that."

Melinda caught another cluster of meteors streaking through the sky with their smoky trails. "Thought you were worried about me."

"I am. But I know it means a lot to you. And I like to see you happy."

Swallowing, Melinda smiled and swung their clasped hands. "Can I tell you something? Doesn't go past us?"

"Of course."

"I think Burke was a spy for us."

Wide-eyed, Lash turned. Her mouth hung open. "Why? What do you mean?"

Melinda wrinkled her brow. She was pretty good at keeping secrets, but the possibility Burke had been using her to drive a wedge between herself and Talus had burrowed into her brain and made a home. She had to talk to someone about it. "I found some transcripts. Phone calls. He was feeding Anthony information."

"I don't think a couple phone calls proves that."

She sat up. "Fine. How about this? I found recordings. Secret recordings from inside the homes in Magnolia. Even my own. Hidden microphones I had been led to believe were placed there by IRF."

Lash sat up with her, meteors falling behind her. "What do you mean? Where did you find this?"

"Anthony's office. And Burke sent it back here. All of it. Everything Jack said. Addy. Everyone else. It's all here. How can it all be here, Lash? And I still don't know how IRF got my vaccine." She jerked her hand free and stood. Pacing, she waved her hands about as she talked. "I can't put it all in a straight line. None of it makes any sense. And it's all so incestuous, I have no idea what's going on."

Lash approached her, laying a warm hand on her shoulder. "If it helps, I'll look into it for you. Or help you. Whatever you need. But you have to promise me something."

Slapping her leg with her free hand, Melinda gazed at her. "What?"

"Don't sneak into Anthony's office. If he finds you in there, there's nothing anyone can do to help you."

"You're the only one who cares about helping me."

"I'm serious, Em. Stop sneaking in there."

She eyed the sky, trying to take in the whole thing at once. She missed the western skies and their clarity. "I wish I could see even half the stars here I could see in the west, Lash."

Leaning against her shoulder and sliding one arm around her shoulders, Lash looked up with her. "Maybe sometime we can go out there. You can show me the glory of the Milky Way."

"I'd like that."

* * *

Dean held out a hand. "Let me help you over the ledge."

In her head, Addy swatted it aside.

She took it. "Thanks."

He clicked on a flashlight with a red beam. "Sorry I couldn't find you a telescope. I tried. Town this big, you'd think I'd run into one somewhere."

Standing on the roof of the lab, she crossed her arms and looked up at the starry sky. Not as much sky as there was in Arizona, but it'd have to do. "That you even tried is sweet. Thank you."

"You're welcome. Got some chairs." He gestured.

Before coming on this ill-advised date, she'd encased her heart in a layer of ice, but looking in his round eyes, the sliver of moon reflected in them, it melted.

She looked past him. "Look, over there." Pointing, she crossed the roof, avoiding a pipe at the last moment, sidestepping, and wobbling on one foot.

Dean caught her. "Careful. Don't forget we're like thirty feet up."

"At least we didn't go downtown where you're staying. Those buildings are dangerously tall." Gripping his bicep, a bicep she'd forgotten was so solid, she guided him to the spot she'd seen at the corner of the roof. "What building are you in?"

"I guess they call it the bank building."

Addy's stomach rolled over. Squeezing between the edge of the roof and a small greenhouse, she yanked a peppermint from her pocket. "Of course they do." She slid down the wall, planting her feet on the tall ledge in front of her.

Dean sank down next to her. Not touching her shoulder, but not far enough away to count as outside her bubble. "Cozy over here. Does it help your heights thing?"

She closed her eyes. "A bit."

His knee touched hers.

She opened her eyes and turned to him. "Look, Dean. This was Jane's idea. I don't know if it was wise." She stuffed the candy cane in her mouth. "I feel like I might be sick. And also. I don't know."

"Hey, I appreciate the invite. If nothing else, we can enjoy this meteor shower together, right? You said it's like a sixty-year peak?"

"Yep. Mom helped me memorize all the peaks. The last peak I remember was the Leonids about eight years ago."

"How do you remember that? Weren't you like…" He trailed off, wide green eyes staring into space.

She nudged him. "I was sixteen. It was amazing. You don't forget thousands of meteors per hour."

Smiling, he leaned his head against the building and stared at the sky. "Guess me and Cameron weren't outside for that one."

The mention of his brother brought her back to earth. Frowning, she pointed out a bright star. "Check it out."

He leaned over, shoulder touching hers so he could follow her finger.

The butterflies made their appearance.

She swallowed around them. "Saturn. It's extra bright. Must be close to opposition, or something."

Breath light in her ear, he asked her how she knew that.

With his face so close to hers, she closed her eyes but didn't move. Point-blank questions weren't always her style, but it was either ask him or not know. Considering Matt, and the baby, and her own confusion, she needed to be as point-blank as possible. "I need you to be straight with me."

He shifted, the heat of his body warming her side. Although the days inched up on summer, the night had grown chilly out here on the roof. "As straight as I can, Addy."

She kept her eyes closed. "All this apologizing. Getting upset about Matt. Coming on this date, or whatever it is. Are you. Do you." She stopped.

He sat up. "I watched Celia put her ass on the line for us in DC. Put her ass on the line for everyone. All of you. You jump in front of bullets for each other. All the time. I realized asking you to not do that for me was, for one, irrational. Unrealistic. It's not who you are."

Eyes hot, she faced him. "How the hell else would we have all survived this if we didn't save each other?"

"We wouldn't have, you're right. But more than that, I can't ask you to change who you are. I don't want to. I like who you are."

Her cheeks stung, the tears drying. "I thought you did. I was wrong."

"I did. I do. What I did, it was a mistake. I was scared." He exhaled through tight lips. "I gotta ask you, though, is Matt gone? Or is he coming back?"

Shrugging, she turned away again. Her throat hurt. Hooking her finger through the candy cane, she pulled it from her mouth before she choked on the saliva. "I don't know."

"Do you want him to come back?"

"I don't know."

"Well, I tell you what, Addy—"

Above them, the sky turned to day.

Addy snapped her head up.

The bright white filled her vision, her eyes screaming as her pupils no doubt fought to keep up with the changing light.

It could only be a fireball, and her mouth fell open as it resolved in the middle of the white light. Purple and revolving, it fell directly at their faces.

She had time to wonder if her last moments on earth would be spent with Dean.

And she had time to wonder if that was OK.

The purple spot shot off to the right, exploding into green and blue pieces that streaked across the sky before being vaporized by the atmosphere.

Catching her breath, she spun back to him. "You—"

He caught her in a kiss.

The butterflies melted into a puddle.

Oh god, and he smelled like Dean.

And he tasted like Dean.

Longing punched her in her slick stomach. But for what, or for who, she couldn't tell.

Breaking away first, she leaned back. "I fucking miss you." Hand flying to her mouth, her eyes wide above it, she lowered her voice. "I don't know where that came from."

He smiled, the corners of his eyes crinkling. "Must have come from the heart."

She shook her head. "I have to tell you something."

"Me too."

She crossed her arms and drew her knees up. "You first."

He wrinkled his brow. "I was the one who told Sly about you and Matt."

She jumped to her feet. Backing away so fast they tangled, she fell sideways. Hands out, she scratched what nails she had along the wooden wall they sat against. A splinter drove itself deep under the nail on her middle finger, and as she fell away from it, she cried out.

But then the edge of the roof was right next to her and she was falling that way. Thirty feet to the ground beside her.

She pinwheeled her arms and lost her balance.

Full-throated scream ripping up and out from her diaphragm, terror of something happening to the baby freezing her brain, adrenaline pounded through her. She scrabbled for purchase.

Hands gripped her. One on the thigh, the other on the new belt she'd gotten from Jane. "Dammit, woman." He tugged, wrapping one arm around her waist and yanking her back onto the roof.

Gripping his arms, she let him sit her down. Pants ripped at the thigh, her leg pounded with roof rash. She'd have to clean it at Dad's, get all the pieces of tar and gravel out of it.

Sighing, she held her head in her hands. "I'm such a mess, Dean. I'm pregnant."

"Is it— How long?"

Shaking her head, she peeked up at him.

His eyes wide once again, brows raised, he searched her face.

"I can't tell you what you want to hear."

"It's not mine." His face fell.

She shook her head.

He stood, arms crossed, and paced. His lips moved, but he didn't make any sound.

Knees drawn into her chest, she wrapped her arms around them and waited for him to calm down. Or storm off. Or whatever.

Finally, he sat in front of her. "I didn't mean to tell him. Sly." He cleared his throat, picking at a spot on his pants. "I was upset after seeing you guys in the rain. And when I came back and talked to you later, it didn't make me feel any better."

The dark hallway, the breaker box, his question about Matt. Her hesitation.

"I guess I complained to the wrong guy. I'm so sorry, Addy. I didn't know it was going to turn out like that." He rubbed her knee with two fingers. "I did not mean for that to happen."

"It's OK. You didn't know. And I think it's a good thing." She met his eyes. So round in the starlight. Meteors fell behind his head, but she didn't watch them. "We need distance. The fact is, he's not over Ella. And I'm. Well." Clearing her throat, she held his eyes. "I still miss you."

"I'm right here, Addy."

The lump crowded her throat again. The longing in her gut spun. "Can we just enjoy the rest of this shower and not make any decisions right now?"

He smiled. "Of course."

CHAPTER 40

A horn honked at her back.

Addy stepped from the street to the sidewalk without looking and turned to watch the truck pass.

Scratch that. Trucks. Plural.

A line of them, ten at least, passed her. The overbearing, military kind like Mom had ridden into town in. The kind that had taken Dad and Jane away. The kind that kept coming in and messing up her life.

Arms folded over her chest, she continued down the sidewalk, stinking exhaust from the trucks gagging her. No doubt they were full of soldiers coming in at Morgan's request.

Back to them, she turned down the street that would take her to the lab.

Dad asked if she would talk to Cassius. See if he'd go speak to the council. Show them the very real effects Talus was having on the city.

In theory, it was a great idea.

In reality, she couldn't even look at Cassius, or Victoria, Rivers, Grey, Talbot, and especially Jim. There'd been nothing to hide from Jim. Addy and Matt both knew that, and yet they'd abandoned them all when they needed them most.

And for what?

Matt had blown town. Left her here to sort out her feelings about Dean.

Who hadn't spoken to her for days. Not since the meteor shower. Not since he found out she was pregnant with someone else's child.

Not since he'd kissed her and she found the butterflies sideways in her stomach. Crooked and trying to find a way out.

Using Mike's knock on the door to the lab, she stepped back and waited.

Celia opened the door, eyes smiling. "Hey, girl. How you feeling?"

"Jane tell you?"

"Tell me what?" She stood aside to let Addy pass and locked up behind her.

"She didn't tell you?"

"Did you ask her to tell me something?"

One side of her mouth raised, Addy shook her head. Even after all this time, and all that had changed, this hadn't. Jane still kept her confidences without being asked. Eyes hot, she rested one hand on the hilt of the knife. "I'm gonna have a baby, Cee."

Heavy lids raised, Celia met her eyes. In the dark of the hall, they were all pupil. "And how do you feel about that?"

"I'm not sure yet."

Celia folded her into a hug.

Shocked, Addy almost forgot to hug her back before she was released. The last time Cee offered a hug was. Well. Never.

Celia led her into the lab. "Got a guest, doc."

At a desk with one of the computers, Huxley stared at a paper in front of his face. "One moment, please, Celia. Michael?"

In his chair, Mike rolled backward from the other desk and snagged the edge of Huxley's before he careened into the doctor. "What do you got, Hux?"

"Is this information correct? Are they growing at that rate?"

Jane walked in, carrying a tray full of shiny metal objects. All sorts of things Addy didn't recognize. "Addy, hey, when did you get here?"

"Jane," she said, "does Mike know?"

"Does Mike know what?" he asked.

Jane shook her head. "Not my news to tell." She set the tray down.

Standing, straightening her shirt, Addy approached the desk.

Like a gunslinger, Mike pulled candy from his pouch so fast he hardly moved. "Got sour apple for you."

"No, thanks," she said, pulling a candy cane from her pocket. "Jane gave me some of these."

Mike watched, eyes round, as Addy unwrapped one end and stuck it in her mouth. "They're pretty good. But I think you made up the name."

Without further prompting, Mike leapt from his chair and caught Addy in a hug that not only took her breath away, it took her off her feet. He laughed. "How exciting, little sister!"

She grinned. "Put me down." As he set her on her feet, she put a hand on her hip. "How'd you figure that out so quick?"

Celia scoffed. "Don't let his pretty face fool you. He's smarter than he looks."

Color creeping up Mike's cheeks, he smiled, peeking at Celia. "Can we do anything for you, bean?"

"I don't know. I have questions." She glanced at the doctor.

Mike popped the sour-apple sucker in his mouth and grimaced. "Forgot I hate this flavor." Nudging the doctor with his elbow, he lowered the paper from in front of Huxley's face. "Doc."

Hux looked around. "Yes, Michael? What do you need?"

"My sister has something to ask you."

"Yes? How can I help you, Miss Cooke?"

She pulled the candy cane from her mouth, fresh breeze blowing over her tongue. "I'm gonna have a baby, Doctor Huxley."

"Congratulations," Hux said, half standing and extending a hand.

Addy shook it with half a curtsy. "Can we find out if the baby is immune?"

Brow wrinkled, teeth protruding over his lip, he sat and wiggled the mouse on the computer. "I'll need some information." He clicked the mouse a few times, adjusting his glasses with his other hand. "What is the due date?"

Addy told him.

He typed, frowning. "I'm afraid even if we could do the test"—he stared over the top of his glasses—"which is not my recommendation, it is too early. You need to be at least eighteen weeks and it seems you are." He paused again, typing numbers. "Approaching eight weeks."

"What does the test involve?"

Huxley folded his hands and leaned toward her. "It's complex. I could not perform it. A specialist would be needed, in order to take a blood sample from the baby."

Her knees buckled.

Mike slid his chair under her ass before she fell.

She sat. "Blood from the baby? How would you"—she slid her hand around her abdomen—"how would you even do that? Would it hurt the baby?"

Huxley's upper lip raised. "Guided by ultrasound, a needle is inserted through the amniotic sack and directly into either the baby's heart or liver. This is not something done lightly, and even under the best of circumstances in the past, it carried the risk of harm to the mother, to the baby, and even the possibility of fetal death."

Addy covered her mouth. Her gorge rose, and her eyes flew about the room. They landed on a trash can on the far side of Mike, and she jumped to grab it. Hanging her head inside, she dry heaved a handful of times. When her stomach and throat stopped trying to revolt, she set it down and bit off a piece of candy cane to crunch between her teeth.

Kill the baby? It wasn't worth that. Not at all. No test would be worth that.

"Is there any other way, doc?" Mike asked. Round blue eyes, just like and not at all like Dad's, looking her over.

"I have been working on a method, Michael, thank you for asking," Hux said, going back to the computer. "It involves blood samples from both parents. I may even be able to predict immunity, if I have a large enough sample base." He stopped and looked at Addy. "Is the father available?"

She shook her head, swallowing both the candy cane and the lump in her throat. "No. He's. Morgan sent him away."

"Ah. Well. Perhaps when he returns. Would you give me a sample, Miss Cooke?"

Thoughts of a needle sticking into her and puncturing the baby's lung or heart or brain speeding through her head, she swiped at the tears crowding her eyes.

Mike rounded the desk and folded her into a hug, laying the side of her face in his chest. "It's all right, bean. We're here." He petted her hair. "Whatever you need, we're here."

* * *

"You sure you're ready to do this, little girl?" Jack squeezed Addy's shoulder.

She shook her head. "No."

He'd told her a hundred different ways not to feel guilty about her friend. She still did. It was all over her creased face.

There was only so much you could do for your kids. Every once in a while, they had to figure it out on their own.

He lifted a hand toward the fence. "Let's get it over with."

Reaching through the fence, she jiggled the inner handle of the gate and let them in. "Shouldn't be doing that. But there's nobody out here to let us in. I wonder if they're here." The edge in her voice said she hoped they weren't.

Jack closed the gate behind them and followed her to the loading dock. "Why aren't there stairs?"

She smiled with one side of her mouth, one hand fidgeting with the handle of the knife.

He doubted she even knew she was doing it.

"We asked that on like the third day. The explanation we was hazy at best. These guys are. Interesting." She scrambled up. "I think it comes down to defense. There's no doors or windows at ground level, and Dead Heads can't climb."

"Can't argue that logic. That door is open," he said, jerking his chin. "Do you think that means there's someone home?"

Planting her feet, she held her hand out. "Someone's here, all right. Let's go find out."

He gripped her hand and pulled himself up. "Thanks for the assist."

Walking in glued to his side, she laughed. "Did you know that's a basketball term?"

He chuckled. "Yeah. What a memory."

Behind the bar, a young man in dark aviator glasses looked up. "Addy, Mr. Cooke, welcome back."

Jack approached the bar as Addy hung back. "Jim, right?"

Jim shook.

A good handshake, like most bartenders who saw everything and heard more.

"You got it." He lowered his glasses to peek over the top of them. "Addy, I'm not going to bite you." Smoke from his rolled cigarette crossed in front of his narrowed eyes.

Giving him a crooked smile, she sat on one of the stools as if it belonged to her. "Thanks. What about them?"

"They," he said, setting a glass in front of her and reaching under the bar, "are still trying to convince Cassie to at least sit on the stage." He opened a bottle of vodka.

She laid her hand flat over the top of the glass. "No alcohol, thanks, Jim."

Tapping his smoke in a hidden ashtray, he replaced the lid and stowed the bottle. "You OK?"

Addy shook her head. "Can I get some water, please?"

Jack sat on the stool next to her. "Make that two. Is Cassius getting a prosthetic?"

Taking their glasses down the bar, Jim filled them both from a tap and dropped ice cubes in. The cubes tinkled against the glass.

Jack smiled. One of the best sounds in the world, the ice tinkling. A relief to enjoy it again. He took the water from Jim and gulped down two large swallows. Summer in the South was coming, the humidity already thick in the air by nine a.m.

Jim leaned on the bar. "I don't know. He won't talk much. It's unnerving."

Addy sighed. "This is my fault." With a weak hand, she slapped the bar. "He'll never act again, and it's entirely my fault."

"Addy—" Jack began.

"I hear you say that again," Jim said, speaking over Jack, "I'll hit you myself. I know we were upset in the hospital. We said some things we didn't mean." He shook his head and took off his glasses, green eyes sparkling. "It was no one's fault but Talus. Not yours, mine, Matt's, or Victoria's." Stabbing his finger into the bar, he scowled. "I won't have any of you blaming yourselves for this. Not when I need you to help me." He slid his glasses back on and pointed into the other room. "Go fix him. We'll call it even."

Jack waited. With her mouth and eyes round, she looked at least five years younger. Almost like a child. But she wasn't. She was about to have her own child. She could deal with this. He'd only come along because she asked, and to make sure Cassius and Victoria said yes. But it'd be best if he kept his mouth shut.

She slid off the stool, heading into the next room.

Jack slid off his own stool to follow her.

"Mr. Cooke."

He stopped. "Call me Jack."

"Like the old whiskey."

"You too, my friend."

Jim chuckled. "True. Jack, Jim, and all their friends. Listen. She's a good woman, your kid. We love her."

Warmth hit Jack's chest. "You should. She is."

"I heard Matt left. Out to the perimeter. We're pretty fond of him too."

"He did. I don't know how to feel about him."

"Don't be too hard on him. I know you're inclined to, considering"—he tilted his forehead toward Addy, who'd disappeared into the dark of the next room—"but he's a good man. We trust him with our lives. And he lights your girl up like the moon and stars."

"I'm not trying to stick my nose in. What is it you want, Jim?"

"Sorry. Wanted to stick up for my man. Why are you here?"

He explained.

Pulling up his own stool on the other side of the bar, Jim sat. "I don't know if he'll do that. Vic, maybe. But I don't know about Cassie. He's a kind soul, Jack. I don't think he'd condone violence."

Stomach sinking, Jack gazed into the other room. The only light shone on the empty stage. "I need his help, Jim. Without him, without this assault plan, I'm afraid this will keep happening." He faced him, brows raised. "Don't you think the city deserves peace? That no one else should have to lose limbs or loved ones or get their hearts broken because of this damned company?"

"And Addy's mom? Your ex-wife?"

"What about her?"

"That's what I'm asking you."

He sighed. "She's part of the company. A big part. She has to be stopped. If I told you half the things she's done in search of a vaccine, or immunity, or even the Cure, it'd curl your nose hairs."

"How does Addy feel about that?"

"She agrees." He crossed his arms. "Seriously. What are you getting at?"

He held a hand up toward the other room. "Just making sure everyone is on the same page. Let's go see if she needs our help."

As he rounded the bar, Jack frowned. "So you agree?"

"I agree we need to stop them from hurting more people. I don't agree with asking Addy to do this."

Jack grabbed his arm. "What the hell do you mean by that?"

He looked down at Jack's hand but didn't ask him to move it. "I know you love her. She's your daughter. But you're missing what's right in front of you. She doesn't want to do this. She's had her heart broken. Twice, now, in what? The last six months?" He huffed. "She's not sleeping well. Have you seen the bags under her eyes? I mean, I haven't seen her all week, not since the hospital, but she looks awful." Laughing, he shook his head. "And she refused vodka. Now that's weird."

Jack tried to penetrate the dark in the next room. "She's got her reasons." He lowered his hand. "Do you really think she's not on board with this? She didn't say anything."

"She glowed when she talked about you. She doesn't want to let you down."

Blowing a breath through his lips, Jack shifted gears in his head. She'd been less than enthused when he asked her to speak to Cassius. He'd thought it was because she felt guilty. "I don't know what else to do, man. We have to do this."

Jim raised an eyebrow behind his wide glasses. "Then let's get in there and rescue her. And you can convince them, instead of making her do it."

* * *

Leaving Dad and Jim talking by the bar, Addy approached the stage room. The big lights off, and the rolling door closed, only the stage lights gave any illumination. Shrouded in darkness, she rushed through approximately a thousand memories she'd made in this room with the Troupe and with Matt.

A low murmur from the other side of the room called her.

Less of a decision and more of an instinct, her feet took her that direction. The low voices tilted down, like Matt's parenthesis pointing at the ground.

"Someone approaches in the dark," Tal said. "Who comes to pay our broken band a visit?"

"'Tis I, good sir," she said, stopping in the shadows. The Troupe sat in a semicircle in the half-dark next to the stage.

"Dear woman," Grey said, standing, "we have missed you. Ere nearly two weeks you've been gone." He stepped away from the circle and offered his hand. "Please do join us."

Eyes stinging, she took his hand and followed him into the light.

Rivers sat on her basketball, rolling it around under her. Grey took his seat next to Tal, picking up his hand and interlacing their fingers. Vic sat apart, legs crossed. Her elbows resting on her knees, she held her forehead with her fingertips.

Back leaning against the stage, Cassius followed Addy with his eyes as she sat.

Addy cleared her throat, hole in her stomach. "Um. You guys know Morgan sent Matt to the perimeter?"

"We heard," Vic said. Her head didn't move.

Palms sweating, Addy resisted the urge to grab her stomach. "Why aren't you working…on…the." With the full intention of asking about the play, she glanced at Cassius and stopped. What an absurd thing to say.

Swiping her palms on her pants leg, she put down a foot and moved to stand. "That was foolish. I'll just. I'll go." She lifted her ass from the floor.

"Sit, Adelaide," Cassius said. Nothing moved but his mouth and eyes. "While the question itself needs no answer, you should not feel compelled to leave because of it." He cleared his throat and leaned forward, light hitting his hair and forehead. "Did you come here for a purpose?"

Swallowing, she nodded.

"Then get to it," Vic said. Her affectation gone, plain speech fell from her mouth like a growl.

Addy cleared her throat. Swallowing, she cleared it again. "Listen. Um. My dad is working with Morgan and—"

"We know."

"I. Yeah. So. They want to strike the Molehill, but they need council approval."

Cassius sat back. "What has that to do with us?"

Victoria stood. "I'm in, if you think it will help."

With a grimace, Addy stood. "That's—"

"Thank you," Dad said, coming from the dark. "Victoria, that'll be a huge help. My source mentioned you, specifically. But you weren't the only one. In fact, we need your help too, Cassius. We need you to speak to the council."

He closed his eyes, sinking into the shadow. "I cannot."

Victoria knelt. "Cassie—"

Lifting one finger, he placed it across her lips. "There are things one would do for love. This is not one." He smiled, his teeth appearing. "For you must know, I do love you. I love all of you. But do not ask this. I cannot."

Dad opened his mouth and drew in a breath.

He could be convincing when he needed to be. Addy had been on the receiving end of that plenty of times. Had seen it in action. But this wasn't the time for him to save the day.

Brushing past him, she slid down the side of the stage until she sat next to Cassius. "I don't want to do this," she whispered, leaning into his shoulder. "I want to have this baby and live in peace. And forget my mom exists."

You could have heard a mouse fart in the silence.

Then they all began to talk at once.

Rivers rolled off the ball and fell in the floor. Grey leapt to his feet and walked circles around Talbot, holding his hand as he went around and around. They all talked so fast, Addy couldn't catch a single word.

Except Cassius. He sat, with his hands in his lap, his eyes round, and stared. Leaning close, he whispered back, "Adelaide, my dear woman. I must congratulate you."

She shrugged. "I guess. It's kinda fucked up. I don't know what to do, Cass."

He put an arm around her. "What do you want to do?"

Again, she shrugged.

The Troupe continued to speak, words flying around them like a shroud.

Inside their bubble, Addy and Cassius spoke in hushed tones.

"It's so… When I got together with Matt, it was because I missed Dean."

"But."

"But now Dean's here and." She sighed.

"You miss our good gentleman, Matt. Of course."

Head on Cassius's shoulder, she nodded. "My mom. Talus, the Molehill, they kill people. Steal their lives. Look what they did to Vic's boyfriend. My dad's friend, Andrew. So many others."

"But."

She lowered her voice so far, she wasn't sure he could hear her. "But she's still my mom."

He hugged her close. "I shall do whatever you ask. But you must promise me something in return."

She looked up at him.

Eyes soft, he smiled. "And you must do one thing."

"What?"

"First of all, promise me you will think about what it is that Adelaide wants. Upon this, my promise rests."

She chewed her lip. "And what is it you want me to do?"

Giving her a squeeze, he glanced at Vic. "My dear Victoria, have you the new monologue?"

"Of course, Cassius. Why?"

"Please do give it to our Adelaide. I would like her to perform it."

Addy leaned away. "In front of people? On a stage?" Trying to duck from under his arm, she scooted.

He clenched her shoulder. "Just on this stage. Just for us. Right here, right now, performing for one night only."

Everyone else stopped their chatter.

"Oh yes, please, Addy," Rivers said.

Cassius released her, handing her a folded paper.

Standing, she unfolded the paper. On it, a monologue at least as long as the one she'd seen Victoria give on their first visit to the Tree covered the page. Notes in the margins, each line filled from side to side.

Wind knocked out of her, she shook her head. "I can't do all this, guys."

"You got this, little girl," Dad said.

She rounded the stage and started up the stairs. As they rocked and tried to dump her off the side, she couldn't help but feel Matt's hands on her hips from when he'd grabbed her to keep her from falling. Something else from the first time they'd visited the Tree.

Pinwheeling her arms, she regained her balance and hopped onto the stage. She tiptoed to the center of the light and narrowed her eyes, heart hammering in her chest. "Where are you guys?" She shaded her eyes with the flat of one hand.

"We are here, my lady," Cassius said from somewhere in front of the stage. "Anxiously awaiting your performance."

She lifted the paper, focusing on the words printed on the page. Imagining Victoria's first monologue, she spoke to the spotlight, shaking so hard she was sure her words would come out bumpy.

Tell me, my dears, that this place is where
We could have our dreams and hopes come to bear
What love we could find in the corners and nooks
The life we could live, that which we could share.
Must we do what we will to fight to the end

Or love what we have and hold on to our friends?
For the chances we take lead us on the path
That life which I spoke from the ground we do rend
Well met with the beauty of creatures unknown
Left to stretch to the light, a path of my own.
A brave new world of fire, breath, and life
Choices unheeded of pain, death, and strife.
For my only choice is built upon thee,
My heart, my soul, the fire inside me.

As the last word trailed away and she lowered the paper, silence deafened her. "Sorry. I know it was awful."

Someone sighed.

"That was absolutely beautiful, Addy," Rivers said. She sniffled. "Even my grizzled sea captain would be weeping like a babe."

Blood creeping into her cheeks, she smiled with one side of her mouth. "You really think so?"

"Dear woman," Cassius breathed, "I knew there was a reason I kept trying to get you into our next show. Now, there will be no more shows, and that you will not be part of what will not exist gives me unutterable pain."

Ducking from under the light, she sat on the edge of the stage. "You asked for my word on another issue, Cassius. I've got a condition."

"What is that?"

"Get your ass up here."

Silence fell again. As if it were a physical curtain. Tension sang in the air.

Someone shuffled.

Cassius cleared his throat and dropped his affectation. "I'll never grace the stage again, Adelaide."

"Bullshit. Get up here, or I'll come down there and drag you up."

He forced air through his nostrils. "Help me up, Victoria."

Although Addy could see only shapes, the exhalations and grunts were enough to tell her they had their work cut out for them getting him to his feet.

Foot.

One hopping footstep followed another as he leaned on Vic and rounded the stage. The footfalls stopped, and he spoke in a low voice. "I'll never make it up these stairs."

Crossing the stage, Addy descended the first two stairs. "Nonsense. If anyone can tell you how to get upstairs when you're broken, it's me. Sit on your ass and scoot up them. If I could do that," she said, pointing to the spotlight, "you can do this."

The stairs creaked as he sat and used his hands and foot to push up the stairs. When they wobbled, Addy caught him under the armpit and helped him haul himself up the last stair and onto the stage.

Panting, he scooted till he could extend his leg. He stared at the circle of light, eyes glistening. "It's my favorite thing, Addy. And I can never do it again."

She sat next to him. "If you love it, you'll find a way to do it. I promise to do what you asked me, if you promise me you'll figure out how to get back up here and do what you do best."

He laid on the stage and interlaced his fingers over his chest. "Agreed."

* * *

Leaving Dad to figure out the time and place for the council meeting and what Vic and Cassius were going to say, Addy gathered up what belongings she had left there, and with one last look in their office with the musty couch, she put the Tree at her back.

Pack over one shoulder, she kicked rocks and wandered down the sidewalk. Vaguely in the direction of Dad's house.

It'd been nice of him and Jane to let her crash their party. There were times, when she sat on their couch and talked to them, wondering at how good they were together, she remembered when Jane helped her pack the last of her boxes. As Dad grew smaller in the rearview, she vowed never to come back home.

And here she was, outside his gate.

She opened it and stepped inside the fence.

The front porch creaked.

The pack dropped to the ground. She pulled her machete.

"Glad you got that back," Dean said. "It'd be weird to see you without it."

"It's been a weird road, Dean."

Crossing his arms, he stepped down onto the top stair. "That it has. Need a hand with that pack?"

She thought about telling him no. But since that would accomplish next to nothing, she picked it up and handed it to him. "Thanks. Bring it inside. I'll sort it out later."

Following her in, he set it in the floor and milled about next to the door as she locked it. The proximity alarm reset, she sat in Jane's chair.

He sat on the couch, leaning his elbows on his knees and pursing his lips. "Sorry I disappeared for a few days."

Without a proper response that wasn't the height of snark, she nodded.

"The fact that you're pregnant kinda took me off guard." He eyed her sideways, hands clasped between his knees.

"Me too. But there's no changing it."

"I know," he said, "I know. I mentioned Celia before, but losing the train is just as much a part of what got me thinking I should try to rectify my mistake." He crossed his arms over his chest. "Watching it go up in flames, my only memento of Cameron inside, it finally hit me."

She sank back into the chair, image of the train in flames burned into her brain. Although she hadn't seen it, she could imagine well enough. "I'm so sorry. It breaks my heart to think it's gone."

"Yeah, well it is. Like everything else we love in this world. It can be taken away in a blink." Sliding down the couch, he leaned over the arm and plucked her hand from her lap.

Limp, she didn't fight as he lifted her hand and kissed her palm. Couldn't.

Rubbing the inside of her palm with both thumbs, he lowered his eyes to their hands. "I realized what I should have known all along. The things we have, we gotta hang on to them for as long as we can. No matter how scared that makes me, if I don't enjoy what I've got while I've got it, what am I going to do when it's gone?" He met her eyes.

She pulled her hand free. "You should have thought of that before you—"

"I know. I'm sorry."

"Before you broke my heart. My trust. I don't know how to start over from that." She stood to pace. "I mean, I told you I miss you, I told you that. But I miss what we had. And I don't know if we can ever get it back."

He met her in the center of the room. "I understand," he said, smiling down at her. The corners of his eyes crinkled. "I get it. Believe me, I do." He grabbed her hand again. "But I swear to you, if you give me the chance to, I will love this baby as much as all the water in all the oceans in all the world. The same way I love you." Squeezing her hand, he erased all the space in her bubble.

Closing her eyes, she breathed deep. His scent, magic and musk and a little bit of sweat, mingled in her nose with the slight bit of leftover peppermint already up there in her sinuses. Clutching his hand, she leaned into his shoulder. "Can we just take it slow, see what happens?"

Sliding one arm around her, he kissed her on the head and rocked back and forth with her. "We can do whatever you want." He leaned back and lifted her chin.

Meeting his eyes, she stamped on the crooked butterflies and tried to smile.

"You tell me no, and we'll be done for good and for all. But unless or until you do, I'm not making the choice easy on you. I'm sorry if that's not OK."

"No you're not."

"You're right. I'm not sorry."

CHAPTER 41

Knapp descended the stairs with his hand out. "Mr. Cooke," he said, shaking with Jack while staring at Cassius and Victoria at the bottom of the stairs, Cassius arriving in a wheelchair. "Thank you for coming." Dropping Jack's hand, he nodded to the actors. "And thank you. The city thanks you."

Cassius stood. Leaning on Victoria's arm with one hand and a crutch with the other, he nodded back. "Let us go do this so that we may be done. I cannot stand for long, my friend."

"Right. Please, this way," Knapp said, climbing the stairs.

Smoothing the tie, Jack rounded Vic and Cassius and met Addy behind them.

Her wide eyes and the way she gnawed at each fingernail like it had committed personal offense hit him in the gut.

"You all right, sweetheart?"

"Cassius is right. Let's get this done. I'll feel better once they're back home."

Cassius and Vic struggled up the stairs. "Anyone else coming down?"

Addy grunted. "Dean said he would. I don't know."

Speaking of the devil, he opened the door at the top of the stairs and strode out from inside the cool depths of city hall. "Hey guys, let me help you." Taking Cassius's crutch, he ducked under his arm. Not before he dropped a wink at Addy.

Stuffing a candy cane in her mouth, Addy grimaced and followed them all.

Jack walked with her into the building. "You sure you're all right? You look green around the gills."

"I guess. Whatever. Maybe I shouldn't have come." She shrugged, staring ahead of them. "I hate to see him do this to himself. He shouldn't be doing this. None of us should be."

Stone settling into his gut, Jack eased an arm around her. Hormonal and sad could turn any woman into a ball of rage or tears in a moment. Even his little girl wasn't immune, and he spoke with caution, his voice low and modulated. "We'll get him through this and back to the Tree before you know it. All he has to do is speak to them. If they try to question him, I'll answer." He gave her a ginger squeeze. "I won't let them abuse him."

She ripped a nail off with her teeth. The finger spurted blood. "Shit." As they entered the cavernous building, her curse echoed off the sides and ceiling. Flushed, she lowered her voice. "Sorry."

He rubbed her shoulder. "Don't worry. We're all nervous."

Knapp opened the door to the inner chamber. "You may all come in, but I'll have to ask everyone except Cassius, Victoria, and Mr. Cooke to remain silent."

Handing Cassius his crutch, Dean dropped back to walk in with Addy. He leaned into her ear. "You all right?"

Jack released her shoulders and let Dean take over. Addy hadn't told him what she thought of Dean this go around, but Jack had seen more than enough of his remorse to be OK with him trying to make it up to her.

Knapp closed the door behind all of them and strode to his seat at the front of the room.

The rest of the council, nineteen of them total, fell into a hushed silence as Victoria and Cassius made their way to the center of the floor. The benches inside the door creaked as Addy and Dean took a seat, and Jack followed the actors to the front.

His palms began to sweat. It was like he was a nervous teen all over again, trying to be cool on that first date with Melinda.

Swallowing, he flattened his tie. "Good afternoon, council. Thank you for having us."

A stern, paper-white older woman in the center leaned over and stared down a pair of glasses. She had to have been at least as old as Paul had been, her grey hair twisted into a bun on top of her head. Her mouth twisted into a scowl under her thin nose. "I am not sure what you think this will accomplish, but I have allowed it since we could not come to a unanimous decision on whether or not you could."

Setting a chair behind Cassius, Jack put a hand on his shoulder as he sat. "I appreciate the opportunity. We, Morgan and I, feel we must be proactive when it comes to Talus. Our options become slimmer the longer we wait."

A pale, balding man cleared his throat. Though he frowned, his small brown eyes held a softness behind his round glasses. "We'd very much like to hear from these wonderful people. Your last play was truly inspired," he said, speaking to Victoria and Cassius.

Cassius waved a hand.

Victoria stood and bowed. "Thank you. Two of our other members, Grey and Talbot, wrote the adaptation."

"They got engaged during opening night," a young woman on the end said. Her straight black hair hung down her back. Her skin, a smoky bronze color, made Jack think of Renzo in the firelight. "That was the cutest thing I've ever seen."

The grey lady in the middle, who appeared to be the mouthpiece for the council, sniffed. "I didn't think people bothered with marriage anymore. I'm not sure why you would." She leaned back. "It seems useless in this age."

Jack cleared his throat and opened his mouth.

"Love cannot be denied, even in these times," Cassius said. His chair creaked. "In fact, it is more important now than ever it was when you were young."

"And Talus destroys it every chance they get," Victoria said, pacing to the middle of the round area before the council. "They stole our Adam from us, you remember him?"

Most of the council nodded. The black-haired woman put a hand over her heart. "He was lovely."

"He was. And now he lives out his days underground, chained to a wall, in hopes we can Cure him."

An image of Andrew, his eyes wide as he fell from the tower, socked Jack in the chest, leaving a hole the shape of a fist.

The grey lady sniffed. "Your point, girl."

"My point," she said, stalking up to the rounded stand where the council sat in a semicircle, "is that we cannot allow this company to continue to rob us of the only thing that really matters." Hands behind her back, she swept from one end of the stand to the other. Her silvery blonde hair flowing behind her, her voice projected to the ceiling. "I have known these people. I have been among them. I have been one of them. They are hungry. They are intelligent. They are driven." She stopped and locked eyes with Cassius.

He sat, enrapt, and stared up at her.

She knelt next to him. "They will stop at nothing until they find a perfect Cure. Until they find a perfect vaccine. Until they find a perfect solution." Hand lying on the thigh of his injured leg, she let tears spill over her lower lid. "They will steal the very heart of us and give it to their demons as an offering."

The man with glasses and kind eyes cleared his throat and glanced down at his papers. "To be as fair as I can, I must say, the raids stopped for the better part of eight months. And now that they've begun again, we have suffered some losses, it's true. While—" He stopped and cleared his throat, eyes shifting to the council members on either side of him. "While I agree with you, the numbers do not."

Jack flushed. How dare they talk about people like numbers. The way Melinda did. He stiffened, readying himself to stand.

Cassius's chair creaked. He pushed up with his arms, standing and fiddling with the crutch until he could lean on it.

Victoria reached out to help him.

He shooed her and limped to the middle of the room.

"Were it simply a matter of numbers, I would be in agreement with you, my good man." He swept his free arm around the semicircle. "I would be in agreement with all of you. The precarious position in which we find ourselves has no easy answer." He swallowed, Adam's apple bobbing. "And would that I could tell you something that, like a fine bandage, could cover the wound until it heals as the skin of this leg."

Lifting the leg, he raised the cut-off bit of pants to expose the healing skin below his knee. "Pink and raw, like the wound Talus has inflicted upon this city. Yet as it heals, so too do our hearts. Although the skin is stretched tight, and the scar will ever be visible, it shall heal." He held a finger up. "That, I do promise." Hopping on the crutch, he approached the center of the desk. Stopping short of touching it, he stared directly at the grey lady. "My dear woman, you are right to question. For what are the few lives they have stolen to this city of thousands?"

She stammered. "It. Yes. It's such a low. Bill, do you have the numbers?"

The bespectacled man ruffled his papers again. "The last group were their own people. Formerly. It was, um."

"And when they tried to come get our Victoria," Cassius interrupted, pounding the desk with a fist, "I stopped them with my very limb." Raising his voice to deafening levels, he shouted. "My very limb!" Lowering his voice, he leaned on the desk in front of her. "I placed my heart and soul before them and laid them bare and asked them to take me rather than my dear Victoria. For my friends are my heart and soul, and without them, there is no life."

Jane's face creeping into his mind without asking, Jack glanced at Victoria.

Cross-legged, she sat on the floor and cried in silence, face turned up to watch Cassius.

"I ask you to stop them. For you are fine and reasonable people, and you know as well as we do, without each other, we are nothing. We must be willing to do what it takes to save one another, each and every soul, before we lose all that makes us who we are. Before we lose the love which binds us all together." He sighed, dropping his head. "Before we sacrifice to the demons of progress our own selves. For we have only so many limbs to give."

Chest bound, Jack watched the council.

The grey lady wiped her cheek, chin trembling.

The bald man's kind eyes reddened behind his glasses.

The young woman cried with her face in both hands. Sobbing.

The rest of the council shifted in their seats, some looking down, some still watching Cassius, most a little teary-eyed.

Fighting the smile that tried to creep on his lips, Jack turned to check on Dean and Addy.

Dean sat alone. Addy had disappeared.

* * *

Over the following weeks, more soldiers arrived. Addy watched each truckload of arrivals with hooded eyes and crossed arms.

She helped in the lab, keeping watch with Celia but also hanging over Jane's shoulder and learning what she could about Huxley's methods.

Clean. Sterile. Just as he said.

He'd learned to synthesize the Cure using cloned human tissue, but the research was in its infancy. He didn't have the kind of facility or staff he needed to make it a real go. He'd also come close to the vaccine but needed Mom's research to make it past a wall he'd hit.

He analyzed pairs of samples from at least a half dozen immune children's parents, Katie included, to see if he could find the markers for immunity. If so, he could tell two people if their child was likely to be immune.

But he couldn't tell Addy if her baby was immune because he was missing Matt's part of the equation. He catalogued her samples for later.

All of it made Addy's head spin, but Mike loved it. Dug into it with both heels and both fists and ate it all up. She never gave him enough credit. He really was smarter than he looked.

And taken with someone again, though Addy couldn't put her finger on who. It was a lot like he'd been about Jane.

One morning about three weeks after the council decided to run with Dad's plan, the troops slowly choking the life out of Talus's supply chain, she found herself sitting alone with Mike in the lab. For once.

He leaned over a tray, doing something clever with petri dishes. "Dad say how long until the actual attack?"

"At least another four weeks. Morgan still hasn't gotten the cannon, and they want to make sure the supply chain is entirely cut off. Dad says it wouldn't do any good to go in there if they could still get reinforcements and supplies. Which makes sense."

"Sure," Mike said, leaning closer to the samples. "He who has the supplies wins the war."

She stood, arms folded under her breasts. "Can we not call this a war?"

He glanced up. "What should we call it?"

"A fucking debacle," she said, slouching into a chair across the room. "Unbelievable. Impossible."

Sighing through his nose, he leaned back. "I know, bean. I wish it didn't have to be like this. But Mom—"

"But Mom. I know." She picked at a fingernail.

"How's things with Dean? Making any progress?" He leaned back over the tray.

Continuing to pick at the nail, she shrugged. His crinkled eyes popped, uninvited, into her brain. "He's. You know. He's Dean."

"And you?"

"What do you mean?"

"Do you want him to keep being Dean in your general vicinity, or go somewhere else and be Dean?"

"Ah hell, Michael. I don't know."

"It's been a few weeks now. If you still don't know, maybe you're coming at it all wrong." He rested his elbow on the table.

She sighed. "What's that supposed to mean?"

Laughing, he raised both hands. "I can't tell you how to think about it. I'm just saying, turn it over sideways and see if you can find the way it fits in your brain."

"I don't know if I get that, but it's better than nothing." She stood, rubbing a belly more convex than concave. She'd read the baby was moving around in there all the time, but she couldn't feel a thing. "I'm supposed to be figuring it out, and the more time I spend with him, the less sense any of it makes."

He smiled and offered her a sucker.

She unwrapped it and stuck it in her mouth. Sour apple. "Thanks. That's really good."

"Good. Best to make pregnant girls happy, I've found."

"Hey, Mike. Speaking of girls. Who is it that's caught your eye?"

The speed with which he turned brick red would have been alarming if he weren't already sitting.

"What, uh, what do you mean? I don't, um." Standing, he pulled out his own sucker but struggled to unwrap it.

He'd never been so shy to talk about Jane. Had never hidden his feelings behind a wall. Addy didn't even think he had a wall.

Finally, he got the sucker in his mouth and sat, crossing his arms. He opened his mouth, cleared his throat, and tried again. "And what makes you think someone has caught my eye?"

She pulled the sucker out and pointed with it. "You can't bullshit me, big brother. I can see right through you. Who is she?" Smiling, she leaned closer and lowered her voice. "Do I know her?"

Addy wasn't even sure he meant to nod, but he did.

Half her mouth raised, and she popped the sucker back in. "All right. I've got to consider this."

He laughed. "Consider Dean. Don't worry about me. I can handle her."

Doubling over, she laughed until the laughter came in hoarse gasps and her cheeks burned. After catching her breath, she wiped her eyes. "If she's anything like Jane, I sincerely doubt you can handle her. Whoever she is."

The front door unlocked, and Celia called out. "We're back, you guys." Hux, Jane, and Celia spilled into the room.

"You better have a sucker for me, Mike," Celia said, laying her long-handled knife on the desk next to him.

He dug one out, nose turning red. "Your favorite."

Celia leaned on the desk and unwrapped it. She shook her head. "How did you even figure out my favorite flavor of every kind of candy? Are you some kind of magician?"

He leaned into her space. "Yes."

Hitting him on the shoulder, she stuffed the sucker in her mouth. "You're something else." Glancing at Addy, she shook her head. "You people." She laughed and went into the next room, where they'd set up a bunch of couches and chairs. And a TV just for Addy.

Dean had even brought her a little memory stick with the entirety of *Trek* on it. However he'd found that.

But before she got lost thinking about him and those crinkling eyes of his, and moved on to what Matt was doing out there and how maybe they could watch some "cheese central" together when he returned, she looked at Mike. That conversation with Celia in the doorway added to what she'd just seen. "You're in more trouble than I thought."

He blushed again. "That's not true."

She leaned on the table. "I've got something to take care of. But one thing. You have to promise me one thing." She held up a finger, pointed skyward.

He lifted his brows, eyes round. That bit of dark curly hair resting on his forehead. "Sure."

"Do something about it, before you lose her too. She likes you, you know."

"I don't, uh. I don't." He shook his head.

"Celia," she called.

"Yeah," Celia answered from the other room.

"My brother has something to tell you."

Celia walked into the doorway. "Yeah?"

Addy leaned into Mike's ear. "Make it good." She dropped a half curtsy at Celia. "I gotta run. Tell me how it turns out." Before Mike could stop her, she stepped down the hallway.

Celia's voice followed her. "How what turns out?"

"Lock up behind me," she said, opening the front door and checking the street. She shut the door and stepped into the sun.

Not that she had anything to actually take care of, but she'd wanted an excuse to give them privacy.

So here she was, on the sidewalk, alone.

The Tree a block away, she could go say hi. She hadn't seen any of them since the council. But she'd heard Cassius had begun sitting on the stage and delivering lines.

And there was whatever happened inside. Mike and Celia?

Well, it made sense when she thought about it.

Her feet turned her toward Dad and Jane's. Funny how they'd found each other in all this. How they hadn't let a thing like fear keep them apart for too long. It could be such a fierce enemy, fear.

What was she afraid of with Dean? Why hadn't she let him do any more than kiss her? He constantly and in a thousand different ways told her and showed her he loved her. It hadn't dimmed when he'd been away. If anything, it had grown.

And her guilt at letting her own love for him fade threatened to take her over at night. When she lay alone and wished it weren't so, wished she could let go of whatever it was that was keeping her from him and stop being so lonely.

Letting herself into Dad and Jane's, she searched for pen and paper.

CHAPTER 42

Sunset falling over the city like a shroud, Jack swung Jane's hand back and forth. "How do you like the ladies at the nursery?"

"You met them. What do you think?"

"I know they're not like you." He stopped, catching her eyes. "No one is like you. I mean, do you think they're all right to watch the baby for a few hours at a time?" He put a hand on Katie's back, where she rested against his chest in her sling.

Red creeping into her cheeks, Jane kissed him on both of his. "They'll do. For brief periods." She rubbed the baby's head.

"Good," he said, swinging her hand and heading home.

"How are things with the defense force?"

"Morgan has them running pretty good. There's a few bad eggs, but for the size of the force, I think I can get them weeded out."

"Addy told me about Sly. That guy needs gone. Yesterday."

"Already handled. He's a farmer now. Seemed almost relieved when I told him."

Stopping, she tugged him in and gave him a real kiss.

Leaning over the baby, he floated in a blissful moment of falling into her. He hadn't taken enough of those moments in the last few busy weeks. Funny how quickly they could go from frightening to amazing to regular.

She curled her fingers in the hair at the nape of his neck. "I love you, Jack Cooke."

"I love you, Jane Doe. Say, when you wanna go about changing that last name?" He tugged her toward the house again.

"Let's get through this damn attack and we'll talk about it."

After they went through the gate, he pulled thick links of chain through and snapped the padlock. If Addy wasn't home yet, she had a key. He tugged the lock and joined Jane on the porch.

"Weird," she said.

"What's that?"

"Only the doorknob is locked. Top lock is undone." Pushing the creaking door open, she stepped inside and reset the proximity alarm. Line between her brows, she unwrapped the baby and took her off Jack's chest without asking. Eyes distant.

Her unease seeped into his jaw. "Addy?" He kissed Katie on her fuzzy head. Her hair grew out in teeny tiny increments. He raised his voice. "Adelaide?"

The house ticked. The fridge kicked over. A single, dim light fell into the living room from the kitchen.

"I'll check her room," Jane said, disappearing down the dark hallway with Katie before he could answer her.

Something had gone sideways. The empty feeling in his gut was sure of it. And he couldn't feel his feet as he slipped through the shadowy living room and into the kitchen.

On the table, a folded piece of paper lay under Addy's Bowie knife.

Scrawled on the blank side of the paper, one word. "Dad."

If he could have breathed, he might have. As it was, he couldn't suck one down, so he sat at the table and tried again. Scooting the knife away, he unfolded the paper.

Dad,

I was going to start this off with an apology, but I'm not sorry. I hate that this is going to hurt you, but that doesn't mean I'm sorry.

So much has happened in the last year, I hardly know where to begin. I'll be gone several hours by the time you read this, so I guess I've got time to explain myself as best as I can. I don't want you to be angry. I can't control that, but if you're going to be angry, you should at least know why.

Ever since that day at the hospital, when my miraculously alive mother punched me in the nose, I've lived with a broken heart. I can't even come close to understanding how you must feel. I know you're angry. So am I. But you have a choice in whether or not to move on. With everything that happened with Dean, I get that now. You can move on from Mom. I can't.

I won't.

You know I love you. You're amazing. I wouldn't be who I am without you. I wouldn't even be alive. You're my superhero, Dad. And you're the best man I've ever known.

Mom might have her flaws. I mean, I know she does, but she's the one who taught me to hope. Even when the night is dark, it's full of stars. If she can't see their light, I have to help her. I have to try.

Listen, I don't know if I'll come back from this. I believe Mom can change. I believe she can be the woman who raised me. But I'm not foolish enough to think she will. The thing is, with me about to be a mom, I can't see raising my baby and telling him or her that I condemned their grandmother to die without giving it one last shot. Or that I gave up on her and let it happen. You didn't see her face last time I saw her. You didn't see the hurt. You didn't see Mom.

And that's not your fault, but it's not hers either.

Cassius asked me, before he spoke to the council, to figure out what Addy wants. At first I thought if I could just choose between men, I'd be OK. But the truth is, what I want is to feel better, to love myself and my choices. None of you can make me feel OK or heal my broken heart. I'm the only one who can do that.

So I've got to try. I'm not sorry.

Addy

P.S. If Matthew comes back, tell him the knife is his if he wants it.

His eyes fell on the knife, blade gleaming in the thin light.

"She's not in there. Do you— What's that?" Standing next to the table, Jane pointed at the letter in his hand.

Covering his eyes, he held it out to her.

"Here," she said, sliding the baby into his arm.

He settled her into the crook of his elbow and nuzzled her nose. Her warmth covered the hole in his midsection, reminded him this little one still needed him. Much more than the one who'd left the note and the knife and gone her own way.

"Oh my fucking god, Jack. We have to go. We have to stop her." Flinging the letter onto the table, Jane spun.

He caught her hand. "Jane. Wait."

Eyes blazing, she tore her hand free. "Don't you tell me wait. We have to catch her. If she went on foot, she's probably not there yet." Her breath hitched. "She nearly took you from me. She's not getting Addy." Sniffing, she leaned on the chair next to him. She swiped at an eye. "We can't let her do this."

He covered one of her hands with his. "We can't stop her, Jane." Holding little Katie close, he met Jane's eyes again.

Red, they glistened as the edge of the knife had.

He smiled. "I don't want to stop her. This is what she feels she has to do." He squeezed Jane's hand. "I did the best I could with her. But she's grown now. I have to let her go. Let her make her own choices."

Pulling the chair out, Jane sat and covered her face with her hands. She shook her head. "This is a damn ridiculous choice. If she lives through it, I'll kill her."

"Look," he said, sitting back, "we'll go ahead with the plan. It's going to take another couple weeks at least to get everything together." Shifting the baby, he picked the note up and read through it again. "If she comes back before then, maybe we won't have to go through with it."

"You think that'll happen?"

He shrugged, giving Jane a weak smile. "No."

* * *

Dinner plates stacked in the sink, wine poured, lights dim, Melinda sat on Ilasha's plush couch and rolled the wine glass in her fingers. "I still don't understand how those recordings got here."

Sliding so close the heat radiating from her leg warmed Melinda's thigh, Lash plucked the glass from her hands. She finished off the wine in it and leaned across Melinda to set it on the end table, her breasts pushing up under Melinda's chin.

Melinda grinned. "You did that on purpose."

Settling back on the couch, Lash lifted one corner of her mouth. "Did what?"

"You know," Melinda said, sliding one arm around her waist.

Lash scooted closer, leaning into her leg. "Fine. I know. Got something to say about it?"

Shaking her head, she slid her other hand up the side of one of Lash's breasts and around her back. Although she wanted to keep bantering, she couldn't not kiss this woman. Not when being with her was a bit like coming home.

Kissing her back with soft heat, raking her over hot coals, Lash pushed her into the couch and slid her shirt over her shoulders. She smiled and covered the side of her neck in kisses.

As much to find out the answer as to turn the heat sideways and make it cool a bit, Melinda frowned. "What are you smiling about?"

Sitting up, shifting between her hips, Lash ran light fingers down the side of Melinda's face. "Took us a hell of a lot longer to get here than I wanted it to. I'm glad to see you like this again, is all."

Melinda tugged at her shirt. "This is unfair. I'm not seeing as much of you as you are of me."

Lash tweaked a nipple with her tongue and sat up. Tugging her shirt from the hem up, she pulled it off and giggled when Melinda helped her. "Still ticklish, woman."

Grinning, memories of the last time they'd been here fuzzy but pink, Melinda explored Lash's hips and waist till she found the right spots to tickle.

Laughing, Lash slapped her hands away. "Don't you start. Or I'll tease you without mercy." She slipped one hand between Melinda's legs and pressed.

Heat rose from Melinda's toes to her head. Her cheeks tingled. Blood rushed through her, pain and pleasure rising at once. She licked her lips.

The phone on the coffee table buzzed.

Closing her eyes, Melinda arched her back. "Leave it."

Hips pressing into hers, Lash leaned over and kissed her again. "Didn't intend to touch the damn thing. Got my hands full," she said, busying the other hand with a breast.

The ringtone started.

The pink feeling rising in Melinda's chest deflated. "It's Anthony."

Ilasha cursed. "Fuck him and fuck his phone call." She buried her face in Melinda's neck and pressed harder between her legs, warm skin setting Melinda on fire.

The ringing stopped.

Melinda exhaled. "What if he comes here?"

"He's got no business at my door. Not tonight."

Buzz and ringer coming in quick succession, the phone began again.

"This son of a bitch," Lash said, snatching the phone.

Holding out her hand, Melinda frowned. "I'll make it quick."

Sitting up, Lash cut her eyes at her. Mashing the call button with enough force to break the damn phone, she blew a gale through her nose and put the phone up to her ear. "Could have sworn I told you to leave us the fuck alone tonight, Anthony."

Melinda's mouth fell open. The tone Lash took cowed even her. It was a Voice Not To Be Fucked With. How she dared speak to Anthony like that, after the fear she'd demonstrated for his bosses, blew Melinda away.

That she'd take such a chance, just to be with her.

The pink feeling returned, making her light-headed.

Lash shook her head, her legs tense. She clutched Melinda's knee. "Charles, listen to me. I don't care if the pope himself—"

The phone squawked.

Full lips pressed together in a thin line, Lash held the phone out without looking. "You're going to want to fucking take this."

Pushing into the couch to sit up, stomach a sudden mass of knots, Melinda took the phone. "Yes?"

"*General. I am so sorry to bother you. Please accept my sincerest apologies.*"

Why? Why did he sound so scared? "What is it?"

"*I am aware it's highly unusual to involve you in the business of defectors, but there is one at the gate, and I'm afraid we require your attention.*"

Lash's jaw bunched and loosened. Her long, thick eyelashes brushed her cheek as she closed her eyes.

Melinda blew out her nose, hitting the phone's mic on purpose. "What could you possibly need my attention for at this hour?"

"General, it's your daughter."
The bottom fell out of her stomach.

RECONSTRUCTION

CHAPTER 43

The lights from the guard tower shone in Addy's eyes. The forest rustled behind her, a foul smell coming closer. She sniffed.

The odor more like a skunk than a 'Head, she shifted on her feet. Tenting a hand over her eyes, she tried to peer through the lights.

"Please don't move, ma'am." The disembodied male voice spoke from the other side of the double gate. Metal clinked. Maybe the barrel of a gun against the chain-link.

"Sorry," she said, lowering her hand. "Just trying to see you. Those lights in my eyes kinda make it hard. There's something out here with me. Can I come in, please?"

"Negative."

She shifted her feet again and grasped her abdomen. The dark at her back, the lights in her eyes, and the tower above her. This had been a terrible idea.

The air shifted ahead of her. Like someone stood up straighter. Metal clinked again, and the voice commanded her, "Lower your weapons."

With slow and deliberate movements, Addy held one hand up while she unsheathed her machete and laid it on the ground. Next to it, she set her bow down. She stood.

"All of them, please, ma'am."

She slipped the quiver off and laid it down. "That's it."

"Where's your knife?" Mom asked.

Chin trembling, the sound of Mom's voice out there in the dark, and asking about the knife no less, took her off guard. Like stepping on black ice. "I gave it away."

The gate in front of her rolled back. The man spoke again. "Move forward."

Hands raised, she stepped past the gate.

It rolled closed, hooking up with the fence with less than a slam and more than a sigh. An innocuous sound for such a gate.

The inner gate rolled open, chain-link clinking. The light jittered but didn't leave her face. "Remain where you are. Do not move."

"Stop," Mom said. "Why are you here, Adelaide?"

Throat thick, she spoke around the lump in it. "I came to." Voice trembling, she stopped and swallowed. "I came to see you, Mom."

"Come to start a fight? Again?"

She narrowed her eyes, the movement causing tears to fall. Cheeks wet, she shook her head. "I came to look at the stars with you."

Melinda stepped into the light, chewing a nail. "That's a nice sentiment, Adelaide. I don't think it's sincere though." With her other arm, she patted Addy's sides and lifted her pants legs to check her boots. "Really, no knives? I raised you better than that."

"Can I put my arms down now?"

Waving the voice over, Mom pointed. "Cuff her."

As he approached, Addy caught sight of his cheek. A crooked scar traveled from his cheekbone to his jaw.

He frowned. "I know you."

"Gian. I remember you. You flipped me off the first time we met."

"Not very polite, Gian," Mom said. "But she probably deserved it."

Grasping her wrists, he clicked the cuffs into place. He pushed her through the gate and leaned close. "She's your mother?"

Mom turned. "What gave it away? The fact she has my eyes or that she called me Mom?" She clicked her tongue. "Less talk. Bring her inside."

"Yes, General. Sorry," Gian said, pushing Addy again.

She stumbled, sweat popping out on her upper lip. If she tripped over her own feet right now, nothing would catch her on her way to the ground. Focused on remaining upright, she almost forgot to take one last look at the stars before Gian shoved her through the recessed door.

They glittered like diamonds tonight, the moon riding high and about a quarter full. "Wait," she whispered.

He did.

Staring at the moon, eyes wide, she took in every bit of the sun it reflected at her. It wasn't enough, but it'd have to do.

Mom stepped up next to her. "I wasn't sure you still liked to look up. You've been looking at your feet so long, I was afraid you forgot everything I taught you."

Still staring at the moon, she shook her head. "I could never forget everything you taught me. Never."

A low chuckle floated from Mom's throat. "Could have fooled me. Let's go."

* * *

Celia opened the lab door, gun drawn. Lids at half-mast, she smiled. "Hey, Jack." She glanced at Jane. "Is it bring your man to work day?"

Jane chuckled. "I couldn't stop him. He insisted."

Standing aside, Celia ushered them in and holstered her gun. She followed them up the hall. "Something up?"

Jack nodded. "Do you know where Dean is?"

"No. But I can get him on the radio."

"Please do."

Stopping as they entered the main lab, Jack took in the room. He'd seen more than he wanted of Melinda's facilities. But what Hux and Mike had set up here was warmer, smaller, and somehow many times less sinister than the lab Melinda and IRF had made. Maybe that was based more in his perception than reality, but he rode the feeling anyway. He pulled a chair up in front of Mike's desk. "How are things around here, son?"

Mike grinned at Celia and offered Jack a hard candy. "Good. Hux is scary smart about this virus."

"So I've heard. I've also heard you're no slouch."

He flushed when Celia walked past him, running her hand along his shoulders. She left the room, disappearing into the back.

Eyes narrowed, Jack popped the candy in his mouth. He considered asking Mike what was going on, then decided he'd been too involved in his love life already.

"Don't let him fool you, Jack," Jane said, bringing a stack of papers out from the other room. "He's just as smart as Hux."

"So you're the one who's been lying about me."

Winking at Jack, she disappeared into the back again.

"You guys seem busy," Jack said, standing. "Maybe I should come back when Dean gets here."

"What do you need Mr. Ross for?" Hux asked, squinting at the computer screen. He typed a few lines, two fingers flying over the keyboard.

"I need to speak to all of you, and it's easier if you're all in the same place. Only have to go over it once that way."

"As defense force leader, or as Jack?"

"Both."

"Hm. Michael, talk to him about what we need while we wait."

"Sure. Hey, Dad, do you think you could talk to the council for us?"

"What about?" He tried to shift from worry about Addy to business. A hard shift when all he could do was imagine what hell Melinda could be inflicting on her right now.

"We'd like to expand to a larger facility. Get some more doctors working on this."

"Why?"

Mike leaned over the desk. "If we can get Mom's research about the vaccine when we run this raid, we can start making it. But we need more supplies and more doctors. A bigger facility." He shook his head. "Hux thinks he knows what they were doing with Andrew and those other people. He thinks they were incubating the virus to make the Cure and vaccine."

Jack covered his mouth. "What? Why?"

"You must grow the virus to use it for an antidote," Hux said, typing. "And for a vaccine, an inactive virus is a necessary component. Before NMZM infected the world, we manufactured most vaccines using chicken eggs. That is not possible with this virus." He stopped typing and fixed Jack with a glare. "This virus is unusual in so many ways, Mr. Cooke. And so we must come at it with unusual methods." He smiled at Mike. "One of the best things your son is good at doing. Thinking of things in new ways."

Mike flushed. "Sometimes." He cut his eyes at Jack. "Sometimes my head gets stuck too far up my ass to see anything straight."

Jack shook his head. "Sorry. You get it from me."

"Got that right," Jane said, breezing through the room from one door to another.

Celia laughed, coming back in. "The only thing you Cooke men can't see is how good you both are."

Jack's turn to flush, he spoke to Hux. "What are you doing about this? How do you plan to grow the virus?"

"Cloned human tissue," Hux said, going back to the computer. "It's quite easy. If we have the right facilities. I need more room. And a bigger staff. And better computers."

Jack crossed his arms. "I don't know what resources this city has, but I'll ask. See what we can do."

"I am excited by the population. Its size."

Jack opened his mouth to speak, but a knock at the door interrupted him.

He stood.

Celia held up a hand. "You sit. I get the door here." She drew her gun and disappeared down the hallway.

As he waited, Jack's mouth ran away with him before he could stop it. He leaned over the desk. "What's going on with you, Mike?"

His easily embarrassed son flushed again. He shook his head, but when he opened his mouth, his forehead lifted his hairline. His ears raised. In fact, everything about him lightened. "Just me being slow on the uptake. Again."

"What does that mean?"

"Means he blames himself too much for shit that's not his fault." Celia walked back through, holstering her gun. "I'm the one who wouldn't take Oren's advice."

Narrowing his eyes, Jack cast his mind back. Through the haze of pain, he pictured Oren's bouncing red mustache. His smart mouth and well-timed off-color jokes. "What advice?"

"Oh, no shit," Dean said, coming in from the hall. "Somebody tell me Celia's not dating."

It hit Jack in a rush. All the little touches and blushing and banter he'd seen in the last few weeks between his eldest and Celia added up. The way they'd fallen asleep leaning on each other in the hospital after the last raid. His brain tried to point it out then, but he'd been too tired to connect the dots.

Celia crossed her arms. "Whatever. We're all here. You had something to say, Jack?"

With a sigh, brain floating down from the happy cloud that'd developed for Mike, he pulled Addy's letter out of his pocket. He flipped the folded letter in his hands. "I'm not going to read this whole thing for you. Suffice it to say, it explains her motives in enough detail for me to believe she did this on her own."

Dean, who'd been about to take a chair on the other side of the room, shot to his feet. "Oh god. Addy. What's she done? Is she all right?"

Jack shrugged. "She surrendered herself to her mother."

Mike covered his face. "Oh. Fuck."

The fact Mike found it necessary to use such language told Jack about all he needed to know about the trouble Addy was in. But he had to ask. "Michael, you spent a lot of time with your mother last year. What kind of danger is Addy in?"

Dropping his hands, Mike's bleak stare told Jack all the rest of what he needed to know, everything he didn't already know.

"My god, Dad. The worst kind."

* * *

Curled into the tiniest ball possible, Addy opened her eyes and stared at the inside of her knees. The cell they'd put her in had a bed with a thin mattress and even a blanket. Which was good. It was cold underground.

She breathed into her knees, wondering how long it'd be until she couldn't curl into such a tight ball. Mom hadn't come to see her, hadn't done more than accompany her and Gian to this cell. She hadn't said a word after they walked into the Molehill. Not one.

The tumblers of the heavy lock turned and the door opened. "Breakfast, Miss Cooke."

Releasing her knees, she stretched and rolled over.

Light surrounded someone in the door.

Addy threw the blanket off and wobbled toward them. "I think I'd like some coffee today."

A woman an inch shorter than her, skin a touch lighter than Cassius's, stood in the door. "Coffee can be arranged. My goodness." She smiled, holding a hand out into the hallway. "You truly do look like her."

Addy glanced down the hall. More doors like this one lined it. Metal, with a small window at eye level. "Is this a prison?"

"You could call it that. Are you hungry?"

She see-sawed her hand. "Eggs are back on the menu. Still can't do bacon though."

Leading her out another door, the woman took her through rounded hallways. "Back on the menu?"

"This place looks a lot like I imagined," Addy said, trying to peek in the open doors they passed.

"Is it now?"

"Smells like earth. One of the only pleasant odors I've smelled in weeks." Her hands crossed her stomach.

"I see." The woman stopped. "Miss Cooke. I have to ask. Why did you come here? What do you hope to accomplish?" With a sudden step forward, she filled her bubble and met her eyes. "Is this part of a trick? Are you setting us up for an attack? I know our supply lines have been hit several times in the last few weeks. Are you part of that?"

Tears crowding her throat, Addy fought the immediate desire to back up. She held her footing and stared down into the woman's dark eyes. "Yes and no."

"Which?"

"I'm not setting you up. You know who's responsible for the supply lines."

She gripped Addy by the arm and shook. "Why did you come here?" Her fingers dug in, nails biting into her arm.

Gritting her teeth, Addy stared. Not the torture she expected, she tried to shift the woman's focus. "Who are you? Why should I tell you?"

Full lips peeling back in a predatory smile, the woman yanked her arm and brought her down to her eyes. "I'm the one you don't want to fuck with. You hurt your mom, you'll answer to me. You get me?" She released her arm, pushing her away.

Addy massaged her arm. "We both want the same thing."

The woman scoffed. "Doubtful."

"I just want my mom to be happy."

"What makes you think she's not? You mean you want her to be like you." Lifting her chin, she looked down her nose. "Your mom isn't like anyone else. I wouldn't want her to be."

Head shaking, Addy followed when the woman walked again. The scent of coffee and bacon crowded the hall. Her stomach rumbled. "I don't want her to be like me. But I want to make sure she's considered all the angles. Maybe there are things she doesn't know."

"Like what."

The tickle in the back of Addy's mind leapt up. "I've seen you," she said, stopping. "You were outside last time I was here. Watching."

She stuck a hand out. "That I was. Let's be formally introduced. My name is Ilasha Livingston."

Chewing her lip, Addy shook. Ilasha crushed her hand, arm like a steel bar. She grimaced. "Adelaide Cooke."

Frowning, Ilasha released her and led her the rest of the way to the food.

* * *

Tray in her hands, Addy faced the tables.

Silent people in grey jumpsuits like the one they'd given her last night ate listless oatmeal with equally listless hands.

A woman whose eyes matched the jumpsuits caught her eyes. Her eyebrows raised, and she drew in a breath as though about to speak. Before a sound escaped her lips, she lowered her head to her food and rubbed her belly.

Slightly rounded, well enough to tell she was pregnant.

"Kendra." Addy smiled and sat next to her. "Thank goodness. Are you all right?"

Thin lips pulled into a frown, she shrugged. "It's been a long three months." She made eye contact with Addy's shoulder. "You?"

"You don't sound the same. What have they done to you?" Addy mashed some of the sloppy oatmeal between her teeth. Which, surprisingly, was the best thing she'd eaten in weeks.

Kendra shrugged again. "Besides forced me to have feelings about an abomination? Not much."

Addy laid her hand over Kendra's free one. "I'm sorry. I'll help you get free of them."

She picked up a spoonful of oatmeal and dripped it back into the tray. "Is that why you came here? To free me?"

Shaking her head, Addy shoveled another spoonful in. Why hadn't she thought of oatmeal before? This was fabulous. "No, to be honest. But I can still get you out."

Stirring her oatmeal, Kendra met her eyes. "I'll never be free." She sniffed and left the table. Stopping at the trash, she dumped most of the food in, set the tray on the used stack, and left the room, shoulders hunched. She never made eye contact.

Addy polished off the oatmeal, drank a small cup of coffee she'd stirred up with at least half cream, and ate the apple they'd sat on the tray with the oatmeal. Her appetite had returned with a vengeance once that oatmeal hit her tongue. It was like she hadn't eaten in a month.

Dropping her tray on the used pile, she considered the plastic silverware before trashing it. They'd had plastic a few times, when she was little. Eventually they'd picked up some real silverware somewhere and stopped using the plastic. Mom had been sure it was going to run out, and besides that, she said it was bad for the environment.

Yet here they were, giving plastic silverware to prisoners of war. It seemed appropriate. This company thought people were as easy to throw away as plastic utensils.

She stood by the door, searching for Ilasha.

A man with a rifle approached. "Miss Cooke, if you would, please."

"Where are we going?"

"The general would like your information catalogued. She's ordered a full workup."

"I'm sorry. A workup?"

He guided her down a maze of earthen tunnels. There was no way she could keep up with all the turns. "Blood tests, hair samples, etcetera."

She stopped in the middle of a hallway that looked identical to the last five and backed into the cold wall. "No."

He slung the rifle off his shoulder and held it to port. "Afraid I have to insist, miss. The general was specific."

"I want to see her."

"She said you'd say that. Please follow me." He held a hand out again.

Arms crossed, she started walking again. "Are you going to take me to her?"

"After we have the samples she ordered, I will inform her of your compliance."

"And then she'll come see me?"

"I don't know, Miss Cooke. All I know is what I was told in my written orders from Mr. Anthony's secretary."

"And who's Mr. Anthony?"

"He's in charge here. Through this door, please." Re-slinging his rifle, he reached into a recess and pulled a door open.

Preceding him into the room, her toes curled and tried to turn her around. Needles, vials, microscopes, all the things she'd come to associate with the virus, both good and bad, crowded the tables in the room. "Did the orders come from this Anthony, or from my mom?"

The guard drew in a breath.

Ha. He didn't know. Well, now the whole place would know within hours.

"Are you one of us? Why haven't I ever seen you?"

A slow smile lifted her lips. "One of hers, are you? Look at me. You tell me."

His jaw dropped open. "You don't have the same last name…you're kidding." He laughed.

"What's funny?"

"Some of us used to talk about you. Wonder if you were alive, what you were like."

She flushed. "You're kidding."

He laughed again.

Realizing she'd copied his own words back to him, she grinned. "Some of you?"

"Yeah. Me, guy named Matt. Couple other dudes. Wonder what ever happened to that guy." He pointed to a chair. "Have a seat."

She did, breath caught around the hole in her chest. Matt mentioned that before, back in Magnolia. She'd forgotten. Nice of this guy to reach right through her ribcage and rip out her heart though.

Lost in thought, she hardly noticed them drawing blood.

CHAPTER 44

Dean charged down the hallway. The bar clanked to the floor, and the door banged open.

Mike stood.

Jack held a hand up. "You stay. I'll talk to him. Anybody else want to come scream at me?" He turned a circle.

Mike encircled Celia's waist with one arm. "I wish I could tell her how sorry I am. I should have talked to her about Mom. Should have told her what I knew."

Lump rising in his throat, Jack nodded. "You and me both, son." He spun on a heel, following Dean down the hall.

"Jack," Jane said, following him.

He stopped in the door. "Yeah."

She kissed him under the ear. "Luck."

Squeezing her shoulder, he motioned to the door. "Lock up after me. I'll be back later."

"You better." She closed and latched the door.

Standing on the sidewalk, he searched for Dean.

He walked with his hands shoved in his pockets, beating feet in the direction of the Tree.

Jogging to catch him, Jack called out.

Without turning, Dean stopped and waited. When Jack caught him, he started walking again. "I can't believe she did this." He glanced at Jack. "I'm so pissed I can't fucking see straight."

"I get that. Where do you guys stand?"

Stopping, Dean shrugged. He pulled his hands from his pockets and folded his arms. "I tried. I tried to fix it. I fucked up, Jack."

"Pretty sure we all knew that. But," he said, hand on Dean's shoulder, "no one's perfect."

Dean laughed. It didn't hold a lot of humor, but it was better than a frown.

"Thanks. I don't know. I thought we had a shot. She didn't even tell me she was doing this." He watched the horizon. "I guess that doesn't say too much about where we are. Or maybe it does."

"I feel pretty lucky I got a note. But she made sure to leave well before I'd have a chance to stop her." He leaned on the half wall next to them. "It's a hell of a punch in the gut."

Dean leaned next to him. "You seemed pretty calm about the whole thing."

"Good. I was trying to. Didn't want to worry Mike." He shook his head. "I thought, after everything Melinda has done in the last year, Addy had written her off. I thought we were on the same page about that." He paused. "I really did."

"It doesn't mean she doesn't love you, if that's what you're thinking."

"No. But thanks for the reminder. I guess it… I don't know."

"Can I ask you something?" Dean shifted on the wall, leaning his shoulder against it and glancing at Jack's belt.

He followed his gaze. "This?" He rested his hand on the pommel of the Bowie knife.

Dean nodded, throat working, lips pressed together.

"She left it for him, yeah. If he wanted it."

He narrowed his eyes and stared off down the sidewalk. "I won't make any assumptions. But something happened to the woman we last saw on the island."

Jack's chest tightened. "Yeah?"

"Yeah." He continued staring at the horizon. "She's different now, Jack. I can't put my finger on it. Seems like she. She trusts herself a lot more than she did when we met." He gave him a crooked smile. "She doesn't need me."

Dean's sad smile punched Jack in the bleak gut. "I know what you mean, man." He clapped him on one shoulder. "We'll get her back as soon as we can."

Meeting his eyes, Dean tensed. "And how soon is that? Today?"

Jack scuffed the ground with his foot. "We won't be ready to move on Talus for another three weeks. Minimum."

"You sure we can't move that up?"

"That is moved up."

"Shit."

Jack clenched his jaw. "I just have to hope Melinda doesn't hurt her before then. There's nothing else we can do."

* * *

Ilasha hovered by Melinda's elbow. "You don't need to do this."

Melinda kept walking, stuttering heart threatening to crawl up her esophagus and puke itself all over her shoes. "She came to see me, Lash. I should at least say hi. Besides." She ruffled the papers in her hand. "I've got all the test results here. I haven't looked them over yet, but now's as good a time as any."

Lash snatched at the papers. "You know Anthony is going to want those. What are we even doing down here?"

Melinda stopped in the middle of the hall. "She's my daughter, Lash. I know she's done some shit, and this is probably a trick, but I can't push her off on Anthony like any other test subject." She sighed, stomach a tight ball. "I have to look her in the eye at least once. I have to know." She started walking again.

"Know what? Is there something you aren't telling me? Is it about why you didn't come back to my place after she got here?" Lash took twice as many steps to keep up. Her breath came in short bursts.

Stopping in front of Addy's cell door, she faced Lash again. "Why did you come with me?"

"You might not be telling me everything, but I can tell when my woman needs moral support." She gripped her arm with a warm hand. "I'm not upset with you. I am worried about you, though, Em."

Insides gone from stone to a mess of snakes, Melinda faced the door. "I don't think she can hurt me any more than she already has, if that's what you're worried about." She lowered her head. "She turned on me, more than once. I believe there was a time when she would have tried to kill me herself, if she had the chance."

"Jesus. Let me get you a guard."

Eyes closed, Melinda smiled. "Isn't that why you're here?"

"I won't let her hurt you, that's for sure."

"Let's get through this. I don't think she's here to hurt me." She peeked over her shoulder. "I do think Jack is planning to come. Maybe to kill me. Maybe to destroy this place. And this might all be a diversion. Addy could be part of an intricate plan."

Lash lifted her chin. "I was beginning to think the brilliant woman I knew had disappeared. Good to see you're as crafty as always."

In her heart of hearts, buried beneath layers and layers of aloof cool, she wanted to believe Addy told the truth last night. But given everything that'd happened in the last year, it didn't seem likely.

It's not like she'd given her family any reasons to love her. With her damaged brain, she'd come back into their lives like an EF5 tornado and destroyed everything in her path.

She opened her mouth to ask Lash if the Cookes were better off without her.

Instead, she clamped her lips together and unlocked the door.

* * *

The cell door creaked open. Light fell in from the hallway.

Squinting at it, Addy sat up. She prepared to ask, again, to see her mom. It'd been almost a full day.

But outlined in the light stood the woman whose frame had haunted her dreams for a decade. Who'd taught her to catch rabbits bare-handed and how to navigate using Polaris. And that Vega would one day be the new North Star.

Who'd punched her in the nose and left her bleeding in the snow. Had killed Ella and Dean. May as well have pulled the trigger or dropped the grenade herself.

Addy cleared her throat. "I guess you didn't have to strangle me to get me in here after all."

Mom stopped, one foot in the cell. Papers rustled. "You're right. I didn't. You continue to be a surprise, jellybean."

The words "don't call me that" surfed to the edge of her lips. On the verge of spitting them out, she caught a breath. She didn't come here to be mad. Or mean.

As though stepping through an invisible wall, Melinda pushed into the cell. The woman from the morning, Ilasha, followed her, arms crossed. She disappeared into a dark corner of the cell and said nothing.

Melinda looked around the room. "It's not much. Maybe we can get you something nicer."

Addy scoffed. "I didn't come here to argue with you, Mom, but I honestly don't think being nice to me is high on your priority list. You tried to kill me last time we met."

She perched at the far end of the bed. "I wasn't trying to kill you." She glanced around. "It's damn dark in here. Lash, is there more light?"

Silent, Ilasha stepped out of the cell. Seconds later, the lights came up.

Mom smiled. "Better. I thought we could talk. Go over your test results together," she said, riffling the papers.

"Why don't we get right down to what it is you really care about?"

"And what's that?"

Pointing with her forehead, Addy frowned. "The tests." She sighed. "You used to talk so much about human ingenuity. About science and exploration. I just didn't realize it meant more to you than family."

For a split second, Mom's face crumpled.

Ilasha walked back in and retreated to her dark corner.

Sitting straight, Melinda inhaled and shook her head. "That's ridiculous. But it's equally ridiculous to think I'd give one up for the other." She flipped back the first page.

Without thinking about it, Addy slid closer and peeked over Mom's shoulder at the test results. As the scent of her mother flooded her nose, an all too brief moment flooded her memory.

The day she and Mom took a speeding boat down the coast to look at illuminated pictures of stars.

Stomach grumbling and slick, she backed away. "What does it say?"

"Well," Melinda said, head bowed, "you're not immune." She side-eyed her. "I didn't think you would be, but we have to check. We can easily give you the vaccine, of course. It is now one hundred percent effective."

"Do you use living humans to grow the virus for it?"

Mom looked up. "I'm sorry?"

"Living humans. To incubate the virus. Huxley says you could use cloned tissue, but you don't." She drew her knees up and sat cross-legged on the thin mattress. "Why don't you? Do you like killing people? Creating monsters?"

Face pinched closed like she'd eaten a whole lemon, Mom pulled out a pen and wrote a note on the test results. "We'll schedule you for a dose of the vaccine in the morning. Let's see." She flipped a page.

Crossing her arms over her baby and leaning forward, Addy shook her head. "You can't give me the vaccine right now. I think. I can't—"

"Oh, see here." Melinda turned to her, mouth open, finger pointing at the page. "You know you're pregnant, don't you?"

Addy's mouth snapped closed. Her teeth clacked. Chin trembling, throat thick, she nodded. "That's what I was trying to tell you," she said, voice low.

Melinda made another note. Emotion flickered across her face, but whatever it was came and went so fast, Addy couldn't decide what it was.

"The hCG levels indicate you are either in the middle of or near the end of the first trimester. Is that correct?" She didn't look up from the paper.

Addy pressed her back into the wall. If there was one person Addy needed to be happy about this, it'd been Mom. Yet here she was, making notes and check marks on her papers as if Addy was just another number. "I don't know what that means. How long is a trimester?"

"The first is twelve weeks."

Addy brushed a tear from the corner of her eye. "Yeah. That sounds right, I guess."

"In that case, I can use you for a control."

From the shadows, Ilasha cleared her throat.

Frown lines deep, Melinda peeked into the dark. "Cormac. Whoever is running the immunity trial. Can use you as a control. Or at least gather some good data. You're nearly even with our first pair." She twisted, frown still deep. "We will need information about the father. As much as you can provide."

Her vision doubling, Addy sank into the despair coming for her with its black fingers. "Whatever you want. Your grandchild deserves the best you can give it. Whatever you think that is."

Mom raised her pen. "What can you tell me?" Expression flat, eyebrows raised at the simple interrogative.

"It's Matt's baby, Mom."

Finally, a real emotion flickered across her features. Her mouth dropped open. "What about Dean?"

Tears falling down her cheeks, Addy shrugged. "It's complicated."

She'd never wanted a hug from her mother as bad as she did right now.

Melinda stood, pocketing her pen. "I'm certain we have his records around here somewhere. And at some point in the near future, he should be available to contribute to testing, if necessary."

Swallowing the tears, the need for comfort, Addy mustered all the command she could. "You leave him out of this."

"This is his home, Adelaide. He will be back." Without a single backward glance, she strode to the door. Hair flying behind her. Stopping in the door, she spoke over her shoulder. "It is nice to see you, child. We will have to speak about your father soon."

"Mom, wait."

"Sleep well."

"Mom."

Melinda strode through the door.

Ilasha peeled herself from the dark corner and followed, throwing one look at Addy, her eyes repeating the threat from the morning.

The door closed, and the lights inside the cell dimmed.

Backed into the corner of the bed, Addy lifted her knees and wrapped both arms around them.

What had she gotten herself into?

CHAPTER 45

Raised voices floated through the roll-up door. Jack's heart rate increased, and he hurried to the loading dock. Sounded like he'd arrived at the Tree just in time to break up a fight.

He scrambled up and peeked through the door.

Cassius limped around the stage on two crutches, a new prosthetic attached to his leg with a few belts. The skin tone didn't match, and it didn't fit him perfectly, but it was enough for him to learn how to be up on two legs again while they found one that did. Papers clenched in one hand, he stopped and faced out.

"Sir, she is mortal.
But by immortal providence, she's mine.
I chose her when I could not ask my father
For his advice, nor thought I had one."

He stopped, lifting the paper and staring at it. "Talbot, my dear, I am not certain about this bit."

His voice echoed from the dark beyond the stage. "Cassius, stop whining and finish the scene. Rivers—"

"Oh, hello, Addy's father." The green-eyed man with shaggy black hair—Grey, if he remembered right—stepped out of the shadows in the back of the stage. "Come to check our progress?"

"Yes. No. Sorry, I didn't mean to intrude."

Cassius lowered himself to the stage and sat, dangling his legs over the front. "You are quite welcome, good sir. We do miss our Adelaide. Tell us, how is she?"

He sighed, heart rate still humming along. He approached the stage, and the rest of the Troupe appeared from wherever they'd been hiding.

Victoria hopped up the stairs and landed on the stage like a bird alighting. She sat next to Cassius. "Your expression does not bode well for the answer to Cassie's question."

Leaning on the stage, Jack crossed his arms on it. He rested his chin on a forearm. "She left town."

A couple of the actors murmured.

Victoria leaned forward, white hair falling out of the bun on top of her head and hanging in her eyes. "Where did she go, Jack?"

"To see her mom. She surrendered herself to Talus."

Cursing, Victoria stood and paced.

Her repertoire of curses impressed even Jack. It'd been a while since he'd heard most of the words she'd drug out and dusted off. He fought a grin.

Cassius laid a warm hand on his arm, brown eyes round. "Can we help her?"

"It'll be a few weeks before we can get to her. I have to believe she'll be all right until then because, frankly, I don't have a choice." He frowned. "Any attack on Talus or attempt to get her back right now would be suicide."

The waif of a woman, Rivers, sat on his other side. "What are we to do?"

"I wondered if you guys could tell me more about what she was like with you. What you did the last few months. The girl who left Harkers Island to come here is not the same woman I found when I got here."

Cassius smiled. "What would you like to know?"

"I thought it got quiet in here."

Jack spun.

Jim stood in the door, rolled cigarette hanging from his mouth. "If we're going to chat, why don't you guys come in here and take a break. I've got lunch ready anyway."

Grey appeared on the other side of Cassius, and he and Rivers helped him up. Once they reached the stairs, Victoria stood to the side and spotted him as he hopped down. "I myself am almost all the production we need these days."

"You will improve, Cassie, my dear," Rivers said, floating down the stairs as if she hardly touched any of them.

Jack followed them into the next room. They filled every inch of space between here and there. His mouth lifted in an unbidden grin. He took a seat at the bar as they took their food to various corners.

"Want a drink, Jack?"

"Sure, Jim. What's your specialty?"

"Make a mean dirty martini."

"Damn, getting fancy up in here." He waved a hand. "Yeah, one."

Jim set to work, smiling with the corner of his mouth. "I see you eyeing this smoke. You want one?"

Jack grinned, corners of his mouth turned down. "Yes. No, thank you."

"Suit yourself."

The Troupe fell into silence as they ate.

Jack pulled the smoke through his nose. "Are they always this quiet when they eat?"

"No. It's a little weird. What'd you ask them before I got there?"

He crossed his arms on the bar. "Did you know Addy left?"

Jim tapped his ashes and stuffed the cigarette back in his mouth. "No. She go to be with Matt?"

"What makes you ask that?"

Jim lowered his glasses with one finger and peeked over the top of them. Green eyes sparkled. He didn't say a word.

Jack went on as though he'd spoken. "You're right. I know. But no, it's more than that. I helped pull her through the death of her mom. My daughter is strong enough to withstand a little heartbreak."

Shrugging, Jim stirred the drink and strained it into a long-stemmed glass. "Sorry this glass isn't right. Beggars can't always be choosers." He produced a jar full of olives. "But olives, we have in abundance. The Greeks basically worshiped olives. I don't disagree."

Jack sipped the drink. It'd been easily decades since he'd last tasted one. Though his dad had been more of a tea drinker, he'd liked the occasional fancy drink. This one, he introduced Jack to when he was about fifteen. When Jack thought there was only high school and maybe college and some protesting in his future.

"That's good, Jim." He tapped the glass. "Thank you."

"My pleasure," he said, smoke lifting. "Where'd she go?"

"To rescue her mom."

Jack might've been expecting glass to break. The smoke to fall to the ground. Something. Anything.

As though frozen in time, Jim stood stock-still. The only thing that moved was the smoke as it floated past the front of his glasses, through his bushy hair, and up to the ceiling.

"Jim?"

Mouth falling open, Jim plucked the smoke out from between his lips and stubbed it out. He mouthed a silent curse and lit another smoke. He took a drag and pointed with it. "She came here, uncertain. She didn't know where she fit in, I could see it all over her. You know what happened?"

Again, Jack shook his head. He didn't. But he was beginning to get an idea.

"She found it, the place where she fit."

Smiling, Jack looked around at the Troupe. "With these guys. I can see that. They seem like they can be fun."

Jim shook his head. "No. She found that sweet spot inside. These guys"—he pointed with the smoke again—"most of them live in that sweet spot. Were born to it. They're easy to learn from."

Pushing the drink away, Jack leaned back. "Ah hell, Jim. That's not good."

"Why not?"

"Now I know why she left. Given." He stopped, swallowed, took a drink, and swallowed again. "Given what she wrote in her letter, and what you're saying. I can't save her from her mother, even if I physically pull her out of there. Whatever happens in there now will either kill her or heal her."

A plate clattered to the ground.

Jack's pulse took off at a gallop as Victoria wove between the couches and came to lean on the bar next to him. "She can't fucking do that. We have to get her out of there. We have to destroy everything Talus stands for." Hair in her eyes again, she scowled.

Jack shook his head. "Everything? Even the Cure?"

"Everything." Vic straddled a stool. "It started out good, with the Cure, but they've changed. They've become synonymous with corruption. With devastation."

"What do you mean?"

"After the general left, and we were forced to work in the lab, I saw how bad it had gotten. Not just the remnants. Do you have any idea what those are?"

In the back of his mind, Jack heard a ping. Narrowing his eyes, he stared up at the ceiling and let his mind wander toward it.

Melinda whispered to him from that hospital on Emerald Isle. *"Shit, Jack, it's the remnants."*

The memories washed over him. The death of Tim and escaping to the roof with Melinda. "I've seen them before. I thought they were Dead Heads."

Vic chuckled from behind her hands. "I wish. No, Jack." Her eyes widened. "The remnants were the ones they used to incubate the virus."

"Victoria, stop," Cassius said. "I cannot bear it."

Pressing her lips together, she lowered her head. "They give and take the virus until there is nothing to give and take anymore. It's how we have such an excess supply of the Cure. It's how we were even able to begin vaccine testing." She sniffed. Her bright, white-blue eyes caught him. "Those are the kind of people who now have control over our Adelaide. Worse than kill her or turn her into one of their experiments, what if they." Her eyes welling, she stopped. Her throat worked.

Cassius finished for her, his voice hushed and shaking. "What if they convince her their way is right? What if she becomes one of them?"

* * *

The lights came up in Addy's cell.

Sitting up, she squinted into them and rubbed her face. Had it been a day? An hour? A week? Without the sun, it was impossible to tell.

A short man with deep brown hair and eyes walked in, clipboard in hand. He extended the other. "Miss Cooke. Pleasure."

Standing and tugging the jumpsuit flat, she shook. "Thanks. Who are you?"

"Cormac McNamara. I appreciate the opportunity to work with you." He lifted the clipboard. "There's a lot to get you up to speed on."

She crossed her arms. "I'm sorry? What are we doing?"

"If you'd come with me, we'll go down to my office. We can talk in more detail. Get you something more comfortable to wear." He checked the clipboard. "Do you need maternity clothing?"

She walked past him and into the hallway. "I don't know. I guess so."

Joining her in the hall and walking with short, quick steps, he led her away from the hallway she'd come to think of as the jail.

"Sorry it took me a while to come rescue you from the cell. Mr. Anthony, my boss, is nothing if not a stickler for paperwork. Everything has to be in order."

She pinched her lips. "How many days have I been here?"

He checked his clipboard. "Four."

Half a week. Still two and a half or three until Dad came. Would it be enough time? Mom hadn't come to see her again after the first visit. If she hoped to do anything about her, she had to see her.

"Where's my mother?"

He shook his head, greased hair glinting in the low light of the earthen halls. "They don't tell me. In here, please." The door he pulled open looked like every other door.

She inspected it. "How do you tell one door from another?"

He smiled. "Lucky guess." Shaking his head, he pointed to the outside of the door before closing it. "And the little plaques next to the doorknob."

She caught sight of the edge of the small plaque before he shut the door, something it surprised her to have missed. Without being invited, she sat in the chair before the single desk.

He sat behind the desk, dropping the clipboard onto it and smiling. "Let me tell you about us."

"Oh, I think I know everything I need to know."

"I doubt that. Your information has been…tainted."

She inspected the ceiling. "If you say so."

"I've had a brief rundown of the past few months and your interactions with the general. Not all of it has been pleasant."

Narrowing her eyes, she inspected him instead. "How do you know about any of that?"

"The general is required to report in." He consulted the clipboard. "As well as recordings from Magnolia. Phone records. Additional information."

They had access to the recordings from Magnolia? Interesting. But a more pressing issue popped to mind. "What additional information?"

"I'm not at liberty to say. What I can tell you is there are many of us here who have been anxious to meet you for some time."

She laughed without humor. "Sure. Sure." Leaning on the desk, she stared at him with half-lidded eyes, doing her best impression of Celia. "Am I what you expected?"

He sat back. "N-no. You, uh. You're surprising, Addy."

"You can call me Miss Cooke." She crossed her arms.

He pulled a key from his desk drawer. "This is for your room. I'm giving you free rein."

"Why?"

"If you don't want it, I won't give it to you. I'd ask a couple things in return though."

"Here it comes."

He fidgeted with the key. "Voluntary participation in our research. That's a requirement."

Her head began shaking before she even opened her mouth. "No."

He held up a hand, palm out. "Hear me out."

"No."

"In your case, the tests would be noninvasive. This isn't something we can afford all of our incubators," he went on, as though she hadn't spoken, "but, of course, you aren't just any incubator."

Black, icy feet walked down her spine. "Incubators? They have names, you know." She stood. "One of them is named Kendra." She leaned on the desk. "They have names, and families, and lives. And here you are, forcing them to die for your supposed research."

"That's not—"

"Don't give me that bullshit. Take me to my mother."

"I'm afraid I can't. Please, hear me out." He stood.

"I'm not—"

He rounded the desk and gripped her arm. Leaning in, he spoke into her ear. "Listen, Addy, please. There's a lot of us. OK, the ones of us who grew up here. We're not all about the way they've been doing things. We want to change." He jerked her arm. "Things can't keep going the way they've been. We could use your help."

She glared. "The hell would I want to help you? You're as much a part of this as her, as far as I'm concerned."

Letting her go, he looked at his feet. "I know. I've done a lot of things I wish I could take back." He glanced at her from under his brow. "Tell me about your doctor. Does he really think he can do what we do without hurting people?"

Although all she wanted to do was storm out of this office and wander until she found her cell again, she nodded. "He does. He thinks he can use cloned tissue."

"How long would it take him to get to where we are?"

"I didn't ask him."

Cormac's brown eyes glossed over as he stared at the ceiling. "Years, probably." He leaned in again. "I hear IRF is different. Didn't your doctor come from there?"

"Are you talking about partnering with IRF to take this place down?"

Eyes darting back and forth, he stepped closer again. "Lower your voice. It's already in the works."

* * *

Melinda ambled down the hall, hands clasped behind her back.

"General," Anthony said from behind her. "May I walk with you?"

She shrugged. "Not like you needed permission before."

"Even so," he said, falling into step with her, "I'm not always a rude asshole."

She shrugged again. "If you say so."

"Your daughter belongs to us now?"

Ah. The rude asshole getting straight to the point. "She's here, if that's what you mean. Ours? No."

"Indeed. I could see where she gets that kind of stubbornness."

"Do you have a point?"

"While I cannot put you back on immunity, not if I want to answer to my own boss, it would be foolish not to have your input. Please work with McNamara. Let him know what your theories are." He stopped, hand on her arm. "I hear there's an IRF doctor in town, the one from your mountain town, if I'm not mistaken, who has some different ideas than we do." Leaning in, he looked left and right. "What are your thoughts on this?"

She stepped back. Fought herself to keep the questions about his relationship with Burke behind her lips. "I need more evidence. As for now, it sounds like a pipe dream. A fluke. Not a long-term answer."

"My thoughts as well." He walked away.

And not like she'd had a destination in mind, but she walked with him. "Since I've been back, I've heard very little about IRF. After you scolded me about Burke, I don't think I've heard you mention them at all. What's going on with them?"

He shook his head. "I'll have to go over the most recent intelligence reports. A few of our spies think they're going to try and mobilize on us soon. I think they've been responsible for our supply lines being cut in half."

Melinda was sure it was more to do with Jack than IRF, but she kept her own counsel on that. Though it might be worth it to bring it up to Lash and find out what the intelligence reports said. "Do we need to be concerned?"

Corners of his mouth turned down, he caught her eye. Narrowed his own. "I don't think so. They've never attacked headquarters before. I have no reason to believe they will now. No. It's far more likely they're just running some exercises. Finding out our weaknesses. It's fine." He stopped. "It's not like we aren't always doing the same."

She laughed. Although she tried to tamp it down, pride swelled in her chest. Wandering into that clearing, receiving the prototype Cure, waking up here, it was some kind of divine blessing. The work they did here was the most important work that could be done. Saving humanity. She was lucky to not have awoken in a different sector. The company had its own army, and she was glad to not be a part of that.

But while he was being talkative, there was something that'd been on her mind. She rested the tips of her fingers on his arm. "Charles."

He looked up, eyes wide. "Yes?"

"Tell me about your bosses."

Even in the low light of the hallway, the color drained from his face. His piercing blue eyes sharpened, and he swallowed twice. He started walking, almost a sprint. "That's not wise, Melinda."

"Why are you so scared of them? What do they have on you?"

His tongue darted out and touched his lip. "It's not that. It's. I can't discuss this with you."

"We can help each other. Tell me what you need from me."

"If this is about immunity, I can't—"

"It's not about immunity, but I'd be a liar if I said that didn't matter to me. What can I do to help you with them, and help myself?"

"Without convincing evidence or a major breakthrough, I cannot get you back on immunity. Other than that, I cannot continue this line of conversation, General." Spinning on a heel, he stalked away and turned the first corner he came to.

Melinda wasn't even sure he knew where that hallway went. He was just trying to escape her.

A major breakthrough, huh?

Arms crossed, she took off in the opposite direction. She had a destination, now.

CHAPTER 46

Addy's cell door opened, light spilling in from the hallway. Mom stood silhouetted in the doorway. "Good morning. How are you feeling?"

Sitting up, Addy wiped the drool from the side of her face. "Less nauseated. Less tired." She scratched her head. "Usually." Swinging her feet over the edge of her bed, she shook both legs. "It's been over a week since you came to see me. What do you want?"

"I have to want something?"

"I had the chance to get out of this cold, uncomfortable cell."

Melinda walked in. "Oh? Why didn't you?"

The nausea returned, but she was sure it was less the baby and more Mom. "What do you want?"

"I need to find Mr. Lyburn's records and thought you could help me dig them up." She held her hand toward the door. "Plus, I wanted to see you."

Addy's stomach flipped. His blue eyes, his smile framed by those parenthetical dimples, skipped through her consciousness, and her stomach flipped again. Definitely not the baby. "I don't know. Maybe I should stay here."

Mom frowned, scuffing the floor with her toe. "I thought you came to see me." She glanced up. "Isn't that why you came?"

"Fine," Addy said, grimacing so hard it hurt her teeth. "Lead the way."

Leading her into the hall, Mom leaned over. "Are you hungry? We can stop by the mess hall before going downstairs."

"Let's get this over with. I'm not hungry right now."

Which was true. The past few minutes left her feeling like she'd been punched in the gut with an iron hammer. There was no way she could put food on top of that, baby or no.

But speaking of the baby. "Mom, can I ask you something?"

"Sure."

"When you were pregnant, when did you first feel the baby moving?"

Stopping at the top of a staircase, hand on the rail, Melinda smiled. Her eyes softened. "With your brother, it took forever. I was over halfway through before I knew that's what it was." Reaching her fingers toward Addy without touching her, she gave her that crooked grin of hers. "With you, it was harder to count in those days, without calendars and doctors and such. But it was much earlier." She cocked her head. "Why?"

Addy shrugged. "Just curious. I didn't intend to get pregnant, but now that I am, I'd like to know more about it. Being stuck in a cell isn't helping."

Mom started down the stairs. "I'm sorry, honey. I should talk to you more. You probably want to ask your mom all kinds of questions. I know I did." She chuckled. "She was so mad at me. But it was the one thing we could talk about. She hated she could only have one baby."

"And you disappointed her when you got pregnant with Mike."

"Yeah." She smiled over her shoulder. "I guess we have that in common. Being disappointments to our mothers."

Addy balled a fist in her stomach. "Jesus Christ, Mom. Thanks."

She continued down the stairs. "You want me to lie to you?"

"I guess not." She sighed. "What does it feel like?"

"Being a disappointment to your mother?"

A giggle bubbled up. Addy stuffed it down. "No. The baby moving."

"Oh. Like a teeny tiny bird right here." She stepped off the last stair and touched Addy on the abdomen. "Sometimes like gas. But mostly like a butterfly."

Addy exhaled a humorless laugh. "Appropriate."

"Why?"

Because its father gives me butterflies. Whether I want to admit it or not.

She waved her hand. "Nothing." Tears threatened, so sudden her eyes stung.

Mom touched her shoulder. "Are you sure you're OK?"

Shaking her head, Addy swiped at her eyes. "I don't want to talk about it with you."

Sniffing, Mom led her down the hall, clicking on a giant flashlight. "There's lights down here, but if someone sees them, they'd come ask what we're doing. That's the last thing I want."

"Why?"

"I don't want to talk about it with you."

Apparently two could play the petty game. "I already told you, it's complicated," she said, following her mom into a dark room.

"Here, hang on. Hold this. Point it at the bottom of the door." Mom handed her the flashlight, pulled a scarf from her neck, and stuffed it under the door. "That should help. Thanks," she said, taking the flashlight back.

In the moment between when she turned off the flash and turned on the overhead lights, Addy spun through a second of vertigo. A cavernous vacuum of air behind her, the room could be full of anything. Knowing Mom, literally anything.

She pulled her arms close, hugging her own shoulders.

The overhead lights glared to life.

Squinting, Addy took in the room. Filing cabinets, for as far as she could see.

Mom motioned to the right side of the room. "There's a bunch of files here on Magnolia. Some more upstairs, but I can't show you those."

Addy wandered toward the cabinets. "What kind of files?"

"Mainly my own reports. Not much of interest."

"Don't be so sure." She considered. "Anything about Matt? Did he make reports from Magnolia?"

Melinda chuckled, moving deep into the room. "When I arrived, he came to see me two or three times. He tried to tell me he was too busy to make regular reports. I think he belonged to you the moment he saw you."

Addy covered her mouth with the back of her hand. "That's ridiculous. He still belongs to Ella."

"Sure." Melinda weaved between filing cabinets. "Ah, here we are." Sweeping a hand across the top of a dusty cabinet, she showed her palm to Addy. Blanketed in dirt. "Looks like these haven't been disturbed in some time."

Addy pulled it open.

Mom clicked her teeth. "I shouldn't let you see these names."

Addy shrugged, thumbing through the files. Memorizing as many names as she could before she hung up on Tim's. "Too late now." She tugged Tim's file loose.

Mom put her hand on it. "Let's stick to Matt's for now."

Addy stuffed it back in the drawer and riffled through the others. Spotting Matt's in front of Vic's, she yanked both out.

Melinda laughed again. "How is it you go straight to some of my favorites? Even Timothy turned on me, in the end." She cut her eyes at Addy.

Addy wandered away. "Have you ever considered it has less to do with me than you?"

"Ouch, kiddo."

Stopping, Addy closed her eyes and swallowed as acid crept up her throat. "I'm sorry. That's not what I came here to say. I'm sorry."

"You're right. It's been a difficult couple years." She closed her eyes. "Sometimes, I'm not even sure who I am anymore."

Shifting her feet, Addy crossed her arms over her stomach. "Mom. That's."

Inhaling, Melinda opened her eyes. "I'm not sure why I told you that."

Addy crossed to her again and laid a hand on her shoulder. "It's OK." She'd already gone over all this in her head, so why was it so hard to say it? Why had she come all this way?

"Look. I've been pissed at you a lot the last few months. We had some good times on Harkers, and that's made the rest of it even worse. I." She stopped.

Mom's brown-hazel eyes met hers, corners turned down. "You what?"

"I've wanted you to be who you were. But that's not who you are. And I have to accept you, I do accept you, for who you are."

The rock in Addy's gut lifted. It didn't fall away, but it stopped pressing on her. Finally.

Melinda's face melted. She snagged the files and slammed the drawer. "Why do I feel like that's conditional?"

"It's not. I don't agree with what you're doing and the choices you've made. But I accept you're different than I remember. And I want you to know that's OK." She stopped, heart beating in her throat, surprised her voice didn't shake with each thump. "I love you as much as I ever did, Mom."

Mouth trembling, Mom grabbed her in a hug and crushed her. "I love you too, jellybean."

Closing her eyes, Addy hugged her back. Surely there must be something else to say, but she didn't know what.

Mom pushed her away. "There is one more file I want to look for. It's from Magnolia." She pointed. "You look that way, I'll look over here."

Addy wiped her eyes and stepped back. "What are we looking for?"

"It's to do with the vaccine. If we find it, I'll explain."

Addy tried a cabinet next to the wall. The drawer stuck. She jerked it. "And if not? You'll keep it a secret?"

Mom spoke to the drawer she'd just opened. "I'm afraid it's complicated and something I don't want you involved in. For your own protection."

Jerking the next drawer down, Addy opened her mouth to question Mom's motives. Instead, the cabinet popped open, and she fell on her ass. "Ouch."

"You all right?"

With a grin, Addy stood to her knees and wiped her ass. "Yeah, I just—"

A cool breeze ruffled her hair.

Mouth still open, she looked at the cabinet. Instead of files behind the front of the drawer, black, open air greeted her.

"You just what?" Her voice approached.

Fingertips on the back of the fake drawer front, Addy pulled the cabinet open. The entire front opened as one piece.

Behind it, dark, cold air greeted her.

"What the hell have you found, jellybean?" Kneeling next to her, she clicked on her giant flashlight and aimed it at the dark.

Some kind of tunnel extended into the wall.

Addy lowered her voice. "You know," she whispered, "when I dreamed about finding a secret tunnel, I always thought it would be cooler than this." She narrowed her eyes. "Is that cobwebs?"

Mom shook her head. "Let's find out." Her eyes sparkled. That explorer's spirit she'd raised Addy with lit her face and lifted her mouth into a true smile. Without waiting for Addy to agree, she crawled into the dark tunnel.

"Mom, wait," Addy said, crawling after her. She spotted a handle inside the false front and closed it behind them, plunging them into dusty, suffocating, spectral darkness.

On her hands and knees, she followed Mom. The only blessing about being in the rear that she didn't have to clear the cobwebs with her own head, she sneezed after getting a nose-full of dirt.

"Bless you," came Mom's voice from somewhere up ahead.

As the light dimmed, Addy's chest closed. Her throat tight, she tried to keep crawling with dust in her eyes. They watered, and she stopped to clear them.

She closed them both, attempting to find a relatively clean spot on her sleeve with which to wipe them. As she did, she called out to her mom.

Silence returned.

Opening her eyes, she blinked in the now pitch-dark tunnel. She couldn't see which way was forward and which way was back.

"Mom?"

Rustling.

She stretched out her arms, hands reaching for the sides of the tunnel. Both hit rough, damp dirt. The dark pressed on her lungs.

Clenching her jaw, she put her palms back on the ground and crawled toward what she thought was the right direction.

Lights flared to life before her, the uneven edges of the tunnel carved out of darkness.

Mom leaned into the tunnel. "Come on, kiddo. There's a whole room down here. Check it out." She walked away.

Addy forced her memory away from the story Matt told about the first time he'd met Melinda. The hard dirt floor pressing into her knees, she crawled the rest of the way. Attempting to stand in the room at the end of the tunnel, her knees gave. She staggered.

Mom gripped her under the armpit and steadied her. "The hell do you suppose this is?" She spun a circle, hands on her hips.

The room, its sides not as smooth as the cell Addy spent a week and a half in, was a quarter the size of the one they'd left. The way they'd come the only way in and out.

Each of three sloping sides held a bank of computers, their flat screens hanging from the walls above their keyboards. One screen on each wall was lit, each with some kind of graphics bouncing from edge to edge.

Mom walked to one of the screens. She tapped the keyboard in front of it.

A screen came up with a little box in the middle.

"Damn."

"What?" Addy asked, joining her and looking over her shoulder.

"Password protected." She lifted and dropped a hand.

Addy pointed at some plastic boxes at the end. "What do you think those are?"

Melinda crossed to them. "These labels are fairly cryptic. 'Main,' 'Green,' 'North.' Huh."

"Locations, maybe?"

Finger on her chin, Mom nodded. "Maybe. They look a bit like routers." She waved her hand. "I was never the best at this." Her fingers slipped across the tops of the boxes. Her eyes wide, the green light reflected off her face and made her look like a resurrected 'Head. Like one of her experiments.

Addy's stomach finished its crawl up her throat. "If you don't know what this is, who does?"

Mom frowned. "I don't know, honey. But I intend to find out."

* * *

Staring at the high-rises, Jack strolled through downtown.

Knapp walked beside him, chattering about the history of the Queen City. "And that's how it became known as 'The Hornet's Nest.'" He bounced on his toes.

Jack chuckled. A fitting nickname for this bustling city full of people. Since Cassius had convinced the council to approve the attack on Talus, the attitude of the whole town had shifted. Readying themselves for the attack, taking in the soldiers who arrived every day now, they continued to provide whatever the defense force needed. And Jack couldn't help but notice extra fortifications around and inside every yard, home, and building. These people might have had it easy, living in this community together, but they weren't soft. Even if they didn't do most of their own fighting, they didn't back down from challenges before them.

Not a bad place to raise kids.

He frowned at the bank building. "It's been two weeks since Addy left. We're about ready for our assault, and if the council is all right with it, I want to move it up to next week."

"Why so soon?"

He shrugged. "I know she went of her own will, but I'd feel better if my daughter was back here. Or at least away from her mother."

Knapp smiled. "I've got a two-year-old. I can't imagine what you must be feeling, but I can sympathize. Are you sure you'll be ready?"

He shook his head, heart beating in his temples. "I'm never sure. And this is. Well. I don't intend to allow Melinda to escape unscathed."

"You intend to kill her?"

"She's going to see the end of this either dead or in prison." He swallowed the lump in his throat, calming the harsh edge he'd found in his voice. "We'll be as ready as we'll ever be, I suppose. The only thing we're missing at this point is the cannon and armament Morgan wanted to bring."

"A cannon would be a useful thing against an underground bunker."

"It would. But a lot of these units came pretty heavily armed. Lots of explosives." He stopped, meeting Knapp's eyes. "We'll just have to plan this to be more guerrilla than I wanted." He shrugged. "Necessary evil. Talus must be stopped."

"A couple of us have some questions about that, Jack," Knapp said, motioning to a convenient bench under a tree.

Jack took a seat.

Knapp sat next to him, thin fingers straightening his tie. "You may not be aware of this, but they are the leading producers of the Cure."

Jack shook his head, already not liking where this was going. "I didn't. Is that why the council was hesitant?"

"One reason." He leaned back, flattening the tie against his chest and crossing one leg over the other. "What do you know about IRF?"

"Hux used to work for them. He says their methods are not as barbaric as what he's seen from Talus."

Knapp clicked his tongue. "It's commonly accepted, by those of us who keep up with these things, that Talus is more brutal but gets faster results. In the business of saving lives, doesn't fast equal better?"

Jack stood and paced. "No, no it doesn't. Look. The first Talus hospital I saw was run on the blood of the people they experimented on. An entire horde, hundreds, maybe even thousands. And they were responsible for most of it." He met Knapp's eyes. "Melinda admitted as much."

"And if they were destroyed, who would produce the Cure? Don't they have a vaccine now, too?"

Lifting his hands, Jack sighed. He dropped them, slapping himself in the thigh. "Sure they do. But at what cost? At some point, the cost has to be too high." He sat again and leaned into

Knapp's face. "Trust me. The general does not care about human cost. Neither physical nor emotional. She cares only about results."

"Understood. But do you think she speaks for the whole company?"

"She has bosses. She answers to someone. I know that for a fact." He shook his head. "Do you think IRF can produce the Cure?"

"They already do, though their production is far, far below Talus's." Knapp laid a hand on his knee. "We're concerned about the Cure. If the supply were to run out."

Jack stood. "We may have to prepare for that eventuality. Did you speak to the council about getting Hux a bigger lab?"

"We don't currently have the facilities, but we can make a call to those interested in helping. If you can find facilities for him, we can provide people."

Jack stood. "Thanks. And we'll get prepared for this assault. Whether we're ready or not."

* * *

"Hey, Dean, thanks for coming," Jack said, opening the door wide. "I know this isn't something you'd like to talk about."

Dean shrugged, hands in his pockets. "You asked. What am I gonna do, say no?"

Jane laughed from her plush chair. "Yes. He'd do well to hear a no or two from time to time."

Half a grin lifting his mouth, Jack sat on the couch next to her chair and motioned to the other end. "Have a seat. We need to go over this before the invasion. It's creeping up on us."

Dean sat. "Yeah, only a few days now, huh. I gotta admit, Jack, your restraint is kind of amazing." He leaned forward, resting his elbows on his knees. "It's been hard to think about anything else except getting in there and pulling her out."

"I don't like it any more than you. But it is what it is. If we go in too early, we won't be able to help her." He glanced at Jane, his face tight.

"It wouldn't matter anyway, Dean, and you know it. She's got something in her head. She's going to see it through." She squeezed Jack's knee. "Didn't get her stubbornness from nowhere, I'll tell you that."

Chuckling, Dean threw an arm over the back of the couch. "So. IRF."

The tightness extended from Jack's face to his chest. "IRF. We haven't talked about them in a while."

"True. But I've been thinking about them lately too. I've run across their chatter a bit here and there while I've been working on this town's comms. God, what a mess."

"How much work do you have left?"

"Months. If I'm lucky." He frowned. "I'd honestly love to have IRF's help at this point. But."

"Given our involvement with Burke's murder and everything that happened in Magnolia, yeah. That's not going to happen," Jack finished for him. "Still. Tell me what you know about them."

"They do a lot of work on the infrastructure, not just the phones. A ton of what they do is aimed at getting the power grid back up. Lot of their guys are responsible for most of the working power plants. Fourteen, I think it is."

"That many? Wow," Jane said, standing with the baby. The little angel, asleep on her mother, wiggled. Jane sat her in the swing and turned the crank. "I didn't know there were enough people to warrant that many plants." As she sat again, she plucked her needles from the side table and settled them in her hair.

"We could get another half dozen or so going if need be. There were over sixty nuclear plants in operation when this shitstorm happened," Dean said, "and in some cases, we're lucky they didn't spontaneously melt down."

Jack's hair crawled away from his forehead. He'd never, not once, considered that could have happened. His stomach jittered inside his abdominal cavity, pushing his guts out of the way. "Why didn't they?"

"Most of them were shut down safely before they became a problem. Probably they hoped to get them back up and running in a few weeks." He leaned forward again. "IRF has been all over that. Roads, they've worked a lot on that. I've come to realize." He stopped, smiling. Eyes cloudy.

"Come to realize what?" Jane asked.

Starting, Dean smiled at them. "Sorry. I've come to realize I didn't have all the intel available when Mike and Addy and me hopped in that train to come after you guys."

Jack grimaced. This was likely to cause some friction, but there was nothing for it. He couldn't let personal issues be greater than the city. "I hope—"

The proximity alarm beeped once, a red LED flashing over the front door. The air clicked, like his old one in Arizona, only this sound came out of the fireplace.

In one fluid motion, Jane popped the baby from the swing and held her close. Sliding a needle from her hair, that fiery mane falling around her face, she crept up next to him with silent feet. "It's the front," she said, voice breaking a whisper.

Dean drew his machete. "I'll get the left side," he said, stalking to the side of the door and holding the blade ready.

Jack crept to the other side of the door. "The next thing I want is a spyhole like I used to have."

Jane hooked her chin at the door, sleeping baby still clutched to her breast. "We'll get it done tomorrow, if we're still alive. See who it is."

Her crack about dying tonight skimming past him, he crouched to peek out the window. "Damn," he said to the glass. "They're already on the porch."

The porch creaked.

Jack might have jumped out of his boots if he were wearing them. As it was, he'd have to fight barefoot.

He looked across at Dean. Mouthed, "Ready?"

Dean nodded, machete raised.

Spinning each of the five extra-long bolts one at a time, he held his breath. He'd love to ask Jane to move away, maybe go to another room, but he thought his head looked best where it was.

The door eased back.

"Oh man, I didn't even have to knock," the voice on the other side said. "Jack?"

Dean's mouth disappeared into a white line.

Jack pulled the door open. "Matt. Thanks for coming back to town. You got here a lot faster than I thought you would. I was expecting you tomorrow." Throwing the door wide, he ushered Matt in. Jane slid the baby back in the swing, and Jack reset the proximity alarm.

Matt walked through the door, opening his mouth to say something Dean interrupted.

"Oh, look who the fuck it is," he said, machete still held at the ready.

Jumping sideways, Matt's hand fell to his side and gripped an empty scabbard. He backed into Jack. "Sorry, I. Sorry, Jack asked me to—"

"Oh he did," Dean said, eyes wide. He lowered the machete. "Could have told me that, Jack."

Matt held up both hands. "What's with all this hostility? And where's Addy?"

Pointing the end of the machete at him, Dean lowered his brow. He growled. "You know what it is. And she's fucking gone, you son of a bitch."

The blood drained from Matt's face.

Jack replayed what Dean said. Saw how it could be misconstrued. Opened his mouth to clarify.

"She went to talk to her mother. Weeks ago. We haven't seen her since," Jane said, cranking the swing handle. "Now get your ass in here so we can talk about the things Jack needs from you. Or get the hell out. Whatever you think will best serve Addy." She planted herself in the chair again, arms crossed.

Stepping fully into the house, Matt shut the door behind him. "What do you mean, she went to see her mother? About what?"

Jack shook his head, stomach full of snakes. Twisting, writhing through one another like that one *Indy* movie. "I guess they had unfinished business. She thinks her mom is worth talking to. I don't see it, but." He shrugged, sitting next to Jane again.

Matt crossed his arms and gave half a grin, his deep smile lines framing one side of his mouth.

"Don't you fucking smile. This is your fault," Dean bristled.

The grin slid off Matt's face. "How do you figure?"

"You could have stopped her. But where were you, huh? You just left her, pregnant, to go off and cry about your dead girlfriend." He threw his hands in the air. "You got Addy right in front of you, man."

Matt stepped closer to him. "You, you're one to talk. You dumped her on her ass for saving *your* life. Do you have any idea what you put her through? How many nights I had to dry her tears?"

"I fucked up."

"You're damn right you did."

Torn between the need to talk about IRF, the desire to punch them both for hurting her, and a touch of pride that two such men were literally about to come to blows over his eldest daughter, Jack stuck his arm in the middle of them. "Guys, please," he said, glancing between them. "I'd be proud to call either of you son. But can we put our dicks away for a minute and talk about what we're really here for? We can't help her if you're fighting."

With a huff, Matt took the end of the couch.

Dean pulled a chair in from the kitchen. He crossed one knee over the other and pretended not to glare at Matt.

From her chair, Jane watched Jack as he sat. "This should be fun."

Resisting the urge to rip a nail off with his teeth, he tilted his head in agreement. "Matt, you know why I called you back?"

"I've got a pretty good idea, yeah."

Jack stood to pace. "I once told Addy I thought it was a bad idea we killed Tim. I still think it was, but looking back on it, I realize it wasn't us who killed him."

Matt sat forward, elbows on his knees. "What did happen with him? Addy only ever told me half the story."

Dean spat the words. "Your boy tried to rape her, then tried to kill Jack and your general."

Eyes hard, Matt leaned back. "Jesus Christ. He was always a dick. But damn. No wonder she didn't want to talk about it." His lips pulled back from his teeth. "Who killed him?"

Jack stopped pacing. "Melinda. Emptied a full clip in his chest. I had to end it."

As he spoke, an idea hit him full force in the chest. He staggered under it. "She killed him so he wouldn't blow her cover. Oh my god, why didn't I see that sooner."

Matt's jaw bunched. "That's as likely as not."

Jack sat again. "He knew about both sides. He knew Talus, and he knew IRF. At some point, IRF convinced him to work for them, and playing double or triple agent or whatever drove him a little nuts."

Matt waved his hand with a chuckle. "He was a little nuts to begin with. But I know what you're driving at. You want me to tell you what I know about them both."

"Think you can tell the truth for once?" Dean asked.

"I promised Addy no more lies. It's a promise I intend to keep."

Jack cut Dean off before he retorted. "From what I've been able to gather, IRF's science department isn't as far advanced as Talus's. But their infrastructure department is the best this country has. Is that your assessment?"

"I'd say so," Matt agreed. "IRF's primary goal isn't science. In fact, I'd say their science department leaves a lot to be desired. I'm surprised they had someone like Huxley working for them."

"Why do you say that?"

"He'd fit right in at the Molehill. Lot of geeky Poindexters there. More soldiers than anything at IRF."

Jack chuckled. "I don't want to know how you know that word."

"What?"

"Poindexter." He waved his hand. "That sounds a lot like what we've heard from Dean."

Matt gave Dean a nod. "Yeah, their phone network is outstanding. I would have met Dean a lot sooner if I hadn't met Ella first."

Dean leaned forward. "What do you mean?"

"Addy tells me you were out in the Mojave when they got the first ground station up and running. I would have been there with Burke, too, but he'd already made the mistake of taking me to his house. I don't think I left her side for months after that."

Dean sat back in the chair, all the wind knocked out of him. "She talked about me?"

Matt scoffed. "Of course she did. What do you think we talked about? Puppies and daisies?"

Jack waved his hand. "Let's get back on track, guys. What else can you tell me?"

They spoke for hours, mostly Dean and Matt alternating. In the end, Jack's conclusions didn't amount to much. IRF was the muscle, the rebuilder. Talus was made of scientists, risk-takers in medicine, and they were damn good at spying. Although some of the details interested him, such as the upper echelon structure and what kind of chaos IRF must be in without Burke, most of it was information he'd already guessed. And he wasn't at all sure they'd help with the invasion.

Dean stood to leave.

Matt looked at his feet. "I didn't mean to pop off at you like that, Dean."

Dean crossed his arms. "OK."

"I don't think Addy would want us to fight. So. Um."

"Yeah," Dean said. "I'm sorry too." After an awkward moment of silence, he shook with Jack, hugged Jane, and made his way to the door.

"I appreciate you coming," Jack said. Opening the door for him, he clapped him on the back and leaned into his ear. "And thank you for not killing him."

Dean sketched a salute, yawned, and saw himself out. He chained the gate and disappeared into the dark.

Jack closed the door and leaned on it.

Eyes wide, Jane angled her forehead at Matt.

Who'd covered his face with both hands.

"Matt," he said, sitting next to him, "do you have somewhere to go?"

Without lowering his hands, he shook his head.

"We've got an extra room. Why don't you stay here tonight, and tomorrow you can sort everything else out."

He leaned forward. "You want me to stay in town? I can go back out to the perimeter."

"I don't think that's necessary. I'd like to have you with us during the assault, if it's all the same." He pulled Addy's Bowie knife from his belt. "I think someone else would too."

Matt stared at the knife. Eyes round, breath short.

"She left me a note when she went. Talking about her mom. But the P.S. said"—he closed his eyes, trying to remember her words—"'Tell Matthew the knife is his if he wants it.'" He held it out.

Matt reached for it.

Jack pulled it back. "Be careful with it."

Matt's Adam's apple bobbed.

Jack held it out again.

Matt took it, turning it over in his hands. After inspecting it, he wrapped his fingers around the haft and slid it into the empty knife holster on his hip. His voice came out barely more than a whisper. "Thanks, Jack."

"Come on, Matt," Jane said, sliding the baby out of the swing again. "I've got to put this girl down. I'll show you the room."

CHAPTER 47

"I don't know, Ilasha. Is this a good idea?" Lash quick-stepped to keep up with Melinda as she charged down the halls. "Tell me what Anthony said, again?"

"He said without a major breakthrough, I'd never get back on immunity." She stopped. "Do you think Addy's results will have anything earth-shattering to say?"

"Em," Lash said, laying a hand on her arm. "I know you're worried about your decision-making. I think you're as sharp as ever. You tell me."

Backing into the wall, Melinda chewed a fingernail. "Well if the baby isn't immune, it would be useful to compare its DNA sample to the immune child. See what markers they have in common, for starters. They are related, it could be incredibly important."

"And if it is?"

"If it is, that lends credence to the biological standpoint. We can easily gain access to the father."

"One of yours, right?"

"No. Yes. He used to be." Fucking traitors, all of them. "A DNA analysis of all three of them, mother, father, and child, would be a good place to start. It could be monumental."

"Wouldn't that mean it wasn't you who created immunity, though?"

"I don't have enough data to answer that question."

Lash started walking again. "So what's the problem? Sounds like the sooner we get this information, the better."

After a beat, Melinda followed. "The test carries a risk for mother and fetus."

"Never bothered you before. You let me help you with this decision. It's the right one, OK?"

The question about cost bounced around Melinda's skull. But Lash was right. Her own thinking had been disrupted by this virus. Diluted. If she could find the answers to these questions, she could help the world. They wouldn't have to go through this. And she'd finally have complete and utter control over the thing that had killed so many. Had ripped so many apart.

Including herself.

She stopped in front of Addy's door and smoothed her hair. Tugging the front of her shirt down, she knocked.

Addy opened the door. "Hey, Mom. Ilasha. Come in?"

Tugging the front of her shirt again, stomach churning, Melinda preceded Lash into the room.

A pillow and blanket lay scrunched on the couch. The TV had been set up for her, Melinda had even dug up some *Star Trek*, but the remotes sat untouched. Dusty.

A book lay on the coffee table, spine cracked.

Melinda pointed as she sat on a small chair. "Watership Down?"

Addy sank into the couch and covered her legs with the blanket. Her knees didn't curl all the way up. "Matt recommended it."

"He reads?"

Addy picked at a spot on the blanket. "What do you want?"

"I have to want something?"

Lips tight, Addy caught her eyes and stared.

Those eyes that were so like hers. Only deeper. Richer. Softer.

Melinda cleared her throat. "I want you to get an ultrasound."

Addy sniffed. "Some of that noninvasive testing Cormac talked about?"

Lash drew a sharp breath through her nose.

Melinda danced around the answer. "Let's get that ultrasound. It'll assure us of your and the baby's health."

Addy stood and stretched. Her shirt lifted, and Melinda made out the shape of a round belly. Her grandchild, in there.

Swallowing, she stalked into the hallway, waiting for Addy to slip on some shoes by the door.

Lash gripped Melinda's shoulder. "I gotta go, woman. Let me know how it turns out."

Swallowing the stomach crawling up her throat, Melinda gripped her hand. "You're not going to stay and help me?"

"Duty calls," Lash said, stepping back. "Good to see you again, Adelaide. Hope we can talk soon." She disappeared down the hall.

Chewing her lip, Melinda led Addy the other direction. "How far along are you, again?"

Addy shrugged. "I don't even know what day it is."

"When was the date of your last menstrual cycle?"

"What month is it?"

"June."

Raising her fingers, Addy ticked them off. "Four moons."

Melinda did the mental math. "March. So that makes you…" She trailed off, numbers tumbling through her head. "About fourteen, fifteen weeks. Ideally, I'd like to wait another few weeks before we do this te—uh, ultrasound, but we must proceed now."

Addy hurried to keep up. "Why?"

Without thinking about it, Melinda had been racing down the halls. She slowed. "Your father. You know as well as I do he's not going to sit out there forever. Not with you in here."

"You got me there. So, will you be able to tell if it's a boy or a girl? What's this ultrasound for? What's an ultrasound?"

"Yes," Melinda said, stopping outside the ultrasound room. "We'll be able to tell the sex of the fetus. An ultrasound is a picture of the baby. It's made using sonar waves. Interesting technology. It was more complex before all this"—she raised her hands—"but at least we still have it."

"A picture? You mean I can see the baby?"

Extending a hand toward the door marked "ULTRASOUND AND TESTING," Melinda nodded. "And hear their heartbeat."

Smiling, Addy twisted the doorknob and walked into the room.

Melinda hesitated in the hallway. She'd gotten her in there without any fight. Any argument. She'd hardly answered any of her questions and had deflected the trickier ones. And her poor, sweet girl fell for every word.

Following her in, she closed the door and latched it.

The domed roof of the room sloped to meet the floors, interrupted by two doors. Ilasha had stationed two men in the inner office, ready to help Melinda if she should need to restrain her daughter.

Who currently slouched in the middle of the room, arms crossed over the baby. "What's all this?" She gestured to the medical equipment.

Smiling, Melinda patted the table. "Hop on up here, kiddo. This," she said, pointing to the monitor, "is where we'll watch the picture." She flicked it on. "It's got speakers for the heartbeat too." She lifted the ultrasound wand and pushed Addy's shoulder to get her to lay down. "And here we have the picture taker. Lift your shirt and undo the button on your pants."

Addy complied, brow wrinkled. "Will it hurt the baby?"

Melinda pasted the smile to her lips. In the bright light of the room, brighter than most of the rooms down here, she couldn't allow her expression to shift. "No. This won't hurt the baby at all." She got out the gel and squirted a good amount over Addy's abdomen.

Addy lay on her back and fiddled with the hem of her shirt. "What's that for?"

Melinda sat and lowered the wand but didn't touch her yet. Once she started the ultrasound, the rest would follow after like dominoes. Maybe she didn't want to start.

"Mom?"

"Sorry, sorry, baby. It's conductive gel. It helps create a bond between your skin and the wand, so the radio waves can be transmitted more freely through the tissue."

"It's chilly."

Melinda lowered the wand, teeth clenched.

The picture sprang up on the screen in black-and-white.

Melinda moved the wand and approached the heartbeat. A whooshing, hummingbird-quick sound echoed from the speakers.

"That's the heartbeat?"

Melinda nodded, still staring at the screen. "Oh, there it is. See this?" She pointed to the screen. Black sections of amniotic sac surrounded the moving bean. Larger than life on the screen, its actual size was about equivalent to a lemon. Such a tiny thing. Her first grandchild. It flipped, kicking and punching toward the wand.

Addy gasped. "Oh my god, Mom. I felt that."

Vertigo hit Melinda so hard, she tilted on the stool. The first time she'd felt Michael move had been looking at an ultrasound screen. She hadn't known that was him in there moving around. She'd been so busy trying to work on graduating and keeping her belly covered so her teachers didn't give her their damn side-eye, she hadn't taken the time to enjoy her first pregnancy until she saw him on the ultrasound screen.

Her throat thickened, and she struggled to pull breath.

"Can you tell if it's a boy or a girl?"

Melinda tried to swallow. "I can't guarantee, but I can make a good guess." She moved the wand and the picture changed. Like one of those kaleidoscope tubes. Swirling the wand across her daughter's abdomen, she brought her grandchild back into focus. "It looks like a girl. See here?" She pointed. "The genital tubercule still looks a bit like it could be either, but this angle appears to indicate female." She paused, breathing through her nose. The vertigo still trying to grip her, that moment in the doctor's office with Jack next to her when she first felt Mike move, found out he was a healthy baby boy, overlaid on this one like one of those books with the transparent pages. Different pictures printed on each page.

She swam back to this picture. And in this picture, she needed to do her test and get it over and done. "There is one way to know for certain," she said, removing the wand.

Addy covered her mouth with her hand. "I can feel her moving in there now. I didn't know that's what it was. You're right, it feels like a butterfly." She looked up, eyes shining.

Seating the wand in its holder, Melinda stood. She patted Addy's shoulder. "Here, we can do one more thing. Let me get something."

Staring at the ceiling, one hand cupping the curve of her belly, Addy nodded. "Thanks. That was pretty all right."

Grimacing, Melinda crossed to the other door. Behind it, the two guards. Both already wearing their latex gloves. One held a syringe with a long, long needle.

And wouldn't you know it, the guard with the scar on his face was the one holding it.

She waved them both out and took the syringe from Gian. Lowering her voice, she pulled him down and spoke in his ear. "Restrain her. Do not let her move."

He caught the other guard on the sleeve and pointed to his wrists, then to Addy.

The guard nodded.

"What the. Who are you? Mom?"

"Yeah, sweetie," she said, laying the syringe on the tray under the ultrasound screen.

"The fuck are you doing here, Gian?" Addy moved to sit up.

Gian and the other guard pinned her shoulders down. "Lie still," Gian said.

"No. What the fuck. Mom. Talk to me."

"Just one test, Adelaide."

Red in the face, Addy fought to sit up. "Why do I get the feeling I'm not going to like this test?" She twisted both wrists. "Why am I even surprised you lied to me? I should know by now." Lifting her head, she raised her lip in a sneer. "I should know better than to trust you. It's like I keep running into the same brick wall."

Swallowing, the lingering vertigo threatening to tip her over, Melinda frowned. "This test must be done. I'm sorry. Please tie her hands," she said to the guards. She put her back to Addy.

Addy's struggles increased. She shouted things at her back. Melinda did all she could to ignore it. The test had to be done. She couldn't wait until the baby was born to find out about its immunity. She couldn't even wait until next week. Her gut screamed she had to get this done before Jack came and knocked everything sideways again.

She snapped on a pair of gloves. Wand and gel in hand, she faced Addy. "I looked over Matt's file. There are no concerns about RH factor. Both of you are positive. So that's a relief."

"Mom, please," Addy said, voice trembling.

She didn't meet her eyes. Squeezing out more of the bluish gel, she set it on the tray and found the baby with the ultrasound wand again. Its rushing heartbeat filled the room.

Sniffing, voice thick with tears, Addy cried, "Please. Whatever it is, you don't have to. You don't have to. You're still my Mom. You're still—"

"Hold this here," Melinda said, cutting her off. She spoke to Gian. "Hold it steady, keep it aimed at the baby. If you move, I'll give you more than a scar on your cheek."

"Yes, ma'am."

Hummingbird sound of the baby's heartbeat the only noise in the room, Melinda retrieved the syringe and an alcohol swab. She still didn't make eye contact with her daughter when she turned back around.

Addy screamed. "No! You can't. Please don't. Don't hurt the baby. Stop. Stop. Oh god," she cried, voice breaking.

Melinda cleared her throat. Finally met Addy's eyes. Her wide, wet, terrified eyes.

It was a wonder her knees didn't buckle. But this had to be done, and she had to hold herself together to do it. "Listen to me, jellybean. I have to do this. This is my grandchild. Please believe I would never do anything to hurt it. I performed this procedure several times in my maternity ward on Emerald Isle. No one will take better care of either of you."

Panting, Addy shook her head. "Hux talked about this. He said it could kill the baby. Please, Mom. Please don't."

"I need you to stay very still. This will pinch." Watching the ultrasound, Melinda found a place to insert the needle. "Stay still, jellybean. It'll be over soon."

* * *

"What are we all here for, Jack?" Celia closed the door to Morgan's office behind her.

Mike flushed and half stood. "You want this chair, Cee?"

Leaning against the wall behind him, she shook her head, heavy lids narrowed. But she smiled.

"Thanks, everyone, for coming down," Jack said, taking a glance around. Besides Mike and Celia, Jane sat across from him. Dean and Matt shared a corner. Either by talking, or fighting, or just grudging acceptance, they seemed to be all right with each other now. Barring the dead or gone, all his favorite warriors had gathered in one place. With, of course, the obvious exception.

He swallowed, trying to block Addy's face from his mind. It didn't work, but he plunged ahead anyway. "The assault should happen late next week. As you know, I've been working to move it up, but Morgan says he won't be able to get the cannon before Tuesday. And then they have to get it all the way back here." He sighed. "Thursday or Friday at the earliest."

"Can we meet them there, at the Molehill, with the cannon?"

Shifting his eyes back to Matt, he frowned. "Not a bad idea. Would save us at least half a day."

"We're chomping at the bit, Jack," Celia said. "I don't know how you can be so calm. And this is me talking."

He clenched his teeth and balled one fist under the desk where they couldn't see it. "I have to be. There's a lot of people counting on me to make the right decisions for the city."

"Forgive me, Dad," Mike said, "but this is the wrong room full of people to talk about the city with."

The air in the room shifted. They all agreed with him.

Even Jack.

He lifted a hand, palm out, catching and holding Jane's eyes. "I know, I know. None of you know better than I do. Trust me."

Matt shifted. "Got a pretty good idea, Jack."

"We're not ruining our chance to get her back by going in there half-cocked," he said, giving Matt a grimace. "I'm sure you know better than most of these guys, but you also know we need a plan. We need a plan we can execute. There's no sense in going into that rabbit warren without enough information. Look." Tugging open the top drawer, he extracted a folded paper and waved them all over. Chair legs scraped, bodies closed in and towered over him, voices murmured. He unfolded the paper and laid it flat. "This is a map of the place. Morgan's guy on the inside got it to him. Matt, can you look this over and—"

Someone hammered the door like they wanted to knock it off its hinges rather than ask for entry.

Everyone in the room drew a weapon of some kind. Without prompting, Mike crossed to the door.

"State your purpose," he said, voice hard. Crowbar lifted, he stood beside the door.

Celia flanked it.

The voice on the other side wavered, muffled. "I need to see Morgan. I have intelligence from the Molehill."

Mike raised his eyebrows at Jack.

Who gave him one curt nod.

Mike spoke to the door. "Hands up, please. Leave your weapons holstered or otherwise undrawn."

The muffled voice agreed. "Just let me in. This can't wait."

Mike eased the door open and let Celia stick her gun in the person's face.

A young man with a puckered scar running down his cheek stepped through the threshold, head drawn away from Celia's gun and hands pointed skyward.

Mike closed the door, crossed his arms, and smiled at Celia as she herded the young man across the room in silence.

She menaced, with her gun, yes, but mostly her eyes, until he crossed the room and sat before the desk.

"Can I put my hands down?"

Jack narrowed his eyes, mind spinning. It stopped, tumblers falling into their slots. "No. I saw you attack Morgan during the last raid. The hell are you doing here?"

Matt leaned on the desk. "I watched Morgan give him that scar," he pointed with his forehead. "His name's Gian. You were working for him?"

Gian rubbed his cheek. "Had to make it look convincing."

Folding his arms, Matt leaned back. "Fooled us, all right." Half a smile curved his mouth. "He was pretty rude to Addy."

Dean lifted his machete from where it'd been slowly falling to his side. "That right?"

Hands still lifted, Gian shook his head and leaned toward Jack. "Listen, it's about her, all right?" He eyed the map on the desk. "Morgan give that to you? Where is he?"

Jack folded the map. His hands didn't shake, but nothing on the inside was still. Not since this boy mentioned Adelaide. "Tell us what you know. Then we'll see what's what." He crossed his arms on the desk and leaned forward. "Tell me about my daughter, or we'll do something to make that other side match."

Jane laid a hand on his shoulder. She spoke just above a whisper. "Make it good."

"You have to get her out of there. I heard her and the general talking. I know why she came there. But." He stopped, swallowing. He stared around the tight circle around him, eyes landing back on Jack. "The general isn't going to change. And she's started"—he cleared his throat, dropping his eyes—"she's started experimenting on her. I watched her." Voice wavering, he stopped.

Dean's quiet voice slipped through the room like goose feet over a grave. "You watched her what."

He cleared his throat. When his jaw bunched, the scar puckered farther in. "I watched her shove a needle into her and take a sample of blood from her baby." A tear slipped down his cheek. "I've never seen such a thing. And the way she cried." Red, wet eyes meeting Jack's, he shook his head. "I'm so sorry. I've seen and done a lot these past couple years. But this. Broke my heart, man." He crossed his arms over himself, rocking back and forth an inch or two as he did.

Matt's sharp intake of breath was the only other thing to make a sound. Jack's heartbeat was so far away, he couldn't hear it. Couldn't hear the blood whooshing through his head. Couldn't even feel the chair under his ass. There was nothing. No one spoke.

Jane knelt next to Gian, needles glinting in her hair. Pinching his chin between two fingers, she turned his head until he met her eyes. "Is she all right? Is she alive?"

"She was when I left."

"And the baby?" Matt's voice gravelly, he got it loud enough to hear. Barely.

Gian shrugged. "I guess. But I don't know for sure."

Jack pushed the chair back harder than he meant. It slammed into the wall, and he walked to the calendar. There was no way to get the troops already in town together in less than a day. Troops had to be fed and rested before the beginning of a battle. They couldn't assemble, march all night, wait all day, and attack the next night. He'd put out the call tonight, but they couldn't teleport to the Molehill, and they couldn't start until the morning. Earliest.

One thing they'd have to do without was the cannon, and whatever extra men Morgan planned to bring with it. What they had would have to do. It'd been foolish of him to wait this long, and he knew it.

Heartbeat returning to pound through his ears, sock him in the temples, and make his chest jump, he faced the others. "We can't get to her before Tuesday night. But it's a new moon, so at least we'll have the cover of darkness. It'll have to be enough."

Jane stood. "Let's get ready."

CHAPTER 48

Mom walked in and shut the door behind her. At least she was alone this time.

She sat in the small chair she'd sat in last time she was here.

Days ago.

She sighed. "Well."

"Well." Addy didn't make eye contact, but she rested the almost finished book on top of her knees, cracked spine facing out.

"Your test produced some interesting results."

"That so." She rubbed the spot where the needle had pierced her and the baby. It'd been sore for a long while but finally felt better. And the cramping had stopped.

"Would you like to know?"

"Not really."

Melinda's hand snuck over and landed on Addy's knee.

Addy didn't recoil. She pushed a breath out through her nose and glanced up.

Mom frowned but smiled at the same time. An unusual affair. "It doesn't matter to you?"

"Only insofar as it matters to you." She shook her head. "But no. It doesn't matter to me."

Melinda chuffed and withdrew her hand. "Can I tell you anyway?"

"If it'll make you feel better."

Standing, Mom crossed her arms over her stomach. "No, it won't make me feel better. I don't know what to think." She paced. "This whole thing is so…" She lifted her hands and dropped them, slapping herself in the legs. "I can't make sense of it."

Curling her feet farther under her, Addy sat forward. Mom's agitation chafed her moody brain like a cheese grater. "The hell do you want me to do about that? Did you come here for something?"

Stopping, Melinda stared. "Did you?"

"You know I did, Mom. You know that. I came here to forgive you." She cleared her throat. "And myself." She sniffed, shoving a nail between her teeth.

Perching on the couch next to her, Mom scrunched her brow. "Forgive yourself? For what?"

She'd turned this over and over and over in the silence of the last few days. Of the last few weeks since she'd arrived. It was most of what she'd been doing, instead of talking to her mother like she'd planned.

Turned out imprisonment provided unexpected clarity.

"I blamed myself forever for your death," she said, staring at Melinda's chin. "So much so that I didn't let anyone near me for forever."

"What do you mean?"

"I pushed everyone away. Built a wall between me and them. To keep them safe from me." She met Melinda's eyes. "I isolated myself so I could never fail someone like that again."

"Your father and brother, the others in your group, they all seem close to you."

Addy smiled without humor. "Seems that way, doesn't it?"

Melinda sat back. "What changed?"

"You broke my heart." Amazing her voice didn't waver or crack. She pushed on. "Then Dean shattered it. And when I went to pick up the pieces and put it back together, I found they didn't go together the same way anymore."

Covering her mouth, Mom nodded. Her eyes above her hand round, she didn't say a word.

"I get it now. Why Dad didn't want to be with you anymore."

Melinda chuffed again. "Because I'm a terrible person?"

Addy leaned forward and laid a hand on her mom's arm. Warmth coursed from her fingertips to her shoulder, rushing through her heart and pumping out to the rest of her body. "No,

Mom. Your ideas are different from ours. Your execution leaves a lot to be desired," she said, gripping the baby, "and you've made some pretty awful mistakes. I'm not going to lie. But you're not a terrible person. What you are is different."

"Would you feel the same if you lost the baby?"

Adrenaline threatened to launch Addy from the couch. She considered. "I don't know. No. But I've had a few days here to cool off. To do some thinking. Some meditation, like I learned from Yaz." She stopped and cleared her throat, shuffling off the silence of the previous days. "I've lived in so much fear. Basically ever since you died. And you scared the shit out of me with that damn test. But my god." She stopped, tapping her teeth.

"What?"

"I didn't come here to keep doing the same thing and expect different results. I can't let the fear control me anymore."

"What are you getting at?"

Thick tears tried to fill Addy's throat. She took Mom's hand and folded it in her own. "I don't hate you. I can't."

Voice small, Melinda let her hair fall in her eyes. "Why not?"

"I wish you'd apologize. I wish you'd see how awful you've been. But I can't stand in judgment of anyone else. Not without piling it on myself. And I'm sick of doing that." She stopped, swallowing again. "What I can do is forgive you, and forgive myself for my errors in judgment. For my clumsiness. For being myself." She squeezed her mom's hand. So warm. Alive. "And I can ask you to consider that there might be another way for you too."

Mom met her eyes, tears lining the edges of them. She opened her mouth, jaw moving up and down. After trying to speak as the seconds ticked away, she snapped her mouth closed and pulled her hand free. "I—"

Her phone rang.

Snatching it out of her pocket, she flipped it open and answered. The blood drained from her face and her mouth fell open. "Motherfucker. Are you serious? Is she—"

The voice on the other end crackled.

Melinda stood to pace. "Is there no way you can—" Mouth hanging open, she nodded. "I see. Well. That is. Someone is going to pay for this oversight." She snapped the phone closed and charged toward the door. "I'm sorry, Adelaide, I have to leave."

Heart in her throat, Addy stood. Was it time for the assault? Had she done what she'd come here to do? "What's wrong?"

Hand on the doorknob, Melinda spun. "I regret to inform you, your friend Kendra has taken her life into her own hands. Or rather, has chosen to take it from everyone else. And the life of the one she carried."

Covering her mouth, swallowing her gorge, and gripping her abdomen, Addy shook her head. "Why?"

"She left a note of some sort. I don't know exactly what it said, but it was something to the effect of 'I cannot face loving this abomination for the rest of my days. And so I will make those days short.' Very dramatic, from what I hear." She ripped the door open. "I'm sorry, honey. I have to go."

The door closed behind her like a steel trap.

Sitting back down, Addy grabbed the book from where it'd fallen in the floor, covered her legs with the blanket again, and found her place. Curled around the baby doing somersaults in her belly, she stared at the pages but didn't see any of the words.

* * *

Jane pulled a breath through her nose. "Damn. What a beautiful night." She swung his hand back and forth. "We should have done this more often."

Jack took in the graveyard. Its mix of great, marble mausoleums and squat, ancient headstones glowed pink in the last rays of dusk. Rolling, knee-high green grass rippled across the gentle hills and through the scattered trees. "We should have."

"Leaving in the morning, are we?"

"Early. This time tomorrow, we'll be ready to attack."

"Should you be talking to your troops or something?"

"I'll speak to them in the morning. Do you think I could get Mike to stay behind with Hux?"

She scoffed and said nothing.

Jack eyed the city skyline. The highest windows of the skyscrapers reflected what gold was left of sunset. With the moon new tomorrow, the eastern horizon was already inky black. "It'll be nice to have you all with me, at least." He gave her half a grin, butterflies in his belly. "Otherwise, I'd worry."

She tugged his hand and stopped, staring at the city.

As she looked away, he studied the side of her face. Freckles sprinkled her cheeks like ethereal glitter. Her mouth raised in a smile, one slight wrinkle right at the corner. It lifted her face, lashes curved up and framing the sparkling emeralds in her eyes. "We're gonna have another baby, love."

Her smile infecting him, his cheeks raised, eyes prickling. "Yeah?"

She met his eyes. "Yeah. Congrats, Daddy."

He tugged her close.

She stepped into him, curling her fingers in his hair and wrapping the other arm around him. Kissing him, she lit him up from the crown of his head to his toes.

He tingled, fingers sinking into her hair. Pulling her as close as he could get her, he kissed her as deep as the very first time. Her silky lips pressed into his, the scent of flowers filled his nose.

He released her, his lips soft on hers as he backed up an inch. "What does this mean for tomorrow?"

Fingers still curled in his hair, she shook her head. "Nothing. Just thought you should know." She grinned, teeth peeking out in the dark. "If you found out after, I figured you'd be pretty upset I didn't tell you beforehand."

He took her hand again and swung it as they kept walking. "It's pretty here. Good people. What do you say, after we do this thing with Talus and everything, we think about staying here?" He smiled at the skyline again. "Seems like a fairly nice place to raise kids. Good community."

"I thought you hated the whole leadership thing."

"I could get used to it. With the right tools, it's not so bad." He shrugged. "This place has its share of unreasonable assholes, like anywhere else. But at least it's got its fair share of reasonably good people too. And it's, I don't know." He squeezed her hand. "It feels a bit like home, don't you think?"

She laughed. "Home is wherever you are, Jack."

He let her hand go and slung his arm around her shoulder. "It seems like what they're building here is more than a community, if I'm telling the truth. It's got all these good things. Things I didn't think I'd ever see again." Chuckling, he shook his head. "Those actors."

Jane laughed with him. "Something else, aren't they? Addy must have had a hell of a time before we got here."

"You think she's going to be all right, Jane?"

"She's got a damn good head on her shoulders. She'll get it all straightened out. I know that much."

"She's braver than I am. Got a bigger heart. I don't know if I can forgive her mother."

Jane scoffed, low and under her breath. "She didn't get that big heart from nowhere, Jack Cooke."

The blush rushed up his neck and into his cheeks, heart pumping endorphins through him. "You're right. She probably learned it from Michael."

Laughing, Jane swung around in front of him and wrapped both arms around his neck. "Sure. And he learned it from you." She leaned toward him and stared at a spot on his chest. "Are we gonna see these plans for the future? This town again?"

One hand in the small of her back, he brushed the hair from her eyes with the other hand. "I don't know." He paused. She'd know if he lied. "If I have to choose between stopping these horrific things Talus Crest is doing to people, and coming back here, well."

She caught his eyes. "When we get home, marry me."

Heart stopped and clogging his throat, he nodded.

"Jack."

"Jane."

"I love you."

* * *

Exhaustion creeping through her skin and drawing over her forehead, Melinda's eyelids drooped as she stalked down the hall. The night lighting was on, and when had it gotten to be so late?

Kendra had certainly been determined to kill herself. They might never discover where she'd gotten the sharpened animal bone, but she'd been able to use it to slice all the way up her arms and across at the elbows. There'd been so much blood. The last time Melinda had seen that much blood, she'd been dying.

Arms crossed, she stopped in front of Lash's door and knocked. She'd been absent from the cleanup. From the whole scene.

All Melinda could see was the look of anguish on the dead girl's face. They'd gotten there before she turned, and her last expression, arms wrapped around herself, was one of complete sadness. Utterly bereft. A girl with no options.

Lash didn't answer the door.

Knocking again, Melinda leaned on it. "Lash? Are you here?" Nothing. No answer.

The sight of all the blood on Kendra's floor, soaked into the dirt in a dark puddle, invaded Melinda's memory. Her heartbeat sped up. She needed to see Ilasha right this minute. Make sure she was OK. Thank god it wasn't Addy lying dead in there on the floor.

"Ilasha? Please." Hand on the knob, she knocked yet again.

Still no answer, but if she jiggled the handle just right and lifted the door *just so*, it popped open. Amazing Lash'd never fixed that.

The living room dark but for the light over the stove in the adjoined kitchen, Melinda crept into the apartment and latched the door. Clearly Lash wasn't home, but since she also wasn't at the scene with Kendra, where could she be?

Either way, the exhaustion crept over Melinda's eyes, and they closed while she was still on her feet.

She eased across the living room, heels scraping the floor, and into Lash's bedroom. She could lay in there and wait for Lash to come back. It'd be comfortable and warm, and if she went to sleep right away she wouldn't have to think too hard about what Addy said.

How, how, how on earth did Addy end up like that? She'd come in here with her sneaky talk and absolutely destroyed her. Far worse than she'd ever done with her fighting.

The hell of it was, maybe Melinda could see another way. For years there'd been no better way. None. She was on the best path. The righteous one. The one that would save the planet from this damn disease and let humanity get back to its destiny. This virus would not be the end of it, and it would not be the end of her.

But the blood. The blood surrounding Kendra in a rust-colored pool. It screamed this was not the way. What she'd done to that girl, to all of them, was wrong.

What she'd done to Addy could hardly be looked at straight on. But what she'd told Addy was true. She took better care of her daughter and her granddaughter than anyone else would have. If McNamara or some other idiot had done it, they might have killed them both. It had to be done, and it had to be her.

But if what she'd done to Addy had been wrong, she had to look at the uncomfortable fact that what she'd done to Jack was wrong too. So many different kinds of wrong.

Crawling into Lash's bed, she kicked off her boots and curled up under the covers. The sheets and pillows smelled like Lash, and Melinda smiled as she let her eyes unfocus. They didn't want to close yet, and she lay there, eyes open, waiting for sleep to slip in like a cat burglar. Dressed in the black of night and stealing her waking mind while she wasn't looking.

Yet, before the thief came, her eyes focused again. The corner of a file stuck out from behind the nightstand.

Adrenaline pumping through her, she sat up. Eyes wide, sleep receding back over the horizon, she tugged the corner of the file. Remembered that drawer full of files in Lash's desk. More secret files? How much was she keeping from her?

The file caught.

She stopped pulling. With her other hand, she scooted the nightstand away from the wall.

Sliding loose, the file threatened to dump its contents in the floor.

Melinda caught them before they fell. Lots of papers here. The file was so thick, she wondered how it'd fit behind the nightstand in the first place.

A picture fell out onto the bed.

The next inhalation caught in her throat, Melinda stopped.

It was a picture of someone's brain. It looked just like the ones—

No. No, it can't be.

Laying the folder on the bed, legs folded under her, she leaned over the manila file and frowned. She inspected the outside of it, nail between her teeth.

It looked like the one in which her report had been stowed. The one that showed she was brain damaged.

With one shaking fingernail, she pushed back the top flap.

"*TEST RESULTS, SUBJECT M. THIBODEAUX.*

FINAL EVALUATION: NO PERMANENT DAMAGE, BRAIN FUNCTION NOT SIGNIFICANTLY IMPAIRED. SUBJECT CLEAR."

Breathless, lump in her throat, Melinda flipped through the rest of the pages. They looked identical to the ones she'd already seen, but they said something completely different. She'd have to compare them side by side, but the gist of it was, she had no lasting brain damage. None. Not a smidge.

Palms sweating, forehead cold, she folded the file and stared at the wall.

Was this the real file?

If so, why did Lash have it? Hidden behind a nightstand?

Who made the fake report Melinda had been given? And why? And did Lash know the answers to those questions? And if so, why hadn't she said one damn word?

Cramming it back where she found it, she slid the nightstand into place, pinched her boots in her fingers, and crept back out into the hallway.

CHAPTER 49

Sitting in one of the blue seats in a lower section, Jack watched the troops gathered in the stadium.

Jim's aviator shades glinted in the sun. "Think it'll be enough?"

"Give me one of those smokes, Jim."

Eyes flickering behind the glasses, Jim opened up a silver case and plucked a hand-rolled cigarette from it. Getting another for himself, he snapped it closed and flicked a match. He lit Jack's and laughed as Jack choked on the first drag. "Been a while?"

Jack nodded, laughing and coughing at the same time. "About twenty years." His eyes watered. Taking another drag, he coughed it back out again, lungs and throat tight. "It was smoother in my head, that first drag."

Jim shrugged, plucking the smoke from his mouth and tapping the ashes on the concrete steps below them. "I'm kind of hoping these get me before a 'Head does."

"You worry about that here?"

Pulling the smoke across his teeth, he stared across the field. "Not much. Not anymore. Except every night in my dreams."

Jack chuckled, the next lungful of smoke going down easier. Following this smoke with another could be all too easy, but Jim was right. It'd kill him if he let it.

He stubbed it out under a heel. "Tell me again what Victoria said."

"She said she didn't tell you the whole truth about what they did to Adam. About what they did to your friend."

"Andrew."

"Yeah." He took his glasses off, green eyes staring down at the troops milling in the grass. "She said they weren't just using them to incubate the virus."

Jack wished he hadn't stubbed out the smoke. "Some kind of experiments."

"I think it's tied up into what makes her so afraid of thunderstorms. And how she turns into such a different person onstage. It takes her away from the things she did. Lets her be someone else."

"What were they doing, Jim? Did she say?"

"They wanted to take the strength the dead get right after they turn and make it an asset. See if they could give the strength and speed to a human."

Scoffing, Jack held his head in his hands. "That's ridiculous. That's like something out of a comic book."

"They got so close," Victoria said, walking up the stairs. "Even I, for a short time, felt it tantalizingly just out of reach." She tugged the chain over her shoulder, and a hulking man followed behind her, linked to the end of it. "Adam decided he'd like to help." Sitting next to Jim, she pointed to the bare stairs next to them. "Sit here, baby."

With a grunt, the man sat. "Help."

Jack's diaphragm seized, like a rock had been inserted in his gut. Andrew said maybe three words after his transformation. One of them had been his name. One of them had been "hurts." How much thought went on in there they couldn't communicate? Things they wished they could say?

Adam stared up at Victoria with his mouth hanging slack. The beautiful man he'd clearly been lost to memory, the bright future ahead stolen by Talus.

Victoria frowned. "A few of the others have also asked to help. They are gathered inside, chained down once again. The rest..." She trailed off, looking over the troops.

"The others?"

"I told them they could not be cured and gave them the option to come with us, or make a different choice." Sniffing, she swiped at her eye. "They made a different choice."

Jack stood. "I've already talked to these guys for the most part. Let me make a round, and we'll get going. It'll take most of the day to get there, and we'll set up to begin after sunset."

Adam worked his way to his feet and swayed in front of Jack, preventing him from going down the stairs. Brow lowered, his bloodshot eyes grabbed Jack's and held them. "Help. Retribution."

Jack clapped him on the shoulder. "Oh yes. There will be a price to pay. Their bill has come due."

* * *

"Seems like I'm greeting you at my door more and more often," Addy said.

Mom walked in, arms crossed. "Sorry I didn't come earlier in the day. There were. There was, um." Her face contorted.

Although nice to watch her struggle through emotions, Addy saved her. "You had to get everything squared away with Kendra."

"Yes. There was a lot of paperwork. And." She flopped onto the couch.

Addy closed the door and joined her. She'd finished the book and sat staring at the dark TV for hours. Feeling the baby kick, daydreaming about seeing her for the first time, what it would feel like to hold her. What she would sound like crying.

"You ever watch any of the *Star Trek* I brought you, little girl?"

She shook her head. "I wanted to. But it hurts too much. I might leave it behind."

"That's a shame."

"If you say it is." She shrugged. "Why are you here?"

Leaning forward, Melinda rested her elbows on her knees and grasped Addy's hand. "You had a point."

Without warning, Addy's heart took off at a gallop. The baby responded to the adrenaline dump by punching her. If she'd been looking down, she might have seen her rounded belly jump. "I did?"

"You did." She dropped her eyes. "I know there was a time where I told you I'd realized the error of my ways." Lifting her eyes again, she caught Addy's. Her chin trembled. "That was a lie."

Breath caught halfway down, halfway up, Addy nodded. "I know, Mom."

"It took a lot. It took coming back here. It took Kendra killing herself. And." She stopped, squeezing Addy's hand. "What I did to you. The things." She dropped her eyes again and cleared her throat. "The things I did to your father. I don't know what a new road would look like, but how do I even start down it?" Eyes wet, she raised her brow and waited for Addy to answer.

Addy exhaled through tight lips. "I think you just did."

Tears falling freely, Melinda nodded.

Melinda's naked face was more an admission of guilt, a plea for absolution, and a beginning at making amends than any words she could have used. Addy scooted next to her and folded her up in a hug. They cried on each other for a while, drifting in one of the warmest hugs Addy could remember.

"So, listen," Mom said, leaning back, "I'm not sure where to go from here." She pinched her mouth tight, eyes wide. Her lashes wet.

The radio on her hip beeped, and her phone rang. Static crackled over the radio.

Unsnapping them both, she looked from one to the other. What sounded like gunfire echoed through the radio's tinny speaker. The phone rang on, insistent.

Addy sighed. "Dad."

Mom arched a brow at her. "General Thibodeaux," she said into the phone.

Bursts of static-y gunfire crackled through the radio.

Standing, Addy glanced around the room. There was nothing to take with her.

"Come on, baby." Melinda flipped the phone closed. "We gotta get you out of here. First stop, weapons locker. Can't have you running around without at least a blade."

An image of Matt's knife flashed before her, unasked for. She frowned. "Let me get my shoes."

Melinda ripped the door open.

"General! There you are." Someone ran down the hall, feet pounding the tile.

"McNamara, what the fuck are you doing here? Go be useless somewhere else." She slipped her gun out of its holster and stuck her head in the hallway. "Adelaide, let's go."

"Addy," Cormac said, trying to step into the room, "have you—"

"Lay a hand on her and it's the last thing you—"

Addy stepped away from her shoes. "Mom, stop. He's on our side."

Mom goggled. "You're kidding me." She looked at Cormac. "She's kidding me. You're *what?*"

"General." He lowered his voice, leaning in close. "I've contacted IRF. They've arrived and are working to infiltrate the compound. We need to leave. They have a safe place for us, but we must meet them outside for extraction."

Heart leaping into her throat and making breathing difficult, Addy gripped Mom's arm. "Wait, what about Dad?"

CHAPTER 50

Jack's radio buzzed with angry static. He pressed the talk button. "Bravo company, what's your status?"

"*In place, sir.*"

"Great," he said, crouching behind a tree.

Lights scanned the yard, some guards congregating at the gate while some made rounds along the edges of the fencing.

It looked deceptively simple. All these troops at his back would have little trouble with the men in the yard. And Talus's supply train had been choked to death in the last couple of weeks. The final screw turned tonight as one of his companies blocked off the main road.

Another went around the side to flank the compound as Jack and Alpha came at it head-on. They'd break through the fence at the same time, round up the guys in the yard, and infiltrate the interior of the Molehill after that. The map Gian provided would be useful, and Jack had broken Alpha company into two teams; one to free prisoners and one to gather research.

Jane, Dean, and Matt were to stay with him and be his backup, with Mike and Celia set to lead the prison break. The hope being either he or they would locate Addy.

As he watched, Celia brushed the loose lock of hair from Mike's forehead. She kissed the spot where it'd been.

Jack flushed. He couldn't hear them, but he didn't need to. There'd been a time, years ago, when Mike was a young man hardly twenty, and he'd thought he and Celia may have a thing. But it fizzled, if it'd ever been there. Nice to see it'd come back. Celia deserved the smiles Mike could put on her face. And he deserved to put them there.

He leaned into Jane's ear, needles tucked in her hair and knives lined across every space she could get a belt. "If it gets sticky in there, you get your ass out, you hear me?"

"Ordering me around?"

"Yes. Take care of yourself, Jane."

"Don't you worry about me. I'll handle myself. Are we ready to do this?"

He lifted the radio to his mouth. "Yeah. Let me give the signal to—"

The radio crackled. "*Alpha leader, come in.*" The voice on the other end frantic.

"Alpha leader, go ahead, over."

"*We're being surrounded. I'm not sure what's*—" The radio cut out.

Jane stood, eyes cast toward the road. "Talus?"

Jack joined her. "There were no reports of additional troops. I don't know." His mind reeling, he opened his mouth to say something about bad intel. Pops of small arms fire sounded, one or two. Then ten or twelve. Then more than he could count.

The men inside went on high alert. Whoever had shown up in the road complicated things.

Palms cool and dry, he gave the signal.

His men tossed tear gas over the fence. These troops didn't have gas masks, themselves, not all of them, but they had come to them from some settlement to the north where apparently they played with tear gas like fog machines. Many of them could stand in it and laugh like a pirate standing in cannon smoke on the high seas. Swaying with the rolling waves.

As the Talus guards on the other side backed away from it, guns and voices lifted, Jack and a squad of men flanked and cut through the fence. The men on the other side should be doing the same. As Jack snipped away with bolt cutters, focused on the fence in front of him and not the men screaming at one another through the haze of gas, Mike and Celia stepped in and peeled back the sections of fence.

"Watch the barbed wire," Jane said, voice low. "Here." She held out a length of cloth. God only knew where she'd found it. Since having the baby, her skill at carrying more than she possibly could had doubled.

Mike took it, wrapped it around both hands, and stepped in front of Celia. He pulled the barbed wire back. "Go," he said, angling his forehead.

Drawing her blade and taking the bolt cutters for the next fence, Celia ducked under his arms and crawled through. The other men followed, Jane and Jack waiting for them all.

Without words, Jane kissed Jack under the jaw and ducked under Mike's arms.

"Dad, after you."

He stopped. "Michael."

"Yeah."

"I love you."

"Don't do that to me when I can't hug you. Just get in there." He chuckled. "I love you too."

Jack unsnapped his gun strap and crawled through the fence.

With a whisper of metal, Mike joined him. "You sure you guys know where to look for Addy?"

They crept under the second fence, another man holding it up for them. "Whatever the map doesn't know, Matt is pretty sure he can supply. I think we're—"

Something boomed. The air whistled.

Without thinking, Jack ducked, hunched over his stomach.

The force of the impact hit him as the sound did. Not close enough to get knocked over, but his nose got stuffy as the shockwave passed.

He shook his head. "The hell?"

His radio crackled.

Some men inside the fence turned toward him.

He drew his gun. The trusty .45. His troops and his son stepping between him and the armed men coming toward them, Jack suddenly wondered how he'd tell his own men from Talus's.

Well. If they were trying to kill him, they weren't his. No matter to whom they'd pledged their allegiance.

The radio spoke, "*Jack.*"

"Holy shit." He pushed the button. "Morgan, is that you?"

Static whined. "*Yeah, and our goddamned cannon. Good thing too. What's your location?*"

"Myself and Alpha are inside the fence." Entering opposite sides of the yard, the company was slowly but surely closing in on the severely outnumbered Talus guards. He heard one of them recognize Matt, but he turned his attention back to the radio. "Where are you?"

"*There's someone else out here. I'm working my way to you.*"

Jack pushed the button and opened his mouth.

A scream rent the air. Guttural, it ripped through the vocal cords from which it issued.

Victoria, with her Adam unchained and the others behind them, crested the hill.

Some of Talus's soldiers scattered, several of them rolling the gate open. Shouting to get the fuck out of the way.

Not the first time they'd dealt with this kind, clearly.

Morgan's voice wavered through the radio. "*What the hell was that, Jack?*"

"Long story. See you under the hill."

"*Meet me in room 6B for bravo. We'll regroup there. Out.*"

Jack glanced around inside the fence. Once Adam had come over the hill with his friends, the men who didn't escape through the open gate had lain down their weapons and put up their hands. Most of them backed up against the fence.

Snapping the radio to his belt, he pulled his machete and waved toward the lumpy hill in front of them. "Let's get underground."

* * *

"Here, Jack. It's down this hall," Matt said, pointing over Jack's shoulder with the Bowie knife. Gun in his other hand, he helped cover the hall in front while Dean, Jane, and Gian covered the rear. Mike and Celia had gone ahead with a squad to free the prisoners. They went with so little fanfare, Jack almost wanted to stop them and hug them both. And tell them how happy he was for them.

The radio crackled. "*Dad.*"

Jack unclipped it. "Yeah, Mike. Run into trouble?"

"*Not exactly. But Addy's not with the rest of the prisoners.*"

Disappointing, but not entirely unexpected.

Matt stopped. "I may know where to look."

Stopping with him, Jack looked up and down the hall. "Are you sure?"

He frowned, the lines next to his mouth deep in the low light. "Not a hundred percent, no. But pretty sure. And if I can't find her where I think she might be, I've got another few good ideas."

Inclined to keep the rest of them together, Jack opened his mouth to tell him to wait.

The radio crackled again. "*Jack, you at the room yet? I met Vic outside, we're on our way in,*" Morgan called.

"Roger," he replied. Sweat popped out on his forehead. Having Adam within these tunnels on the verge of going berserk sat heavy on his nerves. Clearly Morgan felt otherwise. He locked eyes with Matt. "Go get Adelaide and get her out of here. Dean, go with him."

"You got it, Jack," Dean said. "We won't let anything happen to her."

"Damn right you won't," Jane said, catching Jack's eyes but speaking to Dean. "I'll come with you. Make sure."

He wanted to grab her. Tell her not to leave. Hold her tight.

But whatever motivated her to go after Addy was hers, and he couldn't, wouldn't, take it away from her. "Come back to me, love."

"I always will. You know that." She kissed him on the corner of the mouth.

As she, Matt, and Dean took off the other way, Matt pointing using his giant knife again, Jack spun to Gian. "Lead the way. Let's get to Morgan."

Gian pulled out the map. "Look here. He said six bravo. I don't know what's in that room, my contact made that part of the map. It must be something important though. They outlined it in red."

They set off down the hall, Jack taking the map and looking it over. "You didn't make the whole map yourself? What contact?"

"I don't have access to everything. I'm a peon. I did my best, but there was a woman who helped me fill in the parts I didn't know about."

"What makes you think she—"

"Glad you made it, Gian," someone said, standing inside an alcove next to them, stuck in shadow. "Where's Morgan?"

Footsteps pounded from the other end of the hall. As they neared and resolved into Morgan, alone, Jack let go of the coil in his chest. He'd been doing all right leading this crazy thing, but it'd honestly be nice to hand the reins back over to Morgan.

"In here," the voice said, opening the door.

Swallowing, Jack stuffed the map in his pocket and pulled his penlight. He aimed it at the door. As it swung back, he made out "6B" on the plate.

Gian led, and Morgan clapped Jack on the shoulder. "Good to see you. How's things?"

Jack grinned with one side of his mouth. "Was about to ask you the same. What happened out there?"

Morgan waved his hand. "A misunderstanding. I got it straightened out, and we should be getting air support pretty soon." He winked.

Jack's mouth dropped open, his stomach jumping. "Air support? How'd you manage that?"

"After we get through in here, I'll tell you. But I had a reason to come to this room. Let's go." He held his hand out.

Those nice, cool palms Jack had outside disappeared. His stomach slick, he stiffened his spine and edged into the dark room. What was with all these cagey answers? What was going on? And why had he let himself be alone with all these people he hardly knew?

And who was the woman in the dark?

* * *

Addy slid the machete into her scabbard and wiggled her toes. "Thanks for the weapons, Mom." She glanced around the room and down at her feet. "Do you have any shoes in here, by any chance?"

Melinda shook her head. "Sorry, honey. I can't believe you didn't tell me about IRF," she said, shooting daggers at Cormac.

Frowning, Addy followed her back into the hallway. Lacking bows and arrows, she'd also picked up a handgun. "I didn't exactly have a chance. After Cormac here told me about them, you shoved a needle in my baby."

He drew a breath over his teeth, closing the door to the armory.

Addy grimaced. Her throat worked. "Sorry. That came out harsher than I meant it."

"It's OK, baby. I did. I'm so glad I didn't hurt you. Either of you."

"Me too," Addy said, rubbing her belly. How it'd gotten so rounded in the last few days amazed her. And the baby was all she thought about, lately, when she wasn't thinking about how to forgive her Mom and attempt to move forward together.

Cormac pointed down a hall. "This way, General. I have to say," he said over his shoulder, "I never expected to be leading you out of here. Of all people."

"You're the last person I would have expected help from, so I guess we're even." Her feet slowed. "I have to find Lash. I'm not leaving without her."

"She sure is loyal to you, Mom. I talked to her too."

"Is there anyone you didn't?"

Mom's tone had an edge to it Addy couldn't put her finger on. Sadness? Betrayal? Anger? Who knew. "I'm sure I missed a few people. She threatened me if I hurt you."

One corner of Melinda's mouth turned up. "Did she?"

Nodding, Addy followed mom and Cormac around a corner.

"I wouldn't take two more steps unless you'd like a shiny, new knife handle for an accessory," Jane said, "sticking out of that lung I got last time. Hi, Addy." One hand held a knife cocked over her shoulder.

Matt stared down the sights of his rifle, bright blue eyes flashing. "Step away from her, General."

"Addy, come over here," Dean said, voice deep and growling. "Don't move, Melinda. You touch her again, it'll be the last thing you do."

Cormac held his hands in the air and opened his mouth.

Addy's stomach joined her heart, and they both leapt to her throat. Seeing them all here, now, brought tears to her eyes. "Guys," she said, stepping between her glaring mother and her beautiful friends, all of them strung tight against a hair trigger. "Let's all take a breath, OK?"

The end of Matt's gun dipped.

Neither Jane nor Dean stood down. But Jane did smile. "Think I've still got a maternity knife belt somewhere. I'll let you borrow it when we get back to town."

Grinning, Addy rubbed the baby again. "That'd be pretty useful. Feel like this one's gonna slide right off."

Matt lowered the rifle the rest of the way and flushed.

Dean raised his gun. "General. Stop."

Addy spun.

Mom had been sliding back around the corner, eyes fixed to her. She stopped, raising her hands. "I'm sorry. I have to find my own friend. You understand."

Cormac stepped forward, hall lights glinting off his greased hair. "Listen, guys, IRF is coming. We need to get out of here before the fighting starts. They're bringing everything." He glanced at Matt. "There's a group of us getting our asses out of here. Kids like you, Matt. Your friends."

Dean looked sideways, jaw working. "Here I'd almost forgotten you're one of them."

Matt backed up a step. "I'm not. Not anymore." He shook his head, taking them all in at once. "Cormac's right though. We gotta get out of here. If IRF's coming, Dean, you know, it's not going to be pretty."

Eyes still fixed to Melinda, Jane backed up a step. "Addy, come on. We gotta get back to Jack. We should all make a swift exit."

Addy took a step. "You're not wrong. But Mom, you gotta come with us." She held out her hand.

Her mom reached for it.

Matt raised his rifle so fast, Addy didn't see it move. Eyes skipping between them, he clenched his teeth.

Cold fingers slipping inside Addy's hand, Mom stepped close to her. "You can take my weapons, if it'll make you feel better."

"It's a start," Jane said, cocked knife unwavering. "Dean."

"Hand 'em over," he said, still aiming with one hand. He stuck the other out and stepped closer.

But he took his eyes off Mom and met Addy's. Standing close enough for his scent to mix with the Molehill's constant odor of dirt.

Addy couldn't help but smile. No matter what had happened, or what would happen, the sight of him would probably always sock her in the gut. She couldn't take the time to be distracted by him, though, or by Matt, standing there with his red cheeks and blue eyes. Swallowing, baby kicking against the endorphins it'd just been inundated with, she shook her head. "What is IRF planning, Cormac? For this place?"

He shook his head as they moved down the hallway again, Mom free of her weapons, back the way Jane and the others had come. Addy and Melinda walked in the middle of everyone. "I'm not sure. I didn't ask. They just said they'd help us out of here."

"That's good," a voice said from the dark hallway ahead. "I can come with you."

Skidding to a stop, every armed person lifted their weapons at the voice.

Melinda narrowed her eyes. "Anthony. Great."

CHAPTER 51

The door closed behind Morgan.

The lights switched on, and Jack drew his gun. A woman stood by the door, a blur as his eyes adjusted.

"Welcome, gentlemen. I see my map proved useful."

Her face swam into focus. High cheekbones, perfectly coiffed hair, and flawless deep brown skin. "Jack Cooke," he said, holding out the hand that wasn't holding the gun. "You are?"

"Ilasha," she said, stepping forward and shaking. She crushed his fingers in hers. "Heard a lot about you, Jackson Cooke."

"All good, I hope?"

She shook her head, lips pursed. "Course not. Em's not your biggest fan. Not anymore."

His heart thumped into his ribs. "Where is she?"

"Sorry to interrupt," Morgan said, looking around the room, "but about why we're in this room."

The smile this Ilasha worked through her lips walked down Jack's spine like goose feet. He didn't lower his gun.

She held up a hand. "This way, please. All the files are digital. Did you bring something to download them on?"

He patted a small bag hanging on his hip. "Dug up this external hard drive. It's got a terabyte. You wouldn't believe what I had to do to get it." Smiling sideways at Jack, he pulled it from the bag and laid it in Ilasha's outstretched hand. "Not as bad as the cannon. But close."

Brow arched, she crossed her arms and clenched the drive in one hand. "You got a cannon? You're always a surprise, Morgan." Swinging her hips, she waltzed across the room and sat at a computer. "It'll take a few minutes to get it all. You willing to wait?"

Morgan scoffed. "Do I have a choice?"

"Gian. Make sure the door is secure. Can't be having somebody walk in on us." She winked at Jack. "Wouldn't look proper."

His gun hand itched. This woman clearly knew Melinda and had access to the Molehill's computers. Here she was, downloading something for Morgan and talking to him like she knew him too. He sat, resting his arm across his knee, and draped the gun between his legs. "Can I ask what this is all about?"

She tapped the keys, the blue light of the screen illuminating her creepy smile. "Morgan here didn't know it, but his contact, Gian, was a go-between."

"Wasn't surprised when you turned on that light, though," he said, arms crossed. "I thought Gian was pretty well-informed for someone so low on the totem pole."

"That he is. Well. Here we all are together. I've been passing information to Morgan, through Gian, for months now."

Jack looked between them. "For what purpose?"

"Gonna be defecting to IRF tonight, Jack. Thought it best to have as many allies as possible, if I was going to turn on Talus. They're not to be fucked with, you know."

He grinned, treating her to the same toothy smile she'd given him. "Oh, I don't know. I've fucked with them a time or two."

"How'd that work out, then?" She glanced at him with the side of her eye, smile stretching up her cheeks. "I hear it didn't go too well for you."

He flushed, the blood racing up his neck. She knew Melinda all right, even better than he thought, if she knew about that. Yet, here she was, turning on her?

Not likely.

Tapping her on the knee with the gun as she turned back to the screen, he frowned. "Tell me what you're doing and stop lying about it."

She stared at him with the side of her eye, smile slipping off her lips by degrees. "This thing is more complicated than you realize, Jackson. A lot more. Keeping all the ducks straight is a job in and of itself."

"Keeping the ducks straight? What do you mean? Who does that?"

She met his eyes full-on. "Anthony's boss."

* * *

"I'm serious, General. Take me with you," Anthony said, stepping out of the shadows at the end of the hall.

Every weapon in the hall pointed at him. Except Melinda's, of course, because Dean held them all.

She smiled and squeezed her daughter's hand. "Anthony, it's not up to me. These guys are in charge tonight." She gestured at the group surrounding her.

Approaching Jane, who stood in front of everyone, Anthony held his hands out. "Please, young lady, let me come with you." He glanced behind Jane. "McNamara. You've got to let me come with you. I'll explain everything, just bring me."

Melinda caught her breath, her stomach in knots. Could the answer to the mystery be so close? Would Anthony, could he, answer the questions Burke had set spinning in her head? She dropped Addy's hand and pushed past Matt, who stared at Anthony with wide eyes.

"You tell me right now, and we'll consider it."

"What's this we shit?" Jane asked. "You're in charge of nothing."

Clenching her jaw, Melinda tried to ignore the girl. Jane had a hell an axe to grind, but they didn't have time for that right now. She stared into Anthony's eyes. The ones that twitched back and forth like a cornered rabbit. "Charles," she said, voice low, "you need to tell me what you know."

He swallowed. "About. About what?"

"Why the fuck do I think IRF and Talus are related somehow?" She stopped, chewing her lip. "Why did IRF have my vaccine?"

"They what?"

"Why did they have my vaccine? And why did we have the recordings from the hidden mics in Magnolia?"

Matt cleared his throat. "They did?"

"Yes, they did. You know what else I found?"

He shook his head, eyes round, staring at Anthony again, brow furrowed.

"Transcripts of phone calls between him and—"

"Burke. Oh my god," Matt said, backing into the wall. He slid down. "The day I met Ella. Fuck. Fuck me. Jesus Christ." He landed on the floor with a thunk.

Mouth wide, Anthony stared at Melinda. "The transcripts. You." He switched to Matt. "What about Ella?"

"I should have seen it before," he said, dropping his rifle in the floor and holding his head in his hands. "The day I met her, Burke left us alone to go call someone named Anthony." He stared up, one eye between his fingers catching Melinda's. "He left me alone with her, and I forgot everything about that phone call until just now. For"—he glanced at Addy—"one reason or another."

Even unarmed, Melinda still knew how to intimidate. With one finger, she pushed Anthony into the opposite wall. "You're a double agent. You have been. For years. *Years.*"

"General," Cormac said, "what are you saying? Are you saying Anthony is a traitor?"

"That's exactly what I'm saying, Cormac. I also think he fabricated test results in an effort to keep me confused and under control." Narrowing her eyes, she leaned into his space. "Worked for a little while too."

Anthony tried to back farther into the wall, his head scraping against the dirt. "Please, Melinda. Listen. It's not what it looks like." His eyes darted around her.

Peeking over her shoulders, she found Matt behind one and Addy behind the other.

Half a grin lifting her mouth, she turned back around. "Why don't you explain it to me?"

His eyes clouded. "Ella's mother was a beautiful, overbearing woman. Much like her daughter." He smiled over Melinda's shoulder.

She peeked.

Matt had gone two shades paler, red cheeks and blue eyes popping from his face. His Adam's apple bobbed, but he didn't speak.

Addy gripped his shoulder. "And?"

"And. I saw her first." He smiled. "We dated in high school. But life happened and this damned apocalypse. Long story short, she was my high school sweetheart, but she was in love with Burke when she died."

"Ella was two," Matt whispered. "She didn't even remember her mom."

"It's a shame. She was quite the woman."

Melinda backed up a step and stood between Matt and Addy. She opened her mouth, but Addy beat her to it.

"What does this have to do with you calling Burke? With you having those recordings? What does Ella's Mom have to do with any of it?"

He shrugged. "Not much. But Burke and I both protected her and the small community of military men we'd gathered. We were going through a bad patch when he found us and started this whole thing."

Melinda clenched her fists, nails biting into her palms. "When who did? Charles, who found you?"

Anthony grimaced, brow twisted and mouth curled. "Ilasha's father."

* * *

Before Jack even twitched, Ilasha wrenched the gun from his hand.

Without a word, she fired twice.

Morgan fell. Blood spraying behind him in a waterfall.

She stood, watching Jack as she walked around him, and blew a chuckle out her nose. "Thanks, Gian. Morgan has been a thorn in my side for what seems like forever." She kicked Morgan's body, foot thumping against his lifeless side.

Jack swallowed his gorge. The room stank of copper and gun smoke, and as close as he'd been to the gun, he shouldn't have been able to hear that flat thump. But he had.

Without so much as a warning, Morgan's life spilled onto the floor before he could think to defend himself.

Ilasha laughed. "Well. He's not coming back. Good." She spat. It splatted in his face and mingled with the blood stippled on his cheeks. She glanced at Jack. "Oh, don't look at me like that. He would've killed Melinda if he'd gotten the chance. You know we couldn't let that happen."

Jack wanted to stand. Wanted to back away from this woman whose calm eyes said she would brook no argument. Would accept no pleas. Would do no less than exactly what she wanted.

He looked across the room.

Gian lay in the floor against the wall, bloody arm over his head. He'd landed awkwardly, one of his legs twisted behind him at an unnatural angle, the other foot splayed in a position Jack had often seen on the dead. The leg muscles relaxed, letting the foot fall to the side.

Ilasha sat next to Jack at the computer again.

He fought the urge to back up.

"You can call me Lash, I suppose. We're practically bedfellows." She tapped on the computer. "Soon, all these files will be downloaded. There's two more computers that run on their own network. Can't get to them from here. We'll have to get them downloaded as well." She leaned her elbow on the desk and rested her chin on the gun in her palm. "This is all backed up to my daddy's cloud in Wyoming. But communication issues being what they are, I always like to have hard files." She shrugged.

There were so many things to jump on in that little speech, Jack had trouble picking just one. "What is all this? What are we doing, Lash?"

One hand on the keyboard, she tapped the keys with light fingers. "Did you know this place used to be some kind of graveyard? You wouldn't believe the things Daddy's crew found when they were digging it out."

"That's the second time you've mentioned your dad. Is he in Wyoming?"

"He's dead, Jackson Cooke. Like so many others." From the side of her eye, she looked him up and down. "Should kill you too. Leave you here with these two assholes."

He bit the inside of his cheek, fingers cold. Not like the gun had been his only weapon, but it was faster than his machete, and the other gun was strapped inside his boot. He'd never get to it before she pulled the trigger. He crossed his arms over his chest. "Why didn't you?"

She chuckled. "I brought you to her because I thought you'd make her happy, you know that? I broke her heart, and I tried to fix it, and then you broke it too."

All the spit in his mouth dried up. It'd been her? The whole time? His jaw flapped up and down, but no words erupted from his dry gullet.

"My daddy was a billionaire, before all this," she said, waving the gun at the ceiling. "He dabbled in government contracting, kept us to ourselves. Owned a lot of land."

The computer beeped.

Gun coming back up, black eye trained on Jack's forehead, she removed the external drive. "Got to get to those other computers. Here, you go first." She stood and waved the gun.

Hands raised, Jack stepped around Morgan. His boot heel landed in the blood, stamping a half-moon outline in the pool of it. With a grimace, he opened the door and walked into the hall. "Did he start this company?"

"I found out you and your kids were in Arizona, after she left. It hurt, sending her away like that. I wish I could tell you."

He stopped. "Did you tell her?"

"Keep your nose out of my business." She shoved the gun into the small of his back. "Pretty sure I can paralyze you like this. Then you can bleed out and crawl through the dirt for the rest of your afterlife."

Lifting his hands again, he walked. "So you brought us out here. Did you want to get me killed, or was all that slow torture just for fun?"

"For fun."

Fighting with his gorge, his throat thick, he shuffled down one hallway and continued down the next. She was close enough to spin and grab the gun, if he was fast. Besides that, he couldn't see any reason for her to keep him alive. Melinda hated him. He didn't think he hated her, not anymore, but it wasn't like he was going to send her Christmas cards. He steeled himself to make a grab for the gun.

The ground beneath, above, and beside him rumbled. Dirt sifted down from the ceiling onto his head. Somewhere, tile broke. His knees wobbled on the uncertain ground beneath him.

Stopping, he looked up. "The hell was that?"

"Shit. Sounds like the aerial unit."

He spun, eyes wide. "Aerial unit?"

She nodded. "IRF has an aerial assault unit. Got some bombs and whatnot. Not as fancy as they used to be, thank god, but still enough to blow this place to pieces." She raised the gun to chest level. "We need to get those files and get back to Melinda. I've got to get us out of here."

Jack moved to leave, fists clenched by his sides. "I need to get my kids, Ilasha."

The sight of the gun caught him under the curve of his skull.

Lights flashing behind his eyes, he stumbled.

"You'll do as I say, or next time I'll send a bullet through your brain instead. Let's go."

CHAPTER 52

Addy didn't get her hands up before her mom backed into her.

Mom's voice cracked. "Ilasha's what?"

The man named Anthony nodded, eyes hooded. "Her father. He's the one who started all this and left it all to her. God's sake, Melinda, who do you think my boss is?"

Mom sagged against her. "I always thought it was someone...somewhere else. I never..."

Free hand snaking around Mom's shoulder, Addy glanced at Cormac. "What did you know about this?"

He held up both hands. "Nothing, I swear. I never knew Ilasha was anything more than a secretary." The blood crawled up his cheeks. "Oh god. The things I've said to her."

Spinning to Matt, she lifted her eyebrows. "You?"

Eyes round, he shook his head. "News to me, Addy." He looked around the circle. "I'm at a loss like everybody else."

Staring at a spot on his shoulder, she let her eyes fall out of focus. "If you're in charge here, Mr. Anthony, and Burke was in charge of IRF—"

"Most of it," Anthony interjected.

She nodded, eyes still unfocused. "Most of IRF. And Ilasha is your boss. And her father started this whole thing with you—"

"They *are* connected," Mom said, standing straight. "I fucking knew it." She shook her head.

Addy's mind raced so fast, she lost her breath trying to keep up. The baby spun and kicked, bringing her back to earth. "Are they the same—"

The tunnel rumbled, pieces of it raining down on her head. She lost her footing.

Matt stumbled into her.

Her legs and the ground jelly under her, she fell the other way and right into Dean.

He caught her and stood her up. "You OK?"

"The hell was that?"

Anthony shook his head. "I'm not sure, but I think it's best we signal the evacuation and get out of here ourselves. We're under attack."

Jane brandished her knife. "I know. We're attacking you. But that was no cannon blast."

Anthony took off down the hall, speaking over his shoulder. "You've got a cannon?"

"What can I say. We're resourceful."

He shook his head. "Look, there's a room—"

Rounding the corner, he flew off his feet and backward into them before Addy registered there were shapes in the dark ahead.

A hulking man with scruffy brown hair, dim blue eyes, and too-broad shoulders blocked most of the next hallway. "Son...bitch."

"Hi, Anthony. Wish I could say it was good to see you," a female said from behind the mammoth figure.

Addy started, heartbeat in her throat. "Vic, what the hell? Where did you come from?"

She stepped under Adam's arm, floppy hat on crooked. Wispy white hair floated around it. "That is it, precisely, Addy. Hell. That's where I've come from." Smiling, she brought up a gun. "And where our dear friend Anthony is going."

From the spot where Anthony'd finished up against the wall, mouth bleeding, he tried to sit up.

The tunnel rocked again, more of the ceiling falling down around them. In one of the rooms next to them, glass broke.

Victoria's shot, deafening in the small hallway, went wild. A piece of tile chipped off and nicked Anthony in the raised arm.

Eyes wide, he tried to stand, feet slipping on the tile. "Please, Victoria, let me explain—"

Adam stepped forward, chain dragging behind him. "Retribution." He grabbed Anthony by the ankle and tugged.

Sliding down the wall, Anthony shouted and flailed with both hands. He caught Cormac by the pants leg and Jane by the ankle. "Don't, Adam. Please! I'm sure we can help you! Melinda, please." Kicking, dragging Jane and Cormac with him, he inched toward Adam's open maw.

Adam, saliva dripping from his mouth, snarled and bubbled. "No help," he gurgled.

About that, he was right. There was no help. No help for any of them.

Shoving them aside, Dean pushed through Addy and Melinda. He grabbed Jane and kicked at Anthony's hand.

Anthony gripped tighter, whimpering.

Cormac yanked his leg, falling on his ass. He kicked with the other foot, trying to hit Anthony in the face.

Who continued to whimper, begging Victoria to stop this as Adam dragged him, with inexorable sluggishness, toward his gnashing teeth.

Foam dripped from Adam's open mouth and splattered on the floor tiles. He smiled, three teeth in the front chipped, lips bloody from being chomped between them. With no warning, he gripped Anthony's knee and twisted.

The tearing of cartilage and the snapping of bone turned Addy's stomach in a new direction. She stumbled again, one hand over her mouth as Anthony screamed.

High-pitched, like a teakettle, he screamed and writhed. But at least his hands popped off Jane and Cormac.

Dean and Jane bounced off the wall behind them, and Cormac crawled away.

Matt wrapped an arm around Addy's waist and steadied her. "Fuck's sake," he whispered, gripping her.

Clutching his shirt with her free hand, Addy tried to turn her eyes away as Adam gnawed at Anthony's leg like a chicken bone. She couldn't, and the dry heaves wracked her.

Matt turned them both away.

She shook her head, saliva filling her mouth. If she didn't throw up to the symphony of screaming with accompanying bone-crunching sounds, it'd be a miracle.

"Where is Kendra, General?" Vic asked.

Hand squeezing Matt's shirt and catching skin beneath, Addy spun again. Averting her eyes from the mess in the floor, she clenched her teeth.

Eyes drifting away from Anthony's writhing, Mom faced Vic. "I'm sorry, Victoria. She's dead."

Vic pointed her gun at Mom, her eyes dull and lifeless as she stared at Anthony's contorted face. Her chin trembled, but the end of the gun remained steady.

Mom stepped away from the wall. "I'm sorry I couldn't save her."

A laugh bubbled up from the depths of Vic's stomach, screamed out of her mouth, and bounced off the tile of the walls with such force it hurt Addy's ears.

Matt cursed under his breath.

Addy let him go, unsheathing her machete. "Vic, why don't we, um. Why don't we put Anthony out of his misery and get the hell out of here? We can talk about this outside."

Eyes fixed to Melinda, Vic shook her head. "There's nothing more to talk about, Adelaide, my dear. There is so much I owe this woman. She tried to take you from us, and she's done so many, many unspeakable things." Her eyes drifted to Addy's. "If I could but tell you even half what I know, you would kill her yourself."

"Not that we all wouldn't like a chance," Jane said as the earth around them shifted again and dirt fell from the ceiling, "but Addy's right. Let's get out of here first." She pulled a handgun from somewhere and aimed at Anthony's forehead as he writhed, being slowly consumed by a frightfully blank-faced man.

Melinda edged toward Jane, half her shoulder behind Dean's.

Vic's face tightened. "Don't you fucking move, Melinda."

"Victoria, stop," Addy said, stepping toward her. "I've no doubt she's done all you say and more. But listen to me, please. She has regret. Remorse. The desire to be forgiven. Surely that's somewhere we can start. Do we have to go straight to murder?"

Vic shifted her aim and pointed the black eye of the gun at Addy's chest. "You won't come between me and the end of this nightmare."

Bone crunched, Anthony screamed, Dean and Matt and Melinda and Jane all shouted at once, tile fell from the wall and broke on the floor as the ground rumbled again, but none of it registered. Addy stared at Victoria, and the world slowed.

What could she hope to accomplish by stopping her? She'd never have her mother back, not after all that had passed. She could try to forgive her, but she could never trust the woman again.

Yet despite that, she couldn't condone the killing of someone who essentially had no choice from the time she died until this moment. Who'd been guided down this path by a virus that would never stop and a company that was so full of deceit it might be impossible to ever uncover the truth about them. She deserved the chance to atone for her sins.

"Victoria," Addy said, stepping closer again.

Matt gripped Addy's free arm and stepped up next to her. He brandished his knife in one hand. "Vic. Let's go."

White hair floating around her face, Vic shook her head and took aim at Melinda. "I can never go. I never left. And neither can she."

Before she pulled the trigger, Addy lashed out with her machete and hit the gun with the broadside.

It went off, the bullet singing as it clanged off the tile.

Addy and Matt shouted in unison, and Addy ducked as the baby kicked harder than ever before. As though she were trying to escape the shouting and the pounding of her mother's heart.

"You would stop me? How dare you," Vic said, rounding on Addy. As she stepped forward, Adam jumped halfway up.

Addy held out both hands, machete in one, shaking her head. "Please, we can—"

Vic tripped over Adam's leg. Mouth open, she fired the gun again. It would take Addy at least five minutes to realize she'd been grazed.

Because no sooner had she closed her eyes against the shot, did her blade handle jump in her hand.

In a moment of instinct, she gripped it and twisted.

Vic gasped.

Matt drew in a sob.

Eyes popping open, Addy followed the length of the blade down. She found the end of it buried deep in Vic's right side. Bright red blood gushed around the edges of the wound.

Her hand popped off. "Oh my fuck, Vic. Jesus," she said, catching her friend as she fell.

They both crashed to the ground, Addy's knees bouncing off the tile.

Adam roared, rising to his feet.

Jane shot him, ending his roar, and his suffering. He landed like a felled tree.

Anthony didn't whimper and whine anymore. All he could do now was bleed into the floor. Even that would stop in short order.

But Vic cried, wet eyes searching Addy's face. "I could not do otherwise, my dear Miranda. For I could not see the beauty you so eloquently uncovered." She took a hitching breath.

Addy couldn't. It wouldn't come. As if Vic's last few breaths had stolen the rest of Addy's, all that came from Addy was a dry sob. Blood squished between her toes. Only the baby's frantic kicking made any sense.

Dean sank down next to her. "Breathe. It's OK. It was an accident. You're OK." He rubbed her back, pulling her into his chest. "Breathe for me, all right?"

She nodded, but the black spots took up her vision. It wouldn't come.

And neither would Vic's. They'd stopped.

"Sweetie, breathe," he whispered in her ear.

She nodded again, and all at once, her nostrils opened. Air screamed down them, smelling of blood and Dean and dirt.

Falling sideways, she inhaled again, and the tears crowded the bottoms of her lids. She couldn't see, but at least she could breathe. She closed her eyes.

"No, no, no," Matt said, sinking down on her other side. "You gotta walk now, Addy. We have to go."

She stopped, halfway to the floor. Putting down one palm in a pool of blood, she met his eyes. "Did I make the right choice?"

He shook his head. "I can't tell you that." Blue eyes round, wilted parentheses framing his mouth, he held out one hand. "If it helps, I think I would have done the same."

She took it, blood smearing his palm, and stood.

He released her, and again, she stumbled.

Dean steadied her from the other side.

As her heart rate slowed so did the baby's kicking, and she spoke to her mom. "Which way?"

She stepped over Anthony and headed the way they'd been going. "This way."

Jane paced her, knife in one hand and gun in the other. Cormac kept up with them.

Addy staggered behind, wiping the blood on her palm down the side of her jeans. Scraping her bare feet across the floor to try to dry the blood covering her heels and toes. She opened her mouth to ask Mom to slow down a bit.

The ground wobbled under her feet again, and the ceiling collapsed in front of them.

* * *

Stumbling into the wall, Melinda winced as a rock struck the back of her leg. She threw herself away from the falling ceiling.

Jane grunted, falling next to her.

Covering her head and curling into a ball, Melinda waited for the sky to stop falling. Or to be crushed by it.

Dust creeping up her nostrils, silence descended.

She peeked behind her.

Jane did the same. She sneezed twice.

"Bless you," Melinda said, wobbling to her knees.

The tunnel had collapsed behind them. Only she, Jane, and Cormac were here. Addy and the others were missing.

Cormac moaned.

Shifting her eyes, Melinda stood and frowned. The boy had been trapped by falling debris, pinned next to the wall.

She brushed the hair out of her face. Her hand came away wet.

"Got caught by some flying tile there, Melinda," Jane said. She pulled the needles from her hair and shook the dust from it, lips pressed together. "Unfortunately, it looks like you'll live."

Melinda snorted, turning her ear to the wall of debris behind her. "I can't hear Addy."

Jane shook her head. "And I don't think Cormac is as lucky as us." She clutched the needles in one hand, a knife in the other, and had lost her gun somewhere.

But at least she'd stopped actively trying to kill her for a moment, so that was nice. Jane had every right to see red every time she looked at her.

Taking a few short steps, kicking broken tile aside, Melinda wiped her stinging face again and knelt beside him. "Cormac?"

He moaned, eyes rolling in his head.

What she could see of his legs didn't bode well. One of them curled up behind his back. The other disappeared under a pile of bloody rock. "Well shit, Cormac. I didn't like you, but I don't think I would've asked for this," Melinda whispered.

Head lolling to the side, he focused his eyes on her face. "Can't feel it." He coughed and blood sputtered onto his chin. He wiped it and laughed at his red palm. "Tell IRF I'm sorry I couldn't help them."

"I'm sorry you couldn't tell them yourself."

The ground hummed beneath her again, dirt sifting down from the pile of rock and tile.

"Think we should get our asses out of here, if it's all the same," Jane said, wrapping her hair back into the needles. "I'd rather end him and put one of these needles through your eye, but Addy doesn't want me to do that." She paused, hands on her hips. "She never has, to tell you the truth. While we're on the truth, Jack doesn't want me to either. I guess I can respect that."

Eyes round and heart in her throat, Melinda stared at the girl. Jack didn't want her dead? After all this?

A voice no louder than a whisper came through the pile of debris. "Mom?"

Standing, Melinda pressed into the pile. "Adelaide!"

Addy shouted again. "Jane!"

Jane joined her next to the pile. "I'm here! You guys all right?"

Melinda couldn't make out every word of the next shout, but it sounded like "we're fine." She opened her mouth to shout back, and the ground shifted beneath her feet. Less like the shaking happening at irregular intervals and more like it was giving way beneath her.

And as she and Jane scrambled backward, she saw that was exactly what was happening. A hole opened beneath their feet, dirt and rocks and broken tile falling into it. She and Jane clutched each other for support, and the rounded edge of a skull, long and straight femurs, curved rib bones, they came into sharp relief at the bottom of a pit. Jumbled into a pile by the rocks falling from above.

"What the fuck is that?" Jane said, feet slipping. She slid toward the hole, hands skidding over the dirt and tile, looking for purchase. One of her fingernails bent backward and snapped off, bloodying her finger. She hardly flinched, eyes fixed on the pit of skeletons below her feet.

A chunk of ground gave way beneath her, and both feet dangled over a pit that hadn't been there a moment earlier.

The air thick with dirt, Melinda choked and gagged. As the pit finished falling in, for now, she noted her feet still stood on solid ground.

Grunting, Jane pedaled her feet, looking for purchase. She had nothing to grasp with her hands but broken pieces of tile, and they continued to break as she slid backward. Her wide eyes landed on Melinda, but she said nothing. No begging. No screaming. Her mouth a thin line, she continued to readjust her grip in an effort to pull herself from the pit.

Addy shouted through the debris. Something about finding another way around. But that was far away.

Here, in Melinda's head, a war raged. She could let Jane keep falling. The sides of this pit weren't sheer, but it looked impossible to climb. And it had been some kind of large chamber, its floor at least fifteen feet from where Jane hung over it. The fall wouldn't be fatal, not immediately, but she could be left in there to die. It'd be easy.

Melinda had murdered people in worse ways.

Addy shouted again, asking for confirmation she'd heard the plan.

Eyes glazed, Melinda nodded. She lifted her voice. "OK!"

Jane stopped struggling and slid backward. Eyes narrowed, tears tracked down her cheeks. Still, she said nothing.

That new path Melinda spoke with Addy about opened before her. Bright sun shone down, dappled through green trees and their fresh leaves. If she killed this woman dangling over the precipice before her, she could continue, but it wouldn't be down that fresh, clean path. She could pretend all she liked, but it would be the same, blood-drenched, muddy, dirty path she'd been on.

"Damn," she whispered, reaching out a hand.

She grasped Jane's wrist and pulled.

At first, Jane didn't react. Just kept sliding backward.

"You have to help me, Jane. Otherwise, we're both going to end up in that pit." She tugged.

Jane kicked her feet again and found purchase. She pushed, shoving her weight forward as Melinda pulled her up.

When the side gave way, and Cormac's body went sliding into the pit, along with the rocks that pinned him, Melinda closed her eyes and held onto Jane. With her eyes closed, she tugged.

Jane slid flat onto her stomach and lay on the dirty tile, breath puffing up little clouds of dust. "Thanks. I can't believe you did that."

"You offered not to kill me. We'll call it even." She glanced at the spot where Cormac had been until recently. "I think there's space to get through there." She crawled across the hall, giving the new hole in the ground a wide berth.

Jane lifted to her knees and joined her. "I'm not sure we can crawl through there. What if it collapses again?"

"It's either through there, or past this big hole," Melinda said, pointing. "Pick your poison."

Chuckling, Jane leaned against the wall. "Right where I always wanted to be. With you," she said, eyes narrow, "between a rock and a hard place."

CHAPTER 53

Addy would never know which of them shoved her away from the falling ceiling, but by the time the rocks stopped falling and the dust settled, the three of them had run past where Vic, Adam, and Anthony died and turned another corner.

Crouched against the wall with her back to it, she held one of their hands in each of hers. "The hell is going on out there? World war three?"

Dean shrugged, taking his hand back and standing. "We got a cannon, but I'll be damned if that's just a cannon."

Popping to his feet, Matt dragged her up with him. "If it's IRF, it could be anything. Could be a damn atom bomb, for all we know."

Addy gaped. "Jesus Christ, what?"

"They're well-armed," Matt said, wiping the front of his pants clean of dirt. "Dean knows that."

Stepping into the other hall, Dean pulled his mouth into a frown. "I didn't know they were that well-armed."

Addy crossed her arms over the baby. "Seems like they're trying to take the place apart." She headed back down the hall and toward the caved-in ceiling. "We need to get Mom and Jane and Cormac and get the hell out of here." She glanced over her shoulder. "Dean. Where's my dad?"

"He said something about room 6B and meeting Morgan there. That's all I know. I left to come get you."

Cheeks red, she smiled. "Thanks." Her eyes shifted to Matt's. "Both of you." She stopped at the pile of rock and lifted a tentative hand. "Do you think they made it?" She shouted for them through the rock. "Mom! Jane! Are you there? Mom!"

Breathless seconds passed.

Mom shouted back. Not loud, but there. "Adelaide!"

Addy shook her head, the need to hear Jane's voice overwhelming. After Vic, and after Ella, and after everything, she needed Jane to be OK too. "Jane!"

"I'm here! You guys all right?"

Addy sagged, tears threatening. It'd never been so good to hear her voice. "We're all right! Where can we meet you?"

A rumbling sounded from the other side, Jane and Mom both shouted, followed by several seconds of floor shaking.

"Guys!"

Through the rumbling, Mom shouted what sounded like "OK," but Addy couldn't be sure. Her heart pounded in her ears over the rumbling.

Stepping back, she waited for the ceiling to shift again. With deliberation, she pulled one breath after another through her nose and deep into her lungs. Without thinking about it, she turned the baby away from the collapsed ceiling and put her body between them.

Once the sound abated, she stepped up to the messy heap again. "Mom! Jane! Are you OK?"

Matt and Dean on either side of her, she waited.

When they didn't answer, she tried again. Louder.

"I'll help you," Matt said, "on three."

She held up the first finger. Second.

"Adelaide!" The shout from the other side came through louder. Almost clear. "Addy, over here by the wall."

She crept over, one hand holding her belly, the other held out toward the mound of rock. She knelt in front of a dark hole in the rocks, next to the wall. "Mom?"

Mom leaned into the hole from her side. "I'm OK, baby. Jane too." She leaned back.

Jane grimaced. "Your mom saved my life just then." She cut her eyes at Melinda. "Even though she didn't have to."

Mom leaned back into the hole. "Don't tell anyone."

Warming from her chest outward, Addy stretched her hand out. "I think you guys can fit. Come on."

Melinda shook her head. "We're going to go around. You get out of here."

Addy leaned into the hole. "Let me come with you."

Mom held her hand up at the same time Dean spoke.

"Addy, don't crawl under there," he said. "It's not stable."

Corners of her mouth turned down, she took in the men's faces.

They both stood ready, the air around them tense, as they waited on pins and needles to pull her back.

She considered the rock next to her face. They weren't wrong. This damn rock could kill her if it shifted. And the baby.

Backing up, she met Mom's eyes. "Be safe. We'll meet you outside."

* * *

Holding hands, Melinda and Jane tiptoed around the ragged edge of the hole.

"Seriously, what the fuck is that?" Jane asked, pressed against the wall as they crept along the narrow strip of remaining floor.

"I have no idea," Melinda said. She couldn't help but stare into the hole, jagged heaps of bone protruding from the dirt and Cormac's twisted, bleeding body at the bottom. He'd been impaled on one of the protruding bones, and as his limbs twitched, on the verge of awakening, Melinda looked away.

"Maybe this place used to be some kind of graveyard or something," Jane said. She chuckled low in her throat. "That's not the *only* explanation for a pit full of bones. Especially not when you're involved. But maybe."

Tugging, Melinda pulled them both to the other side of the hole. She frowned, her stomach doing some kind of complicated dance. It'd been so long since she felt guilt, she hardly could put a name on it when she did. "I didn't have anything to do with this. I don't know where this came from."

"Sure. Come on. Let's get Jack and get the hell out of here."

"Do you know where he is?"

"I know where he said he was going. Room 6B?"

Melinda's heart leapt and tried to carry on without her. She rounded a corner. "Why would he want to go there?"

"You'd have to ask Morgan. They were supposed to meet there. I have to assume they did, because Morgan brought Vic down here." She sighed. "Poor Addy."

More to have something to say than anything, Melinda asked what she meant. "I know Addy knew Victoria. Were they close?"

"I think so. They spent a lot of time together while Addy's been here, from what I gather."

"It is unfortunate things turned out the way they did." She rounded one more corner, the room down this hallway.

Jane stopped. "It's not 'unfortunate,' Melinda. It's fucking terrible. Addy doesn't kill people, you bitch." She poked her in the shoulder. "You don't deserve her."

"You're right about that. It's best they left me for dead. So I didn't have the chance to mess her up."

Hands on her hips, Jane shook her head. "Do you always feel this sorry for yourself? Or is this just for my benefit?"

Flame crawled up Melinda's throat. She opened her mouth to spit it at Jane.

Who stood, armed to the teeth, and dared her to do it. Eyes blazing, she waited with her mouth curled in something as close to a grin as a grimace.

"Not always. We're here." She reached into an alcove and gripped the doorknob.

"Here, let me go first. They'll get the wrong idea if you go charging in there." Knife in one hand, she snuck into the alcove next to Melinda and opened the door.

Morgan, someone Melinda knew to run his mouth as much as possible, didn't say a word. Neither did anyone else. Easing into the room after Jane, she saw why.

Jane spun a circle. "Shit. Is this all there is to this room?"

Eyes fixed to the pool of blood around Morgan and the single boot print stamped into the drying lake, Melinda crept to him. She shook her head. "No. This is it. Jesus."

"What?"

Staring down into Morgan's lifeless face, Melinda exhaled through tight lips. One small hole rested above his eyes, the edges lined with a thin sheen of blood. "Morgan's done."

"Where the hell is Jack? Does Morgan have his radio on him?"

Melinda leaned over, looking at his belt. "I don't—"

"They went to some other computer room," a voice croaked.

Guts constricting, Melinda looked to the side of the room.

Gian lay in a crumpled pile, face hidden. Blood splattered on his arm, his legs at awkward angles.

Jane knelt next to him and moved his arm away from his face. "Shit, Gian. What happened?"

"She double-crossed us. Killed Morgan and shot me before I knew what was happening."

Crouching, Jane leaned her arms on her knees. "Who?"

"My contact," he said, eyes shifting to Melinda. "Ilasha."

Luckily, when Melinda's legs collapsed, she fell next to him and avoided the small pool of blood seeping from under him. "What do you mean? Your contact?"

He nodded, only his chin moving. "She was passing me information about the Molehill, I passed it on to Morgan. Of course now I wonder how accurate it all was." He whimpered, the corners of his mouth trying to raise. "I can't feel anything."

Melinda laid her hand on his arm. "You'll be all right. We'll get you to the hospital."

"I can't move," he said, voice small. "Why can't I move?"

Jane fixed Melinda with wide eyes, knowing what Melinda did. As much good medicine as they had now, they couldn't fix this kind of injury, and he was bleeding out fast. "I'm sorry, Gian," Jane said.

The ground rumbled. This close to the surface, the sound of small arms fire reached them as faint *pops*. Melinda couldn't imagine the scene. "Sounds like war out there." She glanced across to Morgan, dead on the floor. "We should go."

Gian whimpered again. Jane picked up one of his limp hands, the fingers drooping.

Melinda caught sight of Morgan's gun, still in its holster at his side. With deliberation, she crossed the room and tugged it free. She opened the cylinder, counted all six bullets, and snapped it closed.

Jane's wide eyes met hers again. She nodded and clenched Gian's hand.

The boy whimpered, but he uttered no pleas. His body lay dying, and all Melinda could do was push it one way. At least he wouldn't lay here, a reanimated corpse, staring at the ceiling until the body broke down completely. It may take years. Even Melinda wasn't sure how long it took a 'Head to starve.

Job done, she slipped the gun into her own holster.

Jane sniffed, laid Gian's motionless hand on his chest, and stood. "So. Do you know where they went?"

Brow wrinkled, Melinda considered. "I have an idea."

* * *

"Do you think Mom and Jane will be OK?"

Matt pointed them all down the next hallway. "Hell if I know, Addy. I don't know your friend well enough to say."

Dean chuckled. "They're as likely to kill each other as not. They'll be fine."

Out of breath, she tried to laugh.

Feet slowing, Matt turned. "You all right? Need to take a break?" He looked her up and down, eyes resting on her belly.

She smiled and patted his shoulder. "The fragile pregnant girl will be fine, thank you."

He grasped her hand. "I know, I just—"

A gun cocked. "Where is Mama?"

Addy's blood pressure shot up so fast, she wobbled.

The color left Matt's face.

Dean drew and aimed his own gun. "You get one warning. Drop it."

Hector fired.

She couldn't see where he'd been hit, but blood flew and Dean staggered into the wall.

Heart in her throat, breath squeaking past her thumping heart, she shouted.

The rifle came off Matt's shoulder so fast, she didn't notice it move. "Addy, get behind me." He stepped in front of her, rifle socked into his shoulder and aimed at Hector's head.

Feet slipping, unable to gain traction against the weight of his body, Dean slid down the wall.

She diverted her attention to him, stepping closer.

"Adelaide. Get behind me," Matt said, taking another step between her and Hector.

"Dean's been shot," she said, reaching for him. "Dean, where were you hit?"

He slid farther down the wall, gun pointed at Hector's feet. "I'm fine. Get behind him."

"Tell me where Mama is and I promise to make it quick," Hector said. He took a step toward them.

Matt matched his step. "Look me in the eyes, you son of a bitch."

For the first time, Hector's dark eyes flickered. "You don't insult Mama like that! You take it back!"

Heartbeat in her ears, Addy stepped to Matt's side and drew his knife from its holster.

Eyes shifting between them both, Hector didn't aim. He just shot Dean again and took off down the hall.

With a grunt, Dean slid the rest of the way down the wall. His gun clattered to the floor, and he held his arm, head nodding to the side, feet splayed before him.

Red, uncontrolled rage clouded Addy's eyes. Head tight, her heart threatening to pound it right off the top of her neck, she went after Hector. "I've had enough of his shit," she said. Mostly to herself.

"Goddammit, Addy, wait," Matt said, pacing her. "Get back there and check on him. He needs help to stop the bleeding."

His voice almost cut through the red racing of blood through her ears. Her mouth drew back in a grimace she couldn't control, contorting her lips and cheeks into a scowl so tense her jaw immediately protested. "Tired of his shit," she said. It squeaked out from between her teeth.

Before she rounded the next corner, Matt grabbed her arm and yanked her behind him.

Hector's shot went wild, chipping the tile next to her head.

Matt fired the rifle from his hip.

With a stumble, Hector dropped the gun from bleeding fingers. "I wouldn't like to kill Mama's daughter," he said, smiling, "but some things can't be avoided." He pulled a knife and advanced on them.

Matt sucked a fast breath through his teeth, so sharp it made Addy's own teeth hurt. "Stay away from her. I am not kidding." He caught Hector in his sights, his finger tightening on the trigger.

"I will kill her the way I did the other bitch, and you—"

Matt fired.

Ears ringing, Addy wished she'd plugged them. As she lifted her hand to the side of her head, a very much still-alive Hector lunged forward with the knife and slashed.

Catching her on the inside of her forearm, he sliced downward toward her abdomen.

The blade seared as it cut through her skin. The cut burned and blood flew, splashing her shirt and face. Her hand seized, clenching the knife handle hard enough to turn her knuckles white.

Inarticulate, Matt shouted and swung the butt of the rifle at Hector's head. It caught him in the jaw. The crunch broke through the ringing in Addy's ears. A large crack, like the rifle had hit bone.

Hector spat blood and pieces of tooth in the floor and smiled, blood smeared across his front teeth. He stepped inside the arc of Matt's swing and lunged with the knife again.

Whatever happened after that happened so fast, Addy couldn't keep track. One moment there were two men fighting in front of her, and the next, the ceiling landed on top of them.

* * *

The wooden stairs to the basement creaked under Melinda's feet.

"What if he's not down here, Melinda?"

She stopped, one foot hanging in space over the next riser. Not once had she ever heard Jane sound scared. Until this moment, Melinda thought she didn't *get* scared. "Hell Jane, I don't know." She glanced over her shoulder, foot still hanging in the air. "But Lash has some questions to answer, and you better believe I will find her so she can answer them."

Jane snorted. "Could have told her to stay off your bad side."

Melinda scoffed. "She knows that. But she did it anyway." Her stomach twisted, dragging her heart down into her intestines. "She did it anyway."

Following the illuminated bottom of the stairs, Melinda stepped into the basement hallway with a frown. "Never seen these lights on before. She's down here." Leading, she aimed Morgan's gun at the floor and stopped in front of the file room. Peeking over her shoulder, one corner of her mouth turned up.

Jane held two knives in each hand, those deadly needles still tucked in her hair.

Melinda spoke over her shoulder. "Sure you don't need a knife in your teeth?"

"Funny you should say that. This whole thing started with a knife between my teeth."

Melinda considered asking what she meant by that, but they didn't have time for it. She let it slip away and lowered her voice. "They probably won't be in this room. Be ready, just in case."

Jane's silence was as good as agreement.

Twisting the handle, Melinda opened the door a couple inches. She slipped through.

Jane followed and closed the door. "I can't hear any of the fighting anymore," she whispered.

Melinda nodded. "From what I can tell, this is directly under the other computer room, but much farther underground. A couple hundred feet at least."

"At least. Where's Jack?"

Angling across the file room, Melinda searched the wall for the false cabinet. "Addy and I came down here a week or so ago. She found this hidden room with a bunch of computers."

"Weird. What were you doing down here?"

Melinda's stomach turned. "Looking for files. So I could run some tests."

Jane stopped. "Run some tests. Yeah. I know about your tests," she said, the edge on her voice ragged.

With the full belief Jane wouldn't stab her in the back, she continued to search the room for the hidden door. Spotting it, she angled through the filing cabinets and knelt before it. "I'm sorry, Jane. You can believe me if you want to, or not. I don't care. But I'm sorry." She faced her. "I'm sorry about all of it. It was." Pausing, she dropped her eyes. "I was misguided. Delusional."

"True." She pushed an exhale through her nose. "Accepted."

That brightly lit path stretched on in Melinda's mind. Sun shining on the top of her head.

She pulled the false cabinet open.

CHAPTER 54

The maze of hallways and tunnels and stairs almost confused Jack into forgetting how to get out. Thankfully, he'd always been fairly decent with directions, and he still had Morgan's map.

Now, he leaned against the wall in a room with banks of screens, Ilasha working on one of them. With her back to him, he likely could have crawled back through the tunnel they entered from. But first.

"I need to know what you meant, you delivered me, us, to Melinda. Were you responsible for the murders?"

"Murders?" She glanced over her shoulder, eye twinkling. "Sounds like my boy Tim got up to some"—she winked— "hijinks."

Jack stammered. "Your...your boy?"

She turned back to the screen. "He didn't know his ass belonged to me. Made him think IRF needed him, didn't give him a way out." She shook her head. "Maybe you didn't figure, but my daddy built both companies." Chuckling, she locked the computer and removed the external hard drive. She bounced it from hand to hand. "And when Tim came back with his intelligence about your kid, her eyes just like her mom. Well. He played things his own way, but he got my job done in the end." Scowling, she crossed to the bank of computers across the room. "You fucked that all up, as men are wont to do." Plugging the hard drive into another computer, she clucked her tongue. "Should have known. Should have damn well known."

"I wish you'd left us there." Chest tight, Jack looked back on the village. It had its moments of discomfort, and Wade had never been easy to deal with, but it had been home. It had been something like normal, finally, again. If he'd stayed there, he wouldn't have Jane, Katie, or the baby he learned about yesterday, but how did that weigh against the murder of his friends? When he put weight on one side of the scale, did it creak back the other way? Did it even out?

Lash pulled a chair out and flopped into it. "Me too. Me too." She turned the creaking chair, and it groaned like the sad sighing of the dead. "Your kid is more trouble than she's worth. I'll tell you that. Crafty, that one." She smiled, and it lit her eyes. Her teeth peeked out in a real grin. "She's smart like her mom. Do you know how hard it's been to keep that woman on a leash?"

"A leash? Is that what you call what you've done to me?"

Jack jumped, chest tight.

Melinda crawled from the tunnel, gun trained on Lash.

Jack swallowed, forehead tight, and backed into the wall. If they were about to face off, now was the time to choose a side.

Jane crawled from the tunnel, knife in her teeth.

Just like when she'd run into the light to save him from being arrested. Armed, literally, to the teeth. Ready to plunge one of the deadly sharp knives directly into the heart of anyone who might try to hurt him.

He'd fallen a little in love with her even then.

Half his mouth turned up. "Jane. Good to see you, even though I wish you were outside and far away already."

Teeth scraping the metal, she slid the knife from her mouth and smacked her lips. "And let you have all the fun? I don't think so." She crouched next to him. "Addy's with Dean and Matt, on her way out. What are we doing?"

"I don't know, Em," Lash said, turning back to the computer, "what are you doing?"

"Trying to get everyone out of this hole before it becomes a graveyard, Lash." She inched closer, gun trained.

Ilasha's own gun hand twitched. "It already is. It's hard to get all this done with a gun in one hand. You gonna shoot me? Or can I put this down?"

Jack stood, hand pressed into the cold dirt wall. "Is what she says true, Melinda? Is she the one who sent for us, who was responsible for bringing us from Arizona?"

Melinda shuffled her feet. "News to me. I thought Tim did it on his own." She eased into Lash's peripheral. "You did that?"

Lash's eyes flicked to the side, and in her sad smile, Jack saw the truth. Her talk about "bedfellows" hadn't been a metaphor. Her regret at breaking Melinda's heart hadn't been hyperbole. She had been, and still was, in love with Melinda. And out of all the things she'd said, that was the only one he could make sense of. The rest required…untangling.

Dirt sifted down from the ceiling.

Jack ducked, covering his eyes and looking up at the same time. "Um. Ladies. We have a lot to discuss, but could we get out of here first? This place is falling apart."

Jane eased next to him, knives aimed. "What's going on out there?"

"Aerial assault, I assume," Lash said, back turned again. "Without Burke to keep them to heel, IRF has come for Talus. And here we're caught in the middle." She glanced at Melinda again. "Need to get out of here, that's not wrong. Let me finish this download and we'll take it all with us to our new home."

Melinda stepped closer. "And where is that?"

"I'm sure she's got some pretty sweet digs set up with IRF," Jack said. "Seems like she's in charge over there too."

"I heard," Melinda said. She shifted on her feet, leaning forward and back.

Bumping Jane with his hip, Jack inched closer to the tunnel and the only way out. Addy may have forgiven her mother, and maybe he had too, but he wasn't going to stay in this room and die while she rooted her future in indecision. He was pretty sure he and Jane could take them, but at this moment, all he wanted to do was get his pregnant woman back up to the surface. They'd arrest Melinda and Ilasha when they got to the top and get this all straightened out somewhere far, far away from this death trap.

* * *

Melinda didn't have to look over her shoulder to know Jack was headed for the way out. Still, he paused, and asked her to come with him.

That he'd even offered had to mean she was doing something right. She stepped closer to Ilasha. "Whatever it is you're doing, stop. Come with me. We can figure it all out, together."

Lash cut her eyes at Melinda. "I know that tone on you, Melinda Thibodeaux. You're upset."

"Of course I'm upset," she said, glancing at Jack anyway. He'd put himself between Jane and them and continued to push her toward the exit. She, of course, peeked over his shoulder with those cool, angry eyes of hers. If Melinda needed to know why Jack favored her, all she had to do was take in that gaze. It said it all.

Melinda faced Lash again. "I'm leaving with them. They're right. What we're doing, what we've done, it's."

Laying the gun on the desk, Ilasha held her head in her hands. "It's no different today than it was yesterday. What it is is necessary. This company, and you specifically, have done so much for the Cure, for the vaccine, for immunity. We're saving the planet, like my daddy envisioned." She spun in the creaking chair. "He set me on that path twenty years ago, and when you dropped into it, it was like I'd been gifted with an angel." She grabbed Melinda's fingers and squeezed.

The ragged edge on her voice tore at Melinda's heart like a dull knife ripping through bread. "I can't keep doing this. Any of this." Lifting Lash's fingers to her mouth, she kissed them. "I have to go." She stepped back.

Lash picked up the gun, pointed it over her shoulder, and fired in one motion.

Jane shouted.

Heart stuck in her throat, Melinda turned.

Hands over her head, Jane ducked, dirt in her hair.

Jack twisted toward the wall behind him.

A bullet hole marked the packed dirt not two inches away from him. It'd just missed him.

Eyes wide, he turned back to her and lifted his machete. "If force is how we're going to play it—"

"I'll shoot your woman right in her pretty face if you finish that threat," Lash said.

Breathless, Melinda backed up. The voice coming from Lash was the same one she'd used that night Anthony interrupted them to tell them Addy had surrendered. The Voice Not To Be Fucked With. Before she gathered a thought, Ilasha spun all the way around in her chair.

"Both of you get out of here. Melinda stays. And I hope to god I never see hide nor hair of you again, Jackson Cooke."

Melinda took a step toward her. "Lash. I have to—"

Ilasha stood and fired again, punching a bullet through the dirt next to Jane's head.

Lifting his machete, Jack charged forward with a shout.

Melinda's breath stuck somewhere around her heart. She couldn't let him hurt Ilasha, but she couldn't move her feet to stop him.

The air whizzed. A flying knife struck Lash's hand.

With a shout, her hand popped open and the gun flew.

"Jack, let's go," Jane said, another knife already in hand.

Lash pointed at him. "This is your fault. I should have known better than to bring you into this. Because she loves you, she's allowed herself to be corrupted by all your high and mighty talk." She scowled. "It's bullshit! There is no high and mighty! There's livin' and there's dyin'." She stepped closer to Melinda, and her eyes softened, the corners pointing down. "And there's what we were doing. We were doing something great. You knew that, once. Not too long ago. I don't understand what changed."

That breath still lodged around her heart, the spit dried in her mouth and her tongue stuck to the roof. "It wasn't what any of them said." She glanced at Jack, his blue eyes round, his machete still halfway lifted. "And it's not because I'm in love with him. I love *you*, Ilasha."

Lash's lips tightened and she closed her eyes for a brief second.

"But I. I could have killed my own grandchild. Murdered for the sake of progress. My only daughter too. They could have both died on that table, Lash." Manufacturing spit, she swallowed and closed her eyes. "I guess it didn't mean enough until it came home to me. Until it brushed up against me. I've turned into something that frightens me. A driven, cold, obsessed machine." She stepped away, hand held out toward Jack. "I'm going with them." Holding out the other hand, she stopped. "Come with me."

A tear rolled from each of Lash's eyes. Her chin trembled.

The stuck breath shoved its way down, churning the acid in Melinda's stomach. It turned around and crawled up her throat, searing her esophagus. As Lash's face contorted through sadness, pain, anger, and resolve, the acid ate into Melinda. Burned in a circle that radiated out from the center of her ribcage to its edges.

Sitting, Lash spun. "Get. The fuck. Out."

Still facing her, Melinda waved her other hand at Jack and Jane, shooing them into the tunnel. She tried on a few words in her brain to see how they'd sound rolling off her tongue.

None of them worked.

She backed up with them, leaving Lash to finish collecting the Talus data she planned to take to IRF. Her last look at her woman was at her back, Lash's head hanging low as she tapped the mouse and waited for the files to transfer.

Her chest a great cavity of burning acid, Melinda knelt and crawled into the tunnel.

Ahead, Jane's flashlight bounced up and down. She crawled so fast, Jack and Melinda lagged behind.

"These old knees aren't the same as hers," Melinda said. She tried on a chuckle, but it fell flat.

"Tell me about it."

She stopped. "Jack."

Stopping, he twisted to look over his shoulder. In the dimming light, his eyes caught hers. In that moment, the first real moment of eye contact he'd shared with her in months, she knew. She knew he'd come to a place of peace, a place she hadn't dreamed he could still find after all she'd done to him.

After she hesitated too long, he knelt before her. "Listen, Melinda. It's important to note forgiveness is for me, not you.

But even so, I forgive you. I know why you did what you did. That doesn't excuse it." His face clouded, the dimming light casting long shadows under his chin. "That doesn't excuse it. But I believe you want to atone. And I want to let you. And I want to say I'm sorry."

She squeaked. "You're sorry? What do you have to be sorry for?"

"Expecting you to be someone you're not anymore. Not giving you a chance to be who you are."

A tear rolled into the corner of her mouth. "You've been talking to our daughter."

Jane crawled closer, the light growing brighter again. "We can talk about all this later, yeah?"

Melinda peeked over Jack's shoulder. "Your daughter is immune because she is, because she was born that way, isn't she? Not because of me."

"Huxley is pretty sure that's the case. But can we talk about this later? I feel like this whole place is waiting to collapse."

"You're right," Melinda said, "let's get out of here."

The light dimmed again, Jack following it. After a bare moment of hesitation, she followed. To her screaming knees, it took hours to reach the end. Yet when she did, she didn't stand to stretch them. Hand on the door, the back of the fake filing cabinet, she stared up at Jack.

Words failed, but she had to have at least a few. Forehead wrinkled, she concentrated on what they should be.

"Tell our children I'm proud of them, Jack."

His eyes clouded, brow knotted. "What?"

"They're better people than us. I love them both so much."

She yanked on the file cabinet door.

"Mellie, wait—"

Slamming it home, she threw the lock she'd noticed last time she crawled through it.

He pounded it with one fist from the other side. "Mellie, don't."

The door muffled his voice, and for that moment, she believed he spoke to her not just through a door, but through time.

She rode out the desire to go with him, and to hug Addy and Mike one more time, like a swelling wave. Closing her eyes and clenching her fists and teeth, she waited for it to break over her and pass.

And when it did, she faced the speck of light at the other end of the tunnel. Loosening her jaw, she dropped to her hands and knees and began back the way she'd come.

CHAPTER 55

The dust from the collapsed ceiling sifted down onto Addy's head, her face covered by her hands. She picked up the knife again, and a cracked tile sliced through the heel of her foot as she took a hesitant step toward the pile of rock and brick.

In the low light, it took more than a moment to make out what was in front of her.

A boulder. Wet with blood, black in this light, part of a head with dark hair under it.

Her heart leapt to her throat, out her head, and slammed back into her chest. It'd never raced so fast as she rounded the boulder to find out whose head she was looking at.

Their features had been crushed beyond recognition.

Her gorge rose, as though her stomach had crawled up past her lungs and sought a way out through her mouth.

Someone coughed a handful of times, sneezed, and sniffled. "Fuck me sideways."

Relief hit her so hard, she dropped to the floor. Her teeth clacked together, tongue caught between them. The taste of blood filled her mouth.

She spat and crawled to him. "Jesus Christ. Are you all right?"

"Yeah," he said, voice weak, "but you don't have to call me Jesus. Matthew will do."

She laughed, setting the knife down next to him and waving the dusty air in front of her face. She tried to clear her vision, but try as she might, it still looked like he was pinned by rock and debris from the waist down.

He ran a hand down her leg. "How's your arm?"

Although forgotten, his mention brought her attention back to the throbbing mess. "Bloody. But slowing. Can you move?"

Blowing through clenched teeth, he pressed the rock trapping him with his hands. "Sure. It's—" He pressed, inhaling and exhaling through his nose. "I can't move my feet, Addy." Laying his head on the ground, he caught her eyes and tried to suppress a wince. A breath whistled through his teeth. "What about Hector?"

She shook her head, trying not to look. "He's dead. I gotta get you out of here."

Rising again, he pushed against the pile of debris. "Here. I'll push. You pull."

Scooting into his shoulders, she hooked her hands under his armpits and threw her back into it.

Nothing. Not so much as an inch.

"OK. That's all right." He laid his head in her lap. "Straighten this leg," he said, gripping the outside of her left thigh, "and push against the rocks. I think it shifted."

She squeezed under him and got as close as she could with her belly in the way.

Tilting his head, he smiled at her abdomen and caressed it with a thumb before reaching around to grip her back. "On three."

Fears working to intrude, looking for a crack in her veneer, she clamped her teeth together and set her foot against the debris.

He counted.

They pushed. Pulled. Struggled.

The pile shifted.

Head snapping back, he shouted through clenched teeth. "Stop! Stop." Chest heaving, his eyes rolled in his head. "That. That stung a little." His fingers tightened, pinning her shirt between them.

Without asking, a whimper escaped her throat. She examined the pile on top of him, looking for a weak spot.

He let her shirt go and reached for her face.

Leaning down to meet him in the middle, she tried to catch his eyes.

They rolled, opening and closing. Sweat glistened on his upper lip. "It's OK. I'm OK. It's—" He squeezed his eyes shut, shifting his torso. "It's all right. It doesn't even." Again, he paused, licking his lips. "It doesn't even hurt."

"Addy," Dean said.

She looked over her shoulder so fast, she wouldn't be able to turn her head that direction again for hours. But the pain didn't hit until later. Adrenaline powered her through.

He limped toward her, leaning on the wall, holding his wounded arm. "Are you OK?"

"I'm fine," she said, turning back to Matt. He'd clamped his eyes shut. "He's trapped. Help me, Dean." She tugged.

Matt moaned, struggling against her. "Stop. Stop." His forehead glistening now too, his hairline shone with sweat. "It's fine." His fingers clenched again, gripping her waist and shirt in equal proportions. "I can go. Go see Ella now. You," he said, releasing her and grabbing his Bowie knife, "you take this and go with Dean. You get out of here. It's fine."

She took the knife because he made her. Stuck it in her hand and wrapped her fingers around it. But the tears obscured his face.

Covering another moan with a smile, he touched her face, fingertips sliding down her cheek like bird feet. "Go with Dean. Get out of here." He pushed at her, one hand landing on the baby.

Who kicked and punched and did somersaults only she could feel.

She backed up, insides empty. Grasping the knife with one hand, she laid his head in the floor with the other. The back of his skull round in the palm of her hand, his hair wet.

Her lungs reported she'd need to take in air again at some point, but all she could do was stare at his chest as he waved her away.

"Houlihan."

The side of her mouth turned up. "Yeah?"

Squeezing his eyes shut, he pushed against the debris. His throat worked. "Tell the. Tell the baby about me."

Before she could think of words to answer him with, he stopped struggling. His head turned to the side, his eyes still closed.

Dean knelt next to her. "Addy. You gotta come with me, sweetie. This place is falling apart."

She turned to him, haft of the knife heavy in her palm and the grip slick with sweat.

His eyes wide in the dark, pupils dilated, Dean tilted his head as if he'd asked her a question.

She put one foot under her to stand. Her stomach turned over.

Breaking eye contact with Dean, she glanced at Ricardo-Hector. His head crushed under a rock. Dead and gone.

She turned back to Dean. "I. He lied to me."

He gripped her shoulder with a bloody hand and frowned. "About what?"

But his question didn't register. She glared at the knife. "He lied to me." Meeting his eyes again, brow creased, she shouted. "It's not fine! He doesn't want to go with Ella. He lied!" She took a shallow breath, top of her head tight. "He's not supposed to lie anymore."

"Sweetie, I don't—"

She chucked the knife at the wall. It clattered to the ground.

Crawling back to Matt's still body, she yanked and pulled at the debris, throwing bricks behind her.

A piece of brick thumped before falling to the ground. "Ouch. You hit me."

"Well then get over here and help me."

"We have to go. This place is coming down around our ears."

"Get over here and help me or get the fuck out. I'm not leaving him here." Surprising herself with the even tone in her voice, she mumbled as she shifted her eyes between the shit covering him and his chest, rising and falling. "He has to apologize for lying, or I'm gonna kill him."

Dean knelt next to her again. "Addy—"

"Help me. Please," she said, removing another piece of brick. She tugged a boulder, what appeared to be the bulk of what trapped him. She'd have to hope it wasn't crushing him to death, or hadn't damaged him so badly he'd fall apart if they pulled him from under this mess.

She'd have to hope.

Pushing her aside, Dean nodded at him. "I'll get this. You pull him when I say."

She crawled to Matt's head and hooked both hands under his armpits.

Dean grunted. "Pull, Addy." Leaning into it, he rolled the boulder up a few inches, and smeared blood all over the side.

As it shifted, she tugged. Bricks and smaller rocks and tile and all manner of debris fell as she tugged, but she kept pulling until Matt's feet cleared the pile.

With a forced groan, Dean set the boulder in the floor and crab-walked to her. He looked Matt over. "I don't know if we should carry him in this state. We might make the crushing wounds worse. Is he breathing?"

Feeling for his pulse, she watched Matt's chest. Although slow, it rose and fell. The heartbeat under her fingers pounded against the pads of her fingertips. "He's alive." She met Dean's eyes. "What option do we have besides carry him?"

He shook his head. Standing, he limped onto his injured leg, checked the bleeding on his arm, and leaned over. "None. Here. Help me get him up." Arms held out, he leaned down. "Matt, if you can hear me, man, think light thoughts."

With a grimace, Addy rounded to Matt's side and shoved her arms under him. Working together, they got him into Dean's arms.

Dean exhaled through clenched teeth. "I hope we're close to the surface."

Addy spun.

She had no idea how to get out.

* * *

"Up here, there should be a left turn," Jack said, pointing.

Jane held the bouncing flashlight. "You all right with Melinda staying back?"

"I haven't had time to think about it. Gut reaction?"

She nodded, rounding the corner.

"No. I wish she'd come with us."

"I thought you might—" She stopped, one foot suspended in the air. "Shit."

He glanced up from the map, where he'd been trying to work out where to go after this hall. They had to be closing in on the surface.

But ahead of them, a wall of debris. Rock, brick, broken tile. And.

He pointed. "Is that a body?"

Cursing, Jane crept toward the body. She shone the light down. "Yeah. Don't think I know them. Though who can tell. Their face is pretty well crushed."

A dry heave tried to visit Jack's throat. He swallowed it down and turned back to the map. "All right. We can go"—he spun the map and pointed—"this way. I think."

Jane set off in the direction he pointed, grabbing his hand and pulling him with her. "Let's go. I don't know how much longer this place is going to stay standing."

As if to prove her right, the floor vibrated. A brick fell from the ceiling and hit him in the shoulder.

"Hell," he said, pain flashing where a small spot of blood spread. "That hurt a bit. Here, let's try to turn left up here." He pointed up the hall.

She interlaced her fingers in his and walked faster. "Not gonna lie. My energy is waning."

"I shouldn't have let you come."

She scoffed, cutting her eyes at him and turning down the next hallway. "That's f..." She trailed off, feet slowing, eyes wide.

"What?"

Shushing him, she closed her eyes and dropped his hand. She turned a circle. "Do you hear a radio?"

He slapped his hand to his belt.

No radio.

Ilasha had taken it once they left the room where she'd murdered Morgan. Had clipped it to her own belt and had been wearing it last time he saw her.

He closed his eyes and Listened as Mellie had taught Addy all those years ago.

Voices crackled over a radio. Bursts of static filled the in-between. He strained to hear what the radio voices said, until a clear voice, this side of the radio, echoed down the hall.

"I don't know, Dean. I think we're lost again. I can't get Mike to stay with me. Must be bad up there."

As Dean murmured something in his deep tenor, Jack's head floated. As though someone had filled it with helium. To hear her voice was almost enough. Without waiting for Jane, he took off toward their voices.

"Addy," Jane called, "stay where you are. We're coming to you."

Her voice floated down the hall. "Oh thank god."

Putting on a burst of speed, the need to see her tightening every muscle in his body, Jack hurried around a corner.

Leaned against a wall, Dean panted. Drenched in sweat, his shirt stuck to him. Blood covered his leg and arms, and he held a limp Matt in a cradle hold.

Addy stood next to him, one hand resting on her belly, the other holding a radio to her mouth. Her lips split into a wide, sunny grin as Jack approached. "You look better than I expected, considering these two." She gestured at Dean and Matt.

Enough emotion raced through him to roil through his stomach like a curling pipeline wave. Jack swept his eldest daughter into a tight hug. "Thank god you're all right." He pushed her back and brushed hair from her face. "You are all right?"

Her eyes slipped sideways. "Dean needs help with Matt." Radio clipped to her belt, she approached Jane.

"You're limping, girl. You all right?"

"Cut my foot. For the record, appropriate footwear is a must for collapsing secret bases."

Chuckling, Jane hooked her arm in Addy's and glanced over her shoulder at Jack. "We ready? Hand me the map, love."

Handing it off to her, he switched Dean for Matt's torso. Matt's pasty pale face was covered in sweat, blood, and dirt. "Dean, is he all right?"

Dean shrugged, lifting Matt's legs and pinning his ankles together with his good arm. "He was under a wall when it fell. He's still alive. That's about the best I can tell you."

As Jane led them through unsteady hallways where the ceiling threatened them in each moment, the lights few and far between now, he considered his feelings on the dying boy in his arms.

He'd questioned his motives time and time again. But now, the truth of the matter was, he was practically his son. A part of the family for the rest of his life. Children linked you to people, bonding them to you forever.

Emerging into the busy night, the breath of fresh air he'd been waiting for stifled by gunpowder and smoke, he felt the tug of the string connecting him to Melinda. He may have tried to deny it, but it was there, and it would never be cut.

"Michael, say again," Addy said, speaking to the radio.

"*Get away from the hill. Anoth*—" The radio cut out.

The night before them lit up, a sound Jack hadn't heard in decades filling the air.

Airplane engines.

"The aerial unit," Jack shouted. "Go! Get away from the hill."

Covering their heads, Jane and Addy ran toward the fence.

Struggling with Matt, Dean and Jack followed. Jack fought to maintain his footing, knowing Dean must have been having twice the issue. And if Matt had internal injuries, they were surely only making them worse running over the uneven ground like this.

"Adelaide!"

She stopped. "Yeah, Dad?"

"Get Mike on the radio. Get him to bring a stretcher. We need to stabilize Matt." He lowered him to the ground with ginger care and stretched his tired arms.

Addy repeated Jack's request into the radio. After holding it to her ear, she tugged him on the shoulder. "He says meet him at the gate. We gotta hurry, there's—"

The bomber dropped its shells.

As the world went white, he covered Addy with his body and cradled her.

The rumbling subsiding, he opened his eyes.

The Molehill noticeably slumped in spots. It wouldn't take many more shots like that. Maybe there was still time to get back down there and bring Melinda out. And arrest the woman in charge of all this.

"He says we have to hurry. All this has called every 'Head for a fifty-mile radius." She shook his shoulder again.

"Right. Right. Let's get out of here." Picking up Matt again, he and Dean hefted him toward the fence as the bomber made another circle in the sky.

"Dad, over here," Mike called.

Jane pointed the light, picking out a disheveled but whole Mike. Celia beside him, eyes everywhere at once. Two men stood next to them, stretcher in hand.

Mike waved them over. "Thank god you're all OK." He hugged Addy. "Mom?"

"I don't know. Dad?"

He shook his head, laying Matt on the stretcher. "She's still in there."

"Jesus." He looked around the field. "Morgan?"

Jack shook his head, eyes cast to the side.

"Here," Mike said, handing him the radio, "tell them to stop shelling."

The question 'why me' on the edge of his lips, Jack stopped. He knew why him. He was in charge here. He took the radio. "All units, stand down aerial attack. By order of Jackson Cooke, Queen City Defense Force Leader."

Someone said, "*10-4*," and someone said, "*Roger*," but the bomber kept coming. And the shells it had already dropped kept falling.

And then came the 'Heads.

CHAPTER 56

Crawling away from the sound of Jack still trying to get the door open, Melinda sniffed. Dirt zipped up her nose. She sneezed.

Ilasha's ethereal voice floated down the tunnel. "I hear you in there, woman. Comin' back to kill me?"

She stopped, closing her eyes against the dark. "Just want to talk to you, Lash. Is that all right?"

Silence from the other end.

Taking that as agreement, she lifted herself to her complaining knees, the floor impossibly hard under them, and crawled back to the computer room. By the time she emerged, her shoulders had joined the complaint line.

She cleared her throat.

Lash's back to her, gun on the desk, she pulled a chair closer. "Come. Sit. Ask me."

Melinda straightened her hair and shirt, adjusted the radio on her belt, and tiptoed across the room.

Lash exhaled through her nose. "I could just send these files to Daddy's computers."

Melinda took the seat next to her, crossed her knees over each other, and wrapped her hanging foot behind her calf. Arms crossed, she hunched over her stomach. "Why didn't you ever tell me about him?"

"It would have brought up more questions. About where he was and what he was doing."

Tightening her crossed legs, she leaned forward. "And what was he doing? What is all this, about him starting both Talus Crest and Iridium Flare?"

"Relax. I'm not going to hurt you. I—"

"You love me. Yeah. Sure."

Blowing air out her nose, Lash tapped one nail against the space bar in front of her. "I might not have been entirely truthful, but about that, I never lied." She faced her. "I never lied about loving you. I did. I do."

Backing up an inch, Melinda frowned. "Tell me about the companies."

Dirt sifted from the ceiling, and the lights flickered. Lash's breath caught in her throat, and her eyes snapped back to the screen. She watched the file transfer continue in its little dialogue box.

Blowing out through pursed lips, she leaned back in the chair. It squeaked and squalled. "He had a lot of money, my daddy. I didn't want for nothing as a kid. He always wanted me to take over his business."

"And that was?"

"Certain government contracts that don't matter anymore. He got the patents on a few things and went into business with whoever he chose." Smiling, she turned the chair. "When I was a teen, we used to visit the place my men found your Jack. Did you know, I probably walked in the same places they did."

Before her, Melinda envisioned a wall. Cracks formed, and a brick fell. "Your men?"

"Sure. Not that they knew that. Tim, for one." She chuckled, finger crossing her lip. "I got him thinking IRF needed him, and in the end, he was so confused I don't even think he knew who he was giving a report to."

Melinda's brow drew down. "You. You."

"I broke your toy. Yeah. It was for you." She laid a hand on Melinda's knee. "It was all for you. I didn't want to break your heart, but I needed you working on the vaccine. And." Eyes averted, she stopped and sighed. "I was scared of us. So I sent you away."

Uncrossing her arms and legs, Melinda brushed her hand away and stood. "Scared. So you sent me away. Then you broke Tim, brought me my family, and what? Now you're sorry?"

Spinning back to the computer, Lash shrugged. "Daddy started both companies. He said if they thought they were enemies, they'd fight each other, rather than try to take power from where it truly was. In the middle. They'd leave him alone to create the Cure and get this country on its feet again." She smiled and glanced at Melinda. "And he did. Now we've got roads again, and power, phones, computers, and best of all, a Cure *and* a vaccine. He and I, and these companies, we did all that."

Knees wobbling, Melinda leaned against the far desk. It cut into her thighs and helped center her. "If there was only one, everyone would focus on the one. On the concentrated power. But if there were two…"

"They'd only ever fight each other. And since they were actually fighting themselves—"

"It was a distraction. IRF was a distraction."

"Don't get me wrong," Lash said, smiling again, "they've been a good distraction. Turns out their military unit is the tits. Thanks to Burke. And their technology unit has really grown. Soon, their science unit will experience a boon. McNamara got our defection all set up." Petting the external hard drive, she tapped the mouse. "There we go. All done." She grimaced at the screen. "You gonna come with me now? I'll put you back on immunity. We'll need more samples, but it's not like your family goes far these days."

Melinda gagged and choked, words sticking to her throat. After all she'd been through, it'd been Lash keeping her away from immunity. And for what? She shook her head. "You're just going to carry on with IRF? Like none of this ever happened?" Gesturing broadly at the room, she lifted her hands and shoulders and glared at the ceiling.

"Honey, it's why my daddy set it up this way. Someone's got to be responsible for all these people, all this Cure. And once we get settled with IRF, I'll get another company started. Already got everything in place, just need to bring it all together. If they don't take this place completely apart," she said, glancing at the ceiling herself, "we can come back."

"It's all the same thing," Melinda muttered, sitting on the desk. "All this sneaking around, and there's not even anything to uncover. You knew it all. All along."

Lash nodded, picking up the hard drive. "So?" She held out her hand.

In a trance, Melinda crossed the room and took it. "You made everything so damn complicated."

Cackling, voice rising an octave, Lash nodded again. "Watching some of these people scramble the way they did was so much fun. They hardly knew their asses from a hole in the ground. Keeping up with my false flags and knotted strings was more than they could handle."

An iron fist socked Melinda in the gut. "You." She ripped her hand free. "You made up that report. Why?"

"Which report?"

"The one about my brain. You lied. You made it up. Signed Anthony's name to fake documents. I found the real one in your room."

Fire spat from Lash's eyes. "You snooped in my room?"

"Why? Why did you make it up?"

"You were the only one who could have figured me out, Em. I needed to keep you off-balance. For what it's worth"—she grabbed her hand and kissed her fingers—"I'm sorry."

Melinda's eyes stung. After everything, all the things she'd done for the vaccine and the Cure and the company, the one person who'd stuck by her was the one who'd been between her and the answers all along.

Again, she ripped her hand free. Pointing a finger at Lash, she backed up. "Y-you gaslighted me. You made me think I was crazy. Told me my family was...you tried to keep me from them!"

The radio on Ilasha's belt crackled. "*Michael,*" Addy said. Her voice shook. "*Mike, Dean and I are lost down here. Walk us through the way out.*"

"*10-4, Addy. Who else is with you?*"

"*Just Matt. But,*" she said, voice wavering again, "*he's hurt pretty bad.*"

Lash turned the volume knob down. Melinda's children continued to speak, their voices issuing from the radio no louder than a whisper. "Look at me, Em. Listen to me. They try to hold you back. Ever since they came back into your life, they haven't seen you for who you are." Her eyes shone. "They don't deserve you. I couldn't let you listen to their bullshit."

Addy's words ran over Melinda with the force of a truck. *"I've wanted you to be who you were. But that's not who you are. And I have to accept you, I do accept you, for who you are."*

She lifted her eyes to meet Lash's. "You're wrong. I'm the one who doesn't deserve them."

Mouth hardening into a scowl, Lash's eyes flicked to the gun she'd left on the desk. "I'm sorry you feel that way, General. We did great work together, creating a vaccine," she said, her foot sliding left, "tracking down immunity. And our successes with the Cure have been unparalleled." Her feet slid closer still to the desk. "Your contributions will not be forgotten, and I regret you will be making none further."

As she lunged the last two feet for the gun, Melinda leapt. She chopped at her wrist in an attempt to knock the gun from her hand.

Lash was quicker and hip-checked Melinda, shoving her away and taking aim. "I'm sorry."

Eyes on Lash's trigger finger, Melinda threw herself to the side before Lash made the final half-inch of pull. She rolled, and the bullet went wild. She slipped a hand down to her ankle and freed the knife tucked in there. The one that'd impaled her in the lung.

But as she unsheathed it, Lash took aim and fired again.

This shot didn't go wild, and Melinda's side screamed. The pain wasn't as sharp as she'd imagined. It felt like she'd been hit by a bag full of bricks. And it was warm. Like the orange coils from inside a space heater pressed into her skin.

A deep-throated shout clawed its way out of her mouth, and as the ground shook under her, she wobbled to her feet. One hand pressed into her side, she lunged for Ilasha.

Lash fired again, and the heat spread through Melinda's shoulder.

Either Lash was a terrible marksman, or she wasn't actually trying to kill her.

But she couldn't take the chance it wasn't the first one.

Jumping, she grabbed Lash's right shoulder with a bloody hand and shoved the knife under her breastbone and through her diaphragm, into her heart.

Ilasha gasped, eyes wide, mouth falling open. The gun thumped to the dirt.

As she fell, Melinda released the knife and held her, lowering her to the ground. Her face doubled and then trebled.

Her lips moved, but she bled out so fast, no sound escaped.

Wiping her eyes with her elbow, Melinda sat back and stared around the dirt room.

The computer Lash had been using was still unlocked, its screen shining bright with the Talus Crest logo in the background. An eagle holding a flaming torch in its mouth. Standing on top of a mountain.

Rocking, holding her bleeding side, she realized it always made her think of Prometheus.

The ground beneath her shifted again, dirt falling from the ceiling.

The radio on Lash's belt crackled, Melinda's children trying to help each other through the dark. She unclipped it, with the intention of guiding Addy the rest of the way out of the Molehill. As she did, her eyes fell on the hard drive, still clutched in Lash's fingers.

Snatching it, she stood.

Black spots danced in front of her eyes. Her head spun, and the floor spun with it.

Holding the hand with the radio to her side, she put her head between her knees and took three deep breaths. "OK, Melinda. Take it easy. You're bleeding." She stepped over Lash and fell to her knees, crawling to the tunnel. As she dragged herself inside, leaving the cold, earthen computer room behind her, dust sifted down from the ceiling again.

Without any more warning, it collapsed in front of her, stones threatening to bury her in the tunnel.

Catching her breath with a mouthful of dirt, she backed up as quickly as her wounded shoulder would allow. Falling backward into the room, she curled into a ball as she had when she and Jane had almost been crushed, waiting for the world to end.

Once the rocks stopped falling, she glanced up.

The tunnel was filled in. There was no way out.

A sob creeping up her throat, Melinda looked at her hands.

In one, the radio. The hard drive in the other.

Addy had stopped calling for directions. Hopefully, she'd found her way out. With Matt.

Without stopping to think about how screwed she was, Melinda crawled back to the computers and inserted the hard drive once again. Calling up the share drive, she began the transfer of files. Once it started, she dropped to her knees and crawled back to Lash. Her shoulder tried to give out, so she used that hand to hold the radio. Hopping on the other hand, side screaming, she made it back to her woman. Lying woman though she was, it's not like Melinda had been all that clean.

With a frown, she yanked the knife from Lash's heart and used it to slice off a piece of her own shirt. Folding it, she considered jabbing the knife into Lash's temple and ending it. But the deeper the thought burrowed, the higher she built the wall in her heart. In the end, for all the hard things she'd done, she couldn't do this last one.

So she folded the cloth over Lash's eyes and tied it. At least Lash wouldn't have to see her. At least, when the end came, the last thing she'd see wouldn't be Melinda's bloody and bruised face.

Blindfold secure, she crawled to the computer as the room physically rocked. It wouldn't be long now.

The line for the file transfer moved steadily up. Every single file they had here, every file from Magnolia, every file she'd sent here from Shanti Station, they all zipped across phone lines and through the air to satellites and back down.

Jack spoke on the radio. "*All units, stand down aerial attack. By order of Jackson Cooke, Queen City Defense Force Leader.*"

Again, the uninvited tears fell from her eyes. "I'm glad it's you out there with them," she whispered. She pushed the radio button. "Jack."

He didn't answer.

"Jack."

The radio blipped. *"Melinda? Where are you? We—"* He cut out.

The ceiling rattled, and more rocks fell. Into the room now.

"Are you all right? Jack?"

"Some 'Heads joined the party. And your men are giving us some trouble."

"10-4."

One more thing.

She unclipped the other radio from her belt. "All units, all men. This is General Thibodeaux. Lay down your arms and surrender to the QC. They will protect you. This fight is over."

As affirmative responses came in from her army, a rattling breath sounded behind her. A foot scraped across the ground.

"Jack. They're surrendering."

"Thanks, Mellie. Now get your ass out here too."

The breathing increased, and Lash bumped into a wall. No doubt the smell of *food* came from everywhere, and without her eyes, she was having a hard time finding it.

The transfer bar full, it disappeared from the screen.

Melinda pushed the radio button again. "Jack, listen. If you want my research, all of Talus's records, and everything from IRF, go back to Emerald Isle. It should be there. I've transferred it all there. If you want it."

"Fine, just get out here. I don't think they're going to stop shelling."

"Tell our kids I love them."

And he shouted into the radio, and cursed, and pled. But she turned the volume down on both radios and dropped them to the desk.

"Lash," she said.

The 'Head stopped and turned toward her voice. Shuffled over.

Catching her outstretched hands, Melinda fought the strong dead woman. Even with her screaming shoulder and bleeding side, she twisted both arms behind her back and forced her to the ground.

Lash pushed with her legs, and Melinda fell, cracking her back on the desk. She crashed to the floor, Lash landing on top of her.

Melinda wrapped her in a hug and linked her fingers together. "Ssshh. Be quiet now. Soon, we'll go look at the stars together. We'll go see them together."

CHAPTER 57

Addy looked at her empty hands. "You got an extra knife, Jane?"

She slipped two from her belt and handed both to her. "Happened to yours?"

Addy watched Matt as Dad and Dean laid him on the stretcher. "Such a long story."

"Looking forward to it." Slipping the needles from her hair, she settled one into each hand. She pointed over Addy's shoulder with one. "Eight o'clock."

Leading with the knife, Addy spun. Inexperienced with such small knives, she still made the best of it when the 'Head reached for her with its grasping claws and jabbed it in the ear. She ripped the knife free as it fell. Backing up to Jane, Dean limping over to make a silent third, she glanced to her dad and brother again.

Mike covered Jack as Jack spoke to the radio. An airplane approached, engines howling, and drowned out his words.

Jabbing another 'Head in the face, she spoke over her shoulder. "I thought he told them to stop shelling."

"Evidently they didn't get the message," Jane panted. "We should get beyond this fence. Try to find the trucks and get the hell out of here." The rotten pumpkin of a Dead Head thunked as she buried one of her needles.

Scanning the dark forest beyond the fence, Addy couldn't catch sight of Matt on the stretcher. She hoped the guys who had him had gotten him onto a truck and headed back to the QC.

The small arms fire that had been a constant background symphony since they'd emerged from the Molehill petered off to nothing.

In the empty air, the rattling cicada buzz of the dead rushed in to fill the silence.

And a voice on the radio. *"...go back to Emerald Isle. It should be there. I've transferred it all there. If you want it."*

Holding her arm over her belly, both knives in one hand, she grabbed a handful of Jane's shirt and pulled her closer to Dad. "Mom?"

"Addy, duck," Dean said, aiming over her shoulder.

She did, eyes fixed to her dad.

He whacked a 'Head with his machete, shouting into the radio. "Fine, just get out here."

Mike swung over Dad's head, knocking a 'Head off course before it got to them. Another came from the side and sank its teeth into his arm before he had the chance to spin.

"Michael!" Letting Jane's shirt go, she sprinted closer. Mom's voice came from the radio one more time.

"Tell our kids I love them."

Dad pressed the button and shouted Mom's name into the radio.

While desire pulled Addy to the radio to shout with him, to beg Mom to try to make it out, her mind knew Mom had accepted her fate. And that it was right to let her go down her own path.

Instead, she rushed to Mike and Celia, wrestling the 'Head off him and burying a knife in each eye.

Dean dropped two 'Heads as they flanked them, one falling sideways and knocking the other over like dominoes.

Mike fell to the ground. He gripped Dad's pants leg. "Dad, no, get her out of there."

Knocking another 'Head off course with the flat of his machete, Dad shook his head. "She's made her choice, Mike. We've got to go."

As if on cue, a truck rumbled up beside them. Men in the back shouted, lowering the tailgate and holding out hands.

Dad backed into Addy. "Adelaide, get on the truck."

Jane and Celia flanked Mike and helped him up.

Dean pushed Addy, gun aimed into the dark. "Let's go."

Celia ducked under Mike and wrapped both arms around his waist. "Get on the truck, pretty boy."

He limped and wobbled, reaching out for Jack's shoulder. "Dad, let's go."

Addy, eyes fixed to them all, backed toward the truck. The fight had gone out of her, and all she wanted to do was crawl into the truck and sleep for days.

A bone-crunching, grinding rumbling began beneath them all.

More shells fell from the sky.

Narrowing her eyes, Addy tracked them from the sky to the ground, where they exploded in a scream of white so bright her pupils contracted to almost nothing.

The Molehill slumped, fell in on itself, and sent a great plume of dust twenty feet into the air.

The shockwave rippled her hair.

"Get in the goddamn truck, Adelaide," Dad shouted, pushing against Mike's back with his own. He swiped at 'Heads as they went, holding back the mini-horde pressing in, trying to overtake them.

Dean jumped in the truck and stuck out a hand.

Fighting a dry heave, the stench of 'Heads and exhaust settling into the back of her throat, she grabbed Dean's hand and hoisted herself into the truck.

Three other guys grabbed Mike from inside, pulling him into the back. His side drenched in blood.

Heart meeting the stench in her throat, she swallowed another dry heave. "Mike, do you have a dose on you?"

He held out a hand to Celia as she joined them. "In my pouch, bean."

Jane's head popped over the tailgate.

"Jack, let's go," she said over her shoulder.

"Get up there, Jane," he answered, out of sight.

The truck rolled.

"Jack, now!"

The next few moments unspooled in Addy's mind.

Dad kept fighting, ensuring their escape.

Jane leapt from the truck, joining him and fighting the approaching horde.

The truck drove away, leaving them alone in the dark to fight too many 'Heads.

In the morning, Addy would be left with three less family members. Her mom, Dad, and Jane, all gone in one fell swoop.

She jumped over Mike, grabbing Jane's arm before she jumped down. "Dad! Get on this fucking truck or so help me I'll come down there myself!"

Half a dozen 'Heads reached for him.

The truck picked up speed.

Jane fought Addy's hand, leaning as far as she could, her other arm outstretched.

One of the 'Heads caught Dad's shoulder and he faltered, meeting Addy's eyes.

Addy narrowed her own, stretching out her other hand.

Mouth set in a firm line, he dropped his machete, took two leaping steps, and jumped.

One hand landed on Addy's forearm and gripped. The other went almost to Jane's shoulder. One of his feet hit the bumper.

Addy all but pulled Dad's arm off as he came up. He cleared the lip of the truck, and her hands slipped, sending her sprawling backward.

Dean caught her and kept her from smacking her head into the cold metal floor. "I gotcha, sweetie."

The truck bumped down the road, thumping as it knocked 'Heads out of the way with its front bumper. Dad tugged Jane the rest of the way onto the truck, lifting her midsection over the lip rather than scrape her over the hard metal corner.

Addy's ears rang. The loud engine drowned out whatever it was Dad and Jane said to each other, but he wrapped one arm around her and the other covered her abdomen. They pressed their foreheads together, eyes closed.

Arms around her own belly, she smiled. It looked like she was going to be a sister again.

CHAPTER 58

The balding doctor flipped a paper over the top of the clipboard in his hand. "Now that we've dressed your wounds, I'd like to get you an ultrasound as soon as we can, Miss Cooke."

Addy swung her legs over the side of the bed and rested one hand on the baby. "Why?"

Staring out the window, the night still holding tight to the sky, she forgot to listen to his explanation. Something about "routine checkup" or something. She wiggled the toes that hadn't been wrapped in a bandage.

He touched her knee. "You've both been through a traumatic week, from what you've said. We just want to verify your health and the health of the baby. Nothing invasive."

Black night threatened to come through the window and grip her heart. She grimaced. The thought of promising bodily harm should he prove a liar flitted through her mind, but when the baby somersaulted, she let it flow through. With an absent nod, she hopped off the bed.

He smiled warmly. "Please schedule an appointment with my nurse. Here," he said, holding out a folded paper, "directions to my office. See you next week." Adjusting the gold-rimmed glasses resting on the end of his nose, he spun on a heel.

"Doc?"

He stopped and turned back to her, eyebrows raised.

"Do you know where they've taken the wounded?"

"Busy night. Most of them are still down in triage. The most seriously wounded are already in surgery, from what I understand. I've been taking care of the less serious injuries." Chuckling, he pointed at her. "Although my specialty is babies, I know a thing or two about anatomy and wound care. It's an all-hands-on-deck kind of night."

She wandered out into the hall. "I imagine. Thanks, doc."

"My pleasure." He clapped her on the shoulder and brushed past her. "Get some rest."

Now, where was triage?

She inspected the closest sign. It only told her about this floor.

Well, he said "down in," so it's probably downstairs somewhere.

Setting off for the stairs, she fixed her eye to the green tile disappearing beneath her feet. So clean. Bright. Unlike the Molehill. That place had been clean, but all the dirt had—

"Addy, wait up."

She stopped, crossing her arms under her breasts and shifting from foot to foot.

Dean stopped next to her. "Where you headed?"

"Trying to find triage. Any idea where it is?"

He lifted his bandaged left arm in a sling, one eye crinkling. "Just left. I'll walk you down."

She gave him her arm, and he led her through a maze of hallways until they found the stairs.

The lights and floor gleamed, as they had in Magnolia. This hospital reminded her of that one, and for a moment, Dean shimmered and became Ella, bopping down the stairs in front of her.

She sniffed. "Are you all right? How's your leg?"

He took the stairs one at a time. "It'll heal. Poor thing hates me. I'm surprised it didn't jump ship, to be honest."

Chuckling, she joined him on the same step and took it one at a time as he did, left hand gripping the rail. "First your artery, then your ankle, then you went and got it shot. Yeah, I'd say it's not your biggest fan."

"I'll try to be good to it from now on."

"Speaking of now on," she said, pausing on a stair, "what do you plan to do?"

He hopped down to the next stair and stopped. His head level with hers, he didn't look up. "A lot of that depends on you, I guess."

Her heart thumped against her ribs so hard she could hear it. Gripping the cold metal railing tighter, she rested the fingertips of her other hand on his shoulder.

He turned slowly. His eyes flitted about her face. Brow knitted, he swallowed, and with a tinge of regret, he echoed some of the first words he ever said to her. "It's my fault." He swallowed again, Adam's apple bobbing. "I missed my chance, didn't I?"

Without words to express how sorry she was, all she could do was nod.

He picked up her hand and kissed the inside of her palm. "I'm sorry."

Cupping his cheek, the stubble there rough under her fingers, she sighed. "I know, Dean. Me too. Me too."

"There'll always be a room in my heart for you, if you ever want to take up residence again."

A warm tear traveled down her cheek. She cleared her throat. "I'll never stop caring about you. I hope you know that."

Letting her hand go, he broke eye contact. "I do. Let's get you downstairs."

* * *

On a wheeled stretcher in the hallway of the ER, Jack sat with his arm around Jane as a nurse bandaged Mike's arm.

"Sorry you had to wait so long, guys," she said, glancing over her shoulder.

Sitting next to him on the stretcher, Celia scowled. "Better late than never, I guess." She glared at Mike, heavy lids purple with exhaustion. "At least we already got the Cure in him. Thank god it worked."

He put his uninjured arm around her. "Of course it worked."

Eyes covered with her dirty, bloody fingers, she leaned into his shoulder.

Hugging her close, he stared across the hall and met Jack's eyes. With incredible calm, he smiled. His eyes flicked to Jane.

She leaned, sliding her hand inside Jack's knee. "You all right?"

"I'll let you know after I get some sleep. It's been a hell of a night."

"Thought we were going to fight to our deaths for a minute there."

He wrapped an arm around her waist. "Me too."

"She saved us. I almost jumped off that truck. Her grip was like iron. If she hadn't held me, we'd be dead in the road right now."

Hugging her closer, he shook his head against the side of her head. "Maybe not."

"Probably."

"Probably. She saved us all tonight."

Jane chuckled, hugging his knee. "She's gonna make a hell of a mom."

He laughed, sitting up. Whatever it was on the end of his tongue, a comment about how he still had a hard time accepting that, or to ask her about their own growing child, sat forgotten in his mouth when Addy and Dean walked around the corner at the end of the hall.

He limped along, uninjured arm hooked through Addy's. Her other hand resting on her growing belly, she wobbled on bandaged feet that were otherwise bare.

Jack frowned. Did she just go through all that barefoot?

He slid off the stretcher as they approached. "You guys look not so much worse for wear. Everything basically OK?"

Addy nodded, releasing Dean and hugging Jack. She drew in breath as though she wanted to speak, but instead, she buried her face in his shoulder and hugged tighter.

He closed his eyes and hugged her back. There were a million words he could put here, but none of them would do as good of a job as a simple hug. So he put everything he had into it, surrounding them both in a moment of white light. He let the hospital fall away. The lights, the smells, the moaning of the wounded faded into the background.

Finally, she released him.

Mike jumped off the stretcher, the nurse chuffing, and dragged a long strand of gauze wrap behind him as he smothered her in a hug.

After she let him go and hugged Jane and Celia, she turned back to Jack, eyes wide. The eyes she'd gotten from Melinda. "What did Mom say?"

His guts wanted to crawl away and hide, his tongue stuck to the roof of his mouth, and a tear fell from his eye. Leading her to the stretcher, he sat with her and relayed his experience in the Molehill, starting with meeting up with Morgan. He told her about IRF and Talus, and everything Lash told him in that room.

Addy supplied the few details Anthony filled in before his gruesome death. Her voice thick, she told him about Victoria. About Hector. About Matt.

And he told her the last things Melinda said through the radio.

Once the nurse finished with Mike, he joined them on the same stretcher. Jack looked between them both. "The last thing she said to me was to tell you guys she loved you."

Mouth drawn into a thin line, Addy nodded. Emotions rippled across her face, and her eyelids drooped.

Jack steeled himself for questions and tried to pull answers down from the ether. He'd tried to save her, again, and had failed. Again.

"How's Matt? Do you know where he is?"

Blindsided, Jack's mouth flopped open. Had no one told her?

Her eyes searched his face. She gripped his arm hard enough to cut off circulation.

Jane had been right about that iron grip.

"What? What's wrong? Is he. Where is he?"

He brushed hair from her forehead. "He's in surgery. They don't know." He stopped, eyes on Jane's.

She took Addy's other hand, avoiding the bandage on her forearm. "They say it's fifty-fifty. Maybe sixty-forty."

"Where can I. What, um." She stopped, throat working.

Dean limped off, stopping at the nurse's station.

As Jack watched him lean over the desk, his posture throwing Jack back to the evacuation of that hospital full of babies and death, he knew. He knew what Addy had chosen, and for once he asked the god he didn't believe in to give something back to her. To be kind to her when all evidence proved otherwise.

Limping back, accompanied by a nurse, Dean stuck a hand out to her. "Come on, Addy. I'll take you where you can wait for him."

* * *

Knees drawn as close as she could get them, Addy lay on her side in the dark hospital room and fought sleep. Dean and the nurse left her here in the empty bed and turned out the lights, saying when Matt was out of surgery the orderlies would bring him here.

Fading in and out of sleep, she tried to picture what would happen if he didn't want to be with her anymore. He could have easily come to that conclusion while he was gone. Look what Dean had done.

And besides that, had she come to a conclusion about him? She'd made up her mind about Dean. That ship had sailed. It'd been clear from the first date, really, when he'd come to the QC. As much as she missed him, and as much pain as she'd still been in over it, she'd already put her back to him. It'd likely still ache from time to time, even now, but life moved on.

But whenever she wanted to grab the thoughts about Matt, they squirted away. Grew fuzzy. She left the knife for him, and he took it, but they'd passed no words.

The baby punched her. Or kicked. Kneed. Elbowed. Whatever. She tumbled and rolled in there.

"What am I going to name you?" she whispered, head under the thin sheet she'd pulled up from the foot of the bed, breath making a warm circle from mouth to belly and back.

The lights flipped on. "For what it's worth, dear woman, I'd take any name you gave me."

She bolted up, squinting.

The Troupe, what was left of them, piled into the room. They filled it from edge to edge, leaving no room for strangers and ghosts.

Her mouth lifted in an unbidden smile as Cassius limped on his crutches, ill-fitting prosthetic leg thumping. He sat next to her on the bed.

Rivers handed her a bouquet of flowers, bouncing on her toes.

Grey and Tal spun about the room, and each presented her with a single rose as they did.

She took them one at a time and smiled wider as they spun away, cheeks hurting.

Jim leaned in the doorway, watching them all from behind those shades of his. He laughed and removed a sucker from his mouth. "They tell me I shouldn't smoke here. Your brother hooked me up with this sucker. How are you, Addy?"

The smile fading, she leaned on Cassius's shoulder. He put an arm around her. "I've been better. Nice to see all of you though."

"You are some of the first good news we've had in this horrid place," Cassius said. "We have been told our dears Kendra and Victoria will not be returning from the debacle under the hill." He sighed. "Our Kendra could not stand the terrors of captivity, so we understand."

"And that our fine gentleman is still in surgery. So says your father," Grey said. His shaggy black hair bounced as he stopped in front of her, arms crossed. "How long have you been here, alone?"

Shrugging, she closed her eyes. Throat thick, she pushed through her quivering chin in order to speak. They deserved to know. "Did they tell you what happened with Vic?"

Cassius wiped a tear as it coursed down her cheek. "Only that she was a casualty of this horrible war."

Addy sat up. Wiping the other cheek, she caught Jim's eyes.

He took his glasses off and pointed to the two chairs in the room. "Guys. Have a seat."

Grey and Tal stopped spinning and sat. For once, not touching everything they saw.

Rivers pulled up a piece of floor at Addy's feet and gazed up at her, white teeth peeking from between her lips.

Chin trembling again, Addy crushed the flowers to her chest and gulped down tears. "She was. She was a casualty of this fighting. When it came down to it, I couldn't." She stopped, lump in her throat stopping her from going on.

Best to rip it like a Band-Aid, Addy.

She went on. "I couldn't let her kill my mom. I defended her, my mom."

Rivers closed her eyes. Crossing her arms, she rocked.

Grey and Tal fell silent, holding hands.

Cassius wiped her cheek again. "Do you know, when she left us, she said goodbye. Our Victoria left, and even if she had returned in body, she had already gone in spirit."

Nodding, tears blinding her, Addy sucked on her bottom lip. Knowing Vic expected to die didn't help her killer feel release. "I was bound to her," she whispered, meeting Cassius's deep brown eyes.

His expressive eyebrows dipped. "That you were. And she to you." Crushing her in a hug, his deep voice booming in her ear, he half laughed. "And I am grateful, for one, that it was you. How terrible if she had been taken by someone who hated her. Or worse," he said, pushing Addy back, "someone utterly indifferent. No. I am glad, if she had to die by someone's hand, it was the hand of someone she loved and who loved her in return."

Unable to block the sob creeping up her throat, Addy let Cassius hug her close. She breathed deep, and sleep began to take over again. Impossible to think she'd murdered one of her best friends, and here she was, almost asleep.

She jerked to sitting. "I wish we could—"

Voices approached the room, and wheels squealed against the tile. The end of a bed appeared in the door. Then, two motionless feet under a blanket.

The room spun. Although her wide eyes couldn't look away, she willed them to with everything she had. What if the blanket kept going? What if it covered his face?

She expected a steel grip, but when Cassius grabbed her hand and enclosed it in warmth, it was like being hugged by a soft bunny. "Look there, dear woman," he said, leaning over, "how his hand twitches."

And sure enough, one of Matt's hands lay outside the sheet. A flashing red light taped to his index finger, tubes full of clear liquid strapped to his forearm, his fingers moved as the stretcher wheeled farther into the room.

The orderlies stopped halfway, discussing the turn into the room.

When they resumed, wheels squealing against the floor again and the smell of antiseptic crawling up Addy's nose, the rest of the bed came into view.

He lay asleep, eyes moving in a rapid back and forth under his lids. Dreaming. And breathing on his own. No tube shoved down his throat like they'd done to Jane in Magnolia.

Addy laid the flowers down. "Excuse me."

The orderly at the head of the bed backed Matt into place and flipped a switch on the wall. "Yes?"

"How is he?"

A doctor in scrubs—how many doctors did this city have?—charged into the room and snagged the clipboard from the end of the bed. She glanced at Addy, eyes resting on the baby before flitting back to the clipboard. "I assume you are his wife or girlfriend?"

Addy flushed from head to toe. If she hadn't still been sitting, she'd have gotten vertigo. Her mouth flapped like a carp. No words found their way out.

Without waiting for an answer, the doctor went on. "He's lost a kidney. A few years ago that might have been fatal, but since the Cure, we've made improvements in surgery standards. He should be fine. He'll need someone to care for the surgical site, and he'll need to schedule a number of follow-ups to be sure his remaining kidney functions properly." She hung the clipboard off the end of the bed again. "Other than that, he appears to have suffered no consequential crushing damage. We will need to run tests over the next few weeks to be certain, but his prognosis is good."

Addy was sure she had questions, and that Matt would when he woke, but the doctor sprinted from the room before she could ask.

"Sorry, she's had a busy night," the second orderly said. "Stop by the nurse's station before he checks out, and they'll tell you more about the wound care and stuff."

Both orderlies slipped out.

Center hollow, she stared at the side of Matt's face as his eyes rolled under his lids.

Sliding his glasses back up his nose, Jim lifted both arms. "All right, you guys. Let's get home. It's been a long day, an even longer night."

Before standing, Cassius kissed her on the cheek. "I am sorry we lost Victoria, but she was only ever on loan to us." Half his smile turned down. "We shall bring you shoes later."

With a smile for Cassius, Addy took the hug Rivers offered. "Soon you will give my basketball a run for its money," she said, grinning at the baby. Ducking under Cassie's arm, she helped him from the room.

Grey sat next to her and leaned in her ear. "Were it not for you and our fine gentleman, I would never have proposed to my love."

She faced him. "What do you mean?"

His lamp-like green eyes shone. He opened his mouth.

Tal gripped his shoulder. "Let's leave her to it. She knows."

With a kiss on Addy's cheek, Grey stood and laced his fingers between Tal's.

Addy grinned at Tal, his spiky brown hair standing straight. "You still got that part for me in *The Tempest*?"

With a laugh, he shook his head. "Performances are officially on hiatus." He blew her a kiss and tugged Grey from the room.

As the door closed on silent hinges, she turned back to Matt.

Eyes open, he stared at her.

Stomach leaping to her throat, she jumped off the bed and stutter-stepped to his. The tile cold under her feet, it temporarily chased the sleep out of her system. "You're awake."

His parentheses dimpled his cheeks. "You're here." He glanced at her belt. "You lost my knife."

"You stole that knife from me." She squeezed around the side bar and sat on the bed.

His eyes sparkled. "Good." Holding her eyes with his, he opened his mouth again.

"You lied to me."

He nodded, smile fading. "I thought the one time would be OK."

"You lie to me again, I'll break each of your fingers one by one." For emphasis, she poked him in the shoulder with every word.

He caught her hand on the last poke. The tape from the lighted instrument adhered to his finger scratched her palm. "Let's start over. Matthew Lyburn," he said, taking her hand and shaking it. "I once worked for your mother, and since I was thirteen, I wondered what you were like."

She chuckled. "Am I what you expected?"

"No." Frowning, he ran one hand up her back. The tape on his finger caught in her hair. "You're a hell of a lot more than I ever imagined. I love you, Adelaide Cooke."

Final tumbler slamming into place with a great clang, all at once she knew what she'd come here to say. She sighed. "I love you." Smiling, she leaned closer. "Even though you—"

Gripping the back of her neck, he tugged her the rest of the way down and sealed her lips with his own before she could finish her good-natured insult. Every bit of kindness and tenderness and heat and fire he'd ever given her poured out of him and into her. An entire herd of butterflies zoomed around her stomach and chest, released from the net in which she'd held them. Warmth spread all the way out to each fingertip.

Applause erupted from behind them.

Jumping, Addy looked over her shoulder.

The Troupe had eased the silent door open and stood right there in the doorway, eavesdropping.

"Bravo," Cassius called, blowing kisses. "Bravo, my dears."

Matt laughed. "The hell are they doing here? I thought they left," he said, tugging Addy close and meeting her forehead with his.

"Apparently not." She closed her eyes.

"All right, show's over," Jim said. "Sorry, guys. They insisted. You know how they are."

Addy smiled and nodded, stretching onto the bed and laying her head on his chest. It rose and fell, heart thumping inside his ribs.

Matt chuckled. "Oh, we know."

With the regular rhythm of his heart in her ear and his warm arm around her, Addy let sleep come and take her. For at least a bit.

CHAPTER 59

A backhoe cruised through the fence, and smoke rose from miles away. Jack narrowed his eyes. "We get the dead pretty well cleaned up?"

Arms crossed over his chest, Mike nodded. "Yeah. Wasn't so bad in the daylight with the right equipment."

He smiled. "Get a few for yourself?"

"Hell no," Mike said, chuckling. "Celia wouldn't let me out of the truck. Said if I got bit again she'd kill me herself."

Jack's smile widened. "Damn."

"What?"

"I wish I'd known it was that easy to get you to stay in the truck. I'd have tried it already."

Mike laughed. "Well you know. She has, um." He turned red almost faster than Jack could snap his fingers. He cleared his throat. "She has her ways."

Chuckling, Jack turned back to the Molehill. The backhoe and excavator had already begun moving the big chunks. They could only get so close, because the ground beneath them was a lot like a sponge. There was no way to know if every tunnel had collapsed, and so the work went slow.

Dean approached from outside the fence. The bags under his eyes hadn't improved, but his step had regained a bit of spring. "There you are, Jack. Hey, Mike."

"Here I am. What's up?"

"Why are we doing this again?"

Rocks ground under the backhoe's tires and dust flew into the air.

Jack waved a hand before his face. "We ought to get it filled in properly and make sure any dangerous samples in their labs are neutralized."

Mike agreed. "Hux was particularly concerned about new strains they had been working on."

"New strains?"

"He doesn't know for sure. But he tested Adam's blood and came up with some weird stuff. So he wants to make sure it's all shut down and not dangerous."

Dean shuffled his feet, adjusting the sling hanging over his neck. "Couldn't we just fill it all in, put some caution tape around it, and call it good?"

Jack shook his head. "Sure. But."

"There's always a but," Dean said.

Mike giggled.

Replaying the last sentence in his head, Jack smiled. Before he could stop himself, he laughed along with his son.

Dean chuckled with them but stopped first. "So."

"So?"

"What's the but?"

"I won't leave her for dead again, Dean. I made that mistake once."

"And not to be crude or anything, but look what came of that," Mike said.

Jack sucked an involuntary breath over his teeth. It wasn't like Mike to put something so bluntly. That didn't make him less right. "Exactly. There are some things I still haven't forgiven her for. But I owe her at least this much." He closed his eyes. The memory of their flight from the hospital on Emerald Isle raced through him, twanging his nerves like an overstrung guitar string.

"I won't leave you to them again."

"You fucking better not."

"IRF is a mess, Jack," Dean said, breaking the silence.

Jack nodded. "That it is."

"They could use some help. Get back on their feet. Keep making the infrastructure better."

"I sure have gotten spoiled on this power and stuff," Mike said, "even if I'm not always sure where it comes from."

Jack grinned. "Nobody knew before either. You're not behind the curve."

"Good to know. I seem to fall behind the curve pretty often."

Someone spoke up. "You've got good looks and charm to spare though."

Who else but Celia, appearing out of thin air?

She stopped beside Mike, less than a grain of dirt misplaced under her silent feet. Lacing her fingers between his, she leaned around him and treated Dean to a heavy-lidded stare. "You gonna get out there with IRF? Make the world a better place?"

Smiling, he shook his head. "The first part, yes. The second part." He paused, squinting through the dust. "Maybe."

Together, they stared out at the smoke from the pyres in the distance and shared a silent moment.

Jack broke the silence. "I expect you'll check in. Let me know if you need anything. Come back for Christmas, that sort of thing."

"If you'll have me."

"It doesn't matter what's happened with you and Addy. You're part of the family now. Sorry."

Thumbs hooked in his belt, Dean met Jack's eyes. "Thanks. I'll show up when you least expect it with some laundry."

Jack laughed. "I'll keep in touch with you about this," he said, pointing at the Molehill with his forehead. "And I'll get someone to consult with you about the city's telephone situation."

"We'll see if we can't get it all squared away." He shuffled his feet. "You're staying here, after this is done?"

"Yeah. I guess I'll take over the defense force. Jane and I spoke about it before. We like it here. Good place to raise our kids."

Dean leaned around him. "How 'bout you, Mike?"

"Hux wants to get the information Mom sent. We'll head out to the island. See what's what."

Celia tugged his hand. "Maybe you guys can use that place like you were talking about. The bigger facility?"

Mike nodded, smile stretching his lips. He popped a sucker in his mouth and offered one to each of them.

Jack stuck his in his mouth, the sweet sugar coating his tongue and throat. Twirling it over his tongue, a feeling so strange tingling over him he couldn't identify it, he watched the fires with them as the excavators worked on digging out the hole.

As he swallowed a mouthful of sugary saliva and let his heart and mind fill with the light working its way out from his center, he found the name of the feeling.

Contentment.

* * *

Passing in a whirlwind of heat and humidity, Addy spun through the summer months as Dad worked to unearth the Molehill. As he also worked to rebuild the city, ushering the surrendered Talus folks in and the soldiers out, she and Matt resumed working with the Troupe.

Though she did less and less as time went on. Not because she couldn't, but because the group of them coddled her to death when she was around.

One thing she did do, though, was set that lamp on a table. Straighten the curtains. Clean up the bodies downstairs and move in a couch. And some loaded bookshelves. She even let Jane teach her to knit, and they passed quiet hours on the couch making blankets and hats and tiny little booties.

If she'd known how soothing knitting could be, she'd have taken it up ages ago.

With the Troupe running open auditions, she went to target practice with Jane every day and learned to throw knives. They still weren't as good as the bow, but there wasn't anything wrong with taking up a new weapon.

And on the longest day of the year, the sun beaming down on the whole event, Jack and Jane wed.

She told Addy over and over again it didn't really mean much. They'd been married in spirit for what already seemed like forever. But when she walked between the lot of them, down a central aisle in the middle of a field overlooking the city, she looked like no less than an angel. Flowers braided into her hair, cream-colored flowing dress blinding Addy as she passed, she smiled and cried.

Addy had hardly seen dresses at all, and she'd certainly never seen Jane in one. It was odd.

And Matt squeezed her and whispered in her ear, asking her if she'd ever put on a dress like that.

Watching Jane and Dad smile and kiss, she said she'd think about considering it.

The whole city turned up to pay their respects to Victoria, filling the theatre where Cassius gave her eulogy on stage under a single spotlight. Addy and Matt cried together and held each other up.

The days began to get shorter again. The hole in the ground that was once a warren of tunnels and dens got deeper.

One day she got the call they had dug deep enough.

* * *

Holding the small wreath she'd made of red, orange, and yellow leaves, Addy stood at the entrance to the great cemetery. She gripped Matt's hand in hers. "Did you know today is the equinox?"

Nodding, one parenthesis turning up, he tugged. "We going in?"

"One second."

Silent, he watched the city in the distance. "I still miss her too."

"I wish I could give her one more hug."

"I know it's not the same, but if it helps, you can hang on to me."

She shrugged, giving him a sideways smile. "It's worth a shot."

Careful of the wreath, he wrapped her with his arm.

They entered the graveyard, her head on his shoulder. The baby still three months out, she wobbled a bit when she walked, her hips and feet turned slightly out.

She stuck her fingers in her pocket, feeling the corner of the paper there. As she did, the baby rolled and kicked. She grabbed Matt's other hand and laid it over the baby. "There. Feel that?"

He stopped and stared at his hand, eyes wide. Parenthetical dimples deep, he looked up. "That doesn't hurt?"

She shook her head. "I thought of a few more names."

"We are not naming her after one of your *Star Trek* characters."

"Dad already beat me to it. Just don't tell him that."

Matt rolled his eyes, laughing. "What, then?"

A voice called from behind them. "Hey, you guys."

Although she contained the startled jump and swallowed a gasp, her heart skipped one beat. But just the one. "Hey, Dean." She replaced Matt's arm around her waist. "You came back for the funeral?"

"I had some laundry to do." His eyes skipped between them both. "How are you?"

"We're all right. Other than…" She gestured with the wreath and lifted her shoulders.

"I hear you. Can I walk down with you guys?"

"Please do," Matt said.

He probably thought she didn't notice him squeeze her tighter. Men were something else.

She leaned her head on his shoulder again. "I don't know if I can do this," she whispered.

He squeezed her again. "You don't have to."

Tucking her hand in her front pocket again, she rubbed the pad of her index finger along the corner of the paper. "Yeah. I do."

"I'll be right there if you need me."

She nodded sideways on his shoulder.

And instead of thinking about where they were headed, she asked Dean about IRF.

He chatted about them, explaining how Burke's second-in-command had taken over after his murder. The man had known he was supposed to report to Ilasha in the case of something happening to Burke, but instead, he took over the company. "He never trusted her. And Burke didn't exactly explain why he should."

"Should he have? She had so many lies going, even Matt couldn't keep up," Addy said.

"Hey."

She chuckled.

Dean breezed past her jab. "It's still a bit of a mess. But I think we can put all the pieces back together. Get things back on track."

"Hux reported in from Emerald Isle last week," she said, lifting her head. "He says it'll take about four years to get back to where we were with Cure production. And the vaccine might take longer."

Matt squeezed her. "We'll all have to learn to be more careful again. Don't get bit. Like before the Cure."

Mom, wailing like a banshee and sprinting through the sporting goods store, flashed through her mind. "That didn't always work."

"But remember," he said, stopping, "Hux can tell us about immunity now. Maybe our kids won't have to worry about Cures and vaccines."

Dean cleared his throat. "Sounds too good to be true."

Addy frowned. She met Matt's striking blue eyes. "I guess we'll hang on to it anyway. What else can we do?"

He kissed her on the tip of the nose. "That's my girl."

Crossing his arms, Dean walked ahead.

Matt took a step.

Addy tugged, feet planted. "Emmaline," she said.

"What's that?"

"Emmaline. That's the name I thought of."

Dropping his eyes, he touched his chin.

"Do you like it?"

Meeting her eyes again, mindful of the wreath, he wrapped both arms around her. "I think it's lovely and perfect. Just like her mom."

Again, it socked her in the stomach she was going to be someone's mom. Her feet like black holes on the spinning Earth, she gripped him until the vertigo passed. "Thought you said you wouldn't lie."

Rather than defend himself against false allegations, he slid a hand under her hair and warmed her from the inside out with a deep kiss.

She returned it, floating with him.

Her feet too close together, she almost lost her balance, and the paper in her pocket poked her.

Breaking away, she eyed the cemetery. They'd almost gotten to the gravesite, and they were the last ones there. Dad was already there with Jane. Mike and Celia had come back from the coast and stood, fingers interlaced.

In all, there were about a dozen people in attendance.

Since Mom had been under the earth for so long, she'd already been mostly gone when they got to her. The blood from her head wound lay on top of the rocks covering her. She'd been crushed by the collapsing room and robbed of any hope of escape before she chose her own way to go. Covered head to toe in a shroud, she now lay in an open wooden coffin next to a fresh hole in the ground.

Addy smiled, pulling the paper from her pocket. Letting Matt go, she walked to the grave and laid the delicate wreath on top of the shrouded body.

Matt joined the others and sat in the grass. Everyone else sat and stared up at Addy.

She glanced at the sky and unfolded the paper.

The dim white sliver of moon, having cleared about a quarter of its nightly trek, hung in the deep blue sky. The trees beneath it an explosion of red, orange, and gold.

She cleared her throat. "We're here for my mom. A wonderful, beautiful, deeply passionate, yet flawed woman." Her voice cracking, she stopped.

Matt nodded, smiling. His eyes glistened.

Giving him half a raised grin, she went on. "She was, at different times, my greatest inspiration and my greatest enemy. She taught me to survive. She tried to kill me. It was complicated."

A murmur rippled through the others. Mike laughed.

Still wearing half a grin, she skimmed the paper, finding her place again. Cassius told her it was best to have notes for the first time she spoke in front of a group of people. He hadn't been wrong. "Despite her flaws, she had vision. She made sacrifices. Sometimes the price was greater than the reward. Sometimes the reward was its own price. I don't know a lot more to say," she said, peeping up at them, "but I found this in one of the books at our library, and I thought it was fitting." She cleared her throat.

"Without rage, we cannot know love,
Without pain, we cannot know happiness,
Without the night, there is no day,
Without death, there is no life.
Great goddess of the night, I thank you."

She kissed her fingertips and laid them on the head of the shroud. "I love you, Mom."

CHAPTER 60

Jack loaded the last box in the truck. "You're sure you won't stay?"

Addy grinned. "For the last time. No."

He kicked a rock, déjà vu sweeping over him in a disorienting wave. "You're always welcome back here, you know." He met Matt's eyes. "Look after each other."

Matt shook his hand. "Of course we will, sir."

Stifling a laugh, he pulled his newest son into a hug. "Thought I told you not to 'sir' me."

Hugging him back, Matt laughed. He stepped away and glanced at Addy.

She gripped Jack's shoulder. "There's the Cure and everything, blah blah, safe, blah blah."

He pointed a finger at her. The heart in his chest wanted to curl into a ball and cry. But there'd be time for that after she was gone. "I can still lock you in your room, little girl."

Leaning over her large belly, she hugged him. "Gonna miss you, Dad."

"I'll miss you too. Call me when the baby's born. We'll come visit."

She hugged tighter. "Of course." She sniffled, burying her face in his shoulder.

Closing his eyes, he squeezed her hard enough to make the tendons in his forearms creak. "It's not that far."

She stepped back and wiped her nose on her sleeve. "At least you know the way."

"All the way east," Jane said, stepping in for her own hug.

Jack almost giggled, watching the two of them navigate around the babies between them. They embraced for what might have been eternity. Murmuring secrets only good for each other.

When Jane stepped back and took his hand, both her cheeks were wet. But she smiled. "Give 'em hell, Addy."

"You know I will," she said, pointing a finger gun at Jane.

"And make sure your brother stays out of trouble," Jack said.

"Yeah. Tell him I said hi," Jane said, half a grin curving her mouth.

Matt glanced around at them all. "I'm not sure what's going on here, but I feel like I'm missing something."

Laughing, Jack shook his head. "Nothing important. You guys have a safe journey."

"Somebody will let you know when we get there," Addy said, taking Matt's hand. "He's driving."

With one more wave goodbye and a few more tears, they climbed into the truck and rumbled down the road.

Eyes prickling again, throat thick, Jack squeezed Jane's hand. "This is just really not how I saw all this going."

Jane laughed. "Honey, you ain't the only one."

Facing her, he met her sparkling green eyes and twisted a lock of red hair that'd fallen over her ear between his fingers. "So, Mrs. Cooke. Would you like to go pick up our daughter?"

Dancing eyes smiling, she nodded. "Then you can take me home and sweep me off my feet."

"For the rest of our lives, love."

EPILOGUE

"**J**esus, catch him before he goes in the water."

"I told you," Matt said, jumping back into the boat and grabbing Cassius by the collar, "you don't have to call me Jesus. Matthew will do." He hauled Cassius up onto the dock.

Cassie lay on the dock, panting. "I am so sorry, my good sir. I have never been on such a boat."

Rivers alighted on the dock from the other boat, Grey and Tal following her.

Jim, green under his jaw, climbed to the dock and sat. He lit a cigarette. "Let's not do that again soon, huh?"

The twins, Kyle and Kaylee, the Troupe's newest arrivals, zoomed up and down the dock.

"Dearest Kyle," Cassius said, "please do help an old man up."

Stopping, the teenaged boy held a crooked arm out. "My pleasure, me fine fellow."

His sister stopped next to him, hands on her hips and glasses on the tip of her nose. "*My.* My fine fellow."

"Just for that, you're going in the sound," Kyle said. He dropped his arm just as Cassius grabbed it and pushed his sister.

She pushed him back.

Again, Cassius almost went in the sound.

Rivers floated past them all, basketball thunking off the wooden dock. "Have you a court on this small yet beautiful island? Perhaps my sea captain could come to play."

Arm in arm, Grey and Tal stopped Cassius from falling in.

Hair bushier than usual, Grey smiled at the youngest members of the Troupe. "Kyle and Kaylee. Please do stop and follow us inland."

Tal shook his head. "Or the very special parts I have written for you in what will be our first performance here shall have to be rewritten without speaking lines."

The twins stopped, mouths open, and crossed their arms. In unison.

Addy wobbled off down the dock.

Matt jogged to catch her, hand in the small of her back. "Careful. It's uneven and—"

"Yes, I know, thank you. I remember." She glanced over her shoulder. "I can't believe they wanted to come with us."

"It'll be nice to have them here. And they promised to train new people for when they leave."

Feet hitting solid ground, she stopped and rubbed her belly. At some point during the journey, her belly button had become the most extreme outie she'd ever seen. "Let's wait until tomorrow to check in with Mike. I'm beat."

"We'll get these guys settled in and get you home."

Taking his hand, she inhaled with wide nostrils. The sound stank of fish and mud. She hadn't smelled something so sweet in forever. "We've got a stop to make first."

Without thinking, she let her legs carry her to the Big House. Its sprawling shape covered in grey wood and green shingles.

She kissed Matt under the ear. "You and Jim stay with these animals. I'll be back."

"You got it, Houlihan."

Muscle memory carried her past the doormat where she'd dropped a dripping Dean, past the fireplace where she'd first seen Scott's holey socks, and through an impossible maze past half a dozen stuffed and mounted mallards.

She stopped before a door deep in the center of the house and knocked. Her heart tripped along in her throat, breath shallow.

Scott opened the door. Below his shocking grey hair, his face lit up like daylight. He swung a prosthetic arm. "Lieutenant! Please, come in. Welcome back."

"Hi, boss. It's good to be home."

THE END

A Special Note

If you or someone you know are a survivor of sexual assault, please know there is help. You do not have to recover alone. This is a work of fiction, and in real life, Jack's recovery should have been assisted by a qualified mental health professional. Please see the below resources:

United States:
Get Help: National Sexual Assault Telephone Hotline (RAINN): (800)656-HOPE; www.rainn.org

Find Treatment: SAMHSA: (800)662-HELP; www.samhsa.gov

International:
Crisis hotlines by country, and other resources: http://www.ibiblio.org/rcip/internl.html

ACKNOWLEDGMENTS

I owe so many thanks to my family—Johnny, Robin, Benny, and my mom. They have been my biggest support and cheerleaders throughout this. Also to my alpha/beta team. I wouldn't be here without them. Shevon, Mel, Nora, DJ, Joe, Judith, Selina, Fred, Ada, Jennifer, Mandy, Venius, Sheri…Thank you guys for sticking with me! If I missed anyone who alpha or beta read the series for me, please blame my horrible memory. It wasn't intentional!

And special thanks once again to Michelle Rascon for the beautiful job editing, and to Mato J. Steger for the superbly gorgeous covers. You guys are the absolute best team an author could ask for!

Thank you, readers, for checking out Addy and Jack's story. I hope you love it. I know I do. More to come? Maybe…

ABOUT THE AUTHOR

Bethany writes sci-fi, horror, fantasy, and is dabbling in romance under a pen name. After *Supernatural* ended, she took some time off. Grief is a thing she knows well, and writing is always something deeply personal. She shares stories with the hope others will be able to use them to heal, as she does.

Her debut novel, *Reclamation*, and its sequel, *Reclamation 2: Revolution* are both available wherever books are sold. Don't tell the others, but *Reclamation 3: Reconstruction* is her favorite in the series. Also by Bethany is *Give Me Grace*, from NineStar Press, available wherever books are sold.

Visit her website to find out more and sign up for the mailing list, where you will be alerted to new releases.

bperrywrites.com